No Wings To Fly

Jess Foley was born in Wiltshire but moved to London to study at the Chelsea School of Art, then subsequently worked as a painter and actor before taking up writing. Now living in Blackheath, south-east London, Jess Foley is also the author of *So Long At The Fair*, *Too Close To The Sun*, *Saddle The Wind* and *Wait For The Dawn*.

Praise for Jess Foley

'A really great tale of triumphs and trials that you won't be able to put down' *Best*

'If all sagas were as convincing and exuberant as this, the world would be a better place. I loved it' Monica Dickens

'Compulsive and well-paced' *Wiltshire Times*

'Jess has really captured the sense of a family united against great odds. The heroine is strong but flawed as all good heroines should be and as we follow her triumphs and trials we see her change from a girl to a woman in the most dramatic and satisfying of ways' Iris Gower

'A gripping saga . . . The author writes with exuberance and style, and the central characters are totally convincing. The climax of the story is superbly etched'
Northampton Chronicle & Echo

'A magnificent, beautiful book . . . exciting, moving and riveting from start to finish' Margaret Pemberton

'An earthy tale of love, longing and tragedy'
Swindon Evening Advertiser

Also by Jess Foley

So Long At The Fair
Too Close To The Sun
Saddle The Wind
Wait For The Dawn

No Wings to Fly
Jess Foley

arrow books

Published by Arrow Books in 2006

3 5 7 9 10 8 6 4

Copyright © Jess Foley 2006

Jess Foley has asserted the right under the Copyright, Designs
and Patents Act, 1988 to be identified as the author of this work

First published in the United Kingdom in 2006 by Century

Arrow Books
The Random House Group Limited
20 Vauxhall Bridge Road, London, SW1V 2SA

Random House Australia (Pty) Limited
20 Alfred Street, Milsons Point, Sydney
New South Wales 2061, Australia

Random House New Zealand Limited
18 Poland Road, Glenfield
Auckland 10, New Zealand

Random House (Pty) Limited
Isle of Houghton, Corner of Boundary Road & Carse O'Gowrie
Houghton 2198, South Africa

The Random House Group Limited Reg. No. 954009

www.randomhouse.co.uk

A CIP catalogue record for this book
is available from the British Library

The Random House Group Limited supports The Forest
Stewardship Council (FSC), the leading international forest
certification organisation. All our titles that are printed on
Greenpeace approved FSC certified paper carry the FSC logo.
Our paper procurement policy can be found at
www.rbooks.co.uk/environment.

Mixed Sources
Product group from well-managed
forests and other controlled sources
www.fsc.org Cert no. TT-COC-2139
© 1996 Forest Stewardship Council

ISBN 978 0 09 946646 8 (from Jan 2007)

Typeset by SX Composing DTP, Rayleigh, Essex
Printed and bound in Great Britain by
CPI Bookmarque Ltd, Croydon, Surrey

For Jenny and John

PART ONE

Chapter One

'Well, you certainly don't think the matter's going to end here, do you? Because I can assure you it's not.'

Lily could hear her stepmother's words through the open casement, hissing, sharp and staccato on the summer air, but she could not see her from her seat on the lowest bough of the apple tree. Lily had taken a bite from the ripe pear in her hand, and the juice had run down her wrist. Now, though, for the moment, the pear was forgotten as she concentrated on trying to hear the exchange coming from the room. She could not go closer in order to hear better and get a better view; she dared not give her presence away and anger her stepmother still further. She could, however, see her brother's form through the glass, albeit dim and shadowed in the shade-darkened room. She could not make out his expression, or indeed any feature of his face. All she could hear was the murmur of his voice when he spoke, mumbled and indistinct. Her stepmother's words, however, were clearly audible.

'Your father's going to learn about this the minute he gets in,' she said. 'Make no mistake about that. Because if you think we've got money to burn, to waste on new clothes for you, when you can't look after what you have, then you've got another think coming. Look at your jacket torn.'

Another murmur from Tom, though once again not loud or distinct enough for Lily to catch the words. She had seen him just a few minutes earlier, sneaking into the house, trying to get by without their stepmother seeing him. He had not been sharp enough, though, and had been caught and brought up halfway across the kitchen.

'And what about your cap?' Mrs Clair's voice again. 'Where d'you suppose your cap is now?'

Tom's faint voice came, mumbling, brief, and then the woman's:

'Is it, indeed? Well, you won't get it back now. It's gone for good, you can bet on that. What are you looking for – to get dismissed from school? Go back next month without a jacket, without a cap and they'll send you packing. It'll be the ragged school for you. That old Mr Neville, that miserable so-and-so, isn't likely to give your cap back. What were you doing in his yard anyway?'

Another mumble from Tom, followed by Mrs Clair's harsh tone.

'Well, then, you'll have lost the ball too, and serves you right. And what were you doing playing and wasting time when you were told to come straight home from the farm?'

Lily shifted slightly on the apple bough, straining to hear, but she still could not catch Tom's murmured reply.

When Mrs Clair's voice came again, it sounded closer to the window. 'Yes,' she said, her voice ringing out, obviously directed at Lily, 'and if you out there have had your ears full, perhaps you'd like to get something done. I know you're there.' She appeared at the casement then, overlooking the rear yard with its strip of lawn and the apple tree rising up out of it. Quickly, Lily scrambled down from her perch.

'And don't run away just because you've been caught.'

At the words Lily came to a halt beside the tree, looking at her stepmother.

Going solely by the strength of Mrs Clair's voice, one might have expected a large person, but she was below average height, and lean to the point of thinness. She looked a little harassed today, but that was nothing new. Her light brown hair, thinning a little, was coming adrift from the pins. At thirty-five, the prettiness that had once been hers was fading.

'Sitting out there with your ears flapping,' she said. 'Just because you've finished at the Mellers' doesn't mean you're done for the day. Your father'll be in soon, and there's water to be drawn and vegetables to bring in, so I suggest you get busy. Or you'll find yourself in trouble too. I've enough to do with your brother.'

'Yes, Mother.' At once Lily turned and started across the yard to the well.

'And what are you eating?'

Lily turned back to face her. 'A pear.'

'Where'd you get it?'

'Mrs Meller gave it to me.'

'Oh, I suppose she thinks I don't feed you enough, is that it? Well, throw it away; otherwise you won't want any dinner.'

Lily did as she was told. She would have liked to take a final bite, but she knew better, and drawing back her hand, she threw the half-eaten fruit into the straggling bit of shrubbery beside the lawn. As she did so, her stepmother turned her back on the window and moved out of sight.

After Lily had drawn a pail of water she stood for some moments beside the well, leaning against the upright. She was a girl of just above medium height. She had dark brown hair, and dark eyes, but a very fair skin, and in her regular features was the promise of a nascent beauty. Of late, her coltish form had begun to soften. She had turned fifteen just a month before, on July the second.

She sighed, absently wiping her juice-stained hand over her pinafore. On the early August breeze she heard the chimes from the church clock striking the hour of five. Her father would be in before too long. From where she stood beside the well she could look to the right and see almost to the end of the long garden path, and the area at its foot that passed for an orchard. She turned her attention to the house again. It was a small, 25-year-old dwelling that had been built in the second year of Victoria's reign. It had red brick walls and a tiled roof, and stood four-square on its little plot in Hawthorne Lane, a lane that went nowhere where horse-drawn vehicles were concerned, for the way ended in a stile, beyond which green meadows stretched away towards the next village.

Her eyes and ears focused on the window, Lily could no longer see or hear anything that passed inside the kitchen, though she could well imagine the tongue-lashing that Tom was still receiving. The worst of it was, it would not end with their stepmother's anger – an anger that often seemed to spring from nowhere, and with the least provocation; the end would come when their father returned from the factory.

'Lily?'

Mrs Clair had appeared at the window again. Lily straightened. 'Yes, Mother?'

'I'd be grateful if you'd finish drawing the water,' Mrs Clair said, her voice full of irritation, 'and sometime today would be as well. Dora's got to have her wash, in case you'd forgotten, and there's the vegetables to be got ready.'

'Yes, Mother – coming right away.'

Later, Lily was setting the table for the evening meal – the main meal of the day. She, her brother, stepmother and small half-sister were in the kitchen, the room where the whole family congregated. Mrs Clair was sitting sewing in the light from the window, a little nest of stockings in her lap. Near her feet her daughter, Dora, a placid five-year-old – now washed by Lily, and wearing her nightdress ready for bed – sat cooing over her doll. Tom was sitting on a three-legged stool beneath the long-case clock, nervously shifting and stretching a piece of string between his fingers. Tension was evident in every sinew of his body.

On the soft summer air footsteps sounded in the yard and after a few moments they heard Mr Clair open the back door and enter the scullery. At the sound of her father's steps, Lily looked across at her brother. Their stepmother did likewise, in the same moment hissing in a whisper, 'Yes, my lad, you might well look concerned.'

Seeing the apprehension in Tom's eyes, it was all Lily could do not to move to him, but she remained standing by the table, waiting.

Tom was five years younger than Lily. Small for his age, he was two or three inches shorter than she. In spite of his small, lean stature, though, he had a particular beauty – Lily had always thought so – with his finely shaped head, well-formed features and thick, dark brown hair. Now, beneath his perplexed brow, his hazel eyes looked wide with anxiety, and he shifted on the stool as if he might rise and run from the room. Reading his discomfiture, Mrs Clair said sharply to him, 'You stay where you are, my boy. You're not to move until you're given permission.'

Next moment the children's father was opening the kitchen door and stepping into the room, glad to be home at last. There was not yet an opportunity for him to relax, however, for as he took off his hat his wife said plaintively, 'Before you sit down, Edwin, I want you to deal with that boy. He's been a wretch today, and has caused me no end of trouble.'

Mr Clair was a tall man, still handsome for his forty-four years, though tending to heaviness about the middle. Usually upright in his carriage, and fairly vital in his mien, there was this evening a look of weariness about him that came from more than having worked a hard day at the tile factory. At his wife's words his look of weariness increased,

7

and he sighed and put a tired hand to his face. 'God almighty,' he said, 'can't a man even get in the bloody door before trouble greets him?' Without looking at Lily he thrust out his hat, and in silence she took it. Then he lifted his hand and pointed at Tom. 'You – get here in this scullery.'

After a moment's hesitation, Tom stuffed the piece of string into his pocket, got up from the stool and scampered across the room, past his father and into the scullery beyond. Mr Clair glared out into the kitchen, at nobody in particular, then took off his jacket and undid his belt buckle. As he drew out the belt he followed the boy into the scullery and closed the door.

Silence in the kitchen. Dora looked at her mother as Mrs Clair moved to the table, her lips set in a grim line. Lily stayed where she was, holding her father's bowler hat, her face turned towards the scullery. Almost immediately there came her father's voice barking out from the other side of the door, 'Don't move! Don't you move, you little wretch.' And then a brief silence, a whimpering murmur from Tom, and then the sound of the belt striking. Lily could hear it through the door. As Tom's half-stifled yelps stabbed into the quiet, Lily pressed her hand to her mouth, and choked back a sob.

'Yes, and *you* can stop that fuss,' her stepmother said, '– unless you'd like some of the same. What I have to go through with you two would test the patience of a saint. You don't see your little sister making such trouble.'

After a while the door to the scullery opened and Mr Clair came through, holding his belt and jacket. In silence he handed the jacket to Lily and she took it into the hall and hung it up along with his hat. As she went back into the kitchen he finished fastening his belt then turned and rapped out over his shoulder, 'Now, Thomas, you get upstairs, and stay there till you're sent for – and let me have

8

no more complaints about you. You won't get off so lightly next time.'

Quickly Tom passed through the room, head lowered so that no one would see his reddened eyes and tear-stained cheeks. After the hall door had closed behind him, Lily heard his footsteps creaking on the treads as he ascended the stairs.

As the boy's footfalls faded, Mr Clair moved to his chair and sat down. 'I need a rest and a smoke, and then I'll go and wash.' Turning to his wife he added, 'Unless, of course there's something else you'd like me to deal with before I do.'

'I had to tell you about him,' she said defensively. 'That boy – he's the end.'

Mr Clair sighed again, then bent to his boots to undo the laces. 'Something happened today,' he said, '– and it's not good news.'

'Something happened?' Mrs Clair sat up straighter. 'What happened?'

'I'll tell you later on, when there aren't so many ears around.'

Mrs Clair nodded and looked at Lily. 'Are you going to stop there all day, miss?' Her voice was all impatience and irritation. 'The table won't get laid with you just standing there. And when you've done that you can take your sister up.'

Lily finished setting the table, and then went to Dora who stood on the hearthrug between her father's spread knees, showing him her doll. As Lily approached, the child grabbed at her father's hand and wailed, 'Oh, have I got to go to bed yet, Papa? Can't I stay up a while longer?'

The response came from Mrs Clair. 'No, dear,' she said kindly. 'You be a good girl and go with Lily, and I'll be up later to tuck you in.' To Lily she said, 'Take her up now, will you.'

This was a task that Lily undertook almost every evening.

It helped her stepmother out, and it was no unpleasant chore for Lily, for she was fond of her half-sister, and had helped care for her since her birth.

Now, as Lily trailed a hand over the child's golden locks, Dora looked up at her and gave a sigh. 'Must I, Lily?'

Lily gave a nod. 'Your mama says so, dear.'

As Dora sighed again, Mr Clair drew her to him and kissed her cheek. 'Goodnight, my pet,' he said. 'You go on up with Lily, there's my good girl.'

Dora moved from her father's embrace, saying to her mother, 'Will you be coming up to see me, Mama, before I go to sleep?'

'Yes, of course, dear, but you close your eyes in the meantime.'

Lily took Dora by the hand and led her into the hall and up the stairs to the room they shared. There was no need for a candle on these summer evenings. The light of the day was bright enough as it filtered through the curtains.

In the bedroom Lily pulled back the covers. 'There, now – into bed with you, like a good girl.'

With her doll in her arms, and helped by Lily, the child climbed into bed. 'I'm not a bit sleepy, Lily,' she said. 'Honestly I'm not.'

'Still, you have to sleep,' Lily said. She gently touched the child's doll on her topknot of curls. 'And I think Millie's tired too.'

'Oh, Millie's *always* tired.' Dora pressed the doll's scratched china head into the pillow.

'Well, I think you should both close your eyes and go to sleep.' Lily looked down at the child. Dora was so like her mother: the same bone-structure, visible in the sharp, pointed chin, the small, high-arched nose. 'I shall be up to bed later on.'

'You're not going yet, are you?'

'No, of course not. I shall stay here with you for a while.'

'Till Mama comes up?'

'Yes, till Mama comes up.' This was a lie, for Lily knew that her stepmother would not come upstairs as she had promised. She rarely did; it was always Lily's job to stay with the child until she dropped off to sleep, and only then, when the child was sleeping, could she creep away. If Dora remembered the next day that her mother had not come to visit her while she was awake, Mrs Clair would always say, 'Oh, I did, my dear, but when I came you were fast asleep.'

Sometimes Lily had to wait a good while till Dora fell into her slumber, and on a few occasions she herself had fallen asleep.

Now, looking up at her, Dora said, 'You've got to lie down too. Not just me.'

Kicking off her slippers, Lily hoisted her legs up on the bed and laid her head on the pillow next to Dora's. After a while the child's eyes closed, and then the rhythm of her breathing changed as she drifted into sleep. Lily remained there; it would be a mistake to get up too quickly. Best to be sure. Her own eyes closed and she gave herself up to the comfort of lying there. This evening she was tired; she had had a long day at the Mellers' house. With the harvest due, there was always extra work to be done. Every summer, for the past few years she had worked as a general maid for the Mellers, a farming family in the village. It brought a little much-needed extra money into the house, and also kept her occupied during those weeks when she was away from school. Her brother worked at the farm also, having started there just this summer. A willing boy, he revelled in doing odd jobs about the place and helping with the stock. He loved to be out in the open air too, added to which, it got him away from his stepmother.

While Tom loved his time on the farm, for Lily it was only a stopgap. All summer long she looked forward to September, and the day when she would be back at school.

At fifteen she was no longer an ordinary pupil. Her elementary schooling had ended soon after her thirteenth birthday. However, she had remained on as a pupil teacher, assisting the schoolmistress. She had completed two years of her apprenticeship so far, and had another three years to go, at which time she would herself qualify to seek work as a teacher. She could not wait for that time to come. Then perhaps, if things worked out, she might even gain a scholarship to go to Chelsea in London and study further at Whitelands, the famous school for female teachers. That was in the future, though, for now not even to be dreamt of.

She opened her eyes. For a moment there she had been in danger of dropping off. At her side Dora was sleeping soundly. Lily waited another minute or two, just to be absolutely sure, then carefully drew herself up. Dora slept on, her little pink mouth slightly open. She would not now waken until the morning.

After putting on her slippers, Lily crept across the room, stepped out and closed the door behind her. On the small landing she moved to the door opposite and scratched at the wood panel with a fingernail. There was no sound from within. After waiting a few seconds she eased the door open and crept inside.

Now she could hear his breathing as he lay on his bed. She could see him too. The curtains had not yet been pulled across the window, and the fading light filled the small room with a soft glow. The space was small, and simply furnished. Against the wall opposite the window stood the single bed. The only other furniture in the room was a chest of drawers, a narrow little wardrobe, and a rather rickety chair. She came to a stop on the worn bedside rug, listened for a moment for some acknowledgement of her presence, then whispered, 'Tom? Tommo, are you all right.'

He replied then, his voice only just there, in a murmuring

whisper, half stifled by his hand: 'Go away, Lil. Please. I don't want to talk to anybody.'

'Tom,' she murmured, and stepped closer. He was lying on his side, his hand up to his face. His frame looked small on the counterpane. She sat on the edge of the bed and whispered his name again. 'Tom . . . Tommy?'

'Please, Lil,' he whispered, 'I'll be better if you leave me alone. Besides, you'll cop it if they find you in 'ere talkin' to me.'

'They won't find out,' she said. 'Dora went off like a dream, so they won't expect me down yet. Anyway, they can't hear us if we keep our voices low.' She was silent a moment, then she asked, 'Was it bad, Tommo?'

He nodded. 'Like it usually is. She's never liked me,' he said, '– not from the start. And it'll never be no different now.'

Lily knew he was right. Where their stepmother was concerned, there was little that he could ever do to please her.

'I know I shouldn't have lost my cap,' Tom said, 'but it was an accident.'

'Of course it was. I heard you lost your ball too.'

'Yeh. It was only an old pig's bladder, but it was a good un. I hopped up on the fence to climb over and my cap fell off. And there I was, 'alf way over the fence when old Neville comes out. Course, as soon as he appears, the other boys 'ave gone. You can't see 'em for dust. I tried to get back but as I did so I slipped. That's 'ow I tore me jacket.'

'I'll mend it for you,' she said. Then she asked, 'How was work today at the farm?'

'Oh, fine. I enjoy it so much. Mr Meller – he's so nice.'

'Yes, I know he is. Mrs Meller too.'

He turned to lie on his back. 'I wish I was as old as you,' he said. 'I'd be long finished with school and I could really

13

earn a livin' for meself. And I don't mean on Mellers' farm either. I'd like to get right away from 'ere. Well away from Compton.'

'Where would you go – Corster?'

'Corster? No fear – I'd go to one of the big cities. One of them up north maybe. They say you can earn lots of money up north in the factories. Or maybe London. They got everything in London. And anything'd be better than this. It'll be all right for you. You'll be a teacher one day.'

'Not for another three years yet, though.'

'Still, it'll come, and you'll be doing what you've always wanted.' He turned to her. 'One day when you're a real schoolmarm you'll have a nice 'ouse, and I can come and stay with you.'

'Yes,' she said, 'that would be nice.'

He fell silent for a second, then said, 'I know I'm a disappointment to 'im.'

'To Father? A disappointment? Oh, Tom – that's a melancholy thing to say.'

'Well, look at me. I'm not big and tall like 'im. I never shall be. And I can't do the things he does. He plays the violin, and he paints so well. And 'e's clever with words and figures and such. The way you are. No wonder 'e hardly ever gets mad at you.' He gave a deep sigh. 'I wish our mam was 'ere.'

He was speaking of their own mother, of course. Their own mother who had died a week after Tom's birth, taken by the Bright's disease that she had suffered from for months. People had said it was a wonder she had lived for the birth of her son, and indeed a wonder that the boy had survived as well.

'Was she nice – our mam?' Tom said. 'Tell me, Lil.'

Lily smiled. 'Oh, yes, she was. I may only have been five when she died, but I can remember her very well. Ah, Tom, she was nice, so nice.'

14

'These things wouldn't have happened if she'd still been alive.'

'No – I doubt they would.'

He winced slightly at a sudden pain that caught at him. Lily said, 'He hurt you bad this time, didn't he?'

'Ah, it 'urt like billy-o.' He shook his head. 'He wouldn't be like he is if it wasn't for her. She eggs 'im on and gets 'im riled up. He gets in knackered from work, and all 'e wants is to sit down and catch his breath, but she greets him with complaints about me. No wonder 'e gets mad. No man wants to 'ear that sort of thing the moment 'e sets foot indoors. And tonight he was madder than ever. Not only angry, though. It was like summat was up, summat was different.'

'He's had bad news,' Lily said. 'He told our mother just before I came up. Though he didn't say what it was.' She stirred on the bed. 'I'd better get downstairs, or they'll start to wonder what's keeping me so long.' She stood up. 'I wish I could bring you some dinner . . .'

'It don't matter.'

'You'll be hungry.'

'It won't be the first time.'

She smoothed down her skirt, moved quietly to the door, opened it and looked back. The August evening light was fading quickly now. Tom was a dim figure on the bed. 'I'll see you tomorrow,' she whispered into the gloom, and then was gone.

As she went back into the kitchen her father and stepmother did not look at her but kept their eyes on one another. She had heard the murmur of their voices as she reached the foot of the stairs, but they stopped talking as she opened the door. If it had not been for the fact that their conversation ceased, she would almost have thought they were not aware of her presence. There was silence in the room but for the ponderous ticking of the clock.

'Dora went off to sleep all right,' Lily said. 'She was tired tonight.'

Her stepmother nodded. 'Yes – she would be. She's been so active all day.' She got up, pressing her hands together. 'Well, this won't get dinner, will it?' And then, turning to Lily: 'We'd best get busy.' To her husband she said, 'There's water in the kettle, so if you want to wash now . . .'

As Lily moved to follow her stepmother, her father said, 'When you've got a minute you can go upstairs and tell your brother to come down and eat.'

'Edwin –' Mrs Clair protested from the scullery door.

'The boy's got to eat,' he said. 'Working on the farm all day, he's got to keep his strength up.'

As Lily went upstairs a few minutes later, she wondered why her father had relented so soon where Tom was concerned. It was not like him to be so quickly forgiving.

When the time came, the four sat down to eat the cold lamb and vegetables that Lily and her stepmother had brought to the table. Neither Lily nor Tom spoke as they ate, and there was little conversation between their parents. Their father, in particular, seemed more than usually preoccupied. Soon after the meal was finished Tom said his goodnights and went upstairs.

When he was gone, Lily and her stepmother started to clear the table, while Mr Clair moved to his chair. When all was in order and the dishes had been washed and dried, Lily went back into the kitchen. Her stepmother had taken up her darning, while her father leant back smoking his pipe. Lily took her own sewing basket from the shelf and resumed her work on the bodice she was making for a new dress. For some minutes there was silence, then Mr Clair said:

'So, Lily, my girl, what kind of a day have you had at the Mellers'? They keep you hopping, no doubt?'

Lily, glad of his interest, said, 'Oh, it went pretty much as

16

usual, Father. These days the men are out in the fields most of the time. They hardly come to the house. Mostly it's just me and Mrs Meller and the other maid. It's a big house and there's always plenty to do.'

'I'm sure there is. She's still lending you her books, is she?'

At this, Mrs Clair gave a breathy little snort, which was enough to make Lily hesitate before replying, but then she said, 'Yes, she is. She lets me take anything I want. She says I should read everything.'

'Read,' Mrs Clair said dismissively without looking up from her mending. 'Who's got time for reading? How some women manage to run a house with their heads stuck in a novel half the time, I'll never know.'

'Oh, but she doesn't only read novels,' Lily said. 'She reads other things too. Last week she gave me a book about the Chartists.'

At Lily's words her stepmother gave a contemptuous little sniff and said, 'Chartists, hmm,' but Mr Clair said to Lily, 'And did you find it interesting?'

'Oh, yes,' Lily said, eyes wide. 'They're trying to make changes. Not only do they want *all* men to have the vote, but women as well.'

Mrs Clair hooted at this, and shook her head in wonder. 'Lord almighty,' she said, 'if that's the kind of thing you're learning at the Mellers', I should think it's time you put your mind to something else. I thought you went there to work, not to have your head stuffed with nonsense.'

'Now, then, Mother,' Mr Clair said to his wife. 'It's nice the woman takes an interest in the girl. She knows she's got a brain.'

'Got a brain, is it?' Mrs Clair said. 'What does a girl want with politics, I'd like to know.'

'Oh, but she thinks a girl ought to know about such things,' Lily said, 'especially me, seeing as how I'm

17

'prenticed to be a teacher. She says there'll come a time when girls are taught as boys are taught. For girls it won't be all needlework and drawing and how to bake a pie. The girls should be taught grammar, she says, and physics and chemistry too, and they should –'

Mrs Clair broke in at this. 'Enough,' she said, flapping a hand. 'No more. You're going to find out, young lady, that a girl needs to learn only as much as'll fit her for her life. Which, if she's lucky, will mean marriage to a decent man and having a decent home. And I'd like to know where physics and chemistry and grammar come into that.' She turned to her husband. 'I'm tired of sitting here listening to such rubbish. I think you'd better tell her what the situation is. We'll all be the better for it. You can't put it off for ever.'

Lily looked across at her father. There was definitely something up.

'Yes,' her father said after a moment, 'I need to have a word with you, Lily.'

Lily waited for him to go on, but he tapped out his pipe, repacked it and lit it with a taper lighted from the range. When he had blown out the taper, he laid it on the edge of the hearth. Then he raised his eyes to Lily again. She sat waiting, her needle and thread held still.

'You know,' he said, 'that I've always wanted the best for you . . .'

'Yes, Father . . .'

'Yes, and I've wanted you to have better than I've had. Your brother, too. Though I'm afraid he'll never amount to anything. Anyway – what I have to say is this –' He came to a stop, searching for the right words, then went on again almost in a rush: 'Listen – it's not going to be possible for you to keep on at the school.'

Lily frowned, her mouth opening in surprise. 'Oh, but, Father –'

Mrs Clair broke in sharply, 'There's nothing to say about

it. This isn't a discussion. It's a fact – and you've got to accept it.'

Lily looked at her father. 'Does that mean – that I'm not to be a teacher after all?' She could scarcely believe she was uttering such words.

Mr Clair cleared his throat, then said shortly, 'Yes, it does.' Then with a slightly softer tone, 'I'm sorry, but it does.'

Lily frowned. 'I'm to leave the school, Father?' she said.

'I'm sorry to say you are, yes.' He paused. 'The thing is – the situation has changed. It's an expense – keeping you there for five years. Oh, I know there's the grant, but that's a pittance. It doesn't keep you, and you know it doesn't.'

Mrs Clair chimed in: 'I'll say it doesn't.' Then to Lily, 'Other girls your age are in service, and have been out earning for two years or more. They haven't got these la-di-da ideas. They're content to get to work, and start bringing in a bit of money. *I* was at your age. It was good enough for *me*.'

'But – but I've finished two years,' Lily said. 'In another three I shall be qualified.'

'Yes, and a fat lot of good that'll do *us*,' Mrs Clair said. 'We put all the money into it, and we get nothing back. You qualify, as you say, and then you'll be off. Whatever you earn we shan't see a penny of it.'

'The thing is,' Mr Clair said, 'the situation at the factory has changed. I was told today that –'

Mrs Clair said, cutting into his words, 'You don't need to go into all that. She doesn't need to know all the ins and outs of the matter. She's got to accept what's what, that's all there is to it. You're too soft with 'em, that's your trouble.'

Mr Clair said, a trace of anger in his voice, 'I'm not soft with them at all,' then to Lily: 'But your mother's right, you've just got to accept the fact.'

There was silence in the room, the only sound that from the clock. Lily said into the quiet:

'Then – what am I to do, Father?'

He lowered his eyes, one hand going to cup his chin. 'Well – that's something that's got to be worked out,' he said. 'We'll talk again in a day or so.'

That night Lily lay in the bed beside the sleeping Dora, while through her mind ran over and over again the words that her father had spoken.

She could still scarcely believe it. She was to leave the school. For two years she had spent every day helping with the children's tuition, loving every moment spent in the classroom, and only dreaming of the time when she herself would be the schoolmistress. Not here in Compton Wells, but in some place where she could begin to build a life for herself. And now it had ended. With just a few words every thread of the fabric of her future had been discarded. The future she had foreseen had been cancelled, as if it had never been.

Before her now lay nothing but emptiness. Was it possible? She had been so sure in her dreams, her expectations; so sure that she was left now with nothing to fall back on. What was to become of her? What was she to do?

Chapter Two

Just over a week later, Lily returned home from her work at the Mellers' and found her father in the kitchen. On Saturdays he worked only half days. He was alone in the house. Mrs Clair had taken Dora into Shearley, a village some little distance away. Tom was at the farm.

'I'm just going down to get a few apples,' Mr Clair said to Lily as she came in. He took up a basket, and an earthenware bowl. 'And maybe a few blackberries too.' He towered over her; she just came up to his shoulder. 'You want to come with me?'

She accepted eagerly, and together they left the house, and with Mr Clair leading, went in single file down the narrow garden path. The afternoon was warm, with a fresh and fragrant breeze. Birds cheeped in the trees, and butterflies danced and tumbled over the shrubbery. In the week since her father had given her the news that she would not return to her apprenticeship at the school, he had spoken no further word on the matter. For her part, she had not dared ask more. She would learn everything in due course, she knew, though in the meantime the disappointment, the doubts and the questions had hung upon her like a cloak. All of it, the change in the family's situation, she felt sure, must have to do with Seedley's tile factory.

Today, as she followed her father's broad shoulders down the narrow cinder path a little trace of her disappointment and sorrow was alleviated. It was for the simple reason that she was with him, alone. And today he did not appear quite so stern; she had discerned a warmth in his manner that she did not often see. But there, the atmosphere around the house was always more relaxed when Mrs Clair was not present.

Very soon they came to the orchard, a narrow strip of land at the end of the kitchen garden with a scattering of fruit trees. Hardly worth calling an orchard, her father would say. Together, Lily and Mr Clair gathered a number of wind-fall apples and put them into the basket, then went to the edge of the plot where the brambles grew lushly over the weather-beaten fence. The berries were thick on the stems, and although most of them were still red, a good number were a deep, luscious black. All the ripe ones went into the bowl, except for one particularly large one, which Mr Clair held out on his palm to Lily. 'There you are, Lily,' he said. 'This un's too good for the pie.' Lily took the blackberry and put it into her mouth. It had the sweetest taste, and for that moment, if she could have held an instant in her life it would have been this one, this moment of being alone with him, with the taste of the blackberry on her tongue.

'When we go indoors,' her father said, 'we'll make us a nice cup o' tea. And we'll have a slice of your mam's apple pie.' His words continued the music in Lily's ears, not for the promise of the pie, but for the closeness that was there. She wanted it never to end.

She was stretching up to reach one of the bramble stems, when he said to her, 'Leave that for a minute. I want to talk to you.'

She stopped her action and turned to him.

'Listen to me,' he said.

She nodded, waiting. It was like the scene of a week before, when on the hearthrug he had given her the news that had proved so disheartening.

'I wanted a chance to talk to you,' he said, 'when nobody

else is about.' He paused. 'Now, Lily,' he went on, 'I told you last week that it's just not possible for you to go back to school in September and go on training for a teacher . . .'

She nodded. 'Yes, Father.'

'And indeed I'm very sorry to have had to tell you such a thing. But as I said, the fact of the matter is that we just can't afford it any more. Not,' he added quickly, 'that we were able to well afford it in the first place, but we got the little grant from the government, and that helped out a bit. And, as I said, I've always wanted the best for you, so we were willing to make sacrifices to see that you got the best. But now – well, it's not so easy. We've got Dora to think of as well, and she's growing fast. She'll be starting school next month. And there's your brother too, of course. He's not cheap to keep, and he'll be at school for a while yet. It all adds up.' He sighed. 'The truth is, times are hard, and are gunna get harder.'

Lily wanted to say, Is it Seedley's that's the trouble? but she did not dare, and kept silent.

Then her father said, answering her unspoken question, 'There's been talk, I know, and you might well have heard it. Fact is, there've been sackings at the factory. I know your mam wouldn't agree with my telling you all this, but you've got to know. You're not a little child – you're old enough and smart enough to understand the situation. And the situation's not the best. I've kept my job, thank the Lord, but at a much reduced wage, and God alone knows whether it'll ever go back to what it was before. I couldn't do anything about it. It was either accept it, or leave and try to find something else – which is out of the question. Times are not easy right now – anyone'll tell you that.'

Lily stood silent before him on the grass. A dragonfly hovered for a moment by her shoulder and then darted away over the brambles. She was astonished that her father would tell her such things, confide in her so.

'I'm lucky to have a job at all,' he said. 'Others haven't been so fortunate. Ted Carwin was one of those to go, as was Mr Dilke.' He added quickly, 'Mind you, what I'm telling you here is not to be broadcast. It's for your ears alone. Don't you go telling the Mellers or any of your friends or anybody.'

'Of course not, Father.' She felt a little touch of pride that he had confided in her, though his words merely confirmed that her dream was irrevocably shattered.

'Anyway,' he said, '– so now you know.'

A few moments of silence, then Lily said, 'So – so what am I to do, then, Father? I don't know if Mrs Meller'd want me all year long. She might, though. I could ask her.'

'No, you won't be staying with the Mellers,' he said shortly. He looked across towards the garden, avoiding her gaze. 'We're making other arrangements for you, your mam and me.'

'Making other arrangements?'

'That's what your mam's doing now. She's gone off to meet Mrs Haskin, from Whitton.'

'Mrs Haskin – who used to live here in the lane?'

'Ah, that's right. Before her husband inherited the share in the carriage company and they moved to Whitton.'

'I remember them. They were old friends of yours.'

'Well, *he* was, in particular. Roger Haskin. Oh, I'll say. We've known each other since we were boys.'

'Yes,' Lily said, 'I remember your saying. You were even in the military together.'

'We were indeed. They were great days, those days in the Fusiliers. He's a fine chap, is Roger Haskin. The best friend a man ever had.'

Lily had been made aware of the couple from time to time, though they had not lived in Compton Wells for a number of years. Middle-aged and childless, they were frequently referred to, and were established as old friends, and on one occasion a few years back Mrs Haskin had returned to the village and called in for tea. Lily remembered her as tall, with a large, plump frame, and a wide, smiling mouth; she had made a fuss of baby Dora. 'What about Mrs Haskin, Father?' Lily said. 'Why is Mother seeing her about me?'

Before Mr Clair had a chance to reply, there came a distant call from the direction of the house, and he said, 'Ah, there's your mother and Dora come back. We'd best get up to the house. Don't say anything more for the present. We'll talk again soon.'

Later, in the scullery, Lily was set to washing Dora and getting her into her nightdress for the hour or so remaining before she took her up to bed. As she worked, she could hear her father and stepmother's low, murmuring voices coming from the kitchen. When she went into the room with Dora, though, their conversation abruptly changed its tone.

Tom came back from the farm a little after six, and when Dora had gone off to sleep upstairs the four of them sat down to eat. Afterwards, Lily carried the dishes out to the scullery and began to wash them. As she stood at the sink, her father came in from the kitchen.

'It's settled,' he said. 'It's all settled now. You'll be going to Mr and Mrs Haskin at Whitton.'

Lily put down the dish she was washing and turned to him. 'Go to – to Mr and Mrs Haskin . . .?' She had begun to fear something like this. 'It's all arranged?'

'Yes. You're to go as general maid. Mrs Haskin needs help around the place. The maid she had has just left and she's lookin' for another one.'

Lily stood in silence, letting the news sink in. 'How long must I go for?' she asked.

'How long? Well, that remains to be seen.' There was a

25

certain brusqueness in his manner, an awkwardness in giving the unwelcome news. 'At least for three or four years, I should reckon. After that we can think about it.'

'Three or four years. But – but a girl's petty place – when she first goes off into service – it's usually for no more than a year. And if – '

'It's not the same,' he broke in shortly 'You're going to friends. It's not the same thing at all.'

'Oh, Father – must I go?'

'Yes,' he said sternly, 'you must. I told you, it's all settled. And it's true what your mam says: look at your old school-friends – those girls were going into service at twelve and thirteen. You should be grateful we let you stay on as long as you did. And what else is there for you to do? You've got to start bringing something in and paying your share.'

'Oh, I want to do that,' Lily said, 'but – couldn't I go somewhere local? Oh, let me ask Mrs Meller – see if she'd keep me on full time.'

'I told you, it's all settled. Besides, the Mellers don't pay enough. The bit extra you get from the Haskins will come in very handy – specially in times like these.'

'But Father –'

'Enough!' he said sharply. 'It's done. You go Sunday, a week tomorrow.'

When the Sunday came, Lily helped her stepmother get the midday dinner, and afterwards, when the dishes had been washed and put away, got into her second-best dress and put on her bonnet. Near the time of her leaving, her father came up to her room and hoisted up the box she had packed over the previous days, and carried it downstairs. It was not so heavy, for she owned little.

Tom was at the farm and not there to see her off, but they had made their sad goodbyes earlier. He had said little in words, but she could see from the way he pressed his lips together, and feel from the hard grip of his hand that he was deeply moved. Now there was just Dora and her stepmother. Lily bent to her half-sister and kissed her on the cheek, and then turned to her stepmother. 'Well – goodbye, Mother.'

'You don't need to look so long in the face,' Mrs Clair said. She made no move to embrace her stepdaughter but stood with her arms folded over her flat bosom. 'You're only going to Whitton, you're not going to Timbuktu. You'll soon have a chance to come back and see us.'

'Yes, of course.'

'And listen – don't write home asking us to send things. And don't forget what we arranged – you remember to send something when you get your first pay.'

'I won't forget.' In addition to her board and lodging, Lily was to receive twelve pounds a year, paid to her in quarterly sums, and it had been agreed that she would send a portion of her wages back home, to help out. The little that was left, she could keep for herself.

When it was time, Lily took her little portmanteau, and with her father carrying her box on his shoulder, they walked to the crossroads where they caught an omnibus to the station and got on the train. When eventually they arrived in Whitton they took one of the station flys, and after a short journey the vehicle turned at a crossroads and slowed in front of an old house.

'Well, here we are,' Mr Clair said, and moments later he and Lily were standing outside the carriage and looking at the house which, for the foreseeable future, was to be Lily's home.

The house, Hollygrove, was situated on the Corster Road, some little distance from the centre of the small town of Whitton. It had a slate roof, and timber and plaster walls that were partly covered by ivy. It stood apart from the dwellings on either side with the space taken up by a small

27

paddock on one side, and a large kitchen garden on the other. In the front garden, shrubbery grew thickly around an area of patchy grass.

'Well, come on, then.' As the fly began to turn in the road, Mr Clair pushed open the gate, and together they made their way around the side of the house to a green-painted door. There Mr Clair set the box down at his feet and knocked.

The door was opened by Mrs Haskin, who beamed at them and said expansively, 'Well, here you are. Do come in.' She stepped back, and Mr Clair, carrying Lily's box, stepped into the kitchen. 'You might as well take your things upstairs at once,' Mrs Haskin said. 'Come along.' Moving ahead of them, she led the way into the main hall and up two flights of stairs to a small attic room at the top of the house. 'Here we are,' she said as Lily came up onto the landing. 'I think you'll be comfortable here.'

Inside the little room, Lily put down her portmanteau, and her father set down the box. Mrs Haskin watched from just inside the doorway, and nodded her approval. 'Good. Now come on downstairs and we'll have some tea.' She turned to Mr Clair. 'I've got the kettle on, Edwin, and I'm sure you could do with a cup.' Mr Clair thanked her, but said he wouldn't stop as he had left the fly waiting outside. 'I told Annie I'd get the next train back,' he said.

'Oh, well, if you can't stay,' Mrs Haskin said, stepping out onto the small landing. 'I'm sure Lily'll want to see you off, then.'

The three of them made their way downstairs to the hall, where Mrs Haskin opened the front door, saying, 'Now you have a good journey back, Edwin, and don't you worry about your girl. She'll be fine.' She turned to Lily, raised her hand and gently pinched the girl's cheek. 'We're going to get along just grand, I know we are.'

The open front door revealed the fly standing by the front

gates. When Mrs Haskin had made her farewells to Mr Clair, she said she would see Lily in a minute and then turned and headed back towards the kitchen. Lily and her father went out to where the carriage waited at the roadside.

'Well, Lily,' Mr Clair said, 'you look after yourself, won't you?'

'I will, Father.'

'And be a good girl and do as you're told, all right?'

'Yes, Father.'

'And mind you're a credit to me – you will be, won't you?'

'I will.'

'Good. Don't you be doing or saying anything that'll reflect badly. But you wouldn't do that anyway, would you – smart girl like you?'

'I'll do my best, Father, really I will.'

'Ah, I'm sure you will, and I'm sure your best'll be good enough – if you want it to be. You've got a clever head on your shoulders, you've got a willing spirit, and a capable pair of hands. I don't think as Mrs Haskin can ask for more.' He glanced back towards the house. 'You'll get on all right with her, I'm sure. She's a nice enough woman, and her husband, Roger, is an absolute champ.' He nodded endorsement of his words, and touched at the collar of his shirt. 'I must go or I'll miss my train.'

He bent and gave Lily a peck on the cheek. 'Well, g'bye, girl. You be good now.'

'Goodbye, Father.'

He climbed in and closed the door after him, and a moment later the vehicle was starting away. As the rough little carriage moved off along the road Lily felt a tightness in her throat and the sting of tears in her eyes. She stood watching until the cab had gone out of sight around the bend.

She was still standing there a minute later when from behind her came Mrs Haskin's voice calling out, 'Well, are you gunna stay out there all day, young lady? Because there's things to be done.'

The words shook Lily out of her preoccupation, and she turned and saw Mrs Haskin just closing the front door. Without wasting a moment, Lily moved around the side of the house to the rear door. As she stepped inside, Mrs Haskin said, 'And if you're looking for a drink of tea, dear, I'm afraid you'll have to wait and make do with water. I'd have made some tea for your father, but since he decided not to bother, we shan't be bothering either. You can have some later with your supper. Now,' Mrs Haskin stood before her, hands clasping the dish towel over her girth, 'I suggest you go upstairs and get changed into your working frock and your pinny. Then you come on down and I'll tell you what your duties are gunna be. Maybe then we can get summat done.'

Lily spent the next hour in chores around the house, and then, shortly after six o'clock, Mr Haskin came in. His shadow darkened the open scullery doorway for a moment as he stepped into the room, his glance at once falling on Lily. 'I reckon there's gunna be some rain,' he said, looking curiously at her. Then with a nod and a smile he said, 'Hello, young miss.'

Lily gave a little bob, and said, 'Mr Haskin, sir.'

He was a broad shouldered man of medium height, thick dark hair turning grey. Looking to be in his mid-forties, he was quite clearly some ten or so years younger than his wife. He was quite good-looking, with a strong nose, heavy dark brows, and a wide, generous mouth. He stood there with his hat in his hand looking Lily up and down.

'Well,' he said, 'so we've got our new little maid. Though not so little really. How old are you, young lady?'

'Fifteen, sir.'

'Fifteen, eh. And you're Edwin's girl.'

'Yes, sir.'

He nodded again. 'You'll have to forgive me if I don't remember you from when we lived at Compton. I reckon you must have been knee-high to a grasshopper when I saw you last.' He smiled warmly at her. 'Anyway, it's nice to have you here. We can do with some decent help after that useless little minx Kitty went off. Have you heard about her?'

'No, sir.'

'No, and indeed why should you? And it's just as well she went of her own accord afore she was pushed.'

Mrs Haskin looked up from the food she was preparing and said, 'The girl don't need to know all our business, Father. She'll have enough to do looking after her own affairs without bothering with ours.'

'And right you are,' Mr Haskin said. 'Right you are.'

Later on Lily sat down to eat with the couple, and was relieved to find that the simple supper of cheese, pickles and cold ham was good. After they had eaten, she set about washing and drying the dishes, and then it was time for her to go to bed.

PART TWO

Chapter Three

As Lily made her way through Whitton's small park, she hitched the basket more securely over her arm and looked up at the heavens. The July sun had made an attempt to shine earlier on, and had succeeded for a while, but now clouds had come drifting over and the sky was turning grey and threatening. She just hoped that the rain would keep off, for she had brought no umbrella.

In her basket she carried a package containing a pork pie, two pickled eggs and some bread and cheese – Mr Haskin's midday dinner which he had forgotten to take along with him earlier that morning. It was not the first time it had happened during Lily's employment with the family.

The year now was 1866, and it would soon be three years since she had come to Whitton to begin her work with Mr and Mrs Haskin. Thinking of it sometimes lately, she could scarcely believe that so much time had gone by – how, almost unnoticed, the days had slipped into weeks, the weeks into months, and the months into years. It had, generally, thankfully, been a painless process.

Following her arrival she had settled fairly swiftly into a routine and was very soon going about her duties as a matter of course. She had been relieved to find also, that after initial misgivings about Mrs Haskin's rather sharp manner, for the most part she got on well with her. As the weeks passed, Mrs Haskin had seemed to relax and soften in her manner towards the girl, and, evidently, to judge her worthy of her bed and board and £12 a year. Even so, Lily had to watch her step, for there were occasions when her mistress would be prone to outbursts and passions, and a slip in Lily's work might result in a sharp rebuke, or on very rare occasions, a quick dig with a hard hand.

As for Mr Haskin, Lily had come to know him little better as the time had passed. He was altogether different from his wife. He appeared an easy-going man and, though not much of a one for conversation, was invariably pleasant to Lily. He seemed to regard her with a rather tolerant amusement, for which attitude she could find no reason. A wheelwright by trade, he owned a third of a partnership in a small carriage-construction company, by name of Silver and Son, on the eastern side of Whitton, making – and also repairing – smart broughams and phaetons for those who could afford such things. He loved his work and was closely involved in all aspects of the manufacture of the carriages, from the setting of the springs to the sewing of the upholstery. He worked long hours, leaving home in the mornings just after seven, and not returning until seven in the evening. Even at weekends he would frequently end up at the factory. Usually he rode on his chestnut cob for the mile-and-a-half journey, though on occasions he would hitch up the trap.

Lily had often visited the factory during her time in Whitton, usually to take Mr Haskin some message, or to deliver some food or item that he had perhaps forgotten or which was not ready at the time of his leaving the house. On her first visit, soon after her coming to Whitton, he had taken pride in showing her around the workshops, and with fascination she had watched the men at their various tasks, observing them at different stages of the carriages' construction, as they built everything, starting with the first basic part, right to the final polish on the woodwork. She had been impressed, and the thought came to her that perhaps one day she too might go and work there. At present there was only one female in Mr Haskin's employ, but Lily reckoned it was only a matter of time before there were more.

Lily's continuing employment with the Haskins was now a matter for some consideration for her. She had turned eighteen earlier that July and had already stayed on longer than was usual in such a domestic position, particularly when it offered no chance of betterment. It was time, she had begun to tell herself more and more, to move on somewhere else. But where was she to go, and to do what? What she had most set her heart upon – becoming a schoolteacher – had been put beyond her reach, and she could think of nothing else that she was fitted for or that she wanted to do.

Going by way of the little borough park saved Lily a tedious walk through the hard-paved streets. The park also offered a more attractive outlook with its wide, smooth sward and trees of poplar, beech and elder. It offered, too, the occasional bench beside the meandering pathways, and as Lily approached one of them she decided to sit for a few minutes and take in the view. She would cool down too; for all that the day was overcast, it was humid and rather uncomfortably warm.

She stepped towards the bench, and as she did so she saw a book lying on the seat. She sat down and in the same moment took it up.

There were not many books in the Haskin household, and the few that there were Lily had read, some more than once. Sometimes she got books from the Munie circulating library, but she wasn't always in the house when the library van came by. She greatly missed the Mellers' crowded shelves at the farm in Compton Wells.

The book was a copy of M. E. Braddon's novel *Aurora*

Floyd, and seeing the title on the cloth-bound cover she felt a touch of disappointment, for she had read it only the year previously.

She flicked through the pages of close-set type and read the odd paragraph, immediately remembering the story and the characters as they appeared again. As the minutes passed she soon found that she had read three or four pages. For all her interest, though, she was conscious of the fact that she had taken up something that did not belong to her. She looked around. A group of boys were playing football some distance away, an elderly couple were strolling along one of the paths, and a small boy came by bowling a hoop, encouraged by his doting mother. There was no one who looked to be in a search of a forgotten book.

What should she do? It was almost certain to rain before the morning was out, and if she left the book behind it would simply be ruined. Also, although she had read it, she might quite enjoy reading it again. With only a moment's hesitation she put the book into her basket beside the little parcel of food. Then, with one last look about her to reassure herself that no one was regarding her with suspicion, she got up and started away.

Fifteen minutes later she had moved across the south-eastern corner of the small town and was turning up the cobbled drive of the carriage factory, towards the workshops.

Apart from adjoining offices where the clerks and the managers sat, there were three main workshops: one where the carriages were constructed, another where the paint and varnish work was done, and a third where the upholstery was fitted. Lily made her way into the first one, where amid the noise and heat from a forge, four perspiring men were making iron parts for the chassis of a brougham. Standing just inside the doorway, she peered to see if one of them was Mr Haskin, but he was not among them. After a moment a man with a hammer wiped a hand across his brow and came towards her. She recognised him from past visits as one of the company's foremen. He smiled at her as he approached and said over the noise of the hammering, 'It's Mr Haskin's girl, am I right?'

'Yes, sir.'

'Mr Haskin's been called away, but he said he won't be long, if you want to wait for him.'

'I brought his dinner,' she said.

'Oh, well, if you just want to leave it,' he gestured with his thumb, 'you can put it in his office.'

Lily thanked him and moved back out into the yard, glad to get away from the heat of the workshop, though the air outside was oppressive too. Above her head the clouds were gathering more darkly than ever. Over the cobbles, she made her way to the low buildings at the side, in which the offices were housed, and opened the door that led into a small ante-room furnished with a small table and a couple of chairs. Crossing the room, she knocked on the door to a room opening off. As she anticipated, there was no reply, and after a moment's hesitation she pushed it and went in. She had been in the room several times during her visits to the place, and little had changed over that time. Mr Haskin's desk, unencumbered except for a few papers and ledgers, faced the window. She took from her basket the package containing his dinner, put it on his desk and started back towards the door. As she did so there came a hard flurry of rain on the window pane, and she turned and saw it furiously lashing against the glass.

Moving from the office, she stepped out into the little ante-room and closed the door behind her. Standing beside the small table she looked out into the yard. There was nothing for it but that she must wait. She sat down. A few moments passed while she watched the rain streaming down the glass, and then she thought of the book, and took it out of her basket. Minutes later she was absorbed in the story.

She was disturbed out of her preoccupation by a knock, immediately after which the door opened, and a tall young man stepped into the room.

'Hello,' he said, taking off his hat, and closing the door on the rain-swept yard. 'I didn't expect to find anyone here. I've come to see Mr Haskin.'

'He's gone out,' Lily said.

'Yes, they just told me. They said I should come in here and wait for him.' He put a leather briefcase on the table along with his hat. As he brushed a hand over the rain-dampened shoulders of his light-coloured jacket he said, 'I came out without an umbrella. These summer storms are not to be trifled with, are they?' He gave another flick at his sleeves and ran fingers through his hair. His hair was darker than her own. He had grey eyes, and his face was broad, with chiselled features. He was, she would have said, handsome in a rather angular fashion. He appeared to be somewhere in his early twenties.

'Well,' he said, 'I suppose I might as well sit down.' He moved to the other chair, one with a tapestried back and padded arms. A little silence fell, touched only by the sound of the rain. Not wishing to appear unsociable, Lily closed the book and laid it before her on the table. After some moments the young man said, nodding towards the window, 'It doesn't look as if it's going to let up too soon, does it?'

'No,' Lily agreed. 'It certainly doesn't look promising.'

'If Mr Haskin's been caught in this, it could be any time before he gets back. Are you waiting to see him too?'

'No. No, I just came to bring him something from his home. His midday dinner. He went off without it.'

'Oh, I see.' He smiled, showing white, even teeth. 'And

something nice, I hope. Something worth your getting caught in the rain for.'

She gave a little chuckle. 'A pork pie and some pickled eggs.' How banal it sounded.

He added his chuckle to her own. 'And very nice too, I'm sure. Are you his daughter, may I ask?'

'He has no daughter. No, I work for him.'

'Here at the factory?'

'No, at his home. I'm general maid to him and his wife.'

'I see.' He paused. 'And – may I ask your name?'

'Lily.'

He smiled broadly. 'Well, hello, Lily. My name is Joel.'

She smiled back. 'How d'you do.'

'Have you been working for the Haskins long?'

'Three years now. Almost to the day.'

'Quite a while. Are you a Whitton girl?'

'No, I'm from Compton Wells.'

He nodded. 'I know of it.' He took out his watch and consulted it. 'Getting on for eleven, but I'm in no hurry.' He dropped it back into his waistcoat pocket. 'You're living here now – in Whitton, right?'

'Yes. On the other side of the park. And you? Are you from round here?'

'No, my home's in Corster. I came to see about my father's carriage. It was in an accident and it's being repaired.'

'I see. And did your boss give you the day off to come and see about your father's carriage?'

He grinned. 'My father *is* my boss. For the time being, anyway. I'm down from university for the summer break, and helping him out where I can.'

'Oh, you're a student. What are you studying?'

'Law. I'm at Cambridge.'

She smiled. 'I'm impressed. I hear there's lots of money in being a lawyer. Judging by Mr Dickens's *Bleak House*,

41

anyway. How much longer have you got at university?'

'One more year.'

'And then into the big wide world.'

'Well – we shall see.'

'I was a student for a time,' she said a little wistfully. He was easy to talk to, and she felt the need to tell him. 'I was studying to be a schoolteacher.'

'Oh? What happened?'

She shrugged. 'Things – got in the way. I had to give it up.'

'Oh,' he said, 'that's a pity.'

She nodded. 'Yes – so I came here to Whitton – to work for Mr Haskin and his wife.' She fell silent again; she was telling far too much to this complete stranger. She glanced towards the window. The rain's initial fury was fading. 'It's easing a little,' she said.

'It looks like it,' he said with a nod. Then he added, glancing at the book on the table, 'I see you came prepared for getting caught in the rain.'

'Oh – this . . . I found it, on the way here.'

'You found it?'

'It was on a bench, in the recreation ground. It had just been left there. I thought it would be ruined if the rain came on.'

'No doubt it would. May I?' He got up and picked up the book, looking at the cover. 'Do you like Miss Braddon's sensation novels?'

'Well – I've read two or three – including this one. But I might read it again.'

'I haven't read it – though I believe half the housemaids in Britain have done so.' He set it down on the table. 'What's it about?'

'It's about a rather headstrong woman who commits bigamy.'

'She sounds monstrous.'

42

Lily gave a little laugh. 'Oh, she does it mostly through carelessness, I think.' She shook her head, and added ironically, 'And now I'm beginning to think perhaps I should have left the book where it was – but I get short of things to read.'

With scarcely a moment's hesitation, he turned to his briefcase, opened it and took out a book. 'Here,' he said, 'you can borrow this, if you like.'

She took it from his outstretched hand and looked at the cover. '*Mary Queen of Scots.* I've read a little about her, but not a whole book. Oh, I'd love to read it if I may.'

'Of course. I'm happy to lend it to you.'

She smoothed a hand over the book's cover. 'I can't guarantee how soon I'll finish it.'

'That's all right. I've got other things I can read.'

'But you were in the middle of reading it yourself.'

'I'd only just started it. I can begin again when you bring it back.'

'And how will that be – that I bring it back to you? I can't run up here just when I feel like it, and it's not often I get sent here on an errand.'

'Well, I could meet you somewhere.' He paused. 'Couldn't I?'

'Well – perhaps . . .' Her voice was hesitant. 'I don't get much time off.'

'But you must get *some*.'

'Yes, of course. And I have certain errands that take me away from the house.'

'Oh?'

'Well, for one thing, on Sundays I go to get midday dinner for Mrs Haskin's mother. She's over in Henhurst, and I often get a few hours off during the afternoon.'

'Oh . . . and have you got some time off this coming Sunday?'

'Yes, I have – a little. After going to see Mrs Shalcross.'

43

'What do you usually do with your time off?'

'Well, if the weather's nice, I might go for a little walk in the park. Or on a few occasions I've taken the train into Corster. Just to have a look around – when I've got a bit more time, that is.' She glanced out through the window. 'Look, the rain's just about stopped now.' She still held the book he had given her. 'Are you sure about lending me this?'

'Oh, absolutely.'

'Thank you.' She took up the copy of *Aurora Floyd*, and put both books into her basket.

'Are you going so soon?' he said.

'Yes – I must get back.' She moved a hand to her bonnet strings and adjusted the bow.

'So . . .' he said, 'd'you think we might meet on Sunday? When you're through getting the old lady's dinner.'

Her heart began to beat a little harder in her breast. 'Well – yes – perhaps we can.'

'Good.' He smiled. 'What time d'you finish?'

'By the time we've eaten and I've washed the pots it'll be about half-past two.'

'I could come to meet you there in Henhurst – or wherever you like, come to that. If the weather's fine we could walk in the park.' When she did not answer, he said, 'Well – what d'you think?'

'Yes. Yes, we could.'

'Then I'll meet you at the park, shall I? Is that convenient for you?'

She nodded. 'I have to pass by the gates on my way home.'

'Even better,' he said. 'I'll be waiting by the gates. Say quarter to three?'

Another nod. 'All right.'

'If it rains I'll wait in the bandstand shelter.' He was gazing at her intently, and she shifted her eyes to the window again. 'The sun's trying to break through,' she said. 'I'd better go.'

He reached out and took her right hand in his. 'I'm so glad to have met you, Lily,' he said, shaking her hand.

'Yes . . .' she said, feeling utterly foolish. She was so aware of the touch of him, his skin against hers, the feel of her slim hand held in his broad grasp.

'I'll look forward to Sunday,' he said as he released her.

She could think of no words to say, and merely nodded.

'I'd like to walk back with you now,' he said, 'but I'm bound to wait here to see Mr Haskin.'

'Yes, of course you must.' She pulled on her gloves, then picked up her basket and hooped it over her arm. 'Well . . .' She started towards the door, conscious of each step she took. 'Until Sunday, then.'

He moved before her, opening the door to allow her to step out into the rain-washed yard. 'Yes,' he said, 'till Sunday.'

Lying in bed that night, Lily kept thinking back on her meeting with the young man. She could hear his voice and the words he had spoken. She could see him too, his tall frame, his broad face with the wide smile.

She had said she would see him on Sunday afternoon. Would she? Would she, when the time came, have the courage? Would it matter that much if she did not go to the park as arranged? Oh, he would think poorly of her if she failed to turn up, and just left him waiting, and she would deserve his calumny. In the long run, though, it would not matter. She would not have to witness his disappointment and his displeasure, or hear any hard words that he might speak. It was unlikely that they would ever meet again. They were little other than ships that pass in the night.

*

45

The weekly visit to Mrs Haskin's mother, who lived a little over a mile and a half away, was a regular part of Lily's routine, and one that she quite enjoyed. The old woman was in her early eighties now and finding it increasingly difficult to get about. So it had become Lily's regular Sunday task to take food to her for her midday dinner, and prepare it and eat with her. Mrs Shalcross was very glad of Lily's company, though she never failed to complain that her daughter had not come instead.

The weather had remained fine on this Sunday, and judging by the clear sky looked set to continue so. Lily arrived at the cottage to find the old woman waiting for her. As Lily stepped over the threshold, Mrs Shalcross looked her over and said at once, 'You're lookin' sharp today, Lily. You got yourself a new bonnet?' Lily replied that she had not, that she had merely added some blue ribbon trim to her second-best, at which the old lady nodded approval, and said, 'Well, it looks a treat, dear, it does, really.'

Lily got busy at once and wasted no time in preparing the meat and vegetables, and putting them on to cook. When the food was ready they sat down together. As they ate, Mrs Shalcross spoke approvingly of her son-in-law, and his diligence in his work, but complainingly of her daughter who, she said, did not visit her nearly often enough. For her part, Lily ate her pork and potatoes and greens, and thought of the young man who would soon be waiting at the park.

When the meal was eaten Lily made tea, and afterwards did the washing up and then prepared to say her goodbyes. 'Can't you stay a bit longer?' Mrs Shalcross pleaded, to which Lily replied with a feeling of guilt that she could not, but that she would try to stay longer on her next visit. Minutes later she was out in the lane.

The distance was not so long to the recreation ground, and Lily could have walked it in a relatively short time. She forced herself to move at a fairly slow pace, however, for it was a warm day, and she did not want to perspire. As she drew nearer the park she could hear faintly on the summer breeze the sound of a brass band. Soon afterwards she came in sight of the gates, and moments later she saw Joel as he got up from a bench and started towards her. He was taller than she had remembered.

'Lily! Well, hello!' He stopped before her, his mouth in a wide smile. Lily returned his hello, and asked whether he had been waiting long.

'Just twenty minutes or so,' he replied. 'I've been listening to the band, and doing a little sketching.' He was carrying under his arm what looked to Lily to be a small file or book. He held it up and said, 'My sketchbook.'

'You're an artist.'

He laughed. 'Oh, I wish I were.'

'Are you good?' she said.

'Hmm. Perhaps just good enough to know that I should be so much better.' He turned and gestured towards the park's entrance. 'Shall we go in?'

She nodded. 'We might as well.'

Side by side they walked through the iron gates into the park. There were many other people there, making the most of the fine weather and a day off work, sitting and lounging on the grass in the sun while the band played. The bandstand was not large, but the eight or nine musicians made up for their small number with their enthusiasm.

Joel suggested that they sit for a while, and they chose a spot a little distance from the bandstand, in the shade of a rowan tree. There Lily set down her bag and sat on the grass. Joel sat down beside her. The band was playing 'When You Come Home Again', and some of the sojourners sang along with snatches of the familiar words. Joel sat in silence for a little while, then said to Lily, smiling, with a sigh, 'This is splendid. Really excellent.'

47

'The music?'

'Everything. The music, the sunshine.' He paused. 'Seeing you again.'

She said nothing, and they sat for a while without speaking, just listening to the music, then Joel said, 'I wasn't convinced you'd turn up today.'

In disregard of the doubt she had felt during the week, she said, 'I said I would.'

'Yes, I know you did . . . Still . . .' A moment passed, then he said, 'Do you miss your home?'

'Sometimes. I miss my father and my brother, and my little sister.'

'You don't mention your mother.'

'My mother died,' she said, 'when my younger brother was born. We've got a stepmother – and things are different.'

Aware of a change in her tone, Joel said, 'Don't you get on with her?'

'It could be better.' She paused. 'But anyway, it's not so bad. I shall be going home to see them all again soon.'

'That'll be nice. When did you last go for a visit?'

'In the spring. Just for the weekend. The time before that was at Christmas. That was a short visit too.'

'And when are you going next?'

'In three weeks.'

He nodded. 'I'm sure you'll be glad of the break, won't you?'

She gave a sigh and smiled. 'Well, I have to admit that my life here with the Haskins can really become rather boring at times.'

'Do you get on with them all right?'

'Yes – quite well. Mrs Haskin has her ups and downs, but Mr Haskin's always got a smile and a friendly word. I like him a lot. He and my father have been lifelong friends.' She paused for a second. 'But I've got to think about moving on

48

before too long. I've been there almost three years. I can't stay for ever.'

'What d'you think you might do?'

'I don't know. I told you I was hoping to be a schoolteacher, but that all came to nothing.' She sighed. 'Anyway, tell me something about yourself. Have you got brothers and sisters?'

'I have a brother, Crispin. He's three years older than I.'

'And your parents? Are they well?'

'Oh, yes, they're fine. They're in France at the moment.'

'In *France*?'

'Yes. My father has a business there. He's back and forth a good deal of the time. My brother too.'

Lily was about to ask what kind of business it was that took a man back and forth over the Channel, when Joel said, 'What's happened to the music? The band's stopped playing.'

Lily looked over to the bandstand and saw that the bandsmen had left their seats and that two or three of them were drinking from mugs. 'I guess they need to wet their whistles,' she said. 'I'll bet it's thirsty work.'

They continued to sit there, and as the minutes passed she felt increasingly at ease in Joel's company. The sun was shining, and all around them the air was filled with contented chatter and laughter. She realised that she was glad she had come.

Then, after a while, a group of six youths came and sat a few feet away, and with their arrival the air erupted with their raucous voices and braying laughter. When the noise had gone on for a few minutes Joel leant closer to Lily and said, 'What do you say? Would you like a change of scene?'

She nodded. 'Yes, why not.' Her glance rested briefly on the noisy group.

They got up from the warm grass and moved off across the sward to a ring of trees, in the midst of which lay a pond. On its bank three small boys moved back and forth, sailing boats on the smooth water, while their parents looked on from benches set about the rim.

Joel and Lily walked around the pond until they came to a vacant bench that looked out over the water. There they sat down side by side on the wooden seat, and Lily untied the strings of her bonnet. Further along on the grassy bank a mallard and his mate rested in the shade of a willow. On the summer breeze came the sound of the band starting up again. Joel listened for a second to the melody, then said, 'Ah, that's a grand old tune,' and Lily puckered up her lips and whistled along with it for a few bars.

Joel looked at her in surprise. 'Hey, you can whistle,' he said.

She gave a little chuckle. 'Well, of course I can whistle.'

He laughed. 'I didn't think girls could.'

'It's not that they can't,' she said, 'it's that they're not allowed to.' She joined in, whistling with the tune again, and then sang a few of the words.

'The girl can sing too,' Joel said. 'I'm really impressed.'

Lily laughed. 'No, I can't sing. I wish I could.'

'Yes, you can.'

She laughed again. 'You don't call that singing.'

'Yes, it was nice. Go on, sing it for me – please. I like that song.'

She shook her head and briefly bit her lip. Then, throwing dignity aside, she came in, singing softly along with the band. Her voice was low and light, slightly husky, with a fine little vibrato. A little embarrassed at her own bravado, she sang, avoiding his eyes:

> 'The water is wide, I cannot go o'er,
> Neither have I wings to fly.
> Give me a boat that will carry two,
> And both shall cross, my love and I.'

She broke off with a little laugh. 'That's it. I don't know any more.'

Joel clapped his hands. 'You've got a very nice voice. You really have.'

'Thank you,' she said. 'I can tell you're a man of taste.' Then, with an abrupt change of subject, she indicated the sketchbook that lay on the bench at his side. 'It's your turn to show off now,' she said. 'May I look at your sketches?'

He hesitated. 'As long as you're not too critical.' He held out the book.

'I can't draw a thing,' she said as she took it from him, 'so I'm in no position to criticise.'

Opening the book on her knees she went slowly through the pages, and every now and again gave a little wondering shake of her head. 'They're very fine,' she said. 'They're beautiful.' The pages were filled with pencil sketches. Some were of trees and plants and flowers and horses, and others were of buildings: houses and small cottages. There were three or four figure studies too, and coming upon the drawing of a bespectacled man sitting in a chair, Lily looked enquiringly at Joel.

'My father,' Joel said. 'There's one of my mother there too, somewhere.'

Lily turned a page and saw a picture of a young woman. 'Who's this? This isn't your mother.'

He smiled. 'Oh, no. She's the daughter of my father's partner. Simone Rojet, her name is. She's French.'

'She's very pretty.' Lily studied the fine draughtsmanship of the drawing, seeing how, in just a few lines, he had caught so much detail and feeling. She shook her head in wonder. 'Oh, it's really splendid.'

He gave a nod of gratitude. 'Well – thank you.'

'I don't pretend to know much about such things,' she said, 'but I've always loved to look at paintings and drawings and other works of art. An exhibition of paintings

51

came to Corster last year, and I went twice. It was of some of the works of those new painters, the Pre-Raphaelites. It was so wonderful.'

'Oh, yes,' he said, 'what it must be like to be a really great painter – like Turner, or one of the newer artists. I love them – the Pre-Raphaelites. Frederick Sandys, Millais, and that marvellous Arthur Hughes. Their work is so splendid. If I could ever turn out anything like *The Death of Chatterton*, or Millais' *Blind Girl* . . .' He came to a stop, as if slightly out of breath, and then gave a chuckle, laughing at himself, at the passion in his voice. 'Listen to me,' he said. 'I sound like a madman. Don't worry, it will pass.'

Lily did not laugh. 'No,' she said. 'What's wrong with having dreams, longings? We'd be nowhere without them.'

Along the bank one of the boys gave a little shout of enthusiasm, while further off the band struck up a military march. Lily said: 'And you're studying law. Could you not have studied to be a painter? I've read about famous colleges in London, like the Slade and Chelsea.'

'Ah, yes,' he said, 'but not to be, I'm afraid. That wouldn't be regarded as a real career. For a time, it was something I thought was a possibility, but in the end you have to face reality.' He paused. 'We have – certain courses to follow – and they must be followed.'

'Yes,' she said. 'I understand.' She looked at him in the afternoon light. There was a touch of sadness in the line of his lip, but even as she saw it, it was gone. She turned back to the sketchbook in her hands and turned to the next page, showing the drawing of a woman in a lace cap, sitting sewing. 'Is this your mother?' she said.

'Yes, it is.'

'Well – she looks a nice lady.'

'She is indeed. She's very kind, and very sweet.'

Lily smiled. 'I wonder what she'd say if she knew you were not out sketching, but sitting in the park talking to a strange young woman? What would she say, Joel?'

'You know,' he said, 'that's the first time you've used my name.'

She set the sketchbook down beside her on the seat. 'I don't know your other name,' she said.

'Nor I yours.'

'Clair,' she said. 'Lily Clair. Lily Mary Clair.'

'Ah – Lily Mary Clair.' He smiled warmly. 'Well, I'm glad to know that.'

'And you?'

'I'm Joel Asa Goodhart.'

'Asa – well, there's a famous name.'

'Famous?'

'*Our American Cousin*,' she said. 'The play that President Lincoln was watching when he was assassinated last year.'

'Oh, yes,' Joel said. 'Asa. The American cousin was Asa, wasn't he?'

'But Goodhart,' Lily said. 'I've only heard of one Goodhart – the big draper's stores in Corster and Bath.'

Joel said nothing, and Lily looked at him for a moment, then said, 'Is that you, Joel? Are you *that* Goodhart?'

He gave a little nod and said wryly, 'For my sins, I'm afraid so.'

'Really? And there's one in France too, I read.'

'In Paris, that's right.'

'How is that – that there's one in Paris?'

'My mother is French. She inherited the Paris store from her father.' He looked at Lily's wide eyes. 'You look – so surprised.'

'Well, I am. Of course I am.' She thought about it for a moment. 'So you'll be going into the family business, will you?'

'Eventually, yes, when I finish at university. Though I'm getting my hand in in the meantime, working at the stores during the summer break. Getting experience.'

She nodded. 'And studying to be a lawyer. Mm, I think you must have quite a future ahead of you, Joel.'

He merely smiled at this. Further along the bank the mallard drake and duck took to the water and moved smoothly away.

'If you can't be a schoolmistress,' Joel said, 'what d'you think you might do?'

'I don't know. Mr Micawber always thought something would turn up, but in my case – I'm not so sure. I don't know. Maybe I could go as a companion to a rich lady and travel the world.'

'Would you like to do that? Travel the world?'

'Well, it would be exciting – having never been further than Corster or Redbury. I can only imagine what those foreign cities must be like. I've read about them, of course, and they all sound so different – Paris, St Petersburg, Rome. And what about Venice, where they don't have any roads or turnpikes? The people have to travel on the canals in those two-fronted boats.'

As she finished speaking she realised that the music had stopped again, and then on the air came the sound of a distant church clock striking the hour of five. She sighed. 'Oh, dear, something's telling me that I'd better think about getting back.'

'Oh, must you go so soon? It's early yet.'

'It's time I went.' She retied the strings of her bonnet and picked up her bag. Joel stood up beside her.

From the bench by the pond they set off over the grass, joining a pathway that led to the gates. Out on the street they walked side by side until eventually they came to the Corster Road. A little distance along, Lily came to a stop.

'It's just a short way now,' she said.

'Shall I see you again?' Joel asked.

She had expected the question, part of her mind dreading

it, part hoping for it, and she was in turmoil. But she must say no. She must refuse him. For a while back there she had been a little carried away by the sheer pleasure of his company, and by the music and the sunshine, and for that time she had allowed herself to forget the reality of her situation. But as he had said, it had to be faced. She was a maid, a simple domestic. Whatever her aspirations, that was all she was.

'Shall I?' he said. 'Next Sunday? By the park gates?'

She said after a moment, 'I don't get much time off.'

'But you'll have a little time to spare, surely – after you get the old lady her dinner.'

She said nothing.

'Just a few minutes,' Joel said.

After a second she gave a nod. 'Yes – all right. Just for a while.'

He smiled. 'Good. That's excellent.'

'I must bring you your book back too.'

'Will you have finished it by then?'

'I don't know – but you must have it back.'

'I'm in no hurry for it. Keep it as long as you want.'

She said nothing to this, and they stood in silence for some moments, she avoiding his gaze, which she knew was fixed upon her. Then she gave a little nod, an awkward half-smile, and said, 'Well – goodbye, then.'

He smiled. 'Till next Sunday – yes, goodbye.'

She turned and started away. It was some fifty yards to the house, and over every inch of those fifty yards the repeating thought went through her brain that she was behaving like a fool. How could she have agreed to meet him again? No good could ever come of it.

She came to the gate and, turning, saw him still standing there, watching her. Then, suddenly, she was hurrying back towards him. As she came to a halt before him, she said without preamble, gabbling the words, 'I'm sorry, but

I can't see you next Sunday. I simply shan't have time. I'm very sorry.' A brief pause. 'Goodbye.'

'Oh, wait a second,' he said as she started away. 'What about – well – can't we meet on some other day?'

She turned back to face him. 'I – I don't know,' she stammered. 'Listen – I must go.' She turned away, and then immediately turned back to him again. 'Send me your address,' she said, 'and I'll send you back your book.'

He frowned. 'What? I don't want the book. You can keep it.'

'Oh, but –'

'It's just a book.'

She gave a little nod. 'Well – thank you.' Another little nod. 'I'm sorry,' she said. 'I'm really so sorry.' She turned away for the last time. 'Goodbye.'

As she walked away she could feel his eyes on her back. This time when she got to the gate, she did not look back.

The following Sunday afternoon, returning to the Haskins' after getting Mrs Shalcross's midday dinner, Lily took her usual route past the park. As she drew near the entrance she saw Joel there, sitting on a bench by the gates. For a moment she faltered in her step, and briefly considered changing direction, but he had his eyes on her, she could see, and as she approached, he got up from his seat and came towards her.

'See, you can't get rid of me that easily,' he said.

She stood self-consciously before him. She felt foolish and ill-kempt. Through carelessness in Mrs Shalcross's kitchen she had stained her dress, and now she could feel that a couple of her hair pins were coming loose.

'I began to think you weren't coming,' he said. 'Or maybe that you'd taken another route home.'

'I had to stay on with the old lady. I've been doing jobs for her around the house.' She shook her head. 'I – I can't stop, I'm afraid. I told Mrs Haskin I'd be back in good time.'

'Can't you spare a few minutes? Ten minutes won't hurt.'

When she did not answer, he said, 'Five minutes, then. Come and sit down for five minutes.' As he spoke there came from within the park the sound of the band striking up. 'There you are,' he said, 'here's the music – just for you.'

'No, really, I've got to go. I'm sorry.'

With her words she stepped away, and at once he moved along beside her.

They walked without speaking alongside the park railings, then crossed the street to turn at the corner of Nelson Way, Lily walking at a smart pace, her basket over her arm. The music of the band faded behind them. After they'd gone a little way, Joel said, chuckling, 'Well, you can certainly step it out, Lily. Good job I've got long legs.'

She slowed her pace a little. At the next corner she came to a halt. As Joel stopped beside her, she said, 'You don't need to come any further, thank you.' She felt the skin on her face hot, flushed. She wanted only to get away.

'What's the matter?' Joel said. 'Have I done something to offend you? Have I said something?'

'What? No, of course not.' She looked down, unable to meet his gaze.

'Then tell me what it is – what's wrong. It's like I've become some – some leper, or something.'

'Look,' she said, and took a step away, 'I've got to go, really I have.'

'Oh, no – don't.' His voice held a pleading tone. 'Not like this. I've done something to offend you. You must tell me what it is. Please. We were getting on so well, and then – then you suddenly changed towards me. I thought we were becoming friends.'

She gave a little shake of her head. 'We can't be.'

'No?' He frowned his puzzlement. 'Why is that? Have you discovered my secret past?'

'Your secret past?' She raised her eyes to him now.

'I'm joking, Lily. That's all.' He gave a little groan. 'I'm out of my depth here.'

'No,' she said, 'it is I who am out of my depth.'

His frown was back. 'Are you? How? In what way?'

She was silent for a second, then she said, 'I'm a general maid, a maid-of-all-work, and I can't see my situation changing dramatically. No matter how much I might wish it to.'

'Don't say that,' he said. 'Things could change for you. You could be a teacher one day, the way you want to be.'

'No.' She shook her head. 'This is the real world. No one's going to wave some magic wand. But that's not the point. Joel – I have to think of what might happen . . .' She came to a halt, unsure how to go on.

'What might happen?' he said.

'Yes, with you and me. You said you like me and –'

'Oh, I do. You know I do.'

'Yes,' she breathed, and gave a melancholy little smile. 'And it made me so glad to know that.'

'I thought you liked me too,' he said.

She made no response, and he added, 'I thought you did.'

Looking down at the dusty road, she murmured, 'You must know I do.'

He smiled. 'Then what is the problem?'

She hesitated, searching for words. 'It doesn't matter – if we like one another,' she said. 'Don't you see, it can't do any good. Just the contrary, in fact. I make my living, such as it is, in domestic service. I'm just a maidservant.'

'No!' he said with a note of passion in his whisper. 'You're not just a maidservant. You're a clever, intelligent girl. I think you're absolutely splendid – and you could be the best teacher a child ever had.'

His words gladdened her heart, and for a moment or two she basked in their warmth. Then, putting on a comical

58

little voice, in a heavy country accent, she said, 'O' course, you've got to know as I've been well brought up, sir. To be a good girl, I mean.' She ended the words with a little laugh that rang hollow in the afternoon.

Joel did not join in. Gravely he said, 'I know very well you're a good girl, Lily Clair, and I've never thought otherwise, not for one single moment.' He paused. 'I like you, Lily, so much.' His tone was softly earnest. 'And you know I mean that seriously.'

She was silent for a second, then she said, 'But I'm still a maid, Joel, and you're still the son of a wealthy man, a man with a position. And such a man has great hopes and plans for his son. And I'm sure he's taught you accordingly, and taught you well. Your mother, too. She has her own aspirations for you, and I daresay hers are not dissimilar to your father's. They want you to be happy and successful, and I'm sure that that entails making a good marriage, doesn't it?' Following a little silence she gave a nod. 'Of course it does. I'm quite sure that in their schemes they don't see you getting serious about some little general maid.'

'They want me to be happy, you're right there,' he said. 'And why shouldn't we be friends?'

'Don't you see? There's no future in a friendship for you and me. We move in different circles.'

'Times are changing, Lily.'

'Yes, no doubt they are. But they won't change quickly enough to affect us.' She gave a sigh, eyes fixed on the ground. 'I must go.'

'Lily,' he said, 'don't end it like this.'

'I've got to try and be sensible.' She briefly raised her eyes to his. 'Goodbye, Joel.'

Without waiting for a response she turned away, and left him standing there.

*

The following Sunday when she came by the park he was there again. As she drew closer he came towards her, greeting her with a smile and a hello.

'I didn't expect to see you here,' she said.

'Didn't you? Would you believe me if I said I just happened to be passing by?'

She had to smile. 'Well, no – I have to say I wouldn't.'

'No, and I wouldn't blame you. It wouldn't be the truth.' He paused. 'You said to me that my father would have taught me well, didn't you? Well, he's taught me many things, one of them being that I should never take no for an answer.'

'I'll remember that,' she said, then added, 'Though if you wait for me again next week you're going to wait a very long time.'

'Ah, yes, you're going home – to Compton Wells.'

'For a fortnight. I leave first thing Sunday morning.'

He gave a nod and sighed. 'And soon after you return I shall be off to France – and then come back for Cambridge, for the new term.'

He was studying her intently as he spoke, and she said after a moment, 'What's wrong? Have I got smuts on my nose?'

'I'm trying to read your expression,' he said. 'I'm wondering whether I dare ask you to walk with me for a spell – seeing as how I can't come and waylay you next Sunday.'

Her mouth broadened into a smile, and he put his head a little on one side and said, 'Oh, Lily, I appreciate everything you say, but let's not let a perfectly good friendship go to waste. We can be friends, I know we can. And I'd never see you get hurt, I promise you I wouldn't.'

'Oh, don't,' she said quickly. 'Don't make promises.'

'I mean it.'

'I know you do, but – I'm eighteen years old. Old enough to go through life with my eyes open.'

They stood for some moments without speaking, then he said, 'Well – are we going for a walk?'

Still not answering, she stood reconsidering.

'It's only a walk in the park,' he said. 'It's not a trip to the moon.'

'Yes. Yes, all right. Just for a little while.' After all, she said to herself, what harm could it do? It was just a little walk in the sun. And besides, she had made clear to him her reservations, her awareness of the barrier of their differing situations, and she would not allow anything to sway her from her position of commonsense.

Side by side they walked past the bandstand while the band played a lilting waltz melody. Lily said, 'I don't know this song,' to which Joel replied, 'It's called 'Gardenias for my Lady'. I heard it sung at the music hall.'

Lily listened to the strains of the music for a few seconds, then said, 'It's a very pretty tune,' and added, 'I don't think I've ever seen a gardenia. I wouldn't even know what one looks like. What colour are they?'

'White. They're white.'

'Do they grow in England?'

'I've no idea,' Joel said.

With the music following their steps they walked once more beside the pond, where the mallards again basked in the sun, and then sat for a little while talking and looking out over the water.

There was not much time, though, and only a little later Joel walked back with her in the direction of the Haskins' house. They came to a stop some fifty yards or so from the front gate.

Joel said with a sigh, 'The rest of the summer's going to fly by, I know it. Before you can say Jack Robinson it'll be over and I'll be back at Cambridge.'

'Oh, I envy you that,' Lily said.

'Going to Cambridge? Studying law?'

'Well, not necessarily to study law, but to be able to study – for years even.'

'They don't have ladies there, you know. There are no young ladies training to be lawyers.'

'That's not right,' she said. 'It's not fair. Why shouldn't there be women advocates? After all, Portia did pretty well.'

'Portia – oh, *The Merchant of Venice*. Yes, she did. But she had Shakespeare on her side.'

They laughed together. 'On the Sunday,' he said, 'when you come back – will you be in time to visit the old lady?'

'Yes. I'm getting back in the morning.'

'Then I'll wait for you by the gates – is that all right?'

'Well,' she said, smiling, looking off past his ear, 'it's a free country.'

Chapter Four

The following Sunday morning, the fifth of August, Lily set off to get her train for Compton Wells, sitting in the trap with Mr Haskin holding the reins. Although he often went into the factory for an hour or two on a Sunday, on this day he would be going to Henhurst to pick up Mrs Shalcross and bring her back to the house for midday dinner. It would be no inconvenience, he had said to Lily, to take her to the station first and then call for his mother-in-law. So, late that morning she sat beside him as the vehicle bounced and rumbled over the rough roads, and did her best to relax in his company. It was not so easy. It was not often that she found herself alone with him, and when it happened she invariably found herself a little in awe of him, a little intimidated by his rather jovial way and his teasing questions.

Today as they drove he began to speak of his friendship with Lily's father, recalling times they had shared when they were younger and had fought together with the British army. Lily was fascinated to hear his recollections, and glad of them too, for her father rarely made reference to his earlier days in the military. Afterwards, with one subject leading to another, Mr Haskin went on to speak of his work at the factory, and related two or three anecdotes concerning some of the customers and employees. He had a comical, witty way with his stories, and Lily found herself genuinely amused. As he went on, she remarked on the long hours he worked. He seemed to take so little rest, she observed.

'The work's got to get done,' he replied. 'It's as simple as that. And it's not always possible to get the right people.'

'Have you,' Lily said, tentatively, 'ever thought about employing more women at the company, sir?'

'Well,' he said, keeping his eyes on the road, 'we've got Miss Carter working in the office.'

'Yes, I know, but she's the only one, and she's an older, maiden lady – and your partner is her brother. I meant – would you employ younger women?'

'Such as you, Lily, you mean.' He turned and glanced at her now.

'Well – yes.'

'I reckon you've got tired of bein' a maid, have you?'

'Well – I was eighteen last month, sir, and almost three years I've been with you and Mrs Haskin. A maid's petty place only lasts a year, generally. No maid stays in a post this long. Particularly at my age.' She added quickly, 'No offence, sir, you understand.'

'None taken.' He paused. 'Well,' he said after a moment, 'I don't doubt that you're too smart to go maiding all your working life. You're your father's daughter, and you've got a good head on your shoulders, so it's not surprising you'd be wanting something better. Though I don't mind telling you that Mrs Haskin and I would be sorry to see you go.'

'Thank you, sir.'

'Mind you, I reckon at your age many girls are leaving service anyway, going off and getting married.' He grinned. 'Isn't there some young man for you, Lily? Some nice young fellow with a bob or two in his pocket who's desperate to marry you? Pretty girl like you, there should be. Must be somebody round Whitton way. Not that you get much time for courting, though, I daresay – and it's all very well for you to be reading your books, but there are other things in life.'

Lily said nothing to this, but looked straight ahead. Mr Haskin too was silent for a moment, then he said, 'But as for coming to work at Silver – it's something we can think about. I've no doubt you'd be an asset in the office, and perhaps Miss Carter could do with some assistance. Maybe I'll talk to Mr Carter and Mr Horsham. Leave the matter with me. I won't forget, I promise.'

'Thank you, sir.'

He raised his head. 'Enough of business for now, Lily. Look at that sky – you've got some nice weather ahead for your holiday.'

At the station entrance, he asked whether she wanted any help with her bags, but she gratefully declined his offer. All she carried in the way of luggage was an old carpet bag lent to her by Mrs Haskin, and her reticule. Mr Haskin wished her a good holiday, and a few minutes after bidding him farewell, she had bought her ticket and was making her way along the platform.

There was a delay on the journey, and the train was halted on the tracks for some little time. As a result it was late getting in to Compton Wells. Eventually, though, Lily arrived, and after the short omnibus journey, made her way along the lane to her home. She did so with no feeling of joy. Her two weeks' holiday stretched out before her, and in spite of her hopes, she knew from past experience that it would not be a time of unalloyed pleasure.

Her stepmother was in the kitchen when Lily entered, sorting linens at the table. It had been three months since Lily had last seen her, but in spite of the time of separation there was no warm welcome for her, indeed nothing of any welcome at all. Not that she would have expected such a thing.

'Hello, Mother,' Lily said as she stepped from the scullery.

Mrs Clair flicked her a glancing look and said, 'We expected you ages ago.'

'Yes, the train got held up. There were sheep on the line near Cornley.'

'Sheep on the line.' Mrs Clair shook her head, as if such a thing had never been heard of. 'Well, we've had dinner. We couldn't wait all day.'

'That's all right – I'm not hungry. Is Father about? Tom?'

'Your father's down the garden. Your brother's gone back to the farm. Dora's out playing.'

'I'll put my things away and get changed,' Lily said. 'Then I'll go and say hello to Father.'

When she had changed into her working dress and apron, she went back downstairs and out into the yard. She found her father at the lower end of the garden, near the small orchard, tying back some raspberry canes. He straightened as Lily approached, and gave her a smile.

'Hello, girl,' he said. 'So you got here, did you.'

'Hello, Father. Yes, I got here a minute ago.'

He gestured to the raspberry canes. 'I just want to finish this, then I'll come up. I could do with a cup o' tea, and I expect you could as well.'

'Yes, I could. The carriage was full, and it was so warm.'

After a moment he resumed his task, and Lily bent to help him. As they worked he asked her how she was faring at the Haskins', and she replied that all was well. It was, she knew, what he wanted to hear.

A little later they returned to the house, where Lily found that Dora had come in from her play.

'What did you bring me?' Dora asked her. 'Lily, did you bring me anything?'

Lily replied that she had indeed brought her a little present, and gave her a little flaxen-haired doll, which she had scrimped for out of her wages. Dora was thrilled with the gift, and chattered over it excitedly.

Later on, Lily made tea, which, because it was Sunday, was served in the front parlour. Tom came in from his work

66

at the farm soon after five-thirty, but by the time he had washed, and changed his clothes, the tea things had been cleared away and the parlour was shut for another week.

As the days passed, Lily found herself increasingly eager to get back to Whitton. There had been little pleasurable relaxing, and it was a disappointing time. During the days her father and brother had been out at work, the latter from early in the mornings until quite late in the evenings. On a few occasions, with Dora for company, Lily had gone off on various errands, but for the most part she had no recourse but to remain around the house, helping her stepmother with the chores. So she spent time cleaning, doing laundry, washing dishes, mending the family's clothes and lending a hand in the garden. It was what was expected of her. She was disappointed too, to find that her relationship with her stepmother had not improved in any way. Mrs Clair had not mellowed with the passing of time. If anything, Lily found, she seemed even more prickly, humourless and disagreeable with her stepchildren. Lily tried on several occasions to bridge the gap that was ever there between them, but with no success. Her attempts at initiating a friendly conversation were invariably met with coldness and a certain disdain. As she had done a hundred times in the past, Lily could only urge herself to accept the situation, and acknowledge that it would never be mended.

At least, though, she was able to spend a little time with her brother, during those few hours between his getting in from the farm and going off to his bed. After supper on the Saturday, her last evening, the two of them walked down the garden to the little orchard. It was past Tom's usual bed-time, but he would be up and out of the house the next morning before Lily had risen.

'You hardly get a day off,' Lily observed. 'Going into the farm even on Sunday.'

'I want to,' he said, 'and they need me. Work don't stop just because it's Sunday. The livestock don't know a Sunday from a Sat'day. The cows still 'ave to be milked, the sheep still 'ave to be fed, the stables still 'as to be cleaned out.' He gave a sigh. 'Oh, Lil, it's been grand havin' you back for a while, and I'm sorry you're goin'. I just wish I was goin' too.' There was the shadow of sadness in his face. They had come to a stop beneath an apple tree. Up above their heads bats dipped and soared in the fading light.

'Oh, believe me,' Lily said, 'I'm not going back to anything special. Far from it, and I hope it won't be that much longer before I'm doing something different.'

'Have you given up all thoughts of teaching?' Tom asked.

'I'm afraid I've had to,' she said. Then added, brightening a little, 'But there'll be something else. I live in hopes.'

'Of course you do,' he said. 'Anyway, maybe you'll meet some nice fella and get married.'

'Yes,' she said dryly, 'and pigs might fly.'

He laughed. 'Still, summat good'll 'appen, you'll see. Your time'll come. Mine too. One day I shall get away as well.'

Soon after breakfast the next morning, Lily and her father prepared to set out for the station. As Mr Clair came into the kitchen carrying Lily's bag, Mrs Clair said, 'Lord almighty, you'd think the girl's a child, I swear. She's eighteen years old. Ain't she capable of getting to the station on her own?'

'It's not light, her bag,' he said. 'And it's a longish walk to the omnibus.'

'You mollycoddle 'em, that's what you do,' Mrs Clair said.

Mr Clair said nothing to this, but put on his hat. 'Come on, then,' he said to Lily. 'Let's go, or you'll miss your train.'

He carried her bag along the lane, while Lily walked at his side holding her reticule. At the corner they waited for an omnibus, and so eventually got to the station.

On the platform, in good time for the train, they sat on a bench for a minute or two in silence as other travellers came and went. Lily was conscious of her father's nearness, of their being alone together, and glad of the situation. Throughout the days of her holiday there had rarely been such periods.

'Well,' he said after a while, 'it's back to Mr and Mrs Haskin for you now.'

'Yes. You know, Father, I've been there almost three years now.'

'Is it that long?'

'Three years come the twenty-third.' She paused. 'I can't stay a maid all my life.'

He gave a slow nod. 'No more you can't, I s'pose.'

'I spoke to Mr Haskin on the way here,' she said. 'I was very daring. I asked him about getting a job in his factory. I thought maybe I could work at the books, look after the ledgers, do some accounting, help with the orders and the letters. That sort of thing. He said he'll give it some thought.'

'Well – he's a good man. If he can help you, I'm sure he will. Would you like to work in an office?'

'It isn't so much what I'd *like* – it's what's *allowed*.'

'Allowed?'

'Oh Father, I don't know what a woman is to do with her life. I mean – men can do anything they want, but women can do so little. If they're not wives, then what are their hopes? To be a seamstress? A flower-seller? Maybe slave in some cotton mill or shoe factory? As likely as not a girl will be a domestic somewhere – a servant at someone's beck and call. When I think back to how I had hopes of being a schoolteacher – oh, how improbable it all seems. Do you know, at the universities, such as Cambridge, they don't even allow females to study law?'

After a moment, her father said, 'I wish it had been possible for you to continue with your 'prenticeship at the school, Lily. I do so wish it. It just wasn't. I'm sorry.'

'It's all right, Father,' she said. 'I know you did what you could.' She turned to him and smiled. 'I shall be all right, don't worry.'

'Yes. I'm sure you will. And you know, you've always got a home. If the worst happens, you've always got a home.'

She could think of no response. On the platform before them, people began to stir. Lily drew her bag to her. 'Here comes my train,' she said.

Sitting in the carriage, she tried to read. She had brought with her a book she had borrowed from the circulating library, a copy of *The Small House at Allington*. Concentrating on it was almost impossible, though; not because of the distractions – a very noisy family – but due to her own preoccupations. This day would see her back in her routine, see her going to Henhurst to visit Mrs Haskin's mother to give her her Sunday dinner. And perhaps, afterwards, Joel would be waiting for her by the park. Joel. She had thought of him so often during her stay in Compton Wells. Through all the dreary days with their tedious routines of endless chores, he had come to her unbidden in little vignettes of memory, and she had imagined him in a score of different ways, seeing his face against the light, hearing his laugh, words he had spoken. And today, later this very day, she would see him again.

Lily had hardly been an hour in the house at Whitton following her return, when she had to leave for Henhurst to prepare Mrs Shalcross's dinner. She left with assurances to Mrs Haskin that she would not be late back. On her arrival at the little cottage near the station, she was greeted warmly after her absence, and the old lady asked her about her time in Compton Wells. Afterwards, when the table had been cleared, and the dishes and pots were washed, Mrs Shalcross wanted to sit and continue her gossip over a cup of tea, as was her wont. Lily, though anxious to get away, was forced to comply, and sat at the table sipping from her cup. Eventually, however she could take her leave.

As she approached the park she became aware of the stronger beat of her heart, and was a little shocked by it. Would Joel be there? The question had haunted her, and though she had told herself that if he was not waiting it would make no difference either way, she had known that it would.

As she turned the corner of Charles Street, the park came into view. There was a little knot of people gathered about the gates, and for a moment her beating heart sank a little, for there was no sign of Joel. But then the group moved on, and he was revealed there, sitting on the bench. She quickened her pace and, as she did so, she saw him catch sight of her. In an instant he had got to his feet and was striding to meet her.

'Well,' he said, grinning broadly, standing before her, 'here you are.' He was dressed a little less formally than before, wearing a brown corduroy cap, and a light grey jacket with a blue cravat under the soft collar of his shirt. In the lapel of his jacket was pinned a little white rosebud.

'Here I am.' Lily smiled back.

'At last. At *last*. Oh, those three weeks were *three long* weeks. More like four or five – or six even.'

'Six?' She smiled. 'Not seven?'

'Seven, yes. Eight – whatever you want. They were interminable.'

Her smile grew wider, while her heart beat ever more strongly.

'Anyway,' he said, 'you're here now.'

'Yes. Have you been waiting long?'

'Just half-an-hour or so. And impatient as the devil.'

The music of the band came wafting out of the park, striking up a jaunty tune. The smile on her face felt inane. She said, making conversation, glancing up, 'Well, the weather's kind again.'

'It is indeed. Have you got time for a little stroll?'

She so wanted to say yes, and to walk with him in the park under the sun, but she shook her head. 'No, I haven't, I'm sorry. I promised Mrs Haskin I'd get back.'

'Oh – and I hoped you'd got some time off.'

'Yes, but – being away – there's so much to catch up on. I promised her.'

He gave a nod. 'Ah, well, if that's the case I'll have to put up with it, but I'll walk back with you a way, if you don't mind.'

Together they stepped out, past the gates, with the music drifting behind them. As they walked he asked her about her time with her family, after which she asked him about himself, how he had been spending his time since they had last met. He replied that he had been working in the family business, helping out in the stores, travelling between Corster and Bath. 'And soon, of course,' he added, 'I'll be off to Paris.'

'Ah, yes.' There was a little note of dismay in her voice, a note that she could not hide. 'When are you going?'

'A week come Tuesday, the twenty-eighth.' He paused. 'My father is there, and he wants me there too. A little more experience at the store before I come back for the new term at Cambridge.'

'Which is when?'

'October the second.'

'Oh. And – how long will you be away?'

'It depends on my father's wishes. For several weeks, anyway. I'm going to have very little time here at home before I go back to Cambridge.'

Lily's heart was sinking. Their paths were diverging so soon, so quickly. There she had been wondering and pondering on the wisdom of meeting him again, and circumstances were making the decision for her. Perhaps, though, it was meant to be. Perhaps it was for the best.

They had reached the corner where the lane joined the Corster road, and came to a stop, facing one another.

'I don't want to go to France,' Joel said, 'but I haven't got a choice.' Then, brightening, he added, 'But there's still *next* Sunday. We can meet then, can't we? Please? Don't tell me you've got to work then as well.'

'No,' she heard herself say, 'I should have part of the time free.'

He grinned. 'Good. So – we can meet.'

'Yes – if you wish.'

He smiled. 'Oh, I wish. I do most certainly wish.'

Lily caught his infectious smile, but said nothing.

Joel groaned again, theatrically. 'I'm spinning this out, you realise. I know you've got to go in, but I don't want you to.'

'I know, but I must,' she said.

He nodded and gave a deep sigh, theatrical still. 'Well, I can't prevent it. But anyway – I'll see you in a week.'

'Yes.'

'The longest week it'll ever be.'

She grinned, moved from one foot to another, and shifted the basket on her arm. 'Well – I must go.'

'I know.'

'Yes.'

Neither moved.

'So – I'll see you next Sunday.' He reached out, took her

hand and gently pressed it. 'Till Sunday. Goodbye, Lily.'

She avoided his gaze; she had to. 'Goodbye.'

'Say my name. Please.'

'. . . Joel . . .'

He smiled. 'Yes,' he breathed. 'Yes. That's it.'

She smiled with him. 'Goodbye . . . Joel.'

'Goodbye, Lily.'

When she reached the gate she looked back and saw him standing there, watching her. He raised his hand in a wave, and she waved back, then turned and hurried up the path.

Chapter Five

On Friday afternoon, Lily was working in the scullery with Mrs Haskin when there came a light tap at the door. Mrs Haskin went to open it and revealed there a young boy of twelve or so, standing a little out of breath and touching his hand to his cap. 'Why, it's Willie,' Mrs Haskin said in surprise. 'What are you doing here, lad?' And then, with a touch of alarm: 'Is there something wrong?'

The boy nodded vigorously. 'It's Mrs Shalcross, mum. She've 'ad a fall.'

'A fall?' Mrs Haskin clutched a hand to her bosom. 'Oh, dear God. Tell me what happened.'

'Our mam sent me round next door to see 'er,' the boy said, 'and I found 'er on the floor. So I fetched our mam and she come round, and then sent me to tell you. The old lady's quite poorly, mum.'

Mrs Haskin hovered on the spot, flustered. She thanked the boy for coming with the message, then when he had gone turned to Lily and said, 'Well, there's nothing for it, but I must go to her. As soon as I can. I'll leave you to tell Mr Haskin what's up, and to get his dinner for him when he comes in. All right?'

'Yes, of course.'

Mrs Haskin gave a deep sigh. 'I might well have to stay overnight. We'll see.'

In a few minutes she was ready to leave and, carrying a bag of various foodstuffs and some nightclothes in case she was required to remain, she set off from the house.

That evening, when Mr Haskin arrived home and enquired after his wife, Lily told him what had happened, and said that she would be preparing supper for him.

The meal was an unusual one that evening, for never before since Lily's arrival at the house had Mrs Haskin been absent from the table. Lily served the food and sat in her usual place and ate a little self-consciously. The meal passed almost in complete silence. Lily hoped that Mr Haskin would make some reference to her approach to him concerning work at the factory, but he seemed to have no wish to converse, and she herself could not bring up the matter. She was relieved when the meal came to an end and she could clear the table. By the time she had washed the dishes there was still no sign of Mrs Haskin, and it seemed likely that she would not be returning that night.

When she did appear, it was late the next morning. She came upstairs to the main bedroom where Lily was just finishing making the bed, and Lily at once asked how Mrs Shalcross was.

'I'm afraid she's not well at all,' Mrs Haskin replied. She was still wearing her hat. 'I haven't come to stay,' she added. 'I've only come to pick up a few things, and as soon as I've had some tea I shall start back.'

In the kitchen Mrs Haskin sat at the table and drank her cup of tea. 'Well, I have to say Mother's very lucky,' she said. 'No bones broken, I mean. It could have been so much worse. As it is she's got a badly wrenched shoulder, a bruised arm and a nasty bump on her head. And she's very shocked, of course, and with all that, along with her cold, she's in a poorly way.'

A short while later she prepared to leave the house again. 'Now you tell Mr Haskin I shan't be back till Monday,' she said, standing in the doorway. 'Monday at the earliest. I'll try to get back then, but it'll depend on how Mother is.'

'So I shan't be needed to go to Mrs Shalcross on Sunday,' Lily observed.

'No, that won't be necessary; I shall be there meself. You'll have to get Mr Haskin his Sunday dinner, but you'll manage that all right, I've no doubt. Then you'll be free the rest of the day.'

When Mr Haskin got in from work that evening Lily gave him his wife's message and prepared supper for the two of them. When they had eaten he moved to his chair by the range, lit his pipe and stretched out his legs. Then he took from a cupboard a bottle, poured himself a measure of liquor, and sat sipping. It was not something he did when Mrs Haskin was around.

That night when Lily lay in bed, she thought about the coming day. Joel would be waiting for her by the park gates. It would be the last time she saw him before he went off to France.

As he often did on a Sunday morning, Mr Haskin went into the factory the next day. Before he left, he told Lily that he would return for dinner about one o'clock. Later, as the hour approached, Lily set the table and began to cook the meal. She had started the preparations in good time, so that everything would be ready as soon as Mr Haskin returned. She kept an eye on the weather too, and was relieved to see it remaining bright and fair.

But the minutes went by, and Mr Haskin did not appear.

When he was not there by one-thirty, Lily changed out of her working dress into her best, then put her apron back on. As she moved from her room she heard the sound of the cob's hooves coming round the side of the house. A few minutes later, as she began to busy herself once more in the kitchen, Mr Haskin came through the door.

He was in a jovial mood. He poured himself some beer from the cask in the scullery, and sat back in his chair with a sigh of pleasure. Eyeing his display of ease with a little dismay, Lily said that dinner was nearly ready, to which he replied, 'In a while, girlie, in a while. Let me get my breath for a minute,' and she could do nothing but mark time and wait. At last, to her relief, he said, 'Right, Lily, now we'll have our bit of dinner.'

As he took his seat, Lily set out the food and then took her own usual place. While Mr Haskin ate with a good appetite she ate sparingly, only waiting for the time to pass when she could clear the dishes away. He looked at the small amount of food on her plate and said, 'You ain't eating, girl. Not sickening for something, are you?'

'No, sir,' Lily replied. 'I'm just not hungry.'

'Not hungry,' he said with a little snort. 'You eat like a sparrow on a diet.'

He went on then to remark that the food was excellent, and on how odd it felt not to have Mrs Haskin around. And the long case clocked ticked on. When Lily glanced at it and saw the hands at two-forty-five, she pictured Joel moving to the park gates and sitting down to wait.

At last, however, the meal was over and Lily was able to start clearing the dishes away. As she did so, he said to her with an approving little nod, 'I just noticed, Lily, you're lookin' mighty sharp today. You got on a new frock, have you?'

She felt herself colouring slightly. 'No, sir,' she said, avoiding his amused gaze as she moved to the door. 'I've had it ages.'

'Well, I guess I can't be the most observant man, can I? You've done something to your hair as well.'

With a self-conscious smile she said, 'I just gave it a bit of curl, sir. I did it with the poker.'

'And very nice it looks too.'

'Thank you, sir.' She hovered in the doorway. 'Would you like tea, sir?'

'No, thanks, I shall have a drop more beer in a minute. I'll help myself.'

When she had washed and dried the dishes she carried some of the china back into the kitchen to put it away in the dresser. Mr Haskin watched her working for a minute or two then said:

'I just realised, Lily – it's your time off, isn't it?'

She paused before answering. 'Yes, sir.'

'Course it is. What am I thinking of? There I've been taking my time over everything and it's your afternoon off.' He gave a nod. 'Of course – that's why you're all in your Sunday best.' He waved a hand. 'You better get off, then, girl.'

'Thank you, sir.' She could not show her relief. 'Is there anything else you want before I go?'

'No, I'll manage. You get off wherever you're going.'

'Thank you, sir.'

Upstairs in her room she took off her apron and put on her bonnet and a light linen jacket. A final touch at her hair and she was as ready as she could be.

Downstairs she moved towards the rear door, and reached it as Mr Haskin came from the kitchen to stand in the doorway.

'You're off, then, Lily, I see.'

'Yes, sir.'

He smiled. 'I'm tempted to ask where you're a-goin'. Lookin' like that, I mean. Not to Sunday school I'll wager.'

Lily said nothing, but stood with one hand on the door catch.

'What is it you do on your Sunday afternoons when you leave Henhurst?' he said.

She gave a shrug. 'Well – when the weather's nice I might go for a walk in the park. Sometimes the brass band's playing. That's very nice. Or sometimes I get the train into Corster. I've been to the museum there, and the art gallery.'

'Oh, the museum and the art gallery. Very cultural indeed.' His smile was broad. 'I'm glad to hear you're improving your mind. I'm sure your father would approve.' His smile grew wider. 'Are you sure you haven't got some young fellow out there? You sure there's not some young man waiting for you?'

Feeling her face flushing, she shook her head, and Mr Haskin watched her discomfort and gave a little chuckle. 'Oh, I reckon you're a dark horse, you are, Lily Clair,' he said. 'Well, anyway, I hope he's somebody your father would approve of. But I'm sure he must be. Smart girl like you.'

Moments went by, and Lily remained with her hand on the door catch. Then Mr Haskin said, 'Anyway, you get off, my girl. Don't take any notice of my teasin'. You go and have your walk, or whatever you've got planned. And let's hope the weather stays fine for you.'

She nodded. 'Yes, sir. Thank you.'

'And by the way, that little matter you talked to me about – the possibility of a job at Silver's – well, I haven't forgotten it. Mr Horsham's away right now, but when he gets back we'll have a word.'

'Thank you, sir.'

'Not at all.' He smiled at her. 'Well, then – off you go.'

Seconds later she was outside and walking to the gate.

She passed St Peter's church as she came around the corner into Park Street, and as she did so the clock on the tower struck four. He would not be there, surely he would not be there now. She hurried on. The day had continued warm, and now there was a haze over the sun had brought a little humidity to the air, and had the perspiration breaking out under her arms. She could feel it as she stepped out. She should have left off her jacket, she told herself. She could feel the sweat at her hairline too, under the rim of her bonnet.

She saw him as she came out of Park Street. He was sitting on the bench outside the gates, but facing away from her, clearly expecting her arrival from another direction. From the park came the music of the band.

She had almost reached his side when he turned and saw her approaching. His face lit up, and he rose at once from his seat. He was in his shirtsleeves; his jacket lay on the seat of the bench.

'You got here.' He was smiling, his relief and pleasure evident. 'I was about to leave. I'd just about given up.'

'I'm so sorry. I got held up.'

'Well, thank the Lord I hung on for a while.' He gestured off. 'And you came from the wrong direction.'

'I know. I didn't go to Henhurst today. I've come from the Haskins'. I couldn't get away any earlier.'

'It doesn't matter. You're here now, that's the important thing. I'm just glad to see you.'

His smile shone into her face and she lowered her eyes. She was conscious of the beating of her heart, not due only to her hurrying through the streets.

Next to his jacket on the bench where he had been sitting lay his small sketchbook. She glanced down at it and said, 'Well, at least you haven't been idle while you were waiting, I'm glad to see.'

'No, not at all.' He picked up the book. 'I actually managed to do a little work. Though I can't say my concentration was that special.' He lifted his hands. 'Well? So give me the good news or the bad news. Are you free for a while, or have you got to go rushing off again?'

'No, it's all right,' she said, smiling back. 'I'm not expected back at the house for a while yet.'

'Well, that's excellent. Just excellent. So – what would you like to do? Shall we walk a little?'

'Yes – all right.'

'To the pond, yes?' He looked up at the sky, where the

81

sun lurked behind the cloudy haze. 'Is there rain up there, d'you think?'

She followed his glance. 'Perhaps, but not just yet, let's hope.'

They went through the gates into the park, the music coming louder as they moved on towards the bandstand. This time, though, they did not linger to listen, but passed on by, continuing at a slow pace down towards the pond. All the benches about the pond's rim were occupied, but Joel at once laid his jacket on the dry grass, and after a second's hesitation Lily sat down on it. He sat beside her, then took his cap off and laid it with his sketchbook. He sat hunched over, with his arms round his knees. She would have liked to take off her jacket too, but she was afraid there might be damp patches under her arms.

'I was so afraid you weren't coming,' he said, turning to her. 'The minutes were going by and there was no sign of you. I began to imagine all kinds of happenings. The worst of all being that you'd decided not to come.'

For fear of saying too much, she did not know how to reply. The music of the band drifted over the grass, filling in the little silence between them. 'You hear what they're playing?' he said. 'That song – 'The Water is Wide'. Time for you to sing again.'

She gave a little laugh. 'Oh, no! No more singing – and no more whistling either.'

He groaned. 'Not even by special request?'

'Not even by special request. Once was one time too many.'

There were other young couples around them, lounging in the grass, some of them sweethearts, sitting or lying with their arms entwined. There were children there too, running about in the course of their play, or moving about at the water's edge with their boats and sailing ships.

Joel asked Lily why she had not been to Henhurst to get

Mrs Shalcross's dinner and she told him of the old lady's fall, and that Mrs Haskin had gone to be with her.

'And now you've got the rest of the day off, have you?' he said.

'Well – until half past eight or so. I don't ever get in later than that.'

He nodded. 'Then I'll have to make sure we make good use of the time.'

Into their view there came then a young girl of thirteen or so, with a basket over her arm, halting by the people who sat on the benches or wandered beside the paths. She was selling artificial flowers, and after a little while she came to where Lily and Joel were sitting.

'Buy a pretty flower, sir?' she said to Joel, and he looked up at her and smiled. She crouched on the grass and set down her basket of colourful blossoms.

'You asked about a gardenia,' Joel said to Lily. 'D'you remember? Let's see what we've got here.' He took from the basket three or four little sprays of flowers and laid them on the grass.

'Are they gardenias?' Lily asked. He gave a little laugh. 'Darned if I know.' Then said to the girl, 'Have you any? Have you any gardenias?'

The girl gave a little shrug. She was thin-looking, with pale skin and pale hair. 'I only got what's 'ere, sir, and I wouldn't know what a gardenia looks like.' She touched one of the little sprays that lay in the grass. 'I makes 'em meself. Silk and linen and such. Pretty, ain't they?' Her smile lit up her face.

Joel nodded. 'They are indeed. They're very pretty.' Then to Lily: 'Which one will you have?'

She gave a little shake of her head. 'Really – it's not necessary.'

'Oh, go on,' he said. 'Which one?'

'Well – you choose.'

'Right.' He eschewed the flowers laid on the turf and dipped into the basket and brought out a little spray of mauve blossoms. 'Gardenias or no,' he said, 'these'll do fine.' He held them out to Lily. 'Yes?'

'Yes,' she smiled, and took the flowers and moved as if to hold them to her nostrils, but stopped, while the girl said, 'They ain't got no smell, miss. They ain't real, they're just 'and-made.'

The girl handed Lily a pin then, and Lily fixed the little mauve spray to the lapel of her jacket. As she did so, Joel paid the girl her two or three coppers and she scooped up the flowers from the grass and dropped them back into her basket. Then, wishing the two of them a good day, she went on her way.

'They're nothing special,' Joel said, watching as Lily adjusted the flowers, 'but I couldn't refuse her, could I?'

'I'm glad you didn't,' Lily said. 'Anyway, they're very pretty. And they're very nicely made.'

She glanced up to find him studying her, his dark eyes almost piercing, and she felt herself colouring slightly under his gaze. 'Yes?' she said. 'What is it?'

'Ah, Lily,' he said on a little sigh, 'you talk about pretty – And if you're not the prettiest girl a chap ever set eyes on . . . well, I don't know . . .'

She did not know what to say, and took a breath and said nothing.

'And I don't mean I just discovered that,' he added. 'I thought it from the very first moment I saw you, sitting in that little room at the factory while the rain was tipping down outside. I thought then – my word! here's a champion-looking girl if you ever want one.' He paused and gave a little laugh. 'And a chap does, you know. Oh, indeed he does. Well, this one does, most certainly he does.'

He laughed again, and Lily laughed too, and she felt so close to him, and so admired, and so very happy. It didn't matter that she still felt the dampness under her arms and around the line of her hat band, and that there was dust on her white gloves and her right shoe was scuffed at the toe. She was there with him, and he was so handsome in the grass, and his smile was so white and so warm, and she felt a gladness and a joy and a thrill that she had never known in her life before.

'I can't believe it,' he said, giving a harsh little groan. 'Off to France on Tuesday. Just two days away.' He groaned again and dramatically put his head in his hands. Raising it again, he added, 'I'm not going to see you again for ages – unless I can get back for a few days before I go on to Cambridge. Anyway –' he gave a little shrug, 'we'll have to see.'

He sat for a few moments looking at her while the music of the band drifted on the breeze. Keeping his eyes on her, he ran fingers through his hair. Then, taking up his sketch-book, he said, 'I want to draw you. I want a picture of you, something to keep while I'm away.'

'Now?' she said. 'You want to draw me now?'

'Of course now. There won't be another opportunity before I go away.' He was already opening the sketchbook, turning the leaves to a fresh, unmarked page. From his shirt breast pocket he drew out three or four pencils, looked at them and selected one. From his trousers pocket he took a small pen-knife, opened it to expose the blade, and then sharpened the pencil lead to a fine point. 'There.' He closed the knife and laid it down beside his cap. 'Now – pay attention, please – Mr Leonardo Da Vinci is all set. One masterpiece coming up.'

Lily sat up a little straighter. 'I feel foolish,' she said, 'and very self-conscious. Are you sure you wouldn't rather do a sketch of the pond, or the trees by the bandstand.'

'Hush,' he said, smiling. 'I've got the subject I want, right here. Now – just relax. I'll try not to be too long.'

85

'My hair,' Lily said in mild protest. 'I'm not prepared for this.'

'You look splendid,' he said. 'I wouldn't have you look any other way.' Then, a little sternly, 'Now – please – keep still.'

She remained then unmoving, sitting on his jacket on the grass, while all around them the life of the park went on – illustrated by the shouts of children playing, the voices of adults calling to their dogs, the music of the band. The minutes meandered by. In her own silence Lily sat looking past his shoulder towards the pond. When he raised his head to look at her it was not to make eye contact but to measure, to observe, to absorb the picture before him, to transfer the perception to his pencil. He sighed a little, and groaned now and again, but then sometimes nodded in qualified approval. And so, under his moving fingers the drawing took shape.

Several melodies had come and gone from the band before he gave a deeper sigh, leant back a little, studying the sketch through half-closed eyes, and gave a final nod, saying with the gesture that it was finished.

'Well,' he said, 'for better or worse, that'll have to do for now.'

Lily relaxed, her body bending out of the unaccustomed rigidity. 'Am I allowed to look?'

'I suppose you must.'

He held out the sketchbook and she took it from him. To her the drawing looked quite exquisite. He seemed to have caught it all, even those things that she would rather he had not. There was her slightly pointed chin, her deep-set eyes, there the loosening ringlets of her dark hair, the locks relaxing again into their natural straightness.

'I haven't done you justice,' he said, watching her as she gazed at the drawing. 'You're so much better-looking than that.'

'No,' she said. 'No. You've made me look – beautiful.'

'You *are*.' He leant forward a little. 'I never met anyone so beautiful before.'

She did not raise her eyes; she did not dare. As she continued to study the drawing, he said, 'I've met a lot of young ladies here and there, and there's a few times I've been attracted to them, and –' He broke off, then added, 'Look at me, please.' His voice was gentle. 'Please.'

She looked up, forcing herself to meet his gaze.

'Yes, a few times,' he said. 'Oh – the pretty girls around Corster and Bath, and around Cambridge, and in Paris. But there's none like you, Lily – and I don't only mean the way you look. Though, Lord knows, that's special enough.'

Held in his dark glance, she wanted to say *Oh, I know what you mean*! For she did. It was becoming clear to her; now she was realising it, facing it. Over the past few years she had got a glad eye from several youths in Compton Wells and Whitton or on her trips into Corster. In Whitton the postman's assistant had winked at her, as had the butcher boy, and the baker's boy – and there were times when she had acknowledged that they were handsome, these young men, and vital, and charming. But it had gone no further. She had taken their winks and their sweet or saucy comments, and for moments perhaps they had brought a little thrill, but then she had let them go. But not now. Not with this young man. This Joel.

There's none like you, Lily, he had said, and his words repeated over and over in her brain. And whereas in the past she would have answered a wink, an approach, with deliberate silence or a witty retort, now she could only sit with her heart beating against her ribs, feeling herself held in the spell of his gaze, and the echo of his words.

The band was playing 'In Amsterdam Where the Tulips Grow'. Lily lowered her eyes from Joel's gaze and looked down again at the sketch. After a moment she turned the pages back, looking once more at the sketches she had seen. There was the one of the young woman, Simone.

'She really is very pretty,' Lily said, 'and very elegant too.'

'Oh, yes,' Joel said. 'Elegant indeed.'

'And you say she's a cousin of yours.'

'Second cousin, yes.' He paused. 'I think there were expectations that she'd become even closer in the family.'

'What d'you mean?'

'There were hopes – between my father and her parents, that she and my brother might eventually marry.'

'And it's not going to happen?'

'No, I wouldn't think so. The idea was just in our parents' heads. I guess they rather harboured a wish of the families becoming even closer. Cementing the business ties, and the blood ties, and their very strong friendship.'

Lily nodded, and looked down at the drawing again. 'Well, if your brother did fall in love with her, I could understand it. She's really pretty.'

Suddenly a dog came bounding, leaping between them, so that Lily sat back with a little exclamation of surprise. The dog, a golden retriever, dashed on, a young boy in pursuit. Lily and Joel followed them with their gaze for a moment, then Lily glanced further off and said, 'The music – it's stopped. Ah – shame.'

Joel took his watch from his waistcoat pocket, and said, 'It's after five. They've finished for now I should reckon.'

A gentle commotion had started up some little distance from the bandstand, and Joel said, looking over, 'Something's going on, though.' And then, a moment later: 'It's Punch and Judy, look.'

Lily turned and looked over and saw that a little crowd – many children among them – had gathered in front of a small booth with cheap-looking crimson and gold hangings.

'We should go and have a look,' Joel said. 'What d'you think?'

'Oh, yes, I think so.'

They stood, picking up their things, and made their way across the grass to the crowd of adults and children gathered before the booth, and there Joel once more laid down his jacket for Lily to sit upon. He sat down beside her. The show was about to begin, and the air around them was filled with the murmur of excited, expectant children. The puppeteer appeared, a wiry, round-shouldered, shabby-looking man who went around to the back of the small booth and quickly disappeared from view. Another few minutes and the show began.

Lily was almost as caught up in the melodrama as the children who sat open-mouthed and wide-eyed, all of them spellbound, and shocked, but fascinated by the hook-nosed, hunchbacked Mr Punch who, in his jester's motley, carried out his outrageous acts, dealing with a crocodile, a dog, a doctor and other challenges, each of his triumphs met with his famous cry of, 'That's the way to do it!' They watched as he strangled his baby, then bludgeoned his wife Judy to death; were horrified as he tossed their bodies out into the street and then fled from the arms of the law. And how shocking it was that he got away with his dreadful deeds scot-free – how shocking and delightful for every member of the crowd.

The instant the show was over, and while the applause was still ringing out, the puppeteer's assistant came among the crowd with his hat held out, and pennies and halfpennies and farthings were dropped into it. The crowd began then to disperse. As Lily and Joel rose, a child walked by eating from a piece of sausage wrapped in paper. Joel said to Lily, 'Did you eat luncheon today?'

'Yes. I had a little. Not much. I wasn't hungry.'

'Would you like something now? Would you like to go for some tea and a piece of cake?'

'Well – certainly some tea or coffee would be nice.'

He gestured off. 'There's a coffee house on the other side of the park.'

'Oh, yes, but – oh, but it's sure to be so crowded.'

'Well, then – we'll go somewhere else.' He paused. 'Let's get away from here, shall we? Let's get right away.' His face was bright. 'Shall we?'

'Where to?'

'I know an inn. Just outside the town – at Lettington. It's a nice little place. We can get an omnibus part of the way and then walk. It won't be that far. What d'you say?'

She hesitated, uncertain. She had never entered any kind of inn or public house in her life, and the imminent prospect of doing so brought a little thrill of apprehension.

'We can walk through the fields,' Joel said. 'Come on – summer won't last for ever.

She hesitated still. 'I mustn't be too late getting back.'

'You won't be late. We've got plenty of time.' He waited. 'Well?'

She nodded. 'Yes, all right.'

'Good.' His smile broadened to a grin, and he stooped and swept up his jacket. 'Shall we go?'

Outside the park they boarded an omnibus which took them to the edge of the town. There they alighted, and walked down a tree-lined lane that ended with a stile. On the right, at the end of a track, stood an old barn, and beyond it outhouses and a farmhouse. Somewhere off among the farm buildings a dog barked. Joel climbed the stile and then gave Lily his hand to help her over. She stepped down on the other side with her hand in his, and so it remained for a moment until he released her.

Side by side she and Joel walked along a narrow footpath that threaded through a meadow. It was all new to her, this part of the country. On either side the grass was tall, soon to fall to the haymaker's scythe. Birds sang in the hedgerows, over which the butterflies danced, and the blackberries ripened on the vines. From a distant church a clock struck six. There was no one else in sight, and it seemed to Lily that she and Joel might have been alone in the world.

Reaching the far side of the field they passed over a second stile, walked through an adjoining meadow to a third, and then found themselves on the edge of the village of Lettington. Another hundred yards into the main street and there before them on a corner was the old inn, the Moon and Anchor, with its decorative sign hanging above the door. A minute later they had passed into a small flagged entrance hall and Joel was opening the door to the private bar.

A little nervously, Lily followed him in. The hour was still early, and there was no one else in the room. They sat on a faded, padded bench at a dark-wood table beneath a patterned window, and almost immediately a young girl in an apron came from an adjoining room and asked what they would have.

'What will you drink?' Joel said to Lily. 'I shall have some beer. Will you have some tea or coffee, or perhaps a lemonade?'

'Lemonade,' Lily said. Lemonade sounded safe enough. 'A lemonade would be nice.'

When the girl had gone away Lily had a chance to take in her surroundings. The beams of the low ceiling were hung here and there with old fishing nets and other nautical artefacts. There was a ship-in-a-bottle above the door, while on other parts of the walls hung tinted engravings of seascapes and majestic schooners. Onto the peaceful scene the early evening sunlight was filtered through the window's coloured glass. From the open door through which the maid had gone came the murmur of voices from customers in the adjoining bar. Everything appeared so normal and unthreatening. Having heard stories of the loose living and scandalous behaviour that were bred in such places as taverns and public houses, Lily could now only wonder at them with a sense of growing relief.

The maid came back soon afterwards with their drinks. Would there be anything else? she asked Joel.

Joel looked at Lily. 'You know, I'm hungry as the devil,' he said. 'I've had practically nothing since breakfast. Could you eat something?' When she hesitated, he said, 'Come on, just a little something. Keep me company. You told me yourself you've eaten very little today.' Turning to the girl, he said, 'Could we see the slate, please?'

The maid went away and came back immediately with a slate listing the bill of fare, and after brief consultations with Lily, Joel gave the girl their order.

After she had gone away once more, Joel lifted his glass of beer. 'Well – here's to us, Lily – right?'

'Yes,' Lily said, 'yes,' and raised her lemonade glass.

The time passed, and they talked, and talked. The food came, and they ate, and the hot, delicious venison pie cooled on their plates a little as they talked. Had they stopped to think, it might have seemed that there was not enough time in the world for all they had to say, but no such question entered their minds as the minutes flew by. Joel spoke of his interests, his passions. He told her of his visits to great cities, to London and Bath, to Munich and Brussels, and of his more numerous trips to Paris. He spoke with wonder of the treasures and sights he had seen there. While in Paris he had visited the Louvre Museum; he had walked down the Champs-Elysees, and had stood on the spot where Marie Antoinette and Louis XVI had died on the guillotine. He told also of theatres he had visited, and concert halls. Sometimes, he said, in the concert halls there might be up to a hundred musicians. He had seen operas by Bellini, and Meyerbeer and Rossini, and ballets too, and some of them were breathtaking. He spoke of one particular opera. The scenery was incredible, so spectacular it took your breath away. The performers were dressed in the most fabulous costumes, and not only were there the most wonderful singers on stage, but there were tumblers and acrobats as well, and more dancers than you could count, and even horses. Lily sat listening, soaking up every word.

Moving to more prosaic subjects, Joel spoke of his work in his father's department stores, and of his family. He did not only speak of himself and his interests, though; he was full of curiosity about Lily. He wanted to know ever more about her, and asked many questions. In answering him, she found herself opening to him, telling him of ideas and feelings that she had thought never to divulge.

As they talked together, and sometimes laughed, a few other patrons came and went about the place, but Lily and Joel were barely aware of them. Inexorably, however, the time flew, and Lily remarked with a sigh that the light through the coloured glass was changing. 'What is the time?' she asked, and Joel consulted his watch and told her it was almost seven-thirty. They must go, she said.

When Joel had paid the bill they got up from their seats and left the cosy little room with its occupants sitting over their drinks, and went out into the soft air of the late-August evening. Lily was sorry to leave the place behind. Stepping out onto the road, they realised that the changing light had not only signified the dying of the day, but also the gathering of clouds. 'We're going to get some rain,' Joel observed, looking up at the sky, 'but I reckon it'll hold off for a while.'

At the edge of the village, they came to the first stile, and Joel took Lily's hand and helped her over. On the other side, on the stony path, he released her hand but lifted his elbow, and after the briefest hesitation she slipped her hand through the crook of his arm. And so they continued through the meadow, and all the while she was aware of his nearness.

Another stile to traverse, and then they were in the second meadow. Before them the path wound on, and all through the time of their walk the sky above grew ever more dark and threatening. The promised rain could not be long in coming.

It came on as they were halfway along the path. From the dark grey, heavy clouds the rain began to fall, just a spattering of individual spots at first, and then with swiftly increasing intensity.

In a second, Joel's hand took hers, and together they ran along the path, faces bent against the force of the rain. The last stile was there before them, and they were quickly over. On the left lay the track leading to the old barn and the other farm buildings beyond. 'We'll get shelter there,' Joel said urgently, and together, hand in hand, they turned from the road and started up the track.

They reached the barn's entrance in less than a minute, and found the old door cracked open. The frame offered no shelter, and Joel did not hesitate but pushed the door open wider, and it swung inwards on creaking hinges to reveal the dimly-lit interior beyond.

'Come on, let's go inside,' Joel said, but Lily, fearful of trespass, said, 'Oh, but will it be all right?'

'We're not going to do any harm,' he said, 'and we'll only be here till the rain stops. Come on – there's no one about.'

He stepped through, and Lily, still with her hand in his, went with him. Inside, Joel let go her hand. They stood breathing a little heavily from their run through the rain, while the water glistened on their faces and darkened the fabric of their clothing. On the roof above their heads the rain drummed. They gazed out for a moment while it lashed down, then Joel said, glancing about him, 'Well, I think we're going to be here for a few minutes. We might as well sit down.'

Chapter Six

The floor of the barn was of earth, packed hard over the decades, and covered with bits of hay and straw, detritus from a myriad harvests. Filtered through the small, grimy, cobweb-festooned windows the storm-dulled light showed bales of hay stacked up against the walls. The place was dry, and had a sweet, dusty smell.

'Here,' Joel said, gesturing to a bale of hay that lay further out from the wall, 'let's sit down.' Lily stepped over to it and sat down, and he sat beside her. They did not speak for some moments. Beside the steady sound of the rain there came the faint rustlings of mice. Near to the bale on which they sat, leant an old shepherd's crook. A spider's web clung to the wood, with a huge spider in its centre. Joel pointed to the creature and said, 'Does it bother you, the spider?' 'Not a bit,' Lily replied. 'There's room for all of us. Besides, she was here first.'

He took off his damp cap and laid it down on the floor next to his sketchbook. They were sitting so close, her skirts were touching his thigh. He looked at her intently, his dark eyes fixed upon hers, a faint frown on his brow. Lily took in the intensity of his gaze and almost felt it was too much, that she must look away, but she did not, she could not. He murmured her name. 'Lily,' he said, and then again, 'Lily,' and a moment later his arms were coming around her, wrapping about her slim body and drawing her to him. For two or three seconds the two of them seemed locked, their faces just inches apart, then he drew her closer still, and in the same instant bent his face to hers and kissed her on the mouth.

His lips were firm but soft upon her own, parted slightly, so that she felt the warm moistness of the inside of his mouth, and the faint taste of him, a taste of nothing that she could name, it was merely an extension of all that he was. And, being so close, there was also the smell of his skin, the scent of his hair oil, the scent of *him*. The touch of his mouth on hers was the sweetest thing she could ever have imagined. He breathed with a sigh, 'Oh, Lily. Lily Clair . . .'

Momentarily, in response, her lips formed his name, but she did not speak it. He could sense, though, that it was there unspoken on her tongue, and he said, 'Yes, go on, say my name.' And she said, 'Joel,' and he gave a little laugh, and bent his head and kissed her again.

His kisses were the first lover's kisses she had ever known. She did not know how to respond, and was afraid of making any response at all. So she sat there a little stiff, a stranger in a foreign land, no matter that her heart cried out for her to give in to the sensation that swept over her, and urged her to let go. And he kissed her again, and with his lips upon hers she felt herself melting against him, letting herself, without resistance, be held fast in his arms, fast against the damp cloth of his jacket, smelling the smell of it, of his hair, his skin.

He released her, and leant back a little, the better to take in the sight of her. 'I shall think of you all the time I'm away,' he said. 'I can't bear the thought of being away from you.' He paused. 'Will you think of me, Lily?' When she did not answer at once, he said, putting his head a little on one side, 'Sometimes, Lily? Just sometimes? Tell me you will.'

I shall think of you all the time, she wanted to say. *You'll never be out of my thoughts*, but she said nothing; there was danger in such words.

'Oh, you will, won't you?' he said with a little moan. 'You'll think of me sometimes, won't you?'

'Yes,' she said, and heard herself add bravely, 'of course I shall.'

His smile was wide, showing his white teeth in the gloom. 'Ah – that's splendid. Oh, thank you. Thank you. Oh, Lily, I shan't know a moment's peace while I'm away. And now I know you'll be thinking of me too . . .' He let his words trail off with a little shake of the head. 'I'll write to you at the Haskins'. That'll be all right, will it?'

A little breathless at the wonder of it all, she wanted to say, *Yes, oh yes, I shall watch for the post every day*, but, still trying to hold on to some sense of reason, she said in a little burst, 'Oh, Joel, we're oceans apart, you and I.'

'*No*,' he said at once. 'No, we're not. Don't say that.'

'I must,' she replied. 'We've got to be sensible.' Then with a sad smile she added, 'It's a perennial situation – and a perennial problem too – the rich man's son and the maid.'

A look of sadness darkened his face. 'Is that how it is?' he said. 'Is that how you see it – as simply as that?'

'I – I can't escape from it. It's something I have to face. Something *we* have to face.'

'Yes, *we*. Something we'll face together.'

They fell silent, and the only sounds were that of their breathing, the scratching of the mice in the straw, and the drumming of the rain on the roof, a little fainter now. Then into the gentle quiet, Joel said, a little sound of wonder in his voice:

'I – I think I love you, Lily.'

He was not touching her now. His hands lay at his sides, but his eyes were piercing her own, not allowing her to shift her glance away, even had she wanted to. She looked back at him, held there by his words and his gaze, and feeling her heart beating with joy: so full of emotion and happiness that she felt that, like a cup, it might fill to the brim and spill over.

'No,' he said then, 'I don't *think* I love you. I *know* I do.' He gave the briefest pause. 'I love you. Oh, Lily, I love you.'

She held her breath. His words were the most wondrous sounds she had ever heard, and she wanted to say, *I too. Oh, I love you, Joel.* And even as she stifled the words in her throat she knew that they were the truth.

'I can see,' he said, gazing at her, a faint smile on his lips, 'I can see it in your face. Something . . . Oh, Lily,' he breathed her name, 'if you would say such words to me, I would be the happiest man in England.'

She frowned. 'I – I'm afraid,' she murmured.

'Afraid? Of me?'

'No, not of you. Never of you. Of – our situation. As I said, we're oceans apart.'

'It will be all right,' he said. 'You'll see. I'll make it so.' He leant forward a little. 'Do you believe me?'

'Yes,' she said. 'Yes, I do.'

And then he was holding her in his arms again, and his face was there, his mouth upon hers, and as his lips moved against her own a little voice in her head said yes, everything would be well; it was true what he said, and she must believe. Everything would be all right; he would make it so. And hearing the silent, sweet, comforting words, she took them and embraced them, and gave herself up to his kiss.

For long, long minutes they had remained close together on the bale, arms entwined. Joel had kissed her over and over again, murmuring her name, and, caught up in the spell, she had been for a while almost unaware of anything else. There had been only him. In the whole world there was only the two of them.

But now, turning a little out of his embrace, she became

aware of the changed silence and realised that the rain had ceased. How long had they been there?

'The rain,' she said, 'it's stopped.'

They sat listening to the quiet for a few moments, then, coming out of the spell, she said, frowning, 'I must go. Joel, I must go,' and with her words she stirred, preparing to rise. 'No, wait,' he urged her, 'we don't need to go just yet.' But she got up from the bale, and began to brush the dust and the threads of hay from her skirt.

Minutes later they were outside, and stepping onto the muddy track that led back down to the lane.

Reaching the end of the lane, they waited interminable minutes for an omnibus, and when at long last one came by Joel hailed it and they climbed aboard. Inside the coach they sat side by side without speaking while the other passengers came and went. Lily felt different. She would never, she thought, be quite the same again.

When the vehicle reached the corner of Willow Street she and Joel alighted, and set off towards the Haskins' house. The day was dying, the light fading over the rain-wet landscape. Her hand was held in Joel's as they walked, and she had taken off her glove, so as to feel the touch of him against her skin. Soon, too soon, they reached the corner of the lane that joined the Corster Road. Hollygrove was so close.

When they drew near the house, Lily halted a few yards from the front gate and said, 'Oh, no further. Don't come any further.'

They stood together on the cinder pathway. The light was swiftly fading now. 'I'll write to you,' Joel said.

'Yes. Yes, write to me. I'll wait for your letter.'

He gazed down at her. In the fading light his eyes were shadowed, dark pools. 'How shall I manage?' he said. 'I managed perfectly well before, but now – now that I've found you – everything is different.'

'I know,' she said. 'I know.' And she did.

'All I'll have is my little drawing of you, but it's better than nothing. Though I shan't need to be reminded to think of you.' He smiled gravely. 'In time we shall be together. I know it. For ever.'

'Yes. Yes.'

He bent his face to kiss her, and for a moment she was minded to resist and say, *Oh, no, not here,* but she kept silent, and the kiss came and then she could not have uttered a word.

After a few moments he drew back. Raising her ungloved hand, she touched at her lapel, feeling for the flowers, and said with a little moan, 'Oh, my flowers, my gardenias – I've lost them.' She bent her head to look down. Even the pin was gone.

'I'll bring you a real one,' he said. 'You shall have the prettiest there is.'

She smiled. 'You won't forget.' Half question, half statement.

'No, I won't forget.'

She gave a little nod. 'I must go,' she said. 'I'm so late.' Another moment, drawing out the seconds, and then she was turning away, leaving him standing on the cinders.

Inside the gate she turned up the gravel drive, and at the last minute looked back and saw him standing there. As their eyes locked, he lifted his hand to his mouth, and kissed the palm. She smiled back at him, and then he was gone from her sight.

She entered the house by the scullery door, and went straight into the kitchen. From the front, the house had appeared to be in darkness, but Mr Haskin was there, sitting alone in his chair by the light of a single lamp, a glass and a bottle on the small table at his side.

'Well,' he said, as Lily came in, 'the wanderer returns.' He waved a hand towards the long-case clock. 'Almost half-past-nine, look. I was thinking of sending out the peelers.'

Acutely self-conscious, she felt as if she were drenched in the brightest light, and as if all her words and actions of the evening were written on her face, exposed in the glare for anyone to see. She was at a loss as to what to say. After a moment she asked, 'Did you see Mrs Haskin, sir?'

'No,' he said. 'No, I didn't. I've had a very solitary evening.'

She hesitated on the spot, wanting to go, to be alone in her room, but not wishing to appear rude. She began to untie her bonnet strings. 'Well, sir – I think I'll go to bed if you don't mind.' Then she added quickly, 'Unless there's something you want doing, sir?'

'What? No, nothing. You go on.'

Lily nodded. 'Well, sir – then I'll wish you goodnight.' Another moment's hesitation then she moved across the room towards the hall. As she reached the door, she heard him say:

'As I told you, I shall be having a word with Mr Carter and Mr Horsham next week.'

She turned back to face him. 'Oh – well – thank you, sir.'

He took another drink from his glass. 'Yes, we'll see what they've got to say.'

'Thank you, sir.' She reached for the handle, then his voice came again:

'My God, but you're in a mighty hurry, aren't you, miss?'

She turned back to face him, awkward, uncertain. 'Well – I've got to get up early in the morning, sir.'

'Yes, I know that. It wouldn't hurt you, though, to stay and talk for five minutes.' He smiled. 'You can at least be sociable. Doesn't cost anything.'

'Yes, sir.' She gave a nod, remaining on the spot.

He took another swallow from his glass. 'As I said, I'll have a word with Mr Horsham. Mr Carter too. I'm sure you could be quite an asset to have in the office – smart girl like you. And I've seen for meself that you write a good hand.'

'Thank you, sir.' She could think of nothing to say, and covered the awkward moments in taking off her bonnet.

He watched her in silence for a second, then said, 'Did you get caught in the rain earlier on?'

'Yes, but I – I managed to get some shelter. I was all right.'

'Good. It came on heavy for a spell.'

'Yes – it did.' She hovered there while the moments passed, then, her bonnet in her hand, reached out again for the door handle. 'Goodnight, sir.'

'You're a fraud,' he said. 'You're nothing but a fraud.'

She turned back to him. 'Sir?'

'You – earlier, shakin' your head when I asked if you had a young man.' He was smiling, his eyes twinkling, slightly narrowed. 'And there you are with one – right under our noses.'

Lily felt herself flushing.

'Yes, I saw you, the two of you. Not far from the gate.' He gave a little chuckle. 'Oh, Lily, my girl, you *are* a dark horse, and no mistake.' He chuckled again. 'And it made a very pretty picture, I have to say, the two of you standing there in the twilight.'

Lily remained motionless, her cheeks burning.

'I couldn't help wondering who the young man might be . . .' His words trailed off with the inflection of a question, and when Lily said nothing in reply, he added, 'I just hope he's a decent sort. After all, I've got some responsibility for you while you're under my roof.' He paused. 'I've no doubt the young man's fond of you, isn't he? And why shouldn't he be? – a pretty, personable young woman like you.'

He continued to look at Lily as she stood at the door, her eyes cast down. Then, summoning her will, she said, 'I've got to go, sir. If you'll excuse me, I'll wish you goodnight.'

He nodded. 'Ah, and goodnight to you, Lily. Sleep well.'

She heard his words with the greatest relief, and in moments she had opened the door and was passing through into the small hall beyond.

Later, upstairs in her room, lying in bed, with the candle out, she put away from her mind the awkwardness with Mr Haskin, and thought back on the time she had spent with Joel. It was all there before her, everything, all the images of the day, the sights, the smells, the sounds. She thought of them sitting on the grass while he had sketched her portrait, she remembered the laughter of the spectators as Mr Punch had gone through his outrageous, murderous antics. She saw again the interior of the inn where, in the light through the coloured glass, she and Joel had sat over their venison pie. She saw them in the barn, and smelled again the old hay and straw, heard again the scratching of the mice in the shadows. And she thought again of Joel's kiss, felt his mouth once more on hers, soft and warm, magical.

And now he had gone, and in a very short time he would be in France. But their parting was not for ever. He had impressed this upon her, and she knew it was true. He would have leave from his university, and he would come back and see her, and eventually they would be together, for always.

She turned, restless, feeling that sleep was a long way off. It was likely that tomorrow Mrs Haskin would return. Thinking of the woman, the thought came that Mr Haskin was sure to tell of his discovery about herself and Joel. How would Mrs Haskin react? She would not be approving, that much Lily was sure of.

Interrupting her thoughts came the faint sound of the opening of the Haskins' bedroom door on the floor below. Mr Haskin was going to bed. Several minutes of silence followed, and then she heard the door opening again. After that there came, suddenly and surprisingly, the sound of footfalls on the stairs. Hearing them she listened more intently. Why should Mr Haskin be coming up the last flight?

Listening still, she heard the thin treads creaking as he came on up. She lay quiet, puzzled and a little tense. Then, after a brief silence there came a faint tap on her door.

She made no sound, and another tap came, a little stronger this time, and then Mr Haskin's voice, softly calling out her name. 'Lily? Lily? Lily, are you awake?'

She pulled herself up in the bed. In the quiet she heard the door handle turn, and the next moment, in the faint glow from the moonlight that filtered through the crack in the curtains, she saw the door begin to open. 'What is it?' she said, pulling the bedclothes closer to her breast. 'What is it?'

The door opened fully then, and he stood there, a tall, dark shape. She could not make out his expression in the gloom, but she could see clearly that he was clad in his nightshirt.

'What do you want?' she breathed.

'I just wondered if you're all right,' he said, and she heard the faint slurring of his words. She said nothing. He remained standing there. In the silence she could hear the sound of her own breathing.

After a few moments he came forward until he was standing just a couple of feet from the bedside. She was aware of the beating of her heart.

'Don't take any notice of me,' he said. 'I shouldn't have teased you like that.'

'It – it's all right, sir,' she said at once. 'It's all right. It doesn't matter.'

'Yes, it does. And let me say I'm not in the least surprised you've found yourself a young man. A girl as pretty as you.'

105

He took a step nearer and the next moment Lily felt the mattress dip as he sat down on the side of the bed. She could hear his surging breath as he settled there. She closed her eyes, unable to bring herself to look at him. 'Yes, a pretty girl like you,' she heard him say, 'you should be able to have your pick of the young fellows. And not only the young ones either.' As she opened her eyes again she saw him raise his hand, and a moment later he was bringing it to her cheek. At his touch she flinched and pressed back against the pillow.

'You mustn't be afraid,' he said softly, a little gruffly, 'I won't hurt you. I'd never hurt you.'

Her eyes wide, she shrank from him, but his rough hand remained on her. He began to stroke her cheek, his fingers lingering upon her skin. 'Please,' she muttered. 'Please.'

'It's all right, it's all right,' he said softly. 'It's all right.'

The next moment he was leaning forward and lowering his face to hers, and she could smell the whisky on his breath. And then his mouth was pushing against her own. Under the pressure of his lips she tried to move her head away, but his hand shifted from her cheek and gripped her chin. Held fast she lay there as his voracious mouth covered hers. A second later his wet tongue was pressing against her lips and insinuating itself into her unwilling mouth, moving over her teeth. Apart from the taste of the whisky, she could also taste the tobacco from his pipe, and something else, some sweet, sour essence in his saliva that made her almost gag and choke. Once again she tried to move her head away, and brought up her hands to try to push him back, but he was too powerful, and her efforts were to no avail.

Breaking briefly away, he drew back just long enough to mutter through gritted teeth, 'Lay still. I'm not going to hurt you,' and then pressed his mouth on hers again. The horror was never ending. The next moment his right hand was grasping the bedcovers and yanking them down, exposing her nightdress-covered body. And then he was moving his own body to lay his weight upon her. Tearing her mouth from beneath his, she gave a little squeal. 'No! No! I – I'm a good girl, sir. Please, no!' But he took no heed, and in seconds she could feel the hardness of his sex against her thigh, pressing, pressing.

Gruffly, almost angrily, he muttered, 'Stop resisting, will you? I'll bet you're not so stand-offish with that young fellow of yourn.' She gave another little cry of desperation, and he quickly added, 'There's no sense crying out, there's only you and me.' He kissed her again, while he continued to press against her. 'Come on,' he said in a softer tone, 'be nice, be nice.' And she felt his right hand wrench at the fabric of her nightgown. As he did so she felt the cool air against her bare flesh. A moment later he was pulling up his nightshirt, and the next second was pressing against her once more. This time there was nothing between them, his bare skin was burning upon her own. He lay there for a brief moment, his rampant flesh against her, then put his hand between her thighs. He fumbled there for a second, coarse fingers exploring, and then moved to force her thighs apart. 'No!' she tried to cry out against him, 'No,' but her voice was stifled against his mouth. Another moment and he was manoeuvring his heavy body over her, and in a gasping, tearing thrust he was inside her.

Chapter Seven

When at last he had gone, she lay still for some minutes, as if stunned, and then got up and washed herself. Back in the bed she stared up into the dark, while the tears streamed from her eyes and ran into the hair at her temples.

She did not sleep that night, and the next morning when she crawled out of bed she found that there were a few spots of blood on the under sheet. But it was Monday, and Monday was wash day, and by the afternoon the bedlinen had been washed and, along with the rest of the washing, was hanging out on the clothesline to dry. She was glad of the round of chores that awaited her for she desperately needed to be occupied, though never for one moment while she worked did her thoughts stray from the happening of the night before. First thing that morning she had prepared Mr Haskin's breakfast and served it as he sat, ready for his day's work, at the kitchen table. Throughout, she kept her eyes lowered, and spoke no single word. For his part he gave no word to her either, other than muttering the briefest thank you, and the moment his plate was empty he was gone, riding off on the cob.

Left alone in the house she poured herself a cup of tea and sat with it. She would usually have made a breakfast of some bread and butter, but not today. Today she ate nothing. Over and over again she thought of the events of the previous day and night. How could it have been possible, in so little space of time, to fall from the very pinnacle of happiness to the deepest depths of horror and degradation? How wonderful had been those hours with Joel, and all the things they had done together. Images conjured from the time turned over in her mind, and the afternoon and evening were before her again, in the park, the field, and the barn and the inn, in the sun and in the rain. And what had provided the most wondrous and magical of memories was now all of it sullied, ruined for ever.

All her instincts urged her to run. Every cell in her body cried out for her to pack up her few possessions and get away from the house, but she knew she could not. For the time being she had no option other than to stay. Where could she go? She had no money for lodgings and she had no other prospect of employment. She certainly could not go home to Compton Wells, for if she did, what excuse could she make? She could not tell them the reason, she could never speak of it, never admit the shame of the happening. She was trapped. She could not with comfort stay, but neither could she go.

Mrs Haskin arrived back later that afternoon, remarking to Lily that her mother was much improved, and able to care for herself again. 'Though I shall go back to check on her tomorrow,' she said. 'Just to see that she's all right, and take her one or two things.' She expressed satisfaction that the washing had been done, and asked Lily how things had gone generally in her absence. Lily replied that she had kept busy.

Mrs Haskin regarded her judiciously. 'Are you all right? You look a bit down in the mouth.'

Lily avoided the woman's glance. 'I'm all right,' she said.

'Well, let's hope so. We don't want you sickening for something. It's enough to do with looking after Mother.'

The time dragged by, and Lily lived the days in a fog. On the Tuesday, she thought of Joel leaving England for

France, and all the while she continued with her work, shrouded in a haze of misery and shame, the nightmare of the violation never more than a breath away from her consciousness. Each day she dreaded the time when Mr Haskin would return from the factory and she would have to join him and his wife at the dinner table. At such times she was thankful that conversation was not generally expected of her, and she could sit and eat in near silence without causing comment. When she was called upon to speak, it was almost invariably in response to Mrs Haskin. As for Mr Haskin, he addressed to her only the occasional anodyne remark, and then merely to keep up appearances. At other times the odd jocular comment he threw her way was stilted and awkward, and never did his eyes meet hers.

When Sunday came, Lily went as usual to Henhurst to prepare the midday meal for Mrs Shalcross. She found the old lady much recovered from her accident, and knew a certain relief in spending some time with her. There was no pressure or stress in the old lady's company and, when the meal was finished and cleared away Lily sat with her over cups of tea, and listened to her complaints and her gossip. Today Lily was in no hurry to leave. Joel would not be waiting for her at the park, and in the absence of time spent with him there was nothing she cared to do. She was only sure that she did not want to return to Hollygrove and find herself in the company of Mr Haskin.

When the time came for her to go, she bade the old lady farewell and left the house. As usual her route took her by the park, and she wandered aimlessly through the entrance. The sky was a little overcast today, and there was a September coolness in the air. The band was playing, but to a much reduced audience, and she felt no desire to linger and listen. Instead, she walked on to the pond, and there sat on the bench that she and Joel had shared. She thought of him as she sat facing out over the water. It was only a week since they had been together. Just one week. That day, that last Sunday with him, had been the happiest day she could recall. How swiftly everything had changed.

How long she sat there she did not know, though from the nearby church she was dimly aware of the clock striking the hours away. Before her, at the rim of the pond, two small boys sailed their wooden boats. The time passed, and eventually they packed up their little vessels and left the scene. The bandsmen had long since ceased to play. When a few drops of rain fell, Lily rose and began to retrace her steps. There were relatively few people about now. The rain began to fall more heavily as she neared the bandstand – all deserted now by the musicians – and she stepped up onto it and sat down on one of the seats. Then, while the rain drummed a tattoo on the wooden roof, she sat looking out over the sward.

When the rain stopped, she set off back to Hollygrove; she could think of nothing else to do, and had nowhere else to go.

Mrs Haskin was in the kitchen when Lily entered the house. She was sitting by the window mending some stockings, her sewing basket open beside her. Lily was relieved to find that Mr Haskin was nowhere in sight.

'Well, there you are,' Mrs Haskin said. 'How was Mother? Did you find her well?'

Lily replied that she had, spoke a little about her time with the old lady, and then went upstairs to take off her jacket and bonnet, and put on her apron. Back downstairs, she took her own sewing basket from the cupboard and took from Mrs Haskin two or three of the stockings that needed mending. For a few minutes the two women worked in silence, then Mrs Haskin said, one eyebrow raised slightly:

'I wasn't expecting you back just yet.'

'The rain came on,' Lily said. 'It wasn't a day for walking around much.'

'No, I suppose not.' Mrs Haskin paused, then added, her eyes on her darning, 'And you had no one to meet today?'

The question made Lily's heart sink. So Mr Haskin had told his wife of seeing Lily with Joel. But it was inevitable, she thought.

When Lily did not answer the question, Mrs Haskin said, 'Yes, it seems you've been keeping a few secrets, Lily Clair. All the time we thought that after getting Mother's dinner you were going for a nice solitary walk, or getting the train into Corster, but it seems we were wrong. You had other things to do. And, so I'm told, you were quite late getting back last Sunday night. A case of when the cat's away the mice'll play, I s'pose.'

Lily said nothing, but kept her head bent to her needlework.

Mrs Haskin said, 'Has this been going on for a long time? You and this young man?'

When Lily did not answer, Mrs Haskin said, 'My dear, we're responsible for you while you're in this house. We wouldn't want your father to think we've been derelict in our duties.'

'Two months,' Lily said, without looking up. 'I've known him about two months.'

'Two months, eh? What sort of work does he do?'

'He – he's a student.'

'A *student*.'

'He's studying law – at university – at Cambridge.'

'University. Cambridge. Oh, my dear!' Mrs Haskin pressed a hand to her big bosom. 'This sounds too grand for me. A little too grand for the likes of you too, I have to say. Who is he, when he's at home, this young man?'

Lily wanted to say nothing, but she said after a moment, 'His name is Joel.'

'Joel, eh? And I daresay he's got another name, too. Did you see him today?'

'No.'

'Too busy, was he?'

'No. No, he had to go away.'

Mrs Haskin nodded sagely. 'I see.'

'He's gone to France.'

'*France*?' Mrs Haskin looked incredulous.

'His father – he's got a business there.'

Mrs Haskin gave a wondering little shake of her head. 'It's sounding grander and grander to me. D'you mean it – he's gone off to France?'

'Yes. He went last Tuesday.'

'Ah, so that's why you've been moping around with a face like a wet week.' Now she looked directly at Lily, and when she spoke again her tone was a little softer, a little kinder. 'My dear girl, by what you tell me, this young man is not the one for you. Face it, Lily – you're a general maid. I don't want to sound cruel, but pretty little servant girls are ten a penny. Specially for a man of quality. Take it from me, my girl, there's only one thing young men want, and I don't doubt for a minute that your young man is any different from the rest of 'em.'

'Oh, he is,' Lily breathed. 'He's kind, and he's good.'

Mrs Haskin gave a nod. 'Well, of course you think that, but you're too young to have any experience of life. You'll learn, though. A young man like that will have a bright future ahead of him, and I daresay his folks have higher hopes for him than the kind of understanding he's got with you. And don't take that the wrong way, my dear. You're a well-brought up young woman, but you've got to face the facts: his family sounds a mite grander than yours. But you'll meet somebody else, my dear, and he'll be somebody of your own kind, and believe me, you'll be much better off.' She paused, then added, 'I hope you've been sensible with this young man.'

'Sensible?'

'You know very well what I mean. I hope you have been – sensible. Because I don't want you bringing trouble and disgrace back here.'

On Friday there came a letter from Joel. Mrs Haskin knew nothing of it. Lily was out in the yard when the old postman came up around the side of the house, and seeing her he went to her with the letter held out. Lily knew at once who it was from, and taking it up to her room, she opened it and read Joel's words:

> 27 Rue de Soie, Paris
> 29th August 1866
>
> Dearest Lily,
>   I got here earlier today. My journey was without mishap, but nevertheless I'm quite exhausted, and very relieved to rest from all the travelling. Since my arrival I've hardly had a minute to myself, and I'm writing to you at the first opportunity. Tomorrow will find me at work at the store, as I shall be until my return later in the month.
>   How are you, my dearest? Have you given me a thought since our parting? I've thought of you so many times. You are always on my mind, and I can't wait until I see you again. I hope it won't be long. In the meantime you'll always have the love of
>   Your
>   Joel

She put the letter aside. She would answer it at a later date.

The letter remained unanswered, and the days passed. On the twelfth of September Lily expected her monthly period to make its regular appearance, but it did not, and when

114

three days had passed with no sign, she knew that it would not come. At the same time she began to be aware of certain changes taking place in her body, most remarkably a tenderness in her breasts. Then, some days later, she began to be sick.

The sickness struck at her in the morning, soon after she had risen, and she knelt over her chamber pot retching as if she would bring up her very heart. When it continued so every day, she had no doubt whatsoever of the reality of her condition.

She knew, also, that she would not for long be able to hide the truth from Mrs Haskin, and she dreaded the confrontation that she was sure must come.

It came on Friday morning, soon after Mr Haskin had left for the factory. Lily had just cleared away the breakfast things when Mrs Haskin came to her in the scullery.

'I notice you didn't eat much of anything for breakfast,' Mrs Haskin said.

Lily shook her head, avoiding the woman's gaze. 'No,' she replied, 'I wasn't that hungry.'

'So it would seem. And it would also seem that you haven't been hungry for the past month. And the way I've heard you retching in the mornings, it's a wonder you've got as much as a stomach in you.'

Lily kept her eyes on the plate she was washing. 'I think I must be a little out of sorts,' she murmured.

Mrs Haskin's eyes never left Lily's face. 'Oh, out of sorts, is it.' She paused. 'Are you sure there's nothing you want to tell me?'

When Lily did not answer, Mrs Haskin gave a nod and said, 'Well, if you ask me, your silence says it all.' She fell quiet for a second, watching Lily's averted face, then added, 'Your monthly – as far as I've learnt while you've been here it's about the middle of the month. And regular too, if I've observed correctly.'

115

Lily remained silent.

'Yes,' Mrs Haskin said, 'and I'll bet I'm right in thinking you haven't had it this time, is that so?'

Lily gritted her teeth, and briefly pressed shut her eyes.

'I'm not surprised you can't answer,' Mrs Haskin said. She paused. 'Have you written to the young man?'

Lily turned to her now. 'What?'

'Your young man. Your Joel, as you call him. Does he know about the pickle you're in? Because he ought to be told. Men get away with too much. He's got you into the state you're in and it's only right that he does something about it.' She gave a withering shake of her head. 'You young people, you're so foolish, so stupid. You never think of the consequences of what you do. Have you written to him?'

A sob burst from Lily's mouth, and she put her hands up and covered her face.

'Yes, you might well cry, my girl,' Mrs Haskin said. There was no trace of sympathy in her tone. 'You've got yourself in a right old mess and you'd best think of what you're gunna do about it.'

'I don't know,' Lily said, the words breaking between her sobs. 'I don't know.'

'Well, you'd better think of something, because you can't go on as you are. You realise that, don't you?'

'Yes.' The tears were streaming down Lily's cheeks.

'Yes, indeed. And I'll put your mind at rest over something else – and that is that you surely don't think you're going to stay here, do you? You'll have to leave here, young lady, there's no question about that. What you do about your Mr Joel is up to you, but you can't stay here. Your father and Mr Haskin have been lifelong friends, but I'm afraid that doesn't count for anything in a situation like this. There's no way I'm having you here in your condition. You must try to get that young man to do the right thing by you. Who knows, he might be willing. Though I doubt it. If he's a man with a future, then a poor marriage and a child would really put a spanner in the works. Still – he must at least be informed of the situation, it's only right.' She continued to fix Lily with her unsympathetic gaze. 'Does anyone else know?'

Lily shook her head. 'No.'

'Well, your folks will have to, and before too much longer. Though I shall be writing to your mother myself, you can depend on that. She's got to know, and soon.' She slapped down a tea cloth on the table. 'You've got till the end of the month, and then you'll have to go. I'm sorry it's got to be like that, but there's no choice.' Her voice rose a little, indignant. 'And I want you to know that it's a great inconvenience for me, too. It means I've got to find a new girl and break her in. Not something I look forward to doing.'

The following Wednesday Mrs Haskin, tight-lipped, asked Lily whether she had yet written to her parents. Lily replied that she had not, but that she intended to do so.

'Well, I might as well tell you that *I* have,' Mrs Haskin said. 'I wrote on Monday. I told them you've gone and got yourself into a state and I told them also that I can only keep you a while longer, and that they must expect you home at the end of the month.' She gave a little snort, her fury growing. 'I can't imagine what they're going to say to you when you get back, but you've only yourself to blame. You were stupid enough to get yourself into this pickle in the first place so you deserve all you get. Bringing shame and disgrace like this onto your parents – how could you? Where did you get such behaviour from? Certainly not from your stepmother.' Her lip curled. 'Perhaps you take after your own mother, is that it?'

'Don't you say that,' Lily burst out, the anger and hurt

flashing in her eyes. 'Don't you speak that way about my mother.'

Mrs Haskin's mouth fell open at the passionate outburst. Then she said, grinding the words out, 'You watch yourself when you talk to me, young woman. I won't be spoken to like that by some chit of a girl who gives herself up to the first man who gives her a wink. And *he's* no better than he should be either, that so-called Joel of yours. He deserves all he gets.'

'It wasn't him,' Lily said, the tears starting in her eyes. 'It wasn't him.'

'What d'you mean, it wasn't him? You mean to say you've been going around with more than one?'

'No, I haven't!' Lily cried. 'And if you want to know who it was, it was *Mr Haskin*.'

There fell a moment of complete silence. Mrs Haskin drew in her chin, frowning, bewildered. '*Mr Haskin*? What are you talking about? *What do you mean, it was Mr Haskin?*'

'Exactly that,' Lily said. Her heart was thumping against her ribs. 'It was Mr Haskin. Your husband. *He* did it.'

Mrs Haskin was staring at her, eyes wide as saucers. 'I don't know what you're saying, girl. What are you talking about?'

'Mr Haskin. *It was Mr Haskin*. On the Sunday night while you were staying with your mother. While you were away that night in Henhurst he came into my room. He – he did it to me. It was Mr Haskin.'

A brief moment of silence passed, then the older woman's hand flashed out and caught Lily a stinging blow on the cheek, so hard that she staggered back, the pain bringing tears to her eyes. As Lily put a hand up to her smarting cheek, Mrs Haskin cried out in a passion:

'How dare you say such a thing!' As she spoke, little flecks of saliva flew from her lips. 'Shut your filthy mouth, you little slut.' She raised her hand again. 'And get out! Get out of my house. You're not staying here another day. I want you gone – *now*.'

Chapter Eight

Lily was in her old bedroom, the one she shared with Dora. It was Saturday, just turned two o'clock. She sat at the small table that, years ago, her father had set there, to aid her in her studies towards becoming a teacher. Such a distant dream. There was no one else in the house. Her father was not yet back from work, and her stepmother and Dora had gone out to visit friends. Her brother Tom was, as on most days, out working on the farm.

The table was set near the window, and from her vantage point Lily looked out over the back yard and up the path of the rear garden. It was the old familiar scene, part of her very first memories.

Today, the October scene before her spoke of the ending of summer. In the border beside the small lawn the nasturtiums and the roses were still bright, but the vibrant shades of the green foliage were fading. The leaves of the distant tall elm were already turning yellow. Autumn had arrived and was not to be turned away. She observed it dispassionately. Perhaps in other years it might have brought a momentary melancholy, but not this time; she was already so steeped in unhappiness, and a mere dying of the summer barely touched her mind.

The house was still. There was not a sound. She sighed into the quiet. She felt lost. She had been back in Compton Wells for three days now, and was completely without anchor, without direction, without any knowledge or hint of what was to be. She only knew that things could not continue as they were. That had been made clear to her at the start. 'I wouldn't bother to unpack much if I were you,' her stepmother had said. 'You won't be staying long.'

Mrs Haskin's letter had preceded Lily's return to her home, so when Lily arrived, all was known. And if her stepmother had been cold to her in the past, it was nothing to what she was following Lily's return from Whitton. Since Lily's arrival, Mrs Clair had spoken to her only when it was absolutely necessary, added to which, she had given instructions to Dora not to speak to her at all. 'I mustn't talk to you,' Dora had said. 'Mammy said I mustn't.' And then: 'Did you bring me anything, Lily?' Tom had been given the same instruction as the child, and, like her, was given no reason for the injunction. Of course he ignored it, and talked to Lily whenever they had the chance to be alone.

'But, Lil, what have you done?' he had asked her soon after her return. 'Nobody'll tell me. They won't even talk of it, and they treat you in such a cold manner.'

'I can't speak of it,' she had said. 'Not yet. Someday. In the meantime, just – just believe that I'm not a bad person. I haven't done anything wrong. Believe me, I haven't.'

As for Mr Clair, since her return on Wednesday not one single word had he directed at his daughter, and this was the most affecting of all.

She sighed into the quiet. Before her on the little table lay her writing slope, and beside it the letter that she had received that morning, forwarded from Mrs Haskin in Whitton. It was from Joel. He had written:

The Hazels,
Greenbanks Road,
Corster
28th September 1866

Dear Lily,
    I have heard nothing from you. All the time in Paris I

looked for a letter, but there was not a word. Is
something wrong? As you see from my address, I am
now back in England. I had so hoped that there might
have been a chance for us to meet again in Whitton
before I resume my studies. Sad to say, that now looks
unlikely, as I leave for Cambridge on Monday next.
However, you can write to me there at Clare College.
Please – let me hear from you.

    With love,

    Your

      Joel

For many minutes she sat bent over the table, unable to
think of a single word to write. Then, at last, urging herself
to action, she dipped her pen and wrote:

                  Compton Wells, Wilts.

                    6th October 1866.

Dear Joel,

    As you will see, I am no longer residing at Whitton,
but have come back to my family home in Compton
Wells.

    I received your earlier letter from France, and have
now just received your letter from Corster. I am sorry
that it has taken me so long to write back. With such
great delays, you must be wondering at the cause.

    It gives me no pleasure to do so, but I have to tell you
that this will be my first and last letter to you. I did say
to you during our meetings that I could not see any
future for us together, and this is what I believe. We are
oceans apart, I said, and truly I can see no means of our
ever bridging that gulf.

    I am sorry to say it, but I cannot continue my
friendship with you. I know I said certain things which
may have led you to believe I cared for you, but you

know as well as I that people say things in the heat of the moment which are not true, and which in later, cooler, moments they regret. I'm afraid this has been the case with you and me, and the time has come to disabuse you of any hopes you might have had where I was concerned.

We two shall not meet again, but I wish you happiness, and hope that you meet someone who deserves to have you for a friend.

Lily Clair

She read through the tissue of heartless lies once more, then took an envelope, and addressed it to *Mr Joel Goodhart, Clare College, Cambridge*, and sealed the letter inside. She affixed a stamp, then put on her bonnet and cape and left the house. She must waste no further time. The post box was situated only two hundred yards away, set in the old church yard wall, and on reaching it, she held the letter in the slot, suspended, reluctant to let it go. She knew that the parting of her fingers would spell the end of the dream. But it had to be. She no longer had any choice in the matter; that had been taken from her on that August night. What Joel would think of her on reading her cruel words, she would not dwell upon, and she thrust any hint of such conjecture from her mind. As for her feelings for him, she could not afford to consider them, not even for a moment. She must not. They must be consigned to the past, they must be locked away, never again to see the light of day.

She realised that she was gripping the letter tightly. She took a breath and, briefly closing her eyes, she opened her fingers and let the letter fall.

Before she set off to return home, she went into the church yard and stood beside her mother's grave. It looked well kept, and in the old earthenware pot that was set into the earth were some white roses. It was Tom's work, she knew. Needing comfort, she stayed there for several minutes, and then moved to an old wooden bench set beside the gravel path and sat down. In the branches of a nearby yew tree, jays and mistlethrushes picked at the scarlet berries. A peacock butterfly came dancing over the headstones and lighted on the arm of a small marble angel. Lily continued to sit there in the October sunlight. She had no wish to return home; she had no wish to be anywhere at all. After an hour she rose and started back.

Inside the house she entered the kitchen and saw her father's hat on the chair by the clock. She stood still, listening for some sound from above, but there was nothing. After she had hung up her bonnet and cape she stood for a few moments undecided, then went out into the yard and started down the garden path.

She found him in the small scrap of orchard, stretching up to a sprawling elder tree, picking its berries. She stood in silence on the grass, waiting for him to acknowledge her presence. As she did so, she thought of that other day, three years past, when they had picked the blackberries together. Even now the brambles were festooned, the blackberries heavy on the vines.

After a few moments she took a step forward and said softly, 'Father . . .'

He hesitated for a second, then resumed picking the elderberries and dropping them into a basin.

'Father,' she said again. 'Say something to me, please. Don't subject me to this awful silence.'

He continued with the berries, hands moving carefully from branch to basin. Then he said, without turning, 'These are the last. They'll make fine jelly, and if we don't take 'em now the pigeons'll get 'em.'

'Father . . .'

He dropped another handful into the basin, then halted in his movements, gazing ahead into the foliage of the tree. 'Oh, Lily,' he murmured. His voice came out in a little broken sound.

'Father –'

'Oh, girl, if you knew what this has done to us.' When he turned to her she could see his eyes glistening with unshed tears. With an angry gesture he wiped the back of his hand across his eyes. 'You can't imagine what it was like, getting Mrs Haskin's letter. To bring this upon your family – after the way you've been raised. How could you do such a thing?'

'Father –' she began, but he overrode her.

'What does *he* have to say about it – the man?'

When she did not reply, he went on, 'Susan Haskin said his name's Joel, and that he's from a comfortably-off family. Which ain't such good news. Rich man's son getting involved with the servant girl – it's the oldest story in the world, and never one with a happy ending. What did he say when you told him?'

'I haven't told him.'

'He doesn't know?'

'No.'

'Mrs Haskin said she believes he's in France.'

'He was. He's back in England now.'

'Then you must write to him, at once. You got an address?'

She nodded.

'Then he's got to know. He's got to do the right thing by you. And if he won't marry you, then he's got to help in other ways. He's got to see sense over this, and if he doesn't, then I'll make him see sense meself.'

'Father, it's finished with him,' she said. 'It's over. I'll never see him again.'

'But he's got to be *told*. He can't just get off scot-free. He's got to be told.'

'No. No, please. It's got nothing to do with him.'

He frowned. 'What d'you mean? You're not making sense.'

'Father – it wasn't *him*.'

'What?' There was astonishment in his tone. 'It wasn't *him*?' Then outrage came. 'Are you saying you've been seeing more than one man?'

'No,' she burst out, 'it wasn't like that.' And now her tears welled up. 'Father, I've done nothing wrong. I swear to you. Joel and I – we did nothing wrong together.'

'Then – then *who*?'

She paused for a breath, then whispered, 'It was – Mr Haskin.'

Silence met her words, and there was no sound but for her muffled weeping. Her father stood gazing at her while the basin tipped in his hand, spilling some berries into the grass.

'Are you telling me that he – he took advantage of you?' There was cold disbelief in his voice. 'Is that what you're saying?'

'It's the truth.'

He continued to gaze at her, then slowly shook his head. 'I never dreamt, in all my days, that you'd turn out to be such a disappointment in my life.'

'Oh, but Father – '

He did not let her finish. 'Such a disappointment,' he said. 'And that you should lie in this manner just makes it so much worse. How could you do such a thing? Lie about a man, in order to save your own reputation and this ne'er-do-well you're protecting. Roger Haskin is my oldest and most trusted friend. The most trustworthy man you could ever hope to meet. That's why we sent you there. We sent you to a place where we knew you'd be safe and not

126

exploited in any way.' His expression was a mixture of anger, puzzlement and hurt. 'I don't understand how you can say such a thing of a good man. May God forgive you, for I can't.' He looked down at the half-empty basin in his hand, as if suddenly becoming aware of it, then upended it and watched the remaining elderberries fall. 'You had a whole life ahead of you, and you've thrown it all away.'

She said nothing, but stood with head bowed, the tears cooling on her cheeks.

'Well,' he said, 'you can't have it here, the baby – you realise that, don't you?'

She did not speak, did not move.

'No, you'll have to go away till it's over. If you're set against involving this man who's responsible, then so be it. Your mother and I have already talked it over, and during the next few days we'll decide on where you'll go.'

The days dragged by, while Lily worked in the house, rarely going further than the front gate. When she volunteered to go to the butcher's or the post office her offer was coolly declined. It was as if her stepmother did not want the local neighbourhood to be reminded of her presence. Tom, observing it, was distressed. 'I can't bear to see it,' he said. 'The way they treat you.'

'Don't be upset,' Lily told him, 'it won't go on for much longer. I shall be going away again soon.'

'Where?' he said. 'When?'

'I don't yet know where, but it'll be very soon.'

'Why are you going?'

'I – I can't talk about that.'

He was bewildered. 'How long will you be gone?'

'I don't know. A good few months.'

'But you'll come back and visit, won't you?'

'Not for a good while.'

'Maybe you won't ever come back. Maybe this time you'll go for good.'

She gave a little shrug. 'I don't know. Perhaps.'

'If you go away, we shan't ever be together again, Lil.'

'No, Tom, you mustn't say that.'

'D'you think we shall, then?'

'One day. You wait and see.'

He sighed. 'Oh, I wish I wus going with you. Sometimes I think I'll never get away from here.'

While Lily remained in the relative seclusion of the house, her father and stepmother set about making the arrangements that would eventually take her away again. Aware of it, and waiting, she thought she would not be so sad to leave. Her life as she had known it was finished, and although the future lay uncharted before her, this present limbo where she was treated almost as an outcast was unbearable. Then, one evening, just under three weeks after her return from Whitton, she was told that the arrangements were complete.

Supper was finished, and as soon as the dishes were cleared away and washed and dried, Mrs Clair turned to Tom and suggested that it was time he was off to bed. He went at once, saying his goodnights and leaving Lily and her father and stepmother sitting in the tense quiet of the kitchen. Lily, guessing that something was to be said, could see the awkwardness in her father's demeanour as he prepared himself to speak. Wasting no time in prompting him, Mrs Clair looked up from her mending and hissed, 'You'd better get on with it, then, or we'll be here all night.'

Mr Clair tapped the dead ash from his pipe and prodded the bowl with his fingertip. 'Yes,' he said. 'You're going away. It's all settled. Your mother and I have made the arrangements. It's all done.'

Lily waited but he said nothing further. She looked from

her father to her stepmother, then back to her father again. 'Where am I to go?' she said.

'You're going to Sherrell, not far from Corster. There's a lady there, Miss Balfour. You'll be going to stay with her.'

'Miss Balfour?' Lily said. 'Who – who is she?'

Mrs Clair answered the question. 'She's a lady who's dealt with a few girls in your situation before. Not that she advertises the fact.' She shot a look at her husband. 'Go on, tell her.'

'You'll stay with Miss Balfour,' Mr Clair said, 'and you'll help her out in any way you can, while you're able to, while you're fit enough. As I understand it, you'll do work for a local factory or do needlework. You won't receive any wages for your work, but you'll get your board and lodging, and she'll see you over the birth of the child, and through its adoption.'

'And if you think,' Mrs Clair said, 'that this is going to cost *us* nothing, you can think again. The lady's not a charity institution. The bit of work you do for her won't be enough to keep you, so we've got to pay her something too.'

Mr Clair nodded. 'Yes. Not a fortune, but we've got to pay her nevertheless. Even a shilling a week is a lot to find when times are hard.'

'You don't need to go into detail,' Mrs Clair said impatiently. 'It's neither here nor there how much we pay. The fact is, the lady's not doing it for nothing, and that's all the girl needs to know.'

'You won't, of course, be coming home during your time,' Mr Clair said.

'Indeed not,' said his wife. 'You're not even to show your face in Compton. We're sending you to Sherrell because it's far enough away, so there'll be precious little chance you'll bump into somebody who knows you. But just because you think you're out of the way, doesn't mean you can go gallivanting around. You'll stay close to the house and do

129

as the lady tells you. If you don't, there'll be trouble. She won't put up with any of your nonsense.'

'Quite,' Mr Clair said. 'We want no complaints about your behaviour.'

'No, we don't,' Mrs Clair snapped. She jabbed a sharp finger in Lily's direction. 'And you can take that miserable look off your face. Think yourself lucky. Other girls in your situation get locked away, sometimes for years, in the asylum, or at best go to the convent.'

Silence fell in the room. 'What is to happen to me – afterwards?' Lily said.

'Afterwards?' her father said. 'After your confinement?'

'Yes.'

'Well – you'll have to find employment somewhere.'

'Yes,' her stepmother said. 'Don't go thinking you can come back here and expect to be kept.' She tossed down the shirt she was mending and got up from her chair. 'I'm going up to bed,' she said to her husband. She stood for a moment with her mouth set in a thin line, then turned back to Lily. 'You've brought disgrace on this family, and I'll never forgive you for it.' She continued to glare at her for a moment, then turned and without any further word crossed to the door and went out.

Lily waited until the sound of her stepmother's footfalls had faded on the stairs, then said to her father in a low voice:

'When am I to go?'

'On Saturday,' he said. 'I'll take you to the train.'

The following morning Lily was out sweeping the path, when the old postman came by in his red jacket. Seeing her there, he wished her a cheery good morning and handed her a letter. It was addressed to herself and again had been redirected from the Haskins' house at Whitton. It could only be from Joel.

She opened the envelope, withdrew a single sheet of notepaper and read:

Clare College, Cambridge
19th October 1866

Lily,

I received yours of the 6th. As I had not heard from you for weeks, you can only imagine my happiness at receiving a letter from you. And if you can imagine that, you can also imagine the distress with which I read your words. I never thought to know such unhappiness at your hands, and if I had not the words from your own pen I would not accept them. But I have, and accept them I must, though I cannot believe for one moment that you are right in what you say. I ask you, therefore, to please reconsider your decision.

I will not try to contact you again, but will just hope to hear that you have had second thoughts, and that you realise that you can indeed have a future with one whose aching heart is still yours,

Joel

She held the letter pressed to her breast, while tears stung at her eyes. His words brought pain to her, as she had known and feared they would. But she had had to write as she did, there had been no other way. She put the letter back in the envelope, and slipped it into her pocket. She would not write again. Now, at last, it was truly over.

On Saturday morning, the last in October, Lily and her father left the house to take the omnibus to the station. Lily had said her goodbyes to Tom the night before, and there had been tears in his eyes as he had embraced her. That morning she had kissed Dora goodbye, and exhorted her to be a good girl. There had been no farewell from her stepmother. Indeed, Mrs Clair had not even been in the house when Lily had left it; she had chosen to be out on an errand to the shop, carefully timing her journey so as to miss the parting from her stepdaughter.

Later, on the station platform, Lily stood waiting at her father's side. In his face she read a mixture of emotions, hardly hidden by his frowning brow and tight-set mouth. When the train appeared, rounding the bend and coming towards them with the smoke rising up, he turned to her and said gruffly,

'Well, goodbye, girl. I don't know when I'll see you again, but I hope it'll be in happier times. You be good, and do as Miss Balfour tells you.'

'Yes, Father.'

'And for God's sake don't bring any more misery home.'

The train was grinding to a halt beside them. As soon as it had stopped, Mr Clair wrenched open the nearest door and climbed in with Lily's box, stowing it under the seat. Then he stepped back down onto the platform and helped Lily on board. Setting her portmanteau down, she stood and faced her father as he remained on the platform. With a sudden movement he reached up, and with one large hand pressed her own gloved hand as it rested on the edge of the open window. 'G'bye, girl.' He did not meet her eyes as he spoke.

'Goodbye, Father.' Her voice broke on the words.

Another moment and he was turning, striding away along the platform without a backward glance. Seconds later the train was on the move.

The journey to Sherell took just under two hours. When the train had pulled to a stop, Lily dragged her box out from under the seat and down onto the platform. As she straightened, her luggage at her feet, she saw approaching her a short, middle-aged man. As he drew nearer he looked at her questioningly and said, 'Miss Clair? Are you Miss Clair?'

'Yes, I am,' Lily replied, and tentatively returned the smile he gave her.

'I'm sent to meet you, miss.' He had a slim, wiry body, and a face lined like a walnut. He bent and hoisted up her box and swung it up onto his shoulder. 'You can manage your case, can you?' He gestured towards her portmanteau and she replied, 'Yes, of course.'

He set off then at a smart pace along the platform, with Lily walking at his side. Outside the station he moved to where a pony and trap stood waiting. 'Here we are. Not a grand carriage, but it'll get us there.' He pushed the box into the well of the trap and then followed it with Lily's portmanteau. 'You want to sit up front with me?' he said.

'Why, yes. Thank you.'

He helped her up, then unhitched the pony and climbed up himself. 'Come on, Sal,' he called out. 'Let's be off.'

As they moved away along the street he said, 'The young ladies who've come here call me Mr Shad. My name's Shadrak, but it ain't a name I cares to dwell on.'

Lily said tentatively, 'How d'you do, Mr Shad,' and put out her hand. He took it and briefly pressed it. 'Pleased to meet you,' he replied.

They continued on. Lily had never been this far from home before and the small market town of Sherrell was quite new to her. It looked a pleasant place, not too large, and with many of the old buildings characterful and attractive. After a while of journeying the houses thinned and the trap was driven onto a country road, bordered on either side by fields.

'Not far now, miss,' Mr Shad said. 'Rowanleigh's on the edge of the town, near Kepple.' He nodded his head towards the pony. 'I'm afraid old Sally takes it at her own

133

pace. Like the rest of us she's gettin' on in years.' He chuckled. 'And like most women she won't be 'urried.'

Lily had to smile. 'Have you been with Miss Balfour long, Mr Shad?' she asked.

'Oh, a good few years. Long before she come to Rowanleigh. I wus with her and Miss Beecham beforehand when they 'ad the school in Shalford. There was plenty to keep me busy there, as you can imagine, but I got enough to do 'ere as well. I got more than the 'orse to keep me busy. I'm groom, gardener and general 'andyman. I can turn me 'and to just about anything, I s'pose.'

Lily, liking the man, and feeling more at ease in his company, said, 'I don't mind telling you, Mr Shad, I'm a little nervous, I have to confess.' There was no point in pretending that the situation was anything other than it was. The man had seen other young women come and go at the house, and he knew well what they were there for.

He nodded. 'Well, I should think that's to be expected, miss, though I don't reckon you got anything to be nervous about. Anyway, the mistress'll put you right, sure enough.' He flicked the reins with his weathered, brown hands. 'Come on, Sal old girl,' he called. 'Not far to go now.'

For a while they drove on without speaking, and then Mr Shad was pointing ahead to a house that stood beside a little grove of trees. 'There we are, miss. There's Rowanleigh.'

A minute later they had reached the house, and Mr Shad was down and opening the gates. Behind a well-kept lawn was a solid-looking yellow-brick dwelling of three storeys with a red-tiled roof. A flagged path ran up to the front door, and a gravel driveway to the stable buildings at the rear.

Mr Shad led the pony through the open gateway, then climbed back up and took the reins again. Moments later the trap was coming to a halt in the stable yard and Mr Shad was jumping down onto the gravel. Reaching up, he helped Lily to alight. As she stepped down beside him the side door to the house opened and a tall woman stood there.

'So, Shad,' she said, 'you've got the young lady.'

'Yes, ma'am.'

Lily had been reaching out to take her portmanteau, but the woman said at once, 'Leave those for Mr Shad. He'll take them.' She spoke rather gruffly, with little warmth in her tone. She looked to be somewhere in her early sixties. Her impressive height was set off by the plainest and most severe grey skirt that Lily could have imagined, atop of which was an unadorned white blouse with, at the throat, what looked to be a man's cravat. She had a strong, unsympathetic jaw, a wide, thin-lipped mouth, and pale eyes framed by steel-rimmed spectacles. Her greying hair was pulled back and secured in a bun at the nape of her neck. 'I'm Miss Balfour,' she said, then added, turning, 'Come with me. I'll show you to your room.'

Leaving Mr Shad to handle her luggage, Lily stepped across the gravel and into the house, finding herself in a rear passage with an open door to a scullery or wash-house to one side and a kitchen on the other.

'Don't dawdle,' Miss Balfour said ahead of her, and Lily quickened her step. Following the woman, she went from the passage into the main hall and then up two flights of stairs. On the second floor the woman stopped outside a door and turned the handle. 'Here's where you'll stay,' she said.

It was not a large room, but it was comfortably furnished. Aside from the bed – a little wider than her bed at home – there were a narrow wardrobe and a small chest of drawers. Under the window stood a writing table with a chair.

As they moved inside a knock came at the open door and Lily turned to see Mr Shad with her box on one shoulder and her portmanteau held in his hand. 'The young lady's things, ma'am,' he said and stepped into the room and set the luggage down next to the bed. Miss Balfour thanked him briefly and he went away again.

'Now,' Miss Balfour said when Mr Shad's footsteps had faded on the stairs, 'there are certain things you need to know.' She looked at Lily with a frankness of gaze. 'I hope you're a sensible girl. Though if you were that sensible you wouldn't be here in the first place. But be that as it may. If you behave well and do your work properly we'll get on all right.' She nodded in confirmation of her words, giving the message that there would be none wasted. 'There are rules for the house, but they'll keep for a while. Are you hungry?'

'Well, ma'am . . .' Lily said hesitantly. She had eaten no breakfast and was indeed rather hungry, but she was nervous of saying so.

'I'll arrange for Mary to make you a sandwich,' Miss Balfour said shortly. 'That'll keep you going till we have dinner at seven.' She waved a hand to indicate Lily's luggage. 'I'll leave you to unpack your things now and have a wash, and then I'll see you downstairs in a little while. I'll send Mary up to fetch you when it's time.' She turned and went out, closing the door behind her.

Lily had just finished packing away the last of her things in the chest of drawers when there came a tap at the door, and it opened to reveal a young woman dressed in a maid's cap and apron. She looked to be about nineteen or twenty. She had pale reddish hair, with freckles over her nose, and carried a laden tray. With a nod she deposited it on the writing table. 'I brought you your sandwich, miss,' she said and Lily thanked her. Moving back to the doorway the maid said, 'When you've et it, miss, I'm to come and take you to the mistress.'

When the door had closed behind the maid, Lily washed her face and hands, and then sat at the small table and ate the sandwich. It was cheese, with a tomato pickle, and was very good. Ten minutes after it was finished there came a knock at the door again, and the maid was back, ready to take her to see Miss Balfour.

The girl led the way down the stairs. As Lily stepped down beside her, the maid half-turned to her and asked, 'What's your name, miss?'

'Lily. Lily Clair.'

The girl nodded. 'I'm pleased to meet you, miss. I'm Mary.'

Reaching the first floor, the maid led the way to a room off the landing where she knocked and opened the door. 'Go on in, miss, if you please.'

Lily stepped over the threshold and found herself in a large, cluttered room with tall windows. Near to the door was a wide table, the surface of which was almost hidden by a number of pencil sketches and half-finished water-colour paintings. A small easel was there, and littered about were the tools of an artist: paints, mixing trays, and jars of pencils and paintbrushes. At the other end of the room by the far window stood a desk where Miss Balfour sat smoking a cigarette. The walls behind her were lined from floor to ceiling with shelves of books and files. The smell of tobacco smoke hung in the air.

'Come in and shut the door.'

Lily did as she was told, and moved across the room to the chair that Miss Balfour indicated.

'Did you finish your unpacking?' Miss Balfour asked.

'Yes, thank you, ma'am.'

'And you got your sandwich all right?'

'Yes, thank you.'

'Good.' Miss Balfour drew on her cigarette and blew out the smoke in a plume over her head. There was a photograph on the desk, Lily noticed. Set in a silver frame, it was a head-and-shoulders portrait of an attractive young woman who looked to be in her thirties.

Taking Lily's attention from the picture, Miss Balfour asked, 'Did you have a good journey from your home?'

'Yes, thank you.'

'Good. How are you feeling?'

'I'm feeling well, thank you.'

'No discomfort?' She patted her own stomach.

'No, I'm quite all right.'

'Are you having morning sickness?'

'I was. It stopped a week ago.'

The woman nodded. 'That must be a great relief. How far along are you?'

'Nine weeks.'

Miss Balfour nodded and made a note on the page of a ledger that lay open on the desk before her. 'So the date was . . . ?' She waited. When Lily did not reply, she said with a note of contained impatience in her voice, 'I'm not asking this for any gratuitous pleasure; I need to keep my records. Just let me have the date.'

'The twenty-sixth of August.'

Miss Balfour made another note in the ledger. 'And what was the date when your last menses came on? Can you remember?'

'It – it would have been near the middle of the month, say the twelfth or thirteenth. I'm very regular.'

'Right.' Miss Balfour did some swift calculations with pen on paper, counted off some months on her fingers, then said, 'I should think we can expect the birth sometime in the third week of May. Round about the nineteenth or twentieth.' She made further notes, then looked up at Lily again. 'It isn't my purpose to moralise with you,' she said. 'I'm not one of the sisters up at the Heart of the Virgin. I've no interest in going into the whys and wherefores as to how you came to get into your present condition. That has to be accepted. You're in this situation, and I have made an agreement with your parents that I'll see you through it with no added shame to them. Unless they come here to visit you, you won't be seeing them again until after the birth. If you're one to suffer from homesickness you're going to have to get over it, because I can tell you now that, although you'll be looked after, you're not going to be pampered. We've got no time for that and no inclination for it either. You're not ill, you're in a very natural condition, a condition that's necessary to make the world continue. So you're not going to be treated as an invalid. Do you understand that?'

'Yes, ma'am.'

Miss Balfour nodded. 'Good.' She took a drag on her cigarette, and the grey smoke streamed out of her mouth and nostrils. 'What you do once you've left my care is entirely up to you, but while you're here you will do as you're told.'

'Yes, ma'am.'

'Your parents have made a certain small allowance for you, while you're here, to help towards your expenses, but it won't cover them. So you'll be expected to work. Is that clear?'

'Yes, ma'am. I'm not afraid of work.'

'I'm glad to hear it. Your stepmother tells me you're good with your needle, are you?'

'I – I don't know.'

'You must know whether you are or not. Are you, or aren't you?'

Lily nodded. 'Y-yes, ma'am. I do consider myself to be.'

'Fine. Because if you are, there'll be no shortage of needlework for you.' Here she stubbed out the end of her cigarette in an ashtray. 'I have an arrangement with a draper in Corster, and those of my young women who have suitable talents are pleased to keep him supplied with certain items he needs. Although more and more sewing these days is done by machine, so many ladies only want hand-stitched goods, even going as far as plain seams.' She gave a grudging nod of satisfaction. 'Good. So if you're capable of doing some fine needlework you'll do well. Otherwise it's a matter of homework from the local button factory. That's what my young women tend to do if they are not up to the sewing. Though some of them have been hardly capable of any kind of work at all. Born with silver spoons in their mouths and hardly fit for any kind of work at all. But they learnt. No place for indolence here. By the way, if you're wondering if there will be any other young ladies with you, you'll be the only one. To tell you the truth, I had decided to have no more, but then your parents got in touch with me.' She sighed. 'I'm afraid I don't have the energy I once had. Besides,' she waved a hand towards her cluttered painting table, 'I do have other interests in life.'

As Lily sat there, Miss Balfour went on to tell her about what she could expect in her time at Rowanleigh. There would be no going out of the house without permission, and though it was customary for the young women to run certain necessary errands, these would be arranged. There would be no meetings with members of the opposite sex, there would be no indulgence of cigarettes or alcohol. As she finished saying this last, she took a cigarette from a small silver case on the desk and lit it with a match. After blowing out the flame she said, 'This of course does not apply to myself, as you can see. I am neither in a certain condition, nor am I a guest in someone else's house.'

So she continued. Meals would of course be served at set times, and strict bedtimes would also be observed, as would early risings in the mornings. 'Until you're well into your seventh month you'll be expected to be up by six-thirty,' Miss Balfour said. 'You'll also, in addition to your needlework, be expected to give a hand around the house. I keep a live-in maid, and a part-time cook, and of course Mr Shad. There's enough to do about the place.' She drew on her cigarette. 'Of course,' she added, 'once you've recovered from the birth you'll be expected to leave.'

Lily nodded. 'Yes, of course.'

'Do you have any idea what you might do then?'

'No.'

'Well – you'll have to give it some thought sooner or later. Fortunately, it's no concern of mine.' She tapped off the ash from her cigarette. 'Have you given any thought to the birth of the child?'

'I – I'm not sure I know what you mean, ma'am,' Lily said.

'I hope you're not foolish enough to entertain ideas about keeping it.'

'No. Oh, no.' Now Lily's response was swift. 'No, I'd never want to do that.'

'I'm relieved to hear it. Adoption is the only course for all concerned – the mother *and* the baby – though not every young mother is so ready to realise it. In the past I've had a couple of young women who, once the child was born, had a complete change of heart and decided they wanted to keep it. I'm glad to say I managed to dissuade them. They couldn't have managed on their own. What kind of life would it have been for them? They'd have ended up on the streets or in the workhouse.'

'No,' Lily said again, 'I'd never want to keep the baby. Never.'

Chapter Nine

It had rained heavily during the night and the ground was sodden. The December sky was grey through the bare branches of the rowan tree. Moving about its foot a hopeful blackbird turned over the saturated leaves in a search for food.

It was just after twelve. The house was quiet. Miss Balfour had driven out to visit one of her old friends who was ill in bed with influenza. Mrs Nessant, the cook, was occupied in the kitchen. Mary was somewhere in the house busy at her cleaning. Lily sighed and leant back in her chair, her hand unconsciously moving to the slight swell of her belly. Through the window she could see the blackbird busy beneath the tree; he was there most days.

She was seated at the small writing table in the sewing room. The room being small, it took relatively little fuel to keep it warm, so was a well-used spot in the house when the weather was cold, not only for sewing but for any task that did not require a great deal of space. Lily found it a comforting place, and for most of the morning she had sat working at the sewing that had come from the Corster draper. Now, having completed work on the lapels of a velvet jacket, she had spent some minutes writing a short letter to Tom. She had not heard from him in several weeks, and although he was not much of a one for regularly corresponding, she had been expecting to hear something from him before now.

As was her wont since arriving at the house seven weeks

ago, she spent several hours each day alone, but she did not feel her solitude adversely. For the most part she was kept well occupied, not only with the sewing for the Corster draper, but also making garments – sewn, knitted or crocheted – for the expected baby.

She saw Miss Balfour usually only at breakfast and then at dinner in the evening. Sometimes she would also take tea with her in the drawing room. At all their meetings, Miss Balfour kept her distance, volunteering little about herself, and showing little curiosity about Lily beyond her health and her sewing work. While Lily would have liked their conversations to have been a little less reserved and cool, she was relieved that the woman did not ask too many questions. Not once had she asked Lily about the father of the child she was carrying, and how Lily would have responded had such questions come, she did not know.

There were times in the quiet of her room when she lay unable to sleep, feeling hatred for Haskin and what he had done to her. His assault had changed her life. Not only had it caused her to give up the man she loved, but it had left her expecting a child. She thought again of Miss Balfour speaking of the one or two young women who had expressed a wish to keep their newborn babes. There was no chance of that happening where Lily was concerned. She did not want the child she carried or anything to do with its upbringing. She had no feelings of love for it and could not for a moment dream that any would manifest themselves.

Many times, too, she thought of Joel. Did he ever think of her? If so, did he think of her with bitterness? She tried to picture him at his studies, imagining him as she had never seen him in actuality, leaning over his desk, frowning over the work before him, long legs bent under him, mouth set in concentration. Perhaps he had forgotten her and never gave her a thought. But she could not truly believe that to be the case. After all, he had said he loved her, and even a love that had not lasted must leave a few scars.

'The second post just arrived, miss. This came for you.'

Disturbed out of her reverie, Lily turned as Mary came into the room with a letter in her hand. When the maid had gone again, Lily looked at the handwriting on the envelope and saw that it was from her father. She regarded it with mixed feelings. Whilst she was so glad to hear from him, she did not want any of the coldness that often accompanied his letters, a coldness that came with a lingering, unspoken blame.

She opened the envelope, took out the two folded sheets of notepaper, and read:

Compton Wells
11th December 1866

Daughter,

I'm hoping this finds you well, and that you are escaping the flu. I'm afraid your little sister has the sniffles, and is a little bad-tempered as a result. But your mother and I are as well as can be expected.

I hope you're getting on all right and are doing your work as you should. I hope too that you fully appreciate the great kindness Miss Balfour is bestowing upon you, and that you suitably show your gratitude. Perhaps when this is all over you can make a new start and begin to make something of your life. Though I have to tell you, with regard to your future, that it will have to be forged somewhere other than in Compton. I can make no pretence but must tell you that your mother is not willing to have you home again.

In your letter you asked after your brother, remarking that you have had no word from him recently, that your last letter has gone unanswered. Your last letter to him is lying here still unopened. I must tell you that your brother has gone, almost two weeks since. He went off for work at his usual time in the morning, but never returned home that evening. When I later made enquiries at the farm they said he had not turned up for work that day. We have heard nothing from him since. In the event you're so disposed, I would advise you against wasting sympathy on him. He had a good home here, and he has chosen to turn his back on it, no doubt thinking that other pastures are greener. He'll find out the truth soon enough, I daresay, and will be more than ready to come on back with his tail between his legs. Thomas has been the greatest disappointment to us. Your mother always said that he'd never amount to anything, and she's been proved right. Indeed, with my two elder children having brought me such grief, I can only pray that my daughter Dora will show herself to be of better stuff.

 Your loving
  Father

Lily gave a sigh. Nothing had changed where her father and stepmother were concerned, though in truth she had not expected it to, and in addition it had now been made clear to her that she was no longer welcome in the family home. How hurtful were her father's words. But so be it, she said to herself, she would make her own way; and her future was never in Compton in the first place.

Saddening as the letter was, what was more disturbing was the news of Tom's disappearance. She would wait. She would wait and he would write to her, she was sure of that.

The days of winter dragged on. Christmas and New Year's day had come and gone, causing little more than a ripple in the routine at Rowanleigh. The annual scourge of influenza had come early and severely this winter, and many were becoming affected.

Lily seemed to be cocooned in the house, not only by the snow that had lately fallen, but by the lack of contact with the outside world. She had heard again sparingly from her father at Christmas, but of her brother Tom there had been no word.

Sitting at the table in the sewing room, she sighed. Her back ached slightly, and she put a hand to it and stretched. She was in her fifth month now. Beyond the window the garden was bleak and colourless. Touches of the snow still lingered on the iron-hard earth around the lawn's borders. The sun hung low in the sky, pale and watery, giving no hint or promise of warmth. The blackbird had not been in evidence for several days. How long and drawn-out the winter seemed, and spring still so far away.

The house was very quiet. She had worked for hours at the sewing that had come from the draper, but had put it aside for a while in order to read a little. From Miss Balfour's well-stocked library she had taken a history of the American War of Independence. Fascinating as the story was, though, she found it hard to concentrate, and eventually put it aside too. That morning had seen a visit from the local midwife, Mrs Toomley, a jolly, sharp-faced little woman in her fifties who, under the watchful eye of Miss Balfour, had come in and bustled around, feeling and prodding Lily and asking her questions in connection with her condition. She had gone away declaring herself well satisfied with Lily's progress, adding that she would be visiting again soon.

Into the quiet of the room came the faint sound of activity from the hall where Mary was brushing down the stair-carpet, singing as she worked. She alone had come in today. Mrs Nessant had not put in an appearance as her elderly mother had come down with the influenza and the cook had remained at home to care for her. Lily looked at the clock on the mantel and saw that the time was just coming up to four o'clock. Miss Balfour was out of the house, having gone into Corster to collect the rent on two small houses she owned there. She was expected back soon.

Lily remained in the sewing room for a while longer, then rose from her seat and went down to the kitchen. There she took up the basket of vegetables that Mr Shad had left and began to prepare them at the old pine table. With Mrs Nessant absent, Lily was expected to help with the cooking. When she had finished she set the table in the dining room. That done, she went back to the sewing room where she worked with her needle until the light was gone. Shortly afterwards she heard the closing of the front door, marking the fact that Miss Balfour was back.

Dinner that evening was an even quieter affair than usual. Miss Balfour seemed subdued and ate very little, in the end pushing her unfinished plate aside. When Lily asked politely if she was well, the woman frowned and put a hand up to her head. 'I've got a bit of a headache,' she said. 'I hope I'm not coming down with the flu. We don't need *that* in the house – especially with you in your condition.' A few minutes later she had laid down her napkin, made her excuses and gone up to her room.

As Mary was so busy the next morning, Lily prepared breakfast for herself and Miss Balfour, but Miss Balfour did not appear. Lily ate alone, and when she had finished she went to Miss Balfour's room and knocked on the door. After a moment there came a call to come in and she turned the handle and entered. Miss Balfour lay in bed, the gloom of the room only lightened by the pale light that crept in beside the edge of the curtain.

'You didn't come down for breakfast, ma'am, and I wondered about you,' Lily said.

'No.' Miss Balfour's voice was little more than a croak. Her grey hair was held tight to her head with a close-fitting cap. 'I don't want anything.' She coughed. 'I ache all over, and I've got this awful catarrh and cough. I think I must have that dratted flu.' She coughed again, partly raising herself up off the pillow, then sank back down.

'Are you sure you wouldn't like just a little something? I could get you a lightly scrambled egg, or some porridge.'

'No, I don't want anything.' She paused. 'I keep shivering. I can't seem to keep warm.'

'I'll get you another blanket,' Lily said, 'and light the fire.'

Miss Balfour thanked her. 'I don't think I shall be getting up today,' she said.

Two days passed, and Miss Balfour remained in bed, uncomplaining but showing no inclination to move, and telling Lily and Mary all the while, 'Don't fuss, don't fuss.' On Sunday morning, however, under Lily's tentative persuasion, she agreed to have the doctor, and Mr Shad went off to summon him. Dr Hanbury, a slight man with spectacles and a thin beard and a thin voice to match, called just before three that afternoon. After seeing Miss Balfour he said to Lily, who waited in the hall, that he would send his boy round with some medicine. 'This influenza,' he added, 'it's a most virulent strain, and we don't want it to turn to pneumonia.' Taking in Lily's obvious condition, he gazed at her for a moment then said, 'What about you? Are you feeling all right?'

'Yes, thank you, sir.'

'We don't want you coming down with it as well. When is your baby due?'

'In May, sir.'

'Well – you must look after yourself.'

A while later the doctor's boy came to the back door with a little package of medicine. Mary took it in and handed it

148

to Lily. There was a bottle of quinine and some phenacetin powder, both of which had to be mixed with water. Lily did what was required and carried the medicines upstairs and stood by while Miss Balfour swallowed them. Later, she made some cabbage soup and tried to tempt Miss Balfour with a little, but she wanted nothing of it.

In spite of extra blankets and the fire being well banked, Miss Balfour shivered. Dr Hanbury, calling again the next day, recommended to Lily that a goose grease or mustard poultice on the chest might help, as well as camphorated oil applied to the neck. After he had gone, Lily asked Mr Shad to ride to the butcher and the chemist, and when he had returned with the goods, she warmed up the grease in a basin, and carried it upstairs along with the oil and some pieces of flannel. Informed of the doctor's recommendations, Miss Balfour at first would have none of it, but after a little persuasion she reluctantly agreed to the camphorated oil. When it came to the goose grease poultice, however, she refused point blank.

Gently, Lily massaged into the woman's neck a little of the camphorated oil, and then laid around it a piece of flannel. When she had finished she went down to the kitchen and heated the soup, then, back upstairs again, held the bowl while Miss Balfour took a few spoonfuls. Afterwards, as Lily settled her back, and straightened her pillows, Miss Balfour said haltingly through her dry lips, 'You shouldn't . . . be doing this. It's not your job.'

'It's all right, ma'am,' Lily said. 'It's no trouble.'

'Trouble or not . . .' Miss Balfour panted for breath, 'you should be keeping well away. You don't want to catch it in your condition, and you could, so easily.'

'I'm all right. I'm strong.'

'It isn't a matter of being strong. Mary can help me.'

'Mary's got other things to do. Especially with Mrs Nessant being away.'

The next morning Miss Balfour's condition was even more alarming. Bending at her bedside Lily saw the perspiration standing out on her brow and saturating the hair at her temples. She would have nothing to eat, and would take only a few sips of water.

Dr Hanbury came again that afternoon, and at his request Lily went with him to Miss Balfour's room. With his stethoscope he sounded Miss Balfour's chest and remarked that it was still heavily congested. 'You must keep giving her the quinine,' he said to Lily, 'and applying the goose grease poultices.'

'She won't have the poultice, sir,' Lily said.

'Not have the poultice? But she must.' He looked down at Miss Balfour as she lay with her cracked lips parted, breathing heavily. 'You hear that, Miss Balfour? You must have the poultice. This is no time for being shy. You're very sick, and if you won't let this young lady do it, then I'll have to send round a nurse – and heaven knows they've got enough to do already.'

When the doctor had gone, Lily heated the goose grease in a basin and then took it upstairs along with some pieces of flannel. This time, Miss Balfour ceased to object and, though with obvious misgivings and no little embarrassment, gave herself up to Lily's ministrations. By the light of the lamp Lily drew back the bedcovers and pushed Miss Balfour's nightdress up to her shoulders, exposing her pale, large-boned body and small breasts. All the while Miss Balfour kept her eyes closed and never spoke a word. Lily got the basin of warm grease and, scooping some up into her hand, gently spread it over Miss Balfour's chest, above and between her breasts. Once it had been smoothed in, she took pieces of flannel and laid them over the grease, gently pressing them in place. When she had finished, she pulled Miss Balfour's nightdress down and drew up the bedcovers. Still Miss Balfour spoke no word.

When Mary arrived the next morning it was apparent at once to Lily that the girl was sick. In between coughs, the maid told her that she had a fever and had hardly slept the previous night. 'You shouldn't be here,' Lily told her. 'You should be in bed.'

'Oh, but how'll you manage without me, miss?' Mary said. 'What with the missus being ill and Mrs Nessant bein' away.'

Lily looked at her with a shake of her head. 'Go on home, Mary,' she said. 'I'll manage. Go on home and don't come back till you're well. The cleaning and washing will have to go hang, and if I need anything from the shops Mr Shad will get it. Go on – put your bonnet and cape back on and go home.'

When the maid had gone, Lily gave Miss Balfour her medicine, and then prepared for her a little dish of eggs and milk, of which Miss Balfour took a few spoonfuls. Afterwards, Lily applied a fresh poultice and then helped Miss Balfour – now so weak – to get out of bed to use the commode. 'I never dreamt,' Miss Balfour said hoarsely as Lily helped her back into bed, 'that I'd rely on another for such needs.'

On the evening of the next day, Lily went upstairs to give Miss Balfour her medicine and found her tossing and turning in the bed while muttering disjointed phrases in her dry, cracked voice. After Lily had calmed her and persuaded her to take her medicine, she sponged her brow and neck. 'You're so good to me, Aggie,' Miss Balfour murmured brokenly, her head resting against Lily's arm. 'I don't know what I'd do without you.'

*

Miss Balfour's delirium only subsided when she lapsed into a coma.

Lily found her unconscious when she went upstairs to give her her medicine the next morning. She spoke to her but there was no response, and there was no flicker of animation in the still face. When Lily took up the woman's hand it remained seemingly lifeless. Downstairs, heedless of the cold, she ran out into the yard, calling for Mr Shad. Minutes later he had saddled up the cob and was riding off for the doctor.

Dr Hanbury arrived just after three and at once went up to the bedroom where Miss Balfour lay, moving not a muscle in her stupor. He lifted her eyelid, sounded her chest, and gave an unhappy sigh. With this form of the disease, he said, the influenza poison sometimes affected the brain. He pushed his spectacles up on his thin nose. 'We can only hope,' he said, 'that she'll come out of it in a few days.'

In the morning Lily saw no change in Miss Balfour. It was pointless to prepare food for her; she could not even take her medicine.

Lily herself was running out of energy. Nevertheless she had to look after Miss Balfour and keep the fires banked and burning. She also had to give a thought to Mr Shad. He, who was usually fed by Mrs Nessant or Mary or Miss Balfour, was in danger of missing his meals, and Lily was obliged to provide for him. So she prepared food and set it out on the kitchen table. At other times, she supplied him with a basket of bread and pickles and cheese to take back to his room over the stable and make a meal for himself.

In the late afternoon of that Saturday, when the skies darkened with threatened rain, Dr Hanbury called again, and shook his head over his patient's prostrate form. The rain, a cold icy rain, began an hour after his departure, and set in, falling steadily. Up in Miss Balfour's room Lily closed the casement and built up the fire. Later in the evening Mr Shad came with fresh supplies of firewood and kindling, and Lily gave him some soup and a plate of cold cuts for his supper, along with a jug of beer. When he had eaten and gone, she locked the door against the cold, wet night. Remaining in the kitchen she set out for herself a little of the food left over after providing for Mr Shad. She had no appetite, but she knew she must eat to keep up her strength, and keep illness at bay.

When she had eaten what she could, she washed the dishes and cutlery. Standing at the sink she leant back, stretching. She felt exhausted. Her back ached and her feet ached and her breasts ached, and all she wanted to do was rest. Against the window the rain fell, the rivulets that ran down the panes reflecting, fractured, the glare of the gaslight. She put the kettle on the range and sat down again at the table. When the water had come to the boil she made a pot of tea, and while it was brewing went upstairs to look in on Miss Balfour. There was no change.

Back in the kitchen she poured a mug of tea, added a little milk, and sat sipping it, her left hand resting on the swell of her belly. As she sat on the hard kitchen chair she felt the child inside her give a kick. It was not the first time, nevertheless it filled her with a sense of wonder. Moving her hand on her swollen form, she felt a kick again, now moving against her palm. 'It's all right,' she murmured. 'You don't have to tell me; I know you're there.' It would not be so much longer, she thought, and the child would be born and she would be free again. Free to get on with her life, to make a fresh start.

An image of Joel came into her mind, and she saw him, smiling, sitting beside her on the bench beside the water, while the music of the band drifted across the grass. The maverick thought came that when the baby was born and gone from her, she might see Joel once more. The wild thought lingered in her mind. He knew nothing of the child, and was there any reason that he should ever know? Once the baby had gone from her she would be as if it had never been born.

A sudden flurry of rain, driven by the wind, threw itself at the pane, breaking into her thoughts and bringing her back to the here and now. No, she told herself angrily. Joel had gone out of her life, and she would never see him again.

There was a clock on the dresser, and Lily's eyes moved to it and took in the time. It was almost eleven. She would look in on Miss Balfour and then go to bed. She straightened on the chair, arching her spine, hands to the small of her back, caressing the ache there. As she relaxed she caught a movement at the window. She stiffened, alert. She had seen a figure there, a shadowy form, moving across beyond the rain-streaked pane.

She rose and moved to stand at the window. Beyond the dark gardens the stables were black against the sky. Not even the window of Mr Shad's room was lighted.

Then, suddenly, with an abrupt movement that made her start, made her heart leap and begin to thud in her chest, a dark form lurched up from below the window sill. She gave a little cry, her hand leaping to her mouth, and jumped back. The figure moved closer to the window, and as he came to within the circle of light thrown by the flaring gaslight she saw who it was.

'Tom!' she gasped. 'Tom, is that you?'

Chapter Ten

She had brought him in from the rain and closed the door against the wild night. On the kitchen flags she embraced him and kissed him, her lips against his wet, cold cheek. Standing before her he took off his saturated hat and put it on a chair. The rain had soaked into his shirt and jacket, and his sodden boots left wet prints on the floor. She took his hand in hers and felt the coldness of his flesh. 'You're wet through and you're shrammed,' she said. 'Come and sit by the stove.'

She pulled a chair up and he sat down and leaned towards the heat, stretching out his hands to it. She got him a towel. 'Here,' she said, 'dry yourself off a bit.'

He rubbed at his face and neck, shivering, and as he did so he took in the shape of her body. 'I had no idea,' he said as he handed the towel back. 'You're gunna 'ave a baby. Why didn't you tell me, Lil?'

She shook her head. 'Oh – Tom, let's not go into that now.'

'Is that why you left home? Because of that?'

'Yes, it is, but we'll talk of it later. Have you eaten today?'

'Nothing 'cept a piece of bread.'

'God, you must be so hungry. I'll get you something.'

She put some soup on the hob and while it was warming fetched a blanket. 'Get your clothes off,' she told him, 'and put this round you.'

She turned away then while he stripped down to his drawers and wrapped the warm woollen blanket about him. His boots she stuffed with newspaper and put in the hearth, while his clothes she hung on a clothes-horse in front of the range. In addition to being wet through, his trousers and coat were stained and torn and his stockings were full of holes. When the soup was hot she poured some into a bowl and he sat at the table and ate voraciously. When the bowl was empty, she put before him a plate of ham and cheese and cold potatoes with mayonnaise. 'I'm sorry it's nothing more exciting,' she said. 'We need to get to the shops.'

'It's just fine, it's excellent. It'll keep me goin' for a while.' He briefly put down his fork to pull the blanket more closely about his lean shoulders. 'I'm feeling better already,' he said.

He looked small, slight, sitting there enveloped in the blanket. There were many questions she wanted to ask him, but for the moment she held back. She checked that the stove was well fuelled and that his clothes were on the way to drying, and then fetched from her room a pair of cotton stockings. 'Here, put these on,' she said. 'They'll keep you warm till your own are dry.'

He had finished the food, the plate cleared, and she watched as he pulled the stockings on over his bare, chilled feet. 'Have you got anywhere to go?' she asked.

He shook his head. 'No, I haven't.'

'Then you must stay here tonight.'

'Oh, Lil – you reckon I can?'

'Of course you can.'

'What about the owner of the place? The lady – won't she mind?'

'You leave me to worry about that. I'll make up a bed for you down here.' She gestured to the old sofa in the corner. 'You'll be comfortable there, and no one'll disturb you.' She glanced over at the kettle standing on the heat. 'I'll make some tea in a minute. I could do with a cup too.'

He looked at her in silence for a moment, then pushed his plate away, leant forward and laid his head on his arms. Lily was suddenly aware that he was weeping, and the realisation brought a sob to her own throat. At once she went to his side, bending over him, her arm around his thin shoulders.

'Don't cry, Tom. Oh, please don't cry. Everything'll be all right, you'll see.'

He gave a muffled sob and raised his head and she saw the streaks of his tears on his cheeks. 'Oh, Lil,' he said, his voice breaking, 'why did you ever 'ave to leave 'ome? Why did you ever 'ave to go? I could've managed all right if you'd been there. I always could. But with you gone – oh, everything was so different. I used to look forward to your letters so much. They were never enough though. I needed you there, Lil. I needed you.'

'I'm sorry, Tom.' Gently she stroked the back of his neck, his soft, damp hair. 'Father wrote and told me you'd gone,' she said.

He nodded. His tears had ceased now. 'I had to. I couldn't see any change 'appening. Nothing was gettin' any better.'

She pulled out a chair and sat down facing him across the table. 'Where did you go?' she asked. 'What did you plan to do?'

He gave a sigh. 'Aw, I was so foolish. I 'adn't made any plans. I 'adn't thought it out, I just knew I wanted to go. But what did I know of other places? I only knew Compton and Corster, and a few places round about. I 'aven't been anywhere else in my life.'

'Did it get really bad? Is that why you went?'

His lip quivered as he held on to his control, the tears once again so near the surface. 'No matter what I did, I was wrong,' he said. 'In the end he'd go for me like anything. I was black and blue afterwards.'

157

Lily felt the tears prick behind her eyelids. That her father, someone she loved, should be the one to inflict such pain, was beyond her understanding.

They sat in silence for a little while. When the kettle came to the boil she got up to make tea. Tom kept his eyes on her as she busied herself and brought the teapot and mugs to the table. 'Here you are.' She passed a full mug to him and he took it and sipped at it.

'Where did you go,' she asked as she sat down again, 'when you left home?'

'I didn't get no further than Corster,' he said. 'Well, I had next to nothing. Only the little money I'd saved from workin' at the farm. Mother never allowed me much from my wages. It took ages to get anything put by.'

'What did you do – in Corster?'

'I tried the villages round about first of all – to see if I could find any farm work. There wasn't much goin', though. Well, of course, it was the wrong time of year. I managed to get a little 'ere and there but it didn't last long. In the end I went back into the town to try there. Trouble is, I've only ever worked on a farm. I ain't got any experience of anything else.'

'So what did you do?'

'Whatever was goin'. Whatever I could get. I ran errands for people. I swept yards and crossings. I cleaned out cess-pits. I did odd jobs wherever I could, earnin' the odd penny 'ere and there.'

'How did you manage about eating?'

'I picked up scraps where I could, scavengin' round the coffee 'ouses and restaurants. I wusn't the only one, though; there was competition for everything. Sometimes I was given food for 'elping out with some odd job or something. But it wusn't easy to come by. I slept wherever I could find some place that was dry. When I was in Corster I slept under Tennon bridge. There were other men there; it

158

was a popular place. I wrapped meself in old newspapers and an old coat that I found. I was cold but at least I was dry.'

'Oh, Tom,' Lily said, 'I can't bear to think of it.'

'Yeh, well, there's no goin' back 'ome now. I've just about burnt me bridges there, that's for sure. They wouldn't 'ave me back again now, even if I wanted to go.'

The thought flashed through Lily's mind that in that respect she and her brother were in the same boat. 'So what will you do?' she asked.

He didn't answer at once. In the quiet the clock ticked on, and the rain fell against the window pane. On the clothes-horse a faint veil of steam rose from the sodden clothes. He sat with his hands clenched around the warmth of the mug.

'You'll think I'm mad,' he said after a moment, 'but I thought I might go to London.'

'*London.*'

'There'd be plenty of work there, I reckon.'

'I don't know, Tom – I've heard some very sad stories of people who've banked on that.'

'Well – I don't know what else to do,' he said.

'Oh, but – there must be something. You can't go on like this.'

'I don't see how it can change.' He shook his head and added quickly, 'Oh, Lil, I shouldn't 'ave come 'ere, bringin' my troubles to you. You, in your condition – you got enough on your plate.'

'Don't worry about me. It's you we've got to think about.' She glanced at the clock and rose from her chair. 'I've got to go upstairs. Miss Balfour's sick, and I must go and see how she is. I shan't be but a minute.'

She went up to Miss Balfour's room, which was faintly lit by the small flame of a nightlight. There was a candle on the chest, and Lily lighted it with a match and held it aloft. Standing beside the bed she looked down at Miss Balfour's

159

form beneath the covers, still and quiet. She bent and touched a hand to her brow and whispered her name. There was no response. The flesh of her forehead felt damp. The doctor would be calling again tomorrow; in the meantime there was nothing she could do.

Downstairs in the kitchen she found Tom still sitting hunched over in the chair. She sat at the table again, picked up her mug and sipped from it. The tea was growing cold.

'What's the matter with her, the mistress?' Tom asked.

'It's the flu.'

'Ah, there's so much of it about.'

'She's been ill for days. Really very ill, I mean, and now she – she's in a kind of coma. She's been unconscious for two days, and she's taking nothing in the way of food or drink.'

'It sounds bad.'

'It is. I'm so worried about her.'

'You been lookin' after her, 'ave you?'

'As well as I can. The maid's away ill herself, and the cook's off too, looking after her mother.'

'Yeh, and on top of all that, 'ere I come, turnin' up like a bad penny. That's rich, that is. Oh, I'm sorry, Lil.'

'No,' she said, 'don't say you're sorry. I'd want you always to come to me if you're in trouble. Promise me you will.'

He said nothing. She leant a little closer across the table. 'Promise me, Tom.'

'Yeh.'

She nodded. 'Good.' Turning to the window she said, 'I think the rain's stopped. About time.' Looking back to him she asked, 'Have you had enough to eat? Would you like some more tea?'

He shook his head. 'No, thanks. I've had plenty.' He paused briefly, then said, 'You're gunna stay 'ere till you've had the baby, are you?'

160

'Yes. Mother and Father arranged it.'

'And then you'll be going 'ome again, right?'

She hesitated. 'No, I shan't be going back to Compton. To tell you the truth, I don't know what I'm going to do. I'll have to leave here come the summer, but where I shall go I don't know.'

'Maybe – maybe we could go somewhere together. We could get a house. Wouldn't that be grand?'

She smiled. 'Oh, Tommo, yes, it would be grand. But you need money for a house, and I've got nothing. Like you, I shall have to find work.'

Tom gave a sympathetic nod. Then after a moment he said, 'Your babby, Lil . . .'

'Yes? What about it?'

'Who . . .? Whose is it?'

She gave a brief shake of her head. 'Please – don't ask me that, Tom. Please don't.'

'Sorry.' He dropped his glance, then raised his eyes again to hers. 'What'll you do, once you've got it? Who'll look after you both?' When she did not answer he added quickly, 'Oh, I wish I wus rich, then I'd look after you all right. Both of you. You'd see if I didn't.'

She gave a little smile and sighed. 'I'll manage all right. In any case I shan't be keeping the child.'

'You won't?'

'It's to go for adoption.'

'With who?'

'I don't know. There's a society, a church society. They'll take care of it all. They'll find the baby a home.' She did not want to talk about it.

'And you'd never see it again? Oh, Lil, that's awful.'

'Awful,' she said sharply. 'Why is it awful?'

'You mean you wouldn't want to keep it?'

'No, I wouldn't.' She got up and moved to the door. 'I'm going to get a couple of blankets.'

A little later, when Tom was lying snug on the sofa, she fed the stove and turned off the gaslight. Holding a flickering candle in her hands she stood and looked down at him in the pale light.

'You have a good sleep, Tom,' she said. 'We'll talk again in the morning.' She gestured to a chair she had placed near the sofa. 'I've left a candle and matches in case you need to get up in the night.'

'Thanks.'

She paused. 'Well – goodnight now.'

'Goodnight.'

As soon as Lily awoke early the next morning she went to look in on Miss Balfour.

The nightlight had burned out and the room was lit only by the pale daylight that crept in between the curtains. It was enough, however, for her to see that a change had ensued. As she crossed the room towards the bed she was aware of movement and then she heard Miss Balfour's voice.

'Is that you, Lily?' The voice sounded a little rusty and unused, but to Lily's ears it was the most welcome sound.

'Yes, ma'am,' Lily said, coming to a halt at the foot of the bed. 'Oh – what a relief – to hear you speaking again, to see you awake. Oh, ma'am, it's wonderful.'

Miss Balfour lay on her back with her eyes open. 'Help me to sit up, will you?' she said.

At once Lily moved to her side and helped her up, settling her against the pillows. Miss Balfour, obviously weak, breathed a sigh of thanks. 'I'm so thirsty,' she said. 'My mouth is so dry. Is there some water?'

'Yes, of course.' Lily poured a glass and lifted it to the woman's lips, helping her to hold it as she drank. Miss Balfour took several swallows and then nodded, indicating that she had had enough. As Lily put the glass back on the side table, Miss Balfour said with a frown, 'What day is it? I've lost track.'

'It's Sunday – January the thirteenth.'

'Sunday the thirteenth!' Miss Balfour's voice was incredulous. 'What happened to all those days?'

'You've been so ill, ma'am,' Lily said, 'and senseless part of the time. Dr Hanbury's been in to see you nearly every day. It's been very worrying.'

'And who's been looking after me? You and Mary, I suppose.'

'Not Mary, ma'am. She took the flu as well. She was that poorly, I told her to go back home till she was well again.'

'So it's just been you, has it?'

'Yes, ma'am.'

Miss Balfour sighed. 'I hope I haven't been too much of a trial for you, Lily.'

'I managed all right, ma'am.' Lily bent and tweaked at the blanket. 'I'll put some water on to heat, so we can get you washed and changed. I'll make up the fire too. After that I think I should get you something to eat.'

On the way downstairs she wondered how Tom had spent the night. She had thought about him constantly before eventually falling asleep, but she had no idea how she could help him out of his difficulties. She would give him what little money she had, but as for helping him find work or somewhere to live, such feats were beyond her.

As she entered the kitchen she said in a little whispered call, 'Tom? Tom, are you awake?'

There was no answer. As she drew nearer the sofa she saw the blankets, neatly folded, lying on the seat. Turning to the stove she found that his clothes were gone from the clothes-horse. There was a small piece of brown paper lying on the table, and she moved to it and took it up. Written in pencil in his familiar hand, were the words:

Dear Lil,

Thank you for everything. I'll find something somewhere so don't worry about me. I'm sorry to have come to you in trouble when you already got so many things on your mind. I'll write again soon.

Your loving brother
Tom

The January days had continued icy cold, etching Rowanleigh's window panes with frost pictures and lengthening the icicles hanging from the eaves. In the middle of the village green the pond froze over, and the villagers put on their skates and their coats and mufflers and glided about on its surface. Miss Balfour continued to make progress, and recovered sufficiently to get out of bed. After a while the doctor ceased to make regular calls, while at the same time Mary and Mrs Nessant returned to their duties – much to Lily's relief, so pleased was she to see the restoration of some sort of routine in the life of the household. With Mary available to take over the care of the mistress, Lily was freed once more to apply herself to needlework tasks.

For a time, with the two servants back in the house, Lily saw much less of Miss Balfour, for the latter rarely ventured far from her room. What little food she wanted she ate in the morning room or her study, leaving Lily to eat alone in the dining room or the kitchen. Then, towards the end of the month, the pattern changed again.

Lily was in the sewing room, working on a nightdress frill, when Mary came and said that Miss Balfour would like to see her in her study. Lily got up at once and went to her. She found Miss Balfour sitting behind her desk, writing in her ledgers. A bright fire burnt in the grate, and the room was warm. Already the daylight was fading.

'Oh, ma'am,' Lily said at once, 'it's so good to see you working again.'

Miss Balfour put down her pen, and looked at Lily over the top of her spectacles. 'And not before time,' she said. 'I've spent enough days being unproductive, and letting things go to pot. High time I stirred myself.' She paused, while Lily remained standing before the desk, feeling a little awkward, and not knowing for what reason she had been summoned. Miss Balfour added, a little gruffly, 'But sit down, do. I've asked Mary to bring us some tea.'

Lily sat in the chair on the other side of the desk. She noticed that there was a small glass of something at Miss Balfour's right hand.

'You've been working at your sewing, have you?' Miss Balfour said.

'Yes, ma'am, I have.'

'I'm afraid it all got rather interrupted with my illness.'

'Yes.' Lily ventured a smile. 'But I'm catching up.'

'Good. I have to say they're very pleased with your work so far.'

'Thank you, ma'am. I'm pleased to hear it.'

'Indeed.' Miss Balfour picked up the glass, sipped from it, then added after a pause, 'And how *are* you? All the attention's been on *me*. Are *you* all right?'

'Oh, yes, ma'am. I'm very well, thank you.'

'Thank heaven for that. Have you been looking after yourself? I mean – there's not just one of you to consider, you know.'

'I know. I'm fine – really.'

A knock came at the door, and Mary entered carrying a laden tray. Miss Balfour cleared a space on the desk, and the maid set the tray down and went out again. Gesturing to the teapot, Miss Balfour said, 'You pour, Lily, will you?'

Lily poured the tea and passed a cup to her. The dying light deepened the shadows in the room. Outside the window the bare branches of the rowan had melted into the dark of the sky. Miss Balfour sipped at her tea then put her cup down and said,

'I owe you a great deal, young lady.'

Lily frowned. 'Oh, but, ma'am . . .'

'A great deal. You did so much for me.'

'Oh – but I did nothing that no one else wouldn't have done.'

'Ah, but there was no one else,' Miss Balfour said. 'I know now how sick I was – not even conscious for a time. Dr Hanbury's spoken of it to me, so I know.' She paused. 'I've got so much to thank you for. Don't think I'm not aware of it.'

Lily did not know what to say, and so said nothing.

'It's been a dreadful thing, this flu,' Miss Balfour said, 'but thankfully we all got over it. Though Dr Hanbury tells me there've been two deaths in the village.'

'Yes – one of the blacksmith's sons, and the postmaster's assistant.'

'Sad. It's very sad.' Miss Balfour sighed. 'But now things are getting back to normal again, thank God.'

On the mantelpiece the clock ticked the minutes away. Miss Balfour finished her tea, then leant down to her right and brought up a bottle which she placed on the desk. After pulling the stopper she added a measure of amber liquid to that in the glass. 'I'll take a little more brandy too,' she said. She lifted the glass, sipped from it. 'I have some now and again – at Dr Hanbury's recommendation. Though I don't think I could ever get a taste for it.' She gave a sigh, and then, a rarity, showing her large teeth, smiled, and added, 'Not so with my tobacco, though. Oh, I would *so* like a cigarette now, I tell you. I could commit murder for one – and that shows how much improved I am – but Dr Hanbury says it's too bad for my lungs. A woman smoking? My God, what next! The devil with my health, he doesn't approve – that's the truth of it.'

She sipped again at the brandy while the sky deepened to black and the fire flickered and crackled in the grate. 'Agnes didn't care for it, my smoking,' she said. 'In fact, there was nothing at all that Agnes liked about it.' She set down her glass and picked up the framed photograph of the young woman. 'It's been eight years,' she said. Her voice had taken on a gentler, musing quality. 'We ran a school together, did you know that?'

Lily nodded. 'Mr Shad mentioned it – in Shalford, I think he said.'

'In Shalford, yes. It was very successful. Miss Chambers – Agnes – had a gift for it.' She sighed. 'I couldn't run the place on my own after she passed on – so I sold it and came to live here at Rowanleigh. This is the house I grew up in. I was born here, and then eventually it was left to me by my father.' She gazed into the face in the photograph then set it down on the desk again. 'Those days in Shalford – they were the best days.' Picking up her glass, she gave an ironic nod. 'Brandy loosens the tongue. Sometimes too much. Though when you get to a certain age you don't bother so much about what people think. You can't walk on eggshells all your life, and if you lose friends through it, then those friends were never truly friends in the first place. That's something we discovered, Agnes and I.'

A flaming log shifted in the grate. Lily got up from her chair, and with the poker set the burning wood back in place. Before her eyes the flames danced, sending sparks reeling up the chimney. She took another piece of apple wood and set it on the fire. As she sat back down, Miss Balfour said:

'Have you ever cared for anyone, Lily? Have you loved anyone in your life?'

After a moment Lily nodded. 'Yes,' she said.

Miss Balfour nodded. 'You loved him.'

'Yes, I loved him.' A pause. 'I still do.'

'But – you're no longer together.'

'No.'

'And is there no hope – of your being together?'

'No. No hope at all.'

Miss Balfour gave a sigh. 'That is sad.' She paused. 'I've heard some stories of love. Oh, indeed. Some of them from the young women who came here to have their babes. Some of the stories were quite foolish, while others were quite tragic. And so many of them were the same. Love – whether you're a housemaid or a duchess – it's a great leveller.' She lifted the brandy glass to her mouth, then set it down again, untouched. 'No,' she said, 'I've had enough for now.' Turning back to Lily, she said, 'I think you understand, then.'

'Understand?'

'What it is to lose someone you love.'

'Yes, but not in the devastating way you do.'

Miss Balfour briefly closed her eyes and gave a little shake of her head. 'Oh,' she breathed, 'it is the most terrible thing – to see the death of someone you love. To watch someone you love deteriorate, waste away. To watch the flesh fall off their bones, and see them in pain and be able to do nothing. In the end you almost pray for death to come, so that the dreadful suffering will stop.'

She sat staring off for some moments, then, coming out of her preoccupation she said, 'It was after I got back here to Rowanleigh that I took in the first of the young women. After the school I needed to be occupied, to have some kind of purpose, to be of use, and I'd seen what could happen sometimes to girls who got themselves into such a predicament. I had a sister. Rose. She fell in love with a fusilier, a tall, handsome young man, but he went off and she was left in the lurch. When she found she was to have his baby, our parents cast her out.'

'What – what became of her?' Lily asked.

Miss Balfour looked towards the fire. 'She . . . she jumped into the millpond.' Then with a sigh she said, 'All these sad memories. It does no good to dwell on the past.' She lifted her teacup and sipped from it. 'Gone cold,' she said, and set it back in its saucer. Turning to Lily again, she said, 'What is his name, this young man whom you love?'

'Joel.'

'Would it be – painful – to tell me about him?'

Lily hesitated a second. 'No,' she said. 'Though there isn't a lot to tell.'

Miss Balfour waited, and after a little pause Lily began her brief story. She told of how she had met Joel in the carriage company's office, of their walks in the park, of their last day together, when they had sat on the grass and he had sketched her portrait. She told of how they had gone to the inn in Lettington and had later got caught in the rain.

'And that was the last time you saw him?' Miss Balfour asked.

'Yes.'

'Does he know – that he's to become a father?' Miss Balfour asked.

'No,' Lily said at once, her voice sharp in the quiet room. 'The child is not his, and he knows nothing of it.'

'The child is not his?' Miss Balfour could not hide the puzzlement in her voice.

Lily's hands were clasped tightly before her, her face lowered into shadow. After remaining silent for some seconds she began, hesitantly, to tell of the happening. 'My employer,' she said, '– at the house where I was maid. He was my father's friend, a trusted man . . .' And so she went on. She had not spoken of it before, other than when she had told her father, and then it had been in the most terse manner, simply stating the bare fact. Now, sitting facing Miss Balfour across the desk, it was like a kind of release, like water surging through a fractured dam. The story poured out, and with it her tears, and she could stop neither.

At last she came to a halt, the tears drying on her cheeks. She felt drained. Miss Balfour sat looking at her, her mouth set. 'Oh, my dear,' she said, and leant forward, touching her fingertips to the back of Lily's hand. The little gesture of sympathy threatened to undo Lily again, and she had to hold on to her control.

The clock ticked into the quiet, along with the faint crackle from the burning apple logs. After a while, Miss Balfour turned towards the window and said, 'Look at that – the sky is black. Oh, I'll never get used to winter.' She got up from her chair. 'Shut out the night, that's the best we can do.' At the window she stood for a moment looking out onto the winter-dark garden, then pulled the curtains closed.

Coming back to resume her seat at the desk, she said after a moment, her voice a little more brisk, 'So – what are your plans for tomorrow?'

Lily was grateful for the change of tone, and glad that the laying bare of her heart was behind her. 'Well,' she said, 'I've still got a good bit of sewing to do.'

Miss Balfour smiled. 'Yes, but tomorrow's Sunday. I should think you've earned a day off.'

Lily shrugged. 'Well, I hope to do some reading also, if I have time.'

'Looking in at the sewing room,' Miss Balfour said, 'I see you've been reading von Sybel's book on the French Revolution. Have you found it interesting?'

'Yes. It's fascinating.'

'You have other books there too. I saw a French grammar, a study on the Tudors, a book on the Pre-Raphaelite Brotherhood . . .'

'Oh, there's so much to learn,' Lily said. 'I hope you don't mind – my taking the books from the library.'

'Of course not. That's what they're there for. It gives me pleasure to see that you do.' She looked steadily at Lily, frowning slightly. 'I realise,' she said after a moment, 'that until now I've known hardly anything about you.' She paused. 'The young women have come here over the years, and have stayed for seven, eight, nine months – whatever. And although I always tried to do my best for them, I never sought to – to get involved, to get close – in any way.' Briefly she came to a halt, and then, as if she had perhaps said too much, added briskly, 'But they were no worse for it. They had their babies and – and went away to get on with their lives – with whatever they had planned.' She paused again. 'What about you, Lily? What have you got planned?'

'I?' Lily shook her head. 'Oh, ma'am – I've got no plans.'

Miss Balfour studied her. 'You were working as a maid.'

'Yes, a general maid.'

'You could do better than that, surely.'

Lily was at a loss. 'How?' she said.

'Well – for a start, you've got a brain. There must be some way in which you could use it. You must have had some ambitions at some time. I'm sure you didn't set out to be a maid-of-all-work.'

'No,' Lily said at once, 'of course I didn't. I wanted to be a teacher.'

'A teacher?'

'Yes.' Lily leant forward in her chair. 'I wanted to be a teacher, like you.'

She told then of how she had begun her apprenticeship, and of how, due to her father's financial situation, that apprenticeship had been curtailed. 'So,' she ended with a melancholy shrug, 'I was sent to Whitton as a maid.'

'And you would still wish this, I assume, to become a teacher.'

'Oh, yes,' Lily said, 'but there's no chance of it happening now. None.'

Miss Balfour continued to gaze at her over her spectacles. Then after some moments, she said, 'There might be a chance. Perhaps it isn't too late. Perhaps it isn't too late after all.'

Chapter Eleven

At last the bitter January went out, the ice on the village pond thawed, and the first green points of the crocuses pushed through on the Rowanleigh lawn. February came, dank and drear, and gave way at last to gusty March, and the fields quickened under the chill spring sun with the first signs of the harvest to be. Lily, from her seat in the sewing room, watched the changing seasons and wondered what lay before her. Under Miss Balfour's tutelage she now spent most of her time studying. No more sewing work was delivered from Corster, and none would be in the future. Now, all Lily's energies were directed into her resurrected aim of becoming a teacher, and it was, of course, all down to Miss Balfour. Since her illness, and Lily's nursing of her, she had changed towards Lily, and was now doing all she could to help her. It might no longer be possible for Lily to go and study to teach in a school, Miss Balfour said, but that was no reason why she should not become a governess.

Lily had leapt at the suggestion, and with one aim in mind she and Miss Balfour had set about using the remaining time available. Miss Balfour, glad of the chance to exercise her knowledge and experience, took to the endeavour with enthusiasm. Each day under her supervision Lily studied English grammar, English literature, history, geography, mathematics, physics and French, the tuition in each subject taking her far further than had any lessons at the school she had attended in her younger days.

Giving Lily added pleasure was the fact that her

173

relationship with Miss Balfour had blossomed. One sign of Lily's growing status in her tutor's esteem came with the suggestion that Lily should henceforth address her a little less formally. From now on, she said, Lily should address her as Miss Elsie. There remained in the older woman's manner a certain bluntness, but there was no hiding the innate warmth of her nature, and as the weeks passed Lily's admiration and respect for her grew.

Early in May came news of Tom.

Lily had heard nothing from him and nothing of him since he had vanished into the morning that past January, and she had never mentioned to anyone the fact that he had come to the house. There was no need to; the incident was over and finished with, and revelation would serve no purpose. Then, one bright spring afternoon there came a letter from her father. In the sewing room, sitting before her little table with its books and papers, she read:

Compton Wells
30th April 1867

Daughter,

Your mother and I trust that you are going along healthily, and that all is well with you. Things remain here much as they were. We are enjoying the spring weather and are making the most of the fine days.

I am writing at this time to inform you of sad news concerning your brother. As you know, he left home last year, and we have heard nothing of him since. Until now, that is. I regret to have to tell you that your brother is now, alas, no longer a part of this family. We have just today received a communication with the information that your brother has been arrested and convicted by the courts. The information we have received tells us that he has been committed to

Wentworth prison in Redbury, there to serve a sentence for theft. I hasten to add that I have no intention of going to see him. As a son he is quite lost to me. Although from his youngest years he has been the greatest disappointment to me, even I did not expect such a blow. That he should turn out in such a way is a tragedy, and has brought shame and disgrace onto those who had his best interests at heart. I cannot imagine that, in the condition you are in, you will wish to visit him. But of course, if you do then that is entirely your own affair, and you will do so without any kind of support or endorsement from me. I have washed my hands of him and intend to have nothing more to do with him. Should you decide to visit him or contact him in some other way, then please make it clear to him that he no longer has a family home, and will never again be welcome here.

Your loving
    Father

ps: In case you are interested, I'm also informed that prisoners' visiting times are daily except for Sundays, for one hour, starting at two o'clock, but that prisoners are allowed only two visits per month.

Lily read through the letter and then set it down on the table before her. Tom, in prison. After a moment she got up from her seat and began to pace the room. She would have to go to him, she would *have* to. She could not bear to think of him languishing in some cell without any word of comfort from his family.

Miss Balfour – or Miss Elsie as Lily now thought of her – was in her study. Lily knocked on the door, waited for the response – 'Come in,' – and entered. She carried the letter with her. Miss Elsie sat at her desk.

'What is it?' she enquired, frowning. She could see from Lily's expression that something was wrong.

Lily said at once, 'Oh, ma'am, I have to go to Redbury.'

'To Redbury? What for?'

'It's Tom – my brother. I've got to see him.'

Miss Elsie frowned. 'Really, I don't think you should consider going anywhere – not in your condition. The baby's due in less than three weeks.'

'But I must go. He – he's in Wentworth prison.'

'Oh, my dear.' Miss Elsie lowered her glance to the letter in Lily's hand. 'And you've just learnt about it, have you?'

'Yes. A letter from my father. It just came. He writes that Tom has been – convicted of theft. I must go to him.'

'Well, of course – but are you sure you feel up to it?'

'Yes, really, I shall be all right.'

'When do you want to go?'

'At the very earliest. Tomorrow. I must go tomorrow.'

Miss Elsie nodded. 'We'll get Mr Shad to drive you to the station. Would you like me to come with you? Just for the journey, I mean.'

'Thank you so much. But no. I shall manage all right.'

It was decided that Lily would take the 11.55 from Sherrell, and she had long been ready when Mr Shad came knocking at the kitchen door to say that the trap was waiting. She was dressed simply and practically. These latter months, as her figure had changed with her advancing pregnancy, she had taken to wearing some of the clothes that Miss Elsie had kept in the house, left by the young women who had come and gone before. Now, ready for her first real journey abroad since her arrival at Rowanleigh, she cut a less than fashionable-looking figure.

In the back yard Mr Shad helped her up into the trap, and moments later they were setting off for the station.

It was fine and looked to remain so. There had been no rain in several days, so the road was firm and the horse and vehicle made good time. Before too long they reached the railway station and Mr Shad helped her down. Did she know what time she would be returning? he asked, and she replied that she could not be sure, but that she would take a fly from the station back to the house.

Not long afterwards she was on the train and bound for Corster, where she eventually made her connection for Redbury. On her arrival there she hailed a fly, a rather battered old brougham, to take her to Wentworth prison.

The prison was situated on the very outskirts of the city, and she glanced about her at the unfamiliar surroundings as the carriage made its way along the highways and byways. After a time, the larger buildings were left behind and the old carriage moved through narrower suburban streets where the houses were smaller and set further apart. And then at last she saw before her what could only be the walls of the prison.

She was not prepared for her first sight of the gaol. She had seen pictures of such institutions in books and newspapers, but she was not ready for the reality. The building was vast. Rearing up beyond high brick walls topped with metal spikes, it was a great, grim monolith of grey stone, with belching chimneys. She had little time to study it, however, for the cab had come to a halt and the driver was tapping on the door with his whip. 'Wentworth prison, ma'am. We're here.'

Gathering up her skirts, she got out and paid him the fare. Then, as the driver turned the vehicle to make its way back, she stepped towards the prison. Beneath a large clock showing the time at half-past-one, dark grey wooden doors loomed, forbiddingly closed. She turned her head towards a small door set in the smoke-grimed wall where a number of persons stood waiting in a line, mostly women. Many of them were in coarse, shabby clothing, and spoke and laughed in rough accents. Others, a few of them quite well-dressed, stood quiet and grave. Many held packages or bags. Uncertain, Lily hesitated for a second and then moved to join them. A minute or so later an omnibus pulled up nearby and a number of women, children and men alighted and got in line behind Lily. While she felt tense and nervous she could not help noticing that many of the others there appeared to be quite relaxed and accepting of the grim situation.

Then, causing a stirring of interest and anticipation, came the sound of voices from behind the door, and of heavy bolts being drawn back. At once the waiting people shifted and eased forward. A moment later the door was opening and the first of the women began to pass through.

Moving with the others, Lily shuffled her way towards the door, on either side of which uniformed men stood with truncheons strapped to their wrists, their belts heavy with keys. Some of the women, clearly regular visitors, greeted the men light-heartedly as they passed by, and the guards exchanged casual greetings with them. Lily, going with the flow, went through the doorway and found herself in a vast cobbled yard.

Keeping up with the rest of the visitors, she moved from the yard into the prison's interior, making her way along a low-ceilinged passage with a flagged floor. There were open doors at the end, beside which male and female prison officers were searching the visitors, smoothing and patting with practised hands over their bodies, and looking in the bags and packages they carried.

When Lily got to the door she stood still while a grim, unsmiling wardress ran her hands over her and looked at the contents of her bag.

'All right, pass on.'

Lily moved on among the straggling throng, her way

now taking her through a wider corridor where the voices of the people echoed against the stone walls, their faces lit by flaring gaslights. Now and again she came upon some of the inmates in their garb printed with broad arrows. Usually carrying piles of sacks or other items, they passed silently by without raising their eyes to the visitors.

Another queue had formed at the end of the corridor, so Lily took her place within it, and soon found herself standing beside a long desk at which sat male officers with ledgers in front of them. Here the visitors were registering their names and the names of those they had come to see, at the same time giving up the gifts they had brought with them.

After she had waited a while, one of the officers beckoned to her and she went to him. He asked her whom she was there to see and she gave him Tom's name.

The man turned the pages of his ledger and then, one finger moving on the page said, 'Clair, Thomas, number 119426.' He looked up at Lily again, his glance taking in her pregnant condition. 'Are you related to him?'

'I'm his sister.'

'Name?'

She hesitated for a second and then said, 'Clair, Miss Lily Clair.'

He made no acknowledgement of her single status and her pregnant state; dealing with the dregs of humanity, he had seen it all before, and was not one to be easily surprised. He wrote down Lily's name in his register and then raised his pen and gestured with it along the corridor. 'Go into the room at the end there and wait. You'll be called when he's been brought in.'

The room the officer had directed her to was wide and lined with plain wooden benches, on which sat the visitors who had already preceded her. The walls themselves were stained, and marked with initials and words and slogans, some of the words obscene and to Lily very shocking. She took a seat on the bench beside a woman in her twenties who sat with a small boy. The boy's clothes were untidy and dirty, his face and hands looking unwashed. The woman had rouged cheeks and gave off the stench of stale sweat.

Gradually every seat was taken and a number of visitors were forced to stand just within the doorway. Murmuring voices filled the room.

Suddenly a bell rang out and the voices went quiet. All eyes were directed to the officer standing there with the bell in one hand and a ledger in the other.

He then began to read out the names and numbers of prisoners, and as he did so those visiting the said prisoners went to the warder who ushered them through into the room beyond. At last Lily heard the name she had waited for and quickly stepped up to the man in the doorway.

'Here to see Clair, Thomas, 119426?' he said to Lily, and she nodded and said, 'Yes, sir.'

'Go on through.' He gestured with a movement of the ledger. 'Seat number twenty-six.'

She passed on and found herself in a very long room with small, narrow windows, divided down the centre by a partition of wood in which were set iron bars that went up nearly to the ceiling. There was a long row of rough wooden benches set before the partition, and many of the visitors were already seated there. Lily saw that there were numbers painted on the bench seats, and she moved along until she saw twenty-six. She sat down, finding herself between a middle-aged woman and an elderly man, and waited, while more visitors came in and found their allotted seats.

The minutes ticked by and the benches became full, while the room hummed with the visitors' voices. And then the tone of the voices changed, and looking through the screen Lily saw a line of prisoners filing in. One by one they took seats on the other side of the partition and leant forward to talk to their visitors. In a short time the people who sat on either side of Lily were rewarded with the presence of the men they had come to see, and were soon talking to them through the bars. Lily, still waiting, kept her eyes fixed on the ones who were still coming in. And then she saw him.

'Tom,' she breathed, and half rose from her seat.

She saw how he hesitated halfway along the row, his eyes roaming down the line of the visitors' faces. Then he caught sight of her, and she saw his face light up, his eyes widening as they met her own. A moment later he was there and sitting down to face her.

'Lil – Lil.'

She could see his mouth form her name, and she leant forward on the bench. 'Tom,' she said softly, and then again, 'Tom – oh, Tom.' She wanted to reach out and touch him, but the space between them was too great, and there were the bars also, added to which there were uniformed guards standing against the walls, ready to intervene should there be any flouting of the rules.

Peering at Tom, she studied him in the gloomy light. She was shocked to see that his hair had been shorn close to his scalp. It made him look even more slight and vulnerable. And his clothing. Although she could see the uniform on every other prisoner in the place, to see it on him was too shocking, and she felt sudden tears spring to her eyes, and a lump form in her throat. Even worse, the uniform was too large for him and hung on his frame, making him look smaller than he really was. She saw too that his left eye was a little swollen and discoloured. The sight of him sitting there, so young, caused her to tighten her mouth and cling on to her resolve.

'Tom,' she said, her voice strained, one hand half raised, as if she would reach out to him, 'are you all right, my dear?'

He gave the shadow of a nod. His listless eyes looked dull and hollow, and without a spark of life. His mouth was drawn down at the corners, lips tightly compressed, as if he was fighting to keep back tears. She felt that she would have done anything to have been able to hold him, to press her cheek to his own, but she could only sit there and look at him through the bars.

'Tom,' she said again, again raising her voice slightly against the surrounding din, 'are you all right?'

He gave another nod, but still did not speak.

'I heard from Father,' she said. 'He wrote and told me that – you were in here. It was a shock – to read his letter. I came at once.'

Tom said nothing. His mouth stayed fixed, lips together in a line, as if he did not trust himself to speak. On Lily's right the woman had burst into tears and held an old handkerchief to her eyes. The noise of her sobbing was momentarily loud. Lily waited a few moments for the noise to subside then said:

'Father told me so little. What happened to you, Tom? Please, tell me.'

And now he spoke, leaning forward on his seat, his dark eyes fixed on hers, his brow creased in a frown beneath his close-cropped hair. 'You shouldn't 'ave come, Lil. Oh, Lil, you shouldn't be 'ere. I didn't want you to see me 'ere.'

'But I had to come. I've been so worried about you, wondering where you were, what you were doing.'

'But – but that you should see me like this – see me in this place.' As he spoke, his voice cracked and tears welled up and spilt onto his cheeks. The sight brought the tears to Lily's own eyes, and she choked back a sob. Seconds passed. She dabbed her face and sat with her handkerchief

182

gripped in her two hands. 'Why have they put you here?' she asked when she felt calmer.

A bitter smile now touched his mouth, and he gave a little shake of his head. 'I was caught,' he said. 'I got caught.'

'But – but what had you done?'

'I – I stole.'

'What? What did you steal?'

'I was 'ungry, Lil.' His voice was deep with sadness.

'Oh, Tom.' Hearing his words her tears threatened again, and it took all her composure to keep them at bay. Somewhere in the room a small child began to cry, the wailing sound ringing out against the voices of the people. When the child's crying had ceased, Lily said, 'I can't bear to hear that you were so desperate.'

'I wus. I took some celery.'

'Celery? You took some celery? That's what you stole?'

He nodded. 'From a barrow in the market place.'

She put a hand to her throat. He had stolen *celery*. 'For that?' she said, scarcely able to form the words. 'They put you in here for that?'

He nodded.

'But – you're only a boy,' she said. 'For God's sake, you're not thirteen till June.' She knew well that the punishments meted out by the courts could be harsh in the extreme, but surely not with Tom, not like this.

'How long?' she said after a moment.

'How long? My sentence?' He paused. 'One month. With four days 'ard labour.'

'A month,' she repeated dully. 'With hard labour.'

'I was lucky. I was told it could be more.' After a moment he added, 'I had a whipping too. On the day I got in.'

'Oh, Tom.' His name burst out on a sob. She could not bear to think of him suffering so. Moments passed. 'What happened to your eye?' she asked.

'Oh – that.' He raised a hand and gingerly touched at the discoloured flesh around his eye socket. 'I – I run into a door.'

She frowned. 'Really – is that the truth?'

'It don't matter,' he said.

She wanted to say, *It does matter*, but instead she asked, 'Are they – are they kind to you in here?'

'They're all right. I work in the kitchens, and there's one man – Jake – he's good to me. He looks after me a bit – so it's not so bad.'

'Oh – well – that's good.' She felt relief at the small mercy. 'I'm glad you've got a friend.'

'Yeh.' He nodded. 'Don't worry about me, Lil. I'll be all right. It could be a lot worse. I peels potatoes and washes the pans. It's all right.'

Looking at him through the bars, she could not get over his appearance. It wasn't just his cropped hair; it was his whole demeanour. In spite of his positive words he looked beaten and cowed, without a spark of light in his eyes.

Breaking into her thoughts, he said, 'Anyway, our Lil, 'ow are you? You keepin' well?'

'Yes, I am,' she said. 'I've nothing to complain about.'

'And your babby – when do you expect it? Must be soon.'

'Yes – not long now.'

'I wish I could be there to see 'im.'

'Him?'

'Well – whatever.'

Lily said after a moment, 'I've thought about you so much, Tom, since you went off that morning.'

'I'm sorry I went off without even a word,' he said, 'but you 'ad so much on your plate. If I'd known the situation I'd never have called in the first place. Then, seein' you like that – with you expecting a baby – I had to leave – I couldn't add to your troubles.'

'I worried about you so – not knowing.'

Suddenly a bell rang out, briefly bringing a temporary halt to the conversations, then a man's voice bellowed: 'Five minutes. Just five minutes.' The bustle started up again. Lily was aware of the seconds, the minutes, passing.

'So,' said Tom, 'Father knows I'm here.'

'Yes, they wrote and told him.'

He nodded. 'I 'ad to give my next of kin.' He paused then asked, 'D'you think – d'you think he'll come and see me?'

Lily did not know how to reply. When she said nothing, Tom gave a little nod of understanding. 'It don't matter,' he said.

Another bell rang out, jangling harshly against the sound of the voices, signalling the end of the allotted hour. At once the waiting guards straightened at their posts while the voices in the cavernous room changed their tone, as their owners protested against the passing time and the ending of their visit with their loved ones. One of the guards behind Tom stepped forward and touched him on the shoulder.

'Goodbye, Tom,' Lily said, leaning forward. 'I don't know whether I'll be able to come and visit you again before you're out.'

'That's all right. It don't matter. You look after yourself.'

The guard behind Tom had stepped back, allowing them a few final moments. Lily could see a glistening in Tom's eyes, and felt tears threatening her own once more. All around, the other visitors were getting to their feet, while murmurs and cries of 'Goodbye,' and 'God bless you,' were heard from all corners of the room.

Tom looked at Lily for one last time then turned away and joined the other prisoners who, watched by the guards, had begun to file out of the room. Lily stood there, watching until he had gone out of sight, and then made her way towards the exit. Minutes later, along with all the other visitors, she was outside the prison walls, back in the bright May sun.

She was anxious to get away from the scene of so much unhappiness and stepped out briskly into the street. As she walked, a couple came hurrying by, a burly young man and a young woman, laughing and talking loudly. As they came past Lily in their rough eagerness to get ahead the woman stumbled, and, staggering on her cheap, flimsy heels, she gave a shriek and reached out wildly as she fell. In another second her desperate hands were snatching violently at Lily's arm and Lily was thrown headlong onto the cobbles.

She did not cry out loudly as she fell, emitting nothing more than a little gasped 'Oh.' Then she lay there, the breath knocked from her body. For a few moments she remained quite stunned and hardly able to take in what had happened. She was vaguely aware of a dull ache starting up somewhere on her right hip, and another on her right elbow. Her reticule lay on the cobbles a couple of feet away.

As she tried to catch her breath she was aware of voices erupting all around her, with expressions of sympathy and concern as people gathered about. 'Oh, I'm sorry, dear,' said the young woman who had brought her down. Having herself recovered, she helped Lily up into a sitting position on the cobbles while someone picked up Lily's reticule and set it down at her side. Lily's hat had fallen so far over her eyes that she could hardly see, and she reached up and pushed it further back on her head. She realised that she was being supported by a tall, stoutly built woman. Briefly leaning back against the woman's body, Lily put a hand to her swelled belly. The fall had jolted her so badly she could feel the wrench of it even now.

'How are you feeling, love?' asked the young woman who now bent over her. 'Are you gunna be all right?'

Lily nodded. 'I – I think so.' In her belly the baby kicked, and she nodded again and said, 'Give me a minute to catch my breath. I'll be all right.'

'You went down with such a wallop,' another woman said, and the one supporting Lily at her back, agreed, 'Ah, you did that an' all.

One of the uniformed guards had come over and stood looking down at her. 'You want to come back inside, ma'am?' he asked. 'We got a chair if you wants.'

'No, thank you.' Lily shook her head. 'I just need to get my breath. I'll be all right.'

'D'you think you can stand, dear?' asked the woman supporting her back.

'I – I think so.' The soreness on her hip was sharper now, the numbness from the impact wearing off and letting the pain come through. She shifted around, and with help from two of the women, got to her feet. The stout, motherly woman put a hand under her elbow. 'Where are you going to, dear?' she asked.

'To the station,' Lily said. Her reticule was in her hand now. 'If I can just get a cab . . .'

With Lily on her feet, the sensation of the moment was over, and the people began to drift away. Lily walked with the stout woman's hand under her elbow. She could feel her heart beating from the shock of the fall.

There were three cabs waiting outside the gates and the woman saw Lily safely installed in one of them. Lily thanked her and sat back with a sigh of relief as the fly started away.

At Redbury station she caught the train to Corster where she changed for Sherrell. She was nearing Sherrell station when she felt the first contractions.

187

Chapter Twelve

By the time Lily got back to Rowanleigh she was near collapse. With assistance from the driver she somehow got out of the fly and went inside, the pains stabbing at her so that she staggered, clutching at her belly and catching at her breath. Miss Elsie met her as she entered, took one look at her and went off calling for Mr Shad to go and fetch the midwife. He went as soon as he had hitched up the trap, and returned half-an-hour later with Mrs Toomley on board. Ten minutes after her arrival, with Mary on hand to fetch and carry, Lily's son was born.

The baby came into the world the frailest-looking creature with a head of wispy fair hair and tiny hands stretching out as if reaching for a life that lay almost beyond him. At first he made no sound, but then Mrs Toomley, holding him by his ankles, gave him a sharp little slap on the buttocks and he gave a sudden twist in her grasp and began to squall.

The midwife clucked concernedly over him and said, 'Well, he's the tiniest little mite, there's no getting away from it. I doubt he weighs more than five pound, but he's absolutely perfect for all that.' Then she added, a note of conviction in her voice, 'And he'll pick up, you'll see.'

Lily, lying back exhausted, looked at the baby's glistening, scrunched-up face and could only feel relief that the birth was over. Miss Elsie, who had also been present at the baby's coming, pressed Lily's hand and said, 'Well done. You've come through it.'

The baby was quickly and efficiently bathed, then wrapped in a warm blanket and laid on Lily's breast. She was not prepared for the sudden closeness, and for a moment felt at a loss. But then her arm came up and wrapped around the tiny form and held him to her. The midwife was tidying the room, putting away her things, straightening the bedclothes, humming as she worked. Miss Elsie, standing close to the bed, said to Lily, 'I'll go and make you some tea. I daresay you could do with it.'

As Miss Elsie left the room, Mrs Toomley looked over at the baby who had now started to cry again with a thin, pathetic, wailing sound. '*He's* the one who needs somethin', dear,' she said. 'The poor mite's hungry.'

The baby's head was lying on Lily's breast. Almost without thinking of it, she put up her hand and untied the ribbon that held closed the neck of her nightgown. She pulled it down, her soft breast and nipple exposed, feeling the air upon her skin. And then the baby's lips were there, and the crying stopped as his mouth closed over her nipple. She felt the drawing of her milk into him and gave a sigh.

The midwife, glancing over in the course of her busyness, nodded her approval. 'He might be small but he's big enough to know what he wants,' she said. 'Thank God, *they* knows it even when *you* don't.'

Lily lay back while the child suckled at her breast, milk from the side of his mouth dribbling out and running down on her skin. As he fed, she studied him. She had never seen an infant so small and so vulnerable-looking. She had clear memories of her half-sister as a small baby, but Dora had been born at full term and had been lusty and a good size. How different from this little creature. She looked at the tiny fingers, the minute fingernails, the perfect, flawless skin. Her gaze moved to his head and took in the fine hair and the features of his face. She looked at the button of his nose, at his rosy lips around her engorged nipple. There was a tiny dark mark on his cheek, shaped like a crescent moon, lying close to his left ear. She touched it softly with her fingertip as if she would wipe it away, and then realised that it was a birthmark.

Mrs Toomley came to the bedside and looked down at Lily and the infant as they lay there. 'All right, my dear?' she asked. 'Are you feelin' all right?'

Lily nodded, and gave a faint smile. 'Yes, thank you.'

'Be you in any pain, dear?'

'Not really. No – it's not too bad.'

The baby, having suckled for only three or four minutes, released Lily's nipple and fell asleep. Gently, Mrs Toomley lifted him up and laid him in the cradle. He did not wake. Standing over the infant, the midwife looked down at him and gave a sigh. 'He's a poor, nesh little thing,' she said, 'and he's gunna need some real lookin' after. But as I say, with the right care he'll pick up.'

She prepared to leave then, saying that she would call back later in the evening. Soon after she had gone, Miss Elsie came in with a tray bearing two cups which she set down at the bedside.

'Here – drink some tea,' she said to Lily, 'and then try to get some sleep. You must be exhausted.' She helped Lily to sit up against the pillows, and then watched as she took up her cup and drank. 'I'll write to your parents now, and tell them of the birth,' she added, 'and at some time I'll have to get in touch with the Society. Let them know the baby's here. They're not expecting to be notified yet. Not for several weeks.'

Lily nodded. 'How soon after – do they come and take the baby?' she asked.

'In three or four weeks or so. Providing of course, that the baby's well enough to go.'

'So soon.'

'Oh, as soon as possible. It's the best way.'

'But what about feeding them? Don't they miss their mother's milk?'

'Oh, usually they've gone on to a bottle by then – and if not, the folks at the Society will often have a wet nurse on hand.'

Mrs Toomley came back later, and while she was there Dr Hanbury called. He murmured satisfaction over Lily's condition, but said she must not over-exert herself. As for the infant, he said, 'He's a poor little thing, but once he puts on a bit of weight he'll be fine.'

Lily tried to sleep after they had gone, but she was disturbed by the plaintive crying of the baby, which continued on and off during the night. Sitting on the side of her bed, she held him to her breast. He wanted none of it, however, and continued his miserable weeping, his toothless mouth opening wide. It was not until the small hours of the morning that at last his crying ceased and he slept.

Throughout the days and nights that followed, Lily cared for the baby and tried her best to get him to feed. He awoke and cried so often she got no rest. At such times she held him in her arms and put her nipple to his mouth, but then groaned and sighed when he turned his face away. Weary and exhausted, she whispered to him, 'Please – you must be hungry. You've got to have food.'

As she watched the days and nights drag by, her every moment was governed by the baby's moods and needs. Then, slowly, to her great relief, she began to discern a change in him. He began to take his milk more regularly, and to put on weight. She could feel him heavier in the cradle of her arms. He was getting stronger, there was no doubt of it. His breathing too sounded healthier, and he slept more deeply, and for longer periods.

Lily began to relax a little more and to worry a little less, and as the baby continued to make progress, Dr Hanbury suggested that the breast-milk feed might soon be supplemented with a prepared bottle. This, she knew, would pave the way for the infant's eventual departure, which could not now be very far off.

Almost six weeks after the birth, on a bright, warm June afternoon, Lily took the baby out in the perambulator for a walk in the fresh air, the hood of the carriage lifted to shield him from the sun. It was good to be out of the house for a while. The last time was when she had gone to the prison to see Tom.

She had thought of her brother many times as she lay in her room with the baby at her side, and she thought of him now as she pushed the perambulator along the hard, rutted road. She had no idea where he was. She had heard nothing from him, though he would have been free to write, for he would have been released from prison two weeks ago. She could only wait, and hope that he would get in touch.

As for her father and stepmother, she had had only the merest contact with them since the baby's birth. Miss Elsie had written to inform them of it, and some days afterwards Lily had received a brief letter from her father. With no mention of the baby beyond vaguely acknowledging its existence, he had simply expressed the wish that Lily was recovering well. From her stepmother there was no word.

Her stroll took her along the road and onto a lane, on either side of which lay fields where the young wheat and barley were reaching up in the warm sun. Walking on, she came to a spot where a little copse grew beside the road, and here in the shade of oaks and silver birches she came to a halt. There was the trunk of a fallen tree close to the roadside, and she brushed the dust from it and sat down, turning the perambulator so that she could see into its interior. The faintest breeze stirred the leaves around her, and the sound of birdsong filled the air. Sunlight streamed through the branches, dappling the foliage. The grass around the tree boles was starred with vetch, buttercups, dandelions and daises. She could smell the scent of all the sweet growing things. Leaning forward, she peered into the perambulator. The baby was awake and his eyes at once latched onto her gaze. 'Hello, little baby,' she murmured.

He knew her voice, and he lifted his tiny right arm and stretched out his hand, fingers moving, as if reaching for her. She gave a breathless little laugh. 'Oh, baby,' she cooed. 'Little Georgie.' Where the name had come from she did not know, but she spoke it again. 'Georgie,' she said. 'Little Georgie.' As she smiled down at him his mouth opened into a wide grin, while his steady eyes remained fixed on her own. The sight made her catch at her breath, and her own smile grew broader. She studied his face as he lay there – something she was wont to do. It was not always for the simple pleasure that came from looking on his small, handsome features, but to see – with some touch of fear – if she could detect in him any sign of his father. However, to her saturating relief it had never happened. Each time she gazed into the wide eyes with their thick lashes, or took in the neat, perfect nose and the pink little flower of his mouth, she saw only some faint trace of her own father.

Now, bending closer, she cooed to him again, making foolish mother's sounds, then said, her voice soft and caressing, 'Are you a darlin'? Are you the most beautiful boy in the whole world?' And at once, as if she had shared a joke with him, and he had understood it, he gave a little laugh. It was a brief sound, a little breathless chortle, but it seemed to hang in the summer air, so that she felt she could have held it in her hand and kept it always.

She was aware of a kind of peace coming over her, and she sat back on the log and briefly closed her eyes. In the perambulator the baby lay, smiling, his tiny hands moving on the coverlet. She did not know what was to become of her, but for this moment she knew no unhappiness. Perhaps, after all, everything would be all right . . . but then, suddenly, like a dark cloud coming over the sun, the knowing came to her that it could not last. This little sense of peace and happiness that she had felt so briefly, it could not continue – not in the face of what was real. She got up from her seat. 'Come on, Georgie,' she whispered, 'it's time to start back.'

On her return to Rowanleigh, she laid the baby in his cradle and then rocked him as he drifted off to sleep. Not that his sleep would last for long, she knew; he would soon need feeding again. With this in mind, she went downstairs, heading for the kitchen, to prepare his bottle.

As she went through the hall, Miss Elsie, glimpsing her as she passed by, called out her name, and Lily went into the sitting room.

Miss Elsie, holding a piece of paper in her hand, smiled at Lily as she entered. 'I wanted to have a word with you. Did you enjoy your walk?'

'Yes, thank you, it was very pleasant,' Lily replied. 'Georgie enjoyed it too.'

In the silence that fell, Lily was at once aware of what she had said. It was too late, though, the words were out. She felt herself flush slightly. 'Oh, ma'am,' she said, 'I – I can't always just think of him as *the baby*. It doesn't seem right. I can't leave him just nameless.'

Miss Elsie's expression was one of sympathy. She was silent for a moment, then she said, 'You've spent many weeks with your baby, Lily, and it's not something that can be overlooked. He has been so weak, and so dependent on you. You haven't had it easy – not by any means. None of the young women who came here in the past cared for her child for such a long period, but even so, it was still a wrench for them, to part with their babes. I do understand what you're going through.'

Lily said nothing. The past weeks since the baby's birth had left her increasingly confused and unsure of her role. Now, with her life on the verge of being returned to her, she realised that it would not be the life that she had known.

Suddenly, into the quiet came the distant sound of the baby crying in Lily's room on the floor above. Immediately she turned and started away. 'I must get his feed,' she said. 'I was on my way to the kitchen to prepare his bottle.'

'Leave it. I'll get Mary to do it,' Miss Elsie said at once. 'You don't let her do enough. She's a very capable girl.' As she spoke she moved across the room and disappeared into the hallway. From up above the sound of the baby's crying drifted down.

Miss Elsie was back in a couple of minutes. 'Mary will see to him,' she said. She raised the paper that she still held in her hand, and Lily saw that it was a letter. 'I just today heard from the Society,' Miss Elsie said.

'The Society? Oh. Oh, yes.'

'St Paul's Society of Friends. I wrote to them a few days ago – and told them the baby is now strong and thriving.' Her tone was quite matter-of-fact, and she did not meet Lily's eyes. 'So – I'm glad to say that it's all now arranged. They're coming tomorrow. The Reverend Iliffe and his assistant, Miss Cannon.'

Lily frowned. 'Tomorrow?'

'In the afternoon, some time after two.'

'To – to see the baby . . .'

'Well – yes . . . They're coming to – to take him away.'

Lily's mind was spinning. She had known it was inevitable, but it was hard to take in the words. They were coming tomorrow. 'But – it's so soon,' she said. 'Surely – it's *too* soon. Isn't it?'

195

'No, my dear, the time is good.' Miss Elsie's tone was soft. 'It's the right time.'

Lily stood in silence, dimly aware that the baby's crying had ceased.

'He's fine, Lily, believe me,' Miss Elsie said. 'You heard what Dr Hanbury said when he came to see him the other day. He's very pleased with his progress. He says he's strong now and doing really well.' She smiled. 'And all due to you, of course. The wonderful care you've given him.'

Lily gave a worried little shake of her head. 'He – he's not used to strangers,' she said.

'Lily – he'll be all right, I assure you. He's going to be loved and well cared for. You know that. My dear, we only want the best for him.'

'Yes. Yes, I know.'

'Of course you do, and the Society will find him a good home. He'll have loving parents, and he'll have a good life. Isn't that the best thing for him?'

Lily nodded. Earlier, sitting in the sunshine with the baby, she had felt for a few moments something like a real sense of peace, a feeling that she had not known in a long time, but hardly had the feeling touched her than there had come that swift realisation that it could not last. And of course it could not.

Miss Elsie said, breaking into her thoughts, 'I know what you're going through. But you knew it would happen, Lily. Sooner or later it had to happen.'

'Yes.'

There was silence in the room, and then came the renewed sound of the baby's crying. Lily turned. 'I must go to him.'

'Mary's getting his milk,' Miss Elsie said. 'He'll be all right.'

'I know – but *I* must go to him.' With her words, Lily started to the door.

That night she lay awake in her room. The sky was not yet dark, and in the faint light that crept in she looked into the baby's cradle just two feet away. He was sleeping. For a few moments she held her own breath in an effort to hear the sound of his breathing, something she did so many times in the night. And in the quiet the thought came to her, again, like a new realisation, shocking her, that she would lie like this no more. Tomorrow night when she lay down to sleep, she would be alone.

The Reverend Iliffe and Miss Cannon arrived just after two-thirty the following day. Lily, watching from a window in the drawing room, saw the carriage come to a stop and observed the pair as they got out. She saw the clergyman exchange some words with the fly-driver who at once relaxed in his seat and took out his pipe. Obviously, Lily thought, he had been asked to wait while their business was conducted, so clearly the visitors saw no protracted business ahead of them.

Miss Elsie herself answered the door to the reverend's knock, took his hat and ushered them into the room where Lily still stood near the window. Lily was introduced to the couple, and they shook her hand and smiled at her benevolently. Reverend Iliffe, in his late fifties, was a man of medium height with fine bones that had not a lot of flesh on them. He had smooth, pink skin that looked as if it had rarely seen strong sunlight, and a small, thin-lipped mouth. His pale, watery eyes looked at Lily through the thick lenses of steel-rimmed spectacles. He was carrying a black leather briefcase, wore a dark grey suit, and his scrawny neck disappeared into his cleric's collar. He had a kind air about him, however, and when he smiled the severity of his expression was transformed.

Miss Cannon, standing at his side, was a short, stout

woman in her forties, and wore a grey cape and a dark brown bombazine dress. The hat on her grey hair was a no-nonsense affair of black straw. When she smiled at Lily she showed small teeth with an expanse of pink gum.

Following the introductions, Miss Elsie asked the visitors if they would care for some tea. Reverend Iliffe gave a shake of his head, and said no, thank you; it was a kind offer, but they would have to start back again before too long.

He turned then to Lily. 'And this young lady . . . is the mother?' he enquired, putting the question both to Lily and Miss Elsie.

'Yes,' Lily said, 'I'm the baby's mother.'

The clergyman nodded and smiled, Miss Cannon nodding and smiling along with him. 'And is everything ready?' he asked.

Lily, who had been ready for hours, flicked a glance at Miss Elsie and picked up a coarse, straw basket. 'These are his things,' she said. 'He doesn't have very much. His clothes, his bottle, his rattle – a few other bits and pieces . . .'

'Good, that's splendid,' the reverend said. 'Is the baby here?'

Lily put the basket down. 'I'll go and get him,' she said.

Upstairs in her room she stooped low over the crib, looking into the little face. He was awake and, seeing her, at once connected his gaze with her own, his solemn eyes fixing intently, like a magnet, on hers. As he did so she felt her heart lurch in her breast, and briefly she closed her eyes in pain. In spite of the fact that all through the day she had tried to ready herself for this moment, she knew that she was as unprepared as she had ever been.

Bending her face lower, she smiled at him. 'Hello, my darling,' she whispered. He smiled back at her, and as he briefly turned his face on the pillow she saw the tiny crescent moon on his cheek beside his ear. She bent closer, and kissed the spot, kissed the little moon. He smiled more broadly, as if amused, and her own mouth moved in a tender, sad little smile. Adjusting her skirt, she lowered herself to her knees on the rug. She knew that downstairs the clergyman and the lady would be waiting, anxious to get back into the fly and return to the station, but these were precious moments and they would not come again.

Reaching into the cradle she drew back the light covers and lifted him out. Gently she wrapped him in his shawl then sat back on her heels, holding him in her arms. Putting her mouth to his tiny ear, she said, 'You're going on a journey. I don't know where, but you're going somewhere – maybe to some thrilling, exciting place far away from here.' She held him as close as she dared, drinking in the look and smell of him. 'You'll have a new mother,' she said, 'and you'll have a father too,' making the discoveries as she spoke, little revelations that took her by surprise and all but stopped her in her tracks. 'You'll have a whole new family. Perhaps brothers and sisters.' She paused for a moment as her breath caught in her throat. 'You won't remember me,' she said, 'but that's the way it should be. You'll have a new life, a better life than I could ever give you.'

She wanted to say so much more; there would never be time enough for all the things she wished to say. Outside the window in the rowan tree a thrush began to sing. Hearing the sweet song, Lily said, 'Listen. The thrush is singing. He's singing for you.' The baby looked up at her from the nest of her arms. 'Come,' she said, choking back the tears that filled her eyes. 'Come, my darling. The nice people – they're waiting.'

The clergyman and Miss Cannon turned at Lily's entrance and observed her as she came in.

'Ah,' said the reverend, his smile expanding across his pink face, 'here comes the little mite,' and Miss Cannon, her smile as embracing as the vicar's, said, 'Is he ready to go?'

Lily nodded. 'Yes, he's ready.'

Miss Cannon went to Lily, held out her arms, and Lily laid the baby in them. 'Be careful with him,' she said, as she released the tiny bundle into the woman's grasp.

Miss Cannon gave a little nod. 'Don't worry, Miss Clair, we have much experience of looking after such precious little creatures.'

The reverend spoke up. 'Oh, yes, indeed, you have absolutely no reason for anxiety.' He pressed his hands together. 'So – everything seems to be going along very well. We just need to complete the paperwork and the matter will be settled and we can be on our way again.' He bent then and took up his briefcase, opened it and took out some papers. As he did so, Miss Elsie gestured towards a small writing table on which lay a blotter and ink-stand.

'Ah, yes, thank you.' The reverend nodded, then moved to the table and sat down. As Lily watched, he laid out the papers before him, glanced over them, then turned to her. 'If you please, Miss Clair . . .'

Lily moved to stand by the table. As she did so he uncapped the inkwell, took up a pen and dipped it in.

'Your full name is Lily Mary Clair, is that correct?'

'Yes, sir.'

He wrote on the paper. 'And you were born in Compton Wells, Wiltshire on the second of July 1848.'

'Yes, sir.'

'Thank you. And you're resident here at Rowanleigh, in the village of Sherrell.'

'Yes.'

He nodded, wrote again, then held out the pen to her. 'If you wouldn't mind – we need your signature.'

She took the pen from him, and he pointed to a place on the paper. 'Just there, if you please . . .'

Lily became aware of her heart beating. She stood with the pen in her fingers, hand poised above the paper.

'Just there,' Reverend Iliffe said again, pointing.

As Lily hesitated, the ghost of a nervous little laugh broke in her throat. It was hardly more than a breath, but it rang in the quiet room. The clergyman turned his smile upon her. 'It's quite straightforward, my dear. It's the usual procedure. It's just to say that you willingly give up the infant for adoption.'

Lily did not move. The Reverend Iliffe looked at her and then after a moment switched his glance to Miss Elsie.

'Lily . . .' Miss Elsie said.

Lily nodded, eyes fixed on the paper where the reverend's fingertip was set. He prompted her. 'Just here, Miss Clair . . .'

Lily stood for another second, unmoving, then bent and put down her signature.

Reverend Iliffe smiled and let out a little breath of satisfaction. 'Well done, that's splendid. And now here on this one . . .' He moved the top paper aside to reveal the one below. He pointed, indicating where Lily was to sign. She did so, then straightened and handed him back the pen. As she took a step back, the man turned his head to Miss Elsie. 'If you please, Miss Balfour . . . Your witness signature, please, if you wouldn't mind . . .'

As Miss Elsie moved to the desk to sign the papers, Lily looked across at Miss Cannon holding the baby. 'Oh,' she said, before she could stop herself, 'he doesn't like to be held that low down. He likes his head higher.' Miss Cannon adjusted the position of the baby in her arms and said with a smile, 'I've handled many babies, miss. I'm very experienced, really.'

While the reverend packed the papers away in his case, Miss Elsie set a ledger on the table, an old-looking thing with a brown binding and a loosening spine. She opened it up and wrote in it, and then asked the vicar and Lily to add their signatures. And it was done. The reverend picked up the straw basket holding the baby's belongings and turned an enquiring eye to his companion. 'Miss Cannon?'

Miss Cannon said at once, 'Yes, we're ready to go, Reverend.'

The man and the woman turned to Lily. 'Thank you, Miss Clair,' the reverend said, 'and don't worry about the baby – he'll have a good life – and he'll be well provided for.'

Then they turned, heading for the door.

Chapter Thirteen

The warm days lengthened into high summer, and the first scarlet poppies were seen in the rising corn. At Rowanleigh, Miss Elsie spent hours, day after day, working with Lily at her studies, instructing her in everything she thought might be required in her future work as a governess. In what spare time she had, she turned to her painting, working with her watercolours and brushes. On a few occasions, when the weather was exceptionally fine, she would take her small easel out into the nearby fields. Lily, left alone, tried to concentrate on the projects that Miss Elsie set for her. While the baby had been there, so demanding of her time, she had had no opportunity for such work, nor, indeed, any inclination for it. Now, though, her time was free, and she must make use of it.

It was not easy. Everything had changed. Just a short time ago her child had been there in the house, his very presence demanding her attention, her constant thought, so that she had never been without awareness of his being, his nearness.

And now he was gone. For two days after his departure the cradle had remained in her bedroom, empty and haunting, but then Mr Shad had come and taken it away. Lily had stood and watched as he had carried it through the door, and she had wanted to cry out, to stop him, but she had made no sound. Any protest was useless: her son was gone, and the cradle would remain empty.

She found herself weeping, the tears coming upon her at

the most unexpected times, when she would be totally unprepared. She would see his little body, his face. She could see him in all his detail; his soft hair, his tiny, perfect hands, every feature was there. Sometimes when the pictures came, she would stand stock still and catch at her breath.

Miss Elsie was well aware of it. Emerging from her studio to join Lily for dinner in the dining room, she saw the shadows behind her eyes.

'It will pass, Lily,' she said. 'Believe me, it will.'

Lily had written and told her father and stepmother of the baby's departure. However, she said, she would be staying on at Rowanleigh, where Miss Balfour was preparing her for a position as a governess. Her father had responded saying that she was fortunate to have been given such a chance, but that he could no longer afford the allowance that had previously been sent to Miss Balfour. Lily wrote back to say it would not be necessary, that she would be earning her keep while she was there, but received no reply.

So, the sewing work came again from the Corster draper, and Lily divided her time between the needlework and her studies. The summer days fled by and the nights drew in. She watched as the leaves turned to gold and brown, and there was no further word from her father in answer to her letters. She kept her mind occupied with her work, and always with feelings of gratitude to her benefactress. Any expressions of such gratitude, though, were quickly dismissed. 'You cared for me when I needed it, and when there was no one else,' Miss Elsie said one day when Lily brought up the subject. 'There's nothing more to say.'

Working on the various projects set for her, Lily continued to make good progress, aware herself of the strides she was making as her learning increased by the day. She was glad too, for anything that distracted her from her preoccupations concerning the child, Joel, and Tom.

She had learnt nothing of Tom since the third of May when she had visited him at Wentworth gaol, so when she saw his familiar handwriting on the envelope after the postman's call one morning in November, her heart gave a surge of joy. With eager fingers she took out the single page letter. He had written:

> Fellowes Farm
> Halls Haven, Nr Corster
> 3rd November 1867

Dear Lil,

I know you will have wondered about me, but you have had your own problems to deal with. A few things have happened, but I'm glad to say that life is a bit better now, which is why I'm writing. You'll be glad to know I've got a job, and I'm working and living at Fellowes Farm, so not wandering the streets and getting into trouble. I've wrote to Mother and Father twice but got no reply, and so much time has gone by now that I don't expect to hear.

I wonder about you, Lil, and I think about how you are. And your baby too. I don't even know if you're still staying at Sherrell, or when or if you'll get this letter.

Do you think you could come and see me? I don't get much time off, and I haven't got much money for fares, but I can get to the Woolpack Inn here in Halls Haven next Saturday, the ninth, if you can manage it. I know you won't want to sit in any of the bars, but they got a little room at the back where the old ladies sits and drinks their coffee and tea, and we can go there. I can get away for an hour or so, say from three o'clock, if that's all right.

Your loving brother
Tom

As soon as Lily had finished reading the letter she sat down to pen a reply. She would be there on Saturday, she wrote to him, and would meet him soon after three in the tea room of the Woolpack Inn.

Mr Shad drove her to the railway station on Saturday, for which she was very grateful, for the way was treacherous underfoot. It had rained during the night and the road was muddy and in parts thickly carpeted with fallen leaves. At the station she caught a train for Corster, and on arrival there hired a fly to take her the rest of the way to Halls Haven, and the Woolpack Inn.

It came on to rain as the carriage reached the inn, and she hurried inside. Enquiring of the landlord, she was directed to a room at the end of a short passage. On entering, she found its only patrons were an elderly couple sitting at one of the tables. There was no sign of Tom. The old clock over the mantelpiece showed the time at two-fifty-five.

She moved to a small table near a window, and after laying her bag and umbrella on the padded bench, she undid the collar and buttons of her coat and sat down. As she did so a young girl appeared in the aperture of a serving hatch and looked over at her with a smile. 'Yes, miss, what can I get for you?' Lily replied that she was waiting to be joined by someone and would order when he arrived. The barmaid nodded, 'Right you are, miss,' and disappeared from sight.

The minutes ticked by while the rain increased and ran down the window pane. From the adjoining public bar came a continuous hum of voices. The elderly couple sat murmuring over their drinks. Then, at long last, there was movement at the door to the passage, and Tom looked into the room, saw Lily and entered.

'Tom. Oh, Tom.' She got to her feet and reached out as he

came towards her. He wrapped her in his arms, a little damp from the rain, and briefly held her to him.

'Ah, Lil,' he said. 'Oh, you're a sight for sore eyes, and no mistake.' He bent his head and kissed her awkwardly on the cheek.

As she sat down again he took off his coat and laid it on the bench, putting his cap down beside it. 'I'm sorry I'm late,' he said as he sat down at her side, 'and I can't be out for long. I've got to get back soon.' She took hold of her bag and got out her purse. Handing him some coins, she said, 'You get yourself whatever you want. I'll just have some coffee.'

'I'll 'ave coffee too,' he said. He took the money and moved to the serving hatch. As he stood talking to the barmaid, giving her the order, Lily studied him. He was thirteen now. He did not appear to have grown very much, and in his bearing there was still almost the callow rawness of a child. For all his lack of physical stature, though, he was just as handsome, she thought, but his face was not a face that was content. For one so young there was too much shadow in the cast of his eye, too little lightness in the curve of his lip.

'Oh, Tom,' she said as he came back to the table with the steaming mugs, 'how good it is to see you again.'

He sat down, setting her few coppers of change before her. 'Yeh, and so good to see you, Lil.'

'It's been so long,' she said. 'I haven't set eyes on you since May.'

He lowered his face. 'Ah, that's right.'

Seeing the sudden sorrow in his expression, she realised that he was thinking of the prison, and she said, 'Oh, Tom, those days are over. They're behind you now. There's no need to think about that time anymore.'

'No. No, of course not. That's all past. Let's drink to better times.' He smiled, and lifted the thick china mug. 'Come on. We got better things to think of.'

Lily picked up her mug. 'To the future, Tom.'

'Ah,' he nodded and smiled again, 'to the future.'

They touched their mugs together and drank. From the adjoining bar there continued to drift in the murmur of the other customers.

'How've you been, Lil?' Tom asked. 'Have you been all right?'

'Yes, I've been well.'

'And the baby . . .?'

The baby. The thought of the baby caused Lily's breath to catch momentarily in her throat. Then she said, 'Yes, the baby . . . The baby was born that same day. That same day I saw you in – in Redbury.'

'The very same day?'

'Yes. Soon after I got back to Sherrell. He was early, but he was all right, though.'

Tom smiled. 'He. You 'ad a boy.'

'Yes, I had a boy.' She drew in her breath. 'He's gone now,' she said, trying to make her voice betray no emotion. 'He was taken for adoption.'

'Ah.' Tom nodded. 'So he'll 'ave a good life, then.'

'Yes, he'll have a good life.'

'D'you know where he went to?'

She shook her head. 'They don't tell you such things.'

'No, I s'pose not. It's prob'ly better that way.' He took a drink from his cup. 'And 'ow are you getting on now with the lady, Miss Balfour?'

'Oh – she's been so kind to me. She's teaching me.'

'Teaching you?'

'Teaching me, yes. Every day. Preparing me to be a governess. I'm learning so much. I'm reading Keats and Shakespeare and Milton. I'm even studying French. And I'm learning arithmetic and geography and history – all about the Romans, and the Tudors and the Stuarts. Miss Elsie – she's a very clever woman.' She went on to tell him something of her life at Rowanleigh, and of her work there. At the end of it, Tom said, 'Oh, my, that sounds wonderful, Lil. You're gettin' a real chance to make things better.'

'I hope so. It's what I'm working for.'

'Well, you'll do well, I know you will. And you deserve it too.'

'Thank you. And what about you, Tom? How are you getting on? You said nothing in your letter.'

He shrugged. 'Well, you know me – I never been a one for letter-writing.'

'Oh, I know that all right. Are they good to you here, your employers?'

'Yeh, they're all right. Thompson, their name is. I was lucky to get the job.'

'What are you doing?'

'Assistin' the stockmen most of the time. I like workin' with the animals.'

'And do they feed you well?'

He nodded. 'Oh, yeh, they feed us well enough. I'm comfortable enough too. I sleeps over the stables with a couple of the other lads.'

He went on to speak of his duties on the farm, and of his workmates there, and as he spoke, Lily perceived in him some little growing flame of optimism. Across the room the elderly couple set down their empty teacups, buttoned up their coats and moved to the door. When the pair had gone, Lily said to Tom:

'D'you ever hear anything of your friend?'

He frowned, narrowing his eyes slightly. 'My friend?'

'Your friend from – from that time.'

'At Wentworth?'

'Yes.' Immediately she regretted bringing up the memory. 'You spoke of him when I saw you. He was your good friend.'

He gave a nod. 'Jake,' he said.

'Yes.' She smiled. 'Jake, that was his name. Oh, I was so glad you'd met him, that you'd found a friend.'

'Ah,' he said, and turned his face away.

'Tom,' she said, 'is there something wrong? Have I said something?'

'I want to forget that,' he said. 'That's done with. That's in the past.'

'Of course it is,' she said. 'You'll never have to go back there.'

'I don't just mean that place – the prison. I mean *him*.'

'Jake?'

'Ah.'

Lily peered at him, frowning at his grim, lowered profile. 'Tom, what happened? Did something happen? Tell me.'

He gave a brief shake of his head. Into the quiet that surrounded them a burst of laughter rang out from the public bar. Lily pressed her fingers against the rough fabric of his sleeve. 'Something happened,' she said. 'What was it?'

'It's done,' he said shortly. 'It's over with, and I never want to see 'im again.'

'But – he was your friend. You told me so. You said – '

'Enough, Lil.' His voice was sharp. 'He's no part of it any more. He's nothin' to do with my life! Let it be.' Picking up his half-finished mug of coffee, he drank from it and then set it back on the table. He sat staring down at it while long moments ticked by in silence, then he said in whisper:

'It was 'im, Jake Marchant. It was 'im.' He had turned his face away from Lily again, so that once more she could see only the shallow angle of his profile. 'He should be killed,' he said.

'Tom,' she breathed, shocked. 'What are you saying?'

He turned to her now, and she could see the hate darkening his eyes. 'I mean it,' he said. 'What he did.'

'What he did . . . ?'

His eyes slid away from her, and she saw his features distorted with an anguish that she had never seen there before.

'What happened?' she said. 'Tell me, please.'

He lifted his coarsened hands and covered his face, while his whole body shuddered. After a while he let fall his hands and said, speaking in a harsh whisper, 'He – he was so kind. Just when I needed it, when I needed a friend, and everything was so strange, and so cruel, and I was afraid.' He turned his face to Lily. 'I was so afraid,' he muttered.

'Of course you were,' she said. 'Oh, of course you were.'

'You can't imagine what it's like, bein' in a place like that.'

'No.' She shook her head. 'I can only guess that it must be absolutely – dreadful.'

He nodded. 'Ah – you could say that.'

As he looked down into his mug another little burst of laughter echoed from the public bar. Tom flinched at the sound, and as if suddenly becoming aware of himself, he pushed the mug away and rose from his seat. 'I got to go,' he said. 'I got to get back. I'm sorry, Lil.' He turned to her, leant down and kissed her on the cheek. 'I love you, Lil. You're all the world to me.'

As Lily got to her feet he pulled on his coat and, jamming his cap on his head, turned towards the door. 'Tom . . .' she said, 'wait, please,' but he was gone. Quickly buttoning her coat, she snatched up her bag and umbrella and went after him.

She caught up with him as he reached the muddy pavement outside. The rain had stopped and the air was dry, though dark clouds hung in the sky. A wind had sprung up.

'Tom, wait,' she said urgently. 'Don't go like this.'

'I got to get back,' he said. 'They're expectin' me. They'll moan if I'm not there.'

As he strode out she remained at his side, stretching her stride to keep up with him. Then, reaching a corner where the road joined a narrow lane, he came to a halt and turned to face her. 'Don't come any further, Lil. There's no point.'

'Oh, but Tom,' she said, 'I can't leave you like this. I don't know when I might see you again.'

He hesitated for a second, then said, 'You wouldn't want to see me again – if you knew.'

'If I knew? What are you talking about? What do you mean?'

'Oh, Lil . . .' He gave a groan and turned his face away into the wind. 'I can't tell you. I can't speak of it.'

'Tom, don't say that. You can tell me anything. Anything at all.'

'No.' He shook his head, and when he turned back to face her she could see the pain in his features. 'You'd cast me out. And I wouldn't blame you.'

She was bewildered. 'Tom – my dear, what are you talking about? Is it something you've done? Tell me.'

He shook his head again. 'I can't.'

'There's nothing you could tell me that would make any difference,' she said. 'I don't care what you've done. I know you, and I love you, and you can't have done anything that could make me love you any less.'

'Ah – you say that, but you don't know everything about me.'

Her bewilderment was growing. 'I don't know what you're talking about. Is this something to do with your time in prison? Tom, that's over. You've paid your penalty and it's over.'

'It's not that,' he said. 'It's what 'appened when I was there.'

She frowned. 'Something happened to you while you were in there . . .'

And suddenly tears filled his eyes, spilt over and poured

212

down his cheeks. 'Yes!' he cried out. 'And I'll never be the same again.'

Her own emotion tightening her throat, she looked at him. 'It's to do with him, isn't it?' she said. 'Jake Marchant.'

Tom's silence answered her words.

'Tell me – what did he do?'

Tom hung his head and briefly closed his tearful eyes. 'I can't talk about it.'

'I thought he was your friend,' she said. 'You told me he was good to you, that he looked after you.'

He said nothing.

'Isn't that so?'

'Yeh.' He nodded. 'He was kind. Very kind. And I was new to the place, and like I said – I was afraid.'

'Anyone would be.'

'Everything – it was all so strange and frightening.' He paused, drew a breath then went on: 'And there were some there, two or three of the men, who seemed so – so threatening.'

'They wanted to harm you?'

He hesitated. 'Yeh, but – Jake – 'e stepped in and – and protected me. He was a strong man – big and broad – and powerful too in his general way. The others backed off if 'e faced 'em down. But to me 'e was kind, and I was grateful. He took me under his wing, so to speak, and I guess I loved 'im for it. I felt safe, and I trusted 'im. Oh, I trusted 'im so much. It was almost as if I felt I was with a – a kind father – the sort of father I *should* have had, one who'd look after me. I felt that as long as Jakie was there I'd be all right.'

He came to a stop. Lily waited a moment and then prompted him. 'Go on.'

'You – you don't want to hear no more.'

'Go on,' she said. 'You have to tell me.'

She waited for him to continue. The wind came keening down from the hills, blustered between the trees and lifted

213

the hem of her coat, and suddenly, Tom burst out in a harsh whisper, almost inaudible against the sound of the growing wind:

'He – he did things to me.' He bent his head and put his hands up to his face, while the tears streamed from his eyes. 'He did things to me,' he sobbed, his slim shoulders shaking. 'Dreadful – shameful things. To me – to my body. There was nothin' I could do to stop him. He got me alone in one of the laundry rooms one day, and there was nothin' I could do. He knew that no one would come to 'elp me. He knew they wouldn't dare. And through it all 'e talked to me so kind, so sweet, tellin' me how he'd look after me, and tellin' me 'ow much he cared for me. He said I was like his son. I was 'is boy, 'e said, and nobody would ever dare 'urt me.'

His words came to a halt and he stood slightly bent, his hands still up to his face. Beneath the rim of his cap the wind stirred his dark hair.

Lily stood as if stunned, speechless, her eyes wide with horror as the reality of what he was saying slowly forced its way into her brain. It was all, all beyond her imagining. It could not be so. He was speaking of things that she had never read about, not one word; had never heard spoken of, never heard hinted at.

The seconds passed by while they stood facing one another and the wind swept and gusted. The tears stung her eyes.

'Tom, my dear,' she said at last, her voice breaking, '– this – this dreadful thing. Oh, my dear. It wasn't your fault. Oh, my darling, what happened wasn't your fault. I can't bear to think of you having gone through such – such things. I can't bear to think of you suffering so. But it was *him*, Tom. It wasn't you. It was *him*.'

'But I let him do it! I had to let 'im do it! I couldn't do nothin' else.'

214

'Well, how could you stop him? You couldn't. Of course you couldn't.'

'But it was more than once! It 'appened more than once. Whenever 'e wanted me.' He turned about, letting his hands fall from his face. 'How can you even bear to talk to me? After what I've done. I feel so – dirty. So dirty. I feel I'll never be clean again.' He paused. 'Sometimes I wish I wus dead.'

'Tom, don't speak like that! Don't say such things!' She lifted her arms and wrapped them around his body. Under her touch she could feel him trembling. 'You must go on from here,' she said, her words muffled against the fabric of his coat. 'It's in the past, and you've got to put it behind you. You've got to get on with your life.'

'I can't see anything ahead,' he muttered. 'I never could.'

His words threatened to break her heart. 'Listen . . .' she said, 'the way you're feeling now, things look – look bleak – but it won't always be that way.'

A bitter smile caught at the corners of his mouth. 'Maybe so.' Then, putting his head a little on one side, he said, 'D'you reckon it's possible – that one day we'll be together, the way we talked about it? The way you always said it would 'appen?'

'Yes.' She smiled. 'One day. Who knows when, but it'll happen. We'll find that little house somewhere, and live together.'

'For always.'

The tears welled in her eyes again. 'For always, yes.'

'Yeh.' He nodded. 'You would cook and clean and sew and look after the 'ouse, and I'd 'elp you round the place and work on the land. We'd have a bit o' land, wouldn't we? Two or three acres, maybe. Enough for a cow and a goat and some chickens, right?'

'Yes,' she said.

'Yeh,' he said. He paused briefly, then said, 'You ever 'ear anything from 'ome, Lil?'

'No,' she said. 'I've written but I haven't heard back.'

'No, me neither,' he said. 'Like I said in my letter, I wrote twice but didn't 'ear nothin'. I don't reckon I'll 'ear anything again.'

'Well – give it time. Maybe Father's busy.'

'Yeh, maybe.'

He looked at her steadily for some seconds, and then he said, 'It ain't gunna 'appen, is it, Lil?'

'What? What isn't going to happen?'

'Our little 'ouse. Our bein' together.'

'Why not?' she said quickly. 'It could. It could.'

'Nah.' He shook his head. 'It's just a dream. We're makin' fools of ourselves. Well, at least I am. But there – I reckon I always 'ave done.'

A gust of wind buffeted them. Tom gave himself a little shake, as if coming out of a trance. 'I must go,' he said.

As he began to turn away Lily grasped his sleeve. 'When – when shall I see you again?'

He turned back to her. 'D'you want to? After what you know?'

'Oh, how can you ask such a question? Of course I want to see you. I want to know how you're getting on. I always think about you.'

He nodded. 'All right, then. I'll write you a letter.'

'You won't forget?'

'No, I won't forget.'

He leant down then – only a little, for he was not much taller than she – and pressed his cold cheek against her own. At the same time he embraced her, tightly. Then he was releasing her, straightening and turning away again. 'G'bye, our Lil.'

She watched as he went along the lane, until he had walked out of sight, hidden from her view by a screen of silver birches. He did not look back.

She stood there for some moments after he had gone,

then pulled the collar of her coat about her throat and turned and set off for the inn, there to pick up the fly to take her to the station. As she walked, her feet in the mud of the lane felt as heavy as her heart.

Chapter Fourteen

When Lily arrived back at Rowanleigh she went straight up to her room, where she removed her hat and coat and stood in front of the glass that hung beside the fireplace. She touched at her hair, almost unconscious of her actions. She was only vaguely aware of her surroundings, the room with its simple furnishings, and the window looking out onto the garden, the lawn scattered with leaves from the cherry tree.

Turning from the glass, she moved to the bed, and sat. The silence in the room was complete. From without there came no sound. No birds sang. Beyond the window the sky was grey above the cherry tree, with rain clouds slowly drifting by.

There came a knock at the door, and, momentarily startled out of her melancholy, she called out, 'Come in.' The door opened and Miss Elsie stepped into the room.

'Mary said she heard you come back,' Miss Elsie said. 'Did you see your brother?'

Lily nodded. 'Yes.'

Miss Elsie closed the door behind her. 'And how was it – your meeting?'

Lily did not know what to say. She bent her face, looking down at her hands. Miss Elsie came forward, and stood before her. 'My dear . . .' she said, 'obviously it didn't go as you'd hoped.'

Lily gave a little shake of her head.

'Do you want to talk about it? I'm a good listener.'

When Lily did not speak, Miss Elsie lifted a hand and briefly pressed Lily's shoulder. 'Was it so bad?'

Lily remained silent for a moment, but the gentle touch burst through the dam of her resolve, and she began to cry. Miss Elsie sat down beside her. 'Lily, what is it?' she said.

Lily continued to weep for some moments, but slowly calmed herself. Then, in a rush, it all came pouring out, and she told of her meeting with Tom, of his shocking revelation and his despair. Throughout it, Miss Elsie sat in silence, but there was no hiding the horror that touched her features. When at last Lily's words came to a halt, she said, 'Lily, I can only try to imagine what you're going through – and that poor young man. I only wish I could help.'

They sat without speaking for some moments, then Miss Elsie said, 'I came upstairs as there's something I want to talk to you about – but now I think I should leave you alone for a little time.' She pressed Lily's shoulder again and rose from the bed. 'I'll see you at dinner. I'll tell you about it then.'

Dinner that evening was a subdued affair. Miss Elsie, out of consideration for Lily's preoccupation, kept the desultory conversation rather solemn. Then, after the coffee had been served, she went away from the table, and came back with a copy of that week's local newspaper, the *Corster Gazette*.

'This is what I wanted to talk to you about,' she said as she sat again. Pushing aside her cup and saucer, she set down the paper and turned the pages to the classified advertisements. 'There.' She touched with her forefinger at an entry low on the page. 'This could be just the thing for you.'

She folded the paper back on itself and held it out to Lily, who took it and looked at the small area of text that had been circled with a pencil. Holding it closer to the light of the candelabrum, she read:

Wanted immediately: Governess on daily, visiting basis for two girls, aged seven. Applicant must be young, able, patient, energetic and trustworthy. Please apply with references to Mrs Edward Acland, Yew Tree House, Green Lane, Little Patten, Nr Corster.

Lily read the advertisement over again, while across the table Miss Elsie looked for a response. 'Well?' Miss Elsie said. 'What do you think?'

Lily raised her eyes from the newspaper. 'Do you think I could do it?'

Miss Elsie nodded. 'I wouldn't have shown you the advertisement if I didn't.'

Lily sat with the newspaper before her. She had been studying so hard over these past months – and all with this in view: the possibility of gaining a position as a governess. Now, it seemed, the opportunity was here. She felt a glow of pleasure at Miss Elsie's belief in her, but nevertheless she was full of doubt.

'D'you think I'm ready?' she said.

Miss Elsie nodded. 'I do indeed. You'll make a splendid teacher. You've got all the right attributes. Besides, my name still counts for something around here, and you can be sure I'll give you an excellent character.'

A reply to Lily's letter applying for the position came five days later. Written by Mrs Acland, it invited Lily to come for an interview on Monday, the eighteenth of November, and to bring her character references with her.

When Monday came, Lily set off in the trap for the railway station. The morning was unusually mild for the time of year, and she had about her a more positive air than she had had since her melancholy meeting with Tom. She wore her black straw hat, and her dark grey coat, with a little bunch of papier mâché cherries pinned to her lapel. Taking the Redbury-bound train from Corster, she eventually came to Little Patten, and there set out to walk to Green Lane, which was situated on the edge of the village. Yew Tree House was the fourth house along the lane, a large old dwelling with brick and white stucco walls and a red-tiled roof.

A young maid answered her ring, and Lily gave her name and said she was expected. The girl gave a little bob and asked her to come in, and Lily wiped her boots and stepped into the wide, tiled hall where the maid took her umbrella. She was shown then into a room on the right. 'If you'd please to wait in here, miss,' the maid said, 'and take a seat, I'll go and tell Mrs Acland.'

Lily thanked her and the girl went away. Lily looked around her. The room was quite large, and well furnished. A bright fire flickered in the grate. Lily sat down on an overstuffed sofa, and after four or five minutes the door opened again and the mistress of the house appeared. At once Lily got to her feet.

Mrs Acland appeared to be in her late thirties. She was two or three inches below Lily's height, and rather round and plump. She wore her dark hair with a little fringe at the front, and pulled into a knot at the base of her skull. When she smiled she showed small, slightly inward-sloping teeth. Her smile was warm, though, and Lily felt welcome.

'Hello – so you're Miss Clair. How do you do.' The woman took Lily's hand and lightly shook it. She gestured then to the sofa. 'Please – do sit down.'

Lily did as she was bidden, and Mrs Acland sat in one of the armchairs nearby. After she had politely asked Lily about her journey from Sherrell she began to ask her questions about her background, her schooling and her general experience. Lily told her something of her early history, and then went on to say that she had been lodging with Miss Elsie Balfour for some thirteen months, during which time, under Miss Balfour's tutelage, she had been studying with a view to finding work as a governess.

When Lily mentioned the name of Miss Balfour, Mrs Acland at once gave a little nod of approval. 'Oh, Miss Balfour is remembered in these parts,' she said. 'The school she ran in Shalford with her fellow teacher was highly regarded. It's a few years since she left, but her reputation is still very strong. And you say you're lodging with her, and being taught by her. Well, I doubt that you could do better. Is it she who's provided you with your reference?'

'Yes, ma'am.' Lily took from her bag the envelope that Miss Elsie had given her, handed it to Mrs Acland, then watched as she took out the document and studied it.

'Well,' Mrs Acland said, 'this is certainly a glowing testimonial. Miss Balfour speaks of you as being exceptionally able, and a clever and intelligent young woman.' She gave a nod of approval. 'We had a governess until a few weeks ago, but I'm afraid it all ended very abruptly. The girl fell desperately in love, and one fine day she just upped and went. Left us in dire straits, I'm afraid.' She heaved a sigh, then said with an ironic smile, 'I do hope you're not romantically involved with some moustachioed dragoon, Miss Clair. Best tell us now if you are. I hope there's no one in your life who's planning to come and sweep you away.'

Lily shook her head. 'Oh, no. No fear of that, ma'am.'

'I'm glad to hear it,' Mrs Acland said. She paused, then added, 'I'll be quite honest with you: it's not easy to find a suitable governess. We've advertised twice now, and of the few responses we've had, hardly any sounded suitable. We had no recourse but to keep looking.'

The room had grown a little darker. Mrs Acland looked towards the window, beyond which heavy clouds were gathering. 'Oh, dear, it's going to rain,' she said. Then, turning back to Lily: 'I wonder what are your interests?

How do you spend your time at Miss Balfour's house when you're not studying? Do you go out much?'

'Well,' Lily replied, 'in a small place like Sherrell there're not many places to go. Though on occasion I go into Corster – sometimes on errands for Miss Balfour.'

'My husband works in Corster,' Mrs Acland said. 'He's with a firm of solicitors. Oh, we're very fond of Corster. Well, you've got the theatre and the concert hall, and now there's the aquarium – and all the shops, of course. The children love to go there.' She clasped her hands before her. 'But I haven't told you about the children yet. We have twin girls, Alice and Rose. They're just seven years old, and they're good girls. Miss Trimble sometimes had problems keeping them interested, but I have no doubt the lack was hers and not theirs. Anyway,' she added, her face brightening, 'I think you ought to meet them, don't you?'

'Oh, yes, ma'am, I'd love to.' Lily meant it. She had been looking forward to seeing the children. And it was also a good sign – evidence that Mrs Acland was seriously considering her as a potential teacher for her children.

Mrs Acland rose from her seat, saying, 'I've been trying to teach them myself since Miss Trimble went, but it's not easy with everything else I've got to do.' She started for the door. 'I'll be right back.'

She left the room then, and a few minutes later returned, ushering before her two small girls. They came to a stop not far from where Lily sat, while their mother came to a halt behind them.

'Here they are,' Mrs Acland said, 'my two babies, Alice and Rose.'

They reacted frowning to their being called babies, and sighed and looked long-sufferingly at their mother. Mrs Acland, oblivious, beamed over them. 'Say hello to Miss Clair,' she said.

They looked down at their boots. They looked nothing

alike. Alice was short and plump, with a round face and wispy brown hair, while her sister Rose was of a slimmer build, and had thick curls tumbling to her collar.

'Come along, girls,' Mrs Acland smiled. 'Say good afternoon to Miss Clair.'

The girl Alice turned to Lily, gave a little bob of her shoulders and said, 'Good afternoon, Miss.'

'And you, Rosie,' Mrs Acland prompted.

The other girl also turned to Lily, and shyly murmured a good afternoon. Mrs Acland, watching with approval, said, 'They're a little bashful, but they'll get used to you.' She smiled at them. 'You will, won't you, dears?' They remained silent. 'Miss Clair,' Mrs Acland said, 'is probably going to be your new governess. Won't that be nice?'

They betrayed not by a single flicker of their expressions how nice it would be, but stood unmoving, side by side, their glances directed at the floor. Their mother continued to regard them with affectionate approval, then said, 'All right, my dears, you can go back and get on with what you were doing.'

Without hesitating, the pair turned and headed for the door. As they went, their mother prompted them: 'Say goodbye to Miss Clair, then.'

'Goodbye, Miss Clair,' they called out obediently. The next moment they had gone.

'Well,' Mrs Acland said on a sigh, gazing after them, 'there they are, and as I say, they're good girls. They need a firm hand, of course, but all children do. They need to know their limits, that's all. I'm afraid Miss Trimble's mind just wasn't on her job.' She gave a slow nod. 'I don't think you should have any trouble with them, I really don't. I think you'll do very well.'

After a moment's hesitation Lily said, 'Do I understand from that, ma'am, that you're offering me the position?'

Mrs Acland smiled back. 'Oh, yes, indeed. From meeting

you today, and getting to know you a little – and with your glowing reference from Miss Balfour – I think you might do very well. And I'm sure my husband will feel the same. He would have liked to be here today, but I'm afraid he was called away. He trusts my judgement, though.' She paused. 'So – if you think you could cope with us, then we'd love to have you join us, and see how we all get on for the first year.' She gave a nod in confirmation of her words, then added, 'We did make it clear in the advertisement that we don't require a resident governess, only a daily, visiting. Would that present you with a problem?'

'No. No, not at all.'

'Splendid. You'll need to find a room somewhere nearby, but that shouldn't be too difficult. Miss Trimble had no trouble finding lodgings, and was very well suited. She was with a Mrs Thorne, in Ashway Lane,' she gestured with a wave of her small hand, 'which is just up round the corner on the way to the station. Mrs Thorne is a widow lady – of humble means, but a gracious and pleasant soul, and keeps a very clean house, I understand. Certainly Miss Trimble was very happy and comfortable there, I know, and I should think it very likely that her room is still vacant. There wouldn't be many calls for lodgings in a little place like this. Do you think you might like to enquire?'

'Oh, yes, indeed, ma'am,' Lily replied. 'That could be just the thing. I'll go now, on my way back to the station.'

'Excellent. I'll give you directions.' Mrs Acland pressed her hands together. 'That's splendid – and now we must discuss your salary and conditions.'

Lily was soon ready to set off from the house. With all the necessary business arrangements settled with her new employer, she took her leave of her and made her way back along the lane. Thankfully the rain was holding off, though the clouds remained threatening. Reaching the end, she turned to the left and walked along for fifty yards until she came to Ashway Lane, a narrow, stony little road branching off to the right. Roseberry Cottage was the first dwelling in a row of three, and she turned in at its gate, made her way up the short path to the front door, and rapped on it with the iron knocker. It was opened after a few moments by a short, slim woman in her late fifties, wearing a plain apron over her dark brown dress, and a lace cap on her grey hair. Lily introduced herself and said that she had come to enquire whether there might be a vacant room to rent, for she was looking for lodgings while she taught the Acland children at Yew Tree House.

Mrs Thorne beamed at her. There was indeed a room, she said, the very room vacated by the Aclands' former governess, Miss Trimble. Miss Clair could see it now, if she wished. Lily replied that she would very much like to, and a moment later Mrs Thorne was stepping aside and inviting her to enter.

The room Lily was shown into was up one flight of stairs. Smelling very faintly of beeswax and lavender, it was not large, and its ceiling was low, but the window looked out onto a small vegetable garden at the rear, with the sweeping plains of Wiltshire beyond, along the cloud-hung skyline. The room was pleasantly furnished, and Lily saw that it would offer all she required. She turned to the woman who stood watching her, and saw a little anxiety in her face, a look of hope that the room would do. It would do indeed, Lily was sure. She smiled at Mrs Thorne, and said yes, she liked the room very much, and if the terms were agreeable she would like to take it.

Mrs Thorne returned Lily's smile with relief, barely hiding her eagerness to have a paying guest in the house once more. Miss Trimble, she said, paid one-and-nine a week, with all washing done, and breakfast and supper found. Would that be acceptable? Lily at once said yes. It was then arranged that she would move into the room in a fortnight, on Sunday, December the first, ready to begin her teaching of the Acland girls the following day. All was settled.

Back downstairs in the kitchen, Mrs Thorne asked Lily if she would like to stay for some tea. Lily was grateful for the offer, and thanked her, but said that she must set off back for Sherrell.

She left the cottage a few minutes later with her sense of accomplishment and satisfaction riding high. She had found employment and she had found a lodging. The future was looking brighter.

The clouds remained threatening as Lily set off to catch her train, but the rain held off. Arriving at the station, she went onto the platform and saw on the board that a train for Sherrell was due in twenty minutes.

There was a ladies' waiting room near the ticket office, and she went in and took a seat near the door. There were two other women in the place who sat together beneath the window. Lily took a seat opposite, keeping an eye on the dusty-faced old clock. When the time came she gathered up her bag and umbrella, touched at her hat, and left the room.

She had to wait only a further minute or two before the train drew in and she chose a window seat facing forward. There were three other passengers in the carriage, a middle-aged couple and an elderly woman, obviously travelling together.

Once settled in, she thought back on her meeting with Mrs Acland. It was so splendid that everything had gone so well. She had not dared to hope for such a positive outcome, but it had all come to fruition.

She was so caught up in her thoughts that she was not immediately aware of the train departing. Only when her gaze from the window met the sweeping view of the November landscape did she come out of her reverie.

The fields and woodlands trundled by, punctuated here and there with hamlets, villages and small market towns. After a while the train halted briefly at Church Cresson, and again further along at Stretton, where the three other passengers alighted, leaving her alone in the carriage as the train called at Pippinly, and moved on then towards Hanborough. There a short woman in a dark, plum-coloured coat climbed aboard. As she moved to a seat in the far corner she nodded at Lily, and murmured a little greeting, which Lily returned.

The train rattled on its way, and after a while drew into Corster. Lily sat looking out onto the bustling platform as the passengers came and went to the accompanying sounds of the opening and slamming of the carriage doors. Turning her head to her right, her casual glance was drawn to the window on the other side of the compartment, beyond which a train was just pulling into the adjacent platform, heading in the opposite direction. Idly she watched as it slowed, while some of its passengers rose from their seats, collecting up their belongings, preparing to depart. She turned her head away, and as she did so she heard the sudden flurry of raindrops pattering against the window, and then from the other corner the woman's voice, saying with a sigh, 'Ah, here comes the rain. You could bet the dratted stuff wouldn't hold off for long.'

Lily turned to her, gave a nod, and murmured, 'Yes, indeed.'

And then froze in her seat.

In glancing at the woman, Lily's gaze had also taken in the train on the adjacent, downline track. It had now come to a complete halt, and stood so close that its near carriage window was no more than three feet beyond the window of the compartment in which she sat. From her seat in the corner, she gazed, riveted, into the other compartment, where the passengers chatted to each other or sat reading their newspapers and books. Lily's rapt attention, however, was fixed on one particular man.

Without realising it, she rose from her seat, her taut body leaning towards the far window. Her mouth open, she lifted a hand to her lips, as if to stifle a cry. Then, almost in the same moment, the man turned his head and looked through into the compartment in which she stood. Their eyes met, and in a second the man's widened, and his mouth opened and she could see her name, *Lily*, on his lips.

'*Joel* . . .' She whispered his name without being aware that she was uttering a sound. She watched as he rose up from his seat. He was so close and yet so completely inaccessible. From behind her, out on the platform, a whistle blew. In just a few moments, she knew, her path and Joel's would diverge, and there was nothing she could do to prevent it. She was helpless, standing there looking at him across the carriage, and through the two grimy windows. A few moments more and he would be gone.

He was trying to speak to her, but she could make out nothing from the movement of his lips, and no sound penetrated the two panes of glass and the distance between. Then suddenly the carriage gave a lurch, and she staggered slightly before recovering her balance. As the train began to move off, leaving the other train behind, she saw Joel lift his newspaper and turn its face to the window. In the same moment his right hand came up, moving in a sharp gesture. But how the gesture ended she did not see, for in another second he was gone out of her sight.

As she stood there the rest of the train was left behind and vanished from her view, and then all she saw beyond the rain-lashed window was the collection of smoky railway buildings, and the houses that nestled close by.

Chapter Fifteen

'Excuse me – are you all right, miss?'

The voice came from the woman sitting in the corner seat by the far window, and Lily turned to her, seeing her slightly bemused expression, a little frown of concern on her round, good natured face. Lily's eyes widened as she began to come back to the reality of the moment. 'I – I beg your pardon . . . ?'

'I asked if you were all right . . .'

'What? Oh, yes. Yes – thank you.' Lily half turned and lowered herself once more into her seat. From her bag she took a handkerchief and touched at her forehead and cheeks. Her flesh felt hot, and she could feel herself gasping as her breast rose and fell sharply. She took a few deep, steady breaths and tried to gather herself, but her gloved hands were trembling as she returned her handkerchief to her reticule, and she could feel the faint dampness of perspiration again upon her brow.

Joel. He had been there. Just a few feet away, separated from her by the shortest distance and two rain-streaked, soot-stained windows. Now beyond the glass, the fields, hedges, farmyards and common sights of rural Wiltshire passed by. Seeing it all glide before her, she was only aware that with every yard she travelled, the train was taking her further and further away from him.

The next station on the line was Killetshaw. Lily sat hunched over in her seat as the train pulled into the station then a few minutes later pulled out. Fate had determined that she and Joel should not meet again; it was fate that had played so capriciously, placing him there under her gaze, so close and yet so far, and then sending her on her way once more. A short while ago she had felt so positive. She had had a successful interview with Mrs Acland, and at last had seen a future before her – and then, out of the blue, Joel had come back into her life. He had come back and then as swiftly gone again.

'I couldn't help but see what happened . . .'

Hearing the woman's voice, Lily turned to her.

'What an extraordinary thing,' the woman said, 'to catch sight of your friend like that.'

'Yes.' Lily nodded.

'I felt so sorry for you both – not being able to make contact, not being able to talk to one another, yet being so close.'

Lily, distracted, nodded again. She wanted only to be alone with her thoughts, but the woman was not to be stopped. 'Well, when you next meet,' she said with a smile, 'you'll have something to laugh about.'

'No,' Lily said, unable to stop herself, 'we shan't be meeting again. I don't know where he was going.'

The woman frowned. 'But – he was going to Hanborough, surely.'

'Hanborough?' Lily was at once alert. 'What makes you say that?'

'Oh, but – but I thought that's what he was telling you . . .' She shrugged. 'Wasn't it?'

'Telling me?' Lily's tone was almost breathless. 'I don't know. I couldn't make it out – what he was trying to say. I didn't understand.'

The train had begun to slow, preparing to pull into the next station. The rhythm on the tracks was subtly changing.

'Oh,' said the woman, 'maybe you couldn't see – not from over there – but I could see from my seat here, just as we drew away. He was pointing at the banner of his paper, the *The Hanborough Gazette*. He was pointing at the name – Hanborough. You couldn't see that?'

'No. I couldn't.'

Lily straightened in her seat, and then rose to her feet. The train was pulling in alongside a station platform. She must get back, back to Hanborough. 'Where are we?' she said distractedly, and looking from the window saw that they had arrived at Hardy Chennell. She picked up her bag and umbrella. 'I must get off.' She turned to the woman. 'Thank you,' she said. 'Thank you – so much.'

'You're getting a train back to Hanborough now, are you?' the woman asked.

'Yes.'

'Well, you won't have too long to wait.'

Lily clutched the carriage door-handle and pushed. 'Goodbye,' she said to the woman, and with the woman's cheery farewell, stepped down onto the platform. The rain had stopped now. Closing the door behind her, she stood for a moment getting her bearings, then turned and headed off along the platform towards the narrow bridge that spanned the line.

Not many passengers had alighted at the stop, and they had soon left. In less than a minute Lily found herself alone. Within seconds she reached the stairs leading up to the bridge, and started up. As she did so the train on which she had arrived began to move, the smoke billowing and clouding the air. As she crossed the bridge the train passed beneath and chugged its way along the track. At the same time she saw that a train, the train she wanted, was approaching from the opposite direction.

It was slowing already, the smoke belching up from its stack as it came nearer. She quickened her step, clutching at her skirts with one hand, her umbrella and bag held in the other, while the train passed directly beneath her.

Now it was coming to a stop, and as she reached the top of the steps she heard the sound of its doors beginning to open and close. She hurried down.

Reaching the foot of the steps she started forward, while the guard, ten yards away, and with his back to her, raised his whistle to his lips.

'Wait – please . . . !'

At the sound of her voice, he turned as she came across the boards, and lowered his whistle and acknowledged her with a nod that was half impatience, half good will, then stepped to the train and opened the nearest door.

Another few seconds and Lily, gasping out her thanks, was in the carriage, and the guard was slamming the door behind her. Even as she settled into a seat, the whistle was sounding. Moments later and the train was moving away.

Lily hardly took in the other occupants of the compartment, but sat with her hands clasping her bag and umbrella. Beyond the window on her left the fields and woodland moved more quickly by as the train gathered speed. Her heart pounded.

The minutes passed as the train chuffed its rackety way through the rain-wet countryside. First would be Killenshaw, then on through Corster – where she and Joel had set eyes upon one another – then further on to Vineleigh, and after that, Hanborough.

She sat there while the stations came and went, and the passengers alighted and boarded. Inside her gloves she could feel her palms damp, and a dampness too upon her brow beneath the crown of her hat. Then at last the train was slowing once more, as it pulled into Hanborough station. She picked up her bag and umbrella and got to her feet. The train was running alongside the platform now. She turned towards the door, looking out of the window to where people stood, waiting to climb on board.

And there he was.

He was standing about halfway along the platform, a leather case in one hand, his newspaper in the other, his anxious glance sweeping the length of the incoming train. And in the seconds after Lily had caught sight of him his gaze lighted upon her, and a look of relief and joy washed over his face.

Lily kept her eyes on him as he turned and began to stride along the platform while the train came to a halt. Another moment and she was opening the door, and even as it swung open, Joel was moving towards her. She stepped down onto the weathered boards, and the next second he was there, one hand reaching out to help her.

They stood there while the other travellers came and went around them.

'So,' Joel said, 'you're here.'

'Yes – I'm here.'

'I had no idea,' he said, 'whether you understood what I was trying to say to you – while we were on the train – but you did.'

'Thanks to a kind lady in the carriage with me,' Lily said. 'Were it not for her, I'd still be on the way to Sherrell.' On the periphery of her vision she was aware of the guard moving purposefully with his flag. Then a whistle blew. The train began to move out, its speed gathering as smoke and steam billowed into the autumn air. The guard moved away across the platform, took up a broom and began to sweep. Lily and Joel remained facing one another.

'Well,' Joel said, 'can we go somewhere and talk?'

'Yes. Of course.'

Together they headed across the platform to the exit, and emerged onto the street.

The station was situated on the outskirts of the small town. A tavern stood on the corner across the road from the

234

station, and on the opposite side a coffee house. Joel gestured towards the latter, and they stepped into the road and made their way across.

The coffee house was small, but looked comfortable. Lily followed Joel inside and they took a table by a window that looked out onto the busy Station Road. The only other patrons were a pair of middle-aged women who sat on the far side of the room. As Joel set down his case, hat and newspaper he asked Lily what she would like to drink, and she replied that she would have tea. A young waitress came to them, took their order and went away again. The room was quiet, almost the only sounds being the rumble of carriages from the road outside.

After moments of silence had passed between them, Joel said, 'Where were you heading for, Lily?'

'To Sherrell. And you?'

'Here to Hanborough. On business for the company.'

'I hope this isn't putting you out.'

'No, not at all.'

He leant back a fraction on his seat and took her in with a little nod of approval. 'Well – I have to say you're looking very well, Lily,' he said. 'Is life being good to you? I hope so.'

'Yes,' she murmured, 'things – things are going fairly well.'

'I'm glad to hear it.' He added a moment later, 'It's grand to see you.'

She answered with a faint smile, 'And to see *you* again, Joel.'

'You're going to be a bit late getting to Sherrell now,' he said. 'I hope you didn't have an urgent engagement.'

'No. I'm living there now – staying in lodgings.'

'I see. So you moved away from home again – from Compton Wells.'

'Yes.' She nodded. 'I – I didn't stay there long.'

235

'I see.' A long moment, then he asked, 'Did you get my letter, from Cambridge?'

'Yes.' She could not meet his gaze, but looked down at her hands as she peeled off her gloves. 'It was forwarded on from Whitton.'

'I wondered.' He gave a grave smile. 'But you decided not to answer it.' When she said nothing he gave a sigh and a little shrug. 'Ah, well . . .' Then he added, glancing at her bare left hand, 'I can't help noticing that you're still Miss Clair. You're not wearing any wedding or engagement ring.'

'Oh,' she said, 'no,' and lowered her gaze again.

He smiled. 'I thought perhaps you might be married by now. That maybe you went back to Compton and met some young admirer from your earlier days.'

She frowned. 'No. There's – no one.'

'I'm sorry,' he said. 'I didn't mean to be flippant.' Then he added after a moment, 'I – I've thought of you – so much.'

She wanted to say, Yes, and I have thought of you, but she did not speak.

The brief silence was ended with the arrival of the young waitress with her laden tray. When she had gone away again, Lily, glad of the distraction, stirred the contents of the teapot, giving all her attention to the mundane action. When the tea was poured, she passed a cup to Joel, then sipped from her own. All the while she could still feel his eyes upon her.

'Why did you do that, Lily?' he said after a moment. 'Why did you end it like that? Had I done something so dreadful that you could write as you did?'

She did not answer, but looked down into her cup.

'I was shocked,' he said, 'and bewildered. I couldn't understand what was happening. When you wrote your letter you didn't even include an address. All I knew was that you were writing from Compton Wells. So I had to write to you at Whitton, and just hope that it would be forwarded. And I waited, hoping you'd write back – perhaps saying that it was all a mistake, that you'd had second thoughts – but there was no word. As the time went on I thought I'd never see you again.'

Lily said nothing. She could hardly remember now the words she had written; she could only recall her turmoil at the time that had driven her to write.

'When I didn't hear from you, I didn't know what to do,' Joel said. 'So on my first chance, coming back from Cambridge, I went to the house – the Haskins' house in Whitton, and asked after you. I saw her, the lady – Mrs Haskin, I suppose it was. She confirmed that you'd gone, but wouldn't tell me anything else. I got very short shrift, I'm afraid, so I was none the wiser.' He paused. 'What did I do to you, Lily – that you should write to me as you did? Tell me. I thought, truly, that you were coming to care for me, and I know I wasn't mistaken. But then you wrote ending it all, saying we could have no future together, that we were worlds apart. But that wasn't true. We *did* have a future. I *know* we did. Did you have another reason for writing as you did? Was it me? It must have been.'

She could not keep her silence at this. 'Oh, no!' she breathed. 'Oh, no, it wasn't you at all.'

'Then, what?'

After a moment she turned her face to him. 'Please – I can't talk of that time, not just now.' She shook her head. 'Please – don't ask me.'

He sat frowning, gazing at her with a look of puzzlement, then after a moment he said with a nod, 'Whatever you say. I've got no right to question you.' He picked up his teacup, slowly drank from it and set it down again. 'So,' he said, adding a deliberate, lighter note to his voice, 'tell me what's been happening to you. You say you're now living in Sherrell.'

'Yes.' She was on safer ground here. 'I'm lodging on Aspen Lane with a Miss Balfour. She's an ex-headmistress of a school in Shalford. She's been very kind to me, and has helped me enormously.' She paused, then added with a faint touch of pride in her voice, 'And today I got a position as governess.'

'You're to be a *governess!*' He beamed at her. 'Oh, that's wonderful news. I know how much you've wanted to teach. That's splendid.'

'Yes!' Her joy sounded in her tone. 'I've been to Little Patten just today, for an interview. A lawyer and his wife – Mr and Mrs Acland – they have two children. I'm to start my duties in a fortnight. I found lodgings there too, just a little distance from the house.'

'Oh, indeed that is grand, Lily.' Joel lightly slapped the tabletop with his palm. 'I'm very happy for you.'

'Thank you. But I couldn't have got it without the help of Miss Balfour. I owe her so much.' She paused. 'Anyway – what about you? Have you finished at Cambridge?'

He nodded. 'Yes, I finished this past summer. I'm working for a firm in Corster now. Not for that long, though. I shall be going to work for my father soon, but he wants me to have a little more experience out in the world first. So I'm working with a law firm that my father has employed for many years. They're well established.'

'Are you happy there? Do you enjoy it?'

'Oh, very much. It's hard work, but it's fascinating. There's never a dull moment.'

'Good. Good. Your family – are they all well?'

He lowered his glance. 'My brother, Crispin – he – he died.' His voice cracked on the last words, and Lily could see that tears were not that far from his eyes.

'Oh – Joel,' she breathed, 'I'm so dreadfully sorry to hear that.'

He sat with lips compressed, as if not trusting himself to

speak. Then after a few moments he said, 'He caught pneumonia. Just last winter. We were amazed. A young man, going like that. My father – it all but destroyed him. And my mother. I don't think they'll ever get over it.'

'Joel . . .' Lily struggled to find words. 'I'm so sorry, so very sorry.'

'Thank you.' He said nothing more for a few moments, but sat looking down into his cup. A few other patrons came into the room and took seats at nearby tables. Joel drew a deep breath, then raised his head and smiled. 'We mustn't dwell on sad things,' he said. 'What about your family? How is your brother Tom? Do you hear from him?'

'Well,' she said, 'he writes only rarely. He's in Halls Haven, working on a farm there. He's only ever happy being outdoors. He'd go mad cooped up in an office.' She drank again. 'What is the time? I can't stay too late.'

Joel took out his watch. 'It's quarter-to-five.'

'I shall have to go soon,' she said. 'Miss Balfour will be wondering what's keeping me.'

'*I'm* keeping you,' he said. He smiled, and then his smile faded and his expression became grave once more. 'Oh, Lily,' he said, 'I've thought about you so much.'

His words, out of the blue, took her completely by surprise. 'Oh – Joel . . .'

'I mean it,' he said. 'I haven't changed at all. Not in the way I feel. I've never wanted anyone but you.'

For a moment her breath was held. She realised that it was all she wanted to hear – but she must say nothing. So far she had managed to remain on relatively safe ground, but here the going was perilous and she would have to watch her step.

Joel was looking at her with an intense expression, his eyes fixed on her own. 'No, I don't want anyone but you.' He gave a sad little shake of his head. 'But maybe that's my tragedy.'

She could not look at him, but kept her eyes lowered to her hands as they lay clenched together on the edge of the table.

'I think I've loved you since the day I first met you,' he said. 'When I went into that office and found you with your basket and the book you'd found on the park bench.' Now he smiled, and she could hear it in his voice. 'I'd never met any girl like you, Lily, and I never have since.' Leaning forward, he reached across the table and laid his broad palm upon her upper hand. 'You must know I love you. I don't think that could ever change.'

She sat there, feeling the touch of his hand on hers. Her mind was in a whirl, and she was already in over her head.

'Do you believe me?' he said.

Her nod was barely there. 'Yes,' she murmured.

'Well, it's true.' He gave an ironic smile. 'I thought I'd learnt quite a bit over those years before we met, you know. Like all young men of my age, I thought I had it all worked out. I thought I knew it all.' He paused. 'But I didn't. I didn't know anything about love, Lily. Because I didn't know about you.'

After a few moments he withdrew his hand, and sat back. Gazing steadily at her, he asked, 'I wonder – how you feel about me, Lily.'

'Oh . . .' She hardly trusted herself to speak.

'You told me just now there's no one else in your life. That is the truth, is it?'

She gave the shadow of a nod. 'Yes.'

He smiled. 'Ah, that makes me so happy. And now – being with you here, when I thought I would never see you again . . .' He shook his head. 'We've been brought together in the strangest way, and now that I've found you again – I'd rather not let you go.'

She sat in silence. She could never have dreamt of hearing such sweet words.

He went on: 'I'm twenty-four now, Lily, and I'm doing well. I'm getting experience in the law business and I'm also spending time at the stores in Corster and Bath. Now that Crispin has gone my father's going to expect a lot more of me, and it won't be that long before I leave the law firm and devote all my time to the stores, here and in France, and –' He broke off, frowning. 'You told me, Lily, that we're oceans apart, and that we can have no future, but you must not believe that. You cannot – because you're *wrong*.'

She sat in silence.

'I tell you now,' he said, 'I have a good future before me, and it's you I want to share it with. No one else but you.' He gave a little shake of his head. 'Oh, Lily, you can't imagine the torment I went through today. When I turned in my seat on the train and saw you – saw you in the other train, separated from me by just a couple of windows – well – I didn't know what to do. Then I got off here at Hanborough and began to wait on the platform – hoping you'd understood my message and would turn up on the next train coming in. But I had no idea how you felt about me. You might not have wanted to see me again. Then – then you were there – and I knew you cared. I knew, even after all you'd said in your letter, that you cared.'

She nodded. 'Yes,' she whispered. 'Yes – I do.'

'Ah . . .' he breathed, 'I've so wanted to hear you say those words. It's what I've dreamt of.' He leant forward in his chair. The tea was forgotten, as were the murmuring voices of the other patrons. 'Oh, Lily,' he said, 'I don't intend to let you go – not now that I've found you again.'

She sat silent. These were the words she wanted to hear, but everything was moving so fast.

'I'm going to do well, Lily,' he said. 'It's early days for me yet, with the business, I know, but I've got ambition, and I'm going to do well. My father has great faith in me – in fact he's put *all* his hope in me now – and I know – oh, I know –

that with you beside me I shall be able to do anything.' His smile was broad and joyous. 'Oh, I'm so happy, Lily.' He sat back in his chair, beaming. 'I'm so happy. And listen – I shall soon take you to see my parents. My father is a strict, God-fearing man, but he's fair and good, and once he knows you he'll love you, I know.'

Lily remained still for long seconds while the thoughts and emotions tumbled through her brain and her heart. 'Joel,' she said at last, 'there's something you must know . . .'

'Something I must know . . .?

She nodded. 'Something I must tell you.'

'Yes . . .?' He was smiling. 'What is that, then?'

She did not smile in response; she could not. She continued to sit there, while words formed in her mind and then fled. She picked up her cup and sipped at the cold tea. As she set it down again, she looked up once more to face him.

'Something . . . something happened,' she said.

His smile remained, but was now touched with concern. 'What do you mean, something happened?'

'To me.'

He waited. 'Well – *what*? What was it?'

As Lily took a breath, the door was suddenly flung open, and with loud, raucous voices, three young people burst in, at the same time letting in a sharp draught of cold air. Lily's unuttered words became frozen in her throat. Laughing loudly, the trio settled themselves boisterously at the next table, their voices ringing out in the quiet of the room.

'Go on,' Joel said. 'What were you about to tell me?'

She gave a brief shake of her head. 'No.' She could not speak of it; she should have kept silent.

'What is it?' Joel said. 'What is it you have to tell me?'

'No.' Lily spoke softly under the loud voices of their neighbours. 'It doesn't matter.' Into her mind came the thought, not new, that Joel did not have to know. Why should he? Her son, her boy, was gone out of her life, and would never enter into it again. He was gone.

Leaning closer, Joel said, raising his voice a little, 'What happened that's so terrible? Tell me. Which bank did you rob? Whom did you murder?'

She sat for some moments as if stricken, unable to stir. Then she snatched up her gloves and began to pull them on. 'I must go,' she said. 'I have to get back. Miss Balfour – she'll wonder where I am.'

Joel's light expression faded, and he frowned. 'Are you all right?'

'I must get to the station.' She finished pulling on her gloves and picked up her bag and umbrella. Already she was rising from her seat, turning away. Quickly standing up after her, Joel dropped some coins onto the tablecloth, and moved to follow her. A few seconds more and they were passing out of the warm into the chill November afternoon.

The sky above had grown darker, a cold wind had sprung up and came gusting along the street. Carried on the wind were drops of rain. Together, Lily and Joel stepped into the road and, after waiting for the passing of a slow-moving horse and carriage, set off towards the station entrance.

When they reached the platform Joel made enquiries of an attendant and came back to Lily's side to say that a train was due in fifteen minutes.

She was relieved to hear it. She was desperate to escape from the situation into which she had so carelessly cast herself.

The few drops of rain had ceased, and now only the damp wind blew upon them. Joel moved to the door of the waiting room, looked in and said, turning back to Lily, 'It's too full. Let's go somewhere else.'

Fixed to one of the nearby station offices was an awning,

and beneath it, against the wall, a bench. 'Let's go and sit over there,' he said, gesturing. They moved across the platform and sat down side by side. 'We'll be out of the wind here,' Joel said. He put his leather case and newspaper at his side on the wooden seat, and Lily did likewise with her bag and umbrella. Before them on the platform a scattering of leaves scuttled past. Lily watched as they were blown off onto the track. She could think of no words.

'All right,' she heard him say, 'what is it? Now that we can hear ourselves speak.'

She knew she would have to go through with it, but she sat in silence, not trusting herself to speak a word, afraid of what, once begun, must be said.

'Lily,' he said, 'what is it? Is it something you've done?'

She did not reply.

'Believe me,' he said, 'there's nothing on earth you could tell me that could make any difference. Don't you believe that? Nothing you tell me is going to make you a different girl in any way from the girl I know – the girl I know and love.'

At his words, and seeing the expression on his face, she felt a greater relaxing in her heart and in her mind. Perhaps, after all, everything would be all right.

'Will you believe that?' Joel said. 'Please.'

She gave a slow nod. 'Yes . . .' She paused. 'Do you mean it, Joel? That it doesn't matter – that there's nothing I can say that will change anything?'

'Of course I mean it,' he said at once. 'Oh, Lily, how can you ask?'

She gave a little nod, still so uncertain. 'Well – what I have to tell you . . .' She heard her voice speaking the words as if she were listening to the words of another. 'Joel, it – it wasn't my fault. It wasn't. Believe me.'

'What are you talking about? What wasn't your fault?'

He peered intently at her, but at the same time with a half smile of amusement. 'Tell me.'

She was committed now, and he was waiting, waiting to hear. She dropped her gaze from his and took a deep breath, looking out across the line. 'There is a child,' she said at last.

'A child?'

'A child, yes. A boy.'

Joel gave a nod, frowning. 'Yes . . . ?'

A long moment. 'Mine,' she said, hearing the word escape from her lips.

His frown deepened. 'Yours? I – I don't understand. A child? You say he's yours?'

'Yes.'

'But – how can that be . . . ?'

She did not answer.

Perplexity was etched into his face. After a moment he said: 'Are you telling me that – that you have a child?'

'Yes – I am telling you that.' She spaced the words. 'I have a son.'

'A son.' The words were spoken with a slight note of wonder in the tone.

'Yes.'

In the quiet of the November afternoon Joel's voice broke on a breathless little laugh, a sound full of uncertainty. 'I – I find this difficult to comprehend,' he said. 'You mean it, do you? You're quite serious in telling me this? You have a child.' He was repeating the words as if still he could not take them in.

She nodded.

'You never spoke of this before,' he said.

'Before?' She turned to face him now.

'Well – when we met over all those weeks in the summer of last year – you made no mention of it.'

'I didn't have him then – my boy. He came later.'

He continued to stare at her, his mouth slightly open. 'No,' he said. 'It – it's too much to take in. I know you've never been married – and yet here you are, telling me you've had a child.'

She did not speak. A movement on the periphery of her vision drew her head a little to the right, and she observed a man and a woman approaching along the platform. Oh, let them not come close, she prayed, and was relieved to see them come to a halt some yards away, but then she saw that there were others following them: a woman and two young children, then a stout, middle-aged man. The train must be due, would soon be coming in.

Joel, also aware of the appearance of the other travellers, leaned forward on the bench. 'This is – a shock to me, Lily,' he said. 'I can't take it in. Tell me – when did this – happen?'

'You mean my – my baby?' She turned to face him again now.

He nodded.

'Well, he's just over six months now. He was born in early May.'

'So,' Joel said, peering at her, his brow furrowed, 'you were with the father – the child's father – while you were seeing me.' He gave a slow, disbelieving shake of his head. 'Dear God,' he muttered.

At this Lily gave a little cry. 'Oh, no – don't say that! That's not the way it was. You see – '

'It must have been,' he cut in. His pained gaze did not flinch from her face. 'I think I see now, working out the time. That was the reason you wrote to me as you did, breaking off our – our friendship. Because of your – situation. I guess you couldn't do anything else.'

'Well, yes – that is so. But the rest of it – '

'Your situation with the – expecting the child – and your relationship with him – the other man . . .'

'Oh, Joel – no!' Lily's voice, though soft, was full of

246

passion. She leant forward, one hand reaching out to him. 'You have to let me explain. There was no other man, no other lover.'

A voice broke in: 'Excuse me . . . may I?'

The stranger's voice came from beyond Lily's right shoulder. She started slightly, turned, and saw an elderly woman standing beside the bench with a package in her hands.

'D'you mind if I sit down?' the woman asked.

'No. No, of course not.' Lily shifted along on the seat, and pulled her bag and umbrella nearer, making room. As the woman sat down, Lily noticed that several others were arriving on the platform.

Joel glanced at them. 'The train's due any second,' he said.

Lily shook her head. 'We – we've got to talk. There's more I have to tell you.' She tried to keep her voice steady, while at the same time she felt she might burst out weeping. As she finished speaking there came on the wind the distant sound of the train approaching.

Joel and Lily did not move as the train pulled in. They sat in silence as it came to a stop, watching as the waiting travellers advanced, as passengers alighted from the carriages, and others climbed on board. They continued to sit there while the guard blew his whistle and the train pulled out. With Joel at her side, Lily stared ahead of her as the sound of the smoke puffing from the smokestack faded along the track. She and Joel sat isolated and exposed.

Why had she spoken? she asked herself. It had been madness. She should have kept silent, and Joel would have been happy in his ignorance. True, she would have had to bear the knowledge of his ignorance, but it would have been a price worth paying, if they could have been happy. Yes, she should have held her secret, and with it she would have preserved her image. It had been there, that promise of happiness, coming out of the blue on this miraculous day, and she had wantonly thrown it away. She put a hand to her forehead, bent her head and closed her eyes. How ironic it was. So many times she had dreamt of a chance of finding Joel again, and today it had happened. Fate had stepped in and arranged it in the most bizarre fashion, and at last they had come together again. And now, after all the promise inherent in their meeting, they sat in silence, just two feet apart and separated by an unbridgeable gulf.

'I have to tell myself,' Joel said at last into the quiet, 'that you wouldn't lie to me about such a thing.'

'No,' Lily whispered. 'I wouldn't.' She opened her eyes and gazed unseeingly along the length of the platform. There was no one else about now. Even the station attendant had disappeared from view.

'So – you have a son,' Joel said. 'Since we parted you've had a child.'

'Yes.'

'Where is he now?'

'He – he's with his new parents. I don't know who they are. They adopted him. He was taken away from me soon after his birth.'

The seconds passed, one by one ticking by. Whatever was said now, Lily thought, it would not make any difference.

'What about the child's father?' Joel said.

'What of him?' She spoke without raising her head.

'Well – do you see him?'

Silent, she shook her head.

'Do you?' Joel persisted. 'Do you still see him? Do you still care for him?'

She straightened, turned to him. 'Oh, Joel,' she said, 'you think I've told you all, but you know only a part of it. I'd hoped never to have to speak of any of this – for it can bring nothing but pain.'

He gazed at her. 'There's more to tell?'

She nodded. 'I was in love with no other,' she said, 'but you. I loved you, and only you. I never told you so, but it is true. You're the only man I have ever loved.'

He said nothing. She gazed at him in silence for a moment then lowered her eyes. 'It was Mr Haskin,' she said.

'Mr Haskin?' He looked at her with his eyes wide. 'Of the carriage company? Your employer?'

'Yes. My employer and my father's trusted friend.' Her hands were gripped together before her, while her heart pounded in her chest. 'It was during the night,' she said, 'after you and I went to the inn at Lettington. Mrs Haskin was away from the house, spending the night at Henhurst with her mother. I told you, you remember. She'd had an accident, and Mrs Haskin went to take care of her.' She found it difficult to frame the words, for each one brought the horror of that night nearer again. She had to speak, though.

After a pause she went on haltingly: 'He – came into my room that night, after I got back from seeing you. And he –'

At this her resolve and strength proved not enough, and her voice broke as she burst into sobs, hands moving to cover her eyes as the tears poured down her cheeks. When at last she spoke again her voice was muffled against the fabric of her gloves. 'I could do nothing,' she muttered. She had ceased her weeping now. 'I pleaded with him, but nothing made any difference. And he was just too – too strong for me.' She looked up, her cheeks stained with the tracks of her tears. 'He was too strong. I couldn't stop him.'

Joel was looking at her aghast. He sat gazing at her, his eyes wide, his hands gripping his overcoat on his thighs, blunt fingers digging into the fabric. On the road that ran beside the station a heavy wagon rumbled by, pulled by two carthorses, its driver yelling out to the beasts. On the platform the station master appeared from his little office, looked up at the clock, checked his watch and then retreated inside. Lily sat with her eyes fixed on the floor at her feet. After a time she said dully, not raising her head:

'So you see, I'm not as I was.'

Joel remained rigid, his pained gaze upon her, as if unable to comprehend such a tale.

'I'm not that same girl any more,' Lily said, 'and I never will be again.'

Joel said, his voice deep and husky: 'I don't understand. I can't understand how a man can be so – so wicked.' Briefly he pressed his hands to his eyes. As he lowered them again he said, 'Had you – done anything?'

'What? Done anything? What do you mean?'

He hunched his shoulders, almost a shrug. 'I mean, well – had you said or done anything to – to encourage him?'

She frowned. 'Did I do anything to encourage him?' There was a note of incredulity in her voice. 'Are you asking if I – if I led him on?'

'No, oh, no. Don't think that.' He shook his head in a gesture of distress. 'I didn't mean it to sound that way. I just – wondered . . . Did it – did it just come out of the blue . . . ? Did you have no inkling – no warning that he felt for you in this way?'

'None. There was no warning at all. He was always polite and pleasant, nothing more.' The tears on her cheeks were dry. A dull calm was creeping over her. She realised that with her revelation all was now lost and, whatever her efforts, there was nothing more to be saved.

Along the platform came a woman with two small children, followed by a young girl carrying a basket. 'There's a train due,' Lily said. 'I must catch it. And you – you must go and do your business with your client.'

'Oh,' he said, 'we can't leave things like this.'

She was silent for a second, then she said, 'Listen to me . . .'

'Yes . . .?'

'Listen to me. You said – certain things to me in the coffee house. You spoke of a possible future together, and I know you meant it. But – but things are different now. I've told you certain things – and those things are bound to make a difference. How could they not?' She shook her head and gave a faint, sad little smile. 'Oh, Joel – how I wish that they did not, but they must do – and they have. So – I hold you to nothing. Nothing at all.'

As if she had not spoken, he said, 'I can't – I can't believe what I've heard. And when I think on those times we had together. Oh, how I wish we could go back to them.'

'Yes.' She gave the faintest nod. 'But we never can.'

She sat then in silence, while some part of her brain, and her heart, hoped that he might yet say that all was well, that he would speak some words that would show that their lives could be picked up and resumed, and that they could be together again as if they were once more so young and untouched by the stains of life.

But he did not speak. And as the moments of silence stretched out between them, she knew that all was lost.

Two more travellers had come along the platform, an old man with a younger woman holding on to his arm. Dully, Lily observed them as they drew nearer. If they came close enough they would save her and Joel from any more painful exchanges. Almost with a feeling of relief she saw them come to a halt just two or three feet away – and then the station master was there again, with his flag in his hand, looking back along the track.

'Here comes the train,' Lily said.

The moment after she had spoken there came the faint sound of a whistle, and the train came into view, a tiny shape in the distance, growing larger by the second.

Opening her bag, Lily dipped into it, scrabbling with her fingers, and brought out a small notebook and a pencil. 'Here . . .' Hurriedly she wrote on a page and tore it out, pressing it into his palm.

'Here's my address in Sherrell. Write to me – if you feel inclined.' Now the train was here, slowing alongside the platform. 'Perhaps – perhaps we can still be friends.' She was not sure what she was saying; she was snatching at words in the panic of the moment, while the moment was flying by, irretrievable. Before them on the platform the travellers moved forward, preparing to board. Lily picked up her bag and umbrella and got to her feet. Joel stood up beside her, the scrap of paper in his hand. 'Lily – wait,' he said. 'You can't go like this.'

The train had pulled to a complete halt, and the carriage doors were being opened by the passengers. Joel reached out as Lily took a step forward.

'Lily, wait . . .'

'No, I must go. You can write to me if you want to.'

'Lily – listen to me. This is all a – a shock to me, you know that, but I want to do the right thing. I want – '

'Joel,' she broke in, 'you must not be noble. You need time to think. Now is not the time for hasty decisions.' She hesitated a moment longer, then turned and hurried across the platform to where a carriage door swung open. Joel followed close at her heels, halting at the door as she pulled it shut behind her. There were other people in the carriage, but she hardly noticed them. As quickly as she could, she lowered the window and stood at it, facing him.

'Joel,' she said, 'it's been so wonderful to see you again, to see you so well, and successful.'

There came the sound of the guard's whistle. She put a hand on the top of the open window, and at once Joel put his hand on hers.

'I'll write to you,' he said.

'Yes, write to me.'

As she finished speaking the train gave a jolt and began to move. Joel pressed her hand one last time and withdrew his touch. She stood at the open window until the train had taken her beyond sight of him, then pulled the window closed, and sat down.

Chapter Sixteen

It was well after six when Lily arrived back at Rowanleigh. As she entered the hall she met Mary carrying a tea-tray, on the way to Miss Elsie in her study. 'She's been asking for you, miss,' the maid said. 'She's been wondering why you wusn't back.'

'Yes,' Lily said, 'I'm afraid I got delayed.' Putting down her bag and umbrella, she said, 'Let me have the tray, Mary. I'll take it up,' and took the tray from the girl's hands. Then, still in her hat and coat, she started up the stairs, and a minute later was sitting facing Miss Elsie across her desk and telling of her success at her meeting with Mrs Acland.

Miss Elsie was overjoyed at the news. 'This is splendid,' she said, beaming, 'though I was sure it would go well. When do you start?'

'In two weeks.'

'Excellent.'

Lily went on then to speak of her brief meeting with the two Acland children, and then of having arranged her lodgings with the widow Mrs Thorne. Miss Elsie sipped at her tea and nodded her approval. 'It's all worked out for you,' she said, 'and it's what you've been working for. I'm proud of you, I really am. I've been dying to know how you fared, but you were away such a long time. I was beginning to get a little concerned.'

'Yes,' Lily said, 'I – I met an old friend. Someone I hadn't seen in a good while. We stopped and had some tea together.'

For a moment Miss Elsie waited for her to elaborate, but Lily said nothing more. 'Ah, well,' Miss Elsie said, 'I'm sure that must have been very pleasant. It's nice when old friends meet.'

'Yes.'

Miss Elsie reached out and lightly touched Lily's arm. 'You're tired, my dear. You go on now, and we'll talk more over dinner.'

Up in her room, Lily, still wearing her coat and hat, sat on the side of the bed. About her interview with Mrs Acland she could only feel joy and satisfaction, but at the same time she could not stop reliving her meeting with Joel and what had passed between them. Not only had his feelings for her not changed, but he had spoken of a shared future. In her most self-indulgent dreams it might have been all she could have wished for, but she had had to tell him the truth, the secret that could be a secret no more. And with it, the telling, she had surely spelt the end. Whatever hopes she might have nursed, her confession had surely finished them – and yet, said a small insistent voice in her brain, he had made clear his feelings for her. He loved her still. Perhaps, then, all was not lost. Perhaps . . .

She could do nothing but wait. She would hear from him soon.

After getting dressed the next morning, Lily was standing before the looking-glass touching at her hair when there came a tap at the door. She opened it to find Mary on the threshold, holding out an envelope. 'This just come, miss,' the maid said. 'I brought it straight up.'

Lily thanked her, wondering who the letter could be from. It was too soon to hear from Joel, she had long since given up expecting to hear any word from her father, and, other than Tom, she could not think of anyone else who would be writing to her. Closing the door after the departing maid, she looked at the writing on the envelope, and realised that it was her stepmother's hand. The envelope held a single sheet of notepaper. On it her step-mother's lines were brief and to the point:

Compton Wells
15th November 1867

Lily,

I trust this finds you well. I am very sorry to say that your father is ill, and has been for several days. He is not able to write to you at present and has asked that I write to you for him. It would be as well if you come as soon as possible.

Yours,
Mother

As Lily read the letter through, her heart began to pound in her breast. Her father was sick, and clearly too sick to write. That her stepmother should have been moved to write in his stead was unprecedented – and most disturbing. There was no question but that she must return home at once. She would pack a bag and be ready to leave as soon as breakfast was over.

When told of the letter, Miss Elsie said at once that Mr Shad would drive Lily to the station, and less than half-an-hour later Lily set off.

When the train arrived at Compton Wells she took the omnibus from outside the station and alighted near the end of Hawthorne Lane. A cold wind whipped along beside the hedgerow, and she pulled up the collar of her coat. As she walked she looked about her at the familiar scenery. Thirteen months had passed since she had last been here, but it might have been no more than a day; nothing about it had changed. And still fresh in her mind was her distress on that day of her departure, when she had left in disgrace to go to Sherrell.

Coming at last to the house, she moved round to the back door and let herself into the scullery. Here again all was the same. She stood for a moment listening, then opened the door into the kitchen, and stepped through.

'Father . . . ? Mother . . . ?'

Standing inside the threshold on the worn linoleum, she held her breath, listening again. There was no sound apart from the sonorous ticking of the long-case clock. Then against the quiet she heard footsteps from out in the yard, followed by the click of the latch of the scullery door. She turned as the kitchen door opened, and her stepmother entered.

'Oh – Mother, hello.'

Mrs Clair came to a stop in the doorway. 'So,' she said, 'you got here.' There was no welcoming smile on her face, no warmth in her expression. Even so, there was something different about her manner. Whereas she usually appeared calm and self-contained, now she had a preoccupied air about her, a slightly distracted look; her brow was furrowed, her lips compressed. 'I didn't know what time to expect you,' she said. There was nothing in her manner acknowledging their long separation. Lily might have been away only an hour.

'I arrived just this minute,' Lily said, setting down her things, at which Mrs Clair, as if Lily had not spoken, said, 'I've been up the garden to cut a cabbage.' Her pale hands fluttered. 'We've still got to think about dinner. Life's got to go on.'

'I got your letter this morning,' Lily said. 'It came by first post.'

'My letter – yes.' Mrs Clair nodded. 'I should have written earlier, I know, but there's so much to do, you can't

257

imagine. Thank God, Dora's at school, so that gives me a breather.'

Lily stepped back a pace as her stepmother moved past her and stopped before the kitchen range. Mrs Clair lifted the plate and tipped a few coals into the fire. 'How is he, Mother?' Lily said. 'I was just about to go upstairs. He's in bed, is he?'

Her stepmother turned back to face her. 'Yes, he is. The doctor came yesterday, and will be coming back tomorrow. I don't know how we're going to pay for it all. There's no money coming in.' She gestured towards the hall door. 'Yes, go up and see your father now. He's been waiting for you to get here.' She brushed her hands together, dusting off her palms. 'I've had to leave him for a few minutes – I've got to get things done while I have the chance – while he's quiet. There's so much to do. I'm absolutely worn out.' She wiped the back of her hand across her brow where a wispy lock of hair had come adrift. 'I gave him his medicine not long ago so he ought to be feeling a bit easier at the moment. Trouble is, he needs more and more of the stuff.'

'Mother, what's wrong with him?' Lily said. 'You didn't say in your letter.'

'No – well – it isn't something you can really write about.'

'How long has he been ill? Has he been off work a long time?'

'Several weeks now. For a while he didn't seem too bad, but then he seemed to get worse very suddenly. Just in a couple of weeks. He's gone down very quickly in that time.'

'But what is it? What's wrong with him?'

Mrs Clair waved her hands agitatedly before her. 'Well, it – it's a malignancy, the doctor says.' She lowered her hands to her belly, briefly placing them on her apron. 'In the liver, so the doctor says.' She looked away, towards the window. 'It's the cancer.'

Lily put her hands to her mouth. 'Oh, God.'

'Yes.' Mrs Clair nodded. 'It's bad, I'm afraid. It's very bad. He's so often in pain. Very bad pain at times.'

Lily stood as if frozen. She had concluded that her father's illness must be serious, but the reality behind her stepmother's words was chilling. After a moment she said, 'What does the doctor say about it?'

'Well, there was talk for a while about your father going into hospital – but they can't do anything for him that can't be done at home. Besides, he wouldn't hear of it.'

A pause, then Lily said, 'Is – is Father going to get well?'

Mrs Clair kept her eyes towards the window and compressed her lips into a thin line. Lily needed no further answer. 'Oh, Lily,' Mrs Clair said – and it was the first time she had used Lily's name – 'just go up and see and him. See him while he's peaceful. We'll talk later.'

Lily nodded. 'But I don't want to wake him when he's needing his sleep.'

'I doubt that he's sleeping, but just creep in. Don't knock. You'll probably find him very talkative. It's the laudanum that does it. He'll be thirsty too.'

Lily moved to the hall door, turned and said, 'Does Tom know that Father's ill? You wrote to him too, of course?'

For a moment Mrs Clair did not answer. Then she moved her hands in a little flapping, dismissive gesture. 'Oh, for goodness' sake,' she said, 'just go on up and see your father. We can talk later. Tell him I'll be up in a minute.'

Lily stood for a second in silence, then started up the stairs. On the landing she found that the door to her parents' room was not fully closed, and after a moment's hesitation she gently pushed it open and went in.

The curtains at the windows were half closed, and the silent room was shaded and sombre. In her first glance she took in the familiar wallpaper – entwined vines and leaves on a rust-coloured background – the framed print of a harvesting scene above the chest of drawers. Nothing had changed. Beyond the window the leafless branches of the cherry tree shifted in the burgeoning wind. On the bed her father lay beneath the covers, his head in profile on the pillows. She went to him, and as she did so he turned his head a fraction in her direction.

'Who's that?' he asked, and straight away she heard that his voice was not as she knew it. Just those few words gave away a fragile tone, a light, weak quality that was almost a whisper in the quiet.

'Hello, Father – it's me, Lily.' She trod softly on the bedside rug. 'I've come to see how you are.'

'Lily . . .' he breathed. 'Oh, my dear girl, I'm so glad.'

She was standing right next to the bed now, looking down at him, and she was taken aback at the sight. Even her stepmother's words had not prepared her for his appearance. Faced with it, she was shocked. He seemed so much smaller. All her life he had been a tall, well-built man with strong arms and a broad back, his face full, firm and strong-looking. Now the flesh was shrunken on the bones, his skin had a yellowish tinge to it, his cheeks were hollow, his dull eyes sunken in their sockets. The change in him was so devastating that it brought the pricking of tears to her eyes, and for a moment made her catch at her breath.

'Oh, Father . . . Father . . .' She gasped the words out, hoarsely whispering. It took all her effort to hold back the tears, and she tightened her lips and breathed deeply over the lump in her throat. She wanted to bend and put her arms around him, to kiss his shrunken cheek, but she did not; for too many years such demonstrations of affection would not have been encouraged, and it was too late to begin now.

There came then a little movement at the edge of the bedcovers, and his hand appeared, the thin fingers reaching towards her. As she took his hand in her own she felt the bony knuckles against her palm, and was so glad of the feeble contact.

'When did you get here?' he said, his weak voice quavering a little.

'Just now. I got Mother's letter this morning. I came as soon as I could.'

She saw his mouth move in the semblance of a faint smile, and felt a brief tightening of his fingers within her own.

'Help me . . . Help me sit up a bit, will you?'

Bending to him, she supported his back as he tried to pull himself up in the bed, conscious as she did so of his bony shoulders beneath her hand. He managed to raise himself a little while she rearranged the pillows behind his head, but the effort told on him, and after a moment he sank back again, exhausted from the small exertion.

'That'll do for a minute,' he muttered. His head was a little higher now, and she could more easily see his pale, gaunt face. He moved a hand towards the bedside chest on which stood a pitcher and a glass. 'I must – drink something,' he said. 'My mouth and throat – they get so dry.'

She poured a little water, then, with one hand on his upper back, held the glass to his mouth. When he had drunk enough she set the glass back down. There was a small armchair near the bed, and she pulled it closer and sat. Reaching out to his hand as it lay on the coverlet she laid her own upon it. His skin felt dry.

'Is there anything I can get you, Father?' she asked.

'No – thanks. I'm just so glad you're here.' Then he added, his voice a little querulous, 'Why didn't you come sooner? I wanted you.'

'Oh, Father,' she said gently, 'I told you – I came as soon as I could. I only heard this morning that you were ill.'

'Just this morning?' He frowned. 'Just this morning. Ah, well . . . How long will you be staying?'

'As long as you want.'

A faint trace of a smile touched at his mouth. 'That's good.'

Lily smiled too, a melancholy touch at her lips. 'Oh, Father – I'm so glad to see you again.' And suddenly the tears that she had managed to suppress welled up and ran down her cheeks. With her free hand she wiped them away. She wanted to bring him strength, not upset him further; she must not let him see her cry.

Neither spoke for some moments, and she sat with her hand over his while she held back her tears and tried to be calm.

'You've been away so long,' he said after a while.

'Yes,' she said. 'Too long.'

'Ah, too long, my Lily. Much too long.'

He had called her *my Lily*. He had called her *my Lily*, as he had sometimes used to do. Then she had accepted it as she had loved it, and now it took her breath away.

As she struggled to keep back the tears that threatened again to spring, he moved his hand within hers. 'I've been wanting you to come home,' he said after a moment, his tremulous voice breaking slightly. 'I wanted it – so much.'

'Oh, I too, Father!' she breathed. 'I wanted it too, but I never heard anything. I wrote to you but never got an answer. I thought you didn't want to see me.'

He gave a little moan. 'Well, I didn't – not at first. I – I was so – so distressed, I couldn't see straight. But later – I wanted to see you and – and your letters came and – oh, there was a time or two I thought I'd write back, but it never got done. Your mother was against it. I'm sorry to say that, but she was. She's a very strong woman, your mother.'

Lily said nothing to this, but merely pressed his hand slightly. He took a breath, a hoarse, tortured sound, and said, 'I was so – so unhappy at how it all ended. How we parted. How you – went away.' He paused a long moment, then added, 'I trusted him.' He spoke the words so softly, and at first Lily was not sure she had heard correctly. Then she realised he was speaking of Mr Haskin.

'Yes,' he breathed. 'I trusted him. I couldn't see that he'd ever do wrong.' A slight shake of his head as it lay on the pillow. 'I trusted *him* – and not *you*. I –'

His fragile words broke off and he winced, drawing back his lips over his teeth. Lily tightened her fingers over his hand. 'Father . . .' she said, 'you're in pain.'

'It – it's all right . . .' After some moments he seemed to relax a little, and his breathing became easier again. 'I've got to say it,' he went on. 'There are things I've got to say, and I might not – might not have another chance. There might not be that much – time left.'

Lily bit back the words on her lips and stayed silent, waiting. After a moment he spoke again, the words delivered haltingly in his dry-as-dust tone.

'Yes, I – I trusted him. I couldn't – believe that he would ever do anything to harm you. This was – was a man I'd known since I was a boy. I couldn't – conceive of such a thing as you accused him of. Then – then, of course – when I learnt of your – young sweetheart – that you were seeing the young man – well, that only confirmed it.' His words ceased momentarily while he closed his eyes and breathed in, deeply. Then he continued. 'But later – I thought more about it. I had always – trusted you, and I realised that you had never – never lied to me in your life.' He paused. 'You never did, did you?'

'No, Father.' Lightly she pressed his hand. 'Never.'

The faint smile touched at his dry lips again. 'Never,' he murmured. 'No, I knew that. My girl – she'd never let me down.' With these last words a little broken sob escaped his throat. His pale lips were drawn back and a tear ran down from the corner of his eye to be lost in the whiskers of his sideburns.

Seeing his tears, Lily's own tears were once again so close to the surface, and it took all her strength to keep them down. She took a handkerchief from the pocket of her skirt and gently touched it to his cheek. Then, settling back again, she sat with one hand on his, covering his bony knuckles.

A silence fell in the room, a silence touched only by the harsh sound of his breathing. Then, speaking carefully, as if the words were hard wrung from him, he said, 'It wasn't you – in the wrong. It was *him*. I misjudged you, and I'm sorry. Forgive me.' Then he added, some breath of passion in his tone, 'I would like to kill him. If I could, I would. If I had my strength I would go to Whitton and kill him. I'd kill him with my bare hands.'

'Oh – Father . . .' Lily's hand pressed down on his. 'It's over. It's over.'

'No!' Although he spoke quietly the note of passion was still in the hoarsely whispered word. 'How – how can it be over?'

'It is. It's past.'

'But he ruined your life. That – that monster. That – that viper. He ruined your life and he took you from me.'

'Yes. For a time, but it's all right now. I'm back. And for as long as you want me.'

He breathed a long sigh. 'Well – maybe that won't be so long now.'

Her heart lurched at his words, but she bit her lip, saying nothing. After some time he said: 'Get me another pillow, will you? Behind my head, so I can see you better.'

There was spare bedding on a chair near the window, and she fetched a pillow and eased it down behind his shoulders. Leaning back again, he smiled faintly. 'That's better. Let the dog see the rabbit.' Looking at her now, and catching her glance with his own, he said, 'Your – your baby . . .'

Lily nodded, 'Yes . . .' and waited.

'Miss Balfour wrote – and later you wrote too – about the baby – your baby.'

'Yes . . .'

'Saying your baby had been born. And taken for adoption.'

'Yes.'

'A boy. You had a boy.'

'Yes.'

'A boy.' He paused. 'My grandson he would be.'

'He's your grandson, yes.'

'Yes . . .' His fingers moved again under Lily's touch. 'I wish – I wish I'd seen him. What – what was he like? What does he look like?'

Lily said, 'He is the most beautiful boy you can imagine.' Her smile now was radiant as she spoke. 'And he looks like you, Father.' The words burst from her, while in the same moment the renewed fountain of her tears spilt and started down her cheeks. 'My Georgie – he's got your nose, your eyes. Oh – he's your grandson, and no one else's.'

'Georgie . . .'

'Georgie, yes.' She struggled to force back her tears. 'That's what I called him.' She added sadly, 'Though he'll have a different name now.'

'Yes, no doubt he will.' Her father's voice sounded a little deeper, with a note of resignation. 'He's not with you now, is he?'

'No. As I told you – he was taken – to be with another family.'

'Yes – of course. You wrote to us – and Miss Balfour wrote to us.' He paused. 'It had to be that way. You know that.'

'Yes – I know.'

He managed a slight nod. 'Though I don't doubt it was hard for you – to be parted from him. You hear tell of a mammy's tie to her babby. Like no other bond on earth they say.'

Lily stayed silent, and in the quiet he turned his head a

265

fraction on the pillow, and saw her tears, and read her pain. 'Oh – Lily,' he murmured, 'I had no idea.'

Summoning all her control, she said, 'I miss him so, Father. There's not a day goes by when I don't think of him, and wonder how he is.'

Another faint nod. 'Yes. But, my dear – you couldn't have – have raised him alone.'

She wanted to say, *Yes, I could. I would have worked only for him. I would have given up everything for him.* But even as she made her silent protest she knew that it was unreal. She could never have built for the boy the life he deserved.

Her father spoke again. 'Do you know where he is?'

'No.' It cost her much to say the word. 'I know nothing of him now. I don't know where he is, or who he belongs to. I don't even know his name.'

His head nodded faintly on the pillow. 'Maybe – maybe it's better that way.'

A little silence again. He kept his eyes trained upon hers, their steadiness just occasionally touched by little pulses of pain that went through him, and which he could not hide. 'I'm so – so glad you're here,' he said, 'and I was glad to learn you're still with Miss Balfour in Sherrell.'

'Yes. She's been so good to me.'

'Good. I'm pleased to hear that.'

'Oh, she's been a true friend. She – she saved me, Father. I don't know what I would have done without her help and kindness. She found a good home for my baby, and she's helped me in every other way. She's even helped me find a position.' She paused. 'Father, I'm to go as governess to two young children in Little Patten, the daughters of a Mr and Mrs Acland. I'm to begin my duties a week next Monday.'

'Oh,' he breathed, smiling, 'that's splendid, Lily. I'm proud of you, my girl. I'm proud of you. It's what you always wanted. It's what you worked for, so hard, and now you've got it at last.'

'Yes – and I owe it all to Miss Balfour.'

'Yes – well – she's clearly a good woman. We did hear that she was – quite queer and eccentric – but you must speak as you find – and I've no doubt she's done right by you.' He gave a little sigh. 'Where's your mother?' he asked.

'Downstairs.'

'And Dora?'

'She's at school.'

'It's better for her not to be around. A sickroom's no place for a child.' He paused, then smiled. 'Oh, I'm so glad for you, Lily. Governess. Just fancy.'

'Yes.'

'I – I want you to be happy, Lily. And I know you miss the babby, but – oh, I so want you to be happy.'

She returned his smile. 'I – I get by, Father,' she said. Then she added, 'There are so many with truly dreadful lives. I've nothing to complain about.'

'Good. That's a sensible girl.' He remained silent for a moment, then he asked, 'Is there someone in your life . . .? Have you got a – a special acquaintance? – a sweetheart?'

She hesitated before answering. 'No. No, I haven't.'

'What about that young man you were seeing?'

'No,' she said. 'No.'

'Well . . .' he said, '– in time you'll meet someone . . .'

Neither spoke for some moments, then she said: 'Father, have you – have you heard anything from Tom?'

He gave a sigh. 'Oh, that boy. That boy.'

'Does he know – that you're ill?'

He sighed again and shifted his head slightly on the pillow. 'Oh, that boy. What a disappointment he's been. All his life – and that he should turn out the way he has. Prison. Just think of it. The shame he's brought on us. You'll never know. It affected your mother very deeply.'

Lily said, unable to stop herself: 'It was a piece of celery, Father. He hadn't eaten, and he was hungry.' Anger crept

267

into her voice. 'A piece of celery, and they put him in gaol for that.'

Her father said nothing to this. After a moment, he asked, 'Have *you* seen him – Thomas?'

'Yes. Just over a week ago.'

'Where is he now?'

'He's working on a farm in Halls Haven – but I thought you knew that. He said he'd written to you.'

'Did he?'

'He said he'd written twice, but that he'd got no answer to his letters.'

Mr Clair frowned. 'We haven't heard a word.' He winced and drew in his breath, and Lily said quickly, 'Can I get you something? Shall I go and call Mother?'

Briefly he closed his eyes. 'No – leave her be. It'll pass. She's on the go – from morning till night. What time is it?' As he spoke he half turned his head towards the chest beside the bed, where his watch lay. She picked it up, opened it and looked at the time. 'It's almost two.'

'Not time for my medicine yet.' He sighed. 'I get by on the medicine. God be praised for it. The doctor said it's sometimes referred to as Sister Euphoria. Whatever they call it, I know I couldn't do without it.' He paused, then asked, 'How – how was he?'

'How – ?'

'Thomas. How was he when you saw him? Was he all right?'

At the question she saw Tom as he had stood before her at the corner of the lane. 'He – he's well,' she lied. After a second she added, truthfully: 'He misses you, Father. And – he needs you.'

Mr Clair frowned, gazing off. 'I'd like to have seen him,' he said.

'But why hasn't he been told that you're ill? He should have been told.'

'We don't know where he is. Your mother said – there's no address for him any longer. There's – no way of getting in touch with him.'

Lily said, 'But Father, I told you – he said he wrote to you.'

As she finished speaking a violent tremor went through his body, and she saw the bedcovers rise up as his back arched. At the same time he let out a sound that was half groan and half cry. His mouth contorted, and his eyes briefly rolled back in their sockets. Beneath her fingers his hand convulsed and clenched, while his other hand clutched at his belly. 'Call – call your mother, will you?' he gasped.

Lily needed no second telling. At once she was rising, the rug twisting under her boot as she turned for the door.

Chapter Seventeen

Lily got to the foot of the stairs and turned into the kitchen where her stepmother came towards her, wiping her hands on a cotton towel. 'What's the matter?' Mrs Clair said anxiously. 'Is he worse?'

'He's in pain,' Lily said. 'Oh, Mother, he's in so much pain.'

Mrs Clair shook her head distractedly. 'He's had his drops. He shouldn't be needing more just yet.' She gave a sigh. 'He needs more and more of the stuff to keep the pain away. That's the way it's been going.' She tossed the cloth onto the table and stepped past Lily. 'I'll have to give him some more. It's the only thing to do. Like Dr Helligan told me – there's no point in denying him. He has to have it. He needs it.'

She passed through into the hall and started up the stairs, and Lily went after her. In the bedroom Mrs Clair stopped beside the bed and looked down at her husband. He lay with his eyes screwed up and his lips drawn back over his teeth. The pain he was feeling was written in every line of his face.

'It's bad, is it, darlin'?' Mrs Clair said, bending low over the bed. Hearing the words, Lily was almost shocked. She had never before heard her speak to her father in such an intimate way. Her stepmother had usually addressed him as Father, sometimes Edwin. Now she was calling him darlin', and her tone, though matter-of-fact, was tender. They had a life together, Lily realised, and not just as parents, but as lovers.

As Lily stood by, her stepmother poured water into a glass, then took up a medicine bottle from the top of the chest and carefully counted out some drops into it. That done, she put one hand behind Mr Clair's head. 'There, my dear, you drink that.'

Lily watched as her father, between breaths, gulped from the glass. When it was drained, Mrs Clair eased him back onto the pillow. 'There,' she laid her hand lightly on his shoulder, 'you'll be all right now. A few minutes and you'll feel better. Take that nasty pain away.'

Lily observed the two of them, and their closeness as her stepmother ministered to him both with pragmatism and tenderness. As the minutes passed she watched too as the medicine slowly began to do its work. Gradually the drug took hold, and her father's tight, drawn-back lips by degrees relaxed, as did his bony-knuckled hands that gripped the coverlet. His eyes closed, and slowly his whole body appeared to relax and settle into the bed.

'He'll be all right now. Won't you, darlin'?' Mrs Clair reached down and gently touched her husband's cheek. 'You'll be better now. No more pain for a while.' She remained standing there for some moments, then turned to Lily. 'You going to sit with him for a bit longer, are you?'

'Yes, I'd like to.'

'Good. He'd like that too.' She gave his shoulder the lightest pat. 'I'll just be downstairs, dear. If you need me Lily'll come and get me. All right?'

'Yes – all right.' Mr Clair spoke for the first time following his attack of pain, his voice weak and hoarse. His wife continued to look down at him for a moment longer, then stepped away. In the doorway she turned to Lily and said:

'I should think you'll be feeling dry too. I'll bring you up some tea in a minute.'

Lily was a little taken aback at her mother's words and

271

the unaccustomed slight softness of tone. 'Thank you,' she said.

Mrs Clair stepped out onto the small landing and started down the stairs. Lily remained there for a second then moved to the chair and sat down.

'How are you now, Father?' she asked, leaning towards him. 'Is the pain easing?'

'Yes,' he breathed. 'Yes, it is, thank God.'

He did not speak again for some time, but was still, one hand beneath the covers and the other on top. Lily watched him as he lay with closed eyes. His breathing, though still shallow, now sounded a little more even. He was not sleeping, though, and when she shifted on the seat, causing the chair to creak, he opened his eyes. 'You're not going, are you?' he said.

'No, of course not. I told you, I'll be here as long as you want me.'

'Good.' The faintest nod of his head on the pillow, the faintest touch of a smile.

As the minutes passed it was evident that his discomfort was diminishing, and with a little water to sooth his dry throat, he appeared to relax even more. A while later Mrs Clair appeared with a mug of tea for Lily, and after addressing a few quiet words to her husband went away again to resume her work downstairs.

Lily sat sipping at her tea while the time crept by. After a while her father began to talk again, in a desultory manner at first, but as the minutes passed his speech began to flow, and she realised that it was due to the laudanum. He spoke of several things: of his work at the factory, and his colleagues there, and then of his childhood amid the hills and fields of Wiltshire. He told of adventures he had had and of people he had met. His voice, more animated, was at times almost passionate, and Lily found herself discovering facets of his life that she had never known. At one time he spoke of an incident that had occurred on his wedding day, and she realised with a little thrill that it was his first marriage he was referring to. When he spoke of Ellen, his bride, Lily leant forward on the chair. 'Oh, Father, tell me – what was she like?' she said. 'You never speak of her.'

'Oh, she was a fine-looking young woman,' he said. 'One of the prettiest girls in the village.' He paused, looking directly at Lily. 'And you're the spit of her, you know. Sometimes I see her in you so clearly.'

The words pleased Lily so much, and she hoped to hear more, but he frowned and briefly closed his eyes and murmured, 'Ah, but that's in the past,' and went on to talk of other things. Before long, however, his words began to slow, and his eyelids flickered and drooped. Soon he was asleep, his breathing regular and his hand relaxed on the coverlet. Through the partly open door came the faint sound of footfalls on the stair, and a few moments later Mrs Clair appeared.

'He's sleeping,' Lily said softly as her stepmother came into the room.

Mrs Clair gave a nod. 'Good. He sleeps a lot these days.' She stood looking down at him. 'We can leave him now for a while. He'll be all right – and we'll listen out. Come on downstairs. Have something to eat.'

Lily was aware once again of her stepmother speaking to her in a softer tone than she had used in the past, and was so glad of it. Perhaps, the notion crossed her mind, it had to do with her having been away for so long. She was older now. She had gone away a mere girl, and had come back a woman. She could no longer be seen as the child she had been.

In the kitchen she sat at the table and ate a small slice of cold pork pie with a piece of cheese. Her stepmother ate nothing. The afternoon sky was dark with cloud, and one of the lamps had been lit. Now that the two women were away from the sickroom and face to face, alone, an awkwardness and a tension descended between them. 'So,' Mrs Clair said into the hush of the room, 'how have things been with you? You've been staying on in Sherrell, you wrote, and working at becoming a governess.'

'Yes, I have, Mother,' Lily replied, 'and now I've been offered a position.'

'A position? A position as governess?'

'Yes. With a family in Little Patten.'

'Well – that's something, I'm sure. Have you told your father?'

'Yes.'

'I'm sure he was very pleased to know.'

'Yes, he was.'

'Indeed, and why not? He's always wanted the best for you. So, when do you begin with this new position?'

'A week Monday. On the second.'

'Oh – so soon.'

'Yes.' Lily, a little carried away with the prospect of her forthcoming employment, went on enthusiastically, 'I was there for an interview yesterday. And I met the children, twin girls, Alice and Rose. They seem such a very nice little pair. I'm sure I'm going to love it. Mrs Acland is a charming lady, and the house is –'

She got no further, for Mrs Clair was giving a sniff, and saying, 'Oh – very grand indeed, eh?' and glancing at the clock. 'Look at the time,' she said. 'Dora will be in from school any minute.'

With her stepmother's words, Lily realised that nothing more of her life or progress was to be spoken of. She would not pursue it further. 'How is Dora?' she said. 'How is she taking Father's illness?'

'Oh, I don't like her to see her father the way he is,' Mrs Clair replied. 'She insists he's going to get better, and I encourage her to believe it, but I know she knows the truth.

It'll be bad enough for her when it finally happens, and it won't be long, going by what the doctor says.'

'When did you say the doctor is coming again?' Lily asked. 'Does he come every day?'

'Almost. He'll be here again tomorrow. Though of course I can send for him any time if there's an emergency. Though what he'd be able to do, I don't know.'

'Mother,' Lily said, 'I wish you had let me know sooner that Father was so ill. I should have been here days ago.'

'Well, I'm sorry, but I haven't had a minute,' Mrs Clair said. 'Caring for a sick man – you can't imagine what it's like. You don't get a moment to yourself.'

'What about Tom? Have you written to tell him Father's ill? He should be here at a time like this.'

'Oh, really,' Mrs Clair said in a tired, defensive tone. 'Well, it might help matters if we knew where he was.'

'But he told me he'd written to you,' Lily said. 'He told me himself.'

Mrs Clair put her cup down sharply in the saucer. 'Oh, did he indeed? Well, I'm sorry, but we never heard a word from him.'

'He's got to be told, Mother,' Lily said. 'I know where he is, and I'll write to him at once. I'll tell him he must come home as soon as he can.'

'As you wish. I've got work to get on with.'

As Mrs Clair went out to the scullery with the china and cutlery, Lily brought the writing slope to the table and opened it up. Then she sat down and wrote a brief letter to Tom, telling him that their father was very ill, and that he should come to see him as soon as possible. When the letter was finished she went into the scullery where her stepmother stood at the sink. 'I've written to Thomas,' she said. 'If I go and post it now he might get it tomorrow.'

It took Lily twenty minutes to walk to the post office,

and the November wind was cold in her face, but she was barely aware of it. She paid the postmistress for a stamp and left the letter in the woman's hands. Tom would receive it tomorrow or the day after, though his coming to his father in time was a hope she hardly dared entertain.

On her return home she found Dora there, having just come back from school. It had been over a year since the two had last met and Lily could see a change in her young half-sister. Dora was eight years old now. She had grown considerably taller and was becoming very attractive, with a bright smile and a warm, easy nature. After she and Lily had greeted one another they sat side by side on the settee where Lily asked Dora about her progress at school and told a little of her own life during the time they had been apart. Of Lily's situation with the birth of her son, nothing of course was said, and she realised that Dora knew nothing of it.

Later, at the bidding of her stepmother, Dora went upstairs to see her father and spend a few minutes at his bedside. While the girl was gone, Mrs Clair, having set the table ready for the evening meal, got out her mending basket and sat with it beside the range. Lily sat in the chair opposite, her father's chair, taking some of the mending into her own hands, and the two women faced one another before the fire, their needles moving and glinting in the light from the lamps. Neither spoke. It was only when Dora came back into the room that the silence was broken.

After the meal was consumed – with none of the three exhibiting much appetite – Mrs Clair went upstairs to sit with her husband, while Lily and Dora remained below and cleared the table and washed the dishes. Later, after Mrs Clair had come back downstairs, Lily went up to the bedroom, taking some of the mending work with her.

The room was lit by two softly glowing lamps, one on the chest beside the bed, and the other on a table near the window. The curtains had been closed against the night.

She sat down in the chair next to the bed, looking down at the sleeping man, and she could see that his pain was not that far below the surface. Occasionally his breath faltered, hitching for the briefest moment, and he would wince slightly before he sank back into his slumber. Apart from his harsh breathing, hardly a sound broke the quiet.

That night, as in days past, Lily slept in the same bed as Dora. Dora, who had gone up to the bedroom earlier, was sound asleep when Lily crept in. Lily had agreed with her stepmother that they would share the vigil over the sick man, and in the early hours of the morning she was awakened by a touch on her shoulder and opened her eyes to see her stepmother standing at the bedside, an old coat over her nightdress. A lighted candle had been placed on the chair. As gently as possible, Lily climbed out of bed, while in the same moment her stepmother took off the coat. Lily took it from her and slipped it on over her nightdress. 'How is he?' she whispered.

'I gave him his drops earlier and he's sleeping again now,' Mrs Clair replied. 'He should be all right for a while.'

'What time is it?'

'Two o'clock.' Mrs Clair sat on the edge of the bed and pulled off a pair of men's woollen stockings. She held them up to Lily. 'Here – put these on. It's not so warm in there – they'll keep you a bit more comfortable.'

As Lily pulled on the stockings, Mrs Clair climbed into the bed. Dora, momentarily disturbed by the movement, muttered in her sleep and moved her head on the pillow. Mrs Clair laid a soothing hand on the girl's shoulder. 'It's all right, my dear,' she murmured. 'Go back to sleep now.

Your mama's here.' She turned back to Lily. 'Wake me at six o'clock.'

Lily, the lighted candle in her hand, silently crossed the narrow landing to her parents' room where her father lay in his morphine-induced sleep. No movement came from the figure in the bed. Only one lamp was burning now. She blew out the candle and set it down on the chest then settled back into the old armchair and pulled over her body the warm rug that her stepmother had left. Lifting her stockinged feet, she tucked them under her in the chair and leant her head against the wing.

The minutes and the hours crept by. Later, she looked at her father's watch and saw that it was after six o'clock, well after the hour at which her stepmother had asked to be wakened. Her father was still sleeping soundly. She sat back in the chair and adjusted the rug, necessary against the chill morning air. She would let her stepmother sleep on; with all she had to deal with she must be in need of her rest and a little oblivion.

Over the rest of the day Lily and her stepmother took turns in watching over the sick man. Dr Helligan called late in the morning, but could offer no comfort. As the day wore on Lily kept hoping that Tom might appear, for surely he would have received her letter that morning. There was no sign of him, though.

She slept beside Dora again that night, taking turns with her stepmother in sitting at her father's bedside. After breakfast, Dora went off to school, leaving her mother and Lily working in the house and watching over the sick man. He was in much greater discomfort this morning, and Mrs Clair had had to give him his drops earlier than usual. Even so, when the doctor appeared just after eleven, the effects of the drug were wearing off and Mr Clair was twitching and grimacing with the growing pain.

Dr Helligan took from his bag a hypodermic syringe. Neither Lily nor her stepmother had seen such an instrument before, and they watched, wincing, as the doctor rolled up Mr Clair's sleeve and injected his upper arm. As the doctor pulled the patient's sleeve down again, he turned to Mrs Clair and said quietly:

'He won't have any pain now. This is so much more effective than the drops.' He looked back down at the dying man. 'I'm afraid it's not going to be very long now. His organs are just – just shutting down. The best we can do is try to keep him free of pain.'

After the doctor had gone, Lily and Mrs Clair remained standing at the bedside. Mr Clair was breathing more and more deeply, giving out a harsh, sonorous sound, his body unmoving beneath the covers. There was a difference now in the quality of his insensitivity. Whereas before he had appeared at times to be merely sleeping, now he seemed to be in the very deepest stupor.

Just before eight-thirty that evening Lily sat alone at the bedside while her stepmother went down to the kitchen to fetch some water. Dora was already in bed. All day Lily had hoped that Tom would come, but still he had not, and now she knew that any appearance by him would be too late, for her father would never be conscious again, would never wake to recognise a familiar face.

As she sat there she became aware that her father's breathing had grown even louder, sounding more laboured, alarmingly harsh and stertorous. He lay with his mouth slightly open, his head a little on one side, and as she gazed at him the sound of his breathing changed again, his harsh indrawn breaths beginning to bubble like liquid in his lungs. Suddenly his body convulsed and his eyes opened wide as his head twitched and turned to the side. Lily rose up and bent to him, and as she did so his mouth opened and a stream of dark brown bile poured out over his lips and ran down his chin. She realised that the room had become suddenly silent. His breathing had ceased. Looking into his face she saw that his eyes were dull and the spark of life had gone.

Chapter Eighteen

Eight days later, the church clock was striking eleven, and Lily stood with hands clasped at her waist as the coffin was lowered into the earth. She wore a heavy black cloak that she had borrowed from her stepmother and her hat had been trimmed with black crêpe. The day was bleak and grey and cold, with a dampness in the air that clung to the evergreen leaves of the yew that spread its branches over the wet grass. Her stepmother stood next to Lily at the graveside with head bowed, her broad-brimmed hat and dark veil obscuring her face. There were few other mourners, just three neighbours from the lane – an old man and two middle-aged women – and a stranger: a man who had worked with Mr Clair at the factory. The Clairs had tended to keep to themselves over the years, not encouraging any casual closeness with those living nearby; consequently there were few who felt it incumbent upon them to mark Mr Clair's passing with any show of grieving respect on such an unwelcoming day.

The vicar, coming to the end of his piece, closed his book and, after a moment of respectful silence, stepped back a pace. The ceremony was over. Turning to Mrs Clair he murmured some final words of commiseration, and she thanked him and then turned to Lily, remarking that they had better start back.

On the way to the church Lily and her stepmother had followed the hearse in a carriage hired from a local man, but such a convenience was eschewed for the return journey.

Expenses had to be watched out for, Mrs Clair had said, and they would make their own way home. And so they did, walking side by side through the dreary lanes until they reached the house. There they were greeted by Dora and Mrs McKinner, the neighbour who had come in to keep an eye on the child and also help put out the ale and coffee and bread and ham that the mourners – albeit there were few of them – would expect.

For Lily the next hour passed in a blur, but at last the neighbours had all gone, and she and her stepmother and Dora were left alone. Together they cleared away the few remaining bits of food, and washed the china and glass. When everything was back in its usual order the two women turned to their mending while Dora took a story book and sat before the range.

The hours in the house passed slowly. The lamps were lighted as dusk fell, and the curtains were drawn against the coming night. At six they ate a light supper, and afterwards Lily and Mrs Clair once more turned to their mending, while Dora took up a piece of sewing of her own.

Lily found a certain comfort in the banal process of working with her darning needle, for as time had passed she had become aware of an atmosphere in the room. It was not connected with the family's grief, but something else. It had nothing to do with Dora, but came solely from Mrs Clair, and Lily saw it in a dozen little instances of coolness in manner towards her, of short replies and a marked flintiness in the tone of voice. The faint little show of warmth that had met her on her arrival at the house had quite gone. Lily could not pinpoint a time when the new coldness had begun, nor could she understand why it should be. She was puzzled. Perhaps with someone other she would have asked what the matter was, but she had never in her life entered into any kind of conversation or discussion with her stepmother, and now was not the time to attempt to do so. As she sat there she became further aware that they were so far apart that even in their common grief they could not comfort one another.

The long-case clock ticked on in the quiet. Soon after seven Dora put down the piece of linen she was stitching, kissed her mother on the cheek, and went up to bed. With her departure the strained atmosphere in the room was even more marked.

The time dragged on. Lily, sitting at the table with the darning, felt that she had reached some kind of watershed, some kind of finale as she realised that her ties to her former home had been almost severed. Her father was dead and buried in his grave, and tomorrow she must set off to return to Sherrell.

To her deep disappointment and puzzlement there had still been not a single word from Tom. She had written to him again immediately following their father's death, informing him of their loss, but even this news had brought no response. She had also written to Miss Elsie, telling of her father's demise and saying that she would be returning on Saturday, the day after the funeral. Miss Elsie had written back at once, offering her condolences.

'Well . . .' Her stepmother's voice came into the hush, 'it's time I went to bed. I've been up since half-past-five this morning, and I'm very tired.'

Lily glanced at the clock. It was after nine-thirty. 'Yes, you go to bed, Mother,' she said. 'I'll see to the lamps and the fire.'

Mrs Clair put aside her mending, rose and crossed to the hall door. 'Then I'll wish you good night.' There was no warmth in her tone. Without waiting for a reply from Lily she went, closing the door behind her.

In the silence the click of the door catch seemed to hang in the room. Lily continued to sit there. She too had been up since the early hours, but she felt far from sleepy. There was a tension in her whole body that denied any idea of sleep.

From over her head came the faint sound of movement as her stepmother prepared for her solitary night in her bed alone. From outside came the hoot of an owl, its sound to Lily strangely comforting and familiar. She continued with the darning. She too would go to bed in a while, as soon as she had finished mending the stocking in her hands.

It was almost done. As she put in the final stitch the thought came to her: what was the point in mending it? Her father would never wear it again. No matter. She snipped off the woollen thread, and reached for her stepmother's sewing box where it stood on the table a foot away. The top of the box held a compartment for thimbles and needles and pins and other sewing implements. She put the scissors in one of the trays, and then lifted the tray out. She knew what she would find underneath – a little collection of her stepmother's odds and ends: trinkets and two or three discoloured old photographs, and a few papers that she had kept over the years. She laid the tray down on the tablecloth and looked into the well of the box. There was a bill there from a glover and beneath that a cracked photograph of Dora as a very small child. Idly, Lily took out the sepia-toned picture and looked at the faded image with a fleeting interest, and then went to put it back. As she did so, she saw what had been lying underneath it.

For a moment or two she just sat there, looking down at the envelope. It seemed to fill up the whole scope of her vision. Then she put in her hand and picked it up. Tom's round, carefully-formed handwriting was so familiar to her that she could not possibly mistake it for that of any other person. Then she saw to her greater surprise that there was another, similar-looking envelope lying in the box. She took that out also, and laid the two envelopes side by side on the table before her.

They were letters from Tom. Two letters from Tom, and

each addressed to Mr and Mrs Edwin Clair. On the second she could see a postmarked date: 18 September, 1867.

She sat looking at the two envelopes, both of which had been opened. And the moments went by while the clock ticked into the silence, sounding suddenly loud in the quiet of the room.

Taking a breath, Lily picked up the first envelope. Briefly, very briefly, the concept of privacy and invasion flashed through her mind, but in seconds it was gone and with cool fingers she withdrew the letter and opened it out. On a sheet of cheap, lined paper, in her brother's unmistakeable hand she saw the few words that he had written:

> Fellowes Farm
> Halls Haven
> Nr Corster, Wilts
> 17th Sep 1867

Dear Father and Mother,

   It is a while since I last wrote to you, and an even longer time since I last saw you. I know I let you down, but it was never my wish to bring trouble or shame on you, and I am truly sorry I did. I hope you will be able to forgive me, for I can tell you honestly that I'll never do such a thing again.

   Mr Thompson here at the farm says I can have a couple of days off in a fortnight or so, and I told him I'd like to come home to see you for a spell. I'll have to lose the money, but it will be worth it. Will you please write back and let me know whether I'm welcome. After your last letter to me, it is something I need to know. I shall wait for your letter.

   Your son,
   Thomas

Lily read the letter through again, then put it down and

turned her attention to the other one. Without hesitation she took the letter from the envelope, unfolded it and laid it before her on the table. The address was the same, but the date of it was the eleventh of October, nearly a month following the first letter. In it, Tom had written:

Dear Father and Mother,
    The weather is fine here, and I'm well and hoping you are too, and Dora also. I have been hoping for a letter from you, following my last, but there has been nothing. I guess you're pretty busy with so much to do. When you have time please write. I'd so like to come home and see you. I promise you, I have done no wrong since that time, and I never will again. Please, please write. I am, as always,
        Your loving, obedient son,
        Thomas

Lily remained at the table with the two open letters before her on the dark crimson cloth. The fire in the range had burnt low and the room had grown colder. Still she continued to sit there.

Later, lying in bed beside the sleeping Dora, she felt far from sleep, and turned restlessly on the old mattress, trying to find comfort. So many things were going through her head, tumbling round in her brain. She thought of Tom and his unhappiness and his pleas to be accepted back into his father's heart – for there was no doubt in her mind as to whom the letter was meant for – and also of her father and his last hours. She thought too of her stepmother and the present, sudden coldness in her manner. She could find no accounting for it.

Her thoughts moved on, shifting with the restlessness of her body and her brain. She thought of Joel, and of their meeting and her revelation. Tomorrow she would return to Sherrell, and there would surely be a letter there waiting for her, a letter from him.

At last, in the early hours, she fell asleep.

In spite of having little sleep, Lily was up early the following morning, and when she was dressed went downstairs into the kitchen where her stepmother was preparing the breakfast. When Dora came downstairs the three of them sat down to eat, the meal with her stepmother proving, as Lily expected, to be a very quiet affair. Had it not been for Dora's occasional bursts of chatter it might have passed in silence.

When the the breakfast things were cleared away and washed up, Lily was ready to leave for the station. She was eager now to get away from the atmosphere in the house. Having already said her goodbyes to Dora, who had gone off to call on a neighbouring friend, she was alone with her stepmother.

'So,' said Mrs Clair, 'you're off now, are you?'

'Yes.' Lily stood before the small looking glass beside the chimney, making a last adjustment to the black crêpe ribbon on her bonnet. 'There's a train at eleven-thirty.' Her overnight bag had been packed since early that morning.

'Make sure you've got everything,' Mrs Clair said.

'Yes, I have, thanks.'

'Better not go without this, then.' As Mrs Clair spoke, she put a hand into her apron pocket and brought out an item which she held out. Lily took it from her and saw at once what it was. In her palm lay a small, soft leather pouch which, she knew, held a gold half-hunter watch.

She gazed down at the precious treasure. She had seen it once or twice over the years, stored carefully away in a drawer. 'My mother's watch,' she said in a tone of wonder.

'Yes, your mother's watch.' Mrs Clair's voice was cold. 'Your father insisted it came to you.'

Lily's heart was suddenly full. She slipped the watch from its little pouch and looked at its dull gleam. 'Thank you,' she said. 'Oh, Mother, thank you, so much.'

'There's nothing to thank me for,' Mrs Clair said shortly. 'I just told you, your father said you had to have it.' The briefest pause, and she added, 'Anyway, you'd better get off, or you'll miss your train.'

'Yes. Yes.' Lily took up her reticule and carefully placed the watch inside. Then she bent and picked up her overnight bag. Moving to the door leading to the scullery, she opened it and turned back to face her stepmother.

'Well – Mother – I'll say goodbye.'

'Yes,' Mrs Clair said, and then she added quickly, as if the words had been bubbling up inside her, searching for a way out: 'You'll be hearing from the solicitor in the next week or two, no doubt.'

'The solicitor?' Lily frowned. 'What do you mean? Why should I be hearing from a solicitor?'

'Your father's solicitor. Mr Robson of Cunningham and West.'

'But – but why?'

'Because of the money, of course.'

'The money?'

'The money. Didn't you know?' Mrs Clair's mouth was pinched and thin. 'Didn't your father mention it?'

'I don't know anything about any money. Father never spoke of such a thing to me.'

'No – well – perhaps not.' Mrs Clair spoke dismissively. 'I only learnt of it myself yesterday morning, when I saw his will.'

'Mother,' Lily said after a moment, 'what is this all about?'

'He's left you money, in case you didn't know.' She

almost hissed the words out. 'As if the watch wasn't enough, he left you money too.'

Lily gave a little shake of her head. 'I know nothing about this.'

'No? Well, for your information he's left you fifteen pounds.'

Lily's astonishment showed in her face. 'Fifteen pounds. So much money.'

'Yes, so much money,' Mrs Clair said with a nod, then added bitterly, 'As if his wife and child didn't have need of it.'

Lily saw now the reason for her stepmother's antagonism. So it was this, the money her father had left. It had been eating away at her, festering, for twenty-four hours.

'I wasn't expecting anything,' Lily said. 'Not a thing. I thought everything would go to you and Dora.'

'*Yes*,' Mrs Clair hissed, 'and so it should have. We have so little, Dora and I.'

'But he left everything else to you, didn't he?'

'Oh, yes, he did. He left us the rest of his money, but how far will that take us?'

'But isn't there a pension,' Lily said, 'from his workplace?'

'Oh, how nice of you to mention that,' Mrs Clair said. 'Yes, there is a pension – of sorts – but that won't buy us very much. And I shall get a little help from the Friendly Society, but if I don't have to start taking in washing, or getting a job at the tile factory it'll be a wonder.' She was glaring at Lily, her lip curled. 'And what have you ever done for him that he should reward you in such a way? All you ever did for him was bring him heartache and disgrace, and now he leaves you *this*.'

Lily was so amazed at the hostility that she could not speak. She stood there at the door, taking in her stepmother's attack. Mrs Clair was not to be stopped.

'It isn't as if you needed the money,' she said. 'You're starting in a new post on Monday. You're to become a governess, for heaven's sake. You're nineteen, and you've got your whole life ahead of you. What about Dora? And what about me? My life now is finished. I've got no husband, and hardly any money coming in. What's going to happen to *me*?'

At last Lily found a voice. 'I can scarcely believe I'm hearing this,' she said. 'All this because of fifteen pounds. I could see that something was eating you, but I couldn't imagine what it was. *Fifteen pounds.* Good God, Mother, if it means that much to you, you can have it. Have it and welcome.' She shook her head in disgust. 'As soon as the money comes to me I'll send it on to you. God forbid I should ever take what you see as yours.'

'Well, it's not fair,' Mrs Clair said, her angry voice approaching a whine. 'It's just not fair.'

'Fair,' Lily said. 'You don't know the meaning of the word, and you never have.' After she had spoken, she realised that she had never in her life addressed her stepmother in such a way, and she stood a little astonished at her own temerity.

Her stepmother too was surprised by it. She gazed at Lily for a second or two with her mouth slightly open, then said, grinding the words out, 'I think you'd best be off to get your train. You wouldn't want to miss it.'

'No,' Lily said. 'I wouldn't want to miss it – and I wouldn't want to stay in your company any longer than I have to.' She paused, took a breath. 'But before I go I've got one or two things I want to say.'

Mrs Clair put a hand up to her open mouth. This was a new side to her stepdaughter. 'Oh, listen to it,' she said scornfully. 'If your father could hear you and see you now.'

'Well, he cannot – more's the pity,' Lily said. 'And while we're on the subject of my father, let me ask you something.

Why didn't you let me know sooner that he was so ill? When I got here you said he'd been ill for weeks – so why wasn't I sent for? He told me himself that he'd been waiting for me.'

'I told you,' Mrs Clair said, 'I hadn't got a minute to myself. Caring for a sick man – you don't know what it's like.'

'Yes, so you told me,' Lily said. 'But what about my brother Tom?'

Her stepmother's mouth twisted, the upper lip curving in contempt. 'Oh, now we're on to your brother, are we? I wondered how long it would be before we got round to him. What about him, anyway?'

'Why didn't you let him know? Why didn't you write and tell him that Father was ill?'

'I'll tell you why. Because I didn't have time to sit writing to everybody. I already said – there was so much to do.'

'Tom isn't *everybody*,' Lily said. 'Thomas was Father's son, his only son. And Father was sick, very sick – in fact near to dying, you told me –' She felt tears suddenly threaten as she uttered these last words, but she fought them back; she would not cry; she would not. 'Were you ever going to write and tell him?' she said.

'This is absolutely outrageous.' Mrs Clair glared at Lily. 'I'm not going to be taken to task like this by you. While you've been away you've forgotten your place, miss, and how to show respect. You've forgotten your manners too.'

'You're not getting round it like that, by attacking *me*.' Lily's voice was heavy with scorn. 'Tom loved his father, and he should have been here at such a time. He had a right to be. You should have written and told him.'

'Oh, I should, should I?' Mrs Clair's defensive tone was sharp. 'Well, it might have helped if we knew where he was. We haven't had a word in ages. How were we supposed to know where he was?'

'That is a lie,' Lily said.

Mrs Clair's small mouth opened in renewed outrage. 'How dare you! You – accuse me of lying! You, the greatest liar on earth – to accuse me.'

'I'm not a liar,' Lily said. 'But *you are.*' Putting down her bag and reticule, she stepped to the shelf beside the chimney breast and snatched up her stepmother's sewing box. At the table she set it down. Flinging open the lid, she lifted out the inner tray, then dipped in her hand and brought out Tom's two letters.

'*Here.*' She held them up as she turned back to face her stepmother. 'Here they are, Tom's letters, just where you put them, hid them – safely away from any eyes but your own. Just where you put them – without having the decency to show them to my father.' She put the letters down on the table. Her heart was thumping in her breast.

Her stepmother was standing looking at her, her tight-shut lips a thin line of fury and self-righteousness. 'And indeed why not?' she spat. 'Your father was already ill. Why should he be bothered by such things? Your brother was never anything but trouble. And as for writing to ask for forgiveness, I should think he'd have been ashamed even to show his face here again. In case you've forgotten, he went to prison for being a common thief.'

'He stole a piece of celery!' Lily's voice was full of incredulity. 'He didn't murder anyone or rob a bank.'

'He *stole.*'

'Yes! A piece of celery. He was hungry, and he was desperate.'

'Desperate! In the eyes of the law he's a thief!'

'Yes,' Lily hissed, struggling to hold back her tears, 'and for that – for stealing a piece of celery they locked him up with some of the most evil men in the country.' Now her tears could not be held back, and they ran down her cheeks.

'It was a piece of celery, Mother. He stole it, and my God he has certainly paid the price for it. Would you punish him for ever?'

'It doesn't matter what he stole. He went to prison and he brought disgrace on us.'

'Disgrace,' Lily echoed.

'Yes, disgrace. Which is something that might have concerned you too, in your own behaviour.'

Mrs Clair's words were shocking to Lily. Her father had told her that he no longer blamed her for what had happened, and that he accepted her story of the attack by Mr Haskin. Clearly not so her stepmother. Lily realised now that Mrs Clair would never alter her view.

'Yes,' Lily said, 'and you treated me like an outcast. Someone totally immoral.' Turning from her stepmother's hostile gaze, she took up her bags, and once more stepped to the door. Here again she turned.

'I shall not be coming back,' she said, brushing a hand across her tear-stained cheek. 'We shall not meet again. I shall miss seeing Dora, for she's a dear child and I love her. I can only hope that she takes after her father and not you.'

At these words Mrs Clair opened her mouth to speak, but Lily went on:

'You never liked me, and you never liked Tom either. And while I've come to accept what you did to me, I shall never forgive you for how you treated him. You were a monster to him.' She took a step forward, and Mrs Clair took a step back. 'Yes,' Lily said, 'you were a monster. You are a mean, vindictive, selfish woman, and you are cruel and a liar. I shall send you your fifteen pounds, never fear, and when I've got some money together I'll send you a little so that you can buy something for Dora. But as for you, I never ever want to see you again.'

Her bags in her hands, she turned and passed through

the scullery into the yard. As she did so, she knew she would never enter the house again.

When Lily arrived back at Rowanleigh she met Mary in the hall, who offered her condolences. Lily thanked her and enquired as to whether any post had come for her in her absence. No, Mary said, there was nothing. On learning that Miss Elsie was resting, Lily went up to her room. It was not long, though, before Miss Elsie, having learnt of her return, came knocking at her door to offer her sympathy again and enquire as to how she was faring.

Later that evening Lily made her preparations for the following day when she was to go to Little Patten, and the next morning she was up early for breakfast and soon ready to leave for the station. In the last minutes leading up to her departure she and Miss Elsie were sitting together in the drawing room when Mary appeared. She brought with her a letter for Lily that had just been delivered, and also announced that Mr Shad had the trap ready. Rising from her seat, Lily thanked her, glanced hurriedly at the letter and put it into her reticule.

'Well,' she said to Miss Elsie, 'it's time to go, and I don't mind saying that I'm nervous.'

'Of course you are.' Miss Elsie nodded and drew on her cigarette. 'You're taking a step into the unknown – but you'll be fine.' She gestured towards the door. 'Go on now. Don't keep Mr Shad waiting or you'll miss your train. I'll see you next weekend, and I shall expect a blow-by-blow account of how you got on.'

Lily said goodbye, then picked up her reticule and umbrella and went out into the yard where the trap was waiting. The large bag containing her clothes and books had already been stowed inside it. Mr Shad helped her up, and moments later he was in the driving seat and urging the sturdy cob forward down the narrow drive and out into the lane.

As the little carriage rattled on its stony way Lily took out the letter which she had already seen was from Joel. She sat looking at the envelope for a minute or two, then slipped it back into her reticule.

On their arrival at the station Mr Shad carried her heavy bag up onto the platform and wished her good luck. When he had gone, Lily sat on a bench, all the while sharply aware of the letter. She wanted to take it out and read it then and there, but it was not the time; the train was due, and also she was afraid. Why, she wondered, had Joel not written sooner after their meeting?

At last the train came in and she climbed aboard. In the compartment a young man took her heavy bag and stowed it in the overhead rack. She thanked him and sat down between an elderly businessman and a young woman. As the train started up again she opened her reticule and took out Joel's letter.

She sat there with it in her hand as the train moved from station to station. She was hardly aware of the stops, of the passengers getting on and off.

And at last she could wait no longer. As the train pulled out of Stretton she inserted her index fingernail under the envelope's flap and tore the paper across.

The letter was in two sheets. She smoothed out the pages and read:

The Hazels
Greenbanks Road
Corster, Wilts
29th November 1867

Dear Lily,

I know I should have written before this, and please forgive me for not doing so. I could make the excuse of pressure of work, but that would not be entirely true. The truth, in fact, is that I have not known how to write to you. Even now, as I sit here with my pen in my hand, I am at a loss as to what to say.

It was, of course, just splendid to see you again after so long, and to see you looking so well. Indeed I think that perhaps it was because of my being so thrilled at seeing you, and being so swept away by my pleasure that I perhaps acted rather impulsively, as I know now I did. However, I have had long, long periods of thought about our meeting, and I have come to the conclusion that I must behave with some degree of responsibility, and not, like some impetuous schoolboy, go charging off without a thought of the consequences. I know now, after much soul-searching – and I hope this does not come as the most awful disappointment to you – that I am not yet ready for any commitment such as settling down. I thought I was, but I was wrong. I have much to do in my life – building my career, preparing for a future – and I am simply not in the position of being able to offer the things that a husband should be able to offer a wife. We were very young, of course, when we first met, and by nature youth is allowed to dream and love and have extravagant ambitions, but now, alas, I realise I must be more realistic in my outlook and my desires.

Please forgive me, Lily, if I have hurt you; and I'm sure I have. But believe me, it is the last thing I would want to do. You are a splendid, honest and upright young woman, and you deserve someone better than I. And you will meet him, I have no doubt. You will meet that special person – that certain someone who can offer you all the things that I cannot – and you will be happy with him, as you deserve to be.

Let me say in closing that I hope we can still be

friends. Perhaps, after a time, I might get in touch with you again.

In the meantime please believe that I shall always be
Your loyal and most devoted friend
Joel

Lily sat with the letter in her hand, leaning forward slightly in her seat. Through her pain she became aware of the beating of her heart, and of the sensation that her palms were damp. Sitting opposite was a young couple intent in a conversation about farming, and against the rhythmic sounds of the train Lily caught the occasional murmured words as they spoke of haywains and yields and wagons. In the corner seat on her right, the elderly man polished his spectacles with a handkerchief, while over by the window to her left a young mother brushed a fond hand through her small son's mop of red hair. For everyone else life was going on as usual. For Lily it seemed that in those moments her life had come to a halt.

Steeling herself, she read the letter through again – almost as if she could find different words from those that he had written. But there they were, in black and white, and no matter how many times she might read them they would not change.

So, it was over. And so soon. For a little while she had dared to hope – almost to trust – that the two of them had a future together, but that hope had lasted so little time, blossoming and dying like some exotic flower.

It was what she had feared from Joel's silence after their meeting, and following her revelation. For she did not for one moment believe him when he spoke of not being able to give her all that a wife should have, of not being financially fit for marriage. It was because of the child. Nothing else. Once again the thought went through her mind that she should not have told him of the child. But no, she had had to tell him; he had to know. And of course her revelation had been a shock to him, but he had loved her, he had said, and in her hopeful mind she had clung to that belief. But it had not been enough.

She read the letter through yet again, hanging on the words and phrases, trying to see beyond their banal face value some alternative meanings, some crumbs of comfort. She could find nothing; there were no hidden shades there.

All now was lost. But the realisation brought no tears. Rather, as it took hold, a little tremor of chill touched her body and made her draw in her breath. As she opened her eyes again she became aware that the rhythm of the carriage's movement was changing, slowing again as the train drew nearer to a station. Glancing dully from the window she recognised the scenery that was passing by: a derelict watermill, a row of cottages. They would soon be drawing into Little Patten.

She folded the letter, put it back in the envelope and slipped it into her bag. The train was slowing further now, the carriage rocking with a different tune. She touched at her hat, checked on the fastening of her coat and drew her belongings to her. As the train came to a halt she rose from her seat. The young man in the seat opposite got up and kindly lifted down her heavy bag. Moments later she was on the platform with the carriage door closing behind her.

She straightened, her reticule and umbrella in one hand, the heavy bag in the other, and met the icy-cold wind that came swooping along the platform, its sudden keenness bringing tears to her eyes. She blinked them back and stepped out.

As she walked along the near-deserted platform the thought came to her that she was entering a new phase of her life. Ahead of her was nothing but the unknown.

So little now was as it had been, and she had nothing

to hold on to from the past. In a relatively short time almost everything had changed. Her father was dead, and her ties with her family home were as good as severed. Joel had gone out of her life too, while she had no idea what had become of Tom. As for her boy, he had long been gone from her. She must accept the fact that she was now alone.

Bending her head to meet the wind, she walked on.

PART THREE

Chapter Nineteen

Carried on the breeze came the chiming of the church clock striking the hour of twelve. It was the only sound against the fluting of the birdsong, which came from all around them. In half-an-hour Lily would be leaving her charges to return to her lodgings in Ashway Lane. Under the terms of her yearly contract with her employers, she was allowed free every Saturday afternoon and the whole of every other Sunday. This weekend marked her Sunday off, and she would be spending it in Sherrell with Miss Elsie.

Now, sitting under the tree, Lily touched at the brim of her straw hat, briefly easing it from her forehead. The July day was warm, with the sun blazing from the clear sky. She felt its heat even in the shade where she sat on a small footstool. Just a few feet away were her pupils, Alice and Rose, side by side on an old tartan rug that had been laid on the sparse grass beneath the wide-spreading boughs of the apple tree. In less than two months they would be eleven years old. Lily had been their governess now for three and a half years.

They were in the orchard, at the foot of the kitchen garden, and the lesson was what Lily referred to as *nature study*. The girls had their nature sketchbooks with them, balanced on their laps. With their soft pencils they were making drawings of items of interest around them, and adding little textual notes in the margins of the pages. They had been at their work since eleven-fifteen after finishing a lesson in arithmetic, and Lily knew them well enough by now to tell that, although they were quiet and industrious, their interest was nevertheless flagging. She couldn't blame them; the growing warmth of the day was having an increasingly soporific effect, and she herself was finding it difficult to concentrate.

She fanned herself briefly with her hand, then got up and bent to look at the results of their work. Their efforts were concentrated on a little cherry tree that grew nearby, and although they had drawn the same thing, there was an obvious difference in their abilities. While Alice was the more forthright of the two, the quiet, unassuming Rose was only too evidently the more artistically talented.

Lily made murmured comments of encouragement and approval. She enjoyed teaching them. They were good girls, and rarely gave her any cause for complaint, being generally respectful and well mannered. Like all children they had their moments of being disagreeable, but such occasions were relatively rare.

'Oh, miss,' Alice groaned dramatically, 'it's getting too hot to work.'

'Yes, miss,' Rose added, 'it's too hot. Much too hot.'

'Well, I agree, it is rather warm,' Lily said, 'but there's not long to go now.'

'Thank heavens.' Alice sighed again. 'And no more work till Monday.'

Lily moved back and sat down again on the footstool. The green of the grass was heavily starred with white clover, with bees busy among the blossoms. In one sunlit patch a cock blackbird moved through the grass, followed by two fledglings. As it was relatively late in the season it must, she thought, be the bird's second family. She watched the little act being played out. The two chicks kept only a couple of feet behind their father, waiting to be fed, and every so often the parent found some titbit which he put into one of his offsprings' gaping mouths. They gave him no rest.

As Lily sat taking in the scene, the Aclands' housemaid, Esme, appeared and came to Lily's side. She was sorry to interrupt, she said, but Mrs Acland would like to see her in the drawing room before she left. Lily thanked her and said that she would be there at half-past-twelve.

Watching the maid's departing back, Lily wondered what it was that Mrs Acland wanted to see her about. Following her arrival at the house she had at first been carefully observed – which of course was only to be expected – but the scrutiny had soon relaxed as her employers had found that they had no need for concern, and could have confidence in the new governess. What, then, Lily now wondered, was the reason for her being summoned? Had she, unknowingly, been guilty of some misdemeanour or caused displeasure in some way? She hoped not; she loved her work in the Aclands' household. Not only had her tenure at Yew Tree House been for her a happy time, but it had also been a lifeline, giving her focus and purpose, without which she could not imagine what she would have done.

'Miss?'

From behind her came Alice's voice, and she turned and moved back to where the girls were sitting. 'Yes, Alice.'

'Is this better, miss?' Alice had added some detail to her drawing of the little tree, and also put in the margin a closer view of a few leaves.

'Yes,' Lily said, 'that's much better. Well done.'

And so the rest of the lesson continued for a while longer, until the church clock struck the half-hour, at which Lily said, 'All right, girls, you may put away your things and take them back to the house. I shall see you on Monday morning.'

The pair needed no second telling, and soon their pencils and books had been stowed away. At the same time Lily shook out the rug, folded it and tucked it under her arm and picked up her bag. The three of them then moved off through the orchard and up the garden path to the house where they went in through the back door and into the hall. There the two girls said goodbye, and as they headed for the stairs Lily moved to the drawing room and tapped on the door. A moment later she heard a call of 'Come in,' and she turned the handle and entered.

Mrs Acland was sitting on the sofa with some fabric in her hands and a sewing basket beside her. She smiled as Lily came forward, and Lily was relieved.

'You wanted to see me, ma'am,' Lily said.

'Yes, I did.' Mrs Acland laid down her sewing and indicated a chair nearby. 'Sit down, please.'

Lily took a seat and Mrs Acland beamed at her, her plump face creasing. 'How was your morning?'

Lily smiled in return and said that it had gone well.

'Excellent. It's good for the girls to get out in the fresh air. Particularly Rosie. She'll stay indoors with her nose stuck in a book given half the chance. They've gone upstairs now, have they?'

'Yes, ma'am.'

'Good. Good.'

A little silence passed, while Lily sat with her hands folded in her lap. Then Mrs Acland spoke again.

'Well – now – Miss Clair,' she said, 'I'm sure you're wondering why I asked you to come and see me. The truth is, I'm afraid I have some disappointing news. Disappointing for you, that is.'

Lily waited.

'I say disappointing for you,' Mrs Acland went on, 'as I have to tell you that we've decided, Mr Acland and I, that it's time the girls went off to school.'

Lily nodded. 'I see. Yes.'

'Yes, indeed.' Mrs Acland's smile now was rueful. 'Oh,

dear, I'm so sorry to have to tell you this, but I'm afraid there's nothing else for it. They're coming up to eleven now, and we've decided that a good boarding school is the best course for them. But sadly, of course, that means we shall no longer require your excellent services.'

So, Lily thought, she was not to be reprimanded after all; she was to be dismissed.

'We haven't decided exactly which school the girls will go to,' Mrs Acland went on, 'though we're considering two in particular.' She broke off, her plain face softening with sympathy. 'I'm sorry, dear, to have to give you this news. It must be very disappointing for you. You are disappointed, aren't you?'

Lily nodded. 'I am indeed, ma'am. I've been very happy here.' She paused. 'Would that be in September, ma'am, when the girls go away?'

'Yes. They don't know about it yet. We haven't told them. Please don't mention it to them.'

'No, of course not.'

'I've no idea how they'll take to the idea,' Mrs Acland said. 'I don't think they'll look forward to going away from home, and I'm sure they'll miss you, Miss Clair. They're very fond of you, and they enjoy their lessons. Also I want you to know that Mr Acland and I have no complaints whatsoever with regard to your work, but, as you'll under-stand, we have to think of the girls' future.' She paused. 'I doubt this has come as the greatest shock to you, has it, Miss Clair?'

'No, ma'am. It was inevitable at some time.'

'Of course. You're twenty-three now, aren't you? Is that correct? You had a birthday at the beginning of the month.'

'Yes, ma'am.'

Mrs Acland nodded. 'Well, you're still very young – and I've no doubt you'll soon find yourself another position.' She smiled. 'Of course, you can be assured that Mr Acland

and I will give you an excellent reference. No question about that.'

Lily murmured her thanks, and then asked, 'So – for how much longer will you have need of me, ma'am?'

'Ah, yes,' Mrs Acland nodded. 'Mr Acland and I would like you to stay on for another four weeks. That will take us to near the end of August – Saturday the twenty-sixth.

Lily nodded. 'Yes, ma'am.' She could think of nothing else to say. She had been given very little time.

'Of course,' Mrs Acland continued, 'we're well aware that your contract takes you to the beginning of December – and we wouldn't want you to be the loser with regard to those weeks, so you can rest assured that you'll be paid up until that time.'

Lily was relieved. 'Thank you, ma'am, that's very good of you.'

'Not at all. We came to the conclusion that the girls have to go away, but we only made the final decision a few days ago. I wanted to tell you without too much delay, so that you can start looking out for a new post and get settled again as soon as possible.'

'Yes, I shall have to.'

A few moments of silence went by, then Mrs Acland said, a little note of relief in her voice, 'Well, anyway, that's got that business out of the way. I didn't look forward to having to tell you, but there's nothing for it, is there?' She smiled. 'So tell me now – how have you been getting on lately? We never have the chance to exchange more than two or three words. We're always so busy, it seems. I assume you've been well.'

'Oh, indeed, yes, ma'am. I've been very well.'

'That's good. Have you heard from your brother lately?'

'Not for a little while, no. He writes when he can, but it's not often.'

'He's still in London, is he?'

'Yes, he is.'

Mrs Acland nodded. 'I've been there twice, and that was enough. I don't know how people live there. Oh, good heavens, the dirt, the soot, and I don't-know-what-else.' She shook her head, then, with a pleasurable little sigh said, 'I must say it's nice to sit and chat for two minutes. Esme will be bringing me some tea soon. Would you like to join me over a cup, Miss Clair?'

Lily hesitated. She did not wish to appear rude, but she was anxious to get away. 'Oh, ma'am,' she said, 'at any other time I would be so pleased to, but today I've got to go into Corster for Miss Balfour.'

Mrs Acland nodded. 'Oh, yes, you go in for her rents, don't you.'

'Yes, every fortnight. It helps her out.'

'I'm sure it does.' Mrs Acland clasped her hands before her. 'Well, I suppose you'd better go, then, or you'll be late.'

'Yes, ma'am. Thank you.'

'Fine. And we'll see you on Monday morning as usual.'

'Yes, indeed.' The meeting was over.

From Yew Tree House, Lily made her way to Roseberry Cottage, where she used her latchkey to let herself into the small hall. The door to the little parlour was open and as she closed the front door she heard her landlady's voice call out to her: 'That you, Lily?' – her usual greeting – and Lily replied, also as usual, 'Yes, Mrs Thorne, it's me.' As she moved to the stairs, the landlady came to the parlour door, carrying a letter.

'Here you are, dear – this came just after you left this morning.'

Lily took one glance at the writing on the envelope and saw that it was from Tom. Mrs Thorne noted the gladness in her expression and said, 'You look pleased.'

'Yes. It's from my brother in London.'

'Oh – well, let's hope it's good news.'

Eager to read the letter, Lily started towards the stairs. As she did so, Mrs Thorne said, 'You'll be off to Sherrell a bit later, will you?'

'Yes, but I'm going into Corster on the way. Just as soon as I've washed my face and tidied myself up a bit.'

'Well, the kettle's on the hob, and the water's good and hot. I'll bring it up and leave it outside your door.'

'Thank you very much, but I'll come down and get it.'

'Well, that'll save my old hip. Would you like a cup of tea or something before you go? And maybe a nice little cheese sandwich? Just to keep you going.'

'Thank you, I would.' Lily was glad of the invitation; there was news she had to give to Mrs Thorne. 'Though I mustn't be late,' she added.

Up in her small room she wasted no time but tore open the envelope and took out Tom's letter. He had written:

Hotel Trevin
Camden Town
London E
26th July 1871

Dear Lil,

I'm sorry I haven't wrote in a while, but there's been nothing to tell. And anyway, you know I'm not much of a letter-man. Now, though, I must tell you that I'm leaving London and coming back to Wiltshire. I'm working at a hotel here right now, and I've got just three days to go. Come Saturday, when I've been paid, I can set out. I shall get back as soon as I can and will start looking for work right away. This is a good time of year what with the harvest and everything, and I reckon I'm fairly sure of finding a job. I know a couple of places to try. I'm looking forward to seeing you, Lil, and I hope you haven't been worrying too much about me. I'm well, believe me. I'll write to you again as soon as I'm back so we can arrange to meet.

Till then, I am, and shall always be

Your loving brother

Tom

So, at last, after all this time he was coming back. He'd be leaving today. Another fortnight or so, and they would meet. She folded the letter and put it back in the envelope.

Having fetched up the hot water from the kitchen, Lily washed away the dust from the warm day and then changed into her second-best dress, the dark blue cotton, observing as she did so that it was showing its age. No matter, she had not the money at present for new clothes, and with her employment with the Acland children coming to an end, she must needs watch her spending. The little she had would not last for long.

When she was ready she went downstairs into the kitchen where Mrs Thorne had laid out the tea things.

'Good news from your brother?' Mrs Thorne asked as Lily came in.

'Yes,' Lily said. 'He's coming back to Wiltshire. He's leaving London today. He should be here in a week.'

'Oh, well, that's very nice,' Mrs Thorne said. She moved towards the range where the kettle was singing.

Lily watched the older woman as she busied herself, and in no time the tea was made. Mrs Thorne had also put out a plate of thinly-cut cheese sandwiches and another with a fruit cake that she had baked that day. Lily declined the cake, but gratefully took a sandwich. As she ate and drank she gave her landlady the news that her post at the Aclands' was soon to come to an end, and that she must at once start to look for other employment. It would, she added, almost certainly mean that she would also have to give up her lodgings. Mrs Thorne sighed and said sadly, yes, she was aware of that, and added that she would be very sorry to see Lily go.

When Lily's plate and cup were empty she thanked Mrs Thorne and got up to leave. She would see her tomorrow evening, she said, on her return from Sherrell.

Six minutes after reaching Little Patten station she was on the train and heading for Corster.

On her arrival she set off through the main part of the town towards its edge. Twenty minutes' walk brought her to the river where she crossed at the narrow old bridge and, at the saddlery on the corner, turned into Brookham Way. There she saw ahead of her the two narrow houses, numbers one and two Merridew Villas, owned by Miss Elsie.

Regularly every fortnight, for well over two years now, Lily had been calling on the two elderly tenants of the dwellings, collecting the rent on Miss Elsie's behalf. Miss Elsie, begrudging a rent-collector's commission, had used to do it herself, but since Lily had offered to take over the task it had become an accepted responsibility.

She had come to know the tenants during her fortnightly visits, and it had become her custom to take tea with them, turn and turn about. This pattern was going to change, though, for soon one of the tenants, Mrs Callinthrop, would be going to live with her daughter in another part of the town. It was Mrs Callinthrop on whom she called first this Saturday, and when the rent business had been concluded she drank a cup of tea with the old lady and then went next door to see the other tenant, Mrs Tanner. With more tea politely declined and the rest of her business done, Lily stayed for a while to chat, then said her goodbyes and set off back towards the town centre.

The streets were busy. At a corner shop she stopped to buy copies of two local newspapers, and then continued on, eventually coming to the Victoria Gardens. The entrance

312

was set at the rear of a paved courtyard with benches, a fountain and a horse-trough. One of the benches was vacant, and she sat down on it, facing out across the busy street towards the corn exchange and the museum. The day seemed not overly warm now, and there was a gentle breeze that was pleasantly cooling. From her bag she took one of the newspapers.

The main news on the front page of the *Wiltshire Echo* concerned a case of murder that had taken place in a nearby village, while there was also a report of three cases of smallpox in the town of Redbury. Lily moved on through the pages to those bearing the classified advertisements. In the column listing 'Situations Vacant', there was only one for a governess locally. That was in Little Wickenham, some distance off to the south of Corster. Lily determined that she would write after it over the weekend.

As she sat there, idly watching the carriages moving back and forth and the townspeople going about their business, there came drifting on the air the sound of music. It was coming from the park behind her, from the bandstand. A military march was being played. The sound was stirring and full of vitality as the brass rang out and the drums reverberated on the summer air. With its sound, Lily was transported back to that summer in Whitton when she and Joel had sat in the park while the brass band had played: those summer afternoons, when they had sat by the pond; when he had sketched her portrait; when they had watched the Punch and Judy show; when he bought for her the little spray of linen flowers. She could see the different scenes and images as if they had come from yesterday. She could still hear the murmuring voices and the bursts of laughter that had rung out from the other people out there in the sun. And she and Joel had been among them, caught up only in their feelings, and their growing discovery of one another.

Where was Joel now, she wondered. He too, like Tom, had been out of her life for such a long time. Her last sight of him had been on the station platform at Hanborough, when she had thrust her address into his hand.

Three and a half years. So much time had gone by. And what had she to show for it, that passing time which, although sometimes fleeting, had on so many occasions crawled by in her solitude? Most girls of her age were married by now, or were at least promised – and of those married young women, many were mistresses of their own homes, with babies to care for. Lily, for all her ambitions, had little to show for the time. Granted, she had enjoyed her work at the Aclands', but that would soon be over, and unless she found new employment soon she would become destitute. She had taken so much goodwill and kindness from Miss Elsie, and indeed, she reckoned, she was still in her debt.

The thought came to her of her stepmother. Lily did not correspond with her in any but the most cursory terms. On occasion she wrote a short letter, enclosing a small amount of money for Dora – money that she could ill afford – and her stepmother would reply with grudging thanks, but other than that there was no communication between them. For Lily it was not a matter of regret.

The band played on, but the music had changed. The march had finished and now the tune being played was that of a popular music-hall song, 'The Boy on the Quay', some of the words of which went through Lily's head as she sat there. She looked up at the clock. It was time she set off to catch her train.

Chapter Twenty

'It had to come sooner or later – but you knew that.'

Miss Elsie looked across her desk at Lily, who sat in the chair facing her, an open newspaper on her knees.

'Yes, of course you're right,' Lily said. 'The girls are of an age where they need proper schooling, and to mix with other children. As you say, it was only a matter of time. I suppose I'm lucky I kept the post as long as I did.'

It was almost six-fifteen, and Lily had not long arrived at Rowanleigh. On entering the house she had soon joined Miss Elsie in her study where she handed over the rent money and told of her visits to the Villas' occupants. After speaking a little of the two elderly tenants, she had given the dismaying news of having received notice of the termination of her employment.

'Well, there's no doubt that you were successful in your work,' Miss Elsie said now, 'so you can be sure you'll get excellent references.' She took a sip from a little glass of sherry, then took her tobacco pouch from a drawer. Lily watched as she efficiently rolled a cigarette and lighted it with a match.

'So – you've got four weeks left with the Aclands,' Miss Elsie said, blowing out smoke. 'You can't afford to waste them.'

'No, I certainly can't.'

Miss Elsie shook her head. 'Unfortunately I should think the best posts will have been taken by now, and I don't doubt there'll be other young women in the same boat as you – all desperately searching around to see what's on offer as they lose their pupils to schools. You'll have to look sharp.'

'Yes, I know.'

'Have you told Mrs Thorne you'll be leaving soon?'

'Yes, I have, and I'm sorry for her sake. I know she needs the money.'

Miss Elsie nodded in sympathy. 'Of course,' she said, 'if you find a position around here, and they're happy to have a daily, visiting governess, your room will always be here for you.'

'Thank you.' Lily was, as always, touched by the woman's kindness.

Miss Elsie gestured with her cigarette towards the newspaper in Lily's lap. 'Did you find anything in the *Echo*?'

'There's one that looks a possibility,' Lily said, 'but it's in Little Wickenham.' She picked up the paper, already folded back, and held it out across the desk.

Miss Elsie took it and cast her eyes over the advertisement Lily had marked. 'Little Wickenham's a good way off,' she said, 'but there's not that much on offer, is there? Are you going to apply?'

'Yes. I shall write today.'

'Good.' Miss Elsie put the newspaper down on the desk and got to her feet. 'Come and sit round here and write your letter now. There's no time like the present. I've got to go down and help with the dinner.' She pressed out the remains of her cigarette in a glass ashtray and waved away the lingering smoke. 'There's writing paper and envelopes in the drawer – and stamps too, so your letter can go off right away.' She moved towards the door. 'Now I must go down to the kitchen. Give Mrs Nessant a hand.'

As Miss Elsie opened the door, Lily said, 'I heard from my brother today.'

'Oh, you did?' Miss Elsie turned in the doorway. 'Was it good news?'

'Yes, indeed. He's leaving London to come back to Wiltshire.'

'Well, that *is* good news.'

'He's leaving today. He'll write again as soon as he's back.'

'He'll be looking for a job, of course, once he gets here.'

'Yes – though it shouldn't be too hard to find one, he says. Not at this time of year.'

'Well, let's hope so, and I hope he'll be close by – for *your* sake.'

With her words, Miss Elsie went through onto the landing. Lily heard the click of the latch as the door closed, and then all was silence again.

After a moment or two she sat down at the desk and took from the drawer some writing paper and an envelope. Then, with the newspaper beside her, she set to writing her letter in answer to the advertisement. When it was done she made a copy for her records, then wrote out the envelope. Minutes later it was sealed and stamped.

That task done, she took Tom's letter from her bag and read it again. The address of the London hotel he had given was quite unfamiliar to her. She did not know how long he might have been there – but this was typical of the situation where his time in London had been concerned. She had heard from him only very infrequently since he had gone to the capital. For one thing he had never stayed at one address for any length of time, and in some instances he had written without including an address. Now, though, things were going to be different: he was coming back to his roots. Even now, he was on the way.

She sat back in the chair. The smell of Miss Elsie's cigarette hung in the air. The only sound she could hear was the sweet song of a blackbird, coming from the branches of the rowan tree. Her feelings were a mixture of emotions. In spite of her joy at hearing from Tom again, she had a feeling of melancholy at the uncertainty of her position. Coming back to the present out of her reverie, she took a pair of scissors from a pot on the desk, cut out the advertisement from the newspaper, then dropped the discarded remains into the waste basket.

There were various books and ledgers collected on the shelves beside the desk, some standing on their ends, and others in small piles. Her eyes wandering around the room, she idly scanned the contents of the shelves – and then found her gaze held.

The sudden focus of her attention was one particular volume that lay in the middle of a small stack, a volume holding her with its strangely familiar appearance. It was fairly large in size, with a brown binding, part of which, along the spine, had come loose.

She sat there with her eyes fixed upon it, aware, for some unknown reason, that it held a significance for her. And then it came to her: it was the volume in which Miss Elsie had written at the time of Georgie's going. She could see it again as it had lain open on the table in the drawing room; see it again as Miss Elsie, the cleric and she, Lily herself, had gone to it and written on its pages.

For some seconds Lily continued to sit there, her eyes on the ledger, and then she reached out, lifted it down and laid it on the desk.

A moment later she was lifting the cover, and as she turned the pages she saw that the ledger held records and details of factors and events in Miss Elsie's life, the entries entered in her familiar sloping hand. Each entry was dated, the first pages going back several years. Lily's eyes took in a variety of accounts; notes on employees at the house, the maids and the gardeners; the purchase of a new cob for the trap, and repairs to the trap itself. She found details and information relevant to the painting of the house's exterior, and here and there notes on the Villas and their tenants.

It was not long before she found herself looking at a series of entries concerning the young women who had come to Rowanleigh for their confinements. She read their names and ages, and home addresses, and the brief details that were given of the births of their babies. There, too, were entries dealing with the infants' adoptions.

Several pages on, she came to an entry concerning herself.

As she sat looking at the page before her it seemed that everything around her was stilled. Even the blackbird had, for a spell, paused in his singing. In the silence she sat bent over the ledger, staring down at the page.

In Miss Elsie's angular script she read her own name, her age, her address, and the name of her father. There too was given the date of her arrival at Rowanleigh and an approximate date of the expected birth of her child.

She turned the pages, reading more notes on the Villas in Corster, others dealing with repairs to the roofs, and a brief entry concerning Miss Elsie's illness, and Lily's nursing of her.

And then, on a page headed with the date 3 May 1867, she read of her own confinement, and the birth of her son:

'Lily Mary Clair, delivered safely of a boy. Mother doing well, but baby, though well-formed, presently rather sickly and needing careful tending. No cause for alarm, however, and with his mother is in good hands.'

For some seconds Lily sat riveted by the written words, almost holding her breath. Then, becoming newly conscious of her act of prying, she turned the page. And there she saw – the momentous event reduced to a few lines on the paper – the act of her son's being taken away. There was the name of the cleric, and of the plain-looking woman who had accompanied him and who had taken the baby into her arms and walked with him out of the door. There too were the signatures of herself, and Miss Elsie and the Reverend, Mr Iliffe.

She sat there for long seconds, gazing down at the page, her eyes scanning and rescanning the lines, almost as if she were willing them to tell her more. Then, with a sigh, accepting that there was nothing more to learn, she turned the leaf. To her surprise the next entry also concerned herself. Under the date: 3 July 1867, Miss Elsie had written: 'It is three weeks since the infant was taken, and sorry to say that LC is taking it quite badly. However, still early days yet, and given time she will find acceptance.'

There was a piece of paper lying on the open pages, a small folded sheet. Lily took it up, unfolded it and read what was written.

And as she read it through, her breath caught in her throat, and her heart began to pound in her breast. In a round, careful hand, was written:

The Vicarage
Church Lane
Redfern, Corster
24th June 1867

Dear Miss Balfour,

Further to our business concluded at Rowanleigh on the 12th, the Rev Iliffe has asked me to inform you that all has proceeded satisfactorily in the placement of the Child. He was delivered to Happerfell safely on the same day, since which time Mr Soameson has reported that he is settling in well, and is providing much joy.

I am,

Your obedient servant

L. Cannon (Miss)

Lily sat staring at the letter. So he was living in

Happerfell. Her son, her boy, was living in Happerfell. Georgie – he was so close. He was living so close by. Her eyes moved from the name of the village to take in the name of the man that was written there: Soameson.

She continued to gaze at the letter in her hand, taking in its few, though dynamic, details, and then folded it and laid it back on the page. As she did so she heard from below the faint sound of Miss Elsie's voice. Quickly she shut the ledger and returned it to its place on the shelf. Moments later footsteps sounded on the landing and then the door was opening and Miss Elsie was standing there.

'So,' she said, 'did you get your letter done?'

'Yes, I did.' Lily picked up the envelope. 'All ready to go in the post.'

'Good. Well done.' Miss Elsie pressed her hands together. 'So – now – come on down and let's have some dinner.'

That night Lily lay wakeful, turning in her bed and opening her eyes to look into the dark of the summer night. For so long she had wondered where the child had gone. Now she knew. He was just a few miles away, living with his new family, regarding two people whom she had never met as his father and mother; and not even aware that she, Lily, even existed.

Still with no reply to her letter to Little Wickenham by Friday evening, Lily concluded that the advertiser was not interested. She was relieved to find, however, that there were two positions being advertised in that day's *Gazette*. One was in the village of Upinshall, and the other in Seston, and that evening she sat in her little room and wrote off in reply to both advertisements. She posted the letters on the way to Yew Tree House the next morning.

She had more on her mind, however, than the finding of a suitable post, vital as it was. All through the week there had stayed at the forefront of her thoughts the words she had seen written on the letter in Miss Elsie's ledger. She could not banish them, and throughout that morning they came back to her, again and again.

As the time wore on she found it more and more difficult to keep her mind on her work. Even as it was, Saturday mornings were never the best of times with her pupils, for they were always conscious that the teaching day was short and their leisure time near, and there was always a certain lack of concentration. This morning, though, the lack of concentration was Lily's, and when twelve-thirty came and she said goodbye to the girls, there was no doubt in her mind as to what she would do.

From Yew Tree House she made her way straight to the station and there caught a train to Corster. On arrival, she alighted and after a wait of some twenty minutes boarded a train that would take her to Pilching. From there it was a short journey by fly to Happerfell.

She had never had occasion to go to the village before, though she was familiar with its name. Now, being let down in the centre by the carriage driver, she paid him his fare and stood and looked about her. Not only did she wonder on her best course of action, but she also questioned the very fact of her being there.

Then towards her came an elderly man, walking with the aid of a stick. He caught her eye as he drew alongside, and smiled at her. 'You looks a bit lost, miss,' he said. 'Can I 'elp you in some way?'

'Well – thank you,' she smiled in return. 'I was wondering where I might find Mr Soameson.'

'Mr Soameson, the Scotsman, eh? Ah, well, that's no problem. He lives at The Gables.' He raised a hand and pointed off along the street. 'Just up to the right there, in Bourne Way. Only take you a minute.'

Lily thanked him and set off. Keeping to the footway, she

came soon to the turning indicated, and halted at the corner. The street to her right curved, so that the far part of it was out of her sight beyond a screen of foliage. She stood there, uncertain as to whether to continue. It was not too late to turn back.

Then, after a long hesitation, she stepped forward.

She followed the road for some yards around the bend before she came to The Gables.

Standing back behind a wide, green lawn, it was a fairly large house of three storeys, with white-painted walls, and the gables that gave it its name. It stood partly hidden from view by two oak trees that cast their rich shadows over the grass. A gravel drive curved across the lawn, connecting with the front porch, while a second drive, bordered by a privet hedge, led up beside the house.

At the foot of the drive she stood and stared. The windows showed nothing beyond their dark opacity. There was no sign of life, but she knew they were there, the people. And her son too. Yes. He was there also, some-where behind those walls, those windows. She became conscious of the beating of her heart, and conscious also of how conspicuous she would appear to any casual passerby. And what was she doing there? she asked herself. What did she hope to achieve? She was being a fool; her behaviour was that of a madwoman, some lunatic obsessive. Leave, she urged herself. Leave now, and don't come back.

As the words went through her brain, she caught a glimpse of movement at the side of the house and, looking over, saw the slight figure of a young girl, a maid in apron and cap, approaching from the rear of the building. Lily turned away, hovered there for a moment longer, then started back the way she had come.

On Tuesday, returning to her room in Roseberry Cottage after teaching the Acland girls, she found a letter waiting for her from the advertiser in Little Wickenham. It thanked her for her application, but said the post had been filled. It did not come as a great surprise; having not heard sooner, she had already resigned herself to being passed over. On a note of comfort, she reminded herself that there were still the advertisers in Seston and Uppinshall to give her their consideration.

By the time Saturday morning came, however, there had been no word from either direction; nor had she found anything suitable on offer in that week's edition of the *Corster Gazette*. She would find something in time, though, she told herself, besides which, she would place her own classified advertisement in the paper when she went into the town later to collect Miss Elsie's rents.

That day also, Lily was fully aware, marked a fortnight since Tom had set off from London. He would have been back for well over a week now, she thought, and she would surely be hearing something from him soon.

Meanwhile, at Yew Tree House the twins were restless. They had been told the previous evening that they were to go away to school in Frome in September, and they were full of the news for Lily during the morning's lessons. To add to their excitement they had also been informed that they would be taking a week's holiday in Weston-Super-Mare just before going away to school. It was not surprising to Lily that they found it hard to concentrate on their work, but she had her own preoccupations, and in spite of her fondness for the girls she was relieved when at last the time came when she could get away.

After stopping at her lodgings for a cup of tea and a sandwich, she set off for Corster, and the Villas in Brookham Way. There she collected the rents and drank a last cup of tea with Mrs Callinthrop, who would soon be leaving. After wishing the old lady good fortune, Lily left the house to go back into the town centre.

Her way now took her through the market square and to the offices of the *Corster Gazette*, where she gave to a young, bespectacled clerk the paper on which she had written the wording of her classified advertisement. He took down the details and gave her a receipt for the fee. The advertisement would be in the next Friday's edition, he told her, the eighteenth of August.

Back out in the sun, she moved on along the busy pavement while all around her the air was filled with the town's noise: the rattle and rumble of the carriages, the clatter of horses' hooves, the cries of the street traders. Sweepers were still busy in some parts of the square, clearing away the last of the detritus from the previous day's produce and livestock market. At times she had to pick her way through the debris. On the south side of the square she bought copies of the *Gazette* and the *Echo*, and then stopped outside an ironmonger's to buy a packet of pins from a ragged, middle-aged woman. She tucked the little packet down into her bag, along with her purse and the papers, and continued on her way towards the station.

As she drew near the entrance to the Victoria Gardens, she felt discomfort under her heel and realised that she had somehow picked up a stone. Moving to a vacant bench on the paved courtyard, she sat down and, as discreetly as she could, slipped off her shoe and shook out the small pebble.

With her shoe back on, she was about to rise from her seat, when she heard a voice at her elbow.

'Lily . . . hello.'

Turning, looking up, she saw Joel standing there.

He had his back to the square. He wore a brown tweed suit with a black velvet collar, and carried a brown leather case. As she looked at him his hand reached up to touch at his hat's brim and then adjust his cravat. Lily was so taken aback at seeing him there that for a moment or two she could not speak, then, conscious of her hard-beating heart, she gathered her wits as best she could, and gave him the trace of a smile and murmured a hello.

'How are you, Lily?' he said.

'I'm well. I'm well, thank you. And you?'

'Yes, thank you. I'm very well.'

All about them the people of the town went about their affairs, while he stood in silence, as if searching for words. Then he said:

'May I sit down for a minute?'

'Yes. Yes, of course.'

She drew her bag a little closer to her, and he sat down on the bench a couple of feet from her side. She could see him clearly now without the glare of the sun at his back, and she could see a change in him. Slight though it was, it was there, wrought by the three and a half years since their last meeting. He was twenty-eight now, and the maturing of his years showed in his face. The softness about his cheeks had gone, and there was a leaner, more angular look about his features, the bones showing more strongly beneath his slightly sunburned skin.

All this she took in during a brief glance, and then looked away past the water trough, trying to assume an air of casualness, though every second aware of his gaze upon her, of his nearness once again.

'Have you been well, Lily?' he asked.

'Yes, thank you.'

On a nearby bench an old woman scattered some crumbs from a paper bag, and at once the sparrows were there, pecking about on the flags.

'Did you take the governess post that you were offered that day?' Joel said. 'In Little Patten?'

'Oh, yes.'

'And did it work out all right?'

326

'It did indeed. I'm still there, and very happy. Though it's coming to an end soon, I'm sorry to say.'

'Ah, that's a pity.'

'Yes. Unfortunately for me, my pupils are going off to school. They're of an age now.'

'I see. So you'll be looking out for something else. Or have you already found a post?'

'Not yet. I've written away to a couple of advertisers, and just now I stopped by the *Gazette* and placed an ad.'

He nodded. 'Well – I'm sure you'll find something soon.'

'I hope so – or I shall be in trouble.'

'Do you enjoy it? – being a governess?'

'Yes, I do.' She nodded to endorse her words. 'I've only had the experience of my two pupils in Little Patten, but they're good girls. Oh, yes, I like my work.'

'Good. That's good to hear.'

The conversation, stilted and awkward, and which was going nowhere, tailed off. Moments passed, then Joel said, 'That was such a surprise – seeing you here.'

'Yes – for me also.'

'Are you often in Corster?'

'I come in regularly every fortnight – on an errand for Miss Balfour.'

'Ah, yes, your friend in Sherrell.'

'Yes. I go to Brookham Way.'

'I know it,' he said, nodding. 'Near the river – just over the bridge, on the right.'

'That's it. There's a little saddlery on the corner.'

'Yes, there is. I've been there a few times over the years, mostly on business for my father. It's quite small, but very highly regarded. You've got business there, have you?'

'Not at the saddlery, no. Miss Balfour owns two small houses nearby. The Villas, as we call them.' She smiled. 'They sound grand, don't they? – but they're only small. They're cosy and quite attractive little places, though, and very well kept up – Miss Balfour sees to that. One of them has the loveliest little laburnum in the front garden. It's a picture right now, a mass of golden chain.' She was speaking for the sake of it, she realised, and came to a stop.

'And what have you to do with them?'

'I go and collect the rents, every other Saturday.'

'Oh, so you're a dreaded rent-collector, are you, in addition to being a governess?'

'Yes, I am.' She smiled. 'I've been doing it for a good while now, and I'm into a routine. I come in here to Corster in the afternoon and get to the Villas between four and half-past. Then I sit and have a cup of tea and a chat with the tenants. I'm glad to do it; it helps Miss Balfour out. I don't think she trusts agents any more, and with her arthritis she's not as able as she was.'

'You're very kind.'

'No, it's not kindness,' she said. 'I do it because I'm fond of her. She's been wonderful to me, and if I can do anything to help her in return, then I'm happy to. She's been the most excellent friend. I don't know what I would have done without her.'

'Do you get to see her often?'

'Every other weekend. I'm going there now. For my work I have lodgings in Little Patten, very close to where I teach.' She paused. 'And what about you? Are you still with the law firm in Corster?'

'Not now. I'm working at the stores – here and in Bath.'

'Ah, and are you enjoying it?'

'Most of the time.' He nodded. 'I'm taking on more and more responsibilities.'

'Your father must be pleased with you.'

'Well – yes, he is – and he depends on me more and more, I find. I never foresaw this for myself – becoming quite so involved with the family business.' He gave a shrug. 'But I am, and there's no going back now.'

'No,' she said, 'life has a way of changing things. You find yourself set on a particular course – and you have no option but to go on. You put one foot in front of the other, and soon it's impossible to turn back.'

'Yes,' he said, 'that's right.' He paused. 'And I've come to realise – that I've become my father's son. All those dreams he and my mother had for Crispin – I guess now they're well and truly settled on me. Still, I've nothing to complain about.'

'They're well, are they – your parents?'

'Yes, thank you. I don't know where my father finds his energy. After Crispin's death he put even more of himself into his work. He'd be lost without it. He's involved in every single part – from the manufacture of the goods we buy to the way they're sold in the departments. And if he's not here in Corster, he's in Bath, and if not in Bath then in Paris.' He paused. 'And what about you? Do you get to see your family? Your father and stepmother?'

'My father died – over two years ago.'

'Oh – I'm sorry to hear that . . .'

'Yes – well – anyway . . . I don't go to see my stepmother these days. I'm afraid we don't get on.'

'That's a pity. Still – these things happen . . . What about your brother? Is he going on all right?'

'He's been living in London, but he left a fortnight ago. I'm expecting to hear from him any day.

'Why did he go to London?'

'I don't know. Perhaps someone told him the streets were paved with gold.' She shook her head. 'I don't think he's cut out for life in a big city, a place like London. I've never been there, but I've heard about it.'

'Oh, believe me – it's everything you've ever heard of, and everything you might ever expect. And a lot more too.'

'I'm sure it is.'

He nodded. They sat in silence for a moment, then he

said, 'I've wondered about you, Lily – how you've been getting on.'

She said nothing, but looked down at the flags. Seconds went by. 'It's a great pity you're losing your position,' he said. 'I'm so sorry to hear that.'

'Yes – well – I shall find another one soon.'

'I'm sure you will.' A brief pause. 'What about your – your personal life?'

'My personal life?'

'Well . . .' he shrugged, 'I mean – have you – friends?'

'Friends?' She gave a nod. 'Ah, I understand. I think you're asking if there is – someone special in my life.' She smiled, making light of it. 'Is that it?'

He shrugged. 'Well, I – I have wondered – whether you might have met someone.'

'No,' she said, 'there's no one in my life.'

He attempted a smile. 'Going by what you read, it seems that a governess can sometimes have an interesting life.'

'My employer is a happily married man in his forties,' she said. 'He's not Mr Rochester, and I'm not Jane Eyre.'

His smile faded. 'I'm sorry. I wasn't implying anything. That was crass, and I'm talking like an idiot. It's just that – I've wondered how you are . . .'

'If you really want to know,' she said, 'my life is somewhat dull. I keep busy with my pupils all week. And alternate weekends, as I told you, I collect the rents here in Corster, then go on to Sherrell to see Miss Balfour. We have dinner, and we chat – and the time passes. I stay the night and then I return to Little Patten on the Sunday. So as you can tell, I live a quiet life.'

He gave a little nod. 'And you're managing all right, are you?'

'Managing?'

'I meant financially. I mean – if you're in need of money . . .'

330

Her eyes widened, and she stiffened. 'No, I am not,' she said.

He groaned. 'Oh, my God – Lily, I'm so sorry. I've offended you. I can't seem to say the right thing. Oh, Lily, I didn't mean . . .'

'It's all right; it doesn't matter.'

'It does matter. I'm sorry – really I am.'

Neither spoke for a while. The old woman nearby scattered the last of her crumbs, and watched, smiling and toothless as the sparrows hopped and pecked about at her feet. Joel watched them too, but frowning, preoccupied. Then, turning back to Lily, he said:

'Could you ever forgive me for what I did? Sending you the letter?'

'Ah,' she nodded. 'Your letter.'

'I must have – have hurt you so much.'

She could not look him in the eye. Studying her gloved hands, she said, 'We have reasons for doing things, and we don't always have that much choice in what we do.'

'I had told my father,' he said. 'About you.'

She looked at him now. 'You told your father?' Then she nodded. 'Yes. You would have had to.'

'Yes. I – I suppose I wanted his blessing. Well, I know I did. I wanted to do everything right. It was so important to me. Especially coming so soon after Crispin's death.'

She sat silent, waiting for the next words. Then Joel said:

'He couldn't accept what I had to say – what I had to tell him. He – he just couldn't.'

'It's all right,' she said. 'You don't need to go into it. Of course he couldn't accept it. What father could?'

'I'm sorry, Lily.'

She lifted her head, turning to look at him now. 'It's all right. I understand. Believe me, I do.' Seeing him there, sitting on the bench beside her, she realised afresh how far apart they were. She took in his expensive suit with the pink rosebud in the lapel, the waistcoat, the finely finished shirt, the silk cravat. He looked more removed from her than ever. Yes, of course there was a difference in her status now – to go from general maid to governess was no small step – but in his world she might hardly have moved an inch. They were still oceans apart.

'So – what about you, Joel,' she said. 'What about you?'

'Me?'

'Well, you've told me how busy you are in the family business, but what else has been happening? I'm sure you don't spend all your time behind a desk, or checking on deliveries of goods or the manners of your shop assistants. Do *you* have friends? Is there someone special in *your* life?'

He looked back at her without answering, and in the midst of the surrounding tapestry of sounds his silence was profound.

Of course, she said to herself, there must be someone in his life. There was bound to be. Three and a half years had passed since their last meeting, and he, a handsome, single, talented man, could not have gone through all that time in isolation.

She felt within her a little stab of anger – not at him, but at herself. For she realised now what she had been doing, all along. Like some naïve schoolgirl she had somehow believed that the feelings behind those early, passionate declarations of love would last and see them through; that they would be the answer to any obstacle that life might throw up between them. No matter the signs and the evidence that those obstacles had made apparent, she realised that she had somehow continued to live in hope that one day all would be well.

'So,' she said, forcing a smile, 'has a date been set for the happy day?'

'Lily . . .' He frowned, leaning closer.

'So I should be congratulating you, Joel,' she said. 'And I

do. I wish you all the very best – and the young lady too.' She paused. 'She must be someone of whom your father approves. Are you going to tell me who she is?'

He hesitated for a moment, then said: 'Her name is Simone.'

'Ah.' Lily nodded. 'Simone. The girl in the drawing. The daughter of your father's partner.'

'Yes.'

'And this is serious, is it? You're to be married, are you?' Without waiting for an answer, she glanced up at the clock on the wall of the corn exchange. 'Goodness,' she said, 'look at the time.' She took up her bag. 'Joel, I have to go. I'm so sorry, but I must.'

'Oh, not just yet,' he said quickly. 'Please.'

'No, I really must.'

She got up from the bench, reached out and swiftly shook his hand. 'Goodbye, Joel. It was so good to see you again – and to see you looking so well and so successful – and I do wish you every happiness in the future.' She flashed a brief smile that she somehow managed to summon up from unknown theatrical depths and turned away. Then, forcing one foot in front of the other, she walked out into the square.

Chapter Twenty-one

At Rowanleigh over the rest of that Saturday, and on Sunday, Lily spent a little time with Miss Elsie, the two chatting together over dinner and breakfast and the occasional cup of tea. At other times, Miss Elsie, taking advantage of the warm, dry weather, took her easel into the garden and worked at her watercolours. For her part, Lily planned the coming week's lessons with the Acland girls, and helped Mary in the kitchen. In some solitary moments she found herself returning to thoughts of Joel and their meeting in Corster, but each time such thoughts intruded she tried to thrust them from her.

Late on Sunday afternoon she took the train back to Little Patten, and the following morning resumed her work at Yew Tree House. On returning to her lodgings that evening, she found a letter awaiting her.

It was in response to the letter she had written to the advertiser in Seston, and was inviting her for an interview on Saturday, the nineteenth of August. The writer, who signed himself Lincoln Corelman, had written in a heavy, angular script: 'Laenar House is situated on the south side of Greenbanks Lane, and is a twenty-minute walk north from Seston station. Alternatively, it can be reached by cab. I shall be obliged if you will present yourself with references promptly at four o'clock, and if on receipt of this letter you will at once confirm that we may expect you.'

Lily wasted no time but sat straight down and penned her reply, saying she would be there at the appointed time.

Perhaps, at long last, she said to herself, things were moving and she was making a little progress – and not before time; she had less than two weeks' employment before her. As soon as the letter was finished and sealed, she went along the lane and deposited it in the post box.

The following day, to her great relief, she received a letter from Tom. It had been sent to her at Rowanleigh, and forwarded on to her lodgings by Miss Elsie. Her brother had written to say he was back in Wiltshire, and had found a job on a farm in Wilton Ferres, a village near Corster. He planned to come into Corster on the Friday evening, the eighteenth, he said, and asked Lily to meet him near the entrance to the Victoria Gardens. He would try to be there at six-thirty, and if it rained he would wait in the museum. Lily wrote back at once to say she would be there to meet him.

Friday, when it came, dragged by. From the moment Lily awoke that morning she had her mind set upon her coming meeting with Tom. Then at last the hour came when she was free of her responsibilities for the day, and she took her leave of her pupils and set off back for her lodgings.

On her arrival, Mrs Thorne handed her a letter, which turned out to be in answer to her response to the advertisement placed by the family in Upinshall. It informed her politely that they did not now require a governess until after Christmas, but that they would keep her in mind as the time approached.

After some tea and a sandwich in the kitchen with Mrs Thorne, she set out for the station, carrying her umbrella along with her bag, for there were threatening clouds on the horizon. On arriving in Corster, she bought a copy of that day's *Gazette*, eager to see whether her classified advertisement was in it, and then continued on her way to the square, and the entrance to the Victoria Gardens.

In the flagstoned yard near the Gardens' gate a number of the townsfolk were in evidence and, in spite of the gathering clouds, several of the benches were taken. Lily found a space on one at the other end of which sat an old woman, wrapped up as if for winter and hunched over her fraying basket of belongings. A little distance to the right across the cobbles stood the old town museum, a tall building that dated back to Tudor times, but which had been added to in various haphazard ways over the years. Looking up at the clock on the wall of the corn exchange, Lily saw that it was just after six. She was in good time. Dipping into her bag, she took out the newspaper and scanned the classified advertisements – and there halfway down the column was her own, word for word as she had presented it to the clerk. She read it through with satisfaction, then folded the paper and put it back into her bag. In the square the people came and went. A child with a hoop ran past, then a young lad with a brush and a shovel came cleaning up horse droppings. On her left, the old woman opened a snuff box, sniffed a pinch into her nostrils, and then, muttering to herself, got up and hobbled away. Up above, the sky was darkening by the minute. Half-past six came and went. Lily kept her eyes moving back and forth across the square.

And then, suddenly he was there, coming around the corner of the exchange. He saw Lily at once, and made straight for her, his smile lighting up his face. As he approached, she got to her feet, her own smile answering his. A moment later he was at her side and wrapping his arms around her.

'Oh, Lil . . . Lil . . .' His voice cracked as he spoke her name, and she could feel her eyes fill with tears.

'Tom. Oh, Tommo. Oh, my dear . . .' Her hoarse voice was muffled against the rough fabric of his jacket. For some seconds they held one another, and then she pulled back and looked at him. 'Oh, Tom – it's so good to see you.'

He beamed. 'Ah, it's so good to see *you*. It's been such a long time.'

As he spoke, the first drops of rain fell, and Lily gave a little groan and glanced up at the heavens. 'Oh, here it comes,' she said. She reached out and snatched at his arm. 'Come on – let's get into the dry.'

Without hesitating, they started at a run across the square, heading for the museum. It was only a short distance, but by the time they reached the building's entrance the rain was falling heavily. Laughing and a little breathless, they stepped inside the porch. Briefly glancing back to survey the square, Lily saw that it was now almost deserted. 'Come on,' she said, 'it's not going to let up for a while. We might as well go in.'

Tom pushed open the double doors leading into the foyer and he and Lily passed through. It was warm and quiet inside, the only persons in evidence being the curator who sat reading at a desk, and an elderly couple standing before a carved bust of a prominent local politician from earlier times. The curator glanced up briefly as Lily and Tom walked past him and then lowered his head again to his papers. Ignoring the exhibition rooms on the ground floor, they made their way to the wide stairs and started up. The museum's exhibits held little magic for them now. They had seen them in the past on more than one occasion, and even their first viewing had given no real thrill. Distributed over the building's four storeys, the town's treasured antiquities were, for the most part, a lacklustre collection. Both Lily and Tom knew what they would find in the various rooms: the ancient statues, the fossils, the fragments of pottery unearthed from the surrounding Wiltshire hills, the old tapestries, the collection of sepia photographs of the town and some of its past luminaries.

Passing several other visitors on their way, Lily and Tom

continued on up the stairs. When they eventually reached the top floor there was no one else in sight, not even an attendant – the town could not afford to have them on every floor of the place – and they walked into the wide exhibition room to find themselves completely alone. Looking around at the faded tapestries and ancient Eastern vases and other artefacts in the glow of the lamps, Lily felt glad at the familiarity of it all. Beneath a window on the far side stood an old, mellow-polished bench and she moved to it and sat down. Tom followed and sat beside her. Against the pane behind their heads the rain fell steadily.

Lily put her hands up to her hat, checking it, then whispered with a little chuckle, 'We shouldn't be sitting here. We should be looking at the treasures, not using the place just to shelter from the rain.'

'Ah, it's all right,' Tom said. 'We're not doin' any 'arm.'

She nodded, sighed, then turned fully to him. 'Well, now, our Tom – let me look at you.' She could see in his appearance the time that had passed. He was seventeen now and a little taller, though still with the lean, wiry look he had always had. He was, she thought, no longer a boy.

'Well,' he said, taking off his cap, 'how do I look?'

'How do you look? You look fine.' She meant it. Although his jacket and trousers were worn, his polished boots were scuffed, and he was in need of a haircut, there was nevertheless an air of well-being about him, pointed up by the little white rosebud he had pinned in his lapel. He looked positive and bright, and more vital than she had seen him in years. 'Yes,' she said, 'you look fine, and as handsome as ever.'

He laughed lightly, his voice echoing a little in the quiet. 'Well, you look handsome too, our Lil. Though I'm bound to say you look a little bit older as well.'

'Well, I *am* older.' She smiled at him. 'Oh, it's so good to see you.'

'Ah, you too. Had you been waitin' long?'

'Just a little while.'

'Sorry about that, but I 'ad to wait on Mr Ballantine. He's the boss's brother. He give me a lift in on the wagon. I'm to meet him again at 'alf-seven.'

'Well – that gives us a while.' She gave a little sigh. 'Oh, Tom, you're back, and you've got a job.'

'Ah – and it's a right nice place to work. Mr and Mrs Ballantine are really nice, and I got a neat little bed over the stables. It's not grand, but I'm not after grand anyway. It's fine for me. I'm there with two other blokes. We gets on just dandy.'

'That's so good to hear. I've been so concerned about you.'

'Yeh, I reckon you 'ave, but I'm fine now – really.' He leant back, stretching out his legs in their worn and mended corduroys. 'Oh, Lil, it's such a relief to be back down 'ere again. I don't know why I stayed away so long.'

'Why did you go, Tom?' she said. 'Why did you go to London in the first place?'

He gave a little shrug. 'Yeh, sometimes I asked meself that. I only know I felt I 'ad to get away somewhere.' He paused. 'See – I got dismissed from the farm at Halls Haven.'

'Oh, Tom. You never told me that.'

'Yeh, I got dismissed.' He leant forward, and lowered his head. 'It was the foreman. I was foolish, and somehow I let it out that I'd been in Wentworth, and he took against me.' He shrugged. 'So – I got me marchin' orders.'

Lily looked at his set profile, then said, forcing a smile, 'So – you went to London. Imagine that.'

'Oh, ah, I went to London all right.' He turned to her again now. 'Well, you 'ear the stories about it, London, and I knew of a chap who went there. So – I thought it might be the place for me. They say a fellow who's prepared to work

339

'ard can make a good livin' for hisself. So, I thought, why not?'

'I wish you had let me know, Tom. I didn't know where you were or what had happened to you.'

'I know. I should've told you, but – well, I was moving about from one place to another while I was there. I was 'ardly in one place long enough to send an address. Besides – I wasn't 'appy with it – my situation, I mean.' He sighed. 'The whole thing – it was such a let-down. I so wanted to be able to write and say that I'd made something of meself, but nothin' turned out the way I'd hoped. Still – things'll be better now.'

'Yes, I'm sure they will.'

He nodded. 'Aw, I tell you,' he said, 'London's a remarkable place, no doubt about that.'

'You must have seen some real sights there.'

'You bet I 'ave.'

'And the ladies there have fine clothes, do they? A lot more fashionable than you'd find here in Corster, I'll bet.'

'Well, I don't know about fashion and stuff – you certainly see some finely dressed people – but you see people of all kinds there. Rich people and a lot of very poor people too. And people from all over the world: Chinese people with narrow little eyes and long pigtails; Indian people with brown skins; black people too – black as coal with big lips and fuzzy 'air. You see all kinds – and they dress in the weirdest way and speak very strange languages. You can't understand a word. You wouldn't credit it, believe me.'

Lily gave a sigh. 'It must be such an exciting place. I'd love to go there someday.'

He nodded. 'Oh, yeh. Mind you, it's not all it's cracked up to be. Not by a long chalk. And I tell you something – it's a right filthy place.' He gestured towards the square below the window. 'You think this place is dirty, right? You don't

340

know what dirty is till you've seen London. Well, they call the place the *Smoke* – that's what they call it. The 'ouses are *black*, I tell you. Black with all the soot and the smoke. And some of them fogs you get in the winter – they're as thick as soup, and you can't see your 'and in front of your face.'

'Really?'

'Ah, that's right. You've never seen fog like it, believe me, and when you get indoors afterwards you finds your 'ands and face are filthy. It ain't no wonder they gets diseases there. They got the smallpox now, did you know that?'

'Oh, yes, it's in all the papers. It's not only in London, either – it's getting everywhere – even here in Redbury and Corster and places.'

'It must be bad, then. Still – I managed to stay all right.'

'Thank heavens, yes. What kind of work did you do?'

'Anything. I worked all over the place. I went wherever I could get a job. I worked in 'otels sometimes – odd job boy, or boot boy. Porter sometimes. Then again another time I was 'elpin' out on a market stall. For a few days I worked as a crossing-sweeper. I was a runner once, for some firm in the City, takin' messages all day. Though that didn't last long. Then another time I was workin' in a shoe factory, cleanin' up round the machines. I did work where and when I could. You couldn't afford to be fussy. Sometimes I didn't 'ave any work at all.'

Lily frowned. 'Oh, Tom,' she said, 'it sounds awful. How did you sleep? Where did you live and eat?'

'Well, when I was workin' at the 'otels I got to sleep and eat there too, though the sleepin' wasn't much to write 'ome about. A little cupboard usually, but I was glad of it. At least I was in the dry. Other times I slept where I could. Now and again in some shop doorway – a few times I even went into the workhouse.'

Lily put a hand to her mouth. The workhouse . . . 'Oh,

thank God that's over,' she said. 'That's behind you now. You mustn't go back there again.'

'No, I won't – never. I'm not meant for the city life.'

'How did you come down – from London?'

'Aw, it took me a good while. I walked most of the way, though now and again some kind wagoner give me a ride on 'is cart. I slept where I could – in barns when I was lucky. I managed to get summat to eat too. People were kind generally, and at other times I was able to pick up some vegetables 'ere and there. But it's all right now. It don't matter now. It's over, and I got me a job, ain't I?'

'Yes, you have, and that's wonderful.'

'They're takin' me on at the start just for a couple of months – over the 'arvest, while one of the regular farmhands is away.'

'Only for two months? Oh, dear – that's disappointing.'

'Yeh, I know. I'm told he's been ill and is laid up for a while, but who knows, they might decide they can't manage without me. Anyway, the main thing is, I've got a job for the time bein', and it'll give me a chance to look around for summat more permanent. For I'll tell you somethin' – jobs ain't so easy to come by right now. I reckon I'm lucky to have anything at all – and they been very nice to me at the farm. Mrs Ballantine, she give me a good dinner of eggs and potatoes. She says I need fattening up.'

Lily smiled. 'I'm not surprised.'

'Never mind. I feel fine, that's the main thing, and now that I've got a job, and somewhere to stay, everything'll be all right again.' He paused. 'I got a good feelin' about this place, and I'll tell you summat – I'm not ever gunna give you cause to worry about me again, Lil, believe me, I'm not.'

She smiled. 'Well – just see that you don't.'

Lifting his head he looked up at the clock on the wall. 'I must keep an eye on the time. I mustn't keep Mr Ballantine waiting. That won't be a good start.' On the window pane the rain continued to fall, while from the distance came the faint rumble of thunder. Tom sat in silence for a moment or two, then said:

'I never 'ear anything from 'ome now, you know. I wrote. I told you I wrote, but I never got an answer. I doubt I'd be welcome there any more. I guess they made that clear enough.'

Lily took in his words, then, taking a breath, preparing herself, told him of their father's death. She told how she had been summoned to his bedside, and of how she had written to him, Tom, at the farm in Halls Haven but had had no response. When she had finished relating her story he sat with his head bent, his hand raised to cover his eyes. She realised that he was weeping. She laid her hand on his shoulder, and after a while he grew calmer, and ceased his crying.

'I'd have gone to see him like a shot,' he said softly. 'If I'd only known.' He drew back his lips over his teeth. 'I should've been there.'

She pressed his shoulder. 'You didn't know. You mustn't reproach yourself. It couldn't be helped.'

'Maybe not,' he murmured, and gave a deep sigh. 'I was such a disappointment to him.'

'Oh, Tom . . .'

'It's true. After I come out of Wentworth he never spoke to me again.' He paused, then said hesitantly, 'Did he speak of me, Lil? Did he – did he ask about me?'

The briefest moment, then she said, 'Yes. Of course he did.'

'Did he?' There was a note of barely contained joy in his voice. 'Lil, did he? What did he say?'

'He said – he said he wished – wished you'd been there,' she lied.

'Did he? Did he say that?'

343

'Yes.'

He gave a little groan. 'Oh, God – I wish I'd known. I wish I'd known he was sick. What else did he say?'

'He said – he said he loved you.' The lie came off her tongue with only the merest hesitation, and even as it did she knew she would do it again.

'He said that, did he?'

'Yes, he did.'

'Oh – Lil.' And the tears welled in his eyes again and spilt onto his cheeks. He put up a hand and brushed them away. 'Thank you,' he said. 'Thank you for tellin' me.' He burst out with a little sound that was half sob and half laugh. To Lily's ears it was a sound of joy and relief, and she had no doubt that she had done the right thing.

For a minute neither of them spoke, then Tom said, his voice grave again, 'What about *her*, Lil – our mother? I bet she didn't ask after me, did she?'

Lily could think of no words to say, but her silence was enough. Tom gave a nod. 'Nah, why do I bother to ask? Why would I even wonder about her? She don't change. She never will.'

Lily shook her head. 'No, I don't reckon she will, Tom.'

'Have you seen her since? Since Father died?'

'No. We didn't part on the best of terms. I'm sorry not to see little Dora though, but it can't be helped. Dora and I – we'll no doubt meet again at some time – when she's older maybe, but for now . . . well, I've got no intention of ever going back.'

He confirmed his understanding with a nod. 'You don't need to. You're an independent woman now. A governess yet.'

'That's right. For three and a half years now.'

She went on then to tell him of her teaching of the Acland girls, and a little of her uneventful life in Little Patten. She

344

finished by telling of how she had received her notice of dismissal.'

He gave a sympathetic shake of his head. 'Aw, that's too bad,' he said. 'So you're going to be out of a job soon.'

'Yes, in just over a week. I'm looking for something else.'

'Any idea where you'll go?'

'No, not yet. Though I have an interview tomorrow with a family in Seston. So wish me luck.'

'Oh, course I do. You'll get something soon, I'm sure of it.' He smiled. 'But even better – maybe you'll meet someone and get married. Then you won't need to worry about governessin' ever again.'

'Oh, yes!' she said, with an ironic laugh, 'that'll be the day.'

His expression remained serious. 'Is there – anyone in your life, Lil? Anyone special?'

Her laugh came again. 'Anyone special? No. No fear of that.'

'Nobody?'

'No, nobody.' She wanted done with the subject.

'I thought there'd surely be somebody by now. You're a tidy-lookin' girl, our Lil. I reckon any chap would be proud to be seen out with you.'

She waved a hand, dismissing his compliment and the subject. 'Well, there's no one,' she said. 'Anyway – enough of all that.'

'What you need to do,' he said, grinning, 'is to get 'itched up to some rich farmer. Can't you arrange that? Can't you find some rich widower farmer with a couple of well-behaved kiddies to go and governess for? Then I can come and work on the farm, can't I?'

She joined in his laugh. 'Oh, that would be fine, all right, but don't hold your breath waiting. In the meantime we've got to live.'

Ascending footsteps sounded on the stairs, and soon a

man and woman with a small boy came into view. Probably like herself and Tom, Lily thought, they had come in to get out of the rain. The newcomers moved among the exhibits with the young father pointing out to the child various items which he thought might be of interest. Lily could not take her eyes off the boy. He wore a wide straw hat and a neat little sailor suit, and had golden curls falling almost to his shoulders. He would be about Georgie's age. Tom, also watching the child, murmured softly, 'He's a handsome little chappie, ain't he, Lil?'

She turned to him as if coming out of a dream. 'Sorry?' she said, and then: 'Yes. Yes, he is.'

The young family did not stay long in the gallery, and were soon making their way back to the stairs. The rain was easing off now and the daylight was fading.

Tom said into the quiet, when the visitors' footsteps had died away, 'Your own little fella, Lil – d'you ever 'ear of 'im?'

She did not know what to say. His words touched her gladness for the afternoon like a bruise. She bore the pain for a second, then said, 'No. No, I don't – but let's not talk about the past, Tom.' She forced a smile. 'We've got enough to think about with the present.'

'Yeh.' He gave a little nod. 'You're right, you're right.'

'I'm glad the people at the farm are nice to you.'

'Oh, ah, they are.'

She smiled, looking him over again. 'And you're looking so sharp with your buttonhole.'

He raised a hand and touched at the rosebud. 'Ah, that's what Cissie give me.'

'Cissie?'

'She's one of the dairymaids there. A right pretty little girl too.

Lily gave a slow nod, smiling. 'Oh, is she?'

'Ah, she is.' He grinned. 'I think she've taken a bit of a shine to me.'

'Oh, well, now . . .'

'She ain't been there long either – not much longer than me. I tell you summat – you ain't seen a prettier girl this side of Weston.' His smile lingered for a few moments longer, then he glanced up at the clock again. 'The darned time's gettin' on, Lil. I'm gunna have to go. I mustn't keep Mr Ballantine waiting.' He picked up his cap and put it on, and got up from the bench. Lily stood up beside him.

'Well,' he said, 'I reckon this is goodbye for now, then.'

'But not for long this time, right?' She reached out and pressed his arm. 'I shan't be much longer at my address in Little Patten, but you can always write to me at Miss Balfour's.'

'I know.'

'Shall I walk with you to the square?'

'No, that's all right – I'll 'ave to get a move on. What you gunna do now?'

'I think I'll just sit here for a while, then I'll go and get my train.'

'Right.' Turning to the window, he looked down onto the cobbled square below. Now that the rain had ceased, the townsfolk were out again and going about their business. 'We're so high up 'ere,' Tom said, and gave a little shudder. 'It gives me the creeps. It's like one of the windows at Wentworth – 'cept this one don't 'ave any bars.'

'Tom – don't.' Lily reached out to him. 'Don't think of such things.'

'I can't 'elp it.' He gave a little shrug. 'I still get nightmares sometimes.'

'Tom – oh, my dear, you must try to forget it. You really must.'

'Yeh – I know, but easier said than done.'

'Of course, but – oh, you must try to put all that behind you. It's all in the past.'

347

'Yeh.' He nodded, turning his back on the window and the view. 'That's what I tell meself.'

'Well, it is. You'll never see the place again.'

'No, that I won't.' He spoke with a quiet note of passion. 'I'd never go back there.'

Standing facing him, she reached up and touched at the flower in his buttonhole, then smoothed down his jacket's lapels. She watched his mouth soften again, then said, 'Shall I see you again soon?'

'Well, yeh – I'll try to come in again next Friday if you like.'

'Yes, that would be fine. At about the same time?'

'Yeh, I'll try to get in for an hour or so. Mr Ballantine comes in regular, he says. I reckon he'll bring me.'

'Good. Good. All right, then. I'll see you next Friday. If anything should come up I'll let you know.'

'Ah, right.' He paused. 'I meant what I said just now. I'm never gunna bring you any more trouble. I won't let you down again, Lil, believe me. I want you to be proud of me.'

'I *am* proud of you.'

They stood facing one another. 'Have you got money?' she asked. As he hesitated, she said, 'You've got to have something. You can't go round without a penny in your pocket.'

'That's all right; I'll be gettin' paid tomorrow.'

'You sure? I've got a little if you need it.'

'No, it's all right, honest.' He looked at her for a moment in silence, then put his hands on her shoulders, bent, and kissed her on the forehead. 'It's been real champion to see you, Lil.'

'Yes. Yes, it's been so good.'

'It's only you and me now, right?'

'Yes. Only you and me.'

'Right.' He looked down at her for a second, then turned and started away. Lily watched him as he moved out of the room and disappeared from her sight, his boots sounding hollow on the polished floor, then fading as he descended the stairs. Turning, she moved to the window and looked down, and a minute later saw him appear in the dimming light, walking away across the square.

Seconds passed, and she heard footfalls ascending the stairs and, turning, saw the curator coming towards her. 'Sorry, miss,' he said apologetically, 'but we're just closing up. Would you mind . . .?'

'No. No, of course not.' With her words she picked up her bag and umbrella and set off towards the stairs.

Chapter Twenty-two

As soon as her teaching duties were over the next day, Saturday, Lily returned to her lodgings to get ready for her journey to Seston, and after a bite to eat and a cup of tea set out for the station. After changing trains at Redbury she reached Seston shortly after three o'clock.

Outside the station she asked for directions to Greenbanks Lane, and after a few minutes' walk along the main street came upon it. Laenar House was fifty yards along, a wide, red-brick dwelling of three storeys with evergreens at the front crowding a lawn that looked to be in need of a scythe. Lily's ring at the front door bell was answered by a rather harassed-looking maid who showed her into the drawing room.

When the maid had gone away to fetch Mr Corelman, Lily looked around her at a room that was absolutely crammed with furniture, with the walls likewise festooned with pictures. There appeared to be an abundance of clothes, too; dresses and coats and other items were cast about, draped over the backs of chairs and dangling from hangers on mirrors.

After a few seconds she moved to a sofa and sat down, but as she did so realised that in the midst of all the muddle a woman was sitting there.

'Oh, excuse me,' Lily said at once. 'I didn't see you.'

The woman, looking to be about forty, sat with a quantity of already knitted wool and bags of yarn and needles about her. She wore what appeared to be several shawls and other layers of clothing, and Lily could hardly wonder at not being at first aware of her presence.

'I hope I'm not disturbing you,' Lily said. 'I'm here to see Mr Corelman.'

The woman leant forward a little, her knitting clasped in her two hands. 'Oh, how d'you do?' She had a nervous, tentative manner about her. 'I'm *Mrs* Corelman.'

'How do you. I'm Miss Clair.'

'Miss Clair? Oh – that's excellent. I'm sure my husband won't keep you long. You're here about the post of governess, aren't you?'

'Yes, I am.'

Mrs Corelman nodded. 'We had a young lady here two days ago, also after the position. I didn't meet her, mind you. I leave all that side of things to Mr Corelman. The present governess is Miss Harrison, but she's only here for a little while longer.' She gestured towards a tea tray on a small table nearby. 'Would you like some tea? There's no more cake, I'm afraid, but I can fetch another cup, and add some hot water.'

'No, thank you, really. That's very kind of you.' Lily paused, then said: 'In Mr Corelman's advert he didn't say how many children there are – just that they are between four and eleven.'

'There are five.'

'Five.'

'They're four, six, eight, nine and eleven. They're lovely children, though they can at times be a little boisterous. That's only to be expected.'

'Five,' Lily said again. Perhaps, she thought, it was no wonder Mr Corelman had neglected to mention in his advert the number of children. 'And what are they, ma'am?' she asked. 'How many boys and girls?'

'Four boys and one girl. Gertrude's the youngest at four, and she's my little treasure. They're all out with Miss

Harrison at the moment, and the dogs. The weather's continuing so nice, they've gone out for a picnic in the field and – '

Her voice broke off abruptly as the door opened and a man's voice said into the room: 'Miss Clair? I can see you now.'

Lily at once got up from her seat. As she did so, Mrs Corelman gave her a half-smile, and murmured, 'Good day to you, dear.'

'Good day to you, ma'am,' Lily replied.

Mr Corelman was waiting in the doorway. As Lily went towards him he said, 'You got here very early. It's only just four o'clock now.' Then, before Lily could reply he added, 'Anyway, I'm Lincoln Corelman. Obviously you're Miss Clair.'

'Yes, sir. How do you do?'

There was no question of anyone shaking hands for at once he was turning and starting away along the hall. 'We'll go into the study,' he said shortly.

He was a tall man, and Lily followed his broad back along the hall and into an untidy room. There he pulled out a chair behind a desk and sat down, at the same time gesturing to an upright chair against the wall. 'Bring that over,' he said, and Lily did as she was bidden. As she settled he leant forward and stretched out his right hand. 'Your references,' he said. 'You did bring them?'

'Oh, yes, sir. Yes, of course.' From her bag Lily brought out the envelope containing her references, one from Miss Elsie, the other from Mr Acland, and handed them to him. She watched as he studied them. He seemed to be somewhere in his mid-forties, and had a wide, florid face, with salt-and-pepper hair and bushy sideburns. He wore a soft-collared shirt, and a dark maroon smoking jacket with one of its decorative buttons hanging by a thread. The hand in which he held Lily's references was huge and red.

When he had finished reading the papers, he gave a nod and said, 'Well, your experience doesn't appear extensive, but it looks satisfactory. I see you offer basic French.'

'Yes, sir.'

'What about music? Do you play the piano or the harmonium?'

'I've had some lessons on the harmonium, sir, but I'm afraid I can't say I'm proficient.'

'That's a pity. Miss Harrison plays the harmonium. She's not proficient either. I must tell you now that I'm also considering another applicant for the post.'

'Yes, Mrs Corelman mentioned it.'

'Oh, she did, did she?' He handed the papers across the desk and Lily put them back in her bag. 'I've got five children here,' he went on. 'You wouldn't be expected to teach my youngest daughter, but you *would* be teaching my four boys. And I'm not sure that your teaching of two namby-pamby female twins is going to be of much use when it comes to my sons. Are you resident where you are right now?'

'No, I'm daily visiting.'

'You'd be resident here – and on call pretty much of the time – as our present governess is. Weekends too. Do you work on weekends in your present position?'

'I have every other Sunday off, and every Saturday afternoon.'

He gave a short laugh. 'My God, you've been spoilt. What hours do you work?'

'Nine until four-thirty.'

'Nine till four-thirty. Well, if I were you young lady, I'd hang on to my present post like grim death. You wouldn't get such an easy ride here.'

'I'm not looking for that, sir – an easy ride, as you call it.'

For a moment he looked slightly surprised at her response, then he said, 'Why is it you're leaving your present position?'

'My pupils are going off to school.'

'And how much longer do you have with them?'

'Just till the end of next week.'

'I see. So your time's running out, isn't it?' He leant back in his chair, linking his hands over his paunch. 'Our governess will be expected to help generally with the children, apart from just giving them their lessons. There is a nurse, but she can't do everything.' He paused. 'Mrs Corelman keeps a good deal to herself. She doesn't take a great part in the running of the household, so I'm the one you'd come to if there was any problem, or anything you needed to know.'

'I understand.'

'I hope you do. Our present governess is leaving to get married. Which comes as a great surprise, for she's the plainest wench you can imagine. Anyway, she's hooked somebody, so she must have something. I hope there's nothing similar on the cards for you.'

'No, sir.'

'Well, that's something in your favour. As regards the salary, I pay thirty-two pounds a year, with full board. I assume that would be acceptable.'

There was no tone of question about the words. Lily had been hoping for more, three or four pounds more, but she nodded and murmured, 'Yes, sir.'

'I would expect total commitment for that, of course.'

Another nod. 'Yes, sir. Of course.'

'And absolute loyalty. And punctuality – no sleeping-in in the mornings.'

Lily shook her head.

'Is that a no?' he said.

'Yes, sir. I mean, yes, it was a no.'

'Fine.' He nodded. 'Well – I can't think of anything else for the moment, so I might as well show you the governess's room.' He got up from his chair and

354

strode around the desk. 'Come this way.'

Lily picked up her bag, and followed him into the hall, where he led the way to the stairs. The stair-carpet was worn and stained, Lily noticed, and the banister rail could have used a duster. Going up past the first landing, they continued on up to the next floor. There he stopped at a door, turned the handle and pushed it open.

'There.'

He stood to one side to allow Lily to see into the room. It was neat and tidy, but extremely small and cramped. A narrow little bed was squeezed up against the wall, with a small chest of drawers and a tiny closet crowding in. On a shelf stood a few books and a little china ornament. The whole room had the most pathetic air about it, and Lily, standing on the threshold, felt like the most insensitive intruder.

'It's not what you might call spacious,' Mr Corelman said, 'but it serves its purpose.' He closed the door and stepped back. 'Well, that's about it. I don't think I've got any more questions. Unless you have some . . .?'

Lily shook her head. 'No. No, I haven't.'

'I assume then that everything's acceptable to you?'

Yet again, depressingly, the thought flashed through her mind that she could not afford to be choosy. 'Yes, sir,' she said.

'Very well. I did tell you, didn't I, that I've interviewed another young woman for the post?'

'Yes, sir, you did.'

'Right. Also, I have another one yet to see. They're pretty thick on the ground, governesses, I've discovered. Anyway, once I've made my decision I'll let you know. Whoever I employ will be required to start in just over three weeks. Next month, Monday the eleventh.' He turned and started towards the stairs. 'Come along.'

When they reached the foot he gestured along the hall

towards the front door. 'We don't stand on ceremony here. Can you see yourself out?'

'Yes, of course, sir.'

'Fine.' He gave a nod and walked away, opening the door to the study, and disappearing inside.

Left alone in the hall, Lily stood for a moment a little bemused, then, collecting her wits and her umbrella, she opened the front door and let herself out.

As she sat on the train taking her away from Seston she was filled with a sense of foreboding. She did not want the post in the Corelman house, though at the same time she was only too aware that there was nothing else on the horizon. In spite of her misgivings, if the offer should come from Mr Corelman, she knew she would have to take it.

Halfway through the week she received a brief letter from Tom. In it he told her that he wouldn't after all be able to get into Corster for their planned meeting that coming Friday, but that he would be there for the one following. In his letter he sounded happy, and from a passing reference he made to his situation, Lily was relieved to perceive that he seemed increasingly content. As for her own employment situation, nothing more had come from her answers to the few advertisements she had responded to. Likewise, there had been nothing so far in response to her own advertisement in the *Gazette* – though, she told herself, in an effort at self-comfort, it was still early days. It may have been early days as regards the classified she had placed, but even so her days were running out. This was her last week in the Acland household, after which she would be unemployed.

The week dragged by, and then on Friday Lily received a letter from Seston. In it Mr Corelman said he was pleased to offer her the position of governess to his children at the salary agreed, and reiterated that she would begin her duties on Monday the eleventh of September. He would write to her nearer the time, he said, to make final arrangements. In the meantime she should write back at once and confirm that she would be there on the day.

With no great heart for the task, she replied to the letter that evening and posted it on the way to Yew Tree House the next morning.

This was her last day with Alice and Rose, and although she had prepared lessons for them, she was not overly surprised when not much work was done. Eventually, though, the moment came when she must say her goodbyes to the two girls. It was a tearful time for all three of them, and there were kisses and embraces all round. In the three and a half years that Lily had been teaching them, she had come to be very fond of them, as they were of her. Even so, she was not prepared for the emotional wrench that the parting brought. Afterwards, with her bags packed with her books and other items, she left the schoolroom for the last time and went down into the hall where Mr and Mrs Acland came to meet her and thank her and wish her well for the future. Mr Acland warmly shook her hand, and Mrs Acland did the same and impulsively planted a kiss on her cheek. When her belongings had been put into the trap there came last hugs and kisses for Alice and Rose, and then she herself was climbing up onto the seat. A minute later, with Mr Acland at the reins, Lily was being driven away, leaving the house for the final time.

At the cottage in Ashway Lane, over her tea and sandwich, Lily spoke to Mrs Thorne of her regret at leaving Alice and Rose, and her uncertainty as to her future. With regard to her promised post at Seston, she was unable to hide her misgivings about it.'

'I'm sure it'll be just fine,' Mrs Thorne said kindly. 'It'll all be new to you, but you'll settle in and get used to it in time.'

'Yes, no doubt you're right,' Lily said, unconvinced.

Glancing at the clock, she remarked that she must think about going to the Villas to pick up the rent. This errand too, she thought, would soon be a thing of the past, for once she was in Seston she would be unable to carry it out. In which case, Miss Elsie would have to make other arrangements.

A few minutes later, carrying her umbrella in acknowledgement of the clouds that were gathering, she set off for the station.

Arriving at the Villas in Brookham Way, she rapped on Mrs Tanner's door. Her knock was answered by a pretty, fair-haired girl of about fourteen, who turned out to be Mrs Tanner's granddaughter, Millie, who had come to spend some time with her grandmother. Lily followed the girl into the kitchen where Mrs Tanner was sitting by the range.

As Millie busied herself getting the tea, Lily and Mrs Tanner dealt with the rent money. Afterwards, Lily remarked that this would probably be the last time she would come to collect it, as she was soon to go off to Seston to live and work. Mrs Tanner expressed regret at the news, but wished her well in her new post. When she asked if a new tenant had been found for the adjoining house, Lily said no, that Miss Balfour was not yet ready to rent it out again.

After a while, Lily put aside her empty cup and got to her feet. It was time to set off for Sherrell, she said. First of all, however, she must look into the unoccupied house next door and check that all was well. After saying her goodbyes to Mrs Tanner and Millie, she let herself out, and went down the path under the laburnum tree and the lowering clouds. She was just passing through the gateway when the rain started to fall. In seconds it was teeming down, and with no time to put up her umbrella, she pushed open the gate of the neighbouring house and started up the path. As she got to the front door she heard someone call her name.

She stopped and turned, and as she did so she saw Joel coming towards her through the rain.

Chapter Twenty-three

Joel came through the open gate as Lily looked at him in astonishment. He stopped before her, one hand raised in a vain attempt to keep the rain from his face. His other held a leather briefcase. Lily stood speechless for a moment, the latchkey in her hand, then she said: 'Joel – what – what are you doing here?'

'I had to see you. I've been waiting for you to come out.'

She stood there while the rain poured down, then, juggling her bag and the key, she lifted her umbrella, opened it and hiked it up over their heads. 'You shouldn't be here,' she said.

'I had to see you,' he said.

She shook her head, frowning. 'This is lunacy.'

They remained standing there on the path.

'I had to see you,' Joel said again. 'I've got to talk to you.'

She said, 'How did you know where I'd be,' then gave a nod as memory came. 'Of course – I told you I came here every fortnight.'

'Can I talk to you?' he said. 'Please, I've got to talk to you.'

The heavy raindrops drummed on the umbrella's black canopy, struck the old flagstones on which they stood, and bounced off. The umbrella was not protection enough; the shoulders of Joel's brown jacket were being darkened by the rain.

'We can't stand out here,' she said. A warning voice in her mind told her she should send him away, while another part of her mind embraced his presence and lifted at the sight of him standing so close. There came a loud crack of thunder, so loud and seeming so close that she flinched. The key to the door was in her hand. Joel, standing before her, was getting wetter by the second.

'We can't stay out here,' she said again. Turning from him, she put the key in the lock. 'Let's go inside for a minute.'

Seconds later she was closing her umbrella and stepping through into the tiny hall, with Joel coming up behind her over the threshold. She stood in the hall while he closed the door on the rain, and in a moment all was silent.

'We'll go into the kitchen,' she said, and led the way the few yards along to the kitchen door and passed through. 'Wait here.'

Stepping on through into the tiny scullery, she stood her dripping umbrella in the old stone sink. When she went back into the kitchen a moment later she found Joel standing beside the table with his hat in his hand.

'D'you mind if I take off my jacket?' he said. 'I'm a bit wet on the shoulders.'

'Of course not.' She put her bag on the table. 'Do you need a towel?'

'No, I'll be all right.' He took off his jacket and draped it over the back of a chair, then ran fingers through his hair. They stood facing one another.

He gazed at her. 'You look as if you're poised for flight,' he said. 'Like a bird.'

She said nothing.

'Can we sit down?'

'Of course.' She avoided his gaze as he pulled out a chair from the table and sat down.

'Are you going to take off your hat?' he said.

'I'm only waiting for the rain to stop, then I must leave again.'

He gestured to the second chair at the table. 'Lily, sit down – please.'

'I – I must check on the house,' she said. 'That's what I came here for – to make sure everything's all right. You get these vagabonds roaming about – these wandering navvies. Some of them would think nothing of coming in and making free with the place.'

'Lily, please . . .'

'No – I must.'

She left him then, sitting at the table, and went into the hall, and from there opened the door into the little front parlour and went inside. All was much as she expected to find it, except that the rug had been rolled back from the hearth, and dust sheets placed around the fireplace. Mr Shad must have been here to sweep the chimney, she realised. Everything else was as it should be.

She left the room and went up to look in the two bedrooms. They looked rather cold and uninviting with the mattresses and pillows bare on the beds, but all was in order. In the front bedroom, the larger of the two, she drew out the drawers of a chest and found them empty apart from neat layers of old newspapers. In a cupboard beside the old bed she found a number of items that Mrs Callinthrop had left behind, forgotten or discarded: a few old sheets and blankets, clean but rather worn; a pair of old shoes, some stockings and an old petticoat. She closed the cupboard door on them. Outside the window the rain dripped from the laburnum tree. The deserted street beyond looked sodden under the dark grey sky. Joel would be waiting still in the kitchen. After a moment she went out of the room and down the narrow stairs.

He was sitting just as she had left him, and he looked around at her as she entered. 'Is everything all right?' he asked.

'Yes, everything's fine.'

'Is the place to be let again soon?'

'I don't know.' She came to a stop at the table. 'Miss Balfour doesn't have any immediate plans for it. She's going to take the opportunity to get a few repairs done – that sort of thing.'

He looked up at her as she stood there. 'Sit down, Lily,' he said softly.

After a moment's hesitation she pulled out the chair and sat. 'As soon as the rain stops we must go,' she said.

'I know. I know. I have to go too. There's someone I have to meet.' He took his watch from his pocket, opened it and looked at it. 'I mustn't be late.' He raised himself slightly from the seat and moved his chair closer to her own. Now they were sitting so near. 'I wish you'd take off your hat,' he said.

She looked at him in silence for a second, then put up her hands and pulled out the pins that were holding her hat in place. She lifted it off, stuck the pins back into it and laid it on the table. Taking off her gloves she put them inside the crown. As she touched at her hair, Joel smiled, pleased with the transformation.

'Ah, yes, that's better.'

She did not know what to say, and looked down at her hands. She was so conscious of his nearness, and aware too of the beating of her heart. 'You shouldn't have come here, Joel,' she said after a while. 'Why did you come?'

'I had to. I told you, I had to. I knew you'd be back here today; you told me you would. And I knew where you'd be – one of the houses had a laburnum tree, you said. So I just came along and waited. It wasn't an impulsive move – I've known for days that I had to do it.'

'You could have written to me.'

'If I had, you might have avoided me.'

She raised her head and looked at him now. 'Why did you come?'

363

He hesitated only a second before replying, then said simply, 'I love you, Lily.'

For a moment her breath caught in her throat. His words were like water to a thirsting man, like bread to one starving. She could live on them; she could drink them, eat them, she could breathe them like the very air. 'Don't,' she said. 'Oh, Joel, don't say such things. You wouldn't if you knew what they do to me.'

'I mean it,' he said. He leant a little closer, moved his hand and laid it on hers as it rested on the table top. She could feel the warmth of his palm on her flesh. A pause, then he said, 'I've got to go away, in just a few days, and I had to come and see you before I go.'

'Joel, please,' she said, withdrawing her hand. 'Where is this leading us? For heaven's sake, you come here out of the blue – and you tell me you love me. But it can't lead anywhere. It can only cause more pain.'

'Listen to me.' He gave an urgent little nod. 'I meant it – when I said I love you. I do. I've never stopped loving you.'

'No.' She shook her head. 'You shouldn't be talking like this. It's too late. Too much has happened. We've made our own lives now.'

'No, it's not too late. Listen to me, Lily. Please. I hurt you. When we met again, over three years ago, after we found one another on the train – I wrote to you, and I hurt you. And I want to tell you how desperately sorry I am. I wanted to tell you this the other day in the square – but I couldn't. It wasn't the right time, or the right place. I've got to tell you now, though.' He paused. 'My letter . . .'

'Yes . . .'

'I was cruel. Oh, God, I was cruel.'

'You did what you had to do,' she said softly.

He frowned. 'I – I was so – shocked. Learning of your child. Oh, Lily – nothing prepared me for that.' He groaned. 'As I told you – I'm my father's son in so many ways. I've had to face up to that. There's an old saying that the fruit never falls far from the tree, and it's so true. I'm my father's son, and I've been carefully taught.'

Lily opened her mouth to answer, but he lifted a hand. 'Please – let me speak for a minute.' He paused then went on, 'He's a strong man, my father. A man of strong will and strong principles. He's very sure of his God, and very sure of his morals and the morals of society – what he sees in others, what he expects from others. It's not always easy, being his son. And with the death of my brother my father invested even more in me, demanded even more of me. My brother and I – we were very different – but I don't think my father was ever aware of it, that difference.' He gazed at her in silence for a moment, then gave a sigh. 'I turned from you, Lily, because of what had happened to you, because of your child. I turned away from you. It was something I could not – could not deal with. I just couldn't. It was completely outside my whole – sphere.'

Silence in the little room, silence broken only by the sounds of the rain.

'I thought I would get over it, in time,' Joel continued into the quiet. 'The parting from you, I mean. I thought I would get over you – forget you. It would only be a matter of time. But it didn't happen. I couldn't get you out of my head – or my heart. You've been there, all the time – and in the end I knew it didn't matter about what had happened in the past. In your past. *You* were all that mattered. *You* had not changed. You were the same person that you always were. The fault was in *me* – my narrowness, my bigotry – my own limitations.' He sighed. 'I know it now. Forgive me, Lily.'

She did not speak.

'I've learnt a lot over these months, these years, and I know how wrong I was. About many things. And I know too, what I feel for you. That you're everything to me.'

A sudden gust of wind rattled the pane and threw the rain at the glass. The two people did not move.

'I said just now,' Joel said, 'that I've got to go away.'

She nodded. 'Where are you going?'

'To the Continent.'

'On business for the stores.'

'Yes. Not directly to the store in Paris, though. I shall be travelling around a bit first. Quite a bit. I have to visit suppliers in Italy, in Milan and Florence, also in Brussels. I'm going to be very busy. It's all – most of it – to do with certain fabrics we import.'

'Expensive fabrics,' she said, taking refuge in banality.

He smiled. 'Oh, yes, very expensive. Italian silks, French organzas, Belgian lace. It's a job my brother used to do. I've been learning it as well as I can – with the help of our man who used to work alongside him. He's away ill, though, so it's come down to me. I shall finish the trip in Paris. My father will be there by then. He's going out on business for the store.'

'Paris,' Lily said. 'The young lady, Simone – Miss Roget – is she in Paris?'

He nodded. I intend to see her while I'm there.' He paused. 'Because – because I know now that I must – *must* end it.'

Lily leant back in the chair, one hand rising to her mouth. 'End it,' she murmured. 'With her, Simone.'

'Yes.' He gave a deep sigh and turned his head towards the window. 'I've got no choice now. I know that. I've come to realise that.' He turned back to her, looking earnestly into her face. 'You've been on my mind so much – and I can't go on as I have. It's *you* I need in my life, Lily – if I'm to be happy. I can't live my life for others – my father – Simone. I can't be that unselfish. I can't make myself into what others want of me. I have my own needs. And I need you.'

She could think of no words to say, and sat in silence, one hand still raised to her mouth, waiting.

He went on after a moment, 'Certain things have happened in our lives – in your life and my life, Lily – things we've allowed to keep us apart. But no more. I'm twenty-eight now, and in some way perhaps I've gained enough sense to see that I've been a fool in some of the things I've done. But I'm stronger too. And it isn't too late for us. I know it's not.'

With a little sigh, Lily said, 'I think perhaps it's always been too late for us.'

'No, don't say that. It isn't too late. I can put things right, and I can make it up to you. And I will, believe me.' He paused. 'Of course – it all depends on one thing.'

She waited, saying nothing.

'The big question, Lily,' he said at last. 'Do you – do you love me?'

'Joel –' she began, 'how can such –?'

'Tell me,' he broke in. 'I have to know. Do you? Do you love me?'

She gazed at him, her brow creased. 'I've never stopped loving you. I don't think I ever could.'

He smiled now, a slow smile that transformed his grave expression. 'That's all I needed to know. I can do anything now.'

He took out his watch and consulted it again. 'Five minutes and I shall have to go.' He slipped it back into his waistcoat pocket and laid his hand over hers. This time she did not draw her hand away. 'The next time we meet,' he said, 'things will be different.'

'Does Simone – love you, Joel?' she said.

He gave a reluctant nod, his expression sorrowful. 'Yes – I believe she does.'

Lily gave a little groan. 'Poor woman. This will break her heart. Joel, are you sure about this?'

'Yes, I am. I've got to do it. I must, or I'll regret it the rest of my life.'

Lily was silent for a moment, then she said, 'Your father, too. You'll have to speak to him.'

'Of course, and I don't mind admitting that I'm dreading it. But – but it must be done.'

'He knows of me, doesn't he? You told me he does.'

'Yes, he does.'

'And – he knows of the child too.'

'Yes.' He was silent for a moment, then he said, 'Do you ever hear anything of him, Lily – the child?'

'No.' She cast her eyes down. 'He has a life with others. He's – someone else's son.' Immediately she had spoken she wanted to say, *But I know where he lives. He's with a family in Happerfell.* But the words remained in her head.

A few moments of silence went by. The rain was easing. 'Your father,' she said, 'how do you think he'll respond? He's got his own ideas for your future.'

Joel hesitated, then said, 'He needs me in the business.' Then he added, a faint note of defiance in his tone, 'I can't let him govern my whole life. My life is my own, and I must live it how I wish. He'll be unhappy, of course, and angry and disappointed, but that must be borne. Anyway, it won't last for ever. I'll make my peace with him. I'm his son, and he loves me – and in time, when he's come to know you, he'll love you as I do.'

Lily gave a little sigh. 'If only people didn't have to get hurt.'

'Yes. I wish that too.'

'I keep thinking of her – the young lady – Simone . . .'

'I know. It's going to be the most dreadful humiliation for her, but – there's no other way.'

Lily realised, dully, that the room was slowly brightening. The rain had ceased and the clouds were clearing.

'When do you leave – for the Continent?' she said.

368

'Monday morning. I'll write to you. Shall I be able to reach you at Sherrell?'

'Only for a few more days. I shall be going to live in Seston – in just over a fortnight. I've found a new position.'

He smiled. 'Oh – I'm glad to hear that. You must be very relieved.'

'There are five children.'

'Five. Are you looking forward to it?'

She paused. 'I shall manage.'

'You don't sound that sure.'

'As I say – I'll manage. I'm determined to succeed.'

'And you will. So – can I write to you there?'

'Yes, of course.' She took a small notebook and a little pencil from her reticule, and on a page wrote the Corelmans' address. 'But don't write to me there before the eleventh of September,' she said as she passed the paper to him. 'That's the day I start my duties.'

'I'll remember.' He slipped the paper into his waistcoat pocket. After a moment, he said, 'I meant to ask about your brother. You said you were hoping to see him.'

'I did see him. He's back from London, thank heaven, and working on a farm at Wilton Ferres. Things are looking so much better. I hope to be seeing him again next Friday, if he can get into Corster.'

'Good. And now you've got your position too, in Seston. Things are definitely looking better.'

'Yes, they are.' She nodded as she spoke, but she could not keep the shade of doubt from her voice.

'Listen,' he said, 'in two months I'll be back again. Try to think of that. It's not going to be easy for me over the next few weeks – I've no doubt about that – but once those weeks are over I'll return, and we shall have the rest of our lives together.' He pressed her hands and gave a sigh. 'And now – now I must go.' He looked over towards the window. 'Thank heaven the rain's stopped at last.' Lily's glance followed his, and as she took in the rain-washed back yard a woodpecker flew down and alighted on the edge of an old earthenware pot that sat on the roof of the small coal bunker. Perched on the pot's broken rim, the bird delicately dipped his scarlet-capped head to drink from the collected rain water, then stretched up his throat to swallow. He did it three, four times, and then, lifting his dramatic wings, flew away.

'He was beautiful,' Joel said.

'Yes, he was.'

Joel's glance left the window and moved over the room, taking in the humble furnishings. 'I shan't forget this place,' he said. He leant forward then and kissed her. The act took her a little by surprise, and made her catch slightly at her breath. His lips were soft upon her mouth, his breath sweet and warm, familiar and yet so new. He drew back a little, then put his hands beneath her arms and lifted her from the chair. In a moment they were standing together by the table. His arms were around her, holding her to him.

'Tell me again that you love me, Lily,' he said. 'Tell me again so that I can keep the words with me. Tell me again.'

'Yes,' she said. 'I love you.'

He pressed a hand to his chest. 'I shall keep those words here. I shall need them to keep me going in the difficult times.'

He picked up his jacket, gave it a little shake, and pulled it on. Looking into a small discoloured glass beside the mantelpiece he ran a hand over his hair and adjusted the knot of his tie. He turned back to her and put his hands on her shoulders. 'I'll write to you soon.'

'Yes.'

'And I'll be back by the end of October. Just – just be waiting for me.'

'I will.' She would count the days.

'Kiss me again . . .'

His face bent to hers and once more she felt his lips pressing on her own, while his arms came around her and held her fast. She could have had the moment last for ever, but then he was drawing back, holding her at arms' length, looking down into her eyes again.

'Goodbye, Lily.'

'Goodbye.'

He released her, took up his hat and case, and went to the door. She was still standing there as she heard his footsteps moving through the hall, the opening and closing of the front door and then the sudden silence of the little house.

Later, at Rowanleigh, Lily told Miss Elsie of the offer of the governess's post from Mr Corelman, and that she was to start work for him on the eleventh of next month. When Miss Elsie asked where she planned to stay till she moved to Seston, Lily said she was keeping on her room in Little Patten. Miss Elsie responded saying she would not hear of such a thing, and that Lily must come and stay at Rowanleigh.

So, the following afternoon Lily made her way to her lodgings in Ashway Lane. It did not take long for her few belongings to be packed up, and after she had said her sad goodbyes to Mrs Thorne, she set off back for Sherell.

At Rowanleigh the hours passed slowly. Lily did her best to start planning some lessons for her first week with the Corelman children, but the task was not easy, for she was working much in the dark; she had not met the children, nor yet, come to that, had any discussion with their father about their lessons. Nevertheless, bearing in mind the forceful nature of Mr Corelman, she must do what she could.

Frequently as she worked, her thoughts moved to Joel. She wondered how he was faring and where he was in the course of his travels. So often she thought back to their meeting in the little empty house. She still found it hard to grasp that it had actually happened, that he had been there and said such things to her. She heard again his words, listened again to the tone of his voice, and saw again the tenderness in his face. And while in one part of her mind she dared not hope for too much, in another part she was ready and eager to accept it all. She must believe him, she told herself. He truly loved her; she was sure of it now. With the thought she felt a little surge of happiness that rose and filled her heart.

Of the fact that Joel had come back into her life, she said nothing to Miss Elsie. There would be a time when she could speak of it, but that time was not yet come.

On Tuesday morning the postman came bearing a letter from Tom:

Dear Lil,

I have fixed it with Mr Ballantine and I can get into Corster next Friday. I'll see you by the square again if you can make it about six-thirty. I'm glad to tell you by the way that things are looking good for me here. They seem very pleased with me, so I'm in real hopes of being kept on. I'm making some nice friends too, and Cissie tells me if I'm good I might get another rose buttonhole. Ha ha.

Your loving brother
Tom

Lily read his letter in a glow of pleasure, and immediately sat down to dash off a few lines in reply, telling him that she would be there to meet him. Also, she wrote that she had at long last found new employment, and was to begin in her new position in a fortnight, on the eleventh, with a family in Seston.

Early on Friday morning she received in the post an envelope that had been addressed to her at Roseberry Cottage in Little Patten, and forwarded on by Mrs Thorne. Mary had brought it up to Lily's room and Lily held it in her hand as she stood at the window looking out onto a green lawn that was still almost sparkling under its fading dew. She had known a certain very positive feeling within her on waking that morning. She had thought of Joel once more, and of his promises, and looked forward with renewed hope in her heart to the time when he would be returning from France. There was also the fact that she was due to meet Tom that evening.

The envelope, which she had just opened, held a smaller envelope addressed to her at the *Gazette*, and was surely a response to her classified advertisement in the newspaper. Whatever might be offered now, however, would be too late, she thought; she was already committed to Mr Corelman.

Briefly she took in the writing on the envelope – a casual, dashed-off hand – then tore open the flap and took out the letter. It was with a shock that struck to her very core, that she began to take in the significance of what was before her:

The Gables
Bourneway
Happerfell
Nr Corster, Wilts
28th August 1871

Dear Miss Clair,

I write in reply to your recent advert in the *Corster Gazette*. I realise that you may well have been inundated with responses, and will therefore perhaps find our proposal less than appealing, but I am drawn to approach you, nevertheless. I will not prevaricate, but must announce at once that we are seeking a governess as a temporary measure, for a few weeks beginning this autumn. This is for our daughter Lavinia, whose regular governess has unfortunately had to leave us. We shall be moving to Scotland later in the year, after which time our daughter will be going to school. In the meantime, however, she is in need of tuition, and we cannot see her suffering boredom, as is wont to be her lot if she is left to her own devices for any length of time. This, then, prompts me to write – on the off-chance that you might similarly find yourself at a loose end, perhaps whilst being between engagements. So, if you are interested in such a temporary post, perhaps you would be good enough to agree to come and see us in Happerfell, and learn a little more about us. We are going away for a couple of weeks shortly, but we would suggest that after our return you come to see us on Tuesday, 19th September at, say, three in the afternoon. Happerfell is a small place, and you are bound to find us. The nearest railway station is Pilching. Please let us know if you are interested, and can attend.

Yours truly,
John Soameson

The hands of the corn exchange clock were just coming up to six-fifteen as Lily walked through the square. It was a warm, balmy evening. The shops and offices were closing now, and many of the clerks, deliverymen and shop assistants were making their way back to their homes for their evening meals and what leisure time remained.

Having paused only to buy a copy of the *Corster Gazette* from a newsvendor, she moved on towards the entrance to the Gardens. On reaching the flagstoned area before the gates, she found a seat near the fountain and sat down.

She looked around for Tom, but he was nowhere in sight. She was early; he would be here soon. As her glance moved back and forth across the square she tried to relax, but she was preoccupied. She could not for long escape thoughts of the letter that had come to her that morning from Mr Soameson in Happerfell.

After reading it she had stood holding it in trembling hands, scarcely able to take in the contents. What should she do about it? she had asked herself. And then the answer had come that she had no option but to reply to it, to thank Mr Soameson for his interest, but tell him that she was already engaged for employment.

But she could not so easily dismiss the implications of the letter. Georgie . . . She had been invited to the house where he lived. She could go into the house where he lived as the Soamesons' son . . . But no, it was madness to think along such lines, she admonished herself. Then she told herself that she was fortunate to have her agreement with Mr Corelman – that agreement that prevented her from even considering the offer contained in the letter from Happerfell.

She must not dwell on the matter; it was too tormenting. From her bag she took the newspaper and scanned the first few pages. There was a piece about the formation of the local government boards that were to be set up throughout the country, and a report of alarming outbreaks of smallpox in Bath and Bristol. There was also a report of a fire at a factory in Redbury. She passed over all of it – nothing of it could touch her – and put the paper back in her bag.

A glance at the clock on the wall of the corn exchange showed the time coming up to seven o'clock. Still no sign of Tom.

She continued to wait while the minutes passed and the light faded, but then at last she gathered up her bag and rose from the bench. It was almost eight o'clock. Tom would not be coming now.

Chapter Twenty-four

The early, mellow days of September passed by as Lily waited to hear some word from Tom, hoping every day for a letter, but there was nothing. Friday came, a week to the day since she had waited for him outside the Corster Victoria Gardens, and still there was no word. She would give it until Monday, she decided, and then if there was still nothing she would write to him at the farm in Wilton Ferres. In the meantime she must get on, for that same coming Monday would see her going to her new position at Seston. Mr Corelman had written to say that he would be occupied in Redbury for most of the day, but would expect her at the house at four in the afternoon.

She did not look forward to it. In her room on the Sunday afternoon, she bent over the bed packing into her box the last few items of linen she had ironed that morning. She felt tense and on edge, as if all the time she was waiting for something to happen. She had no sense of ease as she thought about the move to Seston. No matter how much she tried to comfort herself, the prospect was daunting. But then she told herself not to be foolish, and to have confidence in her ability. It was true that Mr Corelman had not appeared to be the most engaging of employers, but she was conscientious and able, and she would succeed.

Joel, too, was on her mind. He would be well into his travels now, though where he might be she could not try to guess. Was he thinking of her? It would be weeks before they could meet again, but she dared not think of that time, that time that existed in his promise.

She straightened from her task and moved to the window and looked down onto the lawn. The blackbird was picking about among the sparse scattering of dead leaves that lay in the margins of the herbaceous border. Her thoughts were in turmoil, and the cause was not only Joel, or her forthcoming employment, or her brother's failure to meet her; there was also the matter of the letter.

It lay in the top drawer of the small chest near her bed, where it had been for over a week. On several occasions she had taken it out and read it through. She knew it now almost by heart.

The letter offered to her the most wonderful opportunity – the opportunity to see her son. However, although her heart surged at the thought of such a meeting, she knew that it could not happen. *Oh, but to see him again* – but she must not even think of it. No possible good could ever come from such an action. Things had changed, and had changed for ever. For a little while she had been his whole world, his everything, but no more. He had a new life, of which she was no longer a part. There was a woman he knew and loved as his mother, a man he loved as his father – and now, she had learnt from the letter, he had a sister too. His new world was complete.

The blackbird was still there, tossing aside the few dead leaves that Mr Shad's gardening had left behind. How simple life was for some living creatures, she thought. With a sigh she turned away from the window and moved back to the bed. A little more effort and the task was finished, the box was packed. She would be ready to leave the next day.

She stood before the glass in the hall to give a final check on her appearance and to twitch at her hat. Miss Elsie was nearby, waiting to see her off. As Lily lingered she could feel her heart beating in her breast. 'Well,' she said, giving a final touch at her collar, 'it's one o'clock. Time I was away. Mr Shad will be waiting and I mustn't miss my train.'

She turned and started towards the rear of the house, Miss Elsie following. Close to the back door her box and valise stood on the polished tiles, waiting to be picked up by Mr Shad, who would be knocking at any moment to say he was ready. Reaching the door, Lily turned to Miss Elsie and said, a note of bravado in her tone:

'Well – wish me luck.'

'Of course I wish you luck,' Miss Elsie said, 'Though you won't need it.'

'I wish I could be as sure.' Lily hesitated for a moment, then stepped forward and tentatively put her arms around Miss Elsie's shoulders. As she did so she could smell the scent of Miss Elsie's tobacco. 'Goodbye,' she said. 'You've been so kind, so good. I don't know what I would have done without you.'

Miss Elsie shrugged herself out of the embrace, a little embarrassed. 'No, my dear, I've done nothing.'

'Oh, yes,' Lily said. 'I couldn't begin to tell you how much.'

Miss Elsie gave a gruff laugh. 'Oh, get along, Lily, do. Such nonsense. You'll be back here again for a weekend before you know it.'

Footsteps sounded on the tiles as Lily moved to open the door, and Mary came towards them. 'Ah, I just caught you, miss.' She held out an envelope. 'Postman's just been, and left this for you.'

Lily thanked her, took the envelope and looked at the writing on it. It was totally unfamiliar. Inserting her fingertip under the flap she tore it open.

It was a brief letter, with a printed heading.

Queen Victoria Infirmary, Grassinghill, Wiltshire

7th September 1871

Dear Miss Clair,

We are writing with the information that your brother, Mr Thomas Wesley Clair, is at present a patient in the Infirmary at Grassinghill. He has given us your name and address with the request that you, as next of kin, are informed of his whereabouts. He has been here since his admittance on Tuesday, 29th August. If you wish to visit him, please be advised that visiting hours are strictly between 10.30 and 11.30 a.m. and 3 and 4 p.m. No exceptions are made to these rules other than in the most exceptional circumstances. If you should wish to visit outside these hours, please apply to the Matron, Miss J. Lavell.

Yours truly,

J. D. Carpenter

Lily stood with the letter in her hand. Any anxiety about her employment with Mr Corelman had vanished. She looked up to see Miss Elsie looking at her with wide eyes.

'My brother,' Lily said, '– he's ill. He's in the infirmary at Grassinghill.'

'Oh, dear. Do they say what's wrong?'

'No – just that he's a patient. He's been there almost two weeks.'

Miss Elsie frowned. 'What are you going to do?'

Lily did not hesitate. 'I'm going there. I must go there now.'

'What about Mr Corelman? He'll be expecting you.'

'I can't help that. I must go and see Tom.'

As Lily spoke there came a knock at the door. 'I come for your things, miss,' Mr Shad said to Lily. 'We'd best get off, if you're to get your train.'

'Oh – Mr Shad – leave them, leave them.' Lily's hands fluttered in her nervousness. 'I'm not going to Seston yet. I have to get to Grassinghill – as soon as possible.'

'Grassinghill, miss?'

'Yes, the infirmary there. I must get there right away.'

She reached the infirmary at Grassinghill at three-forty. She had had to get a train to Corster, where she had changed for one to Wilton Ferres. From there she had boarded a coach that took her almost to the gates.

The infirmary was situated on the outskirts of the village, in a street with few dwellings. Lily had alighted outside an inn, and walked the fifty yards to the infirmary's entrance. Standing at the open gates she took in the building before her. It was a grim-looking place, of three grey-stone storeys, with not one gracious line in all its expanse. From the courtyard, she made her way to the front entrance, over which she read the sign: *Queen Victoria Infirmary and Workhouse*, then mounted the three steps of the wide porch and pushed open the door.

Inside, she found herself in a cavernous hall, with a stone floor and whitewashed walls. A long corridor led from it. Two nurses in starched white uniforms and wide white caps like flying birds crossed through the hall and disappeared through one of the doors that opened off the corridor. A few yards away an old women knelt scrubbing the stone. The pungent smell of lye was in the air. Over to the right was a desk, behind which sat a porter, writing in a book. Lily went to him and he looked up as she appeared next to him. 'Yes, miss, can I 'elp you?'

Lily already had the letter out of her bag as she began to speak. 'I received this letter,' she said, 'telling me my brother is a patient here. I've come to see him.'

The man said at once, 'You'd best go to the nurses' office, miss. They'll tell you where to go.' He pointed off along the corridor. 'Go to the end room on the left. Somebody'll 'elp you there.'

Lily thanked him and went down the corridor. There were people coming and going in all directions. From beyond one of the open doors she passed, a baby cried, its piercing yells ringing out. In another she saw a group of people surrounding a bed. In a third some women stood before water taps, washing out receptacles. The last room lay just yards further on, and she came to a stop at its slightly open door and knocked on one of the panels.

The door was pulled wide and a woman stood there in a white apron over her grey dress, with a tight-fitting head-dress over her short hair. 'Yes, miss?' Her voice was brisk. 'I'm Sister Weston. Can I help you?'

'I'm sorry to trouble you,' Lily said, 'but I've come to see my brother.' She held out the letter and the woman took it and gave it an appraising glance. 'Ah, yes,' the nurse said, 'Thomas Clair.' She nodded solemnly. 'Very unfortunate.' She handed back the letter, and Lily put it into her bag.

'May I see him?' Lily said.

'Yes, of course.' The woman consulted a watch attached by a fine strap to her bosom and added, 'Though visiting time's nearly over for the afternoon. It finishes at four. You won't have very long with him, I'm afraid. Only a few minutes.'

'Oh, but – I've come such a long way,' Lily said. 'Can't I stay with him a while?'

'I'm sorry, miss.' The woman's tone was a little disapproving. 'We can't change the rules for everybody who comes in. We'd never get anywhere. You can come back tomorrow, of course. Visiting in the morning starts at half-past ten. Then in the afternoon again at three. Come with me. I'll get one of the nurses to take you to him.'

Lily wanted to ask what was the matter with Tom, but the Sister was stepping past her into the corridor. Lily followed her to a door opposite, which the nurse opened. 'Simpkin,' said the Sister, to a nurse who was rolling bandages, 'will you take this young lady to patient Thomas Clair, please.' She turned back to Lily. 'The nurse will take you, but as I said, you won't have long with him.'

As the Sister turned and went back across the corridor into her own office, the nurse put down the bandages and got to her feet. 'Come with me, please,' she said to Lily. 'I'll take you to him.'

Lily followed her along the corridor. 'You'll be his first visitor,' the nurse said to Lily who walked just half a pace behind her right shoulder. 'Not that I think it's bothered him. I don't think he's felt much like seeing people. He's in very low spirits, I'm afraid.'

'I had no idea he was sick,' Lily said. 'Not till I got the letter this morning. I mean – well, he's never ill. He might not look that hardy, but he's strong enough. I mean – he came through scarlet fever all right when he was small, and diphtheria too.'

They had come to a stop outside a small ante-room. The nurse gestured towards the door. 'The ward's through here.'

'What's wrong with him?' Lily said. 'Is it pneumonia or something? No, that can't be – not at this time of year. What is it? I've been reading that the smallpox is all over the country, but it surely can't be that.'

The nurse, one hand on the door handle, said, 'Oh, I thought you knew,' then pushed open the door.

'Knew what?' Lily said. 'I only know he's here.'

The nurse looked a little surprised. 'Well – he's not sick in the sense of having a disease or something like that. Though it's made him poorly enough – his accident.'

'His accident?'

'Yes. He was unconscious for days.'

'Unconscious *for days*?' Lily frowned. 'They tell me he's

382

been here almost a fortnight. Why – why didn't anyone let me know before?'

'I told you, miss,' the nurse said, 'he was senseless. Completely. He didn't come round for days. Matron wouldn't have had any way of knowing who to send for. Still – he's getting better now.'

With her words, the nurse stepped forward. Lily, following, found that they were standing in the entrance to the men's ward. It was a bleak, depressing-looking place, and she was horrified at the thought that Tom was a part of it. The roughly plastered walls were whitewashed, and the tall windows, with their half-lowered blinds, let only the coldest light into the cheerless room. Not only that, but some of the windows had bars.

'The windows,' Lily said. 'They've got *bars*.'

'Yes,' the nurse replied, 'this ward used to be part of the asylum.'

Before Lily's gaze two rows of beds stretched out the length of the long, high-ceilinged room. About half were occupied, all by male patients, and of varying ages, from small boys to very old men. At some of the bedsides sat visitors – single persons or couples, never more than two. Over the scene hung a strange mixture of smells – scents of age mixed with urine, bad flesh and sickness, and all overlaid with the strong smell of disinfectant.

Lily was about to ask what was the nature of her brother's accident, but the nurse was pointing down the row of beds, saying, 'There he is, your brother. Down there on the left.' As she spoke she stepped forward, and Lily, following, caught sight of Tom a little way down, nearer the far end. He was lying with his head propped up on the pillows, his face turned away. Lily and the nurse came at last to the bed, and the nurse halted at its foot.

'You've got a visitor, young man,' the nurse said brightly. Tom turned his head and looked at her, and then a moment later saw Lily standing at her side. At once, as their glances met, his eyes welled up with tears, and Lily moved, lightning-quick, to his bedside. As she did so, the nurse said: 'There – you've got a visitor, Tom. Isn't that lovely?' and then turned and started away.

'Oh, Tom,' Lily said, forcing back a sob that rose in her throat, 'what have you been up to this time?' She attempted to smile, but the effort failed and she could only press her lips together while she tried to hold back her tears. The bedclothes were pulled up to his armpits, his right arm exposed as it lay on top of the rough brown blanket. There was a huge bruise on the left side of his forehead, and a wide, dark scab where the flesh was healing. He was wearing a coarse cotton nightshirt in a pattern of light and dark grey stripes. It was darned at the shoulder, and appeared to have been laundered almost to extinction. She had noticed the same garb on other patients in the room. She reached down and took his hand between her own. He lay looking up at her, saying nothing, while tears ran down his cheeks.

She stood unmoving for a moment, then released his hand, looked around her and pulled over a dilapidated old chair that stood nearby. Bringing it to the side of the bed, she sat down. Fiercely she clasped his hand again, and leant closer to him, looking down into his face. 'Tom, my dear. Oh, Tommo, how glad I am to see you.'

He gave a little nod, and moved his fingers in the grasp of her own.

'I came as soon as I could,' she said. 'Though the nurse tells me I won't be able to stay long. But I can come back, of course.' After a pause she added, 'I should have brought you something – some fruit, maybe, or a little chocolate – but I was in such a hurry to get here. I only just heard today – a letter from somebody here in the infirmary.'

He said nothing to this, but after a moment asked, frowning, 'What day is it, Lil? I loses track.'

'Monday.'

His frown deepened. 'Monday?'

'Monday – the eleventh.'

His frown deepened further as he pondered. 'Monday. The eleventh. That rings a bell. It'll come to me.'

A large bluebottle came humming close, buzzing over the bed. Lily released Tom's hand and flapped at the fly ineffectually. From some distance away in the ward came a sudden screeching wail of distress, piercing and loud, and Lily, her blood chilled, turned and saw an old man sitting up in his bed, his mouth gaping, his arms flailing, while a nurse moved quickly to his side.

'Take no notice,' Tom said, 'it 'appens all the time.' He paused then added dully, 'These windows've got bars.'

'I know. The nurse told me it used to be part of the asylum.'

'Yeh, that's what they said.'

The old man who had been screaming began to quieten down. Lily remained silent for a few moments then said, 'The nurse told me you'd had an accident.'

Tom nodded, his lips compressed into a thin line, then on a little gasp he said in a passionate little whisper, eyes glistening, 'Yeh. Yeh, I did.'

She remained silent, waiting, but he said no more, and she held his hand and looked into his eyes. Against the white of the pillow, his thick dark hair looked black. The skin of his face was richly tanned by the sun. From all around them came the murmur of voices as patients talked with their visitors. The nurses in their starched uniforms came and went. In the next bed an old man lying asleep began to snore, his toothless, drooling mouth gaping to the ceiling. Movement beyond the window to Lily's left briefly drew her eyes, and she saw a couple of men in the yard busy with brooms and shovels. The sight reminded her that the infirmary was adjoined to the workhouse. She turned her glance back to Tom.

He was frowning again, but then his frown cleared. 'Yeh, that's it,' he said. 'Today, Monday, the eleventh. Today you starts in your new position, right? In Seston, right?'

'Ah –' She nodded. 'Fancy you remembering that.'

'Well, of course I remembered. You told me in your letter. It's a big day for you.'

'Yes . . . well . . .'

His frown returned. 'So what you doin' here? You should be at Seston. Did they give you the time off?'

'Well, no, but – as I said – I just heard today – about your being here. I came straightaway.'

'But shouldn't you be at Seston?'

She shrugged, making light of it. 'Don't you worry about that. I'll see Mr Corelman – my employer – and he'll understand. For heaven's sake, Tommo, I had to come and see you.'

'Yeh – but it's not right to take you away from your new job.'

She shook her head. 'I told you, don't you worry about that. Everything'll be fine. It's you we've got to think about.' She paused. 'How are you feeling, Tom? Are you in any pain?'

He blinked once or twice. 'It's not so bad. It's nothing to what it was.'

'I must say, that's a terrible bruise – that wound on your forehead.'

'Oh, that – that don't matter.'

'The nurse said you were senseless when you were brought in.'

'Ah, so they tell me. Not that I remember anything about it.'

He fell silent, and Lily waited. Then all at once came the light ringing tones of a bell. She turned at the sound and saw at the end of the ward a uniformed nurse standing, swinging the bell in her hand. At the signal the patients and their visitors stirred, aware of the coming partings.

'Oh, the visiting time's gone,' Lily said with a groan. 'I've hardly been here five minutes.' She leaned closer to him. 'Oh, Tom, I've got to leave.'

As if he had not heard her words, he muttered in a small, broken voice, 'I fell under the cart, Lil.'

'What? What did you say?'

'Yeh, I tripped and fell – and I went under the cart's wheels. So they told me.'

She drew in her breath. 'Oh. Oh, my God. Oh, Tom.'

'Ah.' He gave a little nod. 'It was well loaded up, too. Fair loaded up to the top. Heavy. It was that little dog – Kipper – the ratcatcher – little varmint – he got between my feet and I went down. I don't remember nothing else.'

'Oh, Tom – my dear –' Lily struggled for words. She bent closer over the bed, clutching his hand. All along the ward the other visitors were getting to their feet, putting back their chairs.

'They brought me 'ere,' Tom said. 'In the small wagon. And the doctor did what he could for me. I'm sure they were very kind. They say I was out cold for days on end. Then I come to – and found this.' He shifted slightly, and then brought from beneath the covers his left arm, what was left of it. Lily looked at the bandaged stump just below his elbow, and at the sight her blood rushed to her brain and she felt for a second that she might faint away. She sucked in her breath in a great gasp and clapped her hands to her mouth, her eyes staring out of their sockets.

'Oh, my God! Oh, God!' The words were blurted out between her fingers. 'Tom! Oh, my dear Tom!' Crying out, she fell forward, her arms reaching out to hold him. She lay there, sobbing, one arm across his body, while his right arm came up and wrapped around her shoulders.

She heard, dimly, as from far off, the sound of the bell ringing again. She raised herself, her tears wet on her cheeks. The last of the other visitors were leaving. In the next bed the old man lay snoring, oblivious. She sat there for long seconds, unable to speak, then, brokenly, she said, 'I've got to go.'

'Yeh, you must.'

'But I'll come back tomorrow,' she said. 'Don't worry. I'll be here in good time.' She could barely force the words out. One part of her wanted to draw her eyes to the dreadful sight of his disfigured arm, but another part resisted the horror. 'I'll be here – I will.'

He nodded and gave her the ghost of a smile. 'Ah.'

'And – and you're not to worry – about anything . . .' She was babbling now, and even as she spoke the words she knew how meaningless they were in the face of his tragedy.

His sad smile flickered again. 'It's done now, Lil. It's finished.'

'What? What d'you mean? Oh, Tom – don't say such things.'

'Nah!' Now he looked scornful at his own words. 'Don't take no notice o' me. I'll be all right. You wait and see. They say I'll be well enough to leave very soon.'

'Oh – that's good news.'

'Ah, right, it is.'

Footsteps sounded nearby, and Lily turned and saw a middle-aged nurse approaching. 'I'm sorry, miss,' the nurse said, coming to a halt a few feet away, 'but visiting time's over. I'm afraid you'll have to go.'

'Yes. Yes.' Lily nodded, then, turning quickly back to Tom, said, 'I'll be back tomorrow. Tell me what I should bring for you. What do you need?'

He shook his head. 'I don't need nothin'. I'll be all right.'

'No, really. Tell me.' She waited. 'Do you need money? I

388

know in the hospital it's nice to be able to buy the odd little thing. Cheers you up.'

He did not reply. She looked at his set face for a second, then picked up her bag. Dipping into it she took out her purse, opened it and tipped a few coins into her palm. 'Here . . .' She took his hand in hers and put the coins into it, closing his fingers over them. 'It's not much, but it'll help. If they come round selling sweeties or some other little treats it'll be a help.'

Behind her the nurse took a step forward. 'I'm sorry, miss, but you'll really have to go now. Sorry . . .'

'Yes,' Lily nodded, then turning back to Tom again, said, 'I've got to go, Tommo, but I'll be back tomorrow morning. I promise I will, without fail.'

He nodded. 'Ah.'

Choking back her tears, she leant down and kissed his sunburnt cheek. 'I love you, Tommo,' she said.

Chapter Twenty-five

Weeping, and with her thoughts and emotions in turmoil, Lily made her way to the Plough and Stars inn to pick up the coach for Wilton Ferres. On reaching it found three other people waiting. Dipping into her bag, she took out her little watch and looked at the time. Just after half-past four. She had been due to meet Mr Corelman thirty minutes ago.

There was no direct route to Seston, and it was almost six-thirty by the time she got there, and a further twenty minutes before she reached the house. Her ring on the doorbell was answered by the same maid whom she had met on her previous visit. The girl recognised her at once, and said fretfully, 'Oh, yes, miss. Come in, miss. The master was expecting you much sooner.'

Entering the house, Lily was shown into the large, cluttered drawing room that she had visited before. In the doorway the maid said, 'The master 'aven't finished his dinner yet, miss, and he won't take kindly to having it disturbed, but I'll go and tell him you're here.' Lily was about to say, *Oh, please, leave it until he's finished eating*, but the maid was gone.

After standing there for a moment Lily sat down on the sofa, at the other end of which Mrs Corelman's knitting was much in evidence. In the glow of the gaslight Lily could see a film of dust on the small table at her elbow, while on the rucked carpet near her feet lay a half-chewed bone. On the skirt of her dark blue dress she saw that there was now a quantity of dog's hair, and she brushed at it ineffectually for a few moments and then gave up with acceptance.

The clock on the heavily draped mantelpiece ticked away into the quiet, and then, after some ten or twelve minutes, the door opened and Mr Corelman stood there, one hand holding a dinner napkin, the other on the handle. At once Lily got to her feet.

'Well! Miss Clair,' he said, 'and what a pleasant surprise this is.' His tone was heavy with sarcasm. He stepped forward into the room, glanced at the clock and said, 'It's almost seven. We were expecting you at four o'clock. At least, that was my understanding. I came back from the office especially for your arrival.'

'I'm dreadfully sorry, sir,' Lily said. 'I started with the best intentions, but – but something came up. I'm so sorry.'

'Something *came up*?' His tone now was somewhat withering. 'Undoubtedly, then, that something was more important than your duties here.'

'Well, sir – I received a message that my brother had been taken to the infirmary. I had to go to him.'

'Oh, you *had* to, had you?'

'Yes, sir.'

He nodded. 'Interesting. Did you not perhaps consider that your first duties were to your position here?'

'I – I had to go to him, sir. He has no one else.'

'He has no one else, eh?' Another little nod. 'Well, I must be frank with you, miss, and make it clear that I do not expect any governess in my employ to go running off to members of her family at the first sign of a headache. Her paramount duties are here – to her pupils – my children. Is that clear?'

'Yes, sir.'

'That's something that's understood, then. I might also tell you that the choice between you and the other applicant was not the easiest one to make. She – a certain Miss Parry

391

from Marlborough – seemed ideal in many ways, and it was very little indeed that swung my decision in your favour. I think you should be aware of that.'

He stood looking at Lily with eyebrows raised, waiting for a response. After a moment she gave a brief nod and said, 'Thank you, sir.'

'Indeed. And I might inform you also that Wiltshire has no shortage of young women looking for the post of governess. As I told you, governesses are not thin on the ground, and a great many of those available are, I daresay, extremely well qualified.'

Lily said nothing to this. She knew well that it was only too true. All she could do was lower her glance from his cold, intimidating eyes. She felt wretched. It was the worst possible start to a period of employment that anyone could have imagined. She knew, too, with a greater sinking of her heart, that there was worse to come.

'The children were anxious to see you,' Mr Corelman continued, 'but –' here he broke off and said wearily, 'Miss Clair, please have the good manners to look at me while I'm speaking to you. I have no intention of addressing myself to the top of your head.'

Obediently she forced herself to look him in the face. He paused for a moment, then resumed:

'Yes – your seeing the children will have to wait for the time being. You'll meet them in the morning – and I trust you won't be up late. We're early risers here.'

Her spirits and her courage plummeting even further, she began, 'Sir – about tomorrow –' but he, frowning deeply, broke in over her, saying:

'Have you eaten, by the way? I hope you haven't come at this hour expecting Cook to start preparing dinner just for you. That's not the way we go on here. Where are your things? In the hall? You'll have to take them up to your room yourself. Wait for someone else to do it for you and you'll wait for ever.' He frowned even more deeply. 'Well? Can I get an answer? You've got a tongue, I presume.'

Lily's wretchedness was now so acute that she felt tears of humiliation stinging her eyes. She fought them back. 'I – I haven't got my things with me, sir. I left them at – '

She got no further. 'You haven't got them with you? My dear Miss Clair – it *was* your understanding that you would begin your duties today, was it not?'

'Yes, indeed, sir. What happened was that when I – '

'What's happened, miss, is that you appear to have forgotten your obligations. How do you expect to be ready to meet your charges tomorrow morning when you – '

Now she broke in, saying quickly, 'I'm so sorry, sir, but I can't be here in the morning.'

'What do you mean, you can't be here in the morning?'

'I – I've got to go back to the infirmary. My brother's expecting me.'

He stared at her, for a moment speechless, then said, 'I don't think you're taking this seriously, miss. You have a duty here, or maybe you've forgotten that.'

'I'm sorry, sir,' she said, 'but I have to go back to the infirmary at Grassinghill. I promised my brother. I can't let him down.'

Mr Corelman stood before her with his eyes slightly narrowed, as if weighing her up. 'You've got a choice, Miss Clair,' he said. 'I want you here tomorrow, up and about by seven at the very latest, helping my children with their dressing and bathing and then with their breakfast. You'll be expected to serve them their porridge – though without sugar, no matter what they might request – and then get started with their lessons. If you're not able to meet these simple demands, then we have nothing more to say to one another.'

Lily remained silent. He waited a moment, and then continued:

'Miss Clair, my dinner is now cold. Do I get an answer or do I not? Are you going to be here in the morning?'

She hesitated for only a moment, then said, 'No, sir. I'm very sorry, sir.'

He paused. 'You won't be here in the morning?'

'No, sir. I'm so sorry, but I promised my brother that I would see him. I can't let him down.'

'You can't?'

She said nothing.

'You mean you won't,' he said.

She drew up her courage. 'No, sir, I won't.'

A momentary pause, then he said evenly, 'Make your choice, Miss Clair – your obligation to this brother of yours, or your obligation to me and my family. And think carefully before you reply.'

'I don't need time to think,' she said, steeling herself to hold his gaze. 'My choice is already made.' She half turned, bent to the sofa and took up her bag. As she straightened again, he said:

'I don't think you realise the gravity of your actions, Miss Clair. If you do as you state are your intentions you'll never come to –'

She did not allow him to finish. 'I absolutely realise the gravity of my actions, sir, and I realise also the gravity of my brother's situation. He is lying in a workhouse infirmary having had his left hand and forearm amputated – and you speak to me of your children not having sugar with their porridge. I suggest you get in touch with your Miss Parry, sir, for I shall not be returning to this house.' She did not hesitate a moment more, but turned and, her heart thudding, started to the door. 'I'll see myself out,' she said.

At Rowanleigh, she wept as she told Miss Elsie of her visit to Tom, but her tears dried as she spoke in anger of her meeting with Mr Corelman. Where he was concerned, her bridges were well and truly burnt, she knew, with the result that she was without employment.

It was gone ten o'clock. The two women were sitting in the drawing room, after Lily had picked at a late supper. The room's French windows looked out over the rear lawn, above which the bats swooped in the night sky.

There was nothing for it, Miss Elsie said, but that she must study the classified advertisements again, and perhaps even place another one in the *Gazette*. It was only a pity, she added, that Lily's first advert had brought no response. She knew nothing of the letter that Lily had in fact received, the letter from Mr Soameson of Happerfell.

Perhaps, though, Lily said to herself, the moment had come to reveal to Miss Elsie a little more. After a moment she heard herself say into the quiet:

'But I *did* have a response to my classified . . .'

'You did?' Miss Elsie looked at her in surprise. 'You didn't mention it.'

'It came on Friday.' Lily took a breath. 'It was from a certain Mr Soameson – in Happerfell.' The words, heavy as lead, hung in the air between them. She could not look Miss Elsie in the face, for surely she would see there a recognition of the name.

Miss Elsie remained silent for a moment, then said, 'And what did he offer – this Mr Soameson? Was it of interest to you?'

'It was a temporary post only.' Lily did her best to make her tone sound casual. 'Just for a few months, until the new year.'

She was well aware that Miss Elsie had no idea that she even knew of Mr Soameson's existence. Miss Elsie could have no inkling that Lily had seen the letter in the ledger, the letter telling her where her son had gone.

Outside, over the silhouetted branches of the rowan tree,

the bats continued to dip and swoop in their search for night-flying insects. Above the darkness of the tree the stars were shining. In the soft glow of the lamps Miss Elsie's expression was unreadable. She said after a moment, 'Well, I think you should put another ad in the paper. I'm sure that if you're patient a little longer you'll find something worthwhile,' and added quickly, 'without bothering to pursue the one in Happerfell.'

It was the kind of response Lily might have expected. She could guess what was going through Miss Elsie's mind. Miss Elsie could not let it be known for a moment that she knew the significance of Mr Soameson's name; never could she give away the part that he had played in Lily's life. For Miss Elsie, the idea that Lily should be considering going to work in the household where her son now lived was unthinkable, a possible move that should at all costs be discouraged.

'Yes,' Lily said, 'I must write to the gentleman and thank him, but send my regrets. I should have done so before this. I'll do it tomorrow, and I'll also put another advertisement in the *Gazette*. Something will turn up.'

Early the next morning she took the letter from the drawer of the chest, then drew up her chair to the small table by the window. As she had said to Miss Elsie, she would write to the gentleman and thank him for his interest, but tell him politely that the position he was offering was not for her. The paper was there, as were the envelopes and the pen and the ink – but the words would not come. After some minutes she put the letter back in the chest. He had said he would be away for two weeks; she would answer it later . . .

Over breakfast, the conversation at once turned to the matter of Lily's trip back to the infirmary, and Miss Elsie asked her what Tom proposed to do once he had been discharged. Lily had no answer to the question, though she had thought long and hard on the matter. Although he was a willing and conscientious worker, he had no special skills, and now, with his disability, even simple labouring work would be beyond him. He had no prospective future that she could foresee.

'I've been giving it some thought,' Miss Elsie said after a few moments. 'The young man's got to have somewhere to go when he leaves the infirmary. Well, there's a little spare room – next to Mr Shad's room – which he can have for a while. He'll be able to make it comfortable, and he's welcome to stay there for a few weeks till his injury is better healed. In return he can help Mr Shad about the place. It can't be indefinitely, of course – but he's welcome to stay for a while, to enable him to try to get things sorted out.'

Lily, feeling almost overwhelmed by the woman's kindness, thanked her over and over. 'I shall tell him this morning,' she said.

When she left the house a little later, she carried in her basket some plums and sweet apples, a large piece of cheese, and a fruit cake baked the day before by Mary – all urged on her by Miss Elsie.

At the station Lily bought her ticket and went onto the platform in plenty of time for her train, but it did not arrive. Then, almost half an hour after it was due, the station master announced through a tinny-sounding loud-hailer that there had been a mishap up the line, and as a result the train had been cancelled. The next one, he said, would be the 9.50, calling at all stations to Redbury. Under her breath, Lily groaned. She would arrive at Grassinghill so late. Tom would surely think that she was not coming.

When, eventually, the train drew in she found a seat between a large, uniformed railway porter and an overweight lady who sat with a caged parrot on her knees. Never had the speed of the train seemed so slow, never had it seemed to spend so long at all the many stations at which it stopped, but at last, after a change at Corster, she found herself at Wilton Ferres. There she made her way onto the street and there joined the small group of people waiting for the coach to Grassinghill. She did not have long to wait, and was soon on board and rattling along on the rough, dusty road.

On her arrival at the infirmary she went straight inside. The clock over the corridor arch showed the time as a quarter past eleven and she sighed with disappointment and frustration. She and Tom would have so little time together. She strode on, and eventually came to the ward and pushed open the door. As on the previous day, there were numerous visitors at the patients' bedsides, but she had eyes only for Tom, and at once her gaze sought and found him, down on the left side of the long room, sitting up in his bed. She went to him at once, and saw his eyes light up as he caught sight of her.

'Tom – my dear!' She clutched at his hand as he reached out for her, and bent and kissed his cheek. 'I'm so sorry to be so late. Oh, I'm so sorry!'

'I'd given you up,' he said. 'I thought you weren't coming.'

'There was no train,' she said, 'not for ages. I was in good time, but – but no train. I was feeling desperate.'

He managed a smile. 'Anyway, you're here now.'

'Yes, I'm here – and I can come back to see you this afternoon.'

'But visitin' time's not till three.'

'That's all right. I'll find something to do. I'll go and get myself a cup of tea or coffee. It won't be for long.' She held the basket up before her. 'Anyway – look, I've brought you a few things: fruit – some nice apples and plums – and some cake and some cheese. Miss Elsie sent it.'

'That's very kind of her.'

'Yes, well – that's the way she is.' There was a small tin

locker beside his bed, and she bent to it and opened the door. 'I'll put it in here, shall I?'

When she had put the things in the locker, she pulled the rickety old chair nearer to the bed and sat down and studied him. He looked somehow smaller. His left arm lay outside on the darned blanket, but the long sleeve of his nightshirt obscured any sight of bandages or flesh. The hollow cuff caused her breath to catch in her throat and she moved her glance away. On the wall above his head there was a stain, as if some dark liquid had been thrown. The striped ticking on his pillow, like the blanket, was darned in several places. Glancing down, she saw that there was a split in the linoleum near her feet.

Her glance moved back to Tom, and she gave him a smile. He did not smile back, but just looked gravely at her. 'By the way,' she said, taking up her bag and dipping in her hand, 'I brought you a little more money.'

'You gave me some yesterday,' he said. 'I don't need any more.'

She counted out coins from her purse. 'Tommo, it's as well you have a little something,' she said. She placed the coins on the locker. 'Will that be all right there?'

'Ah.' He nodded. 'I'll keep an eye on it, don't worry, but you shouldn't be bringing me your money – you need it for yourself.'

'It's not much,' she said. 'I can spare that little bit.' She waited a moment, then asked, 'How are you feeling today?'

'Oh, I'm fine.' He nodded. 'Though better for seein' you. And I shall be goin' out of 'ere very soon. They told me this mornin'. The nurse, she said another day or two and I can leave. Maybe tomorrow even.'

'Oh, that's good news, Tom.'

'Yeh, it is.' He lifted his left arm. 'They say my arm's 'ealing up well, and I could have the bandages off later today.'

'Oh – well – that's wonderful. You're obviously making good progress.'

He smiled back at her now, a thin semblance of a smile. 'Ah, progress. Makin' good progress, right?' Then, after a moment, with a little frown, he said: 'What's gun 'appen to me now, Lil?'

His tone was matter-of-fact, but it wrenched at her heart. Drawing a breath, she was about to tell him of Miss Elsie's offer, but he went on before she could speak:

'They won't keep me on at the farm now. Course they won't. They're nice folk, but they ain't daft. A farmhand with one 'and – he'd be a lot o' use.' He looked down at his left arm. 'I s'pose I should be glad it's my left 'and I lost, but it's a small blessin', I reckon. Course, if I was like you, Lil, with your learnin', I could maybe go into some office and spend my time makin' fair copies – and doing sums and that. But I ain't like you. I never had your brain for that sort of thing.' He gave a little shrug. 'I'll have to think of summat, though. I can't go beggin' in the street.'

'Tom,' Lily said, 'I've got some good news for you.'

'Good news?' He frowned. 'What's that, then?'

'Miss Elsie – she says that when you get out of the infirmary here, you can go and stay for a while at Rowanleigh.'

He paused. 'She said that?'

'Yes, she says there's a little room over the stable you can have. You can do it up a bit, so you'll be comfortable there, and she says if you feel like it you can help Mr Shad, the groom-gardener, about the place. There's always a lot to do.'

She expected him to look pleased, but his frown remained. 'Why would I want to do that?' he said.

'Help Mr Shad?'

'No – go and stay at Rowanleigh.'

'But – but it would be good for you. It'll be somewhere for you to stay – till you get back on your feet.'

'Get back on my feet, eh? I wonder how long that'll take.'

She did not know what to say. In the silence that fell between them, she became aware of the snores of the old man in the next bed.

'Well, of course,' she said, 'Miss Elsie says it can't be indefinite, your stay, but – oh, but Tom, she wants to help you. She really does.'

He gave a nod. 'Ah – well, that's very nice of her. Thank her for me, please.' He looked away. 'I don't want to seem ungrateful, Lil, but I don't want charity. I need to make my own way. Besides, what do I do when those few weeks at Rowanleigh are up? I'll have to look after meself then, won't I?'

She sat in silence for a second, then she said, 'Tom, listen – you come and stay at Miss Elsie's for a short while, and then – and then we'll find some little place for the two of us.'

He smiled now. 'Well, that'd be nice.' Then another frown dispelled the smile. 'But how's that gunna 'appen with you being at Seston?' A thought occurred to him. 'Shouldn't you be there now, right this minute? You were s'posed to be there yesterday, weren't you?'

'Well – yes, I was, but . . .'

'What 'appened? Why ain't you at Seston now?'

'I – I'm not going to work there now. Things have changed.'

His frown deepened. 'Changed? What d'you mean, things 'ave changed?'

'Well – just that. I'm not going to work for Mr Corelman after all.'

'But – why?'

When she did not respond he asked again. 'Why? Why ain't you goin' to work for 'im? You told me it was all settled.'

She shrugged. 'Well – yes – I thought it was, but things have turned out differently.'

'How? In what way? You told me you'd be goin' on to Seston when you left me yesterday. Did you go?'

'Yes, I went.'

'And . . .?'

She did not answer.

'Did you see the gentleman – what d'you say 'is name is?'

'Corelman. Mr Corelman. Yes, I saw him.'

He waited for her to go on. 'So? What 'appened?'

She sighed. 'We – we had a disagreement. Put it like that.'

'A disagreement?'

'Yes.'

'What about? Because you were so late gettin' there.'

'Well – partly that.'

'What else, then?'

'Well – I told him I'd be coming back to see you again today.' She paused. 'He didn't – approve.'

Tom looked surprised. 'Well, of course he didn't. Why did you tell him that?'

'Because it was true. I promised you I'd come back today.'

'I know, but – but it was your new position. It was what you'd been waitin' for.' He shook his head. 'Oh, Lil – what have you done?'

She tried to disregard his concern. 'It doesn't matter,' she said. 'I shall find something else. Mr Corelman's not the only father looking for a governess.'

Tom was tight-lipped. 'Ah, maybe so.' With a little nod, he added, 'It was because o' me. You lost your position because o' me.'

'Oh, Tom, really, I –'

'Yes, you did, and now you've got no job.'

'I told you – I'll find something.'

'Yeh, easier said than done, that is. Are there lots of governessin' jobs goin'?' When she did not answer he added, 'No, you see? You're gunna be in trouble.'

'Well, as a matter of fact, there is one,' she said, 'but it's only for a few weeks.'

'A few weeks is better than nothin'. Where is it?'

She paused. 'Happerfell.'

He nodded. 'Over near Pilching. I s'pose it'd keep you till you find somethin' better.'

'Well – we'll see,' she said, 'but don't fret about me, please. Tom, you're the one we've got to worry about.'

'That's what I don't want you to do – worry about me.'

'Listen,' she said, 'it'll all get sorted out. I told you – we'll get a little place for the two of us. Maybe just a couple of rooms at the beginning, but it'll be a start.'

'Oh, right – and where's the money comin' from to pay for these rooms?'

'Well – there are more jobs going than those for governesses. And jobs that pay a good bit more money, I daresay. I can do anything I set my mind to.'

'Ah, I don't doubt you can.'

'I can go as a shop assistant if I want. Get a job in the Corster boot factory. There's work out there, don't worry.'

'Yeh, but governessing, teaching, that's what you want to do. That's what you're cut out for.'

'We have to play the cards we're dealt, Tom. We can't choose them.'

'Ah, you're right there.' He paused, then said, 'That damn little bell'll be ringin' soon.'

'Oh – yes. Anyway, I told you – I'll be back this afternoon. It's not that long till three o'clock.'

As if cued by their words, there came the sound of the bell, and Lily turned and saw the nurse swinging it as she stood just inside the doorway. 'Here it is,' she said with a sigh. She reached out and pressed Tom's hand, then got up from the chair. 'I'll leave my basket here if that's all right. I'll go out and find a cup of tea, and I'll be back at three. And I promise you this time I won't be late.'

Chapter Twenty-six

Some little way beyond the Plough and Stars Lily found herself in the village centre, where there were a few shops. Just past an ironmonger's she came upon a small teashop, and she went inside and sat at a small table by a window. There were only three other people there. When a young waitress came to her side, Lily asked for some tea and a buttered scone; it would be enough to keep her going until she got back to Sherrell.

In the centre of the yard beyond the window was a small patch of earth in which grew a laburnum tree. Looking at it through the warped glass, she thought of the laburnum at the Villa, and of Joel. Before too long he would be in Paris, and he would be meeting again with the young woman, Simone. She reminded herself then that when he wrote it would be to the house in Seston. He could have no idea that she would not be there. Would Mr Corelman forward any letters for her to Rowanleigh? She could only hope that he would.

For the moment, though, there were more immediate matters to contend with. Not only was she without employment, but she also had the added responsibility of her brother's well-being. She had told him that they would find a place together, and she would be true to her word. It was true what she had said: she did not *have* to be a governess. There was other employment for a single woman. She was young and she was strong, and she could turn her hand to anything. She was not too proud. There were factories in

Corster and in Redbury and in other places around. And domestics were always needed. Whatever she did, her place for the time being was at Tom's side. He needed her now as never before.

After spending almost an hour in the teashop, she paid the waitress and left. Out on the footway she stood for a moment, wondering what to do with the remainder of her time. The day had stayed bright and warm and she was content to be outside in the air. Seeing the spire of a church rising up behind some sycamore trees, she made her way to it and entered the yard. There was a little wood-and-iron bench at the side of the pathway, and she sat down. Before her lay the grave plots, the older ones long forgotten, the stones having succumbed to subsidence over the years and now leaning drunkenly in the grass, moss and lichen growing in the carvings. Two or three newer graves had flowers on them, late roses, some fresh, some wilting.

She continued to sit there while the sun traversed the sky. There was barely a sound other than that from the occasional bird and the gentle breathing rustle of the fading leaves of a beech that grew beside the wall. A robin flew down and perched on the top of a little stone angel, red breast flaming, and Lily looked at its saucy, perfect little form and felt a momentary lifting of her spirit. It did not last, however. Even before the bird had abruptly taken off and soared away over the stones, she was already thinking again of the problems that lay ahead.

So, Tom was likely to be discharged from the infirmary over the next day or two. He had expressed himself loath to accept Miss Elsie's offer of help, but until such time as Lily could provide a home for him he would have no choice but to accept it, and be grateful. In which case she must make everything ready for him at Rowanleigh. The room over the stable would need attention, and she must get busy on it, starting today, when she returned to Sherrell.

405

And afterwards? Then she would look about for employment, for she would have to earn enough to keep the two of them until he was out of the woods. *Out of the woods.* The phrase rang in her mind. When would that be? He had lost a hand. And there could be no mending of such a tragedy.

The breeze had strengthened a little. She could hear it in the leaves of the yew and feel it on her cheeks. Looking up at the clock on the face of the church tower, she saw that it had come to a quarter to three. Time to go.

She reached the infirmary with ten minutes to spare, and found that a number of people were already gathered in the courtyard, waiting for admission. She took her place in the line and stood patiently as the minutes ticked by. Two nurses in starched uniforms crossed the cobbles and entered the building, after which a horse-drawn ambulance rattled to a halt before the steps. Two porters appeared and took a laden stretcher from the vehicle and carried it inside. A carriage pulled in, and two distinguished-looking gentlemen alighted, carrying black leather bags. As they vanished into the building two workhouse boys appeared and cleared away some manure that one of the horses had left. More people came to join those already waiting. Then, almost on the stroke of three a stout man in a dark tunic came out and importantly gestured to the crowd. It was the signal to go in, and at once the people surged towards the open doors.

Inside the building Lily did not hesitate, and within a minute or two she was entering the men's ward, and craning her neck to see past the people before her, to catch a first glimpse of Tom.

She could not see him.

Three or four yards into the ward she came to a stop and stood looking down the left-hand row of beds. Tom was not there. Her eyes swung to the right-hand side of the ward, taking in the other occupants; perhaps he had been moved to a different bed. No. He was not there.

After a moment she started down the ward, while on either side the visitors drew up chairs, kisses were exchanged, and the murmur of the chatter grew. As if she could not trust her eyes to have seen at a distance, she walked to the foot of the bed in which she had left Tom just hours before. It lay empty, its mattress rolled up at the head, the pillows stacked. The fleeting, desperate notion came into her mind that perhaps she had come into the wrong ward, but of course she had not; everything else was as she recalled. There was the stain on the wall above the bed, there was the split in the linoleum, and in the adjacent bed the old man still lay.

She turned, looking about her, and saw a nurse approaching. At once she moved towards her. 'Excuse me – please . . .'

'Yes, miss?'

'My brother,' Lily said, and gestured towards the empty bed. 'He was here – there in the bed. I was with him this morning.'

The nurse, a stocky woman in her late thirties, said at once, 'Ah, yes, the young man – Thomas Clair. He's gone, miss, I'm afraid. He left.'

'He – he left?' Lily frowned. 'What – what do you mean – he left?'

'Just that. He left, miss.'

'But – but he can't have. I was here – just this morning.' Lily gestured to the bed. 'I was sitting there, at his bedside. He was in the bed. I brought him some fruit and some cake. I told him I'd be back for afternoon visiting. He knew that. He was expecting me.' This was insane. How could he have gone? She stood there shaking her head, as if by the very fact of denying it she could make it as she wished. 'But – but where – where did he go?' she said.

'I don't know, miss, I'm sure.'

As the nurse finished speaking, Lily stepped beside the bed and opened the locker. It was now empty. 'I put some apples in there,' she said, 'and some plums, and a couple of little packages holding cheese and cake. My basket, too. I left that here. Everything's gone. It's all gone.'

'I wasn't here when he left, miss. It was another nurse he spoke to. Nurse Hesketh.'

'Is she about?' Lily asked quickly. 'May I speak to her?'

'I'm afraid you can't, miss. She was called away a little while ago, to go to the isolation hospital at Biller. There've been more smallpox cases in Corster and she's gone off to help.' The nurse gave a little shrug. 'Though I doubt as she could tell you much more, miss. By all accounts the young man didn't hang about once he'd made up his mind. He went about half-past-twelve. Nurse Hesketh said there was no stopping him.' She gestured to the empty locker. 'His locker was all cleared after he went, of course.'

Lily said, helplessly, repeating herself, 'But – but I was with him. I left him at half-past-eleven. I left him in bed here.'

'Perhaps you'd like to have a word with Sister, miss,' the nurse said. 'If Nurse Hesketh knew anything she'd have told Sister.' She gestured up the ward towards the entrance. 'She'll be in her office, just on the right outside there. Sister James. She might be able to tell you a bit more. You go and see Sister.' With that she gave Lily a tentative smile, and moved past, continuing on her way.

Lily watched her go, then turned and made her way to the Sister's office, where she tapped on the door. There was a call of 'Come in,' and Lily turned the handle and pushed open the door.

Sister James was seated at a desk with some papers before her. She smiled at Lily as she entered, but frowned at the same time, giving the message that she had no time to waste. 'Yes, can I help you?' she said.

'One of the nurses,' Lily said, 'said I should come and see you. It's about my brother.'

'Your brother?'

'Yes, he was a patient here. Thomas Clair.'

'Clair – ah, yes.' The nurse nodded. 'Thomas Clair. Very sad business. Amputation of the left hand. You say you're his sister.'

'Yes, I am.'

'Well, I must tell you that he was in a very bad way when he came in. An accident with him falling under a cart, so we were told by the men who brought him. He was badly concussed and totally unconscious. What was worse, his left hand and wrist had been so completely crushed that there was nothing for it but to amputate – and without delay, before mortification set in. I'm afraid there was no way of saving it. I was there with the young man, Thomas, when he came round later – when he discovered what had been done to him.' She gave a little shake of her head, as if dispelling the memory.

Lily, who had listened to the account with mounting horror, felt tears welling in her eyes. After a few moments, when she had gained a little control, she said, 'I came to visit him this morning, and then came back this afternoon to see him again, but – but he has gone.'

The nurse's frown deepened. 'Oh, dear. And you didn't know he was going?'

'I had no idea.' Lily shook her head. 'When I saw him this morning he had no intention of leaving – I'm sure of that. He knew I was coming back.'

The nurse sighed. 'I'm very sorry for you, miss, I'm sure. All I know is that he left. We couldn't stop him. I spoke to him myself, and tried to persuade him to stay on a while, but he was that set on going. He still had his bandage on.'

Lily said, her throat tight, 'I brought him some cake, and some cheese.'

409

'Yes, he left it all behind,' the nurse said. 'When we cleared out his locker it was all there. Did you want it?'

'No.'

'There was a basket too.' As the woman spoke she leant down to the side of her desk and lifted up Lily's basket. 'This is yours, is it, miss?'

Lily nodded. 'Yes.'

The nurse placed the basket on the desk, and Lily took it up. 'Did he say anything to you,' Lily asked, 'or to anyone else – about where he was going?'

'Not to me. And Nurse Hesketh said he had very little to say.'

Lily put a hand to her brow. 'I just – don't understand it. Where could he have gone? He's got no money – only a couple of shillings that I gave him. He's got nowhere to go. He's got no friends. *I'm* all he's got.' She added plaintively, 'I don't suppose he left any message for me?'

'Not with me, miss. And I'm afraid I can't ask Nurse Hesketh anything further about him as she's had to go off. Which leaves me shorthanded here. This smallpox – it's absolutely dreadful. People are going down like ninepins.' She sighed and shook her head. 'I'm sorry I can't help you, miss.'

Lily nodded her thanks and stood in silence, helpless. There was nothing more to say, and she could think of no further questions. 'Well,' she whispered at last, with a little nod, 'I thank you for your time.'

'I'm sure he'll be in touch with you,' the nurse said. 'He will, I'm sure he will.'

'Yes.' Lily summoned up a sad little smile, then, thanking the woman again, she turned and left the room.

Tom's letter came to Lily at Rowanleigh three days later. Since returning from Grassinghill she had moped about the house with little purpose and not the vaguest notion of

410

what her immediate future might hold. She had had long conversations with Miss Elsie, but, in spite of all the sympathy and understanding she received she had felt no wiser at the end of them. She pondered on what possible work she could obtain, work that would keep not only herself, but Tom also. For many hours over the days she worked in the little spare room above the stable, washing and scrubbing, and all in the half-held belief that Tom would, after all, come there to stay.

His letter was written on the cheapest notepaper and dated the day after he had left the hospital. It gave no address, but simply said:

13th September

My dearest Lil,

It grieves me to have done to you what I did, but I didn't feel I had any choice. I can't come and stay alongside you and Miss Balfour, no matter how kind she is. There's no future to it, you know that, and I've got to stand on my own two feet, or not at all. And the way you were talking you were giving up everything for me, so I reckoned, and I can't let you do that. You already lost your job at Seston because of me, and it can't happen again. I can't have you giving up your work on my account. Your work is as a governess, a teacher, and you can't be stuck in some factory cutting soles for shoes or standing at some vat with your hands dyed black in order to keep me in bread and potatoes. There was nothing for it, Lil, I had to go. Knowing you were coming back in the afternoon, and being a coward, I couldn't say all this to your face. So I got out.

Don't worry about me. I shall find a way to sort things out and make a life for myself. My arm is healing well. It's like I still feels as if my hand is there, but of course it's not. I'll get used to that. There's plenty of

411

soldiers worse off than me, and that's the truth.

Now I got something to say: Take that job at Happerfell, Lil. It might only be for a few weeks, but in the meantime you can look around for something more lasting, and in the end you'll find what you want.

Like I said, don't worry about me. I still got a little of the money you gave me, and I'm not a big spender. I know I got some strokes against me, but I shall make out, depend on it. I shall write to you again soon.

Your loving and devoted brother

Thomas

In her room, sitting on the side of the bed, she folded up the letter. She had no way now of helping him. She had no idea even where he was, how he was living, how he was managing for his next meal or even for somewhere to sleep.

And what of herself? Take the job at Happerfell, Tom had said – but Tom did not know everything. He did not know that the house at Happerfell was the home of her son.

At the thought, her eyes strayed to the chest of drawers in which lay Mr Soameson's letter. She had put off replying to it, but there was still time to do so – still time to write and say that she would be there on Tuesday at the appointed time.

And why should she not? It was true, of course, that taking such a post would give her the chance to look about for something more permanent, which was what she needed, but – and the thought made her heart beat a little faster – it would also give her the chance to see the child.

She got up from the bed, opened the drawer and took out the letter. Then, sitting at the little table, she prepared paper and pen and began to write.

PART FOUR

Chapter Twenty-seven

There was a cool breeze blowing as Lily alighted from the train at Pilching. The signs of autumn were in evidence everywhere now, felt in the keener winds and seen in the yellowing of the leaves of the trees that overhung the far edge of the platform. That morning she had received from Mr Soameson a hurried reply to her letter, saying simply that he would expect her at the house that Tuesday afternoon, the nineteenth, at three or thereabouts.

She found that certain details of the station were familiar to her as she moved along the platform, recognising them from her previous visit. Emerging from the station she found a fly waiting near the entrance, and soon she was seated in the carriage and they were jogging along the road. Happerfell was the next village, and once there the driver made for Bourne Way with no hesitation, and then he was tapping on the side of the carriage with his whip and calling out, 'The Gables, miss. We be 'ere at The Gables.'

Lily got out and paid him, and minutes later the cab was starting away again, leaving her standing in front of the house, looking at it across the lawn. The leaves of the two oaks were turning brown and the summer flowers in the borders had gone. When she had stood here before, she had felt like an intruder, and fearful every moment of discovery. Now she was here by invitation.

From her reticule she took out her mother's little watch, opened it and checked the time. Twenty minutes to three.

She was early, but better early than late. She put the watch back in her bag and pushed open the wrought iron gate. Then, closing it carefully behind her, and aware of her every action, she moved up the flagstoned pathway and up the steps to the front door.

A maid with red hair and a pale skin answered her ring on the bell. Lily gave her name and was asked to enter, and found herself in a wide, green-carpeted hall. The maid took her coat and umbrella, then said, 'Come this way, if you please, miss,' and showed her into a room on the left. 'Please sit down, miss,' she said, 'and I'll tell the master you're here.'

While the maid withdrew, Lily took a seat on a brown velvet-covered sofa and looked around her. The room was spacious, looked comfortably furnished, but though having its share of elegance, was in no way opulent. With its soft earth colours, there was a casual harmony of hues there. Against the coolness of autumn a bright, flickering fire burnt in the grate. Oil paintings hung on the walls: portraits, still lifes, and scenes of Venetian canals. On the closed lid of the piano stood a bowl of white roses, and there was another on the small table before the sofa. A small clock ticked into the quiet.

A few minutes passed, and then the door opened and a man came into the room.

'Ah, Miss Clair.' He came forward, and Lily rose and shook his outstretched hand. 'You made very good time,' he said. He spoke in an unfamiliar accent, pleasantly musical, which she realised after a moment or two was Scottish; she had heard such a brogue once before in her life. As he released her hand he added, 'I'm John Soameson.' Then, gesturing back to the sofa: 'Please – sit down again. My wife will be along shortly.'

As Lily sat back on the sofa the man took the armchair nearby. He appeared to be in his late forties, and had a tall,

416

angular frame. His thick hair was greying, as was the fine moustache that ran the width of his mouth. His features were sharp, as were the grey eyes that gazed at her through fine-rimmed spectacles. He wore a casual tweed jacket with a cravat and a plain waistcoat and brown gabardine trousers.

Sitting back in his chair, he asked a few questions about her journey from Sherrell, then said, 'I don't mind telling you that I'm very pleased to see you, Miss Clair. Though I must say that when we didn't hear back from you before we went away we thought it a lost cause. We assumed that the position was of no interest to you.'

Lily apologised for not writing back sooner, then went on to add that for a time she had been uncertain of her own situation and in no position to commit herself. 'I just didn't know where I was,' she said. It was not the whole truth, but she hoped it would suffice.

'I understand,' he said, 'and anyway, as I say, I'm glad you're here. You brought your testimonials, did you?'

'Yes, sir.' From her bag she brought out her references and gave them to him. After studying them he refolded them and handed them back. 'Excellent, excellent,' he said, then without further pause got up from his chair. 'You stay where you are, Miss Clair. Mrs Soameson will have to meet you. I'll just go and fetch her.'

He left the room then, leaving the door open, and Lily sat alone with the ticking of the clock and the flickering of the fire. The seconds slipped by, and then into the quiet came from the hall the sound of a voice, a small child's voice. Just a few words were spoken, uttered in a high, piping tone. She could not make out what they were, but she was sure who had spoken them. Immediately afterwards came another voice, a young woman's, saying, 'Come along now, dear, you know it's time for your nap.' Then the child's voice came once more, a few words in a little tone of

417

protest, joined again by the woman's, and then the two voices faded away.

A few more minutes passed and there came the sound of movement at the door. Lily got up at once.

'Here's my wife to meet you,' Mr Soameson said, and as he made brief introductions, Mrs Soameson shook Lily's hand and murmured a greeting. Her own accent was English. She was a tall woman, large-boned, with strong features. She wore a light grey dress with a small lace cap set on dark brown hair that was fashioned into coils at either side of her head. While not handsome, there was no doubt that she was a striking-looking woman.

Mrs Soameson urged Lily to sit, and as Lily sat once more, the man and woman took seats in nearby armchairs. Now it was Mrs Soameson's wish to examine Lily's references, and Lily duly handed them over. Mrs Soameson studied them and passed them back a couple of minutes later with an expression of satisfaction.

As Lily put the papers back in her bag, Mr Soameson asked her what newspapers she read. And did she read novels? Which authors? Charles Dickens and Anthony Trollope? Or perhaps she liked tales a little more sensational, such as those by Wilkie Collins and Mrs Henry Wood. Mrs Soameson questioned her too, asking of her tastes in music – did Miss Clair care for the piano works of Chopin? Or perhaps she liked the music hall – which certainly had its place. And what of the theatre and the opera, and the popular painters of the day?

Lily answered as best she could. She often read the *Morning Post*, she said, and as for the novels of Dickens and Trollope, she had read several of them. She had heard piano works by Chopin, and Scarlatti too, on the occasion of a concert given at the Corster town hall, and it was at the theatre in Corster that she had seen Shakespeare's *Twelfth Night* – and wonderful it was. As for the opera, a touring

418

company had come to Corster and she and Miss Balfour had gone to see their production of Verdi's *La Traviata*, which was most moving and beautiful. Of the popular painters of the day, she said, she liked best the paintings of Holman Hunt and Arthur Hughes, whose work she had seen in Bath while on a visit with Mr and Mrs Acland and their daughters.

After going on to ask a few further questions, mainly about the level of Lily's drawing and watercolour talents and her command of French, Mr Soameson said, 'As I made clear to you, Miss Clair, we would require your services only for a limited period. We're leaving in December to go back to Edinburgh, but we need a governess for our daughter Lavinia until that time. Lavinia's teacher, Miss Clemence, has had to leave us – due to a crisis in her family – and will not be returning, sad to say. As I wrote to you, we can't have our girl without tuition all this time, so – if the right person is willing to step into Miss Clemence's shoes for that period it will suit us very well. Do you think you might be that person, Miss Clair?'

'Well – I certainly hope so, sir.'

Mrs Soameson spoke at this. 'Lavinia is eight – coming up to nine in February. She's an intelligent child, but she needs to be kept occupied. When we get to Edinburgh she'll be going to school.'

'We have a son too,' Mr Soameson said. 'Did I mention that?'

'No, sir, you didn't.'

'Yes – Joshua. He's four and a half now. He's a sharp little fellow – and not at all like his sister. Lavinia was born in Edinburgh, but Joshie's a little Sassenach. He'll be ready for some schooling himself before too long.'

Hearing the boy's name, it rang in Lily's mind, and she seemed to hear again the sound of the child's voice as it had echoed from the hall some minutes earlier. Then she became aware that Mrs Soameson was rising to her feet.

'Don't get up, Miss Clair,' Mrs Soameson said, but Lily stood anyway, while Mrs Soameson continued, 'I must go. I have much to do. My husband will deal with any other matters.' Then she asked, bluntly, 'Are you agreeable to coming to teach our daughter?'

'Oh, yes, ma'am. I shall be very pleased to.'

Mrs Soameson smiled. 'Good, that's excellent. When you've finished your business discussions with my husband I'll show you your room. I hope also that you'll be able to meet Lavinia.'

With these words, Mrs Soameson disappeared into the hall.

'Now, Miss Clair,' Mr Soameson said as Lily resumed her seat on the sofa, 'when do you think you could start?'

'Well – as soon as you like, sir. This week if you wish.'

'Yes, indeed.' He looked pleased. 'What about Thursday – would that be too soon?'

'No, sir. I can be ready by then.'

'Excellent. Then Thursday will suit us very well. I shall be in the town, but my wife will be here to receive you.' He nodded. 'Right – and now we must talk about your fee. I think we shall require you to be with us some three months – possibly towards the latter part of December. In which case I would offer you the monthly sum of three pounds fifteen shillings. Would that be acceptable?'

'Yes, sir. Thank you.'

'You will also, of course, have your board and lodging. Miss Clemence had every other Sunday off, and also occasional Saturday afternoons. Are you agreeable to that?'

'Yes, sir.'

'So I take it that you accept?'

'Indeed, sir, yes. Thank you.'

'Very good. Then we shall depend on you, Miss Clair. Can we do that?'

'Yes, indeed, sir.'

'Good. That's grand.' He nodded and faintly smiled. 'Now – as to the time of your arrival here. There's a train from Corster at eleven-fifteen, that gets into Pilching just before twelve. D'you think you could manage that?'

'Yes, sir.'

'Fine. We'll have the trap at the station to meet you.' He pressed his hands together. 'I don't think I've left anything out. If you have any questions please feel at liberty to ask them.'

Lily could do little but give a shake of her head. 'No, sir . . .'

'Very good.' He got up from his seat. 'If you come with me I'll take you to my wife who'll show you your room – and perhaps also you'll meet our daughter.'

Lily rose and, picking up her bag, followed him out into the hall, then along to a room on the left, where he pushed open the door. 'We've finished our business, Edith,' Lily heard him say, 'and Miss Clair will be here on Thursday morning.'

He stepped back into the hall, reached out and shook Lily's hand. 'Goodbye, Miss Clair. We shall look forward to seeing you on Thursday.'

'Thank you, sir. Goodbye, sir.'

As he went back along the hall, Mrs Soameson came out of the room. 'Well, all is settled, then,' she said. 'Good. If you come with me, I'll show you to your room.'

Lily followed her up the stairs to the second floor, the top, where she was led to a room opening off a wide landing. Mrs Soameson pushed open the door and ushered Lily in before her. Lily entered and stood looking around her. Fairly spacious, the room was furnished with the usual bed, chest, wardrobe, upright chair and small table. There was also a comfortable-looking little armchair, while on the bed was laid a colourful counterpane. There were shelves above the chest, and a pot with a geranium on the window sill. The window looked out over the back yard and the kitchen garden.

'I think you'll find it adequate,' Mrs Soameson said. 'Miss Clemence was comfortable enough.'

'Oh, yes, it'll suit me fine, ma'am,' Lily said.

'Very good.' Mrs Soameson stepped back to the door. 'Now – you must meet Lavinia.' She led the way out and across the landing to another door. 'She's in here. Come in.'

Lily followed the woman in, and saw at once that they were in a schoolroom. About the size of the room she had just viewed, it held numerous cupboards and shelves, a table and chair, an easel with a small blackboard, and, facing it, a child's desk. Seated at the desk was a small girl who looked up with curiosity as Mrs Soameson and Lily entered. Mrs Soameson, smiling at her, said, 'Say hello to Miss Clair, Lavinia. She's going to be your teacher till we go back home.'

At the words the girl put down her pencil and got up from her chair. She was a slim child, and rather small for her age. Her mouse-brown hair was drawn back in bunches and tied with yellow ribbons behind her ears. She looked at Lily with a shy half-smile, hardly raising her eyes. Lily smiled back.

'This is Lavinia,' Mrs Soameson said, smiling between Lily and the child, and Lily said, 'Hello, Lavinia, how are you today?'

The girl gave a little nod and murmured, 'Very well, thank you, miss.'

'She's shy,' Mrs Soameson said, 'but she'll soon relax when she gets to know you. I'm afraid she's been a little lost without Miss Clemence – haven't you, dear? She likes to be kept busy.' She stepped closer to the desk and looked down at the paper on which the child had been drawing.

'What is it you're doing, dear? Are you working on your book?'

'Yes, Mama.' Lavinia picked up the paper and held it for her mother to see. On it were some quite well-drawn rabbits with daises and buttercups around them. 'Lavinia's writing a story, and drawing the pictures for it,' Mrs Soameson said, passing it to Lily. Then added to the child, 'Isn't that right, dear?'

'Yes, Mama.'

'I can see you have talent,' Lily said, looking admiringly at the picture. 'I look forward to seeing more of your work.'

She handed the drawing back to the girl, and Mrs Soameson reached out and gently touched the girl's head. 'Right, dear, you get on with your work for a while longer while I see Miss Clair out. Miss Clair's coming back on Thursday.'

As the child took her seat behind the desk again, Mrs Soameson turned to the open door. Lily, following, said, 'Goodbye, Lavinia,' and the child softly echoed her farewell.

Out on the landing Mrs Soameson said, lowering her voice a little, 'You'll meet Joshua tomorrow.' She gestured to a closed door across the landing. 'He'll be asleep at the moment.' She turned then towards the stairs and Lily followed her down.

When the pair reached the hall, Mrs Soameson looked at the long-case clock that stood at the foot of the stairs and said, 'If you leave now you'll be in time to catch the 4.50 for Corster. Would that suit you? Mr Beeching will drive you into Pilching.'

'That would be most kind,' Lily said. 'Though I'm perfectly happy to walk.'

'It won't be necessary. Mr Soameson's already sent to have the trap ready. Did you have an umbrella?'

'Yes, I did.'

'Right, if you'd like to get it, and your coat, we'll go and find Mr Beeching.'

As they emerged into the yard a minute or two later Lily saw a mare and trap standing on the flags. A middle-aged man stood stroking the horse's mane, and cooing to her in a soft voice. As Lily and Mrs Soameson approached he turned to them with a deferential nod and touched at his cap. 'Ma'am.' He was a man of middle height, broad-shouldered and lean.

'This is Miss Clair, Samuel,' Mrs Soameson said. 'She's going to be with us for the next few weeks.' The man nodded to Lily and murmured, 'How d'ye do, miss,' to which Lily murmured a 'How do you do' in return. His Scottish accent was much broader than that of Mr Soameson.

'Mr Beeching's been with us for many years,' Mrs Soameson said. 'He came down from Edinburgh with us – and I know he's looking forward to getting back. He'll see you catch your train, and he'll be waiting for you on Thursday when you come back.' She flashed a brief smile at Lily, showing her large teeth. 'I'll wish you good day, Miss Clair.'

'Good day, ma'am, and thank you again.'

As Mrs Soameson returned towards the house, Mr Beeching stepped to the back of the trap and held out a broad, weathered hand to Lily. 'If ye please, miss . . .' and helped her up. Then, a moment or two later, he was leading the horse down the drive. Outside on the road, when he had closed the gates behind him, he climbed up into his seat and they set off.

He spoke little as they jogged along, beyond making a few observations on the weather and the state of the road, and Lily replied politely. Then after a while they arrived in the village of Pilching, and he pulled the mare to a stop outside the railway station. 'You'll be in good time for your train, miss,' he said as he helped her down, 'and I'll to be here to meet you when you come on Thursday with your things.'

'Thank you – that would be most kind.'

She wished him good day and went into the station, and minutes later was on board the Corster-bound train. As she sat beside the soot-stained window watching the fields and the woodlands go by, she had the feeling of having taken a momentous step in her life. Though whether it was for good or ill she could not begin to guess.

There was no sign of Miss Elsie on Lily's return to Rowanleigh and she went straight up to her room. She was relieved that Miss Elsie was not immediately in evidence, for with her presence there were bound to come questions, and for some questions Lily was not fully prepared.

Later, in the quiet of the evening, she and Miss Elsie sat at the dining table. They were alone in the house now.

'So,' Miss Elsie said at last, 'don't keep me in suspense, Lily. I assume they offered you the position?'

'Yes, they did.'

'And obviously you accepted.'

'Yes.' A pause, then Lily added, eyes down at her soup, 'I need the work, Miss Elsie.'

'Of course you do. How was it – your interview?' Miss Elsie's tone sounded almost casual.

'It went well,' Lily replied. 'Mr Soameson seemed – pleasant. He's from Edinburgh. I met Mrs Soameson too, of course. She's English.'

'And?'

'She was pleasant enough – and the little girl is sweet.'

'What is her name, your pupil?'

'Lavinia. She's eight. A rather shy little thing, but she seems to be a very nice little girl. Imaginative and bright, and creative.'

'Good. And when do you start?'

'Thursday morning.'

'Thursday. So soon.'

'They want me there as soon as possible. I'm to take the 11.15 from Corster.'

'We'll have Mr Shad take you to the station.'

'Do you mind?'

'Of course not.'

A brief silence, then Miss Elsie said, 'He owns the paper mill in Senning, so I'm told. Mr Soameson.'

'Does he?' Lily said. 'I didn't know.'

'Are you looking forward to it – going to live there – work there?'

'Well . . .' Lily said, 'it'll be an adventure.' She nodded. 'Yes, I think I shall enjoy it – and I shall be able to come back some Sundays to see you – as long as I'm welcome, of course.'

'Oh, you're always welcome, you know that.'

Miss Elsie finished her soup and put down her spoon. With her eyes on her plate, her tone casual still, she said: 'And the little boy – did you see him?'

Lily was taken aback by the question. She had never mentioned to Miss Elsie that the Soamesons had a son. After a moment she replied, 'I think I heard his voice.'

Miss Elsie nodded. 'But you didn't see him.'

'No. I heard a small child's voice.' The sound of the voice was still with her. 'I think that must have been him.'

A little pause, then Miss Elsie said, 'Did his parents tell you anything about him?'

'His – his name is Joshua. He's four and a half, so they said.'

A little silence fell. Then Miss Elsie raised her eyes to Lily and said, 'You know, don't you?'

At once Lily felt her heart begin to pound. Playing for time, and control, she said: 'I'm sorry – I don't understand.'

426

Miss Elsie regarded her in silence for a second, then gave a little nod. 'Yes, you do, Lily, you understand well enough.'

Lily said nothing.

'The child, the boy,' Miss Elsie said, and then: 'Oh, Lily, you know about the Soamesons, don't you.'

Still Lily said nothing, though she well knew that silence would not allow her an escape.

'Perhaps I should have guessed earlier,' Miss Elsie said. 'How did you find out? How did you find out where he went? Such things are never revealed. You were never supposed to know.'

Lily hesitated, but could do nothing but confess. 'I know, but I – I found a letter – in your study. In a ledger there. From the woman who came with the cleric that day when they took him away. I'm sorry – I should not have pried.'

Miss Elsie's mouth was set as she gave a brief shrug. 'Well, it's done now,' she said. 'Though I could wish it had never happened.'

'Oh, no, I'm so glad!' Lily said at once. 'I'd so wanted to know. I'd thought about him so much. And there it was – in the letter – saying where he'd gone. Oh, Miss Elsie – it was like – it was as if it was fate.'

Miss Elsie frowned. 'Fate,' she echoed with a faint note of derision. 'Well, if you choose to believe such a thing.' She eyed Lily steadily across the table. 'Is this the reason you took the position?'

'I told you,' Lily said, 'I need the work.'

'Well, no one disputes that.'

'I didn't approach them – the Soamesons,' Lily said, 'although I knew about them. Mr Soameson answered my advert in the *Gazette*. You know that. When it came, his letter, I could scarcely believe it. It just – came out of the blue.'

Miss Elsie nodded. 'Fate again,' she said dryly. Then she shook her head and sighed. 'Oh, Lily.'

'It's all right, Miss Elsie,' Lily said. 'Really, it's all right.'

'Is it?' Miss Elsie sighed again. 'I can't help but think this is a step in the wrong direction.'

'Why should it be?'

'Are you going into this with your eyes open?'

'Yes. Yes, I am.'

'You're going to be in the same house.'

'Yes, I know, but – oh, but it's only for a few weeks. Three months, that's all, and then the whole family will be leaving, going up to Scotland.'

'And you think that at the end of those three months you'll be able to just walk away – with no heart-ache? You think it'll be as easy as that? My dear girl, you're going to be seeing the child every day.'

'Yes, I know, but – oh, it'll be all right. It will. Believe me, it will.'

'I hope so,' Miss Elsie said. There was no note of approval in her voice. 'Though I wonder how they'd feel if they knew who you are. I doubt that takes much imagining.'

'Oh, but they don't know. They can't know. They were never given any clue as to my name, were they?'

'No, of course not. That's never done.'

'Then they never will know. You don't think for one moment that I shall – shall tell them, do you? Oh, I'd never do that. I *am* realistic about this, Miss Elsie, I am. Truly.'

'I hope so.' Clearly, Miss Elsie was unconvinced. 'I just hope you're not building up a lot of unhappiness – for yourself and for others too.' She hesitated for a second then added, 'It's not too late, you know.'

'Too late?'

'You haven't started there yet. You could write tomorrow – or send a message first thing with Mr Shad. Tell Mr Soameson that something's come up, that you can no longer take the position.'

'Oh, no,' Lily said. 'I can't do that. They're depending on

me. They're expecting me. I can't let them down at this late stage.'

Miss Elsie gave a resigned nod. 'I'll say no more.' Then her expression softened a little. 'But – I'll trust you to do the right thing. I can do that, can't I?'

'Oh, of course. Of course. Everything will be all right,' Lily said. 'Believe me it will.'

Chapter Twenty-eight

On Thursday morning, Lily bought a copy of the *Morning Post*, and sat reading it on the train bound for Pilching. Much of the news was given to the rising death toll from the smallpox epidemic. It was rapidly gaining strength, and the paper reported that more hospitals were needed to deal with the sufferers. In London a handful of hospital ships had been moored in the Thames to help cope with the growing number of cases, but these had already been filled to overflowing. Further, the disease had long since spread from the big cities and was now finding victims in rural towns and villages.

After a while she folded up the paper and stuffed it in her bag – there was insufficient room to read it in the crowded compartment, added to which the ink of the newsprint stained her white gloves, and she had only one spare pair in her luggage.

The train reached Pilching on time, and as a station porter deposited her luggage on the platform, she turned and saw Mr Beeching coming towards them, his hand rising to his cap.

'Mornin', miss,' he said brightly, smiling and showing his small, uneven teeth. 'I see you brought some sunshine with you. That's a good start.' He hoisted her box onto his right shoulder and took up her bag in his left hand. 'This way, miss. We've got the buggy outside.'

Lily followed him out of the station to where the horse

and trap were waiting, and soon they were driving away, eventually leaving the village behind and following the road into the countryside.

'So, miss,' Mr Beeching said as the trap rolled along, 'you're about to start your first day as governess.'

'I am indeed, sir,' Lily replied.

'Though I hear tell as you're not going to be with us that long. Just till we go back up north, is that so?'

'Yes, that's right. Just for three months.'

'Aye.' He nodded. 'Three months and we'll be off. Won't be long now.'

'Are you looking forward to it, Mr Beeching – going back up to Scotland?'

He smiled. 'Oh, aye, I am that, although I was very happy to come down here with Mr Soameson.'

'I understand,' Lily said, 'that Mr Soameson has a paper mill, in Senning. Is that so?'

'Aye, that's it. It used to belong to Mrs Soameson's father, and came to her on his death. They came down south to look after it, the mill. Five years back, that was. But I don't doubt Mr Soameson's had enough of it. He tells me he's ready to get back to the family business – making the biscuits and the sweeties.'

'Is that what he does?'

'Aye, the Soamesons have a big company in Edinburgh. Mr Soameson senior's the one looking after things, but he's nay so young any more.'

They were coming into Happerfell now, and soon turned into Bourne Way. Arriving at The Gables, Mr Beeching brought the mare to a halt in the back yard. 'You go on in, miss,' he said to Lily, 'and I'll bring your things up to your room.'

Lily thanked him, and made her way to the rear door where the young maid – whose name she would learn was Lizzie – answered her ring, and said she would go and tell

431

the mistress that Lily had arrived, adding that she was instructed to say that the mistress would see her in the schoolroom in half an hour.

Up on the second floor, Lily made her way to her room, conscious as she did so that just across the landing was the nursery. Was he there? She listened, holding still in the quiet. There was no sound. After a moment she opened the door and went into her room, where she saw at once that a handful of white roses had been set in a vase on the chest, and that a little folded card had been placed on the counterpane. She picked up the card and opened it. It had been decorated with crayon drawings of flowers and two little lovebirds. In a careful, childish hand had been written:

WELCOME, MISS CLAIR.
I HOPE YOU WILL BE HAPPY AT THE GABLES.
BEST WISHES, LAVINIA

Lily was touched by the gesture and the message, and a sudden little lifting came to her heart.

Through the open door she heard the sound of footsteps mounting the stairs, and a few moments later Mr Beeching appeared carrying her box and her bag. He smiled at her as he came into the room and put her luggage down. 'There you are, miss.' Lily thanked him, and he went away again, the sound of his hard boots fading as he descended the stairs.

Over the next twenty minutes Lily unpacked her things and put them away in the closet and the drawers. Her books and the other items she had brought to aid in her teaching she took across the landing to the schoolroom. There she tapped on the door and, getting no answer, pushed it open. The room was empty. Inside, she set her things down on the table beside the small blackboard and looked around her. She had a better opportunity now to see what was to be her little domain for the next few weeks. There was a globe of the earth there, and on the white painted wall a map of the Britain Isles, and another of the European Continent. On the shelves behind the table were dictionaries, an atlas, and books on grammar, history, biology, geography and science. In the drawers of the chest she found paper and pencils, slates and chalks. There were painting and drawing materials too. Everything, it seemed, had been thought of.

Among the items she had brought were some papers on which she had made notes of lesson plans, and sitting at the table she began to go through them, trying to settle in her mind precisely what she should do and where she should begin. She was still sitting there a few minutes later when there came a sound from out on the landing and the door was opened. Mrs Soameson stepped into the room.

'Ah, you're here, Miss Clair. Good morning to you.'

'Good morning, ma'am.'

Lily had at once risen from her chair, but Mrs Soameson said, 'Oh, do sit down,' and gestured for her to be seated again.

As Lily sat back down Mrs Soameson cast her eyes over the books and papers laid on the table. 'Getting things ready, I see. Excellent. Lavinia will be here in a minute or two. She went down into the village with Joshua and his nurse. Have all your things been brought up?'

'Yes, ma'am. Mr Beeching put them in my room.'

'Good. Now, before the children get here, a few things you'll need to know. First – meals . . .' Mrs Soameson then set out to impart to Lily the daily routine that she would be required to follow. When she had finished she moved to the door and looked out onto the landing, listening. As she turned back into the room, she said, 'The children and Nurse will be here any second. Joshua's been a little fractious recently, but he's all right now. He had his

433

smallpox vaccination and it laid him rather low, poor boy. Mr Soameson and I – we weren't absolutely sure whether to go ahead and have him done – one hears so many strange reports – but it *is* the law, after all, and we thought it the wisest course in the end. We must hope the doctors know best, particularly with the situation as it is now in the country. It's dreadful. You read in the papers that hundreds of new cases are being reported every week. Even in Corster the situation is so bad. I hear the isolation hospital's full up and people are having to stay in their own homes. What's it all coming to?'

Now through the open door came from along the landing the sound of children's voices. 'Ah, here they are,' Mrs Soameson said. She turned and stepped to the door, leant out and said: 'Hello, Nurse. Come and meet Miss Clair.' She hovered there for a moment, then stood aside and a second later Lavinia came into the room, followed by a young woman and a little boy. As they came in, Lily got to her feet.

'Good morning, Lavinia,' Lily said. 'Thank you so much for your beautiful card.'

'Good morning, Miss Clair.' The child smiled shyly back. She had taken off her coat and was now in her pinafore and plain brown dress. She had pink ribbons in her hair. The little boy who stood beside her wore a dark grey coat and a straw hat. He looked at Lily with curiosity in his blue eyes.

'And this is Miss Cattock,' Mrs Soameson said, and Lily's attention was taken to the young nurse. She looked about Lily's own age. Somewhat plain-looking and rather plump, she had her pale hair parted in the centre and pulled back and fastened at the nape of her neck. 'I'm sure you two will get along splendidly,' Mrs Soameson said, then turned her attention to the children. 'Did you have a nice walk, Lavinia?'

'Yes, Mama,' Lavinia said. 'We got the cream from the farm.'

'Well done.' Mrs Soameson turned then to the boy. 'And you, Joshie? Did you enjoy your walk?'

He nodded. 'We picked some blackberries.'

'Blackberries – there's a good boy.'

'I scratched myself, look.' He held up his hand, pulling back the sleeve of his shirt to reveal his wrist. 'Look.'

Miss Cattock said quickly, as if perhaps a little anxious that she might be found lacking in her responsibilities, 'Oh, it's nothing, ma'am, really,' at which Mrs Soameson said easily, 'No, I'm sure it's not,' while looking at the child's wrist and shaking her head in sympathy.

Lily watched and listened, spellbound, fixed to the spot on the worn carpet. This child was her son, and seeing him as he walked into the room she had known him at once. Everything about his appearance had fallen perfectly into place. Everything had been so – right, so exactly right. So many times she had wondered, agonising, whether she would know him, but with her first glance as he had come around the door frame she had recognised him. For that first moment, that split second, she had caught at her breath, and held it while her heart had pumped against her ribs. She would have known him anywhere. Over four years had gone by since she had set eyes on him, yet after just an instant it was almost as if he had been out of her sight for no more than a minute.

'Shall we take your hat off, Joshie?' asked Miss Cattock, and the boy stepped to her while pulling at the elastic string that secured it. The hat came off revealing a mop of untidy fair hair falling in curling waves to his collar. The nurse began to unbutton his coat while he shifted from one foot to the other, anxious to be on the move.

'Are you going to say hello to Miss Clair?' Mrs Soameson said to him. 'This is Vinnie's new teacher. Say hello, won't you?'

'Hello, Joshua,' Lily said, smiling down at him, but he

435

would not look at her, instead lowering his head and fixing his gaze on the floor.

'No?' said Mrs Soameson. 'Aren't you going to say hello?'

'He's shy, isn't he?' Miss Cattock said. 'You're a little shy, aren't you, Joshie?' She took off the boy's jacket and smoothed down the folds of his apron. 'You've no need to be shy.'

Lily kept her eyes on the boy. She could not draw them away. Then, as if he had been drawn by her gaze, he raised his head and looked up at her. 'I had a scab,' he said, as if it was a matter of great importance.

'A scab?' Lily was not sure she had heard aright.

'Yes, a scab. It was big. It hurt, too. So much. Here . . .' He touched fingers to his upper left arm.

'He's talking about the scab from his vaccination,' Mrs Soameson said.

'Yes,' the boy said. 'My vaccination.'

Lily gave a little nod. Her heart was full. 'Ah – I see.'

The boy made a little circle with his thumb and forefinger. 'It was that big.'

Miss Cattock smiled indulgently and Mrs Soameson gave a smothered little laugh. 'Oh, Joshie, my dear,' she said, 'I don't think Miss Clair wants to hear about your old scab.'

He looked a little surprised at this. 'Oh,' he said, and then, frowning a little, head slightly on one side, he asked, 'Don't you?'

Lily said at once, 'Oh, indeed I do. Of course I do.'

Taking encouragement from her words he stepped towards her. 'Look,' he said, hiking up the sleeve of his pale blue shirt. 'The doctor scratched me and I had a bad arm.' He tugged on his shirt sleeve, frowning as he did so, as it refused to be pulled up much above his elbow,

'He has to show you,' Mrs Soameson said. 'He won't be

satisfied till he does.' Then to the boy she said, 'But why don't we leave it till another time, Joshie.'

'All right.' He sighed, then said to Lily, 'Another time.'

'Yes,' Lily said, 'another time. I won't forget.' She was mesmerised. He was standing so close to her, and as she looked down at him she could see near his left ear the tiny crescent-shaped birthmark. Of course she had never forgotten it, but seeing it again she was in danger of losing her composure.

Mrs Soameson smiled at the boy, then turned to speak to the nurse. 'I think you'd better take him along now, Nurse. Miss Clair and Lavinia will want to get started with their lessons.'

'Come along, Josh.' Miss Cattock put her hand on the boy's shoulder and together they moved towards the door.

'Goodbye, Joshua,' Lily said as the child was led away, and he turned and said, 'They call me Josh, or Joshie.'

'Oh – right you are, then,' Lily said. 'I won't forget.'

The nurse and the child left the room, and Lily heard the boy's voice fade along the landing.

'I shall leave you too,' Mrs Soameson said. She moved back to the open door as she spoke. 'If you need anything, I shall be downstairs.'

'Thank you, ma'am,' Lily said. 'We'll be fine.'

The door closed, and Lily and Lavinia were left alone.

'Well,' Lily said to the girl, 'we'll make a start with our lessons, shall we?' Stepping to the table, she took up one of the primers she had brought with her. 'I think we'll begin with some English history.'

That evening after supper, and after the children were asleep in bed, Lily returned to the schoolroom and sat at the table to write letters. She wrote first of all to Mr Corelman, informing him of her new address and asking him if he would be kind enough to forward any post that should arrive for her. She was, of course, thinking of correspondence from Joel, for he would assume her to be at Seston. However, given the circumstances of her final meeting with Mr Corelman, she had no great hopes that he would accede to her request.

When this letter was finished, she wrote to Miss Elsie, saying that her first day at The Gables had gone well, and that Lavinia was proving a willing and industrious pupil. Of her meeting with the boy she said nothing. When her letters were sealed in their envelopes she walked along the lane to put them in the post box.

That night she lay in her bed in her new room, her strange room, though growing less strange with the passing minutes. Through a chink in the curtains she could see a sliver of the September moon. The house was quiet and in the hush she could hear the faint creaks and cracks as the timbers settled. A night owl hooted over the gardens, its mournful little cry hanging in the air.

The thought of Joel came into her head. Where was he now? And what of Tom? She could not think of him and his torment without her heart sinking with despair. He must be in touch with her soon.

She shifted on the pillow, listening to the hush. Across the landing in the nursery the children would be long asleep. She pictured the boy lying in his cot, his eyes tight shut, his mouth slightly open as he breathed evenly and untroubled into the quiet. When he had been standing before her she had wanted to touch him, but she had not. He had been near to her, though, and she must be content with that.

Chapter Twenty-nine

On her first Sunday in Happerfell Lily went to church, as was expected of her, along with Mrs Lemmon the cook, Lizzie, and Susie the daily maid, and then in the afternoon joined Lavinia and Mrs Soameson in the morning room, each of them working with her needle. Lily was happy to help out with some of the house mending while the child worked at a piece of embroidery. After luncheon she accompanied Lavinia to the church hall where the Sunday-school class was held for the village children, there leaving her at the door while she herself continued on to take a short walk in the pleasant air. Later, indoors again, she managed to spend a little time with Miss Cattock and the boy. It was something she hoped for each day – being in the presence of the child, for no matter how short a time. At such meetings she would have liked to be close to him, to talk to him, and even, wonder of wonders, perhaps to hold him, but that was too much to hope for. Most of the time he seemed scarcely aware that she was even in the room, preoccupied as he was with his own desires, and any obvious affection that he showed was usually directed to his mother or the nurse. Lily wanted to say to him *Oh, look at me, do*, but she could not, and kept silent. She must be glad of what she could get – and even if he should be sleeping while she and the nurse whispered in conversation together, it was better than not being in his presence at all.

As her days at The Gables came and went, Lily quickly

grew accustomed to the routine in her new employment. She spent hours of each day teaching Lavinia, mostly in the schoolroom, but on a few occasions taking advantage of the lingering Indian summer and going out with her into the surrounding lanes and meadows, there studying the wildlife, taking notes and making sketches. In the evenings too she spent time with the girl, though in more relaxed pursuits, such as needlework or playing Snakes and Ladders. Afterwards, when Lavinia had gone to bed, Lily would be left to her own devices, and after her supper sat in her room or in the schoolroom and read a book or the newspapers, and prepared her lessons for the next day. She saw little of Mr Soameson – he would usually be off early in the morning and not get back till fairly late in the evening – but saw Mrs Soameson quite frequently. Now and again during the day the woman would come up, tap on the door and slip into the room where Lily and Lavinia were at work. 'All well?' she would ask in a loud whisper, and, satisfied, would leave again a minute later.

On Tuesday there came a letter from Miss Elsie. With little news to report, she simply wrote that all at Rowanleigh was well apart from the fact that Mr Shad had injured his back in trying to lift the trap. So, for the time being, she said, she would have to drive herself on any errands. There had not, she remarked, been any letters in the post for Lily, but anything that arrived would be forwarded to her at once.

The following afternoon, Lily received a letter from Joel. It had been sent to Laenar House at Seston, and forwarded on. So Mr Corelman had been the honourable gentleman after all.

Lizzie brought the letter to Lily where she sat at her table in the schoolroom with Lavinia working at her desk close by. When the maid had gone, Lily sat looking at the envelope with the Seston address written in Joel's now-familiar hand, and the Happerfell address scrawled across it by Mr Corelman or someone from his household.

Lily put the letter on the table, and there it lay while Lavinia worked at her English composition, and while Lily tried to give her attention to some French grammar that she had set her mind on studying. Then at last the day's lessons were over and she was alone in the room. In moments the envelope was open and the letter was in her hand. She read:

Hotel Metropole
Ave Rue d'Echelle
Brussels
14th September 1871

My dearest Lily,

By this time you'll be well into your new employment at Seston. I do hope it is going well for you and that you are happy there. I cannot but think that any child would be fortunate to have you for his teacher. Oh, Lily, I think of you so much, and wonder about you, trying to picture you at your work. It seems that you are always with me.

I have to tell you that I have been kept very busy over here. What with travelling about and inspecting and buying new products I am kept hopping and no mistake. My father was due to come here from Paris, but my mother writes that he has been considerably under the weather, so I am having to manage a good deal on my own. I don't think I have ever had to use my own judgement to quite such an extent! Still, now that I'm in at the deep end I venture that I'm learning at a very swift pace.

One thing I am sure of: I should be happy not to see the inside of a hotel room ever again. This hotel is comfortable enough, and I lack for very little, but I miss the familiar comforts of home.

You can write to me here until the 4th of October at which time I am scheduled to leave for Paris. After a brief stay there, I shall return to England, and you. Until that time you will continue to be in the loving thoughts of

Your

Joel

ps Last night I was thinking of the two of us sitting at the table in the little house in Corster. I could see you as you sat facing me while the rain lashed against the window. I remember the woodpecker there too. I said many things to you that afternoon, and believe me, I meant them all.

When Lily had finished the letter she read it through again, anticipating certain words and phrases, and hanging on them. His letter had been written on the forteenth and it was now the twenty-seventh. Having gone first to Seston it had taken almost two weeks to reach her. He would be wondering why he had not had any word from her in reply. She must write at once before he left for France, and inform him of her new situation and new address. It would not be so very long before he was back.

As the days passed, Lily gave Lavinia her lessons and, whenever possible, managed to spend a little time in the company of the boy. She and Emily Cattock were becoming good friends, and Lily frequently went into the nursery for five or ten minutes here or there where the nurse was to be found with the child. On two or three occasions she accompanied them on little walks in the golden autumn weather. The second Saturday – a day a little more relaxed as far as Lavinia's teaching routine was concerned – marked one such time, and Lily and the nurse and the two children left the house to walk into the fields. It was a warm day, though with a haze of cloud that gave a half promise of rain later on. For now, though, it was pleasant. Keeping to the footpaths beside the hedgerows, they moved at a leisurely pace, in keeping with Joshua's short strides. Over on the hillsides some of the fields were black from the burnt stubble, while in others the straw lay in bales.

As the two young women sauntered side by side along the footpaths, the children showed interest in everything around them, and were for ever darting off to look more closely at some miraculous discovery, but when the boy found something of interest it was to his nurse that he turned.

They did not stay out long, for the clouds were darkening, and by the time they got back to the house the hint of promised rain had become a real threat. In the hall they were met by Mrs Soameson, who invited Lily to join her for tea in the drawing room. When Lily went in at the appointed time she found her mistress sitting on the sofa with Joshua standing at her knee, playing with a toy horse. The tea had just been brought in by Lizzie, and as Lily sat in an armchair Mrs Soameson poured out the cups.

'I thought this would be a good opportunity to have a little chat,' Mrs Soameson said as she handed Lily her tea. 'Just to see how you're settling in, now that you've been here for more than a week.'

'I'm sure I'm settling in very well, ma'am, thank you,' Lily said. As she spoke, the boy, oblivious to the conversation, cooed and clicked his teeth, making little galloping noises while he jumped his toy horse along the arm of the chair.

Mrs Soameson said over his little sounds, 'Well, that's good – and the lessons are going well, are they?'

'Yes, indeed, ma'am. I believe they are.'

'Splendid. That's what I expected to hear. I know Lavinia

seems quite settled already – so that's excellent.' She glanced off through the window. 'I hope the rain keeps off. Nurse has gone down to the shops so I trust she took an umbrella. I must say it's not looking very promising.' She lightly touched a kiss to the top of the boy's head. 'Don't you agree with that, Joshie?'

Joshua yawned at this, at which Mrs Soameson nodded and said, 'And quite the right response, indeed. You don't want to be patronised, do you?' To Lily she said, 'He's a little tired. He didn't sleep well last night, and Nurse said he couldn't settle for his nap at lunch time.' She glanced at the clock on the mantelpiece. 'Heaven knows when Mr Soameson will be home. He spends so much of his time at the factory, and he has done ever since we got here. When we came down from Edinburgh it was meant to be only a fairly temporary thing, not more than a couple of years, but it's been five. I think the mill was something of a challenge to him. We could have sold it on, of course, but that would have been too easy. Mind you, he's had enough of it now, and is anxious to get back to Scotland. Well, for one thing, his father's health is not the most robust. He's a wonderful old gentleman, and he's kept the family business going like clockwork, but he can't go on for ever. It's time my husband went back and took over the reins.

'Look . . . look.'

The child's piping voice came as he moved from his mother's knee to Lily, holding up his toy horse as he did so. 'Look.'

'Look,' Mrs Soameson echoed fondly. 'I think that's his favourite word – "Look".'

'Look,' the boy said to Lily.

She smiled at him. 'Yes, I'm looking. That's a most splendid horse, Joshie. Have you got a name for him?'

He nodded. 'He's Mr Charlie Dobbin.'

'Mr Charlie Dobbin, eh? Well – that's a nice name.'

'Yes,' he said gravely. He held the horse a little higher for Lily to see. 'He's got a proper bridle, look.'

'Yes, he has indeed.'

The boy hopped the little horse along the arm of the overstuffed chair, clicking his tongue as he went, then lifted it in a little arc to land on Lily's thigh. 'Look,' he said as he jogged the toy horse along on her skirt, 'he jumps so high.'

'He's a very clever little animal, isn't he?' Lily said, 'and a very handsome one too.'

He nodded, his lips compressed in his concentration. Mrs Soameson said to him, 'Mind you don't spill Miss Clair's tea, Josh,' then to Lily, 'Don't let him be a nuisance, Miss Clair.'

Lily replied at once, 'Oh, he's not, he's not. He's perfectly fine.' She smiled warmly at the boy. 'You are, aren't you, Josh? Perfectly fine.'

As she spoke there came a knock on the door, which opened and Lizzie put her head round and said, 'Mum, I'm sorry to disturb you, but the sweep's here, and I don't know which chimneys you wants done.'

Mrs Soameson got up from her seat. 'I'll come and see to it,' she said. She turned to Lily. 'Will you look after Joshie for a minute, Miss Clair? I shan't be long.'

'Of course,' Lily replied.

To the child, Mrs Soameson said, 'You stay with Miss Clair, Joshie. I'll be back soon.' Next moment she had gone from the room, closing the door behind her and leaving Lily alone with the child.

Lily set down her empty cup and now turned her full attention to the boy. 'Are you going to show me what your horse can do?' she said to him. Every instinct in her being prompted her to reach out and touch him, but she kept her hands clasped before her.

'You know he can gallop too,' the child said gravely.

'He can gallop? Really?'

445

'Oh, yes, look.' He jogged the little horse back and forth along the chair's arm, making the now familiar clip-clopping noises as he went. 'Did you see?'

'Yes, I did. Very good.'

All at once the child stopped the horse's movements and let his hand fall. As Lily looked at him she saw his eyes momentarily droop, and he opened his mouth in a yawn. 'You're a tired little man, aren't you?' she said.

He rested against her leg and shook his head. 'No,' he murmured, and yawned again. 'I'm not tired.' He leant closer, draping himself languidly against her, his horse for the moment forgotten. The room seemed very still. Lily said, 'I think perhaps Mr Charlie Dobbin is a little tired, is he?'

He lifted his head and smiled. 'No, he's not tired. He's never tired.' His lips were soft pink, his skin flawless, his eyes wide and totally trusting. He lifted the toy horse and jogged it two or three times on Lily's thigh, then let his hand fall again. From far off came the faint rumble of thunder, and the boy heard it and at once pressed closer to her, his left hand rising, small fingers clutching at the fabric of her skirt. Sensing his fear, Lily put her hand on his shoulder. 'It's all right,' she said. 'It's just a little thunder. Nothing to be alarmed about.'

He said nothing, but stayed with his arm across her, tense. As the skies had darkened, the light in the room had dimmed. Both she and the boy were listening. Then into the silence came another rumble of thunder, this time much nearer, louder. He pressed closer, and Lily's other hand came up and lay upon him. 'You're not afraid, are you?' she said. 'Don't be afraid.'

He looked up at her again and dumbly shook his head.

'Good,' she said. 'You don't need to be afraid.' Then she added, meaning every breath of each word, 'I wouldn't let anything happen to you.'

A sudden, sharp clap of thunder came, cracking from the heavens as if it might split the lowering sky. It was so loud that Lily was startled, and under her touch she felt the boy flinch and draw in his breath.

'Come,' she said, 'come . . .' and in a second she was wrapping her arms around him and lifting him up, and he was lying in her lap, his face against the softness of her bosom. She thought she might never move again. Moments passed and she began to feel the tension easing a little from his taut form, and then suddenly the room was lit up by a flash of lightning followed by another crack of thunder. He gave a gasp and stiffened in her arms and burrowed deeper into her body. 'It's all right,' she murmured. 'It's all right.'

Long minutes went by. The rain came, driven by a sudden wind. Thunder rolled again and again, but a little more distant now, the storm receding. She looked down and saw that his eyes were closed, and realised that he was sleeping, his mouth slightly open, his sweet breath rising and falling. She looked at the way his fair hair curled from his temples and saw again the tiny crescent mark near his ear. His horse lay in her lap beside him. 'Yes,' she breathed into the sound of the rain, 'you sleep, my darling. You sleep.'

When Mrs Soameson came back into the room some minutes later she put a finger to her lips, as if urging herself to be quiet, and whispered, 'Ah, look, he was so tired, bless him. And he's very much afraid of thunder.' She looked over to the window where the rain fell against the pane, but now less violently. 'What a storm that was.' She stepped closer and looked down at the sleeping boy. 'Look at him, so peaceful now.' She smiled at Lily. 'He must like you, Miss Clair.'

Lily had the Sunday off, and soon after breakfast she set out for Sherrell. The rain of the previous day had gone and the

447

early October sun was shining onto the fields, all stripped now of the harvest, leaving the last gleanings to the crows. She reached Rowanleigh just after eleven, and was greeted warmly by Mary and Miss Elsie. Lily made coffee for herself and Miss Elsie and the two of them sat in the drawing room while Lily told of her first ten days in Happerfell.

Miss Elsie listened attentively to her words – which mostly concerned the teaching of Lavinia – then said:

'And him? What of him?'

Lily did not answer at once. Then she said, 'Joshua.'

'You see him, of course.'

'Yes. The nursery's just along the landing. I see him several times a day.'

'And?' Miss Elsie's question hung in the air.

Lily hesitated a moment, then said, 'He – he's beautiful.'

Miss Elsie's mouth was touched by a sad little smile. 'Beautiful. Oh, Lily . . .'

'He is. He's a splendid, beautiful little boy. Charming and bright and handsome – and loving.'

Miss Elsie studied Lily's face. 'But you know he'll be going away, eventually. Before Christmas, you said, the whole family will leave for Scotland.'

'I know, I know.' Lily spoke quickly, almost as if irritated by the words. Of course she knew. How could she be other than aware of such a fact? 'I'm aware of that. Of course I am.'

Miss Elsie nodded. 'Good.'

A little silence fell between them. Then Miss Elsie said, with a little start, rising from her chair, 'I mustn't forget – a letter came for you yesterday.' She crossed to the door and went out into the hall, returning moments later with an envelope which she handed to Lily.

'Oh – it's from Tom,' Lily said. She looked up at Miss Elsie. 'Do you mind . . .?'

'Of course not. Go ahead – read it.'

Lily tore open the envelope, took out the folded sheets of cheap notepaper, and read her brother's words. In pencil he had written:

Corster
28th September 1871

My dear Lil,

I know you'll have been waiting to hear from me, and I'm sorry I haven't written before. Oh why is it, Lil, that I always seem to be saying sorry for something or other? Anyway, right now I'm trying to think about my future. It seems to me that there's not a lot I'm capable of doing, as things are. But then I look at other people who are worse off and think that in some ways I'm lucky. There are old soldiers from the Crimea who have only got one leg, and sits in the streets begging. Well, that's not for me, Lil. I got my pride, and I've got to do something for myself. But this don't mean being a burden on you. That's not going to happen. I tell you, I've been talking to some fellows, and they reckon that America is the place to go. Would you reckon I was crazy if I said that I'd like to go there? I know I'm hindered now, and there's a limit to what I can do, but I'm getting better every day at handling things. Learning all the time. And I'm told that in America they appreciate a hard worker, and a hard worker can get on and make something of hisself. So, Lil, that's what I'd like to do – go to America. They call it the New World, and maybe that's what it will be for me. You don't think I'm barmy, do you? Anyway, Lil, I want to ask you for your help for the last time. And I promise it <u>will</u> be the last time. I won't ask anything of you again. Which brings me to my question: Is it possible for you to lend me some money? I need it for my passage. I've been to

...s at Bristol, and after asking around I find
...e's a cargo steamer leaving in the middle of October
for Philadelphia. The ship's in dock for repairs right
now, but I talked to the first mate and he says he'll help
me get on board. I can work for part of my passage
money, but I shall need a bit more. Can you help me,
Lil? I promise, I'll never ask you for anything else again,
and in time I'll pay you back. It might take a while, but
I'll do it, believe me I will. I'll work hard, and once I'm
over there I think I'll have something to work for. Here
there seems to be nothing, and I don't seem to be going
anywhere.

I reckon to be here in Corster at the end of next week.
Say Friday, the sixth. Can you meet me in front of the
museum? Say at six o'clock. If you can bring me
anything to help me out I shall pay you back as soon as
I can. And who knows, Lil, one day, when I've become
successful in America you can come out and stay with
me, and live with me. There's space out there, you
know. It's not like Corster or London where people
have got to live so close together with no room to
breathe.

You'll be glad to know that my arm has healed very
well and gives me no trouble. I haven't got any address
right now, so you can't write back, but if you're not
there on Friday I'll understand that you can't meet me.
And if you can't I'll write to you again. I know you
won't let me down, though, will you?

Till Friday, and always

Your loving and faithful brother

Thomas

She sat with the letter in her hand.
'Well, Lily?' Miss Elsie said, 'What does he have to say?'
For a moment Lily was unable to speak. Then a sob burst

from her throat and she leant forward, shaking her head in despair. 'He's living in a dream. He's just – living in a dream.'

'Tell me. What does he say?'

'He wants to go to America,' Lily said. 'He says he's arranged passage on a ship, and of course he needs money to help pay his fare. I can see it now – some unconscionable man selling him a dream – taking him for anything he can get. And how's he going to live in America once he gets there? How will he work?'

Miss Elsie said, 'But – if it's what he wants . . .'

'I know. It's like when he went off to London – he thinks life will be different. And it won't be. But I can't tell him that. I can't destroy what little hope he might have left.' She paused. 'And of course – if he goes I'll never see him again.'

A moment of silence, then Miss Elsie said, 'Have you got some money to give him?'

Lily gave a deep sigh. 'Only the little I managed to save up while working in Little Patten. But – he's welcome to it all.'

'If you need more . . .'

'Oh, ma'am.' Lily was greatly touched by the woman's kindness. 'Thank you so much, but I couldn't take anything else from you.'

'It's not a time to be proud, Lily,' Miss Elsie said. 'If the young man needs it, then he must have it.'

'Thank you. Thank you.'

'I have some cash here in the house.'

'Thank you. I shall pay you back. You know I'll pay you back.'

Miss Elsie nodded. 'Whenever. It's not important.'

When Lily returned to The Gables in Happerfell, Lizzie met her in the hall with a grave expression and a lowered voice.

451

Lily frowned, aware at once that something was amiss. 'What is it?' she asked. 'What's the matter?'

Lizzie glanced quickly around, then murmured: 'It's the master's father, miss – old Mr Soameson. A telegraph come, so Mrs Lemmon says. I'm afraid he's died. Went in the night.'

After the maid had gone, Mrs Soameson came into the hall. 'Ah, there you are, Miss Clair,' she said. 'I thought I heard you come in. Did you have nice day in Sherrell?'

'Yes, thank you, ma'am.'

'That's good.' Mrs Soameson's expression grew a little grave. 'I'm afraid we had some bad news while you were gone. Mr Soameson's father has passed away. We received a telegraph this morning.' She sighed, shaking her head. 'We knew he wasn't strong, but it's still come as a great shock. There's nothing for it but Mr Soameson must go up to Scotland, of course, and arrange the funeral. He's leaving first thing tomorrow. A dreadfully long journey, but there you are, it has to be done.' Another deep sigh. 'I think it will mean our moving back to Edinburgh sooner than we'd anticipated.'

Up in her room Lily took off her coat and hat and stood at the window looking down over the rear garden. She had only just arrived at the house and now suddenly there was talk of the family leaving so much sooner than planned. And Edinburgh – it was a world away.

Chapter Thirty

On Monday morning, Lily asked Mrs Soameson if on the coming Friday she might finish her lessons a little early and go to meet her brother in Corster. Mrs Soameson made no objection, and when the day and the hour came, Lily made ready and left the house.

She arrived in Corster just after five-thirty, and at once went to the little paved yard at the entrance to the Victoria Gardens. There, facing the corn exchange and the museum, she sat on a bench in the overcast light of the pale sun. The air was cool, with a chill breeze blowing. As usual at this hour, there were many in the streets who were going to their homes after their day's work, and they moved past Lily with purpose. She kept her eye on the corn exchange clock, watching the minutes pass until Tom should arrive. In addition to the money she carried in her bag, she had some other items: on the way from the railway station she had bought a bar of his favourite chocolate, and also, from a street-vendor, two ripe pears.

Six o'clock came and went and she scanned the vista about her, not knowing from which direction he would appear. There were not many others in the little paved garden. An elderly man sat on one the benches, his old dog, tethered by a lead, resting at his feet. On another bench sat a middle-aged man in rags, with his belongings packed into a straw basket and two hessian sacks.

The minutes passed, and there was still no sign of Tom. She thought of that other time when she had waited for him in vain, sitting on this very bench, not knowing that he was lying unconscious in Grassinghill Infirmary.

Six-thirty. From the nearby bench the old man got to his feet, and the dog rose with him. As the man passed Lily by he raised his hand and touched it to the brim of his hat and gave her a smile. She smiled back, and he walked slowly away and out of her sight.

Then, suddenly, Tom was there, coming around the corner of the museum at a fast pace, almost running. He saw her at once, and headed straight for her, and in moments was coming to a halt, reaching out to her. As she got up and stepped forward, his arms came up and wrapped her round.

'Ah, Lil – Lil, you're here, you're here.' He sounded a little out of breath.

'Of course I'm here.' She drew back a little from him and gave the whisper of a gentle laugh, part relief, part joy, part grief. His one good hand stayed on her upper arm, while his mutilated arm fell back to his side. The stump of it was hidden, the sleeve of his jacket pinned back, shielding it from view.

'Oh, Lil,' he said, 'I'm *so* glad to see you. I'm so glad you could get away.'

'I'm glad to see *you*,' she said. 'Come, sit down on the bench with me.'

'No.' The word came out sharply, and he took a step back and half turned, looking about him.

'What's the matter?' she said. He looked so ill at ease, so tense. 'Is something wrong?'

He turned again, still looking anxiously. 'Have we got to stay out 'ere? Let's go inside somewhere.' He gestured across the street. 'Let's go into the museum.' Even as he spoke he was starting away.

She joined him, and together they went across the cobbles, he moving at a sharp pace so that she had to hurry to keep up with him. She could not understand why he seemed to be in such a hurry. In moments they came to the museum's entrance. All was quiet as they went in, and as they crossed the foyer the bespectacled curator at the desk merely glanced up and registered their presence. Together they climbed the stairs, the worn, polished treads under their feet giving out the occasional creak. They passed two other visitors coming in the opposite direction, but saw no one else. Soon they arrived on the top floor and moved along the landing past the battered Greek and Roman statues, and the display cases with their old pottery and other ancient artefacts, to the room where they had sat before.

Inside, they moved to the old polished-wood bench that stood beneath the tall window that overlooked the cobbled square below. While Lily sat on the bench, Tom moved closer to the window and looked down. Glancing up at him, Lily thought again how tense he appeared. He was like a rabbit, alert and ready to run, or like a coiled watch-spring, ready to snap.

'Tom, you're making me nervous,' she said into the quiet. 'Please – come and sit down. Come away from the window.'

'This window,' he said, still gazing down, 'reminds me of Wentworth, except there's no bars.'

'I know. You told me.'

'I'll never go back there. Never.'

'Well, of course you won't. You'll never have any reason to.' She paused. 'Come and sit down.'

After a moment he turned from the window and sat beside her.

'How is it now?' she said, lifting a hand towards his damaged arm. 'Does it hurt you at all?'

He touched his left arm with his right. 'No, it don't 'urt. Though it feels a bit – nervy at times – like the nerves are on

455

edge. It's queer. And often it feels like it's still there, my 'and. Like I feel I could move it, move the fingers. It's weird.' He gave a little nod of resignation, then said, changing the subject, 'So where are you staying now, Lil? I 'ad to write to you at Miss Balfour's. Are you back there now?'

She felt that he was speaking not out of genuine interest but merely for the sake of talking, and even though he had moved to sit beside her, she could feel in him that strange tension and agitation.

'No,' she said, 'I have that position in Happerfell – the one I told you about. I started just over a fortnight ago. A well-to-do Scotsman and his family. I'm governess to a little girl there. It was supposed to be for three months before they all go off to Scotland, but now I don't know. It could be a lot sooner.'

'So your work with them'll come to an end.'

'I'm afraid so.' She shrugged. 'But something will turn up.'

'Yeh, it will.' The sound of distraction in his voice was hardly hidden. He forced a smile. 'Good for you, our Lil.'

She smiled. 'Oh, Tommo, I'm so glad to see you again. I've been thinking about you, and worrying about you.'

He nodded. 'Ah, I reckoned you would be. I'm sorry I put you through all that: going off from the infirmary before you got back to see me. I told you, though – I couldn't do nothin' else.' He sighed. 'I been a drain on you long enough.'

'Please – don't talk like that.'

'It's true. I always seem to be askin' for something. And this time's no different, is it?' As he spoke there came a noise from the direction of the stairs and he turned his head sharply and looked towards the door. When no further sound came, he relaxed slightly once more. Turning back to Lily, he said solemnly, 'Yeh, I always seem to be askin' for something, but it won't continue, Lil, I promise.'

'It doesn't matter,' she said. 'I love you. Anything I've got you can have.'

'Oh, Lily, what a sister you are. You're champion, you are.' He gave a little wondering shake of his head. 'You been so good to me. Ever since I can remember.'

She put a hand up to his face, gently, briefly touching his cheek. 'Nonsense. I haven't done anything special – only what any sister would do.' She took him in as he sat beside her. She did not know what she had expected to find, but she was distressed to see him look so unkempt, so dishevelled. His angelic face was as beautiful as ever, but he was in need of a shave, and his ragged, uncombed hair looked dirty. When he lifted his hand to scratch at his scalp she saw that his fingernails were rimmed black. He wore the same clothes that she had last seen him in, though now there was no collar to his shirt, and one of the knees of his corduroy trousers had been torn. His boots were dusty, with crusted mud around the soles. 'Tom,' she said, 'I think you've lost weight. Are you getting enough to eat?'

'I'm all right. I'm getting along.'

'I brought you some chocolate,' she said,' and a couple of pears.'

A slow smile touched his solemn mouth. 'Well, I wouldn't say no to a nice pear and a bit o' chocolate.'

She brought out the bar of chocolate, and the paper bag with the pears. He took them from her and placed them on the bench. Then he took a pear from the bag and bit into it. As he did so the juice ran down his chin and he wiped at it with the sleeve of his stunted arm. 'Boy, that's good,' he said. 'That's very good.'

He finished the pear, core and all. 'I'll keep the other for later,' he said, and worked the wrapping off the chocolate bar. The chocolate was gone in a couple of minutes, and Lily took its paper and put it into her bag. As she did so he got up from the seat and looked from the window.

457

'What are you looking for?' she said.

'Nothing. Nothing. It's all right.' A few more moments glancing out at the scene down below and he stepped back to the bench and sat down again.

'How have you been living?' she said to him.

'Oh, I've managed all right, I s'pose. Nothin' spectac'lar, but all right, considerin'.'

'Have you had any work?'

'Nah. Nothin' to speak of.' He held up his left arm, and added with a bitter little laugh, 'You need two 'ands even to 'old a broom.'

His simple words were like the greatest pain in her heart. She would have done anything to make his anguish go away, but there was nothing she could do. She could not even offer him hope.

'I've managed to earn a bit runnin' some messages,' he said. 'Here in Corster for a firm of solicitors and for some people at the *Gazette*. At least my legs are fit, and I'm a quick runner.'

'And where have you been sleeping?' she said. It was obvious from his appearance that he had not spent the most comfortable days and nights. 'Have you managed to stay in the dry?'

'Yeh, I've been all right. Don't worry about me. I found a little place out on the edge of the town. Just a little shack, a little lean-to, but it keeps the rain off.'

As he finished speaking there came the sound of footsteps on the stairs, climbing, and the murmur of voices, and he quickly got to his feet and peered off through the door onto the landing.

'What's up?' Lily said. 'You're so jumpy. What's the matter?'

He remained standing there for some seconds, gazing off, shoulders hunched. Then a middle-aged couple, a man and a woman, came into view. They wandered at a leisurely pace into the room, looking about them at the exhibits as they came. Tom moved back to the bench and sat down again.

'I can't stay round here,' he said in a whisper. 'I'm gunna 'ave to go.'

Lily frowned. 'Why?'

He did not answer, and kept silent as the couple wandered about the room. They did not stay long. There seemed to be little to interest them for more than a few passing moments, and after a while they drifted back towards the open door.

Tom watched their departure and listened while the sound of their footfalls faded along the landing, then he got up and looked from the window again. Lily said, 'What are you looking for, Tom?'

He turned to her. 'I shouldn't have come 'ere today.'

'Not come here? Why?' She was mystified.

He shook his head. 'No, I shouldn't, but I 'ad to.' He paused. 'Did you bring it, Lil?'

'The money? You mean the money?'

'Yeh. Did you manage to get me any?'

'Yes, I got you some.'

A smile of relief briefly touched his face. 'Ah, you're a good girl, you are. I knew you wouldn't let me down.'

She had her hand in her bag, seeking her purse. 'Miss Elsie let me have it,' she said. 'I didn't have enough of my own.' She took out her purse, opened it and extracted a little wad of notes. 'She let me have thirty pounds for you.'

'Thirty pounds.' He came to stand closer to her, and shook his head in a little gesture of wonder. 'Oh, Lily, she's a good woman, ain't she?'

'She is indeed. Of course I shall have to pay her back.'

'Yeh, of course you will. And I'll pay *you* back too. Just as soon as I've earned a bit.'

'Well – when you can.' She held the money out to him and he took it and looked at it.

'I never seen that much money in me life before,' he said. He stuffed it into the pocket of his trousers.

'I hope it'll be enough,' she said.

'Oh, yeh.' He patted the pocket. 'That'll be grand, and it'll see me through, don't worry.' He stepped back and looked down through the window again. 'Did you see anyone as we came in?' he said, turning to flick a glance at her.

'See anyone? Who? Who are you talking about?'

'Coppers. Did you see any coppers about?'

'What – what are you concerned about the police for?'

'I'm not going back in there,' he said.

'To prison?' She frowned. 'Well, of course you're not. Tom – what is this all about? Tell me. *What* have you done?'

He gave a little groan and said, 'Oh, Lil, don't get on at me. I know I do stupid things at times, but . . .'

As his voice trailed off she said sharply: 'What have you done? Tell me.'

He came back closer to the bench and, his voice low, said, 'I didn't steal it. Honest, I didn't. I didn't steal it.'

'Steal what? What are you talking about?'

'The purse. The gentleman's purse. It was just there, on the seat.'

Her eyes widened. 'What are you telling me, Tom? Have you done something?'

'I told you – I didn't steal it. It was just there, after he'd gone.'

'You took it? You took somebody's purse?'

When he did not answer, she slapped the seat of the bench beside her. 'I think you'd better sit down and tell me what's happened.'

With an air of reluctance he sat down at her side.

'Tell me,' she said, feeling her heart beat at the thought of what he might be about to say.

'It was two days back, 'ere in Corster,' he said after a moment. He lifted his hand and jabbed with his thumb towards the window. 'Down there in the square. I come in durin' the afternoon, looking for work. Doing some runnin' maybe – or anything – but there wasn't anything being offered. Anyway, I'd been 'ere a while, walking round, and I came by and got meself a drink of water at the fountain and sat down. I was on one of the benches near where we met just now. It wasn't that warm a day, and there weren't many other people sittin' around, but there was this old man there, a well turned-out old gentleman, he was. He had a couple of bags with him, and a leather case. At one point he sat there going through his purse, and when he got up to go 'e left his purse behind on the seat.'

At this Lily gave a groan. 'And you took it. Oh, Tom, don't tell me you took it.'

'Well – well, it was just there, on the seat. I didn't see it right away, and when I did he'd gone off out of sight. I didn't *think*, Lil. I just wasn't thinkin' straight, I s'pose.' He gave a deep sigh. 'I just wasn't.'

'So you took it, the gentleman's purse.'

He closed his eyes and gave an almost imperceptible nod. 'Ah, I did.'

'Oh, Tom . . .'

He nodded again. 'I did it without thinking twice. It was there, and I just looked round and then stepped across the gap and picked it up. It was just so easy. One second it was lyin' there on the bench and the next it was in my 'and.' He gave a groaning sigh. 'Oh, Lil, I know, I know – I must've been barmy, and if I could've undone it I would, believe me. But it was too late; it was done.'

'What d'you mean? Surely you could have put it back.'

'I had it in my pocket. And just at that moment the old man comes back round the corner by the corn exchange. And he's got a peeler with him. They come straight towards the bench, I tell you. For a second I just stood there like some rabbit fixed by a stoat, and then I took off. I couldn't do anything else. I 'ad to get away.'

'Go on,' Lily said.

'Well . . .' He turned his head back to face her again. 'I got away. Like I said, I'm fast on me feet, but the peeler, he was fast too, and he almost caught me – but I was faster still and I managed to give him the slip. He came close though – close to catching me – and he saw me all right. Close up, I mean. Oh, yeh, he saw me close up, right enough – and I knew he wouldn't forget me.'

'What did you do – with the man's purse?'

'I threw it away. As I was running. I didn't take anything from it. I didn't even look inside. I didn't 'ave a chance. As I was running I slung it over a wall into somebody's garden. It's still there as far as I know. Though doubtless the police think I still got it.' He shifted on the seat, his fingers clenching and unclenching. Then he got up again and moved to the window. Looking down through the glass he said, just loud enough for Lily to hear: 'He saw me today. That constable. He saw me coming 'ere a while ago. The same one.'

'He saw you? Are you sure?'

'Oh, ah, I'm sure, right enough. I darn near ran into him. I was only a yard away. I got out of his way as sharp as I could, but 'e saw me all right. He made that clear enough.' He turned to face her. 'He's after me, Lil.'

'You think he's followed you?'

'Yeh, I reckon so. Though maybe not on his own.' He moved close to her again. 'I got to go, Lil. It's not safe for me to stay 'ere.' As he spoke he was stepping back, as if ready to run. She got to her feet, reaching out to him.

'Oh, but Tom – you can't go like this. How will I get in touch with you? You're going to be leaving the country. I might never see you again.'

462

'Oh, you'll see me again,' he said, 'don't you worry about that. I'll be turning up, like the old bad penny.' He moved from one foot to another. 'Lil, I got to go. It's not safe for me 'ere.' He put his right arm around her, drawing her close. 'I'll write to you, depend on it. As soon as I get there, to Philadelphia, I'll write and let you know where I am.' His arm tightened even more. There was desperation in his touch. 'Don't think too badly of me, Lil, please.'

'I could never do that, Tom.'

He leant back a little and looked into her face. 'You wait – you'll hear good things of me, once I'm settled.' He smiled. 'And we'll have that little 'ouse together, you just see if we don't.'

Then, with a wrench he was breaking away from her, adjusting his cap securely on his head and stepping back to glance down from the window once more. And Lily, watching his every move, saw him start, saw his body jerk upright, and heard the gasp of his breath.

'Oh, by Christ, they're 'ere!' he cried. 'They're 'ere, the peelers!'

He spun, giving out a little yelp, turning on the spot as if not knowing which way to go. Then he flung himself forward and dashed across the room to the doorway. In seconds he was through it and running out onto the landing. Lily heard his boots thudding on the wooden floor, the sound echoing in the silence of the place. As he disappeared from her view she turned back to the window and looked down, and saw two constables nearing the building. In seconds they had vanished from her sight as they entered through the doors below.

Her own heart was beating wildly as she moved across the room past the unseeing eyes of the stone statues. Reaching the door she looked out. There was no sign of Tom, though she could hear the sound of his hurrying feet coming from one of the galleries on the far side of the

463

landing. Then all at once he burst into view again, dashing towards her. In the same moment two young women appeared from behind him in the doorway and stopped, standing in surprise, watching his progress. He was oblivious to them as he frantically ran forward, his mouth gaping, his eyes starting in terror. As he came to Lily where she stood in the doorway to the gallery he gasped out, 'There's no other way down! Oh, Christ 'elp me!'

She could see that his eyes were glistening with tears of panic. He ran past her into the room, spun, then returned at a run, and came dashing past her again, this time heading for the stairs. She could only stand there, hands up to her mouth, watching as he started down, his boots thundering on the treads. The two young women had come forward a little now, moving nervously from the opposite gallery and, curious and drawn by the drama, stood watching his descent. Lily, like the young women, watched him dash down, and then hurried to the head of the staircase to peer after him. She watched as he reached the next landing, turned, and disappeared from her view. And for a few seconds there was only the sound of his footsteps. Then, all at once he was in her sight, coming back along the landing and up the stairs again. Standing at the top, she watched as he came hurtling towards her.

'They're 'ere! They're 'ere inside!'

He gasped out the words as he came up. Briefly he came to a floundering halt, his good arm and his mutilated arm reaching out. 'Lil! Oh, Lil!' He was gasping for breath, little flecks of spittle spraying from his lips. 'Lil, for God's sake 'elp me! They'll send me back! Lil, don't let 'em. Oh, please, don't let 'em.'

Following his words there came the sound of other footfalls heavy on the stairs below, rapidly climbing. Tom turned and looked down, and then whirled, his eyes wide in terror and desperation. For a couple of seconds he hovered there, as if at his wits' end, and then flung himself forward again. Dashing past Lily, he bolted back into the gallery. Turning in his wake, she started after him.

She watched him, her horrified eyes taking in every desperate move of his body as he skidded past the display cases, the battered statues and the fragments of ancient pottery. She watched him as he ran, without any hesitation in his step, towards the window above the bench. She watched him as he leapt up onto the seat and, in a continuation of the one single move, threw himself headfirst at the pane.

No sound at all came from Tom. There was only the shattering of the glass. One moment he was there, silent, leaping, and a split second later he was gone.

Chapter Thirty-one

For a few seconds after Tom had vanished Lily stood dumb-stricken and rooted to the floor, looking at the window, the sound of the breaking glass still ringing in her ears. Then, turning, she saw the two young women standing with open mouths, unable to believe what had taken place before their eyes. Vaguely she registered this, and then, forcing herself out of her momentary daze, spun and headed for the stairs.

She met the two constables coming up, and they stood to one side to make way for her, somewhat startled by the sight of her as, clutching at her skirts and with all decorum gone, she rushed down.

Outside she ran the few yards to where Tom lay on the cobbles. His body lay strangely doubled up, like some discarded, disjointed doll, and she knelt and bent over his lifeless form. His cap had come off and lay a foot away from his shoulder. From his smashed head his blood ran in thin rivulets between the stones. His eyes, half open, and which had seen so little joy, looked dully up at the sky.

What happened next passed by in a fog, a kaleidoscope of people coming and going, sounds, men's voices asking questions, kindly, sensitively, the feeling of hands touching solicitously at her shoulder. The two police constables who had come so soon to her side learnt from her that the young man was her brother. The ambulance was being sent for, they told her, and he would be taken to Corster General

Hospital, though it was clear to all that he was beyond help. She would wait, she said; she would not leave him here alone. As she stood beside the body her knees buckled and she sank down, only prevented from falling by one of the constables who stepped forward and caught her. From within the museum someone fetched a chair, and she was urged to sit. Someone else had covered Tom's body with an old piece of blanket, and she sat before it, her eyes dull, her lips compressed. When the ambulance wagon came at last, she turned her head away as he was lifted up and placed on board, then, turning back, she watched as the vehicle trundled away over the cobbles. When it had gone from sight one of the senior policeman asked her to accompany them to the constabulary office, where an official report must be made and a statement taken. There, in a bleak room, she sat facing an officer across a weathered desk. While she drank a mug of hot, sweet tea, a succession of questions were asked and her answers duly noted. Later, when she enquired as to what now was to happen to her brother, she was told that there would be a post-mortem examination, followed by an inquest, which she would be required to attend. She would receive notification, they said. She was also informed that all Tom's possessions found on him would be given to her. Two hours later, when she was free to go, she stumbled out into the cool October night and started on her way back to Happerfell.

Arriving at The Gables, she met Mrs Soameson in the hall, and at once it was apparent to the older woman that something was very wrong. After one or two questions, she took Lily into the drawing room and there, weeping, Lily told her what had happened. Mrs Soameson listened for the most part in silence, only interjecting the occasional expression of sympathy. 'Perhaps,' she said, when Lily had come to the end of her story, 'you'd like to go back to

Sherrell tomorrow – to see your friend, Miss Balfour. Stay there, and come back on Sunday.'

So, the next morning Lily made the journey to Rowanleigh, arriving just before noon. She was met by a surprised Miss Elsie, who was not expecting her for another week. Soon, in Miss Elsie's study, Lily was pouring out her heart.

She stayed amid the familiar comforts of Rowanleigh the rest of that day, and until the hour the day following when she started back for Happerfell. She carried in her purse a sum of money that Miss Elsie had pressed upon her for the expenses of the funeral. The thirty pounds that she had given to Tom, Lily had told her, was still being held by the authorities, but she should have it returned to her soon. Mr Shad drove her to the station. Arriving back at The Gables, she eschewed the supper that Mrs Lemmon offered and went up to her room. Next morning, after another almost sleepless night, she was back in the schoolroom again with Lavinia, taking up her teaching duties once more.

That afternoon there came for her a letter from a clerk of the local court in Corster informing her that an inquest into Tom's death was set for Wednesday, the eleventh of October, at eleven-thirty, and that she would be required to attend.

Two days later, therefore, she went into the town, and there made her way to the old civic hall in one of the outer boroughs where the inquest was to be held. At the appointed hour she sat in a large, draughty room and listened as the clerk gave information to the coroner. There were few other people present and it was all over in a very short time. Within half-an-hour the coroner had declared the inquest adjourned, in order to allow the investigating police officers time to gather necessary evidence. Lily was free to go.

With a death certificate issued following the post-mortem, and Tom's body released for burial, she made her way to the Corster Town Hall. There, to a sharp-faced clerk, whose demeanour exhibited not an ounce of sympathy, she registered the fact of her brother's death.

Outside, on the busy street again, she felt a little wave of relief wash over her. Something more had been achieved; now she could see to his burial.

There was an undertaker's not far away – she had noted it on her outward journey – and she went there now. Invited into the director's office, she sat at a desk opposite the solemn-faced, black-suited man and, after receiving his condolences, set about making arrangements for Tom's funeral. When she said that Tom's body was at present lying in the coroner's mortuary, the man was prompted to ask how he had died. Forcing the words out through her tight lips, she said that her brother, in a moment of great despair, had taken his life.

The man looked even more grave at this. He said he was very sorry to hear it, and then added, hesitantly, frowning in sympathy, 'Are you aware that your brother might not be allowed burial in consecrated ground?'

For a moment she was at a loss for words, then she said, 'No – I didn't know.'

'I'm afraid so. It's not a hard and fast rule, however, and sometimes the church incumbent is not so strict – depending on the circumstances. But I should think the burial will have to be in the Shelbourne cemetery.'

'Not in the churchyard?'

'I doubt it – but you would need to ask the vicar. Go and see the Reverend Mr Sillipson at St Michael's.' He gestured with a wave of his hand. 'Just at the bottom of the hill.' He paused. 'He's quite new to the parish, but I've no doubt you'll find him an understanding man.'

She nodded. 'Yes – I'll go and see him. I'll go there now.' She paused. 'I'd like it if my brother could have a little service.'

469

'Well,' the man said, 'that's something you'll have to talk to the reverend about. In any case, I shall write to him today to find out the arrangements. I'll confirm to you, in a day or two, when the burial will be – the day and the time, and exactly where.' He went on then to say that the schedules were more full than usual, owing to the increased number of deaths resulting from the smallpox, numerous cases of which were causing much alarm in Corster and the surrounding areas.

With the arrangements completed as far as was possible, Lily was then asked to choose a coffin for her brother's body. Drawing on the little money that Miss Elsie had provided, she chose the cheapest available and paid the money into the man's hand. Then, her business done, she thanked him and left the building.

Reaching the church, she could see no one about as she entered by the gate and walked up the path between the graves to the porch. Inside, she pushed open the heavy door, stepped into the hushed interior and looked about her. At first she thought the place was empty, but then she noticed movement up near the altar, and saw there a woman in an apron and cap dusting the altar table. She went towards her.

The woman turned as Lily approached up the aisle, and gave her a little smile. 'Hello, miss,' she murmured as Lily came to a stop before her. Lily wished her a good afternoon and asked if the vicar was anywhere about.

'He's in the vestry, miss,' the woman said, and pointed off towards a door. 'Just go and knock.'

Lily thanked her, moved to the vestry door and tapped upon it. A moment later she heard a voice saying, 'Come in,' and she opened the door and stepped inside.

The Reverend Sillipson was sitting at a desk with three little stacks of tracts before him. A number of them he was holding in his hand. As Lily entered the room he got up from his chair and smiled at her over the top of his spectacles. Dressed in his cassock and dog-collar, he was a man of medium height and very slim build, round-shouldered, with dark, thinning, smoothed-back hair. He appeared to be in his late forties, but his face was unlined, his brow as smooth and pale as paper. He greeted her with a friendly 'Good afternoon', after which he added, still with his smile, 'I'm the Reverend Sillipson. And what can I do for you, miss?'

Lily gave him her name, and then, holding on to her control, told him that her brother had died. She had, she said, just come from the undertaker's where she had gone to arrange the funeral. At her words, the cleric's slightly guarded expression changed to one of sympathy, and he said at once, 'Oh, you've lost your brother. I'm very sorry to hear that. And looking at you, I can only assume that he was a young man.'

'Yes,' Lily said, 'he was seventeen.'

The reverend nodded. 'Oh, it's sad – it's very sad.' He was still holding the tracts. He moved as if to put them on the desk, but then, on an impulse, held them out to her. 'Take them, please,' he said. As Lily, a little surprised at the gesture, took them from him, he said, 'You might find they give some solace in this distressing time.' Then he added, 'They're new. They were just delivered from the printer today.'

Lily glanced down at the tracts. There were three of them, each bearing a little coloured picture of the iconic Christ figure. Beneath the pictures, printed in ornate script, were written testaments to Christ's enduring love.

'Anyway,' the reverend said, 'you didn't come here for me to give you tracts – conforting as they are. You're here to talk about the sad business of your brother's funeral.' He gestured to a nearby chair. 'Would you care to sit down?'

Lily murmured her thanks and took the seat. He sat down also, and turned his chair to face her.

'Which funeral director did you go to?' he asked her, and she replied, 'Mr Scrivener, in Maple Street.'

He nodded. 'Excellent. I shall no doubt be hearing from him by first post tomorrow, asking for a time and day for your brother's funeral. I can probably give you that information now. It'll be in about a week, or a little more.' He turned in his chair and pulled a volume across the desk towards him, opened it and scanned the page. 'Yes. Let's say next Wednesday – the eighteenth – a week today. Say at eleven-thirty. Would that suit you?'

'Oh, yes. Thank you.'

'You would like a little service for your brother, no doubt.'

'Yes,' Lily replied. 'Oh, yes, if that's possible.'

'Oh, indeed. And can you tell me where his – his body is lying now? At your home is it?'

She hesitated for a moment, then said, 'He's in the mortuary. The coroner's mortuary.'

The reverend's surprise showed in the slight widening of his eyes behind his spectacles. 'In the coroner's mortuary? So his passing was – unexpected.'

'Yes.'

'Oh, dear. Did he have an accident? Or was it a sudden illness? Surely not a heart seizure at his age.'

'No.' Lily gave a little shake of her head. 'No, he had no seizure, no – no accident.'

The Reverend Sillipson waited.

'I'm afraid he – he took his own life,' she said. 'He – fell – from a window.'

The reverend put a hand up to his cheek. 'He . . . fell?'

'Yes.' A moment's pause, then she added, 'He – jumped.'

Silent seconds passed, while the man sat, his lips pursed. 'I think you should have told me this at the start,' he said after a moment. His tone had changed now.

Lily said nothing. She could think of no words.

'I'm very sorry,' the reverend went on, 'but I'm afraid I cannot preside over any service for the young man – nor officiate at his burial.'

'Please . . .' she said, 'just a few words. He had little time to go to church, but – oh, just a few words, a little blessing. It would mean so much.'

He sat up a little straighter in his chair. 'I'm sorry,' he said, 'but this person has taken his own life, and that being so he has forfeited all right to be received into God's grace. It is for God, in His wisdom, to take and give life; it's not for the likes of us mortals.'

Lily felt her heart contract with pain, while sudden tears pricked at her eyes. 'Oh, but Reverend,' she burst out, 'he was only young. He'd just suffered a dreadful calamity – and he'd gone through so much.' Her throat was so tight that she could barely get her words out. For herself she would not have cared a fig about a service given by this pale-skinned rake of a man, who looked as if he had never had contact with humanity, but for Tom she wanted it. 'Please,' she said, 'don't deny him this. He was desperate – and not thinking straight. He was afraid and – he didn't know what he was doing . . . Please – all he needs is a little prayer, just a little blessing.'

The cleric rose from his chair, at the same time raising a slim hand to stop her passionate flow. 'I'm sorry,' he said, though there was no touch of regret in his tone. 'I cannot spare him one single word. He'll have to be buried in the cemetery – and on the other side of the hedge.'

Lily frowned. 'The other side of the hedge? What does that mean?'

He waved his hand in a dismissive gesture. 'There's a spot there, in the cemetery. It's marked off on the other side of a privet hedge. That's where such as your brother are

473

buried.' His thin, pink lips were tightly pinched. 'There's no room for such a one in Holy ground.' As he spoke, his voice seemed to be full of pride. He was merciless and invincible in his Goodness, his knowledge of what was right and wrong. 'I'm here to interpret God's will,' he added solemnly, 'and I must, and shall, do it the way I think best.'

Lily had also risen to her feet. 'Is – is that your final word?' she said.

'Yes,' he said with a nod. 'I'm sorry, but it is. If you came here with –'

Now, suddenly angry, she drew herself up. She no longer felt obliged to listen to any word he spoke. 'Yes, I'm sorry too,' she said, cutting into his words. 'I'm sorry that you, as your God's representative, have no warmth of under-standing in your soul. I'm sorry that you have no compassion for a young man who was in need of simply such a thing. Such a thing that might indeed have saved him.' She realised that she was still holding the tracts. She held them up, in a glance taking in the pious phrases and the little coloured images of the benevolent Christ figure. She held them out at arm's length. 'Would your Jesus have turned away from him?' And now the tears that she had so far kept at bay came rising up and brimming over. 'Would *He* have turned from a young man who was so desperately in need? A young man who was good and whose only failing was to have nothing, and whose future was bleak and without hope?' Her voice broke on a sob and she added bitterly, 'If this is so then I would want no part of your god.'

The man's mouth opened in disbelief and amazement. 'You are a blasphemer,' he said. 'That you dare to come into God's house and speak in such a way!'

'Yes, I *do* dare!' Lily said through tight lips, tears streaming down her cheeks. 'And I mean what I say. But have no fear – I shall see my brother buried without your mealy-mouthed words.' She was sobbing. 'He doesn't need the likes of you to get into your – your Paradise. If there is a God in heaven then He will see past your mean-spirited little soul – and He will take him to His heart.' With her final words she drew back her hand and threw the tracts at him. They struck him lightly on the chest and fell to the floor in a little scattering of colour. 'Keep your pious words,' she said. 'We don't need them.'

Turning swiftly about, she went from the room, and then, her feet ringing on the stone flags, made her way back out into the grey October day.

The days passed with little to differentiate one from another, Lily living them as in some dull, waking nightmare. She continued to teach Lavinia in the schoolroom, and gave all she could, but always a part of her mind was detached, off in some other world where she relived, over and over, her last moments with Tom. Always, in her mind, she saw him leaping up, so agile in his desperation, one foot on the seat of the bench as he launched himself forward. The images were always the same. When he throws himself through the glass he plunges head first. There was no changing that memory. In that recurring image there is no suggestion of him putting up his arms to shield his head as he goes through the frame. He goes face foremost, his chin jutting, lips drawn back over his teeth, and the lacerating spears of glass slice into the flesh of his face and his throat, and he is already bleeding to death before he hits the ground . . .

The funeral, she had had it confirmed by Mr Scrivener, would take place at eleven-forty-five on Wednesday, the eighteenth. It would be in the cemetery and there would be no clergyman to officiate at the graveside. She had written to her stepmother informing her of Tom's death, but there had been no reply. She was not, after all, so surprised. There

475

had been no word either from Joel since his letter from Brussels. He would be in Paris now. She was sure, though, that she would hear from him soon.

In Lily's grief, the only moments that brought her any relief and allowed her a little, precious, touch of happiness, were those when she saw the child, her son. Such moments might by chance occur anywhere, but they usually came when she went into the nursery at midday. Sometimes he lay sleeping in his cot, while on other occasions he was wakeful and energetic. The prospect of seeing him, if only for a few minutes, drew her like a magnet. When she went there on Tuesday, the day before the funeral, she found him awake and bright and talkative. He was in the process of having his clothes changed. As she came across the carpet he struggled in Miss Cattock's arms and, being let go, ran towards Lily with a smile. At once she crouched, holding out her arms to meet him, and he came to a stop a foot from her outstretched hands. Now she could smile. A few more inches, and he would be in her arms, as he had been on the afternoon of the storm. This time he came no closer, but stayed where he was and looked up at her with his soft smile and his blue eyes wide. He was wearing white linen drawers and a cotton vest that exposed his upper arms. On his naked left arm she saw the half-healed scar from his recent vaccination, the vaccination he had been so proud of. Seeing it, she wanted to draw him to her and press her lips to the little healing wound, but then, with a chuckle, he was turning, moving back to the arms of his nurse. The brief encounter left Lily with a little warmth that touched her aching heart.

The following day, she caught the train into Corster and from the station took an omnibus to the Shelbourne cemetery. She carried with her a little bunch of carnations that Mr Beeching had cut for her and wrapped in paper. On her arrival she called at the office that was situated just within the gates and there made enquiries regarding the burial of her brother. The clerk consulted a ledger and said, 'Due at eleven-forty-five, miss, right?' Lily nodded, 'Yes', and the man gave her directions to the spot where the interment was to take place.

The cemetery was large and Lily made her way along the paths between the graves with their stone slabs, Maltese crosses and carved angels. There were few other people about; she saw only the occasional mourner carrying flowers, and a gardener working here and there. Following the clerk's directions, she left the main part of the cemetery and passed into another, much smaller section. There were no mausoleums here, no stone angels keeping watch, and what stone slabs there were were altogether more modest and humble.

She came upon an open grave with a small wooden spar set in the ground in front of it. On it she read the words Thos Clair. The earth from the grave lay next to it in a heap. She stopped beside it, and stood there, waiting. There was a keen wind blowing, and it crept under her collar. She was oblivious to the discomfort. After a while she caught movement from the corner of her eye, and turned and saw pallbearers approaching, carrying a coffin, Tom's coffin. At a sedate pace the men came to the graveside, followed by an elderly man in a black suit.

There was no ceremony. In a silence broken only by the little sighs of exertion as the men worked, Lily watched as the pine coffin was lowered into the brown earth. When it was in place the men stepped back, gave the faintest hint of a bow, and retreated. Lily and the man in the black suit were left alone. After a moment she stepped to the grave's edge and let fall the carnations onto the coffin lid. Some remained there, while others fell off into the gap at the side. As she stepped back, the man held out his prayer book. There was sympathy in his lined face. Would she, he asked hesitantly, like to say a prayer? She thanked him, deeply grateful for his kindness and understanding, but declined. She did not, she could have said, need prayers from the pens of others; and any prayer that she might make she would make alone.

She thanked the man again, gave one last look down at the plain lid of the pine coffin and turned away.

As she deposited her umbrella in the hall stand on her return to The Gables, Lizzie came to her and whispered that the master was back from Scotland. Then, gesturing to the silver tray on the table, she added that a letter had come for Lily while she had been out. Lily thanked her, and while the maid headed back towards the kitchen, she picked up the letter and saw at once that it was from Joel.

With it in her hand she made her way up the stairs to the top floor, crossed the landing and opened the door to the schoolroom. Lavinia was sitting at her desk writing, working on the history lesson that Lily had set for her, and she looked up with a shy smile as Lily appeared in the doorway. Was all going well? Lily asked her, and Lavinia replied that it was, and that she had nearly finished her written exercise on the Stuart kings of England.

In her room a minute later, Lily took off her hat and coat, then picked up the envelope again and tore it open. Standing by the window, she looked at the words that Joel had written. Under the address he had given: 23 Rue de Soire, Paris, she saw the date: the eighth of October. It had been written ten days ago. Obviously it had been delayed in its passage. She went on to read:

My dearest Lily,
    Well, no matter how time might drag, it eventually goes by. And how I'm longing for the time when I can return to England and see you again. I hope that that

478

time will not be long now. After much travelling, I have eventually come to Paris, where I can at least settle in the apartment for a while, and not have to dash about for another train.

That said, I'm glad to report that things are going as expected here; there are no surprises, which perhaps is a good thing. Routine and dullness are, if nothing else, safe. I am, as before, keeping very busy with the store – and the demands upon me and my time are even greater with my father being less than his robust self. It appears now that he suffered a slight stroke. We are all hoping and expecting that he will make a complete recovery, but the mild debilitation he has suffered has given him food for thought, and as a result we now hope that he is becoming a little more resigned to being less involved in the work, and more ready to delegate. Even so, I should be free to return near the end of the month, so it will not be long now. And as I said above, no matter how the time might appear to crawl, eventually it will pass and we shall be together again.

Believe me, I cannot wait for that time. I must say at this point, though, that I have not yet spoken to my father about us. I shall do so as soon as I feel the time is right, but while his health remains frail I cannot risk causing him further hurt. Have no fear, though, when the time comes I shall put all before him. Likewise, when Simone returns to Paris with her mother I shall make clear to her the change in my feelings and in my situation. I do not pretend for one moment that this is going to be an easy matter, and I dread the thought of causing her distress – which is what will certainly happen. And not only Simone, but her mother too. But I know now that I cannot live for another. I am, when it comes down to it, selfish, and I can only envisage my own happiness in this. I do want to assure you, though, that when I come back to Corster it will be as a free man, a free man who will never stop loving you.

Please write to me here and let me know how you are. I think about you so much. You cannot imagine how pleased I was to get your letter just before I left Brussels, and learnt that you are happily employed in your new situation. Not that I would wish it to continue indefinitely, for it is certain that as my wife you will no longer be a governess to other people's children.

I shall close now, and hope that this reaches you soon. And, please, think of me – as you know I am thinking of you.

Your loving
Joel

A little later, leaving Lavinia at work at her lesson, Lily went downstairs, heading for the kitchen for a glass of water. As she reached the foot of the stairs, Mrs Soameson appeared in the open doorway of the morning room. 'Ah, Miss Clair,' she said, 'I've been watching out for you. Can you come in for a minute?' She was in mourning now, wearing a black bombazine dress and a black lace cap.

Lily went into the room and, at her mistress's bidding, sat in one of the small armchairs near the sofa. As Mrs Soameson sat down facing her, she said with a smile, 'A quiet time of day, thank heaven. Joshie's sleeping, and Lavinia's busy, no doubt.'

Lily nodded. 'Oh, yes, indeed, ma'am. We're doing history. She's working on a written exercise now.'

Mrs Soameson gave a little nod, paused briefly, then asked with sympathy in her voice: 'How did your day go, may I ask? Your poor brother's funeral?'

Lily, prepared for the question, replied that all had gone as expected, though she went into no detail of the day's events. Mrs Soameson took in her words as she spoke, but knowing of the immediate circumstances of Tom's death, did not pry further. After a minute or two, having gone on to speak of everyday matters, she said with a sigh, 'I wanted a word with you, Miss Clair. I'm afraid we're in something of a state of upheaval here. Mr Soameson returned from Edinburgh this afternoon. Did you know that?'

'Yes, I did, ma'am. Lizzie told me when I came in.'

Mrs Soameson nodded. 'Yes, and it's certain now that we're going to be leaving sooner than planned.'

'Oh, really, ma'am?'

'Indeed, yes. Mr Soameson is talking about going in the middle of next month. Probably on the eleventh.'

'Oh,' Lily said, 'so soon.'

'So soon, yes. The business here – the paper mill – the sale is going through very smoothly, and the managers are absolutely reliable. There's nothing really now to stay on for – whereas Mr Soameson is very much needed back in Edinburgh, and as soon as possible.' She clasped her hands. 'Oh, there's going to be so much to do in a short space of time, but now we've made the decision we have to get on with things. The lease on this place is due to end soon, anyway, so that's no problem. Our future is there – in Edinburgh. And for the children too. Lavinia will be able to start school right away.' She gave a little shake of her head, and said, 'I'm really sorry about you, Miss Clair, for it means you won't have so long in our employment as we'd anticipated, but – oh, dear, these things can't be helped.'

'Of course not,' Lily said. 'I do understand.'

Mrs Soameson looked around at the room and gave a sigh. 'A move is such a daunting task – but if we grasp the nettle it'll get done. It has to – we have no choice.' She waved a hand, taking in the furniture around them. 'At a time like this I'm happy to say that not a lot of this furniture belongs to us, so it'll be mostly just our personal things to pack up.' She smiled. 'And we shall be very glad of any help you can give us in that respect, Miss Clair.'

'Oh, of course,' Lily said. 'Anything I can do . . .'

'We haven't told the children yet,' Mrs Soameson went on. 'That'll be done in good time. Lavinia will remember her old home, of course, but for Joshie it'll all be quite new. He was born here and has never set foot outside England.'

Joshie. In a few weeks he would be gone, Lily said to herself. When that happened she would never see him again.

'Anyway,' Mrs Soameson went on, 'I had to let you know without delay, for you'll want to look around as soon as possible for a new position.'

'Yes.' Lily gave a nod. 'Thank you. I'll look in the *Gazette* on Friday.'

Chapter Thirty-two

Immediately following Mr Soameson's return from Edinburgh, the servants and anyone else available were set to the task of packing up the family's belongings in preparation for their transfer on the long route to Scotland. There was an air of excitement that pervaded the whole house.

'We're going back to Edinburgh early, miss,' Lavinia said to Lily as they settled to work in the school room on the Friday morning. 'Mama told me after breakfast.'

Yes, Lily replied, she was aware of it.

'I'm looking forward to it,' Lavinia said. 'Though I'm sorry you won't be coming with us, miss.'

'Well – there you are. I shall stay here in Wiltshire.'

'If you came with us you could be governess for Joshie. He'll need one soon.'

'Yes, he will.'

'What will you do, miss, when we're gone? Go as governess to some other little girl.'

'I hope I shall be able to.'

'Or perhaps you'll get married, miss.'

Lily smiled. 'Who knows. Perhaps I shall.'

The *Corster Gazette* was delivered to the house every Friday, and in the short break between morning and afternoon lessons, Lily left the schoolroom to go downstairs to see if the paper was available for a few minutes. She must needs study the classified advertisements. Notwithstanding that her future was with Joel, she must, before that future was formed, take care of the present, and that meant finding another post for when her employment with the Soamesons came to an end.

She found the newspaper on the hall table and took it back up to the schoolroom where she would be alone until Lavinia returned for her afternoon lessons. The main news article on the front page told of the Corster isolation hospital – which held no more than a dozen beds – being full with smallpox victims, so that more and more sufferers were having to be treated in their homes. She turned to the pages of classified advertisements, and after a brief search in the 'Positions Vacant' column found an advertisement from a gentleman in Little Hawes who was seeking a governess for his two children from the beginning of January. At once she set to write a letter in response.

Later that day she received a letter from the Corster constabulary, informing her that at her convenience she might call at the office and retrieve her late brother's effects. She went into Corster the next afternoon, and at the police station was brought a tray bearing the items that had been in Tom's possession when he had died. There was a pocket knife, a handkerchief, her own last letter to him, a few coppers and an envelope containing the thirty pounds. She signed a receipt for the items, and took them away.

On Sunday she went to Sherrell to spend the day with Miss Elsie. The skies were clear, and the thinning October sun shone down on the autumn landscape. The grass of the meadows was still green, but the leaves of many of the trees had turned to brown and gold. As she walked along the lane towards Rowanleigh she saw that the leaves of the horsechestnut were yellowing, while the brown, shiny conkers, such a joy to children, lay scattered over the grass verge and the road.

Later, sitting with Miss Elsie in her study over tea, Lily

handed her the thirty pounds, along with the money left over after paying for Tom's funeral. She would repay the sum used as soon as possible, she said. She went on to speak briefly of the burial, and then of the news that her employers were to go to Scotland much sooner than originally planned. They intended now, she said, to depart in November, the date being set for Saturday the eleventh.

'So soon,' said Miss Elsie. 'That's only three weeks away.'

'Yes.'

There was a brief silence, then Miss Elsie said, 'You're going to miss the child, I'm sure.'

'Lavinia's an excellent pupil,' Lily said. 'I've been so fortunate in that respect.'

'I was thinking of the boy.'

Lily said nothing, but gave a brief nod.

'You still see him, do you – about the house?'

'Yes.' Lily nodded. Then, in a little quiet outburst, she added, 'Every moment with him is precious!'

Miss Elsie gazed at her, unable to hide the faint expression of dismay on her face. 'You'll have to let go, Lily,' she said into the quiet. 'You'll have to let go eventually.'

'Of course. I know that.'

'Do you?'

'Of course. I'm realistic. I have to be.'

'Once the family's moved away – and so far away – it's doubtful that you'll ever see him again.'

'I know. I know.' Lily spoke quickly, almost impatiently. While she realised the truth of Miss Elsie's words she did not wish to dwell upon them. 'I know he'll be gone,' she said. 'I've known that from the start.' She forced a smile. 'I told you – I'm realistic about this.'

Miss Elsie's expression softened. 'I'm sure you are.' She paused. 'I just don't want to see you hurt – again.'

'There is no fear of that,' Lily said with a touch of bravado in her tone. She could have added, *Anyway – other things are*

485

happening in my life. Joel – Mr Goodhart – is due in England at
the end of the month. And then my life will be changed. But she
held back. Something in her kept her silent. She would
wait, wait until everything was settled.

The letter that Lily had waited for from Joel came on
Tuesday. It arrived by the first post and she read it in
the privacy of her room. It had come from Paris, from the
apartment on the Rue de Soire and was dated Monday
the sixteenth of October. It had taken just over a week to get
there. He had written:

My dearest Lily,
   I am writing this in some haste, as it must get to you
before I return. And as time is of the essence, then it
must necessarily be brief. I am due to leave Paris on the
evening of Friday 27th, and to be back in England on
Saturday, which will leave me no time to contact you
that day once I'm back. Can you meet me on the
Sunday, 29th? Can you have time off on that day? I do
hope you can. In Market Street, close to the theatre, is a
little restaurant called the Crimmond. Can you meet me
there? You will not wish to wait there alone, so I will be
there from the time of its opening at six o'clock. If you
could try to arrive about 6.30 that would be ideal. We
can eat there, or go on somewhere else – whatever you
wish.
   You will not be able to reply to this letter, for I shall
have left France before any letter reaches me. Try to be
there, though, please. In any case I shall wait till seven-
thirty. If you have not arrived by then I shall assume
that you have been prevented from coming, or that you
have not received this letter.
   Before I go I must tell you that it has been done –
what I promised. Simone returned yesterday and we

486

spoke at length. It was the most difficult thing I have ever had to do in my life, and I must tell you that I would never wish to do it again. To see someone suffer so much pain and anguish, and to know that oneself is the cause of that suffering is the most sobering of experiences. I cannot say more at this point. I have not yet spoken to my father on the matter, due to his present frailty, but I plan to do so before I leave. This will be another task for which I have no appetite, but which has to be undertaken.

Think of me, as I shall think of you.

Waiting, longing, to see you, I am, ever and always,

Your

Joel

So it was done. He had gained his freedom. She sighed, exhaling the breath held too long in her lungs as she had reads his words, feeling the tension drain from her body. It was done. And in a short a time he would be back. Just five days and they would be together again.

She held on to the thought, and in all the horror of the past weeks it was the one single ray, the one candle flame, that brought light into the dark.

There came in the post the next day a letter from the Corster coroner's Court informing her that the inquest into the death of her brother would be resumed on November the first, and that she would be required to attend on that morning at ten-thirty.

The next day, Thursday, brought a letter in answer to her response to the classified advertisement in the *Corster Gazette*. In it, the writer, a Mr Arthur Molle, said that he and his wife were seeking a governess for their son and daughter of six and seven years, from the beginning of the new year. He would be away from home for a while, he added, but if Miss Clair was interested he would like her to come to Little Hawes for interview in mid-November. A specific day and time would be arranged. Lily wrote back at once to say she would be pleased to attend, and would look forward to hearing again from Mr Molle nearer the time.

On Friday, the thought was constantly with her that Joel would be setting out from Paris that evening – and on Saturday too, from the moment she awoke, he was there on her mind. She did not know at what hour he would be arriving at his home in Corster, but frequently she pictured him on his journey, stepping off the boat at Dover or sitting on the train bound for the West Country. Each hour brought her nearer the moment when they would be together.

Then Sunday came, at last, and the minutes and the hours dragged by, but eventually, at long last, it was time to get ready to go to meet him.

On the train to Corster she sat looking out at the autumn scenery. Occasionally, when the train passed through areas deeply shadowed by trees or the high chalk banks that marked the route she caught brief glimpses of her reflection. Though these revealed nothing of the shine of anticipation in her eyes, or the touch of anxiety in the set of her mouth, she knew that they must be there.

In Corster when she alighted she felt the urge to hurry, but she held back; it was not yet six o'clock. Near the end of the platform was a ladies' waiting room, and she went in and sat on a bench while fifteen slow minutes passed by. From where she sat she kept an eye on the station clock, and when the hands came to six-fifteen she picked up her bag and umbrella and went out of the station.

The town's streets were not so busy on a Sunday. As she turned into Market Street she heard the clock of St

Margaret's church strike the half-hour. The Crimmond restaurant was well-established in Corster. A wide-fronted Georgian building, it had tubs of evergreens on either side of its oak front door. It was six-thirty when Lily entered, and she was approached at once by the head waiter, who gave her a little bow, and said, 'Yes, madam, good evening.'

Lily politely returned his greeting and said that she was there to meet a friend, Mr Goodhart. As she spoke she was already looking around, hoping to catch sight of Joel. The interior was not spacious, and several diners were already seated, though most of the tables were still empty. Did madam's friend make a reservation, the waiter asked, to which Lily replied that she thought not. Then perhaps, the man said, she would like to take a seat and wait for the gentleman. She thanked him and he took her coat from her and led her to a table over by a window. As she sat down the waiter asked her if she would like to order something while she waited. Although she wanted nothing, she said she would have a little tea.

As she sat there, other diners came in and were led to their places. The waiter brought her tea in a thick white china pot and she poured it out and sat sipping at it, wondering where to direct her gaze. She felt self-conscious sitting there alone, when every other diner in the place was in company. Eventually she heard the sound of the church clock striking the hour of seven. By this time the restaurant was well over half full. She had drunk one cup of tea that she did not want, and now poured a second. She toyed with it merely, though, sipping in a desultory fashion. When the waiter came to her once more he looked at her sympathetically. Did madam wish for anything else? he asked, and Lily replied with thanks that she did not, not for the present. He nodded his head and went away again.

The minutes passed. Almost every table in the place was now occupied. She knew she could not continue to sit there without ordering something more – and now here was the waiter coming to her again, his eyebrows rising slightly as he asked the question he was bound to ask: 'Is there anything else you would like, madam?' No, she said, thanking him, and then added, 'Please – if you'd be kind enough to bring me my bill . . .' Minutes later she had paid, and was taking up her bag and umbrella.

As she stepped out into the street the church clock struck eight. The gaslamps had been lit, and in the gloom she stood looking along the row of shops towards the square, and then up to the left, in the direction of the town hall and the municipal buildings, peering at the shadows of the anonymous figures that moved in the lamps' glow. Where was Joel? What could have happened to him?

She continued to stand there on the pavement, close to the restaurant's entrance. She would wait a further half-hour; she would not move until the clock struck half-past. She stayed there while the evening sojourners strolled past and as the diners in the restaurant finished their dinners and emerged, replete, to head for their homes.

The night air was growing chill now, and a keen wind came whipping up from the direction of the river. She must go. On the church tower the clock struck a single chime. As the sound died away she turned and walked miserably towards the station.

Chapter Thirty-three

In the schoolroom next day Lily continued about her duties, giving Lavinia her lessons, while downstairs the preparations continued apace for the move to Scotland. While Mrs Soameson supervised the sorting and the packing of the things that would go up north, Mr Soameson was out of the house on his own business, only getting home late in the evenings, too exhausted to do more.

When Tuesday came, with no word from Joel, Lily felt increasingly at a loss. She had no way of knowing even where he was. There was no point in writing to him in Paris if he had already left, while at the same time she balked at writing to him at his family home in Corster. She could do nothing other than continue to wait.

She was in turmoil as she lay in bed that night, her mind constantly torn. One moment she would be thinking of Joel, and then, in trying to wrench her thoughts in a different direction, she would find herself thinking of Tom, and the inquest next day at which she must attend. At other times she found her thoughts straying to the small child who slept in his little bed on the other side of the landing. It was close on three o'clock when she eventually fell asleep.

From Corster Junction station the next morning she took an omnibus to the coroner's court, arriving with plenty of time to spare. On giving her name to a clerk at a desk she was directed to a side room and instructed to wait until the court was in session, after which time she would be called in. The room she entered was a shabby, soulless place with marks and stains on the walls, and cuts and scratches in the wood of the centre table and the benches. It was empty when she went in, but after several minutes other people began to arrive. Where some were poorly dressed and coarsely spoken, others were obviously of a higher class. All of them, she assumed, were there as witnesses. Among them she recognised the two young women who had been in the museum that day and who had seen Tom's plunge from the window.

As the clock on the wall ticked the time away, people came and went, while those waiting shuffled their feet, and muttered to one another in low conversations. Some seemed relatively light-hearted, while others appeared grave and preoccupied. Two or three of the men sat smoking pipes or cigarettes, and the smoke drifted in the stale air and clung to the tobacco-stained walls. Every so often an officer of the court appeared at the door and called out the name of someone required in the courtroom. At last, after what seemed an age, Lily's own name was called.

A few minutes later she was in the courtroom, standing before the court officials and a handful of spectators, answering the coroner's questions. In a low voice, halting at times, she spoke of her last moments with Tom in the museum gallery, and also of the accident which had resulted in the amputation of his hand. There could be no question to anyone but that his final act had been anything but deliberate, but the elderly coroner seemed to understand the total desperation of Tom's last moments, and spoke of him in kindly tones.

At last she was told she might step down, and the coroner announced an adjournment until two-thirty. She was instructed to return at that time. Rather than sit in the waiting room she wandered out into the street, and from there to a coffee house where she drank a cup of tea. She was back in the courthouse well before two-thirty, and after sitting waiting for an hour was informed by the clerk that the inquiry was over and that she was free to go. He went on to say that there had been a verdict returned of 'Suicide while the balance of the mind was disturbed'. She nodded and thanked him and went out into the grey November afternoon. It was over.

Returning to Happerfell, Lily hoped that she would find that there was some word from Joel awaiting her, but there was none. Mrs Soameson, however, sought Lily out and asked her to join her in the drawing room. When Lily went in, she found her talking with an aproned workman who was taking down some of the pictures and wrapping them to be packed for transport. Mrs Soameson stayed long enough to give the man further instructions, then left him, saying to Lily, 'Come, let's go somewhere where we can talk for a minute.' She led the way into the morning room, sat down and gestured for Lily to be seated in the chair opposite.

'Was it awful?' she asked. 'I thought of you so many times, having to go through that. It must have been dreadful for you. So very upsetting.'

'Yes,' Lily murmured with a little nod. 'Yes, it was – difficult.'

'And is it – all over now?'

'Yes. There was a verdict. Now it's finished.'

'I see. And the verdict – it was what you expected?'

'Yes. Suicide.'

Mrs Soameson let out her breath on a deep sigh. 'It's so tragic,' she said. 'Such a young life. Wasted like that.'

Lily said nothing, but sat with lips compressed, not trusting herself to speak. After a moment Mrs Soameson said, leaning forward a little in her chair:

'The business – with the inquest this morning – that isn't

493

the only reason I wanted to talk to you now. Something has come up. We're leaving even sooner than we'd planned.'

'You're not going at the end of next week?'

'No, we're not. We're leaving on Saturday.'

'On Saturday? This coming Saturday?'

Mrs Soameson nodded. 'Indeed we are – and it's all such a terrible rush, but it's got to be done. Something has come up in Scotland – all to do with the business and the house – and Mr Soameson says there's nothing for it but that we get there as soon as possible.' Her tone changed a little as she added, 'This whole thing is an upheaval for you too, I know. When you came here you were expecting to stay on at least another month, and now it's thrown all your plans up into the air. I'm so sorry it's happened for you this way.'

Lily said, 'Well – if it has to be, ma'am. It can't be helped.'

'No, it can't be helped. I'm afraid it can't.' A pause. 'However, you won't need to go back to Sherrell any sooner, for we'd like you to stay on for a week or so and help Nurse look after Joshie. It'll give her a little respite when she needs it.'

'But – isn't he going with you on Saturday?'

'Well, we've decided against it. I don't think it would be a good idea at all. I think he's coming down with a little cold, and I don't want him taking that awful long journey if he's under the weather. And the house in Edinburgh will be in such a state – it's going to need all our concentration to get it in order and to find places for our things. Lavinia's coming with us, but I think it's better that Joshie stays on for a while. I thought you might also, while you're here, be able to help Mrs Lemmon and Susie with some of the packing that's yet to be done. If you have time, of course. There won't be a lot, but it would be a great help to us if you could manage it.'

'Yes, of course. I'll help in any way I can.'

'Are you sure you don't mind? Staying on to help with Josh?'

'No, not at all. I'll be glad to do it.'

'He's not a demanding child, as you know, and he's fond of you. Are you sure it's not a terrible imposition?'

'No,' Lily said at once. 'Not at all.'

'Good. That's splendid. I thought also that you might do a little work with him on his letters – now that he's beginning to read. What d'you think of that?'

'Yes. Oh, yes, I'd love to.'

'He's a bright boy. I've been going through his little primers with him – as Miss Cattock has too – and he learns very quickly.'

'Oh, I'd love to help him, if I can,' Lily said.

Mrs Soameson nodded. 'That's excellent. Mr Soameson and I have talked it over – and we'd like you to stay on till the Sunday of next week. That's the twelfth. Would that be all right?'

'Yes, of course.'

'Splendid. Joshie should be over his cold by then and we'll have had a week to get the house in order. Miss Cattock can bring him up on the train, setting out on that day, Sunday. They'll travel overnight and we'll meet them from the train on Monday morning. I hope by then we shall have everything ready for him. He doesn't like upheaval. It tends to make him anxious. Did I tell you that Lizzie will be coming along with us also on Saturday? We shall need all the help we can get, I tell you, though Mrs Lemmon will be staying behind for a few days, as will Mr Beeching. They'll be joining us a little later too.' She gestured to where two large tea-chests stood near the wall. 'All this endless packing. We seem to have accumulated so much while we've been here. A lot of it went off this morning – quite a wagon-load. It's going to be chaos there till we get things sorted out.' She gave a sigh, then added, 'Anyway, that's not your problem. Mr Soameson will see about your wages before we leave, of course.'

'Thank you, ma'am.'

'I don't mind telling you that Lavinia's going to miss you so much, Miss Clair.'

'I shall miss *her*.'

Mrs Soameson nodded, pleased. 'Well,' she said, 'I suppose we must get back to work . . .' She rose from her seat as she spoke, and Lily rose along with her. In the hall they separated, Mrs Soameson to go back to her packing chores in the drawing room, and Lily to return to the schoolroom and Lavinia.

Thursday and Friday passed and there was still no letter from Joel. It was a week since he had been due to return to England, and there had been not a single word.

Lily was up and breakfasted well before the first postal delivery on Saturday morning, but again there was nothing for her. She had no time to brood, however. There were so many last-minute preparations to be made before her employers' departure for the station, and she felt obliged to do what she could to help. Shortly after a hurried and informal luncheon, Mr Soameson came to her in the schoolroom where she was packing away her text book primers and papers. There he thanked her for her work with Lavinia, and presented her with a new reference, remarking as he did so that it was glowing, and should surely help her in securing a new post. In addition, he paid her the balance of her wages, and was kind enough to give her a little bonus in recognition of her employment being terminated earlier than had been anticipated. When it was all done he shook her hand, wished her luck in her future career, and said he hoped that one day they might meet again.

After he had gone, Mrs Soameson and Lavinia came into

the room. Lavinia's eyes were moist as she said goodbye, and impulsively she put her arms around her. Lily bent and kissed the child, and for some moments they held one another. 'I'll write to you, miss,' Lavinia said, a little tearfully. 'Will you write to me?' Lily replied that of course she would.

When the final goodbyes had been said, Lavinia went from the room, leaving Lily and Mrs Soameson alone. After reassuring herself that Mr Soameson had satisfactorily settled everything with Lily with regard to her wages and her reference, Mrs Soameson handed Lily a slip of paper bearing the family's Edinburgh address, and exhorted her to write at once should there be any problem. 'You'll go back to Sherrell when you leave here next Sunday, will you?' she asked, and Lily replied that she would, and would probably remain there until she found a new position.

Then it was time for farewells, and for Lily to wish her mistress a pleasant journey. At this Mrs Soameson gave a groaning little laugh and said, 'Oh, that journey! Almost eleven hours, and I can never sleep on those trains. We shall be wrecks by the time we arrive.' With a final goodbye she moved to the doorway. She must, she said, go and spend some last few minutes with Joshie. 'His cold is worse,' she added, 'and he so wants to come with us. But I can't put him through that exhausting journey – not the way he's feeling.'

It was close on two o'clock, and soon afterwards Lily – now having said her goodbyes to Lizzie too – stood at the window of her room looking down onto the back yard. There she watched as Mr Soameson and Lavinia and the maid got into the carriage, ready to start on the first part of their journey. Mrs Soameson stood with Joshua in her arms until the last moment, at which point she kissed him and then handed him over to Miss Cattock who stood nearby.

Two minutes later the carriage was rattling down the drive and out onto the road.

The atmosphere in the house was strange without its recently departed inhabitants. Later in the afternoon, released from her teaching schedule, Lily helped Susie, the daily maid, with the packing of some linen and a little china, and afterwards went up to the nursery to join Emily Cattock and the boy. The child's cold had well and truly taken hold and he lay in his bed listless and fretful.

Lily ate dinner that evening with Miss Cattock, Mrs Lemmon and Susie in the servants' dining room. Later, she went up to the schoolroom where she sat at her table and wrote to Miss Elsie, telling her that her employment with the Soamesons would terminate on the coming Sunday, and that she would be returning to Sherrell some time that day.

The next day was the fifth of November. Lily spent the day in desultory occupations, helping where she could and also spending time with the boy and his nurse. In the evening there came the sound of fireworks – cracks and bangs coming from the direction of the village centre – and she and Emily Cattock stood at the nursery window and looked out towards the flares of light. Over on a hill through the gathering autumn mist they saw the glow of a distant bonfire where yet another effigy of Guy Fawkes was burning.

Monday came . . . Tuesday . . . Still no word from Joel. The red-jacketed postman came to the house on both days, but brought nothing for Lily. Joel must have had an accident, she told herself. It was the only answer. Either that or he had been taken ill. But where? Was he still in France? Was he in England? Yet again she thought of writing to him at his home in Corster, but when it came to it she drew back. She would be a part of his life one day, and one day soon, but that time was not yet. And yet, if he were sick, would he be so sick that he could not even write a few lines? The questions spun and pounded through her brain.

On Wednesday Joshua appeared somewhat brighter, and in the morning, while Emily Cattock worked at her sewing, Lily sat with the boy on the rug before the fire and spread his coloured bricks before him. They were painted with the letters of the alphabet and simple words, and bright pictures of animals. Together Lily and the boy went through them as he named the letters and words, and then tried to read out the short sentences that Lily composed. He was thrilled to find that he was successful almost without fail, and Lily and Emily applauded him. At the sound of their approval he chuckled, pleased with himself and eagerly asked for more.

In the afternoon, after the boy's nap, Lily and the nurse took him outside to get a little fresh air – advocated always by Mrs Soameson – all three wrapped up against the sharp breeze. Mr Beeching, taking advantage of the spell of dry weather, was cutting the grass of the back lawn, the last cut of the season. He was standing with legs astride, rhythmically swinging the scythe, the hush and swish of the blade sounding keen in the November air. Lily and Emily and the boy walked past him down the central path between the lawns, down wide stone steps into a lower area beyond, where more lawns and flowerbeds were laid out.

Leaving the formal garden behind, they followed the path down through the kitchen garden and into the orchard. In the summer, Miss Cattock said, Joshie had been happy to play among the trees with his sister, and to amuse himself on the swing that hung from one of the apple-tree boughs. Today, though, when asked if he would like to go on the swing he shook his head and said no, he would rather go back indoors. At his words, the three of them turned and started back towards the house.

The accident happened as they were climbing the broad steps that separated the lower part of the formal garden from the higher. Lily was in front, with Joshua and the nurse immediately behind. As Lily moved onto the top step she heard Emily give a little squeal of fright, added to at once by a cry from the boy. Turning quickly at the sounds, she was just in time to see the nurse falling in an awkward heap at the foot of the steps.

Joshua, halfway up the steps, stood with his hands pressed to his face, his expression contorted in horror at the sight as he let out a wail. Stepping down past him, Lily was quickly at the other young woman's side, bending over her as she lay on the path, one leg twisted beneath her and the other at an uncomfortable-looking angle with her boot propped up on the lowest step. She was grimacing in pain, her breath coming out through gritted teeth. All the while Joshua was wailing, shaken by the violent drama of the accident and seeing the pain in the nurse's face. Lily turned to him and said quickly, soothingly, 'It's all right, Joshie. Nursie will be all right. She's just had a little fall. Don't be upset.' She turned her attention back to the nurse. 'Can you get up, Emily? Let me help you.'

With some difficulty she helped the nurse up into a sitting position, though it was not without the young woman suffering considerable discomfort. 'I've hurt my ankle,' the nurse said. 'I don't know whether I can stand on it.'

'I'll help you,' Lily said. 'Lean on me.'

It proved not to be possible. As the nurse, clinging to Lily's arm, put down her right foot in order to stand, she recoiled with a sharp cry. All the while Joshua's crying continued in the background, though his wailing was now subsiding into a little sobbing sniffle.

'I can't,' the nurse said. 'I can't stand on it.'

Lily helped her to sit back on the lower step, then

straightened, looking around for the gardener. He was no longer in sight. 'Don't move – I'll go and find Mr Beeching,' she said. 'He can't be far away.' Then to the boy, gently: 'You stay here with Nursie, Joshie. I'll be back in a moment.'

She was away then, her skirts held in both hands, hurrying up the steps and between the lawns. Racing round the side of the house she saw Mr Beeching cutting the grass near the front gate, and ran to him. Miss Cattock had hurt herself in a fall, she said, and could not get up. Mr Beeching at once laid down his scythe and came running.

Between them they managed to get the nurse into the house, where Mrs Lemmon came and at once took charge and directed them into the morning room. There Miss Cattock was helped onto the sofa, and while Lily turned her attention to soothe the child, Mr Beeching went to wait out in the hall. When he had gone, Mrs Lemmon took a look at the injured leg, taking off the nurse's boot. The young woman's ankle was already swelling alarmingly, and was obviously very painful to the touch. They must, Mrs Lemmon said, send for Dr Sheene, and at once she went out into the hall to despatch Mr Beeching with the summons. That done, Lily took Joshua up to the nursery, away from all the fuss, and there tried to distract him with his blocks.

The doctor came later, and after his departure Mrs Lemmon came up to the nursery where Joshua sat on the rug before the fire with his toys, the trauma of the recent past now forgotten. Mrs Lemmon looked down at him as he played, and said to Lily in her soft Scottish brogue, 'Is he all right here with you? He is, isn't he?'

'Oh, he's fine,' Lily said. 'He's absolutely fine.'

'Good. Poor Nurse can't get up the stairs as things are. She's going to have to sleep down there on the sofa.'

The doctor, Mrs Lemmon went on to say, had pronounced Miss Cattock's ankle very badly sprained. He had bound it up, she added, and instructed the nurse that she must rest it and put no weight on it for several days.

Lily said, 'But she's to travel up to Scotland on Sunday with Joshua. That's only four days away. Mr and Mrs Soameson are expecting them.'

'Well, she can't travel,' Mrs Lemmon said. 'The girl's not capable of walking a step, and she's certainly not going to be well enough by Sunday. That's all there is to it.' She paused briefly, then said, 'I've just been talking about this with her.' Another brief pause. '*You* could take the boy, miss.'

'I? Take him up to Scotland?'

'Why not? The fare's all paid for. The tickets are bought and the sleeper's booked. And he'll go with you happily enough – though he wouldn't go with just anybody, Nurse says.'

'Does she say that?' Lily said, sounding pathetic to her own ears, seeking endorsement of the heart-warming tribute.

'Oh, she does indeed.' Mrs Lemmon nodded, backing up her words. 'Well, what do you think, miss? Can you take the boy? He'll be in good hands with you, and you won't have any other duties.'

'No, that's true, I shall not,' Lily said. She realised suddenly that it was something she wanted to do. It would give her time to spend with the boy – all those hours she would have with him, half the day and all the night . . . 'Yes, I suppose I could,' she said, sounding a little uncertain, as if she were making up her mind. 'Yes,' she said, 'I will.'

Mrs Lemmon nodded, pleased and relieved. 'That's grand,' she said. 'The child will get there after all. Mrs Soameson will have to be told. Will you write to her? I don't think Nurse is quite up to it.'

'Yes, of course. I'll do it now. Mrs Soameson should get it tomorrow, or Friday at the latest.'

When Mrs Lemmon had departed, Lily satisfied herself that the child was safe and content, then hurried across the landing to her room. There she gathered up her writing materials and went back to the nursery. Joshua was still playing happily before the fire, protected from the flames by the fire-guard. Lily set down her things on the little table by the window, then said to the boy, 'You know you're going up to Scotland on Sunday, don't you, Joshie?'

He smiled. 'Yes, I'm going to see my mama.'

'Yes, you are. But Nurse won't be taking you now. Did you hear what Mrs Lemmon said? *I* shall be taking you.'

'Oh. Won't Nursie be coming with us?'

'No, she won't. But she'll come up later – when her leg's better.'

He nodded. 'But you're coming with me.'

'Yes, I shall be taking you. All the way to Scotland. Won't that be thrilling?'

'Yes.'

Lily sat down at the table, and arranged her writing paper before her. 'Now I'm going to write to your mama in Edinburgh. Will you be all right while I do that, darling?'

He gave a laugh, showing his perfect little teeth. 'Of course I will.' Picking up his wooden horse he held it up to her. 'Can Mr Charlie Dobbin come too?'

'Oh, most certainly. We couldn't go without Mr Charlie Dobbin. Besides, the more the merrier.' She adjusted her chair. 'Now – I must get my letter done.'

She dipped her pen in the inkwell and began to write.

When the letter was finished, she gave it to Mrs Lemmon, who arranged with Mr Beeching to have it taken to the post box.

Lily slept in the nursery that night, in Miss Cattock's bed, while the nurse spent the night downstairs on the sofa, an old walking stick beside her to enable her to take a few necessary steps when required. The nurse's accident had changed the whole routine in the house. There was no precedent for such a situation, and it was a matter of doing what was best. While Miss Cattock protested that she was taking a liberty by being in the morning room, Lily and Mrs Lemmon told her that she had no option, and that Mr and Mrs Soameson would certainly want her to have every aid to promote her comfort and recovery. Lily also told her that she had fully informed Mrs Soameson of the nurse's accident, and had assured her that they would manage perfectly well in spite of it, and that she herself would travel with Joshua to arrive in Edinburgh on Monday morning as arranged.

Thursday passed quickly for Lily, for she spent most of it with the boy. It was precious time – time, she well knew, that was all too soon to come to an end.

Friday came. By now she had almost given up expecting to hear any word from Joel, though she was still so hopeful. What possible crisis could there be other than that he was sick or had had an accident?

The *Corster Gazette* had come that day, and that evening, in the nursery, while the child lay sleeping, Lily took it to scan the advertisements for some position that would suit in case the one in Little Hawes did not work out. Among the numerous advertisements for sheep and cattle fairs, properties for sale and offers of music tuition, she studied the instances of employment on offer: calls for brewery apprentices, housekeepers, milkmaids and stockmen. There was no call there for a governess. On the right-hand side of the page there was again a report on the smallpox epidemic and its significance in the area. It made for alarming and depressing news.

The following morning she stayed in the nursery with Joshua, keeping him occupied with his toys and his alphabet blocks, and then in the afternoon took him downstairs to see the nurse where she lay on the sofa, her tightly strapped ankle resting on a cushion. Miss Cattock was glad of the visit, and Joshua was equally pleased to be with her again.

Lily and the nurse chatted together as the boy played with his toys before the fire. He seemed to be recovering from his cold, Lily thought, and would surely be well enough for the trip the next day. With regard to it, everything was now set for the journey; earlier that day she had packed bags for herself and the child, and they were ready to leave. If her assumptions were correct, when she had safely delivered the boy in Edinburgh, she would stay overnight and then set off to return to Corster on the Tuesday. From that time on, her employment with the Soamesons would be finished. Further, she would have said goodbye to the child for the last time.

As she sat chatting with Emily Cattock, there came a tap at the door, and Susie opened it and held out an envelope. The postman had just called, she said, and there was a letter for Miss Clair.

Lily thanked her, took it, and saw at once that it was from Joel.

She stood there with the letter in her hand as Susie closed the door and left. 'Well,' Emily said, 'aren't you going to open it? Joshie and I'll excuse you.'

Lily turned and smiled. 'Later,' she said. 'I'll read it later.'

Chapter Thirty-four

In the early evening Lily and the maid brought up hot water to the nursery and Lily bathed Joshua. He was cheerful, but she could see behind his humour that he was tired, and that his tiredness would soon overtake him. She studied him as she washed him in the soft, warm water, gently smoothing on the soap and sponging it away, taking her time, almost not wishing the pleasure to end. She took in everything about him, revelling in each little observation of this perfect form that she had once miraculously discovered and known, and lost, and now was discovering all over again. It was something she had thought she would never do. She took in the feeling of his skin, like the finest silk, the perfect shape of his little limbs, his exquisite fingers and toes, the blush of his cheek, the texture of his fair hair as it sprang from his temples and curled in the damp. She took in the smile he turned to her, showing his small white teeth, and the subtle dimple beside his lip. She took in the little crescent mark by his ear – and if it was a flaw, dear God, she would not have had him without it. There was a bubble of soap on his chin which she wiped away with a fingertip, and as she gloried in him she remembered the times when she had bathed him before the fire at Rowanleigh. Now it was a different flickering fire, and he was four years older. Without question, though, he was still her son. Perfect and beautiful.

When she had finished she lifted him out and dried him with a towel warmed on the fire-guard, and then dressed him in his little nightshirt.

'I don't want to go to bed,' he said. 'I'm not tired yet.'

'Oh, but Joshie,' she said, 'tomorrow we're going on that long journey.' Before she had come to The Gables she had thought of him always as Georgie. No more. Joshua was his name, a part of him. She accepted it now, fully.

'Tomorrow?' he said, looking at her wide-eyed.

'Yes, tomorrow. I told you.' She sat down and lifted him onto her lap. 'We're going up to Scotland.'

'Scotland. Oh, yes.' He nodded and gave a yawn.

'You're a tired little man,' she said, then added, 'Yes, what an adventure that will be, to go to Scotland.'

'Is it nice there, in Scotland?'

'Oh, I'm sure it is. You're going to be very happy.' She had wrapped him in her arms, her right hand enclosing his two small feet. 'You're going to be living in Edinburgh from now on. A beautiful place, they say. Where your mama and papa are now – waiting for you.'

'And Vinnie too?'

'Yes, Lavinia too. They're all waiting for you.'

He smiled. 'Are they? Shall I see them tomorrow?'

'No, but we'll set out tomorrow. It's a very long journey.'

'Is it?'

'Oh, indeed it is. We have to go to Pilching first, then to Corster. Then we go to London, and from London to Edinburgh. It'll take many hours.'

'Will it?'

'Oh, indeed it will. So you'll need to have a good sleep and be fresh for the journey.'

'Yes, I shall.' He nodded. 'And you must have a good sleep too, and be fresh for the journey.'

'Yes, I must.'

'Will Nursie be sleeping downstairs again tonight?'

'Yes, she will. She can't climb the stairs yet.'

'Not with her leg bad, no.'

'No, poor Nurse.'

'Will you be sleeping here in Nursie's bed again tonight?'

'Yes, I shall.'

'You won't leave me alone, will you?'

'No.' She breathed the word as she smoothed his hair back from his brow 'I won't leave you alone.'

He yawned again, his mouth opening wide. 'Come,' Lily said, 'into bed with you, young man.'

He did not protest as she rose, lifted him onto the bed and tucked him in under the covers.

'Here – have Bunny.' From beside the pillow she took up his stuffed rabbit, a rather sorry-looking creature missing half of one ear and with much of its coat worn away, and laid it in his arms. 'He must sleep too.'

'Is there room for Bunny to come to Scotland? Along with Mr Dobbin?'

'I should think so. You go to sleep now.'

She bent over him as he settled and closed his eyes, and stayed watching him until he had drifted off. It took so little time. In less than a minute she could see his lips part as his breathing became gently rhythmic. She hovered a moment, then bent lower and touched him gently with a kiss on his sweet-smelling hair. Then she straightened and turned away.

Joel's letter, unopened still, lay where she had left it, on the table near the window.

With the child sleeping behind her, she moved to the table, stood there for a moment then sat down. The letter lay in the little pool of light cast by the oil lamp. Since being handed it by the maid earlier that day she had had no opportunity to read it in privacy. Now she had. She took the letter up, slipped the tip of her finger under the envelope's flap, and tore it open.

The letter was dated the twenty-eighth of October. It had taken almost two weeks to reach her. He had written:

My dearest Lily,

There is nothing I can say, no matter what careful and subtle words I choose, that can possibly bring you any comfort. I am so aware of that, and I am aware of how badly I have let you down. You had the right to expect everything from me. Indeed, I made it clear that you had that right, and now I am going back on my promise and have taken that right away. How can you forgive me? And can I even ask you to do so? As you see by the address from which I'm writing, I am still in Paris, and on this day I was supposed to be returning to Corster, ready for my meeting with you tomorrow at the Crimmond. And by the time you receive this you will have been to the restaurant and waited for me, and eventually realised that I was not going to appear.

I must not delay any further, but must tell you the truth. You deserve nothing less. And you deserve so much more than I have ever been able to give you.

When I wrote last I told you that I had ended my understanding with Miss Roget. This was the truth. I told her that I loved another, and could not continue with the relationship as it was. She was, as you can well imagine, distressed by my revelation, but nevertheless she said she understood and would not wish to stand in the way of my happiness, as painful to her as it was. Oh, Lily, I cannot describe how difficult it was for me to tell her such things. She is such a good and upright person – I know you would agree with this if you knew her – and so deserving of someone who loves her and appreciates all her excellent qualities.

Even so, having unburdened my brain and my heart, I thought I was in control of the situation, and that even a similar revelation to my father was something that I could execute. I would have to, for I wished only to be back in England at your side.

Alas, Lily, things have not turned out as I intended, as I wished. Having told Miss Roget and my father, and while making my plans to leave for England, I watched this fine woman fall into a decline and, knowing that I had been the cause of it, I was stricken with remorse. I could not escape seeing the results of my action. Even though she did her best to avoid me, we were thrown together by circumstances, and I could not but see the effect upon her that I had had. I had dashed all her hopes of happiness, and, further, felt I had ruined her chances of marriage to anyone else.

In the end, Lily, I could face it no more, and I asked her to forgive me and assured her that we would go on as we had. I have told my father also, and he is, of course, much relieved by my change of heart. And now I have to tell you that discussions are underway with Miss Roget and her mother concerning a time for our marriage. I cannot say that the new arrangement brings me the greatest joy, but I must take comfort from the fact that I am doing the right thing, as most would view it.

But you, Lily – to you I have brought such grief, I know that. And I have no way of mending it. I have told Miss Roget that I will remain with her and marry her, and at the same time I have deserted you, the one I love above all others, and who deserves love as much as anyone else. I will not ask you to forgive me, for forgiveness is not appropriate nor something I could ever expect. Perhaps, though, you might possibly understand a little of my situation, and see how a weak man can find himself so in a tangle.

I hardly know what else to say. Lily, you are a fine and beautiful and intelligent young woman, and in time there will come someone who is deserving of you, for certainly I am not. And that someone, whoever he may be, will make you happy, and you will find that, in the end, you were better off without me.

I will say only one thing more: that is that I shall never forget you, nor the brightness and the love that you brought into my life. I did not deserve any of it, but I shall treasure it none the less.

Joel

Lily laid the letter down on the table and sat there in the soft glow of the lamp while the time passed and the little clock on the mantelpiece ticked into the quiet. Taking in the clock's face she saw that it was after eight. Mrs Lemmon would have been expecting her downstairs to eat. It did not matter. She remained where she was. She had not drawn the curtains, and beyond her still head the sky was starless and dark.

After a time she folded up the letter and put it back in its envelope. She had no wish to read it over again. She had no need to; every word in Joel's neat hand was engraved in her mind and on her heart.

She was disturbed from her silent sitting by a light tap on the door and, getting up to answer it, she found on the threshold Susie bearing a tray with a bowl of coarse vegetable soup, some bread and butter and a little dish of vanilla junket. 'Mrs Lemmon's sent it up, miss,' the maid said in a whisper, 'seeing as 'ow you 'aven't come downstairs to eat.' She tipped her head a little to one side. 'She was expecting you downstairs, miss, and wondered if you're all right. *Are* you all right, miss?'

Lily assured her that she was, and thanked her. As the maid softly closed the door and departed, Lily placed the tray on the table. And there she left it, for the soup to grow cold and congeal and the bread to go dry. It was still there when she at last undressed and climbed into bed.

*

511

A wind sprang up as the night drew deeper, and Lily, lying sleepless in the nurse's too-soft bed, heard it rattle the window pane, and sigh in the branches of the ash tree. It was not the wind that kept her from sleeping. Her own thoughts did that. They churned around in her brain without cease, giving her no respite, while she turned from one side to another in a vain search for comfort and ease. Eyes open, she gazed unseeing into the room, its darkness relieved by the nightlight that burned on the side table. In his bed on the other side of the fireplace Joshua slept soundly on.

When dawn came she lay and watched as the light crept through the crack in the curtains and stole into the room, slowly giving the familiar objects their shape and colour once again. The nightlight had burnt out. Her head ached, and her eyes felt sore. After a while she got up and pulled on her dressing gown. The child was still asleep, though he would not be for much longer, she knew. The room was cold. In the grate the remains of the fire were ashes. Like her hopes.

In the gloom she stood for a moment over the child's bed, watching him as he slept, so peacefully, his mouth open against the pillow, his stuffed rabbit half-embraced. She turned away, paced the room for a minute and then sat down at the table by the window. Reaching out, she drew the curtains back a little, just a little, and the cold November light crept in and touched the baize table-covering and the envelope containing Joel's letter. It was still there. Of course it was still there. Nothing had changed during the night.

Later, as if hardly aware of what she was doing, she got up from the chair and went to the fireplace and looked into the mirror that hung above the mantelpiece. In the grey light she stared at her face in the glass, as if searching there for some sign of what had happened, as if Joel's words might be engraved upon her brow. Her eyes, red-rimmed, gazed back at her, dry as bone after the sleepless night. Through all the hours she had not shed a tear. Inside her heart, inside her head, she felt empty.

After a little while Joshua awakened, sat up in the bed and called out, 'Mammy?' and then 'Nursie?' and Lily at once went to his side. 'I'm here,' she said. 'It's Lily. Lily's here.'

'Lily?' he said, and then, suddenly comprehending, yawned and gave her a smile. 'Lily,' he said.

'Yes, darling,' she said, 'it's Lily.'

'Is Mammy here?'

'No, but you'll be seeing her soon.'

He looked at her with widening eyes for a moment as memory returned, then said, 'Oh, yes – I'll be seeing her in Scotland. Are we going away today? Is it today we're going?'

'Yes, it is.'

'On the train.' He was sitting up in the bed. 'We're going on the train, aren't we?'

'Yes, a long way. We're going a very long way.'

And suddenly, with her words, there came the almost overwhelming desire to leave, to get away, to escape. She would like to run, to run and never stop running. She would like to go now, this minute.

As if connecting with her thoughts, tapping into the spring of her emotion, the boy said, 'Are we going soon, Lily?'

'Yes, we are.' A little wave of relief swept over her at the thought. 'Yes, soon,' she said. 'We shall be leaving very soon.'

'What will ye do when you've delivered Joshua to his mama?' Mrs Lemmon said. 'Will you come back here?'

'I don't know,' Lily said. 'I haven't decided.' She and the cook were standing in the kitchen, where Lily had gone after she had picked at her lunch in the room beside it. 'I shall probably go on back to Sherrell,' she said. She was already wearing her hat and coat, ready for the journey, eager to depart.

'But you've got your things here, haven't you?' Mrs Lemmon said.

'Well, yes – a few things,' Lily replied. 'Clothes – some books. But I don't need them in a hurry. I can come back and collect them in a few days.' Mr Shad would help her, she was sure. 'If it's not inconvenient,' she added.

'Inconvenient? No, of course not, dear. We shall be here for a few weeks yet, and Mr Soameson will be coming back down to help get things sorted out.' She paused, looking at Lily with a slight frown. 'Are ye all right, miss?'

'All right?'

'Well, you look a little – distracted, if I might say so.'

'No, I – I'm fine. I'm all right.'

'Your eyes are a little red – a mite bloodshot.'

'Oh.' Lily brushed the remark aside with a wave of her hand. 'I – I didn't sleep so well last night.'

'Oh, dearie me, that's a shame – when you've got such a journey in front of you. But I must say, I'm not too surprised. It's quite an undertaking – such a jaunt. It's so long. Endless. And with a four-year-old boy.'

'Well . . .' Lily shrugged. 'It has to be done.'

'Aye, no question of that. From here to London, and then on to Edinburgh.' She shook her head and sighed. 'Have you ever been to London?'

'No, never.'

Mrs Lemmon nodded. 'Well, that's going to be something for you – a new experience. And going across London from one station to another, you'll see something of the place. I've done it a few times – and it's not to be forgotten. You've never seen such sights, believe me.' She shook her shoulders in a little dramatic shudder. 'I couldna live there,

514

I know that much. It's filthy – everything just covered in soot and grime.'

Lily merely nodded. She found it hard to concentrate on what was being said. Her mind was spinning. She did not want to make polite, idle conversation, she wanted only to be alone – alone with the child – and to go, to start out on the journey. 'Well, I don't plan on spending longer there than I have to,' she said, 'and as for the journey, it's got to be done.'

'Aye, it has. Have you everything ready?'

'Yes. I've packed our bags. With advice from Nurse.'

'Good. That's good. I've made some sandwiches for the two of you. Some potted meat, and some cheese, and a little cold beef.'

'So much,' Lily said.

'Not so much – you'll both get hungry on that long journey. What about money? Have you got enough? Mrs Soameson left money with Nurse for any expenses for the trip.'

'Yes, it's all arranged. Nurse let me have it. I've got my wages too.' Lily hid her impatience. 'I don't need anything. We'll manage just fine.'

'Of course you will. How is the child? Is he all right?'

'Yes. He's with Nurse now, saying his goodbyes. He's mostly over his cold. He's seemed so much better over the past couple of days. I'll look after him, don't worry.'

Mrs Lemmon smiled. 'Of course you will. What time are you leaving?'

'Very soon. We have to get the 3.33 from Corster. I just have to bring my bag downstairs and get Joshie into his coat, then we'll be ready to go.'

Lily went to see the boy's nurse then, in the little room where she sat with Joshua on the old couch. Miss Cattock was feeling so much better today, and hoped very soon to be getting about as well as before. After discussing with the

515

nurse what the boy should wear, Lily took him upstairs to the nursery and got him into his outdoor clothes. Over his sailor suit she put on his light grey ulster, and then set his hat on his head and fastened it beneath his chin. The bag holding their belongings was nearby. In it she had packed the things that the child would need on the long journey and for his night's sleep on the Edinburgh-bound train. His stuffed rabbit was in there too; his toy horse he would carry. For herself Lily had packed the things she thought she would need for the next few days, until that time when she had delivered the boy to his new home in Edinburgh, and she was back in England.

'There you are – all ready to go.' Crouching before the boy, she leant back a little to take him more fully into her vision, and gave a little nod of approval. 'And such a very handsome boy too.' She smiled. 'Just one or two things to go into the bag then we'll go downstairs.' As she moved to get up, he said, a little note of anxiety in his voice, 'Did you pack Bunny?'

'Yes, I did, my dear. Never fear. And you've got Mr Charlie Dobbin safe, haven't you? We can't leave them behind, can we? They're yours.'

He smiled. 'Yes, they are. They belong to me, don't they?'

'They most certainly do, and they wouldn't be happy with anybody else.'

'No, they wouldn't. Mr Charlie and Bunny belong to me, but I belong to Mama and Papa. Is that right, Lily?'

'Yes,' she said. 'Yes, you do.'

'Yes, Vinnie does, too. Everybody belongs to somebody. Who do you belong to, Lily?'

She gave a little laugh. 'What? Oh – I belong to me,' she said, and then, glancing at the clock, 'Heavens, look at the time. We'll be leaving soon.'

He was silent a moment, then he said, 'Are we coming back here?'

'No, we're not. You'll be living in Edinburgh from now on. In Scotland.'

He nodded and looked around him, his glance taking in some of his other toys where they lay on the shelf by the chimney and on the chest in the corner of the room, and in a wooden box by the fire. 'What about all my other things?' he said. 'What about my top, my ball, my soldier with his drum? Will they all stay here?'

'Well, only for a little while,' Lily said. 'Later on they'll all be packed up and taken up to Scotland, and you'll get them there.'

'All of them?'

'Yes, all of them.'

'Ah.' He nodded, relieved. He pointed then to pictures that hung on the wall; one depicted some kittens playing with a ball of yarn, the other showed colourful fish among waterweeds. 'My kittens and my fishes – will they go too?'

'Yes, they will. Of course they will.'

'I've never seen fishes,' he said. 'Only dead ones, in the kitchen. Have you ever seen fishes, Lily?'

'Oh, yes, I've seen them. At the aquarium.'

'The what?'

'The aquarium. It's in Corster. Oh, it's a wonderful place. So many different kinds of fish – all swimming about.'

His mouth opened a little in awe. 'And you can see them?'

'Yes, of course. Anyone can go and see them.'

He nodded. 'One day I'll see them too.'

'Oh, I've no doubt you will,' she said. 'Listen, I'm sure in Edinburgh they must have a fine aquarium. It's a big, beautiful city.'

'Is it? Is it bigger than Pilching?'

'Oh, much, much bigger. It's a wonderful place, and I know you're going to be very happy there.'

'Am I?'

'Oh, yes, without doubt.'

'And will you be staying in Scotland? Will you be staying with me there?'

'No,' she said. 'No, I'm afraid not.'

'Oh.' The word had a little dying fall. He sounded disappointed. 'Why not?'

When she did not answer in time, he added, 'I wish you would, Lily.'

'Do you?' she said.

'Yes, I do. We could do reading from my blocks again.'

'Oh, yes, we could certainly do that.'

'Where will you go, Lily?'

'Go?'

'Well, if you don't stay in Scotland with me and Vinnie, will you go somewhere else?'

She nodded. 'Yes – I expect so.'

'Where will you go?'

'What . . .?'

'Will you go home?'

Home. The word seemed to hang in the air.

'Where is it, Lily?' he said. 'Where is your home?'

She remained there for a second longer, crouching before him, then she straightened and got to her feet. 'Come, we must go,' she said. 'Mr Beeching will have the trap ready. We mustn't be late.' She turned, bent and picked up the bag. It was surprisingly heavy. 'Let's go downstairs.'

Minutes later all the goodbyes had been said with Mrs Lemmon, Susie and Emily Cattock. The three had given their good wishes for a pleasant journey, and had kissed the child. Now it was time to go. With Mrs Lemmon and Susie watching from the back door, Lily took Joshua by the hand and went into the yard. As she did so, Mr Beeching came towards them, took up Lily's travelling bag and placed it in the well of the trap. Then, turning, he helped Lily in, afterwards lifting up the boy. She grasped the child and he, holding his toy horse, settled on the seat beside her.

'Are we going to Scotland now?' he said.

'Yes, we are,' Lily replied.

'Good,' he said. 'Good.'

Moments later Mr Beeching had taken the mare by the bridle and was leading her down the drive towards the road.

As the wheels and the horse's hooves crunched on the gravel, Lily looked around her. The wind that had blown last night had died away, but at its height it had stripped the trees of the last remaining leaves and scattered them all over the garden. The sky above was dark, and heavy clouds were gathering. She sat with her arm around the child as he nestled against her, Mr Charlie Dobbin in his hands. She felt a sense of finality as they moved away; her time here at the house was over. She would only see it again when she came back to collect her belongings, and she had told Mrs Lemmon that that might not be for several days. She would never sleep in her room here again, never teach again in the schoolroom. When she returned from Edinburgh she must go on to Rowanleigh. There was nowhere else to go, and once again she would throw herself on the comfort and temporary security of Miss Elsie's kindness. She thought of the boy's words up in the nursery, when he had asked, 'Where is your home?' She had not had an answer for him then, and she did not have an answer now.

The carriage came to a halt as Mr Beeching let go the mare's bridle and went to open the gates onto the road. It would take them an hour to get to Corster, via Pilching, where eventually they would pick up their connection for London. Lily did not care how long it took. In her mind the journey to Edinburgh stretched out ahead, seemingly without end, and she was glad of it. For one thing, she was so relieved to get away from the confines of the house where there was nothing to distract her from her thoughts. More than that, though, and the most important thing of all, this journey gave her time with the child. That, for now, was all that mattered. It was all she had. There were only these immediate hours before her. Beyond them, there was nothing.

The gates were open, and Mr Beeching was moving back to the mare. As he came to her side and caught the bridle, a figure appeared around the tall privet hedge, a young lad in a grey uniform and a cap with a scarlet badge above its peak. The telegraph boy, Lily realised. He came through the gate and said to Mr Beeching as he approached, 'Telegraph for Miss Clair, sir. The Gables. Am I in the right place?'

'Ye certainly are, laddie,' Mr Beeching said, gesturing to Lily, 'The lady's sittin' here.'

'Ah, righto.' The boy came round the side of the trap and reached up and put a small envelope into Lily's hand. Then, with a touch at his cap, he turned and started away. Lily looked at the envelope and Joshua said, 'You got a letter, Lily.'

'It's a telegraph, Joshie,' she said.

She realised that Mr Beeching was standing waiting, still with one hand on the mare's bridle. She tore open the envelope.

It contained one single sheet of paper, an official form with a printed heading and a brief message written in pencil, all in uppercase:

HOPE THIS REACHES YOU BEFORE YOU SET OUT STOP LAVINIA SCARLET FEVER STOP DO NOT BRING JOSHUA YET STOP WAIT WEEK STOP WILL WRITE LATER STOP MRS SOAMESON

Lily sat looking at the words. She was not to take the boy

to Edinburgh after all. He was not to go for at least a week.

So what now? Why, after a few days she must depart from the house, leaving the boy in the care of his nurse, whose ankle was growing stronger and who would, when the time came, be able enough to take him to his new home.

'Everything all right, miss?'

Mr Beeching's voice came as if from a great distance into her tumbling thoughts.

'I – I beg your pardon, sir,' Lily said, coming out of her fog. 'What did you say?'

'I asked if everything was all right, miss. Your telegraph, I mean. No bad news, I hope.' He paused. 'You're all right, miss, are ye?'

'Yes,' she said. 'Yes, everything's fine, thank you.' She paused. 'Please, Mr Beeching – carry on.'

'Right ye are, miss.' He looked up at the sky. 'And I think we'd be well to do so before the rain comes, too. There's a good deal up there.'

Grasping the mare's bridle, he led the horse and carriage out onto the road. As he did so, Lily opened her reticule and slipped the telegraph into it, into the pocket, down beside Joel's letter, Tom's pocket-knife and her mother's watch.

'Shall we be there soon, Lily?' Joshua asked as she put her arm around him once more.

'No, not just yet, dear,' she said. 'We've got a way to go yet.'

When Mr Beeching had closed the gates he climbed up onto his seat. Then, with a flick of the reins he spoke a word to the mare, and the carriage jolted and started forward.

Chapter Thirty-five

At Pilching station Mr Beeching carried the heavy carpet bag up onto the platform, and there insisted on staying until the Corster train arrived. When at last it drew in he saw Lily and the boy safely into a carriage and put the bag up on the luggage rack along with Lily's umbrella. That done, he stepped back down onto the platform, and Lily lowered the window and looked out at him.

'You sure you're going to be all right now, miss?' he asked.

'Yes, thank you, Mr Beeching, we shall be fine.'

He lifted a hand to touch at his cap, wished her and the boy goodbye, then turned and strode away along the platform.

Lily watched him go, then pulled up the window and turned to sit beside the child. There were two other people in the compartment, a middle-aged cleric and his female companion. They looked over at the boy and smiled indulgently at him. Lily asked Joshua if he was all right, and he said yes, and added, a little wide-eyed, a touch of wonder in his voice: 'We're on the train.'

'Yes, we're on the train. We'll be moving soon.'

'I like it on the train,' he said.

The clergyman, who had overheard the brief exchange, said to Joshua, smiling, 'And where are you off to, young man? Somewhere interesting?'

Joshua looked briefly at Lily, as if for confirmation, then said to the man, 'We're going to London, and to Scotland.'

'To London and to Scotland, are you? Well, well, that's quite a journey. Are you looking forward to it?'

The boy nodded. 'Yes.'

'I'm sure you are. It's going to be very exciting for you.'

Joshua gave another little nod, and then his face distorted as he sneezed.

'Oh, dear,' the cleric said, 'somebody's got a cold.'

'Well, he's just getting over one,' Lily said, 'aren't you, Joshie?'

'Yes, I'm just getting over one,' the boy said.

There was a little mucus dribbling from his nostrils, and Lily took out her handkerchief and wiped his nose. 'There you are now, good as new.'

From along the length of the train came the sound of the carriage doors being slammed shut. The noise, signifying that they were about to leave, made Lily tense, and she steeled herself to try to relax. Moments later came the sound of the guard's whistle and then they were moving off.

The clouds overhead gathered ever more closely as the train rattled on through the Wiltshire countryside, and the light in the carriage grew dimmer by the minute. 'We're in for a storm,' the cleric said to the woman at his side, and she nodded agreement. A young mother and two children got on at Sheppey Hart, and they talked in loud voices as they ate sandwiches and drank from a bottle of water. Lily sat looking from the window as the bleak landscape passed by under the ever-darkening sky. As they rode, she marked off the stations on the route, aware that each one was taking her and the child further away. It was not too late, she said to herself; they could get off at any station and take a train back to Pilching. She could take the boy back to The Gables, and make some excuse, and everything would be well, and he would stay there until it was time to leave on another day. But the stations came and went, and she remained in her seat. Close against her side, Joshua chattered for a little while, but then became silent, inhibited by the noisy newcomers, and sat watching them, fascinated, and a little ill-at-ease at their crude manners and boisterousness. He gave a yawn. He had missed his usual midday nap, Lily realised, and he was tired. 'Not long to go now,' she murmured to him.

Then, at long last, the train was drawing into the platform at Corster Junction. She pressed the boy's shoulder. 'Here we are, Joshie. We're getting off now.'

'Are we there? Are we in Scotland?'

'No, dear, we're just coming into Corster.'

The woman and her two raucous children were gathering their belongings together. Lily got to her feet. 'Come,' she said, 'we must get ready to get off.' As she reached up to the luggage rack for her bag, the clergyman rose and lifted it down for her, placing it on the seat. The train was coming to a halt. The woman and her children came pushing by to the door and Lily sat down again, the boy at her side. When the train had come to a stop the door was flung open and the woman and the two boys got out. Lily took up the bag and her reticule and murmured a goodbye to the cleric and his lady. To Joshua she said, 'Have you got Mr Charlie Dobbin?' and he said, 'Yes, I have', clutching the toy to his chest. She stepped down onto the platform, and as she did so, Joshua cried out, 'Don't leave me, Lily!' and she turned, saying, 'Oh, I won't leave you, darling. I'd never leave you.' Setting the bag at her feet, she reached up and lifted him down.

'There.' She bent to him and put a gentle hand under his chin, lifting his head a little. 'Are you all right now?'

He nodded.

'Good. And are you all right to walk a little way?'

He nodded again. 'Yes.'

She smiled and straightened. 'Then we'll go.'

With her reticule and the carpet bag in one hand, and grasping the boy's right hand with the other, Lily set off along the platform. All about them porters moved to and fro with wagons of luggage, and travellers meandered or hurried about. The air was full of the sound of voices, guards' shrill whistles blowing, carriage doors slamming and steam hissing and belching. Joshua observed it all with wide eyes, then after a few yards looked up at Lily and said: 'Are we going to see Mama and Papa now?'

'What did you say, my dear?' She could not hear him clearly above the surrounding din, and she bent a little to him while he repeated his question. 'Come on over here a minute,' she said, and led him over to the side, near the wall, out of the way of the throng of travellers. There she put the bag down and crouched before him.

'Listen,' she said softly. 'Joshie – we're not going to Scotland just yet.'

'Oh,' he said, 'I thought we were. You said we were.'

'Yes, I know I did, but –' She came to a halt, momentarily at a loss. Then she summoned up a smile. After all, this was going to be a good thing, something they would both enjoy. 'No,' she said, 'we're not going up to Scotland just yet.'

'Are we going to London, then?'

'No, we're not going to London either, not yet. In a few days you'll be going up to Scotland, to see your mama and papa, but not yet. Not just yet.'

'Why not?'

'Well, for one thing, Vinnie's ill. She's got the scarlet fever, and your mama doesn't want you to catch it, does she?'

'No,' he said with a little shake of his head. 'No.'

'No, of course not.' She paused, giving him a bright little smile. 'So – I tell you what we're going to do – we're going to have a little holiday.'

'A holiday?'

'Yes. You know what a holiday is, don't you?'

He nodded, but then immediately shook his head. 'No. Is it nice?'

'Oh, yes!' She beamed, wide-eyed. 'It's very nice. A holiday is lovely. On holiday you get to do all kinds of nice things – things you can't do at other times.'

'Oh.' He sounded a little awed, but interested.

'Yes,' she said, 'and that's what we'll do.'

He smiled now. 'Yes,' he said. 'I like a holiday.'

'Yes, you will, my darling. I know you will.' She had her hands on his shoulders, looking into his blue eyes. 'You're going to have a lovely time, I promise you.'

'Am I?'

'Yes, you are. We both will. Only for three or four days, then we'll go back to Happerfell, and when Lavinia's better, Nurse will take you up to Scotland as planned. But first we'll have our little holiday, just the two of us. We'll have a jolly time together, won't we?'

He nodded, solemn, lips pressed together. 'Yes.'

Yes, she said to herself as she crouched before him, they would have a good time. For a few days they would be together. She would have him to herself for a little while – and then take him home again, to get on with his life, his life without her. She smiled, touched a hand to his cheek, and then straightened again. 'Come,' she said, 'we'll go and find a cab, and then get ourselves a nice cup of tea.'

She took his hand, and together they moved along towards the exit, but as they drew closer to it there came a sudden drumming on the roof above their heads. Lily gave a resigned groan and said, 'Oh, here comes the rain,' and then added, coming to a sudden stop, 'My umbrella! Oh, I left my umbrella!' Taking a firmer grip on the boy's hand, she hitched up the heavy bag and turned. 'We must go back and get it.'

They started back along the platform, Lily hurrying now,

for she could see in the distance the guard hoisting his flag. Her effort was useless, she knew; they would not make it in time, besides which, she did not even know which carriage she and the boy had sat in. Seconds later a whistle had blown, and the train was moving on.

'We're too late,' Joshua said as they came to a halt. Lily said with a sigh, 'Yes, I'm afraid we are. Well, there's nothing else for it, but we must run between the spots.'

They made their way back along the platform to the exit, descending the steps into the subterranean way that would take them beneath the upward-bound line. Reaching the end of the underway, they found several persons standing sheltering from the rain just within the station entrance, while others out on the pavement went scurrying by, topped by their black umbrellas. Lily looked out onto Station Street, seeking a cab, but where they were usually lined up, waiting for passengers, there was none to be seen. 'It's the rain,' she said to the boy. 'Everyone wants a cab in this weather.'

'Is this Scotland yet?' he said.

'What? No, my dear, no.' Distracted, she looked up and down the street; if there was no cab then there might be an omnibus that would take them part of the way. 'I told you, this is Corster,' she said. He was looking up at her anxiously and she told herself that she must show no concern in front of him. 'Don't fret, my dear,' she said. 'We'll be all right. Everything's fine. It's just this silly old rain, isn't it? How foolish of me to leave my umbrella behind.'

People pushed past them, running in from the street to catch their trains, closing dripping umbrellas as they came. Clutching Joshua's hand, Lily stood looking out at the dreary scene where the carts and carriages and drays trundled by in the relentless rain, their drivers hunched over, the horses streaming. The station clock showed the time at four-forty-six, and there was deep gloom under the rain-heavy clouds.

Looking up at Lily with wide eyes, Joshua said, 'Can we go home now?'

'What? Oh – my dear.' She bent to him. 'Not just yet. We'll get a cab, then we'll be all right, I promise.' She straightened again. 'Listen – there's a fly-man just along the road. Let's try there. We'll get a cab there, I'm sure. He's only a little way – and if he's not ready we can wait for him in the dry.' She hesitated for a moment longer, hoping that the downpour would ease, and then, renewing her grip on the boy's hand, said, 'Are you ready, dear? Can you be a big boy and run a little?'

'Yes.' He nodded. 'I can run. I can run very fast.'

'Good boy. You're a good boy. Come, then. Let's hurry.'

Clutching the bags and the boy's hand, she stepped out into the rain. 'This way.'

They turned to the left, while the rain beat down. She could not run. The large bag was too heavy, and the boy's steps were too small, but she walked as quickly as she could. Keeping to the paved footway, they hurried up the street. In seconds, it seemed, they were drenched. In no time at all the hems of Lily's skirt and coat were wet with the water that splashed up under their feet. The thin soles of her boots were sodden, and she could feel the heavy drops pounding on the black straw of her hat. A little less than two hundred yards from the station they came to the fly-man's yard. 'Here we are,' Lily said with relief, a little breathless. 'We'll get shelter here, and we'll get a cab.'

Over the entrance to the yard was a fading, painted sign saying 'Rt. Baxman. Fly Proprietor'. Lily had passed by the premises in earlier days. Now she and the boy hurried under the sign, and as they did so she gave another sigh of relief for before them, in the yard outside the fly-man's house, she saw a carriage, a rather forlorn-looking brougham, and a chestnut horse between the shafts. 'Look, we're in luck,' she said. 'The man's here – his carriage is here – and he must be for hire as his horse is hitched up too.'

As they crossed the yard there came all at once a sharp and terrifying flash of lightning. It seemed to crack the dark sky, flashing the heavens whiter than white, lighting up the darkness of the scene with a stark brilliance. Joshua gave a little cry, a yelp, halted in his tracks and threw himself at Lily. She, also startled by the lightning, stood for a moment with the boy's arms clutching her about her knees. Only seconds after the lightning flash came a clap of thunder, and the child cried out again and gripped her tightly through her coat and skirt. Dropping the carpet bag onto the wet ground, she bent to him. 'It's all right, it's all right.'

But his terror could not be assuaged with her words, and he only held her more tightly, his face buried in the fabric of her coat. She crouched, heedless of her hems in the wet, and put her arms around him. Through the thin wool of her gloves she could feel that his coat was saturated. Lightning flashed again, and thunder cracked and growled. He whimpered, trying to press even closer, and she thought of that other time, in the house, when the thunderstorm had driven him into her arms. 'Just be brave for a while longer,' she said. 'Soon we'll be in the dry.' Holding him by the shoulders, she eased him a little from her body. His face glistened with the rain in the dull light. 'Come on, let's get out of the rain.' She straightened, taking his hand.

The fly-man's horse and carriage were standing close to the house's back door. Lily and the boy hurried forward, Lily casting her eyes about for a glimpse of the driver. She could see no signs of life anywhere, though she saw that the door to the house was slightly ajar. Coming to a stop below the step leading to the narrow porch, she called out, 'Hello . . .? Is there someone there . . .? Hello . . .?'

There was no answer. The roof of the porch was so

shallow that it gave nothing but the very smallest shelter from the rain. She called out again, 'Hello . . .? Mr Baxman? Are you there?'

When there still came no answer she said to Joshua, 'Come on, we've got to get you into the dry for a minute.' Leaving the bags on the ground next to the step, she took the boy's hand and led him over to the carriage. After only a moment of hesitation she opened its door. It was, as she expected, empty. She bent and picked up the boy and placed him inside the carriage. 'There you are, Joshie. Now you're out of the rain.' She climbed up after him and lifted him onto the forward-facing seat. 'Now you wait here, my dear. I'll get the bags and see the man. We'll soon be off, you'll see.' She backed away, and he sat looking at her as she stood in the doorway. There was so little light in the carriage interior, and his eyes were dark pools in the blur of his face. The rain was dripping from his boots onto the floor. 'I'll be back in a minute,' she said.

Returning to the porch, she picked up her reticule and the carpet bag and then carried them to the carriage. When she opened the door to place them inside she saw that the boy was lying on the seat. His eyes were closed. He had pulled off his hat and it lay beside him. She deposited the bags on the floor, then stepped back and quietly closed the door behind her.

Back once more at the door of the house, she knocked again. The fly-man had to be around; he was bound to be; he could not be far away; he would not leave his horse in such a situation. She knocked again, and waited, then stepped forward up onto the step and pushed the door open a fraction wider. 'Hello . . .?' she called. 'Hello, sir . . .? Is there anyone there . . .?'

There was no answer. She stood, uncertain, and as she did so she realised that the rain was easing, it was coming to a stop. With relief, she looked up, but saw that the skies were as dark as ever. There was no doubt that the rain would soon be back. She waited another moment, and then turned in the direction of the carriage. She must see if the boy was all right. She would wait with him inside the carriage; the fly-owner was bound to be out soon.

She moved across the cobbles, heedless of the puddles, up to the carriage door again, reaching up for the handle.

'Hey! You there! Get away from that door!'

The man's voice startled her. It came not from the house, but from around the corner of the yard where an outhouse stood. She turned at the harsh sound and saw a tall, lean man coming towards her across the yard. He was clad in a brown waterproof cape and a wide-brimmed, waterproof hat. He carried in one hand a pail, and in the other a mop and some rags. She remained standing by the carriage.

'Get away!' the man barked out as he came on. 'Get away from the coach this instant.'

She was puzzled at the man's behaviour. 'Sir,' she said as he drew nearer, 'I mean no harm. I'm wanting to hire you if you're free. I need to get to Brookham Way on the other side of the town.'

'The cab's not for hire,' he said bluntly. There was no mistaking the anger in his voice. He came to a stop before her and set down the pail. It was full of liquid, and a strong, pungent scent rose from it in the heavy, damp air. Lily recognised the smell as that of Lysol.

'You best go to the station and pick up a cab there,' the man said.

'I couldn't get one,' she said. 'They were all taken. That's why I came to you.' She could not understand his manner. 'Can't you help me, sir?' she said.

'I just told you, miss, I'm not for hire,' he said. 'So be off with you.'

There was nothing more to be said, and feeling on the verge of tears of frustration she reached out and grasped the carriage door handle. Seeing her action, the man stepped forward and roughly brushed her hand from it. 'Get away from that handle,' he said. 'Don't touch anything. Get away.'

'But sir –'

'I told you – get away. Just get away.' Then he added, without pause, 'Well, what are you standin' there for? I told you, get away.'

When she reached for the handle again, he snatched at her wrist. 'You deaf or summat?' he said, 'I told you not to touch nothing. What's the matter with you?'

'The child –' she said. 'My – my boy. He's in the coach –'

'*What*?' The man looked horrified. 'You got a child in there?'

'He's not doing any harm,' she protested. 'He was just – sheltering from the rain while I tried to find you.'

'Dear God!' the man muttered. 'Get him out. Get him out at once.' Throwing the mop and rags down onto the wet ground, he stepped forward and yanked open the door. Past his shoulder Lily could see the boy lying stretched out, his face on the coarse fabric of the seat. 'Get 'im out,' the man said. 'Get the little mite out!'

He held the door open wide, and Lily stepped up into the carriage and bent to the boy, who began to sit up. The raised voices had alarmed him, and she could see the distress in his face.

'Come, Joshie,' she said gently. 'We can't stay here. We have to find another cab.' She pulled him upright on the seat. 'Come on, my dear. Let's put your hat back on and get you out.' She took up his wet hat and put it on his head and adjusted the string beneath his chin. 'There – all ready. Come on, now. There's a good boy.' She moved back to the door and stepped down onto the ground, while at the same time the boy picked up his toy horse. Then she lifted the boy in her arms and set him down beside her on the cobbles.

'Don't forget your bags,' the man said.

'No,' she said. 'Thank you.' Leaning back into the carriage she took up the carpet bag and her reticule.

The man was watching her, an unreadable expression on his face. 'Right,' he said, 'now you get the little chap away, well away.' There was no anger in his voice now. 'I'm sorry I shouted just now, but . . .' His words trailed off.

Lily said nothing, but took the boy by the hand. 'Let's go back to the station, Joshie,' she said. 'We'll get a cab if we wait long enough. If not we'll find one somewhere else on the street.'

Outside the fly-man's yard they turned back in the direction of the railway station, and as they approached, Lily saw that there were still several people waiting to pick up cabs. 'It's no good,' she said. 'If we wait there we'll wait for ever – and I don't think the rain is going to keep off for much longer. Come – let's walk up into the town.'

They set off again. After they had gone a few paces the boy said, tilting back his head to look up at her, 'Why was the man shouting, Lily? Why was he angry?'

'I don't know,' she said.

'Was he angry with me – for being in the carriage?'

'No, dear, he wasn't angry with you. He was angry with me, but I don't know why.'

They walked on a little further, then the boy said, 'I'm tired, Lily. My legs are tired, and I'm cold.'

'Oh,' she breathed, 'poor boy.' She came to a halt and bent to him, putting a hand to his cheek. 'I know you're tired,' she said. 'It's been a long day for you, But soon we'll be indoors and you can rest, and we'll get a nice fire, and be warm again. Won't that be nice?'

'Will you carry Mr Charlie Dobbin for me, please?' he asked.

He held up the toy horse and Lily took it. 'We'll put him in the big bag, shall we?' she said. 'He'll be safe and comfortable there along with Bunny.' Putting the carpet bag on the wet ground, she unfastened the opening and put the toy horse inside. 'There he is.' She gave the boy an encouraging smile. 'All safe and sound.'

He did not smile back. His lip trembled and she could see he was on the verge of tears. The sight brought a lump to her throat and she compressed her own lips, fighting back the threatening emotion. She could not afford for a moment to let the boy to see any hint of vulnerability. 'Let's walk on,' she said.

They set off again, and then, as they reached the corner of Market Street, the rain began to fall once more. Lily groaned under her breath, and led the child into the shelter of the doorway of a disused warehouse. And there they stood side by side while the rain continued to beat down and the townspeople scurried past.

They stayed for almost half an hour, during which time the child hardly spoke a word. Then, at long last, the rain stopped. Lily picked up the carpet bag and, with a sigh of relief, looked up at the sky. Up above the roofs of the town the clouds were clearing. 'Come,' she said, 'we can go now.'

Five minutes later she managed to hail a cab.

Sitting side by side in the carriage, Lily and the boy were driven through the rain-wet streets of Corster, leaving behind the market square, the shops and the factories and crossing the river to the outskirts. Then, at last, the cab pulled into Brookham Way, and Lily saw up ahead on the right, the little row of terrace houses.

'Here. Just here.' As she spoke, she leant forward and tapped sharply on the little window behind the driver's seat, and the vehicle came to a halt.

'Are we there?' Joshua said, and Lily replied, 'Yes, we are, my dear. You stay here a minute, while I pay the man.'

The boy did not demur, and Lily stepped down into the

cinder-covered road and gave the driver his fee. Then, reaching up, she lifted the carpet bag and then the boy down beside her.

As the cab trundled away, they walked to the little gateway of the second villa and up the short path to the front door, where she bent and lifted the larger of the two flower pots that stood there and took up the spare latchkey. A moment later it had been turned in the lock, and she was stepping inside.

With the door closed on the bleak day, she led the way along the narrow passage into the kitchen, and there put down the carpet bag and her reticule. The place was cold, and had an air of dampness about it. She knew that neither Miss Elsie nor Mr Shad had been here for a while. The last time she herself had been here was in August with Joel, just before he had left for the Continent. Then, too, it had rained.

'Well, we're here, Joshie,' she said with relief in her voice. 'We got here at last.'

'Where?' the boy said. 'Where are we?'

'Where? Oh – well, we're in a part of Corster. A nice little part, and we shall be fine here for a few days.' She turned in the room, looking around. 'First of all, I'll get you comfortable, then I'll light a fire, and after that I'll get us something to eat.'

After removing her hat and coat she took off the boy's hat and coat and boots. Everything seemed to be wet through. He was wet to the skin, and his little feet were like ice. In the carpet bag she had packed a few spare items of clothing for him, and when she had dried him with a towel she put a nightshirt and a pair of clean, dry stockings on him. She went upstairs then to the main bedroom and fetched down a couple of old blankets from the cupboard and wrapped them round him, and seated him on one of the kitchen chairs. 'Now,' she said, 'I'll make us that nice fire, and we'll be warm again. I'll get our things dry too.'

There was some kindling near the range, and a thin pile of old newspapers. Moving to the back door, she said, 'I'll see if there's coal or wood,' and went out into the yard. In the small outhouse she found a little firewood, and in the bunker beside the back door some coal. She loaded a bucket and carried it inside, and soon had a fire going. There was a clothes-horse in the corner of the room, and she set it in front of the range and draped their wet clothes over it.

'There – they'll soon dry.' She smiled encouragingly at the boy. 'And look – the sky's quite clear now. What a blessing.'

From the well in the yard she brought in water and filled a kettle, and set it on to boil. While it was heating she took off her own wet stockings and put on a pair that she had packed in the bag. Standing in her stockinged feet she then took out the sandwiches that Mrs Lemmon had provided for their journey. She laid a couple of them on a plate, and put it on the table, then set the boy's chair before it.

'There, Joshie, eat a sandwich, why don't you? Some nice potted meat. You like that.' She smiled at him, but he did not smile back. Instead, he looked down at his hands. 'Aren't you going to eat something?' she asked.

He shook his head.

'No? I thought you'd be hungry. Won't you have even a little bite?'

He shook his head again.

'All right, dear. Would you like a glass of water? There's no milk, I'm afraid, but I'll get some tomorrow. Have a sip of water for now, will you?'

He shook his head.

'Will you have a little tea when I make it?'

Another shake of the head. 'No, thank you.'

'You must have something, Joshie. Just a little? To please me?'

Another shake of the head. Then he said, frowning a little, 'Is this the holiday, Lily?'

'What, dear?'

'The holiday. Has it started yet?'

She hesitated, for a moment at a loss. 'Yes,' she said then, 'but it will be much better tomorrow. The sun will come out, and we'll do something nice. Maybe we'll go to the aquarium. Would you like that?'

He frowned.

'You remember? The aquarium I told you about? Where they have all the fishes? That'll be interesting, won't it?'

Silent, he gave a little nod. Then he said, 'I don't like holidays.'

'Oh – Joshie.'

He began to cry, large tears welling from his eyes and running down his cheeks. Lily, sitting on the adjacent chair, brought him onto her lap, wrapping her arms around him. 'Don't cry, my little sweetheart. Oh, don't cry.' She could not bear to see his tears.

His tears faded after a while, and he lay quiet in her arms. Soon he was asleep. The sandwiches remained untouched on the plate. Night had fallen, and the room was in deep gloom. She wanted to light a candle to relieve the dark, but she could not disturb the boy. She would have liked to take him up to bed, but soon it would be too dark to see her way up the stairs.

Eventually the kettle began to boil, so she would have to move. Murmuring softly to the boy, she carried him to the old sofa by the window, laid him down on it and covered him with the blankets. He stirred, and then settled again, his breathing becoming rhythmic once more. She lit two candles and by their light made some tea. Sitting at the table she sipped at it and ate a few bites of a sandwich. From her reticule she took out her watch and laid it on the table. It gave the time at ten minutes past eight.

She fed the range with more coal later on, and pulled up a chair near the sofa. While the steam rose from the wet garments on the clothes-horse she watched the boy as he slept.

This was not the way she had meant it to be, she said to herself, but it would be better tomorrow. Everything was new and strange to the child, so of course he was not at ease with it. He was so tired, too, so exhausted. For him it had been the longest day, but he would be all right soon. It was just his tiredness. When he had had a good night's sleep, he would be all right again. If the weather was dry they would find something interesting to do in the town. Perhaps go to the aquarium, or do something else that would amuse him.

She continued to gaze down at him in the dim light. The only sound in the room was the occasional crackle coming from the range. There was no sound at all from the night outside. She yawned. For her too it had been a long day, and she felt the exhaustion of all the tense and pressing hours. She was dog-tired, and she needed to sleep. After a time she rose and, taking a lighted candle, went up to the bedroom again and brought down another blanket. After banking up the fire she settled herself on the sofa with him, covered herself and tried to sleep.

Chapter Thirty-six

She was awakened by the boy's coughing, though it would have taken far less to wake her; she had not been deeply asleep. Indeed, neither of them had slept well. Just as she had passed the night in fitful dozes, she was well aware that the boy had done the same.

Casting aside the blanket she sat on the edge of the sofa and put an arm around him as he sat up. 'Are you all right, my darling?' she said. He coughed again and said yes, but there was no energy in his voice, no note of enthusiasm. Picking up the watch from the table she saw that it was just after eight. 'It's going to be a nice morning, Joshie,' she said, turning, looking out of the window over the back yard. 'The sun is out for a change, look.'

Leaving the child under his blankets on the sofa, she washed her face and hands and then got dressed, throwing on her clothes with no consideration as to her appearance. That done, she raked out the hot ashes from the range, then went out into the yard for wood and coal for the fire. There was little of both left, and she would have to get more. The sky was clear, but there was a keen wind blowing, and she was glad to get back into the relative comfort of the kitchen. When she had rekindled the fire she put on a kettle of water to boil. A little later, when it had heated, she poured some into a bowl and gave the boy a wash. The clothes she had draped before the range had quite dried during the night and she got him dressed. He suffered it all uncomplaining, passively and without comment, in contrast to how he usually was with his little protests and obvious impatience to be getting on with something more vital and more interesting. He was rather listless, she observed, and she told herself that it was due to his not sleeping so well, and his exhaustion of the day before. For breakfast, she could only offer him more of the sandwiches that Mrs Lemmon had prepared, and she put one on a plate before him as he sat at the table, and poured a little water into a glass. He took a bite from the beef sandwich and a sip from the glass, and then sat back in the chair, wanting no more. 'No?' she said. 'No more?' He shook his head. She gave a nod; she would not press him. Reaching out, she laid the back of her hand upon his brow. 'Your forehead's too warm, Joshie,' she said, frowning. 'I hope you haven't caught a little chill.'

He said nothing, but looked back at her dully, without interest in her words.

'Here,' she said, picking up his toy horse, 'here's your Mr Charlie Dobbin. Aren't you glad to see him today?'

She put the toy on the table and the boy picked it up, clicked his tongue at it in a half-hearted way, and moved it across the table top in little jerking, galloping movements. Lily said, smiling, 'Oh, that's good. I'm sure Mr Dobbin likes a little exercise.' The boy smiled faintly, moved the toy horse on a few more inches, then set it back down.

Lily watched him for a few moments, then said, 'We need to get a few things from the shops. Let's go round and see Mrs Tanner next door for a second or two, shall we? She'll help us out, I know.'

Taking him by the hand, she led him out of the house to the front gate, and turned up the path of the adjoining house. Her rap on the door was answered by Millie, Mrs Tanner's granddaughter. Invited in without hesitation, Lily and the boy went along the passage into the kitchen where Mrs Tanner sat with her crochet beside the range. The old lady was surprised to see her, and Lily told her that she had come to stay next door for a few days with her mistress's little son. She would not sit down, she said, when invited to, but she would be most grateful if the old lady or Millie could sit with the child for half an hour while she went to the shops to buy a few necessities. Millie spoke up at once; she would go to the shops, she said, and get whatever was needed.

The girl put on her coat and hat and accompanied Lily and Joshua back to the house next door. There Lily wrote a list of things she needed and gave it to the girl with some money, asking her also to call at the coal merchant's yard in the next street and ask for a sack of coal to be delivered to the house.

'There, Joshie,' Lily said when the girl had gone, a basket over her arm, 'Millie's going to get us something nice for our dinner and also for breakfast tomorrow. She's going to get a little tonic for you as well – that'll make you feel better – and she'll go to the dairy too, later on, and get us some milk.'

While Millie was away, Mrs Tanner came in, bringing part of a fruit cake that she had baked, and a large piece of apple pie. She cooed and clucked over Joshua where he sat on the sofa, and tried, briefly, to amuse him, but he showed little interest, and after a few minutes she gave up and settled in the grandfather chair near the range while Lily made some tea.

As the two women sat drinking it a knock came at the front door, and Lily answered it to find on the doorstep a young man selling bundles of kindling. She bought some and set them down in the hearth beside the range. Millie came back a little later, her basket loaded, bringing eggs, bread, potatoes, cabbage, and a small piece of beef. She had also bought some candles, a bottle of Haver's tonic, and a little bar of plain chocolate. As soon as she had unloaded the basket she set off again, this time heading for the nearby dairy. While she was gone, Lily put away the groceries and opened the bottle of patent medicine and poured a little into a glass along with some water. After a few moments' coaxing, she got the boy to drink a little, but he spat it out and turned his head away, refusing to take any more. 'Oh, come, Joshie,' she pleaded, 'do try to take a little. It's good for you. And if you drink a spoonful you can have a bit of chocolate to take away the taste.' He could not be persuaded, however, and Lily put the chocolate and medicine away in the cupboard.

Millie came back shortly afterwards, bringing a quart of milk and a small quantity of butter and cheese, after which Mrs Tanner got up from her chair to return to her home next door. Millie remained, glad of a change of company and someone new to talk to. She was happy also to make herself useful, feeding the fire in the range and tidying the hearth, and fetching in water from the well. She was, she explained to Lily, between employments. She had recently been working as a milkmaid at a nearby farm, but the farm had been sold on and she was now looking for a post elsewhere.

She went at midday, leaving Lily to prepare a meal for herself and the boy. The child wanted little of it, though, and after the first couple of mouthfuls turned from his plate. There was mucus coming from his nose, and Lily wiped it away. His brow was over-warm when she laid her hand upon it.

Up in the main bedroom, Lily lit the fire to air the room and the bed. Back downstairs she got the boy to lie down on the sofa, covered by the blankets. As he slept, she busied herself about the kitchen, tidying the place, washing the dishes and preparing food for the evening, all the time moving as quietly as she could, so as not to wake him. Later during the afternoon the coal merchant came with a bag of coal. Lily was relieved; at least now they could be sure of keeping warm.

She prepared an omelette later for herself and the boy, and was pleased to see him eat a little of it. But it was only a very little, and when she spoke coaxingly to him, trying to encourage him to eat more, he began to cry. He was consoled after a while, but she knew well that any such consolation could only be a passing thing.

That evening she tried again to get him to take some of the medicine, but he would have none of it, and after a few vain, coaxing words, she gave up. She changed him into his nightshirt then and took him upstairs to the bedroom, which was illuminated with one of the nightlights that Millie had brought from the chandler's. Lily sat on the side of the bed as he lay with his stuffed rabbit in his arms. When he had fallen asleep, she continued to sit there for some minutes, then eased herself up and crept back down to the kitchen. There she sat at the table, the door to the passage open so that she would be able to hear him if he should awake and cry out.

Later, up in the bedroom, she put on her nightdress and got into bed beside him. He stirred briefly as she lowered herself onto the mattress, but then settled again. She lay on her side, her left hand light upon his small body, feeling his warmth, his nearness. With his nose congested, his breathing, usually so sweet, sounded harsh in the quiet.

Later in the night he suddenly awoke. 'Mama,' he said in an anxious little cry, and Lily put her arm around him and spoke to him in soft tones. 'It's all right,' she said. 'You'll be going to see your mama soon. Go to sleep, darling. Go to sleep. You're safe, you're safe.'

He moved restlessly for a little while, swallowing and sniffing, and she murmured softly to him with comforting words. After a time he settled again and fell asleep once more.

Lying in the dimly-lit room, she looked up at the ceiling, taking in the cracks and the water-stains that marked the old plaster. In her blind way she had somehow trusted that everything would work out, but nothing was happening the way she had envisaged.

On the seat of the old kitchen chair that stood beside the bed, her watch ticked the hours away into the quiet. Tomorrow, she said to herself, she would pack up their things and they would go back to Happerfell.

Next morning she could see at once that the boy was no better. In fact, it was obvious that he was worse. His nose was blocked so that he was forced to breath only through his mouth, while at the same time the mucus ran down from his nostrils and over his upper lip. Lily wiped it away and soothed his warm brow. There was no question of their travelling back to Happerfell today. She could not take him on such a journey in his present condition. The day was damp, and bitterly cold, and she could only think that he must stay indoors in the warm. If he was well enough tomorrow, they would go then.

Millie came later in the day, and tried to amuse Joshua as he sat on the sofa. He would not be diverted, though, and sat there dull and listless. When she pressed him a little he grew tearful, and she tactfully withdrew her attentions.

The longer Lily observed him the more her concern grew, and in the end she asked Millie if there was a doctor nearby. The girl replied that there was a Dr Trinshaw living not far away, and that he had visited her grandmother on two or three occasions. 'Can you go for him?' Lily asked her. The girl at once agreed, and went back next door to put on her hat and coat and set out on her errand. She returned some twenty minutes later saying that she had left a message at the doctor's house, and that he would be calling round just as soon as he could.

Millie left the house again soon afterwards, leaving Lily and the boy alone. Just over an hour later there came a knock at the door, and Lily answered it and found the doctor standing in the little porch, his carriage in the road beyond the gate. Dr Trinshaw was a slim man of middle height, in his late fifties. He had bushy side whiskers and wore a dark brown ulster. She asked him to come in and led the way into the kitchen where the child still lay on the sofa.

'Are you the boy's mother?' the doctor asked, looking down at Joshua.

She hesitated for the briefest moment, then said, 'No. I – I'm his guardian for now. His parents are in Scotland.'

'How old is he?'

'Four and a half.'

He nodded. 'The girl left the message that he's poorly and has a very bad cold. Is that right? What are his symptoms?'

Lily told of the child's raised temperature, his dry cough, his running nose and lack of energy and appetite, and added that on Sunday the two of them had got wet through in the rain. He had not been well since.

The doctor had put down his bag and taken off his coat, and Lily watched while he bent to the child. 'And what is your name, young man?' he said to him, smiling.

'Joshie,' the child said.

'Ah, Joshie, is it? And you're four and a half, are you?'

'Yes. I shall be five next May.'

'Shall you now?' The doctor indicated the boy's toy horse on the sofa beside him and said, 'That looks like a fine animal. He's yours, is he?'

'Yes.'

'Oh, very handsome indeed.'

The doctor sat on the sofa and gently unbuttoned the boy's shirt. After he had done so he pulled the garment down from the child's shoulder, exposing the scar on his

545

upper arm. 'I see he's been vaccinated,' he said to Lily. 'And not so long ago.'

'Yes, sir.'

The doctor nodded, and continued his examination, taking the boy's pulse and sounding his lungs with a stethoscope. Joshua protested a little at first, giving a plaintive little moan, and Lily thought that he might cry, but the doctor spoke softly to him and called him by his name, and after a few moments the child relaxed and suffered the intrusion without further complaint.

The doctor's brisk examination did not take long. When he had finished, he patted Joshua gently on the head and said to Lily, a little brusquely, that she might button up his shirt again. As she did so, he put his instruments away. There was nothing seriously wrong with the boy, he said, as he got into his coat. He was merely suffering from a chill, and would soon recover. His appetite would come back, he went on, and she should give him easily-digestible foods such as soups and porridge. He added that he would send his boy to the house with medicine for the child, and something to rub on his chest. From his bag he took a small notepad and wrote out his bill, and Lily took some of her precious funds and paid him. From his tone and his manner, she had the feeling all the time he was disapproving, that she had done wrong to call him out.

When he had put his fee away in his purse the doctor put on his hat and moved into the passage. Lily, following, said to him, 'I was so worried about him, Doctor. I was afraid it was something worse.'

At the open front door he turned, shook his head and gave a sigh. 'Frankly, I'm run off my feet,' he said. 'I don't mind telling you, ma'am. With this dreadful plague *everybody's* panicking and fearing the worst. I haven't had a minute. Oh, it's a terrible sickness, of course, but most of the time it's a false alarm – a little croup, a bad chill, a bad cold, a little indigestion – but I have to come out, just the same. All winds and weathers. You can't take any chances.' He paused. 'It's not surprising you were anxious,' he said, 'but there's nothing much wrong with the child that won't be put right with a little rest, a good tonic and some nourishing food. And keep him warm. If you take him out, make sure he's well wrapped up. Believe me, he'll be as right as rain in no time. Of course, if he should get worse, then you send for me, all right?' He touched at his hat. 'I'll wish you good day.'

Lily thanked him, and he turned and strode out to his carriage.

When she had closed the door behind him, she went back into the kitchen. 'Well,' she said to the boy, 'the doctor's going to send his lad with some medicine for you, Joshie. It'll be here soon. Will you be a good boy and take it as the doctor says?'

'Yes,' he said, nodding.

'That's a good boy.' She beamed at him, then said with a sigh, 'I don't think we can go back to Happerfell just yet, Joshie. The doctor says you've got to stay warm, so I think today we'd best not venture out.' She bent over him and gently smoothed a hand over his fair hair. 'He also says you've got to eat something. Will you do that? What do you say if I make you a little junket, eh? A little sweet, creamy junket? I know you'd like that. And maybe afterwards you could have a little bit of chocolate.'

He thought about this for a moment, then said, 'Yes – I'd like some chocolate.'

She made the junket then, flavouring it with a little essence of vanilla from a bottle she found in one of the cupboards. As she set it to cool the doctor's lad came to the door, bringing a bottle of medicine and a jar of unguent. She gave him a halfpenny and he went happily on his way. Back in the kitchen she smoothed some of the ointment

547

onto the boy's chest and then covered it with a piece of flannel she found in the bedroom cupboard. She wrapped him up warmly again and gave him a little dose of the medicine, which he swallowed while pulling a face, and then gave him a small piece of chocolate, both as a little reward and to counteract the medicine's taste.

Later in the day Mrs Tanner sent Millie round with a pot of vegetable soup, and to Lily's joy Joshua took some of it with a little bread. Afterwards Lily read to him from one of his storybooks that she had brought in the carpet bag. When it was time for him to go to bed she gave him a little more of the medicine, then took him upstairs and lifted him into the bed. 'I didn't say my prayers to gentle Jesus,' he said, frowning, and Lily replied, 'That won't matter. Gentle Jesus won't mind, not if you're not well.'

He lay down and she tucked him in under the covers.

'You won't go till I'm asleep, will you?' he said. He pulled his rabbit to him, wrapping it in his arms.

'No, I won't.'

He coughed a couple of times, then closed his eyes, and in the dim glow of the nightlight she sat on the side of the bed and watched over him until at last he fell asleep.

She awoke the next morning beside the boy, reached out and took up the watch from the chair and saw that it was just after seven. He had not wakened in the night, and was sleeping soundly, his mouth a little open. She lay back, listening to his breathing. It seemed a little clearer, she thought, a little easier.

She slipped out of the bed as quietly and as smoothly as she could and, putting her coat on over her nightdress, crept from the room and went down to the kitchen. There she cleared out the ashes from the range, laid and lit a new fire, and put on a kettle of water to heat. When she had washed she went upstairs and got dressed. The boy was lying sleeping as she moved quietly around in the dim grey light.

A little later, when she was down in the kitchen again, she heard him call her name, and she went back upstairs and found him sitting up in the bed. She sat beside him and ran her fingers through his soft hair. 'Did you have a good sleep, Joshie?' she asked.

He gave a little nod. 'Yes.'

'And Bunny too?'

'Yes.'

'That's good.'

She thought he looked better, and was convinced that his voice and breathing did indeed sound a little easier.

'Do you feel like a little breakfast?' she asked, and he nodded.

'Good,' she said, 'then let's get you washed and dressed – and then we'll give you your medicine too.'

He seemed to improve further as the day wore on, and Lily watched him like a hawk every minute of the time. At breakfast he ate a soft-boiled egg with some bread and butter, accompanied by half a cup of milky tea. Also, without protest, he took more of his medicine, and suffered her to rub his chest again with the soothing balm. At one o'clock he took a little more of the soup that Mrs Tanner had sent, and immediately afterwards settled on the sofa under a blanket. Millie called round while he was sleeping, saying that she was going to the shops and would be happy to get anything that Lily required. Lily was grateful for the offer and gave the girl some money and a small list of items she needed.

When Millie returned, Joshua was still asleep, and quietly the girl helped Lily do a little work about the house, bringing in more coal and drawing fresh water from the well. When the child awoke, after sleeping for over two hours, he looked refreshed and brighter. Lily took a flannel, wetted it in warm water and wiped his face. To her increasing relief he seemed to be growing better with each passing hour, and later, when she asked him how he was feeling, he replied cheerfully that he felt well. She could only believe that what he said was the truth, for his improved condition and spirit showed in his appearance and in everything he said and did. To Millie, she remarked, 'There, you see? Like the doctor said – it's just a chill. He's going to be fine in no time at all.' To the child she said, 'Well, there you are, master Joshua, I think you'll be well enough to go back to Happerfell tomorrow. What do you think about that?'

He spoke up quickly. 'I thought we were going to see the fishes,' he said.

Millie frowned. 'The fishes?'

'I spoke about us going to the aquarium,' Lily replied, then to the boy, 'Is that what you'd like to do – go and see the fishes?'

'You said we could,' he said.

She smiled. 'I did indeed. Well . . .' she gave a nod, pleased, 'if that's what you want, then that's what we'll do.'

By the time he went to bed that night his cough had mostly gone, and his breathing was so much clearer. She watched and listened as he knelt and said his prayers. Then she tucked him into bed with his rabbit, sat with him until he had fallen asleep, and went back downstairs. When she joined him in bed later, he was sleeping soundly.

When Joshua awoke, he asked again for his mama, and Lily again explained to him that he could not go to her yet as his sister was ill. 'Don't you remember I told you?' she said, and he replied, yes, he did remember. But it wouldn't be that long, she added, and he would be going up to Scotland to be with his mama and papa again soon. He seemed to accept this, and then asked again about going to see the fishes. She was glad; she had thought he might have forgotten, but clearly he had not.

So it was that after he had taken his usual midday sleep, they set off from the house to go into the centre of the town. The weather was fine. The morning frost had gone and the sun shone down out of a clear sky. Stepping out from the gate, Lily looked down at him. 'All right, Joshie?' she said. 'D'you think you'll be all right?'

He looked up at her and smiled. He was well wrapped up in his overcoat and muffler, and wearing on his head his warm little cap with the earflaps. 'Yes,' he said. 'Are we going now to see the fishes?'

'We are,' she replied. 'We certainly are.'

They walked a little of the way, hand in hand, and then when a cab came by Lily hailed it, and they rode the rest of the way into the town centre.

The aquarium was said to be the largest of its kind in the West Country. It was housed in an elegant, cavernous old building just off the High Street, not far from the theatre. Lily had visited it while governess to the Acland girls, and it had been a wonderful, thrilling experience. Now, as she and the boy entered the first room it all came back to her, not only the sight of the great glass tanks, but also the clean smell of the place, and the silence. There were not that many other visitors, just a few children with adults, and she and the child had unimpeded views of the tanks and their fascinating contents. There were fish of all kinds – some so very tiny that they could barely be seen darting amongst the waving water weeds, others comparatively huge and moving slowly and ponderously back and forth through the still water. So different too in their shapes they were – some like sharp slivers of silver, and others almost as round as an india-rubber ball – and how varied in their colours and markings, some being very dull in appearance, while others were of the brightest hues and the most dramatic patterns.

Joshua was fascinated. Together, he and Lily moved from room to room, going slowly from one tank to another, and he gazed at the strange creatures before him in awe, his eyes wide in wonder. He was full of exclamations and questions, and Lily did her best to give him answers, repeatedly referring to the copperplate legends on display beside each glass tank, giving information on the creatures within.

At last they came to the end, and Lily and the boy made their way back out onto the street. Standing on the pavement, she bent to him, putting her hand on his cheek. 'Was that good, Joshie?'

'Oh, yes, it was good. I shall tell Mama, and Papa, and Vinnie too.'

'Oh, yes, indeed, you must tell them all about it.' Seeing his bright, interested little face turned up towards her own, she could only marvel at the difference in him, at the change wrought in just a day or so. She was so glad that they had gone to the aquarium. It would be something that he might remember.

Further along the street they came across a poster advertising a circus. A picture of a clown was displayed, with a painted face and comical hat. In the background were dramatic studies of a lion and a bear. Joshua came to a stop and looked curiously at the clown's made-up features.

'What is he?' he asked.

'He's a clown,' Lily said. 'He's part of the circus. He's there to make you laugh. Children love him.'

'Would I love him too?' he asked, and Lily said at once, 'Oh, you would, my dear. I know you would.'

'And there's a lion and a bear, look.'

'Yes, they have lions and bears in the circus,' Lily said. 'They have elephants too, and little dogs that perform amazing tricks. Oh, the circus! It's a wonderful thing!'

Joshua was wide-eyed. 'Can I see it?' he asked. 'Can we go tomorrow?'

She looked again at the poster. There was a matinee performance at three. He could have his rest for a while at noon, and they would be in plenty of time for the show. Then they would start back to Happerfell the next morning. After all, what would one day more matter? If she had to make her excuses for five days, she could as well make them for six. And it would be good, so good, to spend a little more time with him, before he went out of her life for ever.

'Can we?' he said again. 'Oh, Lily, can we?'

She stood in silence for a moment, then she said, with a little shake of her head, 'We'd better not, Joshie. I'm sorry, dear – but tomorrow we have to take you back home.'

Yes, there was no question of it now: tomorrow they would set off back for Happerfell. She should never have brought him away in the first place. On receiving Mrs Soameson's telegraph she should at once have asked Mr Beeching to go no further, but she had not done so.

No more. It was over. That evening she must write to Mr and Mrs Soameson. She would tell them that she had brought the child away for a little holiday, but that on the morrow she would be taking him back to Happerfell to be with his nurse. There would be no fuss, surely there would not. On the contrary, she said to herself, they would probably be pleased. Yes, she would ask Millie to get her some paper and envelopes, and she would write tonight.

'Oh, Lily, please?' the boy said, looking up at her. 'Can't we go to the circus?'

'Another day, Joshie,' she said. 'Perhaps another day.'

*

After he had gone to bed that night, she sat alone in the kitchen. The door into the narrow hall was open so she would hear if he called out, but all was silence. She had before her a notepad and pen and ink that Millie had brought round. She turned up the flame slightly on the lamp, then drew the pad to her and began to write:

2 Merridew Villas
Brookham Way
Corster
16th November 1871

Dear Mr and Mrs Soameson,

I received your telegraph, and was very sorry to hear that Lavinia is ill. Still, with the right care – which I am sure she is getting – I have no doubt that she will soon be better. As you're well aware, Miss Cattock is still laid low with her ankle injury, so I have taken the liberty of bringing Joshua away for a little sojourn. The weather has been so bad, and he has been confined to the house so much, that I thought a little respite would not be out of place. I hope you do not disapprove. We have not gone far, only to Corster, where we are staying in a house owned by my friend, Miss Balfour, of whom you are aware. I'm sure you'll be pleased to know that Joshie and I have had a fine time. We have even visited the aquarium – with much excitement. Tomorrow, however, we shall go back to Happerfell. If Miss Cattock is well enough to care for him then, I will leave her to her work, otherwise I shall be more than happy to remain with Joshua until you judge it is safe to have him with you in Scotland. When that time comes I shall be more than happy to escort him in the event that Miss Cattock is still indisposed.

Yours truly
Lily Clair

From the little notebook in her reticule she copied onto the envelope the address that Mrs Soameson had given her. Then, when the ink was dry, she slipped the letter inside. She would post it tomorrow, on the way to the station.

After a while she got up, filled the kettle and put it on the range. Then, returning to the table, she sat down. There was no sound within the house. She sighed deeply. With her firm decision to go back to Happerfell she could feel the tension draining out of her. Soon, she told herself, the problems would be facts of life, and beyond her control. And she would be alone. There was no more Joel in her life, Tom was gone, and soon the boy would be out of it too.

She sat up late that night. When at last she went up to bed she found the child sleeping soundly. Silently and softly she undressed and climbed in beside him, lying against his tender warmth. After some hours she slept.

Chapter Thirty-seven

She left him still sleeping the next morning, and went downstairs into the kitchen. It was icy cold. She slipped on her shoes, put her coat on over her dress and lit the fire in the range and made some tea. When it was brewed she sat hunched at the table, sipping from the cup.

Her decision to return to Happerfell had brought, she found, an enormous relief, and now, having made that decision, she was desperate to keep to it. Of course they must go back. Every hour she kept him away only made her sin the greater. What exactly she would say on her return to The Gables she had not decided, but she would work it out.

Moving into the hall, she stood at the foot of the stairs and listened for any sound from the bedroom above. All was quiet. Back in the kitchen she took off her coat and hung it up behind the door. The room was getting warmer now. She filled the kettle again and put it to heat. It would be ready for Joshua's wash when he came downstairs.

A little later she poured more tea for herself. She had kept the pot hot on the range, and the brew was strong and stewed. She drank it anyway, and ate with it a slice of bread which she spread with a little beef dripping that Mrs Tanner had sent round with Millie.

As she sat there she was attracted by a movement beyond the window, and she turned and saw the woodpecker perched on the edge of the earthenware bowl. He drank there from the rainwater, and then, in an instant, was gone again. He had his own life to live, she thought, and lived it untouched by the little dramas of others around him. An image of Joel came into her head, and she saw him as he had sat at the table before her that day when the wood-pecker had come to drink after the rain. She could see every detail of his features, from the curve of his upper lip to the faintest lines etched in his brow. She could hear his voice too, not only his words, but his tone, his every nuance. She had believed him, when he had said that all would be well for them – but even then, she had been a little afraid.

Her reticule was on the dresser nearby, and she took from it his letter. She had not read it since that morning when she had received it at The Gables. Now she unfolded it and read it again. Though she knew what she must read, at the same time there was one desperate, irrational part of her being that hoped that somehow it would tell a different story. Of course she could change nothing. Every word was there, irrevocable. Afterwards she folded the letter again and put it back in the envelope.

Don't think about it, she told herself. It was done. As recent as it was, it was now a part of the past. Now was the time to think about the present, and the future. Later today she would take the child back to Happerfell. She would remain at The Gables for a few days with him until the nurse was fit enough to care for the boy and then, if nothing more was required of her, she would leave and go back to Sherrell.

And what of Miss Elsie? She would be wondering what had happened. She would have been expecting Lily to have arrived back at Rowanleigh by this time, on her return from escorting the boy to his parents in Scotland.

What could she tell her? How could she admit what she had done? How could she confess to such foolishness, such selfishness . . . ?

The writing paper and envelopes and pen and ink were still there on the table. She adjusted a sheet of notepaper before her, dipped the pen in the ink and wrote:

2 Merridew Villas
Brookham Way
Corster
17th November 1871

Dear Miss Elsie,

I have no doubt at all that you will be most surprised to see the address at the top of this page, and so learn that I am at the Villa. And you will be wondering why I am here. I hardly know how to write this, but write it I must, for you are my only friend, and if I am to unburden myself to anyone, then it must be to you.

Oh, Miss Elsie, I have done a foolish thing – a most foolish thing. As you know, I was to escort little Joshua to Edinburgh at the weekend, taking him there to rejoin his family. I will confess, and it will surely come as no surprise to you, that I had mixed feelings about the enterprise. I looked forward to having those many hours of the journey with my precious child, while at the same time I was only too aware that at the end of that journey I would lose him, for he would go out of my life for ever. Not, of course, that he was ever really mine, except for those few weeks before he went from my side, as a babe, to be taken to his new home.

You said to me, not so long ago, that I would have to learn to let go. I have not learnt, Miss Elsie, oh, I have not learnt. I must now, though. It is long past the time. I would breathe and live for him, but he is not mine, and truly I must accept this. But there, he was never really mine, was he?

I think I am putting off telling you what I have done. You see, I am a coward into the bargain. But I must put it off no longer, and I want to get this posted off to you so that you will know, so that you will know the worst.

The truth is, I did not take Joshua to Scotland after all. At the last minute, through illness of his little sister, our journey there was cancelled. We should then by rights have remained in Happerfell until a later date, but we did not. To my shame, and my growing disgust with myself, I have to tell you that I brought the child away. I brought him here to Corster, to the empty Villa, where we have been since last Sunday evening.

God alone knows what possessed me to do such a thing. I can only say that I wanted that time, some little time, with the boy. It could not hurt, I thought; no other was to be deprived of his company, and he would have an enjoyable time. I could show him the town, and for a few days he would have a change of scene. Well, I must tell you now that things have not turned out quite in the way I had hoped, and later this morning we shall be setting off back to Happerfell. If there is music to be faced, then I must face it – and whatever censure comes my way, then it is due, for I have brought this upon myself. I can only pray that the child is no worse for it.

Please, do not think too badly of me. Although my son was taken from me, I never ceased to be a mother – I know also that I never shall, but that is one thing that I shall have to bear.

When I have taken him back to Happerfell, I shall leave him there with his nurse and come to you at Rowanleigh, if I am still welcome. What happens to me after that is in the lap of the gods, though as things are I have to say that the future is not something that I am inclined to dwell upon.

I expect to be back in Sherrell within the next day or two. In the meantime, please look with kindness – though undeserved – on your most grateful beneficiary,

Lily Clair

She addressed the envelope and stuck on one of the postage stamps that she had brought in her bag. She looked then at her watch on the dresser and saw that it was almost half-past-nine. Joshua, generally an early riser, was usually up long before this time. She would not wake him, though. He needed his sleep, particularly today when they had the journey back to Happerfell before them.

Millie called round a while later, asking if there was anything she could do, and Lily told her that she and Joshua were to leave that day. When the girl left, she took off to the post the letters that Lily had written.

Over the next hour Lily packed some of their things into the carpet bag in preparation for their leaving, and did a little tidying up around the kitchen. She also made for herself a breakfast of a slice of bread with some of the beef dripping. She would keep what was left for the boy. It would be good for him. When she had dried her hands on a dish towel she went upstairs into the bedroom. He was not sleeping, but lying with his eyes open.

'Ah, so you're awake,' she said. 'Did you have a good sleep?'

He did not answer, but just looked at her.

'I've got you some nice dripping for your breakfast,' she said. 'Or if you'd prefer it you can have a lovely fresh egg. How would that be?'

He gave the faintest little nod. She smiled at him, then sat down on the edge of the bed. 'You're going home today,' she said. 'You're going to see Nursie again. Won't that be nice?'

He remained silent for a moment, then he said, frowning, 'My head hurts.'

'Your head? Oh, my dear. It's that nasty old chill of yours. Perhaps it's come back. I'll get you a little of your medicine. You'll feel better then.'

She fetched the bottle and gave him a spoonful. He

pulled a face as he swallowed it, but did not protest. Afterwards she took him down into the warm kitchen, gave him a wash and got him dressed. He seemed quite languid throughout the whole process, and afterwards he climbed onto the sofa and lay back against the worn cushion.

'Do you want Mr Charlie Dobbin?' Lily asked him.

He nodded dully, and she got the toy and gave it to him. He took it in his hands without enthusiasm, and after a moment laid it down on the seat beside him. 'Oh, poor Mr Charlie,' Lily said in a sympathetic voice, smiling, trying to encourage some little vital response from him, but he did not smile in return. Bending to him, she laid the back of her hand on his smooth brow. He was warm. He was too warm. It was his chill, she said to herself. It was still lingering. Perhaps it had been a mistake to take him to the aquarium. But he had seemed quite well, and had been so happy.

'Would you like a little breakfast?' she asked him. 'Perhaps some of that nice dripping? I know you like that. Or maybe that nice little egg. Would you?'

He shook his head, and closed his eyes. Soon he was asleep.

She sat there, watching him.

Millie called in later on, to say goodbye, but Lily said they would not be returning to Happerfell today after all; the child was not well enough for the journey. Millie was surprised to see him lying down, so subdued, so lacking in vitality. It was his chill, Lily said. She should not have taken him out to the aquarium; she should have kept him indoors. But he would be better tomorrow.

Joshua stayed on the sofa all day. Lily kept him warm with blankets laid over him, and gave him his medicine at intervals. In the afternoon he ate a little bread and dripping, but only a little, leaving most of the food on the plate. His head still ached, he said, and he complained also of an ache

561

in the small of his back. Lily turned him over on the sofa, pulled up his shirt and gently massaged his lower back for a couple of minutes. He grew impatient with it, though, and irritable, so she stopped, and adjusted his clothing again.

In the early evening, she boiled an egg for him, cut a thin piece of bread and butter into fingers, and sat beside him encouraging him to eat. He tried a little, but with no enthusiasm, and eventually the plate was abandoned with the egg only half-eaten. When she tried to persuade him to eat more, he began to cry.

That night, lying in bed beside him, she put her arm around his small body, holding him as close to her as she dared. When he fell asleep she lay there listening to the sound of his breathing.

On Saturday she awoke in the morning with her head feeling heavy, dull and woolly. She had not slept well. She had not slept well for the simple reason that the child had not slept well. He had tossed and turned in the night, sometimes talking in his sleep, muttering unintelligible words. On two or three occasions he had briefly surfaced from his shallow sleep and tried to sit up, staring around him at the dimly-lit room. Lily, sensitive to every movement he made, had looked into his wide eyes and put her gentle hands upon him, trying to calm, to soothe. 'It's all right, my darling. It's all right. Go back to sleep.' And after a moment or two he had closed his languid, bewildered eyes, and settled back again with a troubled sigh.

She had lain awake long enough, she decided. She must get up. The boy was silent at her side, sleeping, and she was loath to disturb him. She moved carefully in the bed, easing herself out onto the thin mat that lay on the cold linoleum. She adjusted the bedcovers behind her, then took her clothes and crept out of the room.

Downstairs she went through the usual routine: wash

quickly, get dressed, then rake out the stove, relight the fire and put a kettle of water on to boil. While the water was heating she put on her boots and her coat and went outside into the yard to draw fresh water from the well. She made tea and sat down at the table and sipped from the cup. The tea was scalding hot, but it brought no comfort. Unless the child was so much better, she thought, he would still not be well enough to travel.

The door to the hall was open, as usual, and she got up and stood at the foot of the stairs and listened. There was no sound. Back in the kitchen, she saw that they would need more coal, and she took the bucket from the hearth and went out into the yard, and filled it from the bunker.

She was just coming in through the back door when she heard the boy's cry.

For all that it was fairly faint, the sound of it almost stopped the blood in her veins. For the briefest moment she stood stock still, then she set down the bucket, hurried into the hall and started up the stairs.

The bedroom door was open, and she swung around the jamb into the room and saw the boy kneeling up in the bed.

'Mama,' he said, frowning, as she appeared in his view, his mouth distorted. 'Mama.'

'It's me, my darling,' she said as she hurried to his side, and saw at once that he had been sick, the vomit having spilt down the front of his nightshirt. She cleaned it off and then sat on the bed and held him. He was shivering.

'Oh, my dear, are you cold?' she said.

He gave a little sighing groan and nestled against her, his head lolling as if he was weary. 'My head, Lily. My head hurts so.'

'Oh, darling . . .' With one arm around him, she laid a hand on his forehead. He was burning up, the perspiration was damp on his brow. 'You've got a fever,' she said. She should never have taken him out to the aquarium, but he had so wanted to go, to see the fish, and he had so enjoyed the little outing. 'Here, my darling, get under the covers again.' Gently she urged him down onto the mattress. 'You must keep warm.'

She pulled the blankets up over him, and he lay back on the pillow, looking up at her, frowning. 'My head, Lily,' he said in a little whine, putting a hand up to his temple. 'My head hurts.'

'Poor old head,' she said, and kissed his hot clammy forehead. 'I'll get you some more of your medicine. The doctor left a little valerian too. I'll get you some of that.'

In the kitchen she took up the small bottle of valerian and measured three drops into a glass and added a little water. Then she picked up his medicine and a spoon. Back upstairs, she lifted him up a little from the pillow. 'Now, dear, drink this. This will be good for that silly old headache.' Supporting his head, she held the glass to his lips and watched as he drank down the water and drops. Then she measured out some of the medicine, and he swallowed it without protest.

'There, now. You lie down and close your eyes, and you'll feel better soon. Perhaps later you'd like a little milk or some hot chocolate, would you? We'll ask Millie to go out and get you some.'

He shook his head, and his eyes filled with tears that spilt over and ran down into the damp hair at his temples. The sight tightened her throat and brought tears pricking. Perhaps she should send for the doctor again, she thought. But no, it was only the chill that had come back, and the doctor was busy with serious illnesses. He wouldn't thank her for bringing him out when it wasn't warranted.

'It's all right, my love,' she said, controlling her voice. 'I'll look after you, and you'll feel better soon.'

'I want my mama,' he said plaintively. 'I want my mama.'

She nodded, catching at her breath. 'I know,' she said. 'I know.'

A while later she brought up a little kindling and some coal and lit a fire in the small grate. Throughout her busy-ness the boy lay back in the bed, making no sound.

Come midday, he had not improved at all. If anything, she had to admit to herself, he was worse. From the feel of his brow she was sure that his temperature had risen even further, and he was complaining again of pain in the small of his back. Pulling back the bedcovers, she turned him onto his stomach, lifted his nightshirt and gently massaged his back. His body was so small under her hands. She felt totally ineffectual, and simply did not know what to do for the best. When he complained of thirst she brought him some water. She tried to persuade him to eat a little, too, and prepared for him a small bowl of bread-and-milk, adding a spoonful of sugar. He ate a little of it, then lay back on the pillow as if exhausted.

When Millie came round in the afternoon she was shocked to see him so poorly. Lily said at once, repeating her line like someone whistling in the dark, 'It's that nasty chill of his, that's what it is, but he'll be all right soon. He'll be fine, you'll see, and I'll take him home again tomorrow.'

Millie went out to the shops later, and brought back with her some few things that Lily required, and then stayed a short while to talk. When she had gone, Lily went back upstairs into the bedroom.

The child was lying as she had left him thirty minutes before, his eyes heavy-lidded, half-closed, a dull expression on his face. She moved to his side and bent over him.

'How are you, my dear?'

He did not answer, but just looked up at her. His lips were slightly apart as he lay breathing through his mouth.

Then, as she looked at him, he gave a little cry and tried to raise himself on the pillow.

'What is it –? Oh, my darling –' She bent lower to help him, and put her arm around his shoulders as he struggled to sit up. His eyes were screwed tight-shut and his mouth was suddenly contorted, lips drawn back over his teeth. He gave a heave, and vomited a dark bile over her hand and the white sheet. Then, with a little sighing groan, he sank back against her supporting arm.

A new wave of panic rose in her, engulfing her. She lowered him back onto the mattress. He was shivering now, his body caught in a sudden rigor, and when he opened his mouth she heard his teeth begin to chatter. The faint sound, brief and small, was terrifying in the silence. *Oh, dear God, what is it? What is wrong?* 'Mama,' he said in a small voice. 'Mama.'

'Soon,' she said. She was trembling now in her fear. 'Soon. I'll take you to your mama soon. I promise.' This was nothing to do with a chill, she thought. She must send for the doctor again without delay.

'Lie down and rest a minute, my darling,' she murmured. 'I must leave you for a second, but I'll be right back. I must just run next door and see Millie.' She was straightening, stepping away. 'I'll be right back, my love.'

She hurried down the stairs and a moment later was knocking on the door of Mrs Tanner's house. Millie opened it, and Lily said to her at once, 'Oh, Millie, I've only got a second. I've come to ask if you could please run for the doctor. Joshua's condition is so much worse.'

'I'll get my hat and coat and go at once,' the girl said. 'You go on back to him, miss. I'll call in and see you later.'

Lily went back indoors. The vomit was still on her sleeve, and she took a damp cloth and dabbed it off as best she could. A glance at her watch told her it was almost seven o'clock. She was aware of an empty feeling in her stomach, and realised that she had not eaten all day. It did not matter; she would get something later.

Upstairs, she bent beside the bed. She saw now, with relief, that he was sleeping. Through his open mouth his breath came a little harsh, a little rapid. He had pushed the bedcovers low on his body, exposing the vomit stain on the yoke of his nightshirt. She had no other shirt for him to change into. Gently she pulled up the bedclothes, and under their light movement he shifted and sighed. 'It's all right,' she whispered to him. It was her answer to everything. 'It's all right.'

Millie came knocking at the door a while later. She had come straight from the doctor's house. He was out on a visit to a patient when she had called, she said, but she had left a message with his wife, asking that he come as soon as possible.

'Did his wife say when he would be back?' Lily asked.

'No, she didn't. She said he had several calls to make, and it might be some time.'

When Millie had gone again, Lily went back upstairs. The boy was awake again now, his eyes half open as he looked off into the shadowed corners of the room. The fire was burning low in the grate, and Lily decided to take him down into the kitchen. She could keep him warmer there, she thought, and it would be easier to keep an eye on him.

'Come, Joshie, I'm taking you downstairs,' she said. 'You'll be just as comfortable there, and I can look after you better.' Pulling back the bedclothes she lifted him up in her arms, where he sagged heavily against her. With his head on her shoulder she carried him from the room and down the stairs. In the warm kitchen she laid him on the sofa, and he settled back with a pillow under his head and the blankets over him. Bunny lay at his side. After making sure that enough water had been brought in from the well, and that there was enough fuel for the stove, Lily pulled the old grandfather chair nearer to the kitchen table and, in the light of the oil lamp and a candle, settled down to wait for the doctor.

Her watch, which she had placed on the table, ticked away the minutes, and eventually the hours. And still the doctor did not come.

Every so often she got up from her seat and moved to the sofa where the boy lay. He was asleep again now, but his mouth hung open as he breathed harshly into the quiet. In the soft light she could see how the perspiration flattened his curls to his head, and she watched him screw up his eyelids, and twitch agitatedly as if he was disturbed in his sleep. On the fabric of the blanket his little fingers drummed, and he clutched at the rough material as if in fear.

When the watch showed eleven o'clock she knew that the doctor would not come that night. From the bedroom she brought down another blanket, then she banked up the fire. The boy had not wakened and, although he should have taken his medicine, she would not disturb him. She lit a nightlight which she placed in a saucer, and it cast a pale light in the room. She drew her chair closer to the sofa, and leant back in it, and closed her eyes.

She got little sleep, and when it came it was in brief periods. For most of the time she lay awake, watching and listening. The child, lying so close on the sofa, was restless all night long, frequently waking, murmuring unintelligible words in his fitful sleep, or crying out as he awoke, calling for his mother. Through the long hours Lily did what she could do soothe him, to comfort him. He vomited again in the early hours, and she wiped off the vomit from his nightshirt and held him in her arms. Later she bathed his hot, damp brow with a flannel wrung out in cold water, and gave him sips

568

of water and valerian for the aches in his head and back. Nothing seemed to help him, though.

The cold daylight of Sunday morning lit up the comfortless surroundings and found her sitting in the chair weary and red-eyed through lack of sleep. On the sofa the boy lay on his back, breathing through his mouth, the perspiration drenching his brow and matting his hair. His eyes were closed, but she doubted that he was asleep. The doctor must come soon, she said to herself.

Doctor Trinshaw arrived just after eleven, his sharp rap with the iron knocker heavy on the thin door, and ringing through the narrow hall. Lily, who had been waiting for that very sound, rose from her seat and hurried along the passage. As she opened the door to him he stepped through without hesitation, one hand taking off his hat. He was sorry he had not been able to come the night before, he said, but he had been so busy with his other patients.

She closed the front door behind him and followed him into the kitchen.

'So, how is he?' he said as he put his bag and hat down on the table and took off his coat. 'The girl you sent left the message that he was not improving.'

No, he was not, Lily said, and told how the child had vomited more than once, and that he was perspiring constantly and complaining of aches in his head and his back. He had a fever, and at times he was shivering. 'I thought it was his chill come back,' she said, 'but then I thought it might be the flu.'

The doctor hitched up his trousers at the knees and lowered himself onto the rug before the sofa. He smiled at the boy and spoke softly to him. 'How are you, my little fellow? Not so well today, I understand. Oh, dear, that's not good to hear, is it? We shall have to do something about that, shan't we?'

He took his watch from his waistcoat pocket, opened it

and placed it on the sofa seat. Then he held the child's wrist in his practised fingers and took his pulse. He nodded slightly as he made his count, and then patted the boy's hand and laid it back on his small form. Opening his bag, the doctor took out the case holding his thermometer, shook the instrument vigorously then said, 'Open your mouth, my little man, will you? This won't hurt.' And the boy opened his mouth and the thermometer was slipped under his tongue. When the doctor removed it shortly afterwards he looked at it and gave a grave nod. 'It's a hundred and three degrees,' he said, 'and his pulse is very rapid.' He turned and smiled at the boy, and pulled the blanket up around his shoulders. 'Good boy,' he said. 'That's a very good boy.'

He gently patted Joshua on the head and rose a little stiffly to his feet again. He stood looking down at the child, then moved to the table, pulled out one of the hard-back chairs and sat down. He gestured to another chair at the table and said to Lily, 'Sit down. Sit down a moment.'

She did so, clasping her hands before her.

'You're the boy's nurse, you say. Isn't that what you told me?'

'Yes. Well – yes. In a manner of speaking.'

He was frowning. 'Where are his parents now?'

'In Scotland. Edinburgh.'

'Yes, so you said. Do they know their son is ill?'

She felt her heart give a little lurch at his words. 'No, sir, they don't, but I was hoping to take him back to his home tomorrow – in Happerfell.'

He put an elbow on the table and put his fingers to his chin, his eyes downcast. His brow was deeply furrowed. 'You were right to call me out again,' he said. 'I'm not easy about this. I'm not easy about this at all. You say he's been shivering, and has had a fever, and is perspiring.'

'Yes.'

'With bad headaches and aches in his back?'

'Yes.'

'The small of his back?'

'Yes. I gave him a little valerian.'

'What about a thirst? Does he have a thirst?'

'Oh, yes, indeed.'

'Constipation. Is he constipated?'

'Yes, he seems to be.'

The doctor nodded, his frown constant, his mouth a grim line.

She felt that the answers she had given to his questions were making up for him a picture, one that he recognised only too well. 'Is it not his chill that has just got worse?' she said. 'Or perhaps – the flu?'

'No, it's not the flu. It's not the chill either – though it *was* a chill that he had. I've no doubt about that.' He turned and looked over at the child where he lay under the blankets. 'It's not a chill now, I'm afraid.' He looked back at Lily, his gaze fixed upon her. Then he said, 'Say – going back ten days or a fortnight ago – was the child taken anywhere where he might have been – exposed to anything?'

'He hasn't been anywhere,' Lily said. 'Up until a week ago he was still at his home, in Happerfell. Till last Sunday. We came here then on that day. We came straight here.'

'Only a week ago?'

'Yes. Before that he hardly ever set foot outside his home.'

'And no one else at his home is ill?'

'No. No one at the house. I've been told that his sister has the scarlet fever – but she's in Scotland.'

The doctor shook his head, a gesture almost of impatience. 'This is not scarlet fever,' he said brusquely, and then added with a sigh, 'Would that it were.'

'Doctor,' Lily said, 'what is it? What do you think it is? If it's not his chill, or the flu, then what is it?'

'Only a week ago he was at his home, you say.'

'Yes. I was with him.'

He shook his head and sighed again. 'I'm perplexed here,' he said.

Her puzzlement grew, and her fear grew with her puzzlement. 'Doctor – what is it you're thinking?'

He glanced over at the child once more. Joshua lay oblivious to what was going on in the room. Keeping his eyes on him, the doctor said, 'These symptoms the boy has – they're symptoms I dread to see.' He turned back to Lily. 'And I'm afraid I've seen them a number of times over the past months.'

Lily felt herself go cold. She had feared it, but had not been able to countenance the possibility. 'Do you mean the – the smallpox, sir?' she said.

'It's everywhere,' he said wearily. 'It's the worst outbreak we've ever had in this country.' He looked over again at the child. 'The strange thing is, his symptoms are showing up so quickly. The incubation period of the common smallpox is usually from about ten days to a fortnight – but you tell me that only a week ago he was at his home, well out of harm's way.'

'Yes, he was.'

He lowered his head. 'This is more worrying.'

She frowned. 'Sir . . .?'

He looked up at her. 'There's more than one strain of the disease,' he said. 'One of them is the *malignant* smallpox – or the flat black pox as it's sometimes known. It strikes within days, and very severely. Where have you taken the boy?'

'I beg your pardon?'

'Where has he been – out in public, where he could have picked up the infection?'

'We only went to the aquarium. That was on Thursday.'

'That's only three days ago. No, that couldn't be it. That's too recent. You say you travelled here from Happerfell last Sunday?'

'Yes.'

He nodded. 'Well, that could be it. Perhaps at some point in your journey he came in contact with the disease. That would work out with the incubation period.'

'Oh, I don't think so, sir. He – he didn't touch anyone. I know that. I was with him all the time.'

'You don't need to touch anyone to contract this disease. It's the most contagious we know of. Physical contact can certainly be a factor, but the disease can just as well be carried on the air, or on a person's clothes. It always finds a way, believe me.'

A memory returned to her and she thought of the carriage that Joshua had lain in, and the fly-driver with the disinfectant. But before she could say anything, the doctor said, shaking his head and spreading his hands:

'Well, however the boy might have caught it, it's academic now.'

'But – but he can't have the smallpox,' she said. There was a note of desperation in her voice. 'He's been vaccinated. You saw his scar yourself.'

'Yes, I know that, but it seems that vaccination is not always the answer. You know yourself that it was made mandatory by the government in the fifties, for everyone over the age of two. My God, ninety-eight per cent of the population has been vaccinated, but it hasn't prevented this epidemic one iota. You read the papers, you can see that for yourself. The disease has just rampaged through the country. It's the worst epidemic we've ever had. Look at Leicester. Did you read about that? There've been those protests in the town – protests *against* the enforced vaccination. They're claiming it's only made things worse.' He shook his head and sighed. 'What is one to think? I don't know. I don't know *what* to think. You've been vaccinated, have you? You must have been.'

'No, I haven't, sir. I – I missed it.'

'You missed it?'

'Yes – my father didn't want us to have it done. Me or my brother.'

'And he got away with it, did he? Hmm. Well – personally speaking, I would advise you to have it. And you shouldn't delay. I can send off for the vaccine for you first thing tomorrow.' He paused. 'Would you like me to do that?'

She did not answer. Her mind was spinning. She could think only of the child. 'So you – you think he – he has the disease, sir?' she said. She could scarcely get the words out.

'Yes, I have to think so,' he said. 'And if it *is* the malignant smallpox then the situation is very grave. For one thing he'll have been so weakened by his having taken the chill.'

Tears welled in Lily's eyes like a meadow spring, and spilt over and ran down her cheeks. She gasped, sucking in her breath. Through a throbbing in her ears she heard the doctor as he went on:

'You can't take him home, of course. To Happerfell, did you say? Oh, no, he can't travel. He's not well enough. Besides which – if he *is* infected, then he's extremely contagious. A great danger to others.' He got to his feet, reached out and drew his bag towards him. 'I think,' he said, 'you should wire his parents to come as soon as they can. They have to be informed.'

Lily rose too, and stood there with the tears streaming down her face. After a moment, forcing from somewhere a degree of control, she said, 'But he – surely he – surely he must go into hospital.'

'Oh, miss, I'm afraid that's just not possible,' the doctor said with a shake of his head. 'The isolation hospital was filled weeks ago. It holds so few beds. It was never intended

574

for an epidemic of these proportions. No, the child has to stay here, there's no alternative.' He opened his bag, looked into it as if checking that everything was present, then closed it again. He picked up his hat. Lily, taking a step towards him, said in a little cry of desperation:

'Oh, but, doctor – perhaps – perhaps it is just – just the flu.'

He looked at her sadly for a moment, then said, 'I only wish I could think so.'

'But – but what can be done? There must be something you can do.'

He gave a slow shake of his head. 'There is no cure,' he said simply. 'No cure at all. The disease has to take its course. The common form of it isn't always fatal, not by any means, but the malignant form . . .' he glanced over at the child, 'that's another matter. I've only ever come across it twice. It's quite rare – thank God – and it's *very* different. It strikes quickly and much more severely. And as with the common strain, the old and the young are the most vulnerable, plus of course anyone already with any kind of weakening sickness.' He sighed. 'I'll come back later today, and I'll bring something to ease his pain. In the meantime, keep the room ventilated, and make sure he's warm and comfortable. Though you're doing that anyway, I've no doubt. You could maybe sponge his skin down with a little tepid water, and try to get him to take some nourishment. He's got to eat. A little soup or milk.' He paused, squinting at her. 'How are *you* feeling? Do you feel all right?'

'Yes. Yes, I'm fine.'

'You look tired.'

'Well – a little perhaps.'

'You've got to keep your strength up, you know. We can't have *you* being sick as well – and you're in a very vulnerable situation. You can't be too careful. You look to be a strong and fit young woman, but this disease is no respecter of good living. You must take precautions, you know.'

'Precautions?' She was hardly taking in his words.

'Precautions, yes. You must. I know it's difficult, but for a start you must try not to get too close to the boy.'

'But – but I've been sleeping in the same bed . . . and I must look after him.'

'Yes, of course you must, but you can still take care of yourself. You *have* to. For a start – try not to breathe in his breath. Try to keep your face averted when you're close to him, and have as little skin-to-skin contact as possible. I know that sounds next to impossible, but you have to think of yourself as well.'

She nodded.

'Are you listening to me?' he said, eyeing her sternly.

'Yes, sir.'

'Good. Good. I don't want a second patient on my hands. Anyway, I shall bring the vaccine for you tomorrow.' He turned and looked over at the boy on the sofa. 'Everything depends now on how things go over the next forty-eight hours. We shall know for certain one way or the other before too long.'

Chapter Thirty-eight

Over the following hours Lily rarely strayed from the boy's side, only leaving to fetch water from the well, to make up the fire or do odd jobs around the kitchen. She heated up some soup that Mrs Tanner had sent round with Millie, and tried to get the boy to take a little. He swallowed two or three spoonfuls but would take no more. His mouth looked dry, his lips chapped, and from time to time she gave him little sips of water to quench his seemingly never-ending thirst. Also she bathed his brow and chest with a moist flannel. For most of the time he lay with his eyes closed, seemingly unaware of her presence. All through that night he tossed restlessly in his fitful sleep, murmuring and stuttering words and phrases that Lily, sleeping at his side, could not comprehend.

Millie called later the next morning, and went at once towards the boy. As she did so, Lily said urgently, 'You mustn't get too close, Millie. He's very sick.'

Millie came to a halt and stood looking down at the child, then turned back to Lily. 'What did the doctor say, miss? Did he say what's the matter?'

'He thinks . . .' Lily could scarcely get the words out, 'it's – it's the smallpox.'

'Oh, miss.' Millie put a hand to her mouth. 'Oh, miss, that's terrible. Poor little chap.'

'Yes.' Lily's voice was choked. 'I think you'd best not come round any more, Millie. In case what the doctor says is true. It would be terrible if you caught it too.'

577

'Oh, I won't do that, miss,' the girl said at once. 'I been vaccinated. Apart from that I caught the cowpox when I was back milkin' at the dairy. I'm safe from it, miss. Don't you worry.'

She asked then whether Lily wanted anything done about the house, and offered to go to the shops for whatever was needed. Grateful for her kindness, Lily said there were a few things she would like, and also asked if she would mind going into Corster centre, to one of the drapers there, and buy for Joshua a new nightshirt. Millie agreed at once, and Lily gave her some money, a list of the items she needed, and the girl went off.

The milk wagon came by, and Lily bought a quart of milk, some butter and a piece of cheese. She made tea and, sitting at the table, drank a cup and ate a slice of bread with some of the butter and cheese. She had no appetite and merely ate because she knew she must if she was to keep up her strength, and this she must do in order to care for the child. As for the food she ate, it might as well have been chalk in her mouth, for she scarcely tasted a bite.

Millie returned from the shops with the items she had bought, and then went away, saying she would be back later. Left alone with the child, Lily removed his stained nightshirt, sponged his skin, and then dressed him in the new nightshirt. As she worked he remained passive and uncomplaining. Afterwards, she stayed by the sofa, watching over him and doing whatever she could to ease his discomfort. She was still there when the doctor arrived just after six o'clock.

He saw at once – as was only too obvious to Lily – that the child was much worse. He looked down at the boy with a grave expression on his face, and gave a slow nod. 'It's as I feared.' He bent over the sofa and pulled back the blankets. Lifting the boy's nightshirt, he examined his chest and then lowered the shirt back in place. 'It's not going to be long before the rash appears,' he said.

As the man straightened, the boy opened his eyes wide and gave a little moan, a grunt, and his head jolted back on his neck. In the same moment his body arched and his legs kicked out. They jerked spasmodically for a couple of seconds and then the movement subsided. Lily watched in horror. 'What's happening?' she cried.

'It's a convulsion,' the doctor said. 'It's one of the symptoms. There's nothing to be done for it. It will pass quickly.'

It did pass very soon, and afterwards the child lay back exhausted and gasping for breath. The doctor adjusted the blanket where the boy had disturbed it, then moved to his bag and took from it a small bottle. 'This is opium,' he said. 'If he suffers too badly with his headache and backache, give him one or two drops in a little water. It will help him rest.' He set the bottle on the table, closed his bag and reached for his hat. 'Did you send for the boy's parents?' he asked.

She shook her head. 'No – not yet.'

He sighed. 'Listen – I know how difficult it is sometimes, to face the truth, but it has to be done.' He paused. 'You must send word to them, miss. And a letter is no good. There's no time to lose. You'd best telegraph.'

She nodded. 'Yes, I will.' She knew he was right. There was no escaping the fact. 'It'll go off straightaway in the morning,' she said.

'Fine.' He turned towards the door. 'I'll come back tomorrow. And I'll bring the vaccine for you. I should have it by then.'

That night, as before, Lily pulled the grandfather chair up beside the sofa, and dragged a blanket over her. It was a cold night and a strong wind had sprung up, rattling the window in its frame and slicing in through the little gap under the door. She had fed the fire in the range, though, and it gave out a steady heat, and there was a good supply of coal in the scuttle in the hearth. On the sofa the child lay under his blankets. Earlier he had vomited again, and then had moaned with the pain in his head and back. She had given him a little of the opium. Now, at least for a while, thank God, he was sleeping.

As she sat there she kept thinking of what the doctor had said – that she must inform the boy's parents of his condition. She had put it off, but she knew that it must be done, and at the earliest opportunity. Now that she had made the decision, she could not leave it, and she laid the blanket aside and got up. Sitting at the table, she lit another candle and drew towards her the writing paper and pen and ink. Mr and Mrs Soameson would only just have received her letter, she thought. Nevertheless, she had no choice. She had never had occasion to send a telegraph ever before. On a sheet of paper she drafted several messages, trying to find the right words. Eventually she wrote, carefully, in uppercase:

REGRET TO TELL YOU JOSHUA VERY SICK.
COME AT ONCE TO TWO MERRIDEW VILLAS,
BROOKHAM WAY, CORSTER. LILY CLAIR.

She put down the pen and folded the paper. First thing in the morning, she would ask Millie to take it round to the post office.

Her sleep came in the briefest spells that night. Not only could she find no comfort in the hard, ungiving armchair, but every thought in her head and every emotion in her heart was bound up with the child. If her eyes were open they were fixed upon him in the pale glow from the nightlight, just as her ears were attuned to every sound he made. When dawn came, the first cold light found her sitting stiff and aching, her eyes scratchy and sore from lack of sleep and her head pounding.

He too was awake. He lay there, looking up at her through half-closed eyes, his dry lips apart, his breaths short and shallow, and in the growing light she could see the rash that was sprouting on his neck, creeping up to his jaw. When he moved to push back the blanket from his chin, she saw it too on his arms.

Millie came to the door just after nine, bringing a basin of potato soup. Standing beside the sofa she gazed in horror at the sight of the rash on the child's flesh. Lily, who had watched it constantly, had seen it spread and become darker with the passing hours. Not only that, but the lesions were growing larger.

When Millie asked if there was anything she could do, Lily took up the message that she had written the night before, and a second sheet on which she had written the Soamesons' Edinburgh address. She gave the papers to the girl with a sum of money. 'It must go off as a telegraph,' she said. 'Please, take it to the post office, and see that it goes off at once.'

Millie was back in less than an hour to give Lily her change and say that the telegraph had gone.

Left alone again with the boy, Lily watched, and waited. When he cried out with pain she gave him a little of the opium, after which he lapsed once more into his quiet, stuporous state. From time to time he whispered for his mama, and muttered other words that Lily could not understand. The rash was growing. Now it had spread up from his neck onto his jaw and lower cheek, while on his arms it was creeping lower onto his wrists and hands. At the same time his flesh had begun to take on a reddish hue, and whereas before it had had the texture of the finest silk, now it had begun to take on the appearance of a strange kind of crêpe-rubber.

Doctor Trinshaw came to the house just after three. He came striding through the hall into the kitchen. 'How is he?' he asked. 'Is he any better? D'you see any change?'

In reply, Lily said haltingly that he seemed to be worse, much worse, and that a rash had appeared, and was spreading. Acknowledgement of the boy's deteriorating state was something she had avoided, but now she had to do it, though her words almost froze in her throat.

The doctor nodded. 'It's as I expected.'

Lily stood by in silence then as he pulled back the blankets and lifted the boy's shirt. Not only was the rash still spreading, but the lesions were growing larger yet. After a moment he pulled down the boy's shirt and drew the blankets up over him again. Throughout it all the child had remained with his eyes closed, breathing harshly through his mouth.

'Yes,' the doctor said, 'it's the malignant type, as I thought. The lesions are not producing pus – not as in the common strain – and as you can see, they're under the skin, and quite flat-looking.' He looked back down at the boy. 'Are you managing to keep him comfortable?'

'I've tried to, sir.' She could barely get the words out. 'He hasn't spoken for a good while now. He was crying out in pain with his back, and I – I gave him a little more of the opium. It – it seemed to soothe him.' Her eyes were stinging from her unshed tears. 'I didn't know what else to do.'

The doctor nodded. 'Unfortunately there's nothing you *can* do.' His tone was both sympathetic and practical. 'The lesions will start to join up soon.' He paused. 'I'm afraid then – the end will be near. Did you send for his parents?'

'Yes,' she heard herself say. 'I sent off the telegraph – this morning.' She was trying to take in the implication of the man's words. *The end will be near.* It could not be possible. Everything had been leading up to this, but it could not be. There must be something to be done.

She stood there, hands clasped before her. The doctor was watching her intently. 'You must have realised by now,' he said.

'Realised,' she said dully.

He shook his head. 'I wish I could give you hope,' he said sadly, 'but I cannot. It won't be long now. You have to accept that.'

She nodded, trying to take in his words.

'We've got to think about *you* now,' he said.

She frowned. '*Me*?'

'Yes, you. You've got your life in front of you, and we've got to look after you. As he spoke he stepped to his bag and undid the clasp. 'I've got your vaccine here. I'd hoped to have it earlier, but there's such a demand for it – as you can imagine. Anyway, we've got it now.' He pulled wider the jaws of his bag and then turned to look at her again. 'You must try not to take this too much to heart,' he said. 'D'you understand what I'm saying?'

'Sir?' She was in a daze.

'Listen,' he said, 'I know how it is. Nursemaids – they get fond of their charges, their little boys and girls. They get so close to them. They're bound to. And you're no different. I can understand how hard this is for you. Have you got family of your own?'

'What?' She frowned. 'Family? No. No family.'

'Ah, well . . .' He did not wish to dwell on the subject. 'Anyway, we've got to make sure you're all right.'

From his bag he had brought out a little linen packet, which he now opened up and from it extracted a slim glass phial. He held it up to the light. 'This is the vaccine,' he said. 'Though I have to tell you that we're late already. By rights, this should be administered within four days of exposure to the disease – and it's obviously been much longer where you're concerned. But better late than never, yes? We must do everything we can.' He gave her the trace of an encouraging smile. 'As I said, you're a strong, healthy-looking young woman, so you should have a good chance of fighting this off – and it's not as if you're related to the boy, so his weaknesses won't necessarily be yours.' Carefully he laid on the table the small linen bag, and set the phial on it. 'All I need to do is give a tiny scratch in your upper arm.' From his bag he now brought out a small hard-leather case, opened it up and drew out a fine metal scalpel. 'I do it with this,' he said. 'It won't hurt, I promise you. No more than a scratch anyway.' He set the scalpel down and looked over towards the sink. 'While you roll up your sleeve, I'll wash my hands. Are you right-handed?'

'Sir?' she said dully. Her mind was spinning.

'Are you right-handed or left-handed? This will have quite a nasty effect. You'll be a bit incapacitated for a week or two, so you'd best not have it on the arm that you use.'

'Oh. Oh, yes. Right-handed. I'm right-handed.'

'Fine. You pull up your left sleeve, then, or pull it down from your shoulder.'

He moved away to the sink, took up the large jug from the draining board and poured a little into the bowl. Carefully, thoroughly, he washed his hands and then dried them on a towel that hung on a rail nearby. 'There, now . . .'

As he replaced the towel a little gasp from Lily drew his head round, and he turned towards her. 'What is it? What's the matter?' He took a step forward, coming to a halt with a groan. 'Oh, no! How did that happen?'

Lily was standing with her hands spread on her breast,

looking down at the broken vaccine phial on the floor at her feet.

'What happened?' the doctor said.

'I – I'm sorry,' she said, her head lowered. 'I – I picked it up. I shouldn't have done, I know. I'm sorry. I dropped it.'

The phial was shattered into several pieces, its contents making a tiny wet stain on the floor. The doctor frowned, shaking his head. 'Well, there's no saving it now,' he said. There was an unmistakable note of anger in his voice at her clumsiness. 'It's done for, and I shan't be able to get any more until tomorrow at the very earliest.'

'I'm sorry,' Lily said. 'I'm sorry.'

'Yes, well – it's done now. We'd better get something to clear it up.'

She got a piece of newspaper and an old cloth. Carefully she picked up the fragments of glass, put them in the newspaper and then wiped up the residue of the mess. The doctor watched her for a moment and then put his things back in his bag.

'I'll try to get some more vaccine and bring it tomorrow,' he said. He shook his head. 'It's a great shame that that's happened. Every hour is important in a situation like this.' He turned from her and looked back at the boy. 'I'll call to see him again this evening.'

Millie came round later on, asking if there were any errands to be run, and also bringing good wishes from her grandmother. The old lady would come round in person, she said, but she was afraid to. Millie had no such fears.

Later, when the girl had gone, Lily sat alone watching over the boy. Pulling his nightshirt up around his upper chest she sponged his small form with a soft flannel wrung out in tepid water. He watched her through half-closed eyes, suffering her ministrations without a word. His limbs as she lifted them were like those of a rag doll, without life.

In the late afternoon light she knelt on the mat before the sofa looking down at his exposed little body. The rash now was everywhere. With tender fingers she touched some of the lesions on his thigh. They felt soft and velvety, and they were growing larger all the time. On the inside of his nightshirt, beneath his buttocks, she saw a stain, and realised that it was blood. He had bled from the rectum. Her eyes started from their sockets as she gasped out in horror, the tears springing up and coursing down her cheeks. *What have I done? What have I done?* She lowered his shirt to cover up the dreadful sight, then pulled the blanket back over him. Softly, lightly, she touched at his cheek where the dark lesions were creeping up inexorably from his jaw. The little crescent moon by his ear had been swallowed up, but they had not yet reached his eyes, those blue eyes, now dull, that seemed to watch her every movement through their dark and heavy lids. She leant down and kissed his cheek, kissed the lesions there, feeling their softness beneath her mouth. *You must try to avoid direct contact with him*, the doctor had said. *Try to avoid breathing in his breath.* She could hear the man's words like some distant echo as she kissed the boy again, her parted lips lingering on the lesions, the monstrous disfigurements of his perfection. Her slightly open mouth moved onto his own lips, and she kissed them too and drew in his warm, foul breath.

He became delirious within the hour, thrashing his arms and legs, and groaning and gasping and crying out, his eyes wide and full of fear. Lily, her well of tears having run dry, tried to comfort him and bring him ease. She got him to take a little more of the opium in water, and it calmed him after a while and he fell again into a stupor. The lesions on his throat and face had continued to grow, and, like those on his torso and legs, had now joined together, making one blackened mass beneath the skin.

Late into the evening, in the light of a single candle, she knelt on the hard floor beside the sofa, watching every twitch, every tremor of his face and body, listening to every nuance of every harsh breath.

He died just before seven o'clock.

Chapter Thirty-nine

Lily sat in the old grandfather chair. She had not moved in a long time. Her head was aching, her tear-swollen eyes were sore, and tiredness drenched her body. She had poured water into a glass, and she sipped at it, trying to quench her thirst. Looking at her watch, she saw that it was close on four o'clock. Just before noon two men had come, driving a mortuary wagon, to take Joshua's body away. It would not go to the old town mortuary, they had told her, but to the special, temporary one that had been opened in the district of Hillcot on the outskirts of the city. Everything had been arranged by Dr Trinshaw, who had arrived at the house less than an hour after the child's death.

He had not been surprised, of course, to find that the child's life had ended. He had been expecting it, the inevitable. After making a cursory examination of the body, he had covered the boy's face. Then, sitting down at the table, he had said to Lily, 'The child's parents will want to see me when they come, I have no doubt. Give them my card, will you?'

'Yes, sir – of course.'

After placing his calling card on the table he had glanced back at the covered body and said, 'Those blankets will have to be burnt, of course, and anything else he used. Toys, everything.' He had closed his bag then and got up from the table. 'I'll be back later on with your vaccine, if I can get it.' Frowning a little, he studied her. 'Have you eaten today?'

'Yes,' she had said, the lie coming easily.

'Good.' Then, having taken in her dull, red-rimmed eyes: 'How are you feeling?'

'All right, sir. Thank you, yes. I'm fine.'

'No headache, no ache in your back? No nausea?'

'No, really, I'm fine, thank you.'

'Good. You've got to look after yourself.'

Millie had come in soon after his departure, and hearing of Joshua's death had wept. She had stood before the sofa looking down at the little shape covered by the blankets, the tears running down her face. She had not lingered long.

When the men came to take the child, Lily had turned her head away, not wanting to see them touch him. But even that had not been enough, and she had gone out into the yard. Without a coat in the cold, bitter wind she had stood hunched up in the lee of the old garden shed. Her head was pounding now, her brain seeming to throb against the inside of her skull. Eventually she had taken her courage and gone back indoors. The men's errand had taken little time, and they had long since left. The little blanket-covered form was gone from the sofa. The blankets themselves had gone, too, and so had Bunny and Mr Charlie Dobbin.

Now, still sitting in the chair, she became vaguely aware of the coldness of the room. It did not matter.

When the knock came she started slightly, then rose and went to answer it. Opening the front door she found Mr and Mrs Soameson standing on the threshold, their faces looking grave and gaunt, their mouths pinched with desperation. The cab that had brought them was still in the street, the driver standing beside the horse. She had known that they would come, must come, but the sight of them brought her heart pounding.

'Oh – sir – ma'am . . .' She stepped back a pace.

'We came at once,' Mr Soameson said, taking off his hat. 'As soon as we got your telegraph. We travelled all night.'

589

'How is he?' Mrs Soameson said breathlessly. 'How is my boy?'

Lily did not answer. She could not, but stood dumbly, one hand up to her throat.

Followed by her husband, Mrs Soameson came into the narrow, dimly-lit passage. Her eyes were fixed on Lily's face, searching, reading there what she could. Mr Soameson did the same, and they saw in an instant that all reason for hope had gone.

Mrs Soameson gave a moaning little cry and sagged, leaning against the wall. 'We're too late,' she cried out. Then to Lily: 'Don't tell me – oh, don't tell me we're too late.'

Lily, searching for words, said nothing, and her silence only confirmed their dread.

While the carriage waited in the street, the three sat in the cold kitchen, neither of the two visitors having taken off their coats. After telling them that the boy's body had been taken to the temporary mortuary at Hillcot, Lily told of how he had fallen ill, and of the rapid onset of his sickness. She spoke of Dr Trinshaw's visits and of how he had ministered to the child, but had been able to do nothing to save him. Of the child's suffering at the end she said nothing, choosing to let them believe that he had slipped quietly and painlessly away. Mrs Soameson wept throughout, leaning forward, twisting her wet handkerchief in her fingers, while Mr Soameson sat with a grim expression, his mouth set in a tight line, his eyes glistening with unshed tears. At one point Mrs Soameson straightened a little and protested pathetically, her voice breaking, 'But he was vaccinated! Everyone was vaccinated. We had to be.'

Lily said, avoiding their eyes, 'It was my fault. I brought him away. I should not have done.'

Mrs Soameson responded quickly, her words bursting

out on a little sob, 'No! No, you should not have!' and then leant forward again, her hands to her face.

Frowning, her husband touched her on the shoulder, and said softly, a little hoarsely, clearly struggling for control, 'Oh, Edith . . . Edith, dear . . .' Then to Lily he said, 'No, Miss Clair, you should not have done. But – but you were not to know. And I do believe that what you did was with the best intentions – trying to give him a little pleasure.'

At his words, Lily wanted to say, *But I did it for me. I wanted him with me.* But she kept silent.

Moments passed with only the sound of Mrs Soameson's quiet weeping, and then Mr Soameson opened his coat and took out his watch. After consulting it, he slipped it back into his waistcoat pocket, turned to his wife and said gently, 'My dear, we must go to Hillcot. We can see him there. If we go now we'll get there before dark.' He rose from his seat and put on his hat. 'We must see the doctor as well.'

'He's expecting to hear from you, sir,' Lily said.

She passed him the doctor's card, and he glanced at it and put it in his pocket. 'He'll need to be paid,' he said. 'Has he been paid any of his fee?'

'Very little of it, sir.'

'I'll settle with him.' He turned back to his wife. 'Come, Edith.'

Mrs Soameson rose from the hard wooden chair, her eyes red and swollen, her mouth contorted with grief. Her shoulders hunched, she followed her husband into the passage. When they reached the front door, she spoke no word to Lily but went straight out to the carriage. Mr Soameson, standing on the threshold, turned to Lily and said:

'Well, Miss Clair – I doubt that we shall meet again.' His face was grim, his mouth a thin, tight line.

She did not speak.

He shook his head, then suddenly the remnants of his

fragile composure failed and his chin quivered and tears welled in his eyes. Stifling a sob, he lowered his head, eyes on the ground between them. He remained like this for several seconds, then, raising his head again, some of his control regained, he said, 'You'll be leaving here now, will you? Going back to Sherrell, I daresay.'

'I expect I shall, sir.' She had given the matter no thought.

He nodded. 'Just in case I need to get in touch – about things.'

'Yes, sir.'

He nodded again. 'And how are you feeling? Do you feel all right?'

'Yes, sir – thank you.'

'Good.' He touched at his hat and without another word turned and made his way out into the street. There he climbed into the cab beside his wife. Lily, standing at the open door, watched as the vehicle rattled away.

Dr Trinshaw came back to the house just before six.

'It's mighty cold in here,' he said as he preceded Lily into the kitchen, its sparse interior illuminated now by an oil lamp and a single candle. 'You haven't got any heating,' he added. 'Have you no coal?'

'Yes,' she said. 'I just forgot to light the stove. I'll do it in a minute.'

'I hope you're looking after yourself,' he said. 'I told you, you can't afford to take chances. You're in a vulnerable state. You don't look that bright to me.'

'I'm fine, really.'

He turned and took in the bare sofa. 'When did they come,' he asked, 'the men from the mortuary?'

'Just before twelve.' Her voice was dull, flat.

'Have you heard anything from the child's parents?'

'They came here – just after four o'clock. They went off to the mortuary.'

592

He gave a sorrowful sigh, and set down his bag and hat on the table. 'I've got your vaccine,' he said, 'and perhaps this time it won't get wasted. Better let me have your arm . . .'

While he washed his hands, Lily opened her dress and dragged it down off her left shoulder. The doctor dried his hands then took from his bag a slim glass phial and the container holding the scalpel. As he did his work she stood waiting by the chair. The ache in her head had become all-enveloping, and she was also aware now of a dull ache that had taken hold in the small of her back.

'Sit down,' the doctor said, stepping to her side. She perched on one of the hard chairs, and he bent to her. 'This'll be just a little scratch.' He stretched the soft skin of her upper arm between his finger and thumb and scratched into the flesh with the point of the blade. A little blood appeared and he wiped it away with a bit of cotton wool. 'Now . . .' He took up the glass phial and shook it, and Lily felt the cool touch of the glass against her skin. Glancing down she saw the pus-like liquid come out of the phial's opening. Firmly, the doctor rubbed the vaccine into the wound. 'There you are – all done. Though it should have been done days ago.' He produced a bandage then, and wrapped it around to cover the little wound. 'You might want to wear an armband for a while,' he said, 'till the scab heals and the painful swelling goes down. A lot of people do, for if somebody knocks into you, you'll know it.' He patted her shoulder. 'You can cover up now.'

While the doctor put his things away, Lily pulled her dress back in place and began to secure the buttons of her bodice. As she finished, he put his hand on her brow. 'My dear young woman,' he said, frowning, 'you're on fire.'

Even as she asserted that she was feeling well, he was reaching for his thermometer. Moments later it was in her mouth. Then his watch was out of his waistcoat pocket and he was feeling for the pulse in her wrist.

As he put the thermometer away he said, 'Your temperature is high and your pulse is rapid. Have you been eating? When did you last eat anything?'

'Not long ago,' she lied, then added, 'I don't get that hungry.'

He gave a little snort. 'All living things need food.' He looked at her for a few moments in silence, then drew up a chair. 'I hope you're not taking this too hard,' he said. 'How long had you been with the boy?'

'I beg your pardon?'

'You're employed by the boy's family, you said. How long had you been with him?'

'Two months.'

'Two months. Well, that's not so very long – though one can get attached to children in a very short time. As I said, they can wind their way into your heart. And a dear little fellow like that . . .' He leant forward and briefly touched the back of her hand. 'This will pass, believe me. You mustn't let it – hold too great a sway.'

She was silent for a moment, then she said, 'I took him to the aquarium.'

He frowned, as if a little puzzled, then gave a nod. 'What are you going to do now?' he asked.

She did not know what to say. It came to her that now that the child's body had been taken away, and Mr and Mrs Soameson had been to the house, there was no longer any reason for her to remain.

'I don't know,' she said.

He picked up his hat. 'Well,' he said, a little gruffly, 'I'll come back tomorrow at some time. I want to see how you're getting on.'

'Oh, sir,' she said quickly, 'it won't be necessary, truly.'

'What d'you mean, it won't be necessary?'

'I – I shall be all right. Really. Besides, I haven't the money to –'

He broke in, cutting off her words: 'I'm not concerned only with money.' His voice was sharp with disapproval. 'I'm not in this to make my fortune.' He put on his hat and reached for his bag. 'As I said, I'll come back tomorrow. And I hope, when I do, that I find this place a bit warmer – and that you've had something to eat.'

After he had let himself out, she continued to sit there.

Millie came in later. It was so cold in the kitchen, she remarked. She looked at the sofa in silence for a moment, but said nothing of it. She had brought some food in a basin. It was still hot. She set it down on the table. 'Look, miss, I brought you a little lamb stew. There's not much meat, but the vegetables are nice, and it'll be good for you. Grandma said I was to see that you ate it. While you do, I'll light a bit of fire. Get the place warmed up a bit.'

She set out a plate and a fork and spoon, and stood for a moment as if waiting for Lily to begin eating. Then she turned away and busied herself at the range, raking out the ashes and setting paper and kindling. She soon had a fire going. When she gave her attention back to Lily a little while later, she saw that the basin of food was still untouched.

Millie left the house not long afterwards, and Lily sat alone. The kitchen was growing warmer now. She looked at the watch. It was after eight. Soon she would go to bed. There was nothing to sit up for. The ache in her head was stronger now, as was the ache in the small of her back, and she felt a fatigue that seemed to drain her body of all vitality. A wind had sprung up again, rattling the window and sighing around the walls. She was lulled by it, and when the knock came at the front door she was startled, and sat up in the chair. It could not be Millie, not at this time, and she could think of no one else who might be likely to call.

The knock came again. She waited a moment longer, and then, taking up the candle, rose from the chair and went into the passage. At the door she stopped, one hand on the doorknob. 'Who is it?' she said, her mouth close to the wood.

'Lily? Lily, is that you?' She could hear the voice clearly. 'It's Joel.'

She stood stock still, her breath held.

His voice came again. 'Lily? Are you there? It's Joel.'

She pulled back the bolt and opened the door onto the night. Joel was standing on the step. Beyond him, in the street, stood a horse and carriage.

'Lily,' Joel said, peering in at her through the gloom. 'Oh, thank God you're here.'

She remained as if frozen, one hand on the door, the other grasping the candlestick. He took a step forward. 'Aren't you going to let me in?'

She moved back, and he came over the threshold. As he did so he gestured back towards the carriage. 'I have to keep the cab waiting there. I've only got a few minutes, then I must get to the station.'

She closed the door and turned and moved along the passage. Joel followed. In the kitchen she set down the candlestick on the dresser and moved to stand at the other end of the table. Her heart was pounding. He took off his hat and set it down, along with his leather case, on the table. He wore no gloves. 'I won't take my coat off,' he said. 'I have to get a train to Bath. I feel as if I've been running for days.' He looked at her in silence, then asked, 'May I sit down?'

She spoke now. 'Yes. Yes, of course.'

He pulled out a chair and sat, and then gave a sigh and briefly closed his eyes in a gesture of relief. 'Oh, Lily, you can't imagine how glad I am to see you. To have found you.'

She could think of no words. Through the lingering shock at his appearance she continued to be aware of the ache in her head. For a little while it had seemed to recede. Now it was back, stronger than ever, and filling her skull with a blunt pain that pushed against her eye sockets and pounded in her ears. Her arm too, where she had been vaccinated, was starting to throb.

'Are you alone here?' he said.

She nodded. 'Yes.'

Briefly he smiled his familiar smile, his teeth bright in the glow of the lamp and the candle. She took in everything about him – the shape of his nose, his jaw, the cut of his hair, the angle of his brow. Of course nothing had changed. Had she expected it to? Every tone and shade of his colouring, every inch of his flesh, every line of his tall, rangy form, was the same, unaltered, inevitable.

'Please,' he said, 'aren't you going to sit down? You look as if you're about to run away.'

Obediently she pulled out a chair and faced him across the table. He peered at her in the soft light for some moments then said, 'Are you all right, Lily? You don't look quite yourself. You look a bit – pale.'

'I'm fine, I'm fine,' she said.

'Good.' He nodded. 'You're shocked to see me, I know. And at this hour. But I had to come. I wish I could have written first, but I didn't have the time. I had to see you.'

'How did you know I was here?' she said.

'Well, I didn't – at first. I came back from France late yesterday, and this morning, as soon as I could, I went to Happerfell, expecting to find you there. When I saw the maid at the house, she said you'd gone up to Scotland to take your employers' little boy to join them there. You'd left over a week ago, she said, and you weren't expected to return to the house afterwards, unless it was to pick up your things. She thought you must have gone straight to

Sherrell.' He nodded. 'So that's where I've been now. I've just come from there. From Rowanleigh. I saw the lady – your friend Miss Balfour. She told me you weren't there, but that she expected you in a few days. She wasn't that friendly with me, I have to say. And she was giving nothing away. She's very protective of you.' He paused. 'But after a while she softened a little, and we talked, and in the end – I told her – about us. It was then she said that, as far as she knew, if you weren't in Happerfell, then you'd be here in Corster, at the Villa.' He gave the ghost of a smile. 'Of course, I came as soon as I could.'

When he had spoken he sat looking at her, studying her face in the pale light. 'Are you sure you're all right, Lily?' he said.

'Yes, really, I'm fine. I'm just – a bit tired.'

He nodded. For a moment the only sound was that of the wind as it keened around the house. Then he said:

'What are you doing here, Lily? Why are you in this place? What made you come back here?'

'My – my employment came to an end,' she said, as if that answered the question.

'And you needed a little change of scene?'

'Well – yes.'

'And you chose to come here?' Clearly, it made little sense to him. 'But you'll be going back to Sherrell soon . . .'

'Yes.'

'And what then?'

'I don't know. There's the possibility of employment in January – but I'm not sure about it yet.'

'Miss Balfour – when we spoke, she told me about your brother. Oh, Lily, I was so terribly sorry to hear about that. The poor young man . . . and how dreadful for you.'

She nodded. She could see Tom lying on the cobbles outside the museum. She must not think about him. Her clenched fingers worked.

'After that, and what I did,' Joel said, 'it's no wonder you wanted to get away, have a little time alone.' He looked around him, taking in the room with its sparse furnishings. 'I remember when I came here with you that time. I'd been waiting for you and the rain came on. I don't like to see you here now. It's a depressing place. How much longer are you going to stay?'

'I – I don't know. Not long.'

'I think the sooner you get away, the better. It can't be doing you any good.'

Into the quiet came the sudden, light scurrying of a mouse running round the skirting board, gone again in seconds.

Joel said, 'I came here to say something – but first – I have to ask you if you still . . .' He came to a stop, then said simply, 'Do you – do you hate me, Lily?'

'Hate you?' She frowned, shaking her head. 'Oh, no. No. Never.'

'I wouldn't blame you. I hurt you. I know that.'

'It's past. It's in the past.'

He took a deep breath, then said, almost rushing the words out: 'I have some things I must say, and I couldn't put them in a letter. I had to come and see you – wherever you were. It wouldn't wait.'

She sat with lips compressed. Her head was throbbing, and her left arm was tender to the touch. The ache in the small of her back was reaching up her spine, and now she felt a touch of nausea threatening its own special agony just below her breastbone.

'Oh, God, this isn't easy,' Joel said with a groan. He gave a hopeless little shake of his head. 'When I think back – on our story, Lily – I wonder how it could have turned out differently. I was so happy with you, having met you that summer, and I was sure I could make everything work out for us. I knew I could. I had such faith – but then, you wrote to me out of the blue, and ended it. Of course, I had no knowledge of the reason for it – that – that ghastly horror you had endured – and the result of it – the fact that you were to have a child. I just thought that you no longer cared for me.'

'No,' she said quickly. 'That wasn't so.'

'Oh, yes, I came to know it later, but not at the time.' He sighed. 'And so, of course, I had to try to build a life without you, and I thought I had done it fairly successfully – until that day we met again.'

'Don't, Joel,' she said. 'There's nothing you need to remind me of. You think I haven't been through it a thousand times?'

'Yes,' he said sadly. 'I too. I don't know how it is – you take a step, and then you take another, and then you find you're on a path, and suddenly there's no way of turning back.' He sat gazing at her, a slight frown on his brow. 'I'm sitting here with you,' he said after a moment, 'and I've no idea what's going through your mind. Have I been an idiot to come here? I've no idea what you think about me. You are so quiet, so – so removed. Perhaps you're wishing I hadn't come.'

She hesitated a moment, then said, '*Why* have you come, Joel?'

Now he smiled, faintly. He leaned forward a little into the table, his mouth working, as if trying to frame the right words. 'I'm free, Lily,' he said.

'Free?'

'My – understanding – my engagement with Miss Roget – it's over.'

In the silence between them she could hear the wind sigh. She could think of no words.

'I hardly dare ask how you feel about it,' he said, 'but I had to come and tell you at once. She – she's released me from – from my promise. I didn't ask her to, but she has. She knows that it was no good our going on as things were. I would never be happy – she came to realise that. And so she never would be either. She came to me, two days ago, and told me of her decision. Of course she's sad about it. I think it – it cost her a lot to say it, to do as she did. It was a great step. But she knows things wouldn't work as they were. Not for us to be truly happy.'

Lily sat with her hands clenched before her on the edge of the table, fingernails digging into the flesh. Joel sat looking at her, waiting. 'Say something, Lily,' he said.

She shook her head. 'I don't know what to say.'

'Oh, Lily . . .' He leant forward again and reached out a hand towards her. When she did not respond he let his hand fall again. 'Lily, don't you see? It means we can be together. For always. For always, Lily. Together.'

'Together.' She barely mouthed the word. The pain in her head now was like a physical attack, beating against the back of her eyes, while the nausea stabbed at her, forcing her to swallow.

'Yes, together,' he said. 'As I said, I'm going to Bath tonight, but I shall be back again in a few days.' He paused. 'May I come and see you then, Lily?'

When she did not answer he frowned. 'Don't say no. Oh, don't let everything be for nothing.' His tone had a note of passion in it. 'We've had so many hits and misses, but now at last everything can go right. I know it can.' He waited for her to speak. 'I'll be back on Monday. Will you still be here?'

Still she said nothing. 'I'll be back on Monday,' he said, 'and I'm going to take you away from this place. I'll take you back to Sherrell, to be with Miss Balfour. There's not going to be any need for you to take another governess post. You can stay there with her until we marry. Which can be as soon as you like. There's nothing to stop us now. Nothing to get in the way.' He gave a slow nod. 'I've learnt some lessons, Lily, I promise you I have, and I'm a better man for it. You'll find that out.' He paused, waiting for her to speak, his expression anxious. 'What are you thinking? *Please* – say something. Are you giving me another chance?'

She could not meet his gaze, but kept her eyes fixed on her fingers. Across the table he consulted his watch, then dropped it back into his pocket. 'I have to go,' he said, 'or I shall miss my train.' He got up from the chair and took a step around the table. 'Tell me before I go. Please. Tell me I haven't come here for nothing.'

Still she did not speak.

'I'll make it up to you, Lily. I promise you I will.'

'I don't know what to say to you, Joel,' she said, still avoiding his gaze.

His expression was pleading. 'Just – just say that I'll be welcome.'

As he finished speaking he stepped closer to her, but she put up a hand, palm out. 'No,' she said. 'No – please.'

He halted, stood looking down at her. 'Don't you love me any more?' he said.

She bent her head, briefly closing her eyes. 'I never stopped.'

'Oh, Lily,' he breathed. And now the faintest smile touched his mouth, his eyes. 'I can live on those words – they'll feed me.'

He bent to her, to take her in his arms, but she leant back, hands lifting as a shield. 'Don't touch me, Joel – please – not now.'

'I'm sorry,' he said, straightening. 'This is all very sudden for you, I know. I couldn't prepare you for it, I'm sorry.' He frowned, peering at her in the soft light. 'You look so pale, Lily. You look – drained.'

'Well, I've got a slight cold.' She forced herself to meet his eyes. 'And as I said, I'm a little tired. Nothing to worry about.'

'Then I shall not.' He stepped back, and picked up his hat and leather case. 'Now I must go – this minute.' As she moved to rise he added, 'No, don't come with me. I'll see myself out.' He paused. 'And I'll be back on Monday.'

She remained sitting there as his footfalls sounded along the passage, as the front door was opened and closed. She could feel the perspiration breaking out on her brow, while the pain in her head throbbed against the bone of her skull. Another wave of nausea struck at her, and she lurched from the chair, stepped quickly across the room and vomited into the sink.

Dr Trinshaw came back the following afternoon. As usual, he came in without ceremony, striding past Lily into the kitchen. Lily followed him and went back to her chair near the range. The room was warm. Millie had been in earlier and lit the fire. Without taking off his overcoat, he opened his bag and took out his thermometer. He asked Lily how she was feeling, and she replied that she had a slight headache. He took her temperature and also her pulse, then looked at the site of the vaccination on her tender, swollen arm. When her arm had been dressed again he sat facing her on one of the kitchen chairs.

'You're looking very dark and puffy around the eyes,' he said. 'Did you sleep last night?'

'For a while.' She could not tell him that she had barely closed her eyes, that the presence of the child had been all around her. She had lain on her back, weeping in the dark. Her head had throbbed, and the ache in the small of her back had grown stronger by the hour. Although well covered with the blankets, she had shivered.

'Now you listen to me,' he said. 'Your pulse hasn't come down, and neither has your temperature. I must be blunt with you and tell you that you are ill – and if you don't do something about it, you're going to get worse.

Listen to me – you're a young woman and . . . how old are you?'

'Twenty-three.'

'Twenty-three. Yes, and I daresay you're a strong young woman too. The little boy – he was so weakened through that dreadful chill, but it doesn't have to be that way with you. You've got to eat, and get your strength up.' He stood up. 'I shall come back tomorrow, and I want to see a change in you. I want to hear you've been looking after yourself. You understand me?'

'Yes, sir.'

'If your aches get worse then take a little of the opium that I left with you for the boy. Is there some left?'

'Yes, sir.'

'Take a couple of drops of that in some water. It'll help you sleep too.' He closed his bag. 'If you get much worse you'll need to have someone to help care for you. Is there anyone?'

'Mrs Tanner's granddaughter, Millie – she's very good. She comes in and helps out.'

'I meant someone who could be here all the time.'

She shook her head. 'No, there's no one.'

'Right.' He frowned and gave a sigh, then picked up his bag and his hat. 'I'll be back tomorrow.'

As the doctor went from the front door he met Millie coming up the path.

'Ah, it's Millie, isn't it? Mrs Tanner's granddaughter. How are you, miss?'

'Very well, thank you, sir.'

'You're going in to see Miss Clair, are you?'

'Yes, sir.'

'Good.' He smiled at her. 'You seem like a sensible girl, Millie.'

'Well . . . thank you, sir . . .'

'How old are you now?'

'Fourteen last August, sir.'

He nodded, then glanced back briefly over his shoulder. 'I don't mind telling you, I'm concerned about Miss Clair. The young lady is not at all well, and I'm afraid at this rate she's going to be very ill.'

'She's not eating, sir. I've brought stuff round, but she don't eat it. She says she's not 'ungry.'

'Well, she must eat. And she needs looking after.'

Millie gave a little shrug. 'I does what I can, sir.'

'Oh, I'm sure you do – but if this illness progresses, as with the child, then she's going to need someone here all the time. She's going to need a lot of care. There's no room in the isolation hospital, though, and I know of no nurse to spare in the borough. But when I ask her, she says she's got no one.' He gave a sigh. 'It's a dilemma, I don't mind saying.'

'She's got Miss Balfour, sir,' Millie said.

'And who is Miss Balfour?'

'She lives in Sherrell, sir. She owns these two 'ouses. Miss Clair – she lives with 'er sometimes.'

'I see. D'you know how to get word to her, Miss Balfour?'

'My grandma's got her address, sir.'

The doctor nodded. 'I'll come in and see your grandmother now.'

Lying in the dark that night, Lily could not sleep. Her legs felt as if her blood did not reach her feet, and the pain in her head threatened to split the bone of her skull. Her upper left arm was one swelling ache. She had begun to shiver, though her brow near her hairline was wet with sweat. After a time she half sat up and fumbled for the pack of Lucifer matches on the bedside chair, struck one and lit the candle. By its light she poured a few drops of valerian into a little water and drank it down. She could smell the smell of the child in the sheets. She could smell his sickness and also that sweet fragrance that was his alone. The doctor had said that the sheets must be burnt too, but what was the point of that? She had slept in them already, had slept in them with the boy beside her. The flame of the candle wavered in the draught that needled its way past the curtain.

She was still in bed the next morning when she heard voices coming from below. She dragged herself up to look at her watch. It was just after eleven-thirty.

Her head was pounding with an ache that filled her whole skull, while the ache in her back made her wince as she moved. She had been sick in the night, and her arm was throbbing like a drum. Eyes shut against the pain, she sat up straighter, listening, and then realised that the voice was that of Miss Elsie.

Moments later the voice came nearer as Miss Elsie came to the stairs and started up. Reaching the small landing, she tapped on the bedroom door and entered. A yard from the bed she came to a halt. She had taken off her coat and hat, but still wore a scarf wrapped around her throat.

'Well, Miss Lily Mary Clair,' she said shortly. 'This is a surprise and no mistake.'

'Miss Elsie,' Lily said, her voice sounding stiff and unused, 'how . . . what are you doing here?'

'I've come to see about *you*,' Miss Elsie said. 'Mrs Tanner's granddaughter came to Rowanleigh last evening. Came with the message that you were ill. Bless the girl. I was so grateful to her. So Mr Shad and I – we set off from Sherrell first thing this morning. He's downstairs right now, setting the fire and getting in some water and coal.' She looked around at the plainly-furnished little room and gave a shudder. 'This place is like a damned ice-house. You need a fire up here too.'

Lily groaned. 'Oh, Miss Elsie, I'm so sorry you were dragged out like that. You shouldn't have been. I'll be all right.'

'Well, if you're looked after properly you will.' Miss Elsie's voice had a no-nonsense tone to it. There was a small chair by the fireplace, and she brought it over to the bed and sat down.

'After getting your letter I was expecting you back at Rowanleigh,' she said. 'I couldn't think what was keeping you. Then the young man came, Mr Goodhart, and after that, young Millie.' She looked at Lily in silence for a few moments, then leant forward and laid a hand on Lily's wrist. 'She told me – she told me about the child.' Her fingers tightened about Lily's wrist. 'Oh, my dear . . . my dear.'

The ever-present, ever-waiting tears sprang to Lily's red-rimmed eyes and coursed down her cheeks, and for long moments no words were spoken. Then, at last, with a finger-hold on her control, she said dully, frowning, 'Miss Elsie – I wish you hadn't been put to all this trouble.'

'My dear,' Miss Elsie said, 'you cared for me when I was at my lowest, and when there was no one else. The least I can do is return a kindness.'

'But – but it's not safe for you.'

'Don't you worry about that,' Miss Elsie said. 'I'll be all right. I'll take whatever precautions I think necessary, and I shall be fine. I've had my vaccination, too. So has Mr Shad.' She got up from the chair. 'Now you lie down again. Mr Shad'll come up in a minute and set a fire here, and we'll get the place a bit warmer. While he's doing that I'm going to get you something to eat.'

Lily remained in bed with Miss Elsie tending her. Dr Trinshaw called late in the afternoon, and Miss Elsie stayed in the room while he checked Lily's temperature, took her pulse and looked at the vaccination wound. Lily heard their murmured exchanges as though through a fog. He did not stay long, but patted Lily's hand and went away again.

As the hours passed, Lily slaked her thirst on sips of water, and took the drops that Miss Elsie gave her to ease the aches in her head and back. She tried to take a little food too – soup at one time, and part of a lightly scrambled egg. On neither occasion could she keep it down.

Mr Shad left to return to Sherrell later that day, and Miss Elsie made up the bed in the second bedroom with blankets that she had brought from Rowanleigh. By the light of a candle she sat up late at Lily's bedside, and when she eventually went to her bed in the next room she left the door open so that she would hear if Lily called out in the night.

The next morning, Saturday, Miss Elsie sponged Lily's sweat-drenched skin and dressed her in a clean nightgown. Lily was barely aware of what was happening, and submitted to the ministrations with a dull expression and hardly a word. When Miss Elsie had finished, she had Millie come into the room and set a fresh fire. Later, Miss Elsie sat in the chair at Lily's bedside and gently dabbed at her brow with a damp flannel.

'How are you feeling today, my dear?'

Lily's chapped lips moved as if painfully. 'All right,' she murmured faintly. 'I'm . . . all right.'

A little nod from Miss Elsie. 'Dr Trinshaw,' she said after a moment, her voice low, 'he says you can win here.' Her words sounded deliberate and measured. 'He says you're young and you're strong, and you can beat this thing – and I say that too.' She leant forward and laid her hand with the gentlest touch on Lily's cheek. 'Lily Clair – you're a girl with spirit, you are. You have been ever since I met you.' Her mouth moved in an unaccustomed smile. 'And you're not going to let this beat you, are you?' She drew in her breath. 'If you are, then you're not the girl I knew.'

Lily lay silent for some moments, then she said, her voice faint, hardly more than a whisper, 'My boy and I – we went to the aquarium.'

Miss Elsie leant closer. 'What did you say, dear?' Above the frill of Lily's nightgown she could see the rash that had come up on her throat.

Lily's decline was so rapid as the sickness advanced. It was like a tide that caught her up and swept her on as if she were nothing more than a piece of flotsam. By noon on Sunday, the rash on her body had spread so much further, the flat, dark lesions growing, taking on a blackish hue beneath the skin. Towards evening she became delirious and lay gasping for breath, her limbs twitching, muttering incomprehensible words through dry lips while the sweat poured from her body and plastered her hair to her scalp. After a time even her mutterings fell silent. Miss Elsie sat at her bedside all night long, and when she leant over her in the cold dawn light, she saw that the lesions had spread and joined together, making of her face a blackened mask that ran down to disappear beneath the neck of her nightgown.

Chapter Forty

It had rained in the night, quite heavily, adding to the water in the butt in the yard, and filling up the broken earthenware dish that stood on the coal bunker. Now, though, the clouds had gone and the skies were clear, though it remained very cold. The doctor had come to the house just after eleven, and at any moment the mortuary attendants would be calling. When the knock came at the door, however, Miss Elsie answered it to find Joel on the doorstep.

'Mr Goodhart . . .' Her spirit sank anew at the sight of him.

'Miss Balfour . . .' He was smiling at her, and surprised to see her there. He had just come from Bath, he said, and had come to see Lily. She was expecting him.

Miss Elsie noticed that he carried in his hand a leather briefcase and a small white flower. She looked sorrowfully at him. His face was full of hope and expectation. In halting words she told him then of Lily's passing. She had died that morning, she said, taken by the smallpox.

For a moment he stood there deeply frowning, as if he had misheard. Then he said quickly, 'But – no. No, this – this can't be. Not Lily. I was here with her – just on Wednesday. This can't be.'

'There was nothing anyone could do,' Miss Elsie said.

'No,' he said, still frowning. 'No.'

Miss Elsie did not speak at this, and after a moment he put his head a little on one side, and in anguish drew his lips back over his teeth. Tears flooded his eyes and streamed down his cheeks. He gave a sob, and then said, when he could get his breath, 'But – she was so young, so – so alive. She – she was strong.'

Miss Elsie gave a little nod. 'Yes,' she said. 'Strong, yes – but she would not fight.'

As she spoke, a horse-drawn wagon came into view, and as it slowed at the gate she realised that it must be from the mortuary. She watched as it came to a halt, and two men climbed down. They were dressed in black and came up the path bearing a stretcher.

Joel did not seem to be aware of them until they stopped just behind him. As they did so, the man leading said to Miss Elsie, briefly raising his hat: 'If you please, ma'am – we've come for Miss Clair? Miss Lily Mary Clair . . . ?'

Miss Elsie nodded. 'Yes – indeed.' She stepped back. 'I'll show you upstairs.' Turning to Joel, she added quickly: 'Please – Mr Goodhart – excuse me, just for a moment. I must attend to this – business. But please – do come inside for a minute, will you . . . ?'

He said nothing, but gave a little nod, and remained standing there, as if in a trance. Then as the men came forward he stepped aside to allow them past. Miss Elsie gazed at him for a second longer, at his stricken face, and said, 'I'll be back directly.' Then to the two men she added, turning back into the house, 'Come this way, please.'

She led the way along the passage and up the stairs. At the top, she opened the door to the bedroom but remained outside on the small landing. As the two men came up behind her she gestured into the room. 'Just in here,' she said. 'I'll leave you to your work. I'll be downstairs if you need me.'

She stood aside then as they went past her into the bedroom, and then briefly hovered there, hearing their voices as they spoke to one another in hushed tones. Then she turned and went back down the stairs and along the passage. When she came to the open front door she found that Joel was no longer there.

Standing on the narrow front step, she looked along the street in both directions. He was nowhere in sight. As she turned to step back into the hall she saw a scrap of white down on the flags near the step, and dully realised that it was the flower he had been holding.

She stood there for a moment longer, then closed the door against the cold and went back into the kitchen to wait for the men to come downstairs. Out in the yard the woodpecker flew down and alighted on the rim of the broken pot, dipped his scarlet-capped head and delicately drank.

To find out more about Jess Foley and other fantastic Arrow authors why not read *The Inside Story* – our newsletter featuring all of our saga authors.

To join our mailing list to receive the newsletter and other information* write with your name and address to:

The Inside Story
The Marketing Department
Arrow Books
20 Vauxhall Bridge Road
London
SW1V 2SA

*Your details will be held on a database so we can send you the newsletter(s) and information on other Arrow authors that you have indicated you wish to receive. Your details will not be passed to any third party. If you would like to receive information on other Random House authors please do let us know. If at any stage you wish to be deleted from our *The Inside Story* mailing list please let us know.

So Long At The Fair

Jess Foley

Growing up in a small Wiltshire village, Abbie Morris knows what lies ahead of her – a life of drudgery as a menial servant. But when Abbie's mother casts the family into crisis, her world is turned upside down.

Six years later, the Morrises are rebuilding their lives and when Abbie and her sister Beatie set off for the country fair, the world seems a good place. Until a chance encounter with Louis, a handsome stranger, leads to tragedy.

Abbie struggles to put that terrible evening behind her, and when Arthur Gilmore comes into her life believes she might even find happiness. But then her past catches up with her, and it seems she might never cease to pay for the night she stayed so long at the fair . . .

arrow books

Too Close To The Sun

Jess Foley

When Grace Harper is orphaned, her world falls apart. Life has always been hard, and now she and her little brother Billy are left homeless and alone.

But Grace must put her grief and fear aside, and think practically. Accepting a job as companion to the wealthy, lonely Mrs Spencer means that she and Billy have a roof over their heads, but just as Grace starts to find her feet disaster strikes again.

Things look desperate, and when she is offered the good life for herself and Billy, Grace is tempted. But is she, in search of safety for her little family, flying too close to the sun?

arrow books

Saddle The Wind

Jess Foley

In a small village in the West Country a baby girl is born into poverty. For little Blanche the future looks bleak.

Her life changes one fateful day when her mother is summoned to The Big House to nurse Marianne, daughter of a wealthy mill-owner. But although she and Marianne grow to care for one another as sisters, sisters they are not. And when Blanche meets and falls in love with Marianne's intended husband, her struggle not to betray her closest friend threatens to destroy her happiness for ever.

A powerful saga of passion and pain, *Saddle The Wind* is a thrilling, intensely moving testament to the human spirit, which builds to a spellbinding climax.

arrow books

ALSO AVAILABLE IN ARROW

Wait For The Dawn

Jess Foley

Faced with a future that holds little promise, Lydia Halley longs to leave home. But it is only after her mother's tragic death that she finally seizes her chance of freedom – a freedom she has yearned for all her life.

Taking up lodgings in the bustling city of Redbury, she meets handsome stranger Guy Anderson and so begins a friendship which blossoms into love. Until one day a telegram from Italy brings devastating news for Guy – and their passionate leave-taking has dramatic consequences for them both . . .

arrow books

**Order further Jess Foley titles
from your local bookshop, or have them delivered
direct to your door by Bookpost**

☐	So Long At The Fair	0 09 941576 3	£5.99
☐	Too Close To The Sun	0 09 941577 1	£5.99
☐	Saddle The Wind	0 09 946645 7	£5.99
☐	Wait For The Dawn	0 09 946647 3	£5.99

Free post and packing
Overseas customers allow £2 per paperback

Phone: 01624 677237

Post: Random House Books
c/o Bookpost, PO Box 29, Douglas, Isle of Man IM99 1BQ

Fax: 01624 670923

email: bookshop@enterprise.net

Cheques (payable to Bookpost) and credit cards accepted

Prices and availability subject to change without notice.
Allow 28 days for delivery.
When placing your order, please state if you do not wish to receive any
additional information.

www.randomhouse.co.uk/arrowbooks

arrow books